VIZ GRAPHIC NOVEL

MAISON IKKOKU™
GAME, SET, MATCH

This volume contains
MAISON IKKOKU PART EIGHT #7 through PART NINE #4 in their entirety.

STORY & ART BY RUMIKO TAKAHASHI

ENGLISH ADAPTATION BY GERARD JONES

Translation/Mari Morimoto
Touch-Up Art & Lettering/Bill Spicer
Cover Design/Hidemi Sahara
Layout/Yuki Shimotoku
Editor/Trish Ledoux
Assistant Editor/Bill Flanagan
Senior Marketing Manager/Dallas Middaugh
Senior Sales Manager/Ann Ivan
Marketing Associate/Jaime Starling

Editor-in-Chief/Hyoe Narita
Publisher/Seiji Horibuchi

First published by Shogakukan, Inc. in Japan

Printed in Canada

Published by Viz Communications, Inc.
P.O. Box 77010
San Francisco, CA 94107

10 9 8 7 6 5 4 3 2
First printing, November 1999
Second printing, December 2000

MAISON IKKOKU GRAPHIC NOVELS TO DATE

MAISON IKKOKU
FAMILY AFFAIRS
HOME SWEET HOME
GOOD HOUSEKEEPING
EMPTY NEST
BEDSIDE MANNERS
INTENSIVE CARE
DOMESTIC DISPUTE
LEARNING CURVES
DOGGED PURSUIT
STUDENT AFFAIRS
HOUNDS OF WAR
GAME, SET, MATCH
WELCOME HOME

VIZ GRAPHIC NOVEL

MAISON IKKOKU™ VOLUME THIRTEEN

GAME, SET, MATCH

STORY AND ART BY
RUMIKO TAKAHASHI

CONTENTS

PART ONE
BACK AND FORTH

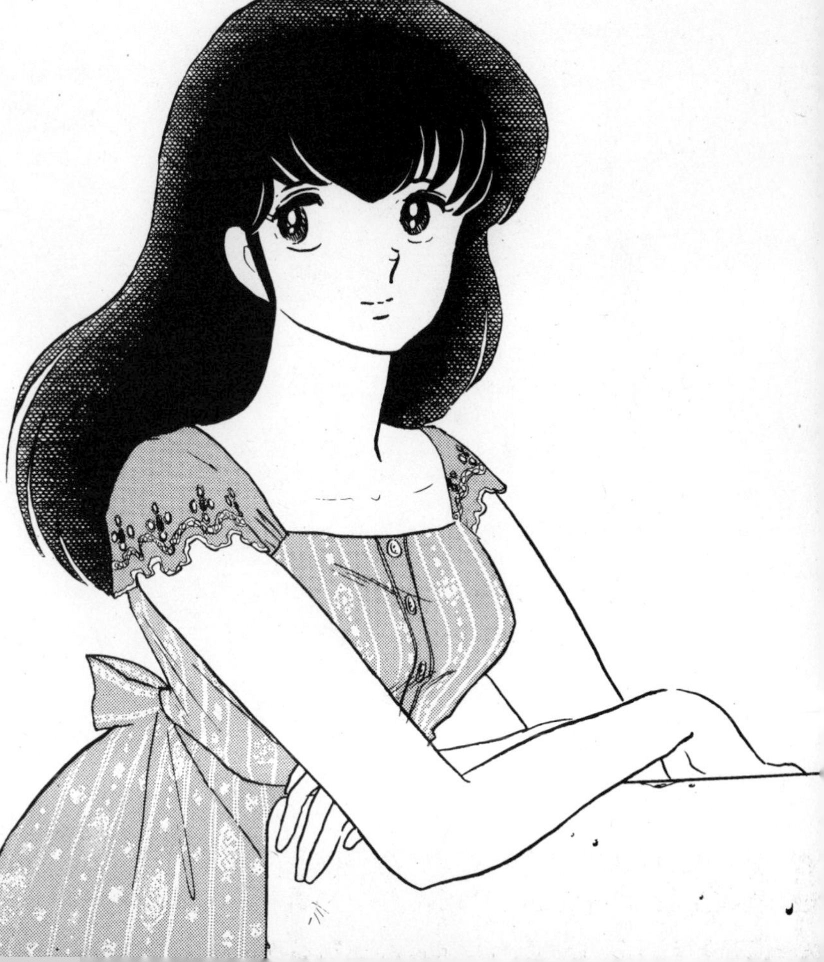

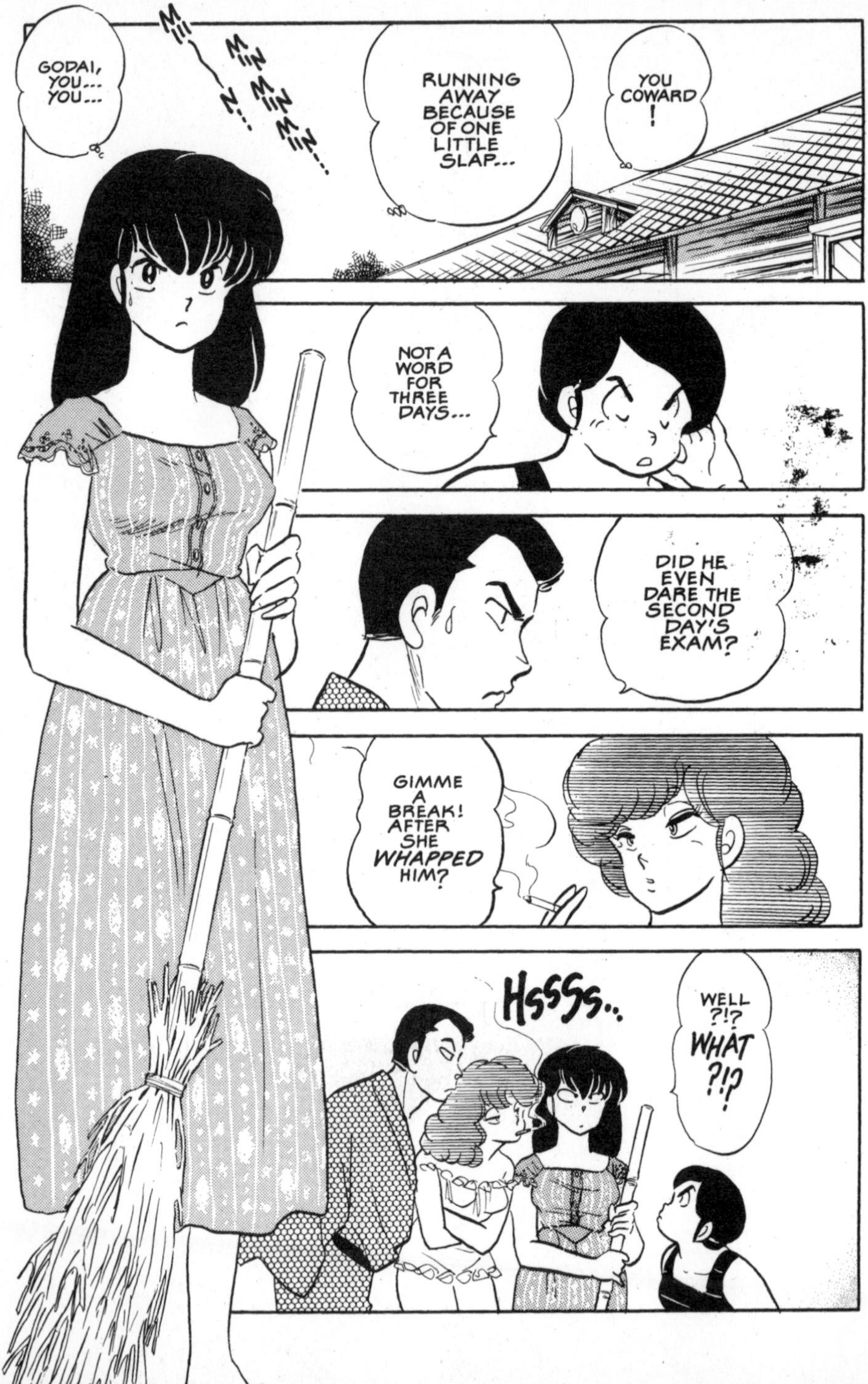
GODAI, YOU... YOU...
MIII—N...
MIIN MIIN MIIN...
RUNNING AWAY BECAUSE OF ONE LITTLE SLAP...
YOU COWARD!
NOT A WORD FOR THREE DAYS...
DID HE EVEN DARE THE SECOND DAY'S EXAM?
GIMME A BREAK! AFTER SHE WHAPPED HIM?
HSSSS...
WELL?!? WHAT?!?

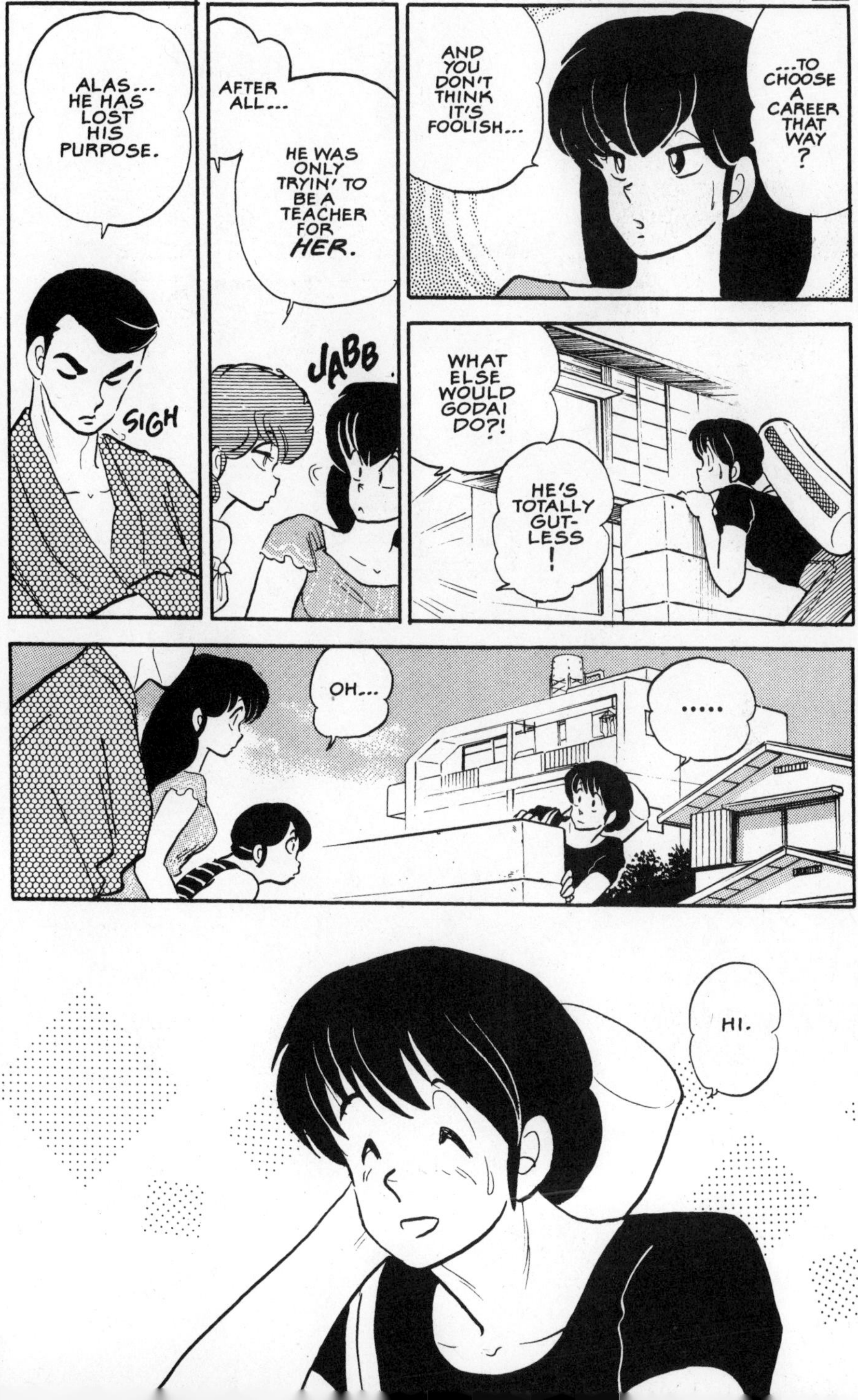
ALAS... HE HAS LOST HIS PURPOSE.
SIGH
AFTER ALL...
HE WAS ONLY TRYIN' TO BE A TEACHER FOR HER.
JABB
AND YOU DON'T THINK IT'S FOOLISH...
...TO CHOOSE A CAREER THAT WAY?
WHAT ELSE WOULD GODAI DO?!
HE'S TOTALLY GUT-LESS!
OH...
.....
HI.

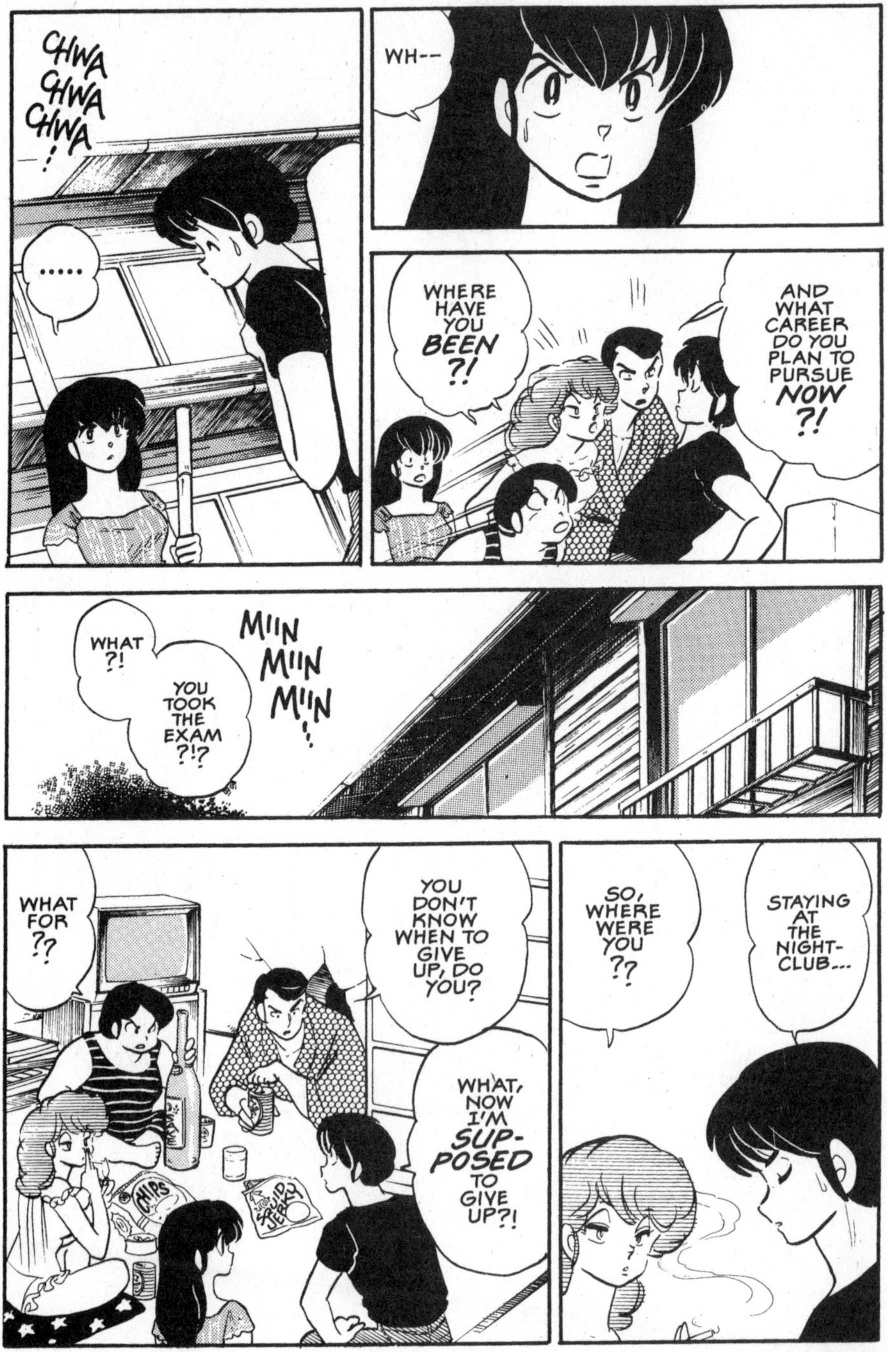
CHWA CHWA CHWA
......
WH--
WHERE HAVE YOU BEEN ?!
AND WHAT CAREER DO YOU PLAN TO PURSUE NOW ?!
WHAT ?!
YOU TOOK THE EXAM ?!?
MIIN MIIN MIIN
WHAT FOR ??
CHIPS
SQUID JERKY
YOU DON'T KNOW WHEN TO GIVE UP, DO YOU?
WHAT, NOW I'M SUPPOSED TO GIVE UP?!
SO, WHERE WERE YOU ??
STAYING AT THE NIGHT-CLUB...

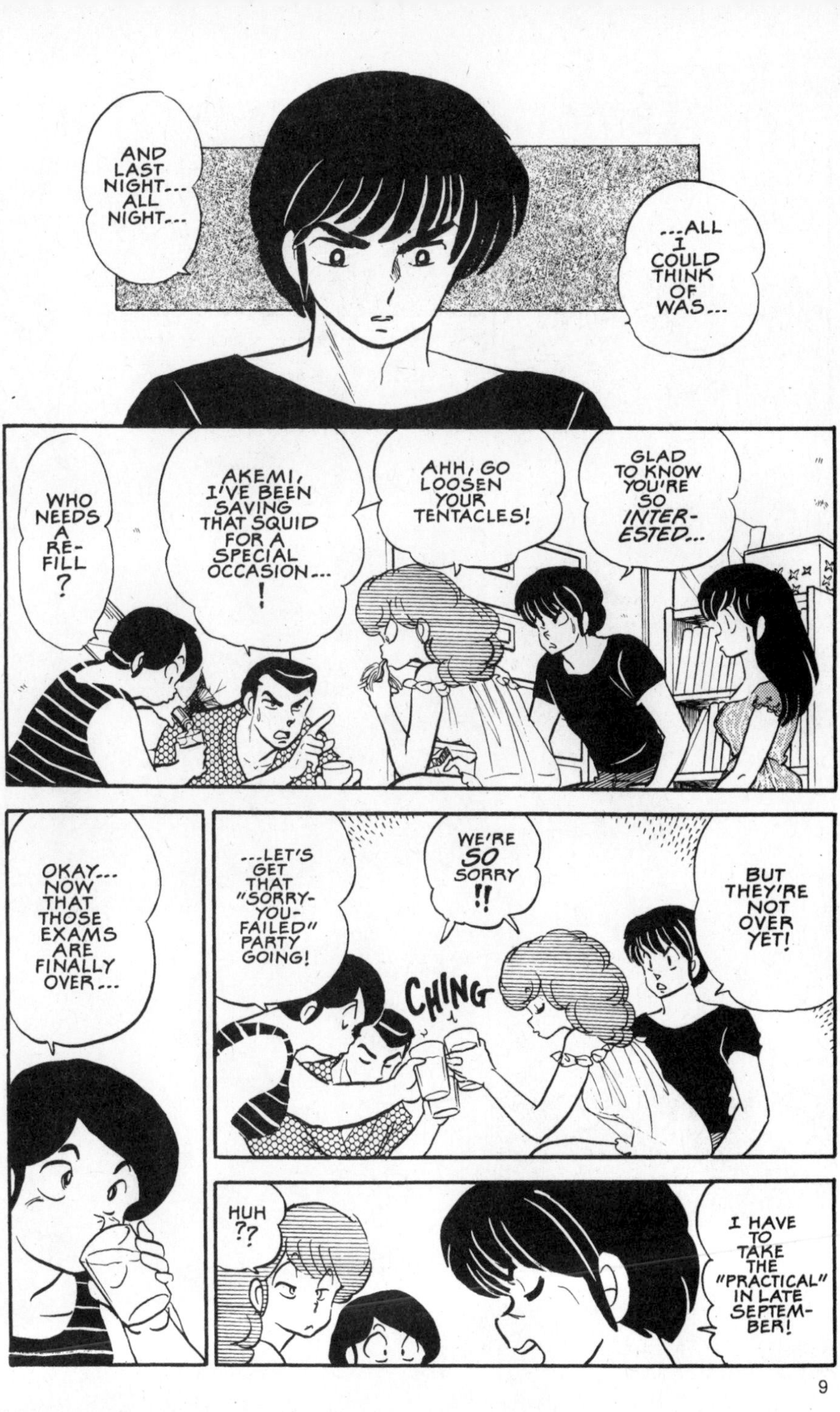
AND LAST NIGHT... ALL NIGHT...
...ALL I COULD THINK OF WAS...
WHO NEEDS A RE-FILL?
AKEMI, I'VE BEEN SAVING THAT SQUID FOR A SPECIAL OCCASION...!
AHH, GO LOOSEN YOUR TENTACLES!
GLAD TO KNOW YOU'RE SO INTER-ESTED...
OKAY... NOW THAT THOSE EXAMS ARE FINALLY OVER...
...LET'S GET THAT "SORRY-YOU-FAILED" PARTY GOING!
WE'RE SO SORRY!!
CHING
BUT THEY'RE NOT OVER YET!
HUH??
I HAVE TO TAKE THE "PRACTICAL" IN LATE SEPTEM-BER!

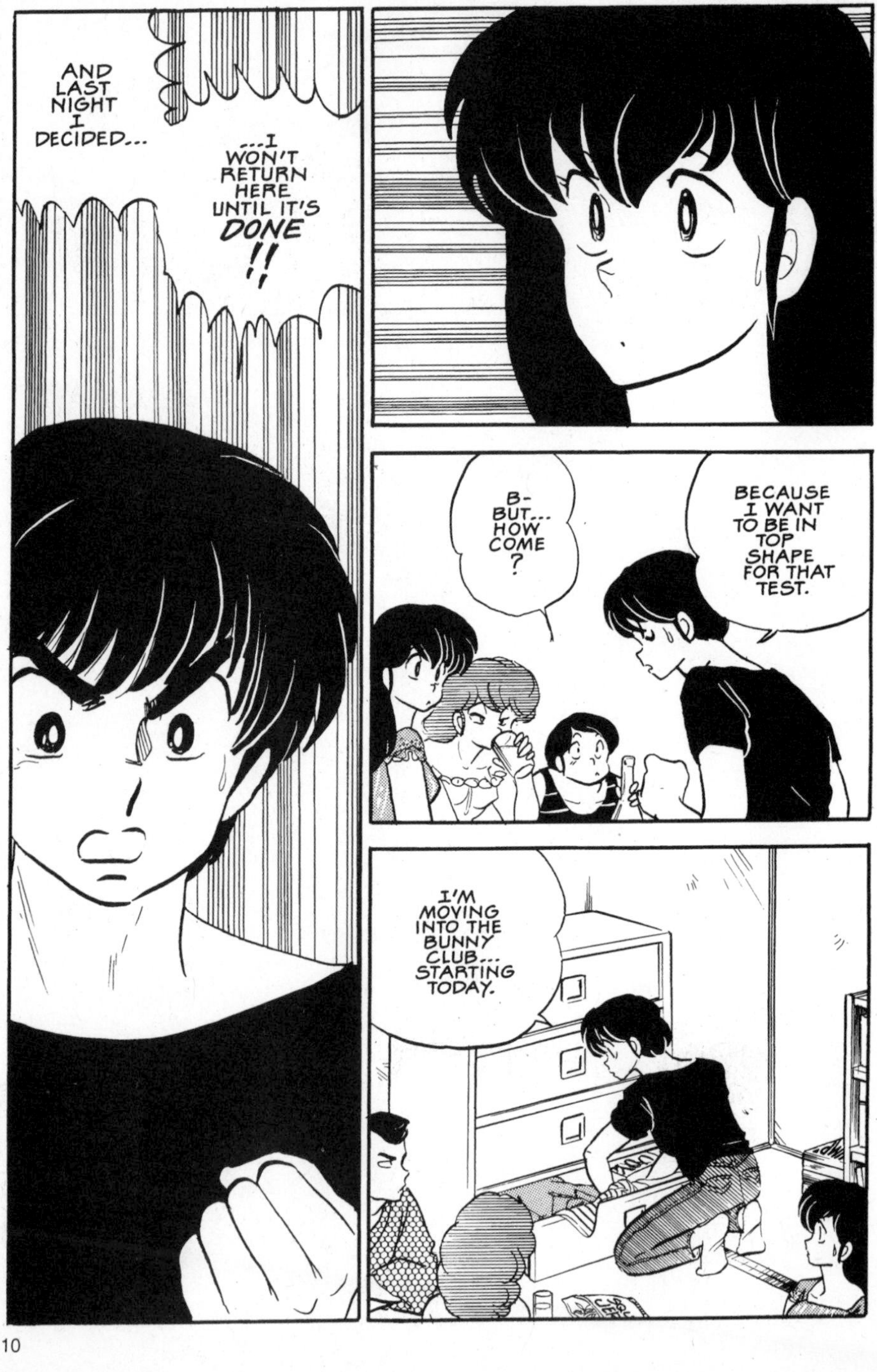
AND LAST NIGHT I DECIDED...
...I WON'T RETURN HERE UNTIL IT'S DONE !!
B-BUT... HOW COME ?
BECAUSE I WANT TO BE IN TOP SHAPE FOR THAT TEST.
I'M MOVING INTO THE BUNNY CLUB... STARTING TODAY.

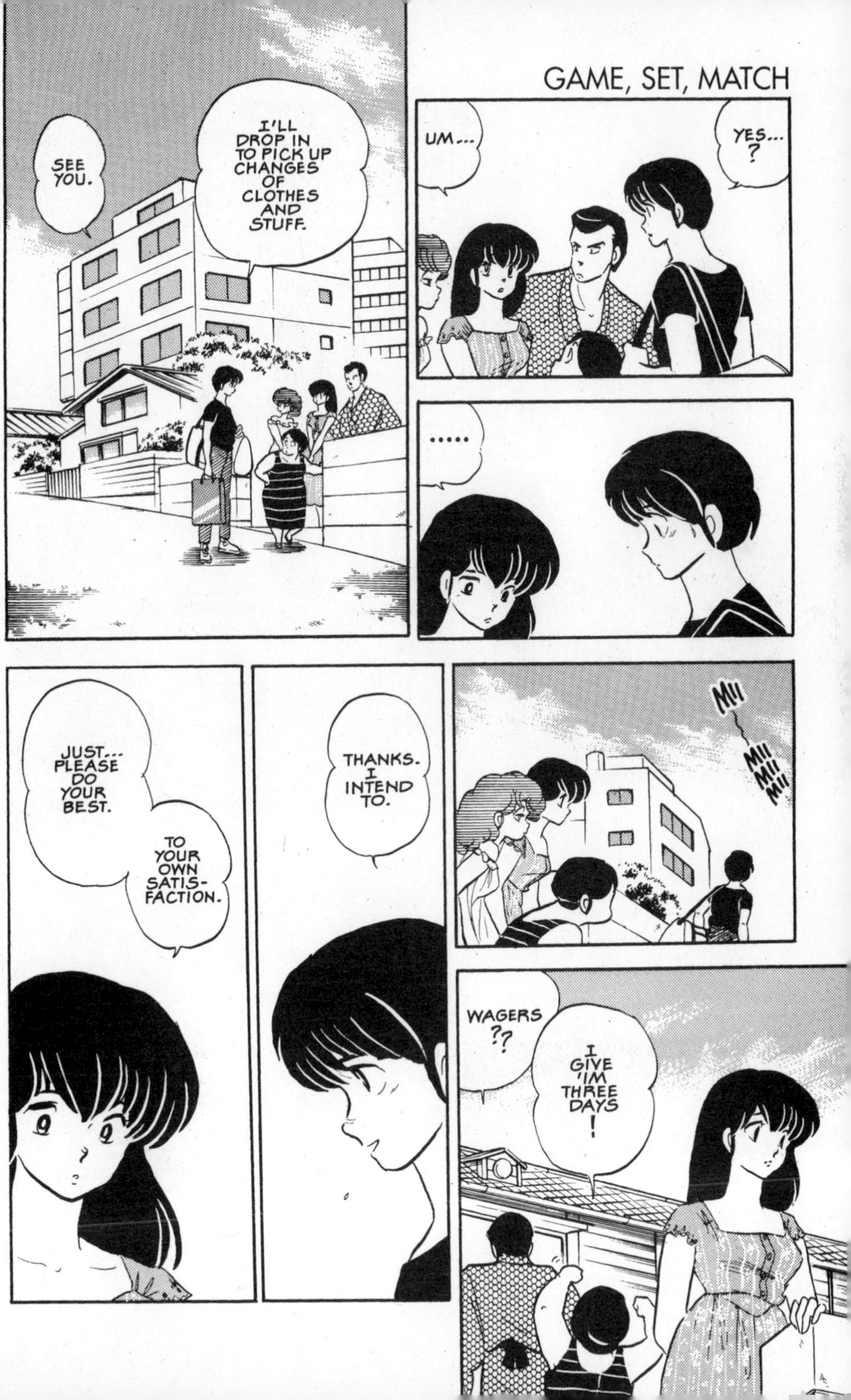
SEE YOU.
I'LL DROP IN TO PICK UP CHANGES OF CLOTHES AND STUFF.
UM...
YES...?
......
JUST... PLEASE DO YOUR BEST.
TO YOUR OWN SATIS-FACTION.
THANKS. I INTEND TO.
MII MII MII MII
WAGERS??
I GIVE 'IM THREE DAYS!

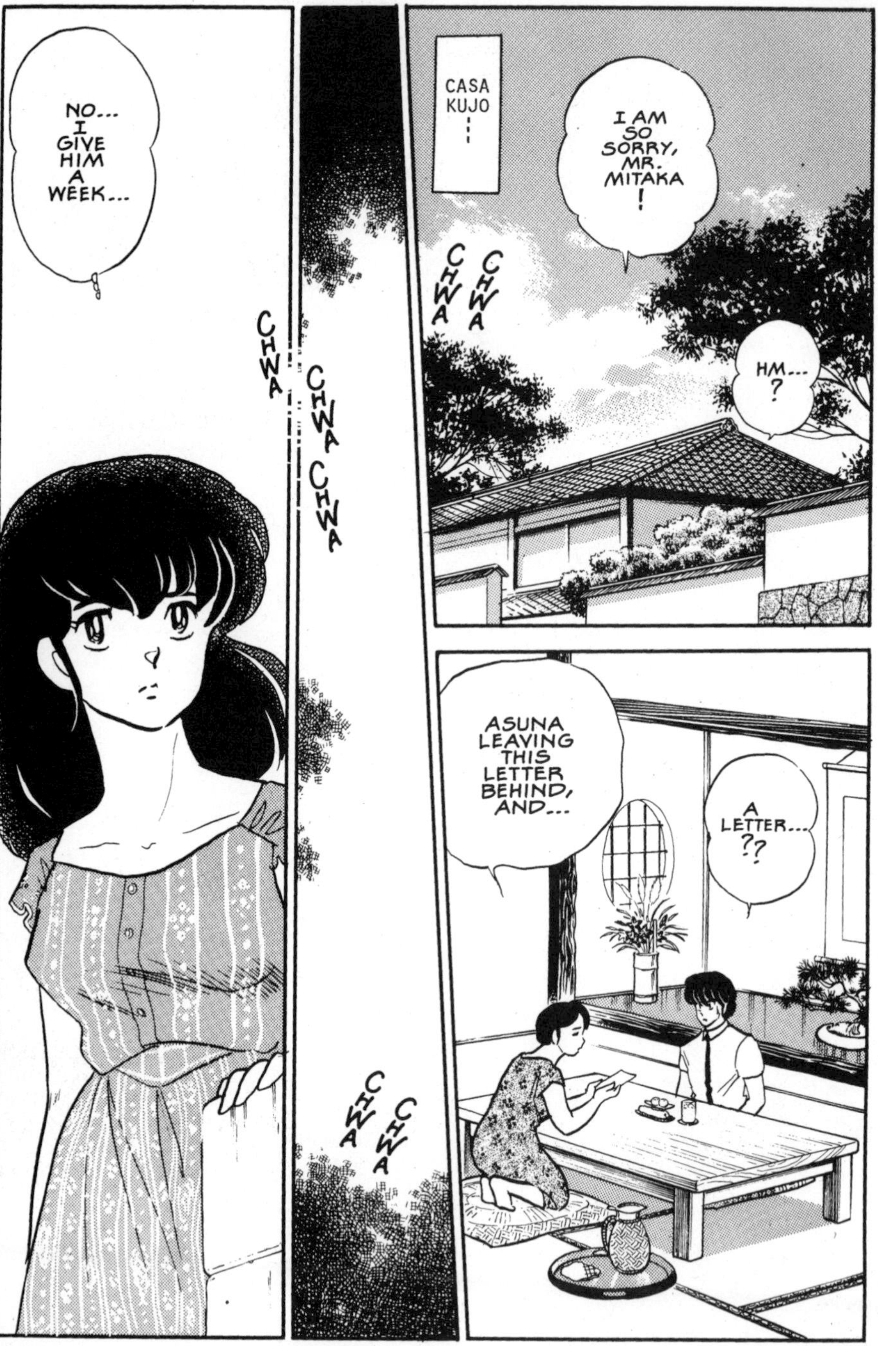

NO... I GIVE HIM A WEEK...
CHWA CHWA
CHWA CHWA
CASA KUJO ...
CHWA CHWA
I AM SO SORRY, MR. MITAKA!
HM...?
ASUNA LEAVING THIS LETTER BEHIND, AND...
A LETTER...??
CHWA CHWA

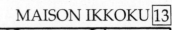

DON'T TELL ME SHE'S RUN AWAY...

OH, NO, NO. SHE'S SPENDING THE SUMMER WITH HER RELATIVES IN IZU...

OH...

W-WELL THEN...

I SHOULD READ...

.....

As neither Mr. Mitaka nor I have yet fully sorted our emotions, I feel it may be premature to formalize our engagement at this time. Please postpone the date of the wedding.
　　　　　　　　　　--Asuna

"POST-PONE"...

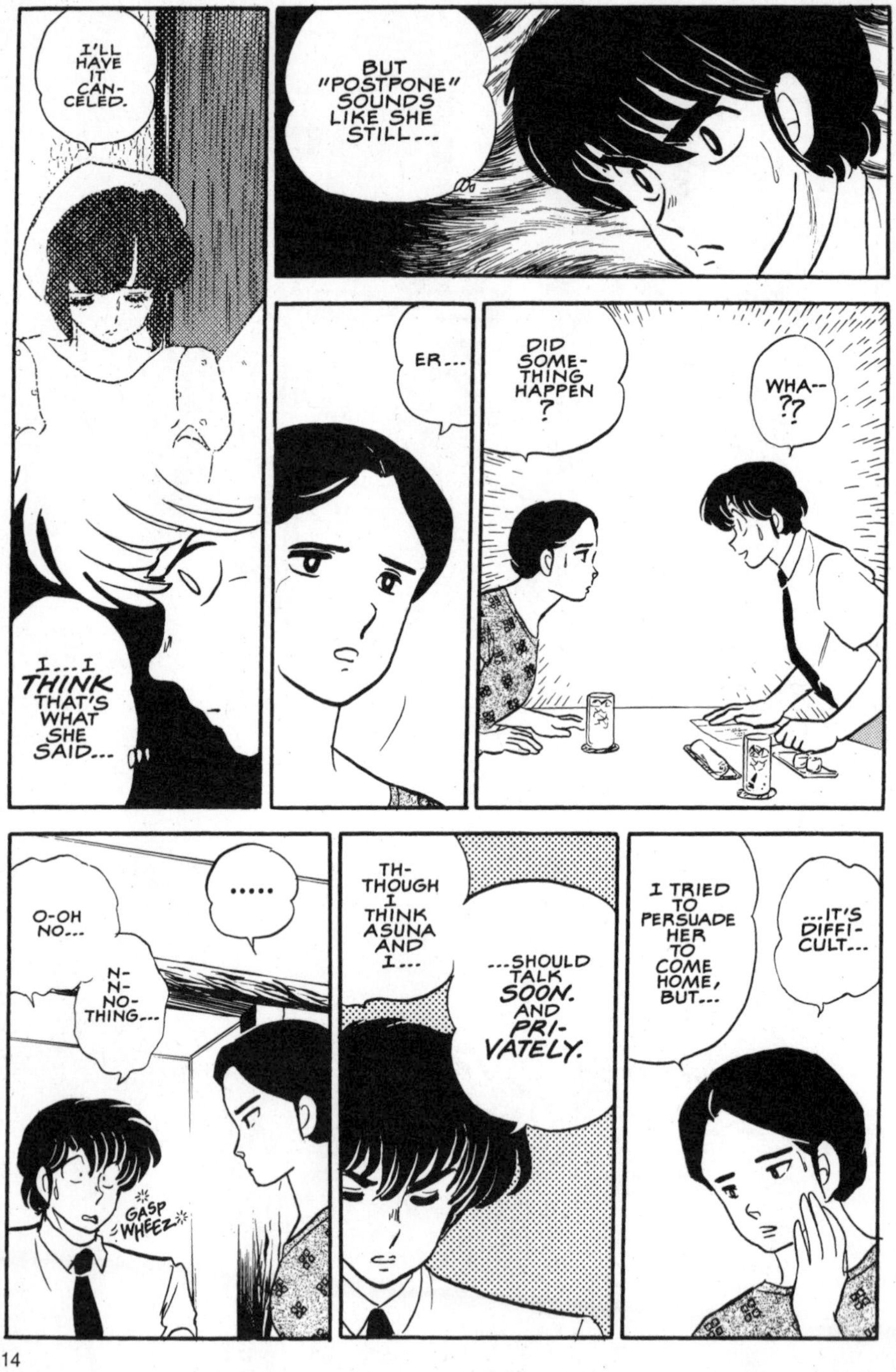
I'LL HAVE IT CAN-CELED.
I... I THINK THAT'S WHAT SHE SAID...
BUT "POSTPONE" SOUNDS LIKE SHE STILL...
ER...
DID SOME-THING HAPPEN?
WHA-- ??
O-OH NO...
.....
N-N-NO-THING...
GASP WHEEZ
TH-THOUGH I THINK ASUNA AND I...
...SHOULD TALK SOON. AND PRI-VATELY.
I TRIED TO PERSUADE HER TO COME HOME, BUT...
...IT'S DIFFI-CULT...

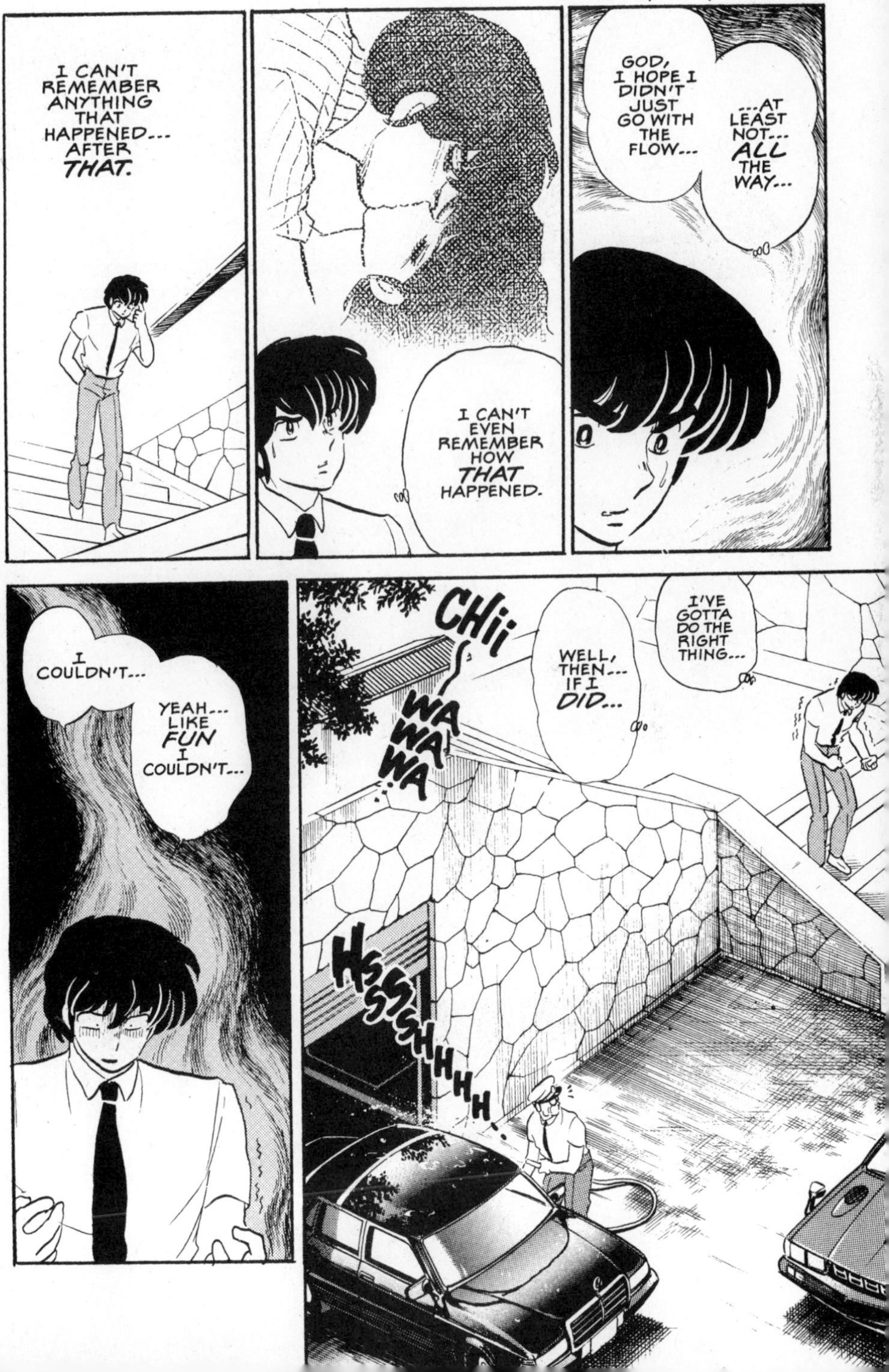
I CAN'T REMEMBER ANYTHING THAT HAPPENED... AFTER THAT.
I CAN'T EVEN REMEMBER HOW THAT HAPPENED.
GOD, I HOPE I DIDN'T JUST GO WITH THE FLOW...
...AT LEAST NOT... ALL THE WAY...
I COULDN'T...
YEAH... LIKE FUN I COULDN'T...
CHii
WELL, THEN... IF I DID...
I'VE GOTTA DO THE RIGHT THING...
WA WA WA WA
HSSSHHHHH

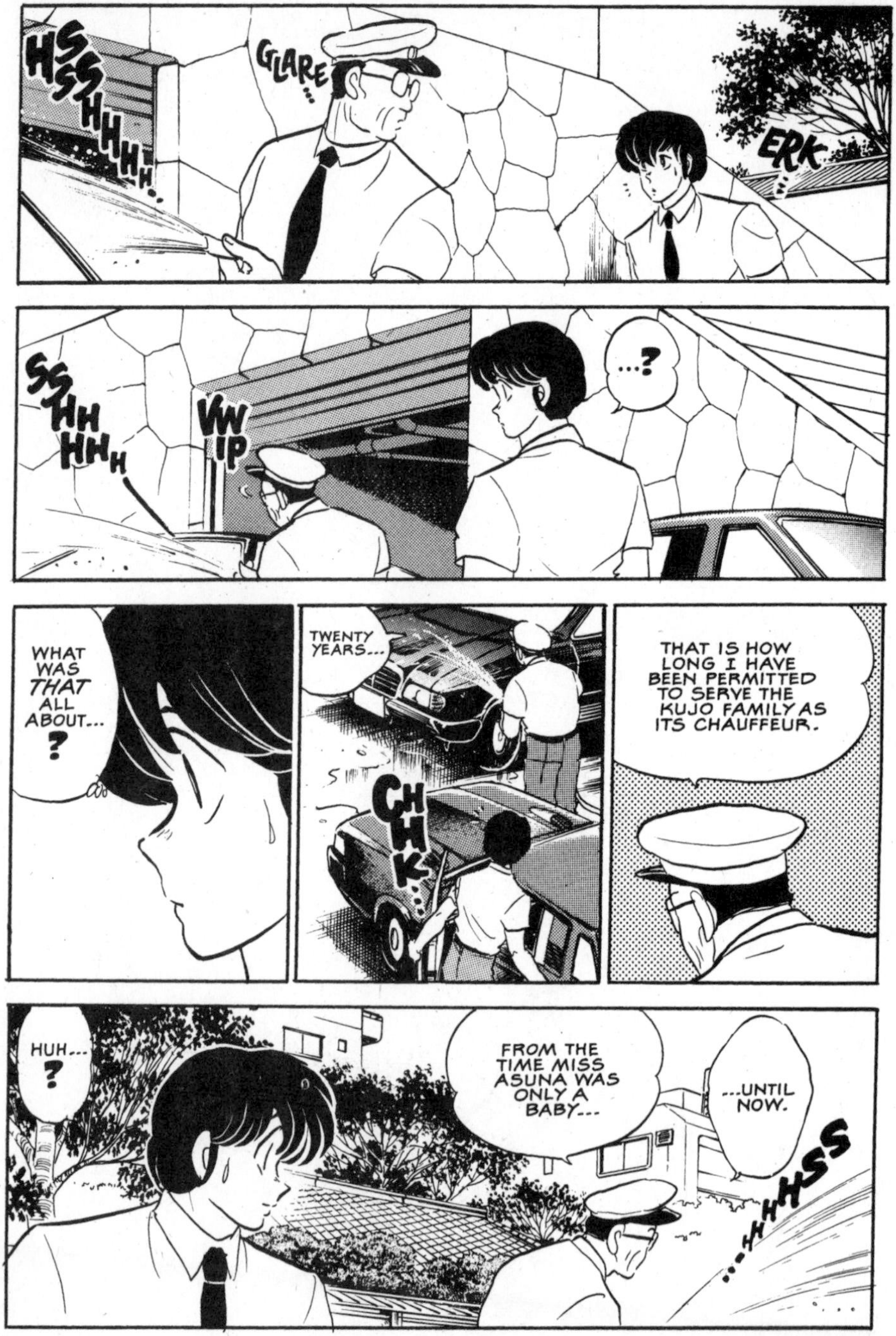
HSSSHHHHH..
GLARE...
ERK...
SSHHHHHH
VWIP
...?
WHAT WAS THAT ALL ABOUT...?
TWENTY YEARS...
CHHK...
THAT IS HOW LONG I HAVE BEEN PERMITTED TO SERVE THE KUJO FAMILY AS ITS CHAUFFEUR.
HUH...?
FROM THE TIME MISS ASUNA WAS ONLY A BABY...
...UNTIL NOW.
...HHHHSS

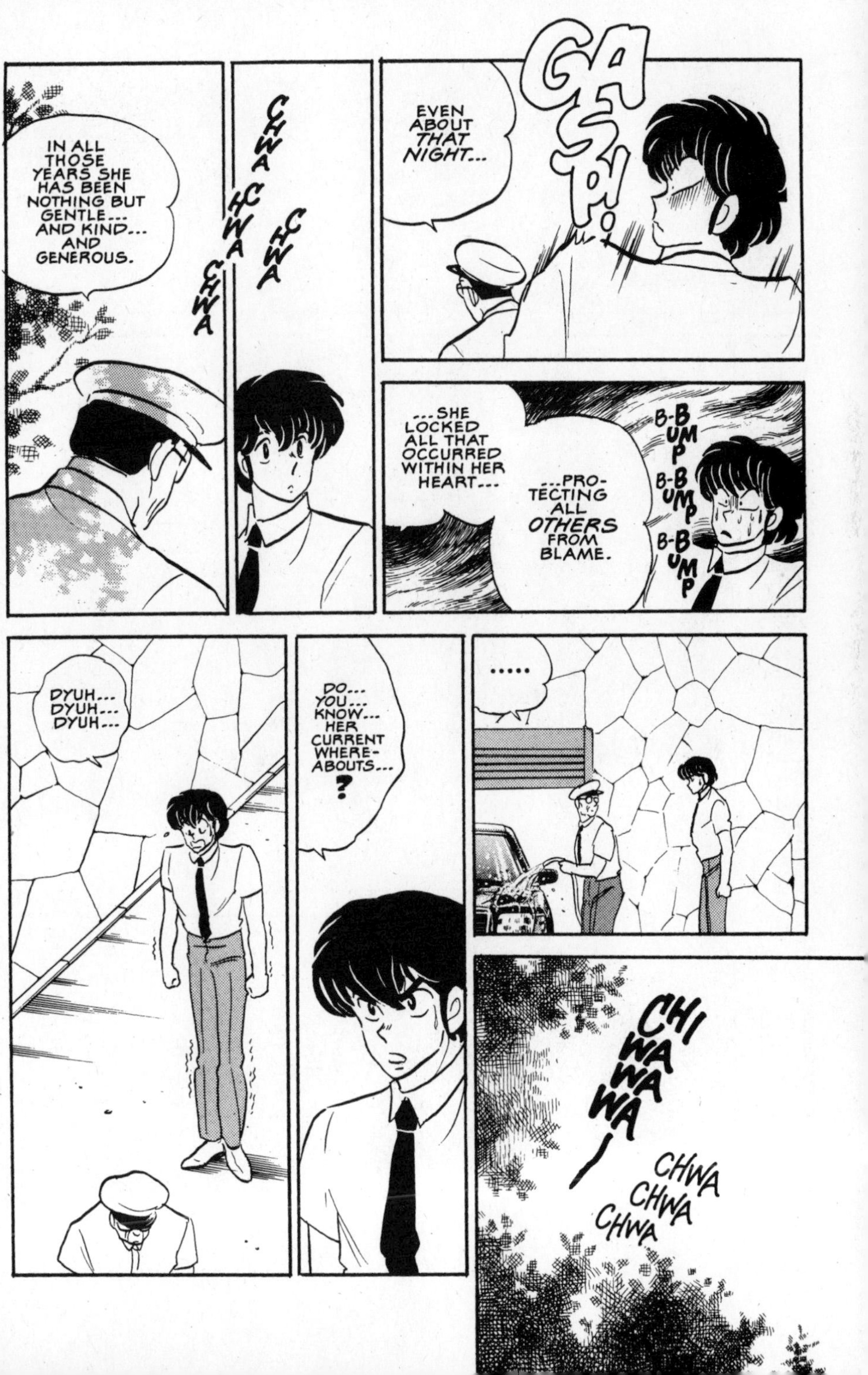
IN ALL THOSE YEARS SHE HAS BEEN NOTHING BUT GENTLE... AND KIND... AND GENEROUS.
CHWA CHWA CHWA CHWA
CHWA CHWA
GASP!
EVEN ABOUT THAT NIGHT...
...SHE LOCKED ALL THAT OCCURRED WITHIN HER HEART...
...PROTECTING ALL OTHERS FROM BLAME.
B-BUMP B-BUMP B-BUMP
DYUH... DYUH... DYUH...
DO... YOU... KNOW... HER CURRENT WHERE-ABOUTS...?
.....
CHIWAWAWAWA
CHWA CHWA CHWA

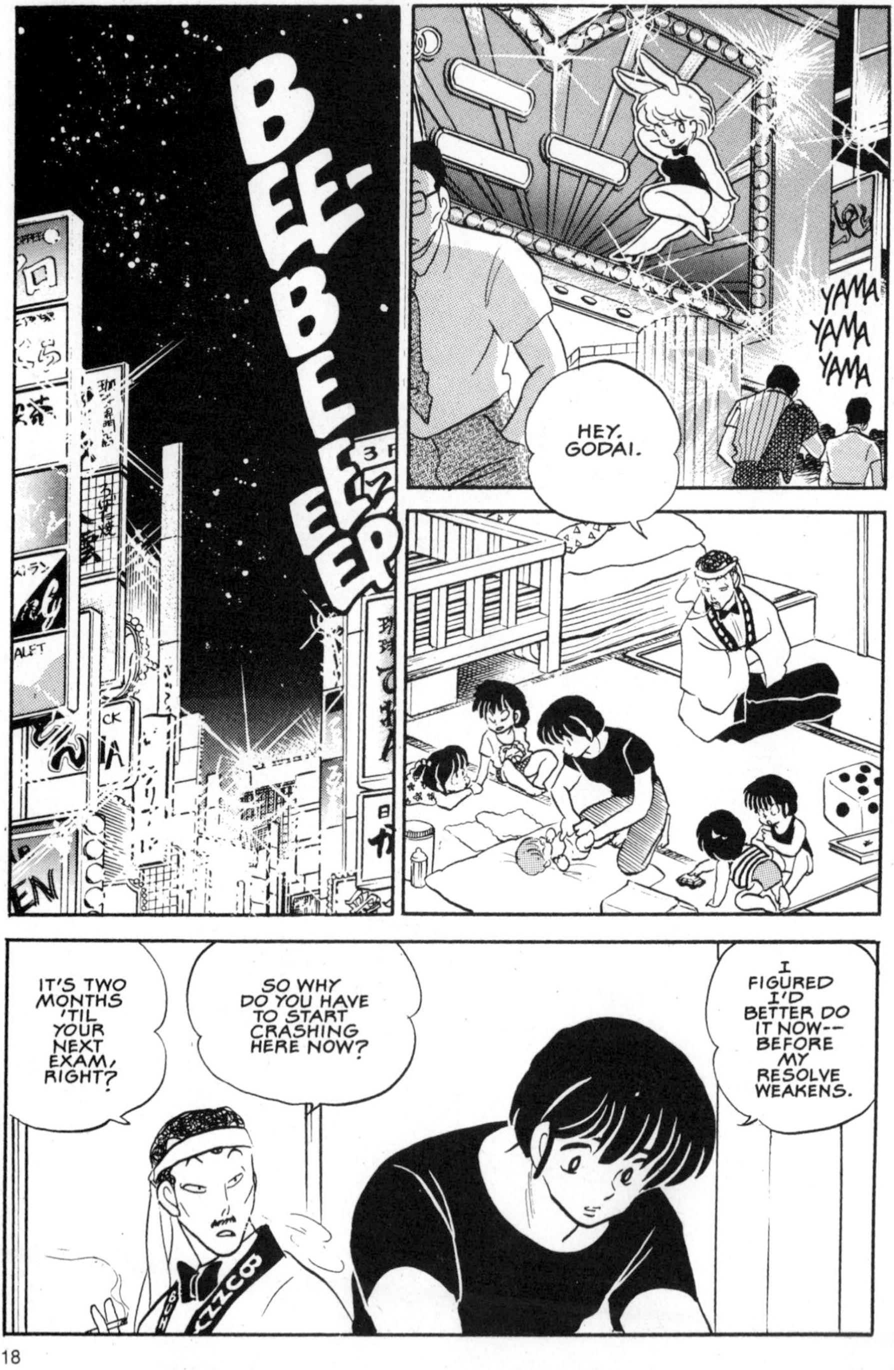
BEE-BEEEEP
YAMA YAMA YAMA
HEY. GODAI.
IT'S TWO MONTHS 'TIL YOUR NEXT EXAM, RIGHT?
SO WHY DO YOU HAVE TO START CRASHING HERE NOW?
I FIGURED I'D BETTER DO IT NOW--BEFORE MY RESOLVE WEAKENS.

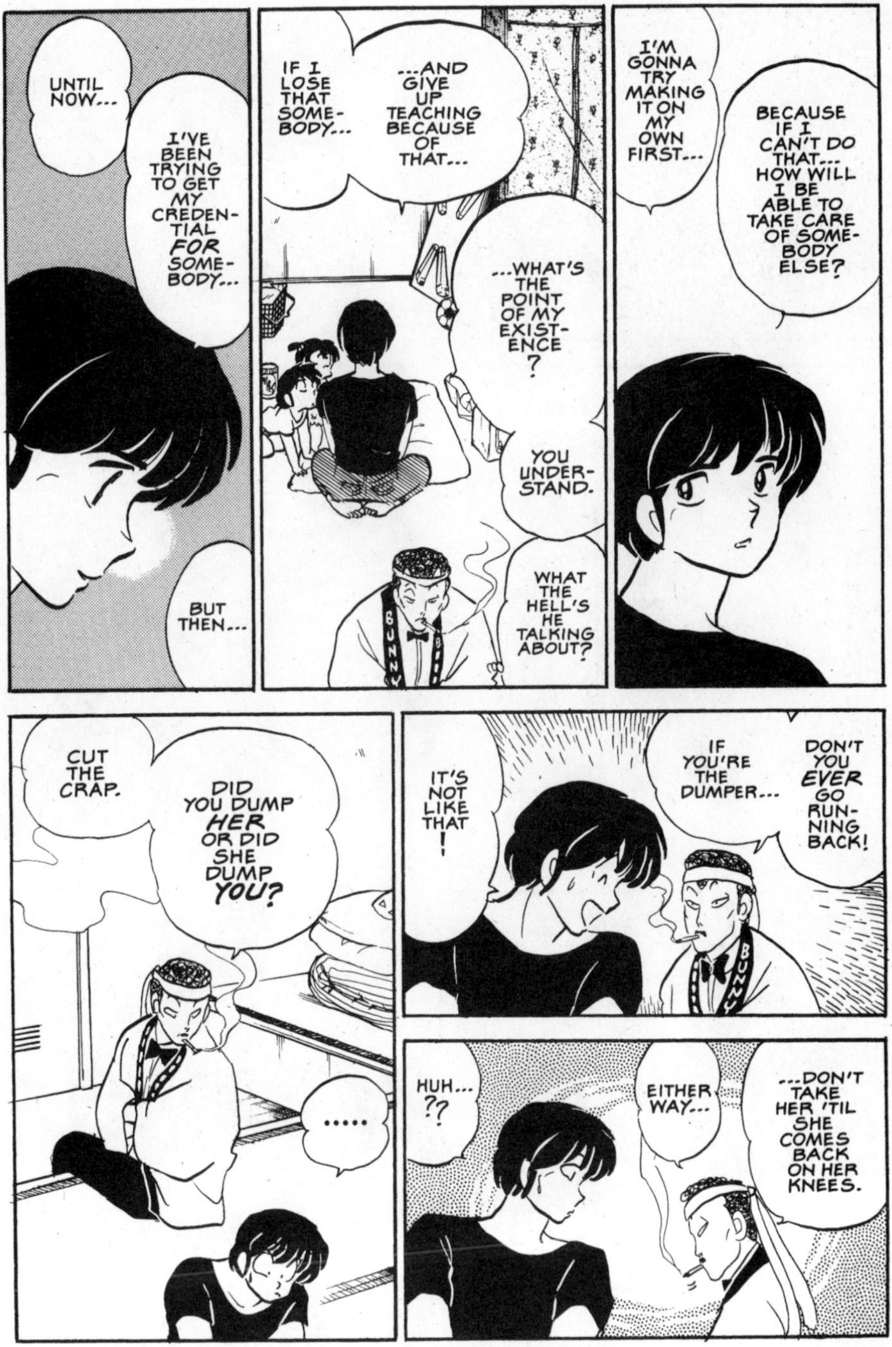
UNTIL NOW...
I'VE BEEN TRYING TO GET MY CREDENTIAL FOR SOMEBODY...
BUT THEN...
IF I LOSE THAT SOMEBODY...
...AND GIVE UP TEACHING BECAUSE OF THAT...
...WHAT'S THE POINT OF MY EXISTENCE?
YOU UNDERSTAND.
WHAT THE HELL'S HE TALKING ABOUT?
I'M GONNA TRY MAKING IT ON MY OWN FIRST...
BECAUSE IF I CAN'T DO THAT... HOW WILL I BE ABLE TO TAKE CARE OF SOMEBODY ELSE?
CUT THE CRAP.
DID YOU DUMP HER OR DID SHE DUMP YOU?
......
IT'S NOT LIKE THAT!
IF YOU'RE THE DUMPER...
DON'T YOU EVER GO RUNNING BACK!
HUH...??
EITHER WAY...
...DON'T TAKE HER 'TIL SHE COMES BACK ON HER KNEES.

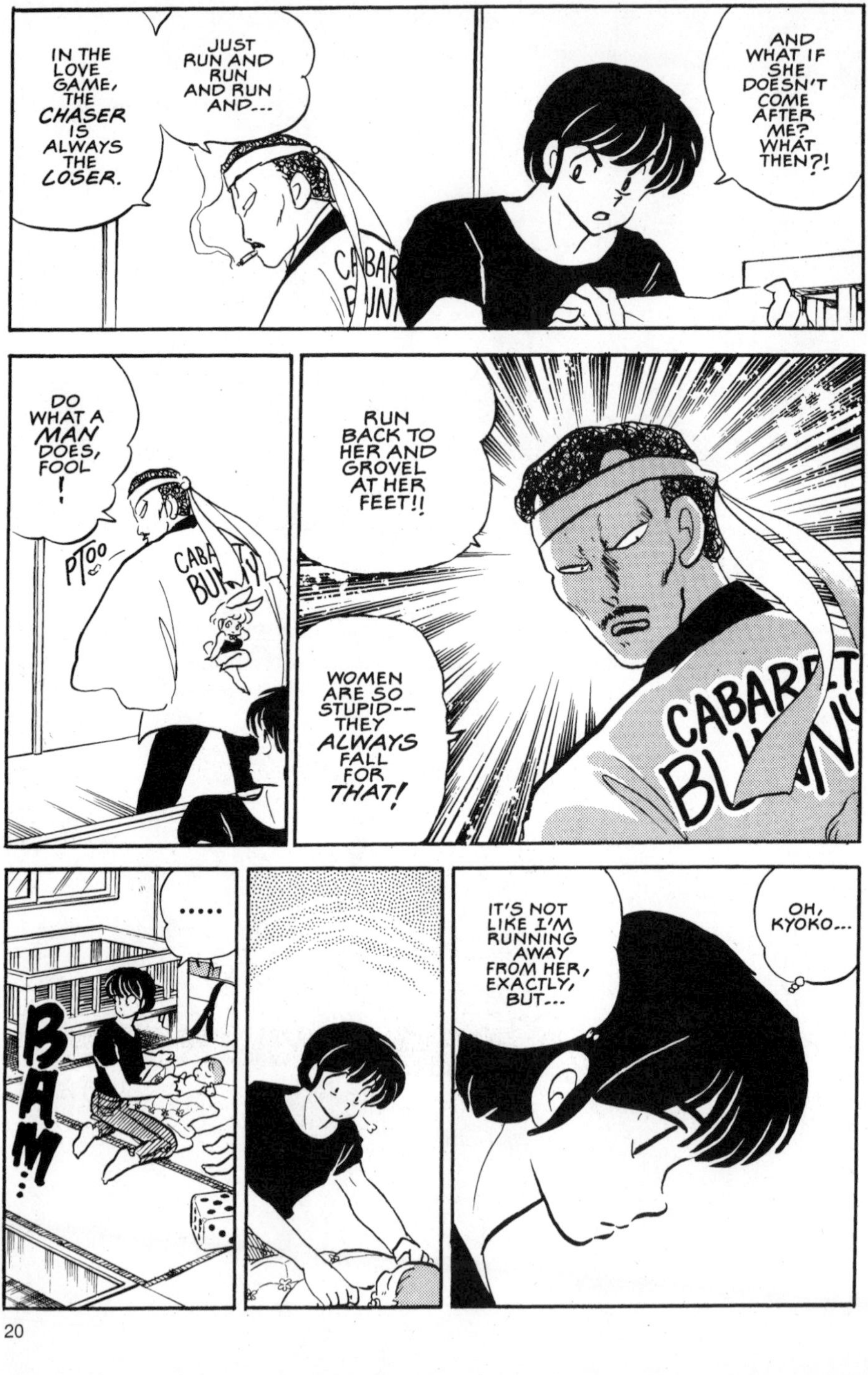
IN THE LOVE GAME, THE CHASER IS ALWAYS THE LOSER.
JUST RUN AND RUN AND RUN AND...
CABARET BUNNY
AND WHAT IF SHE DOESN'T COME AFTER ME? WHAT THEN?!
DO WHAT A MAN DOES, FOOL!
PTOO
CABARET BUNNY
RUN BACK TO HER AND GROVEL AT HER FEET!!
WOMEN ARE SO STUPID-- THEY ALWAYS FALL FOR THAT!
CABARET BUNNY
.....
BAM...
IT'S NOT LIKE I'M RUNNING AWAY FROM HER, EXACTLY, BUT...
OH, KYOKO...

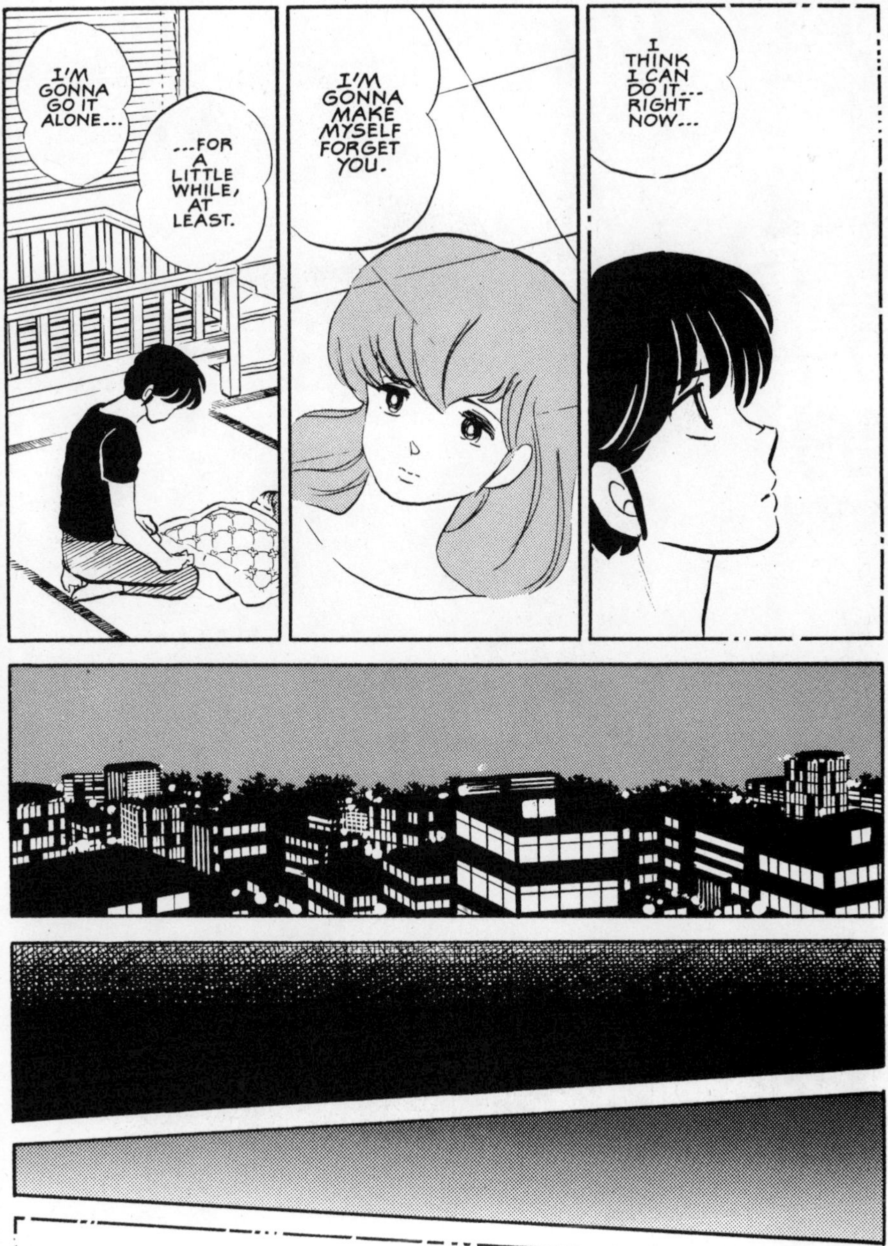
I'M GONNA GO IT ALONE...
...FOR A LITTLE WHILE, AT LEAST.
I'M GONNA MAKE MYSELF FORGET YOU.
I THINK I CAN DO IT... RIGHT NOW...

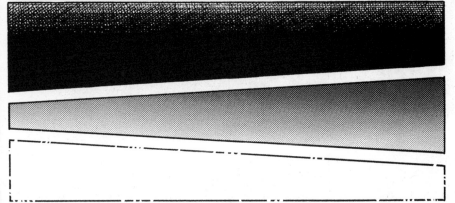

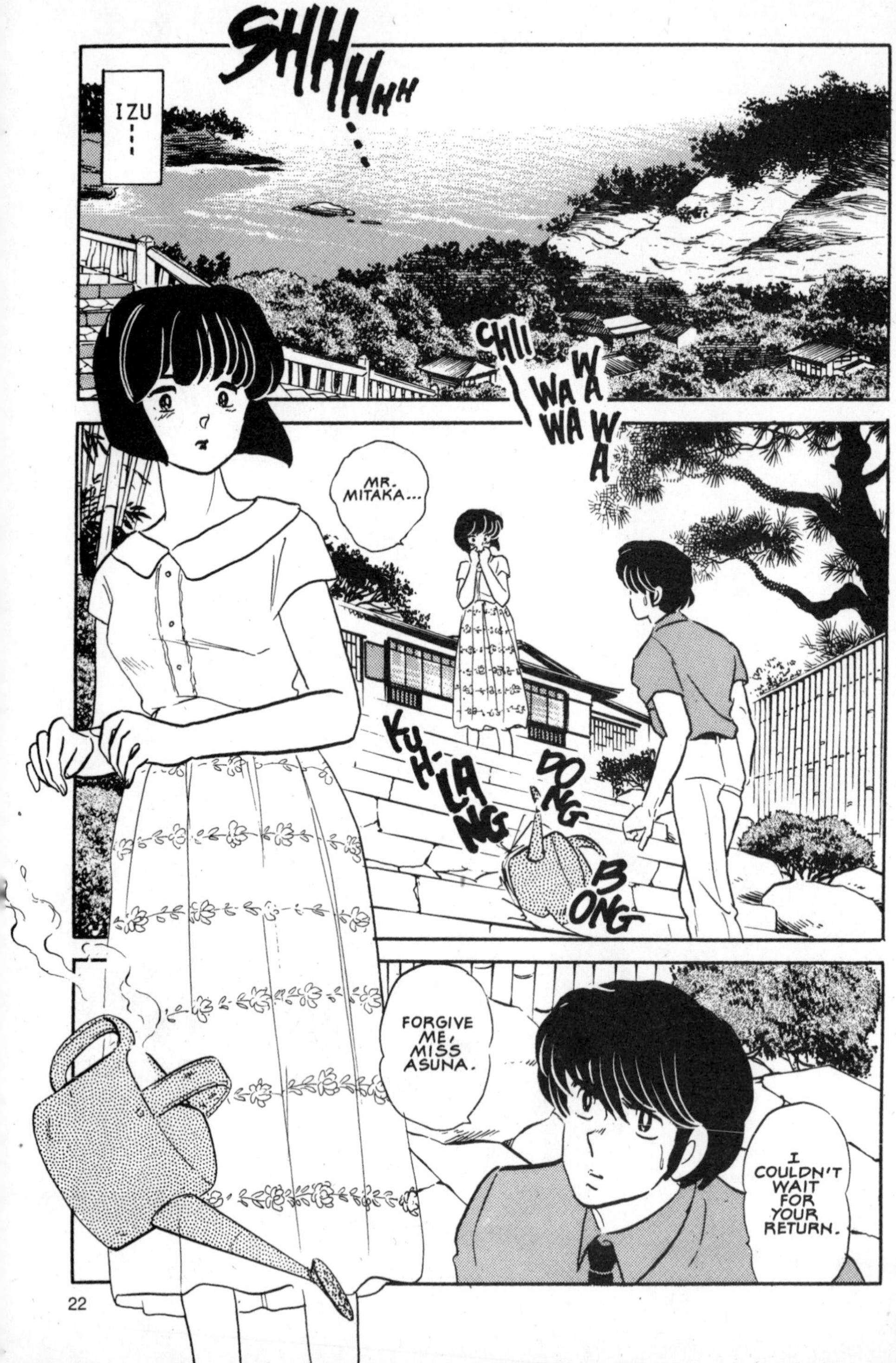

SHHHHHH
IZU...
CHII WA WA WA WA WA WA
MR. MITAKA...
KU-LIANG
DONG
BONG
FORGIVE ME, MISS ASUNA.
I COULDN'T WAIT FOR YOUR RETURN.

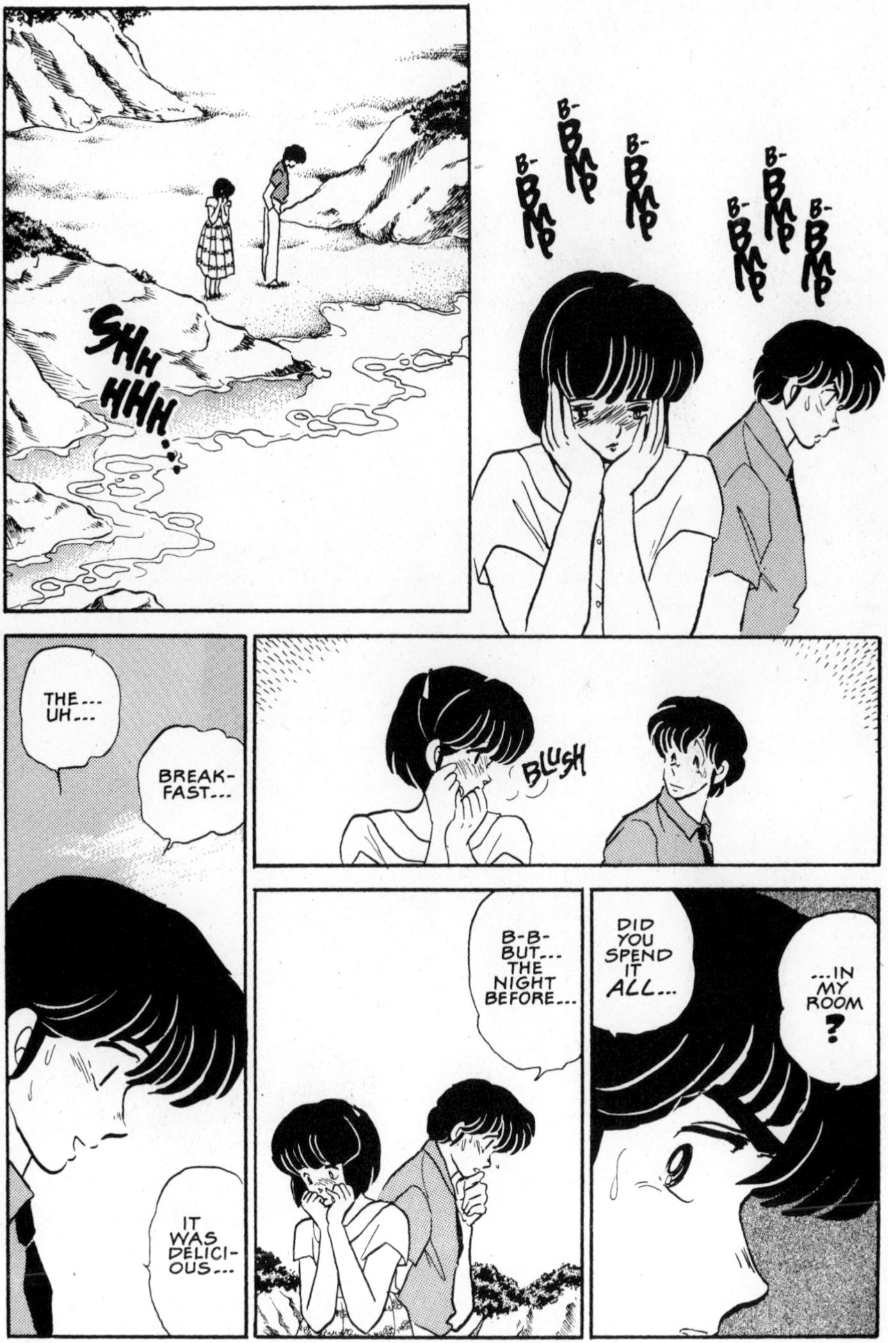
SHHHHH...
B-BMP
B-BMP
B-BMP
B-BMP
B-BMP
B-BMP
THE... UH...
BREAK-FAST...
BLUSH
IT WAS DELICI-OUS...
B-B-BUT... THE NIGHT BEFORE...
DID YOU SPEND IT ALL...
...IN MY ROOM ?

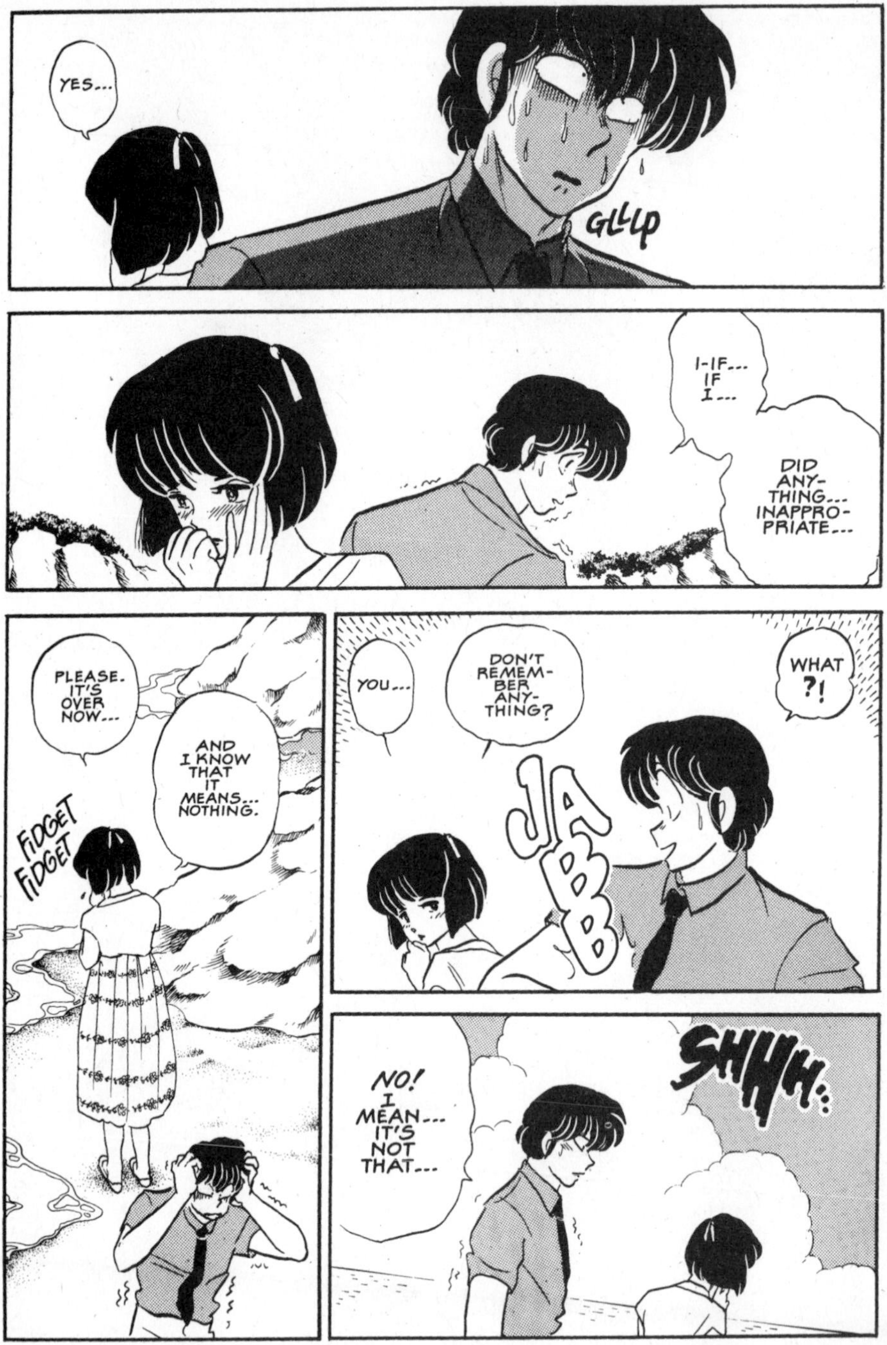
YES...
GLLLP
I-IF... IF I...
DID ANYTHING... INAPPROPRIATE...
PLEASE. IT'S OVER NOW...
AND I KNOW THAT IT MEANS... NOTHING.
FIDGET FIDGET
YOU...
DON'T REMEMBER ANYTHING?
WHAT ?!
JABB
NO! I MEAN... IT'S NOT THAT...
SHHH...

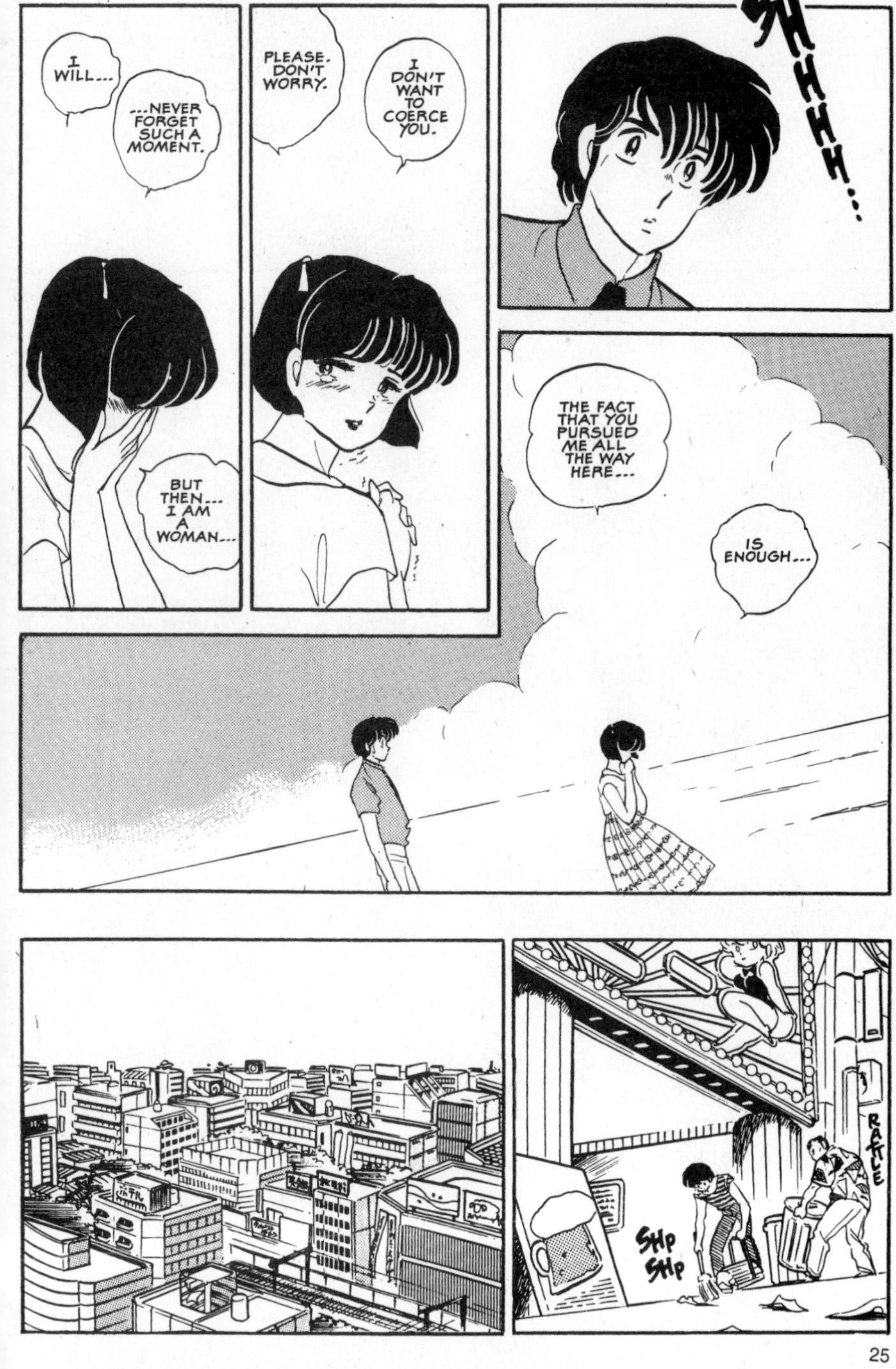
I WILL...
...NEVER FORGET SUCH A MOMENT.
BUT THEN... I AM A WOMAN...
PLEASE. DON'T WORRY.
I DON'T WANT TO COERCE YOU.
SHHHHH...
THE FACT THAT YOU PURSUED ME ALL THE WAY HERE...
IS ENOUGH...
RATTLE
SHP SHP

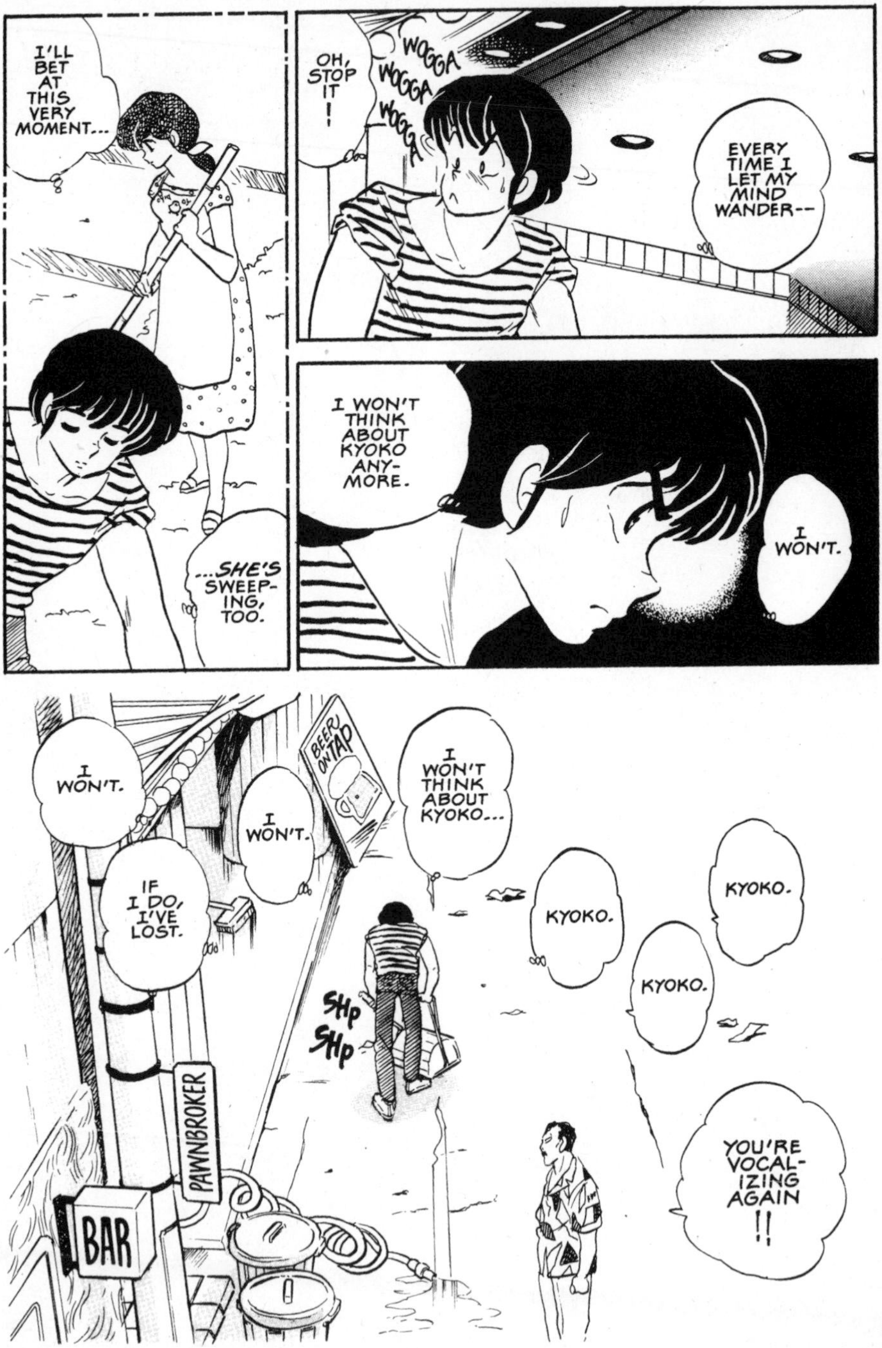
I'LL BET AT THIS VERY MOMENT...
...SHE'S SWEEPING, TOO.
OH, STOP IT!
WOGGA WOGGA WOGGA
EVERY TIME I LET MY MIND WANDER--
I WON'T THINK ABOUT KYOKO ANYMORE.
I WON'T.
I WON'T.
IF I DO, I'VE LOST.
BEER ON TAP
I WON'T.
I WON'T THINK ABOUT KYOKO...
BAR
PAWNBROKER
SHp SHp
KYOKO.
KYOKO.
KYOKO.
YOU'RE VOCALIZING AGAIN!!

PART TWO
THANKS...FOR EVERYTHING

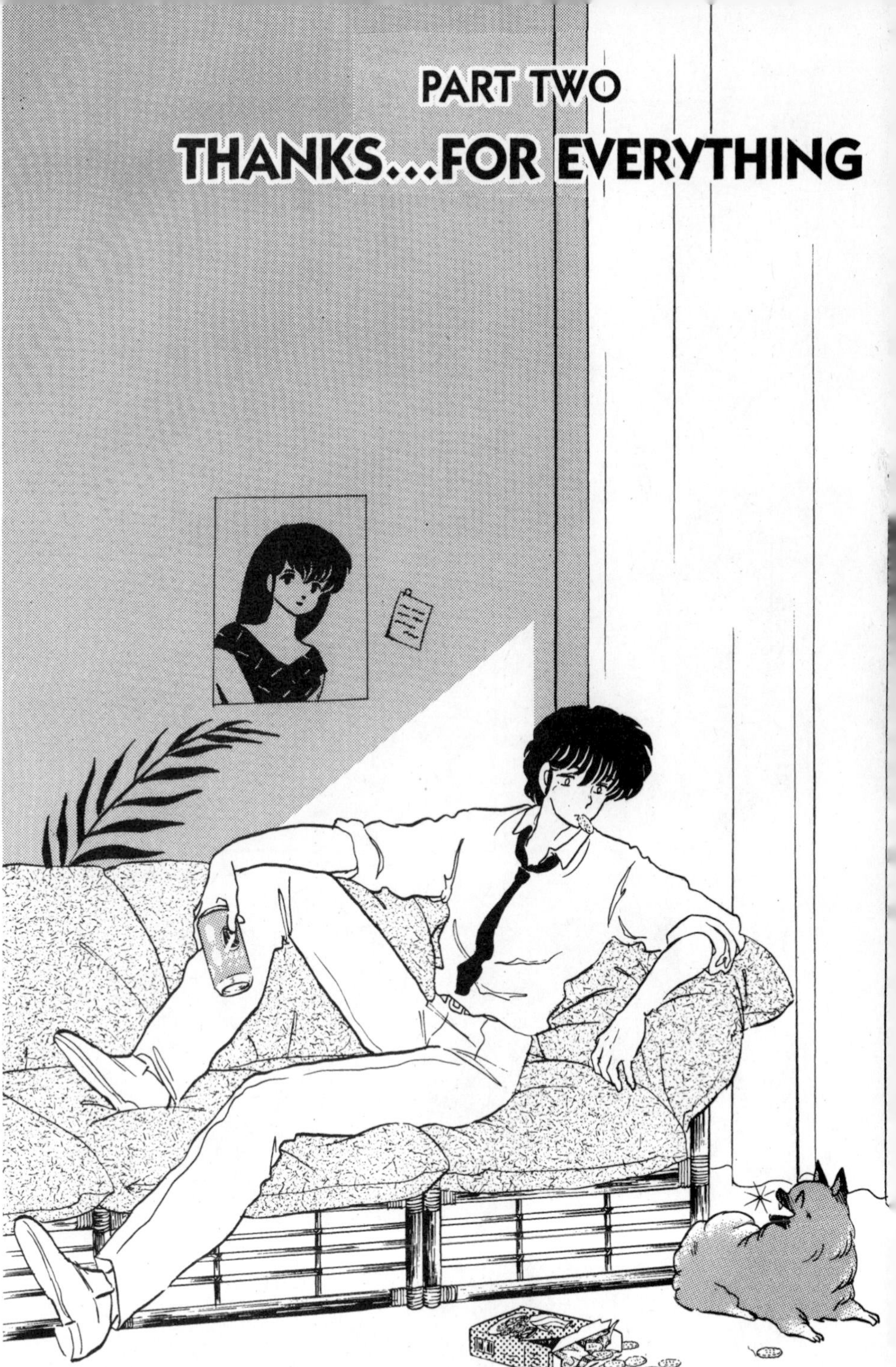

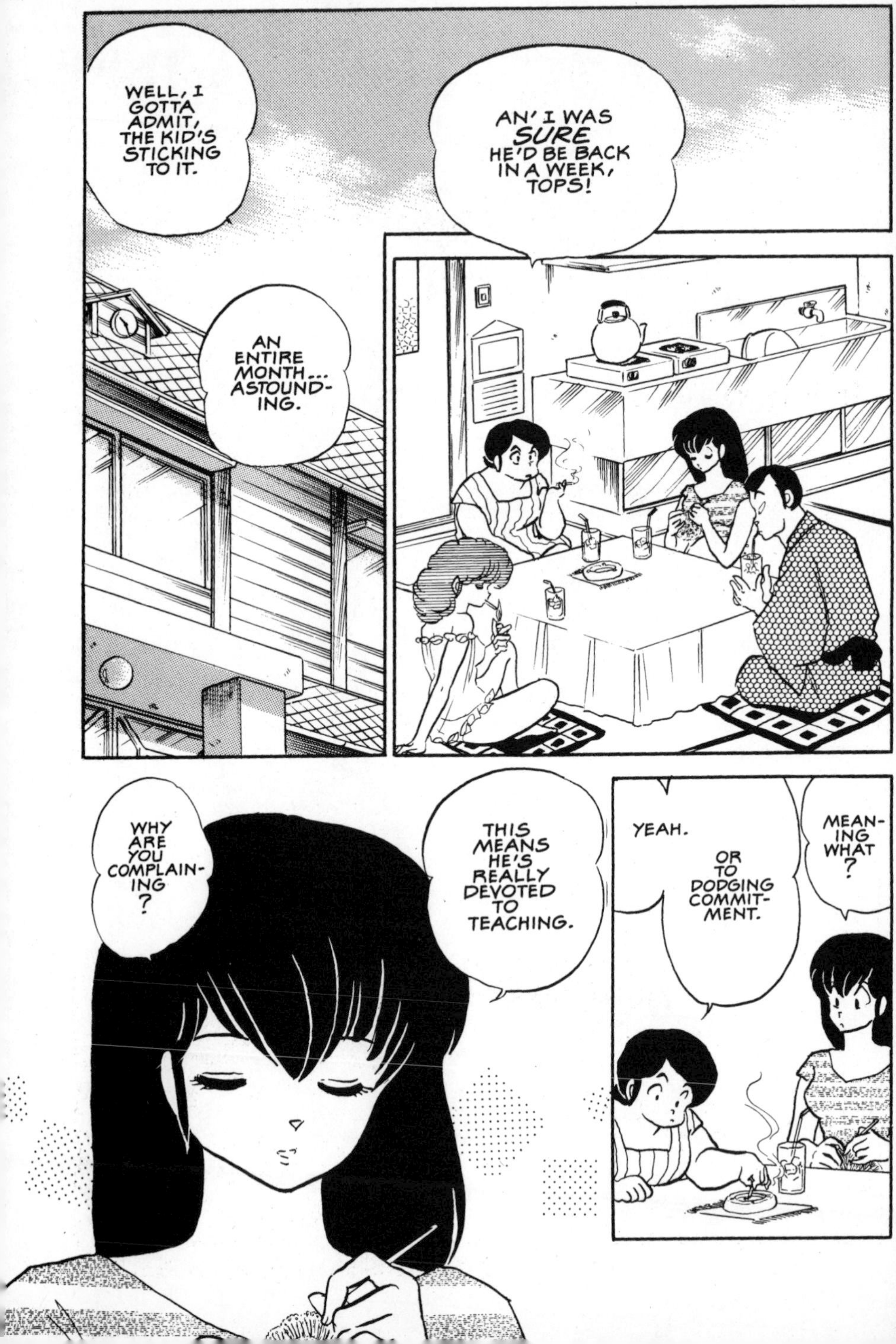
WELL, I GOTTA ADMIT, THE KID'S STICKING TO IT.
AN' I WAS *SURE* HE'D BE BACK IN A WEEK, TOPS!
AN ENTIRE MONTH... ASTOUNDING.
WHY ARE YOU COMPLAINING?
THIS MEANS HE'S REALLY DEVOTED TO TEACHING.
YEAH.
OR TO DODGING COMMITMENT.
MEANING WHAT?

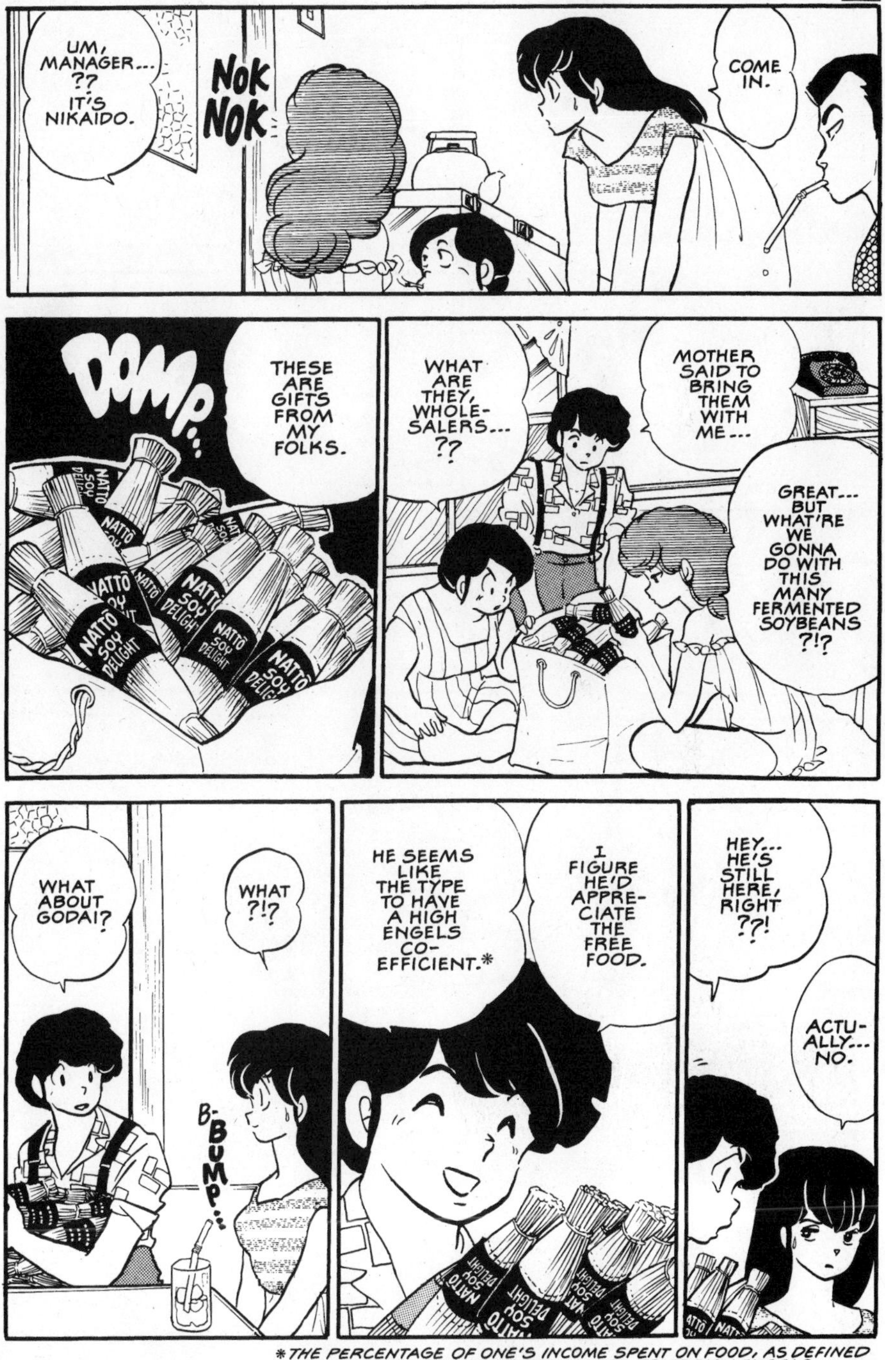
UM, MANAGER... ?? IT'S NIKAIDO.
NOK NOK
COME IN.
DOMP...
NATTŌ SOY DELIGHT
THESE ARE GIFTS FROM MY FOLKS.
WHAT ARE THEY, WHOLE-SALERS... ??
MOTHER SAID TO BRING THEM WITH ME...
GREAT... BUT WHAT'RE WE GONNA DO WITH THIS MANY FERMENTED SOYBEANS ?!?
WHAT ABOUT GODAI?
WHAT ?!?
B-BUMP...
HE SEEMS LIKE THE TYPE TO HAVE A HIGH ENGELS CO-EFFICIENT.*
I FIGURE HE'D APPRE-CIATE THE FREE FOOD.
HEY... HE'S STILL HERE, RIGHT ??!
ACTU-ALLY... NO.

*THE PERCENTAGE OF ONE'S INCOME SPENT ON FOOD, AS DEFINED BY THE GREAT SOCIALIST ECONOMIST, FRIEDRICH ENGELS.

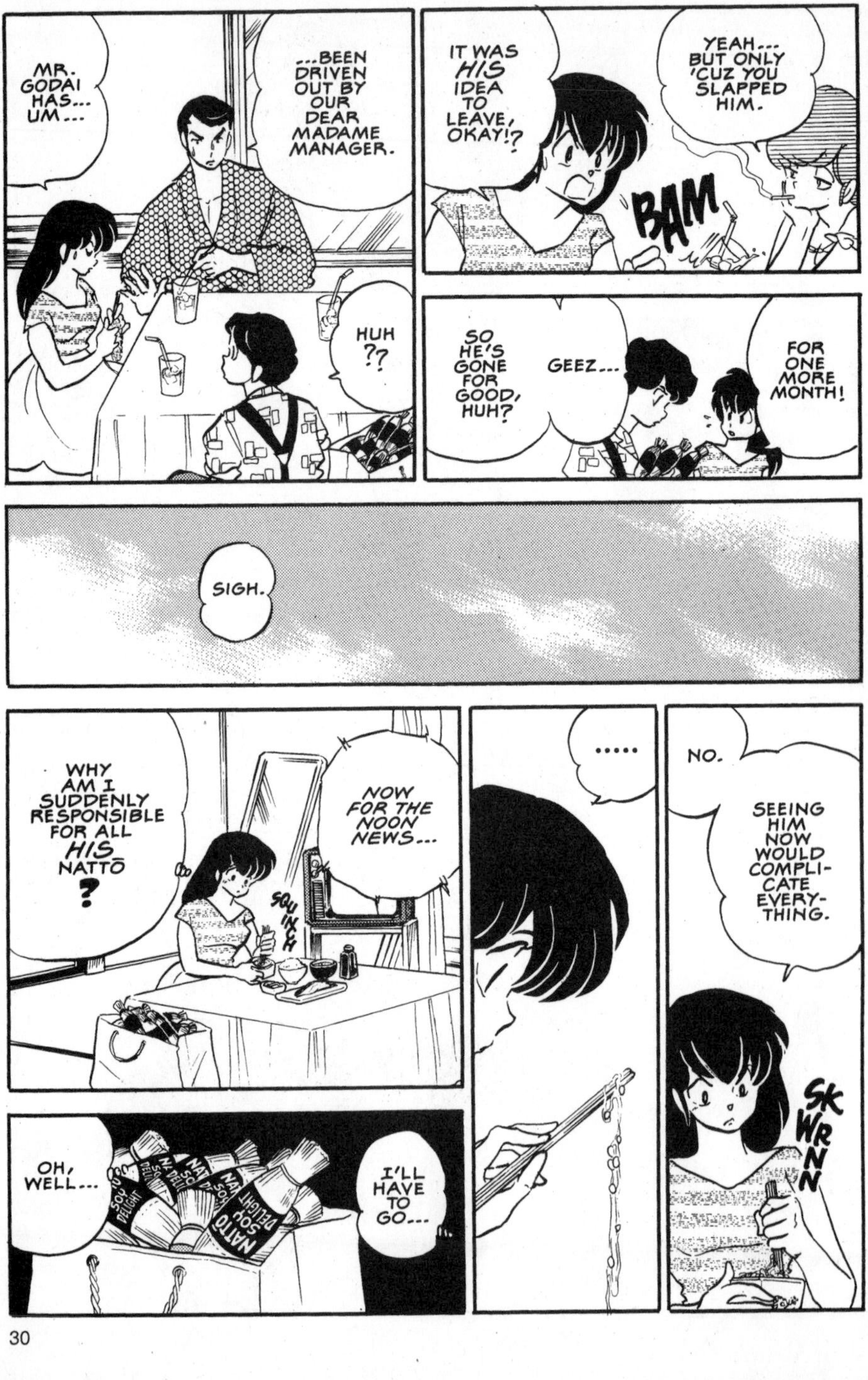
MR. GODAI HAS... UM...
...BEEN DRIVEN OUT BY OUR DEAR MADAME MANAGER.
HUH ??
IT WAS *HIS* IDEA TO LEAVE, OKAY!?
YEAH... BUT ONLY 'CUZ YOU SLAPPED HIM.
BAM
SO HE'S GONE FOR GOOD, HUH?
GEEZ...
FOR ONE MORE MONTH!
SIGH.
WHY AM I SUDDENLY RESPONSIBLE FOR ALL *HIS* NATTŌ ?
NOW FOR THE NOON NEWS...
SQUINCH
OH, WELL...
NATTŌ SOY DELIGHT
I'LL HAVE TO GO...
.....
NO.
SEEING HIM NOW WOULD COMPLICATE EVERYTHING.
SKWRNN

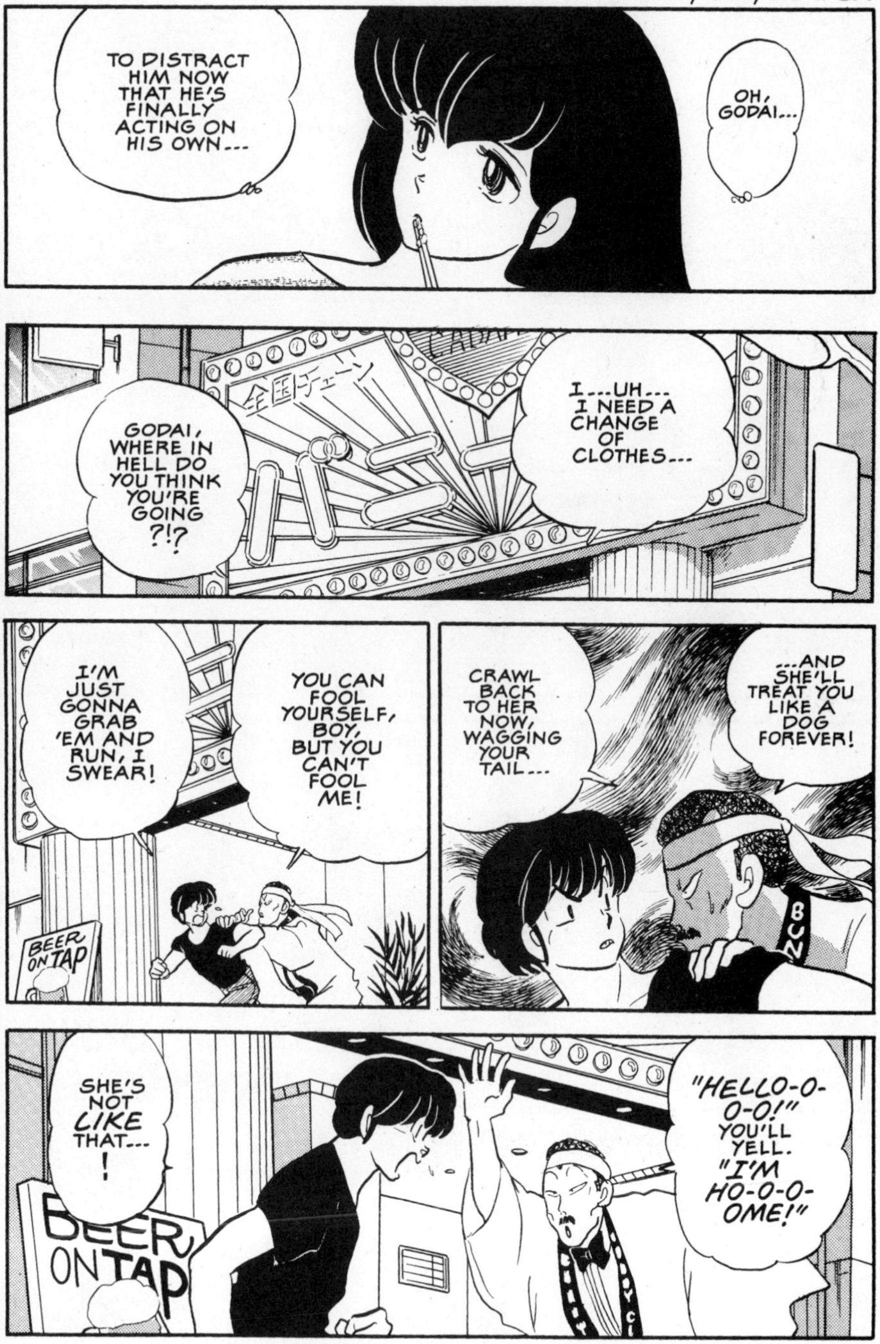
TO DISTRACT HIM NOW THAT HE'S FINALLY ACTING ON HIS OWN...
OH, GODAI...
全国チェーン
GODAI, WHERE IN HELL DO YOU THINK YOU'RE GOING ?!?
I...UH... I NEED A CHANGE OF CLOTHES...
I'M JUST GONNA GRAB 'EM AND RUN, I SWEAR!
YOU CAN FOOL YOURSELF, BOY, BUT YOU CAN'T FOOL ME!
BEER ON TAP
CRAWL BACK TO HER NOW, WAGGING YOUR TAIL...
...AND SHE'LL TREAT YOU LIKE A DOG FOREVER!
SHE'S NOT *LIKE* THAT...!
BEER ON TAP
"HELLO-O-O-O-O!" YOU'LL YELL. "I'M HO-O-O-OME!"

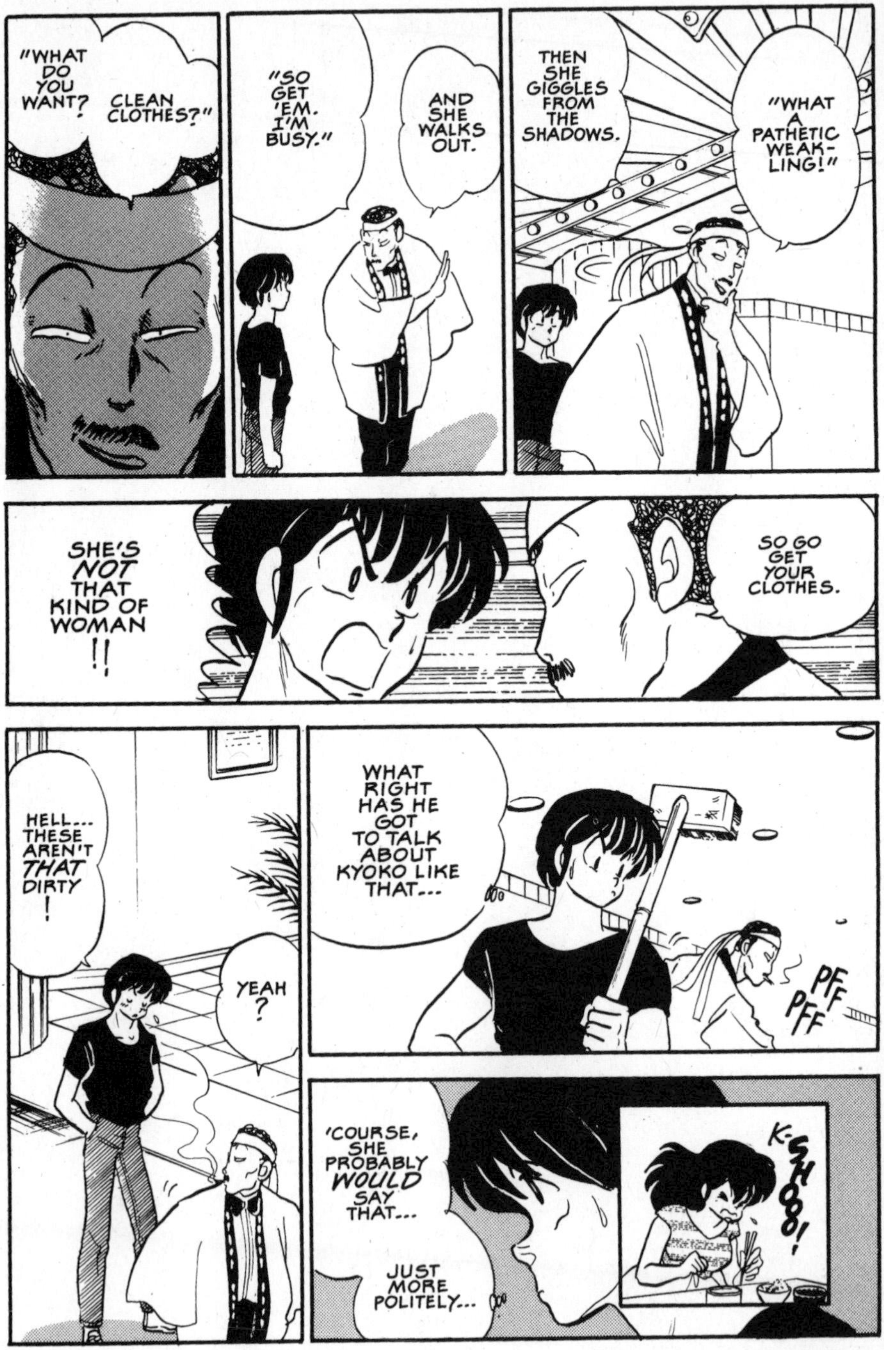
"WHAT DO YOU WANT? CLEAN CLOTHES?"
"SO GET 'EM. I'M BUSY."
AND SHE WALKS OUT.
THEN SHE GIGGLES FROM THE SHADOWS.
"WHAT A PATHETIC WEAK-LING!"
SHE'S *NOT* THAT KIND OF WOMAN !!
SO GO GET YOUR CLOTHES.
HELL... THESE AREN'T *THAT* DIRTY !
YEAH ?
WHAT RIGHT HAS HE GOT TO TALK ABOUT KYOKO LIKE THAT...
PFF PFF
'COURSE, SHE PROBABLY *WOULD* SAY THAT...
JUST MORE POLITELY...
K-SHOOO!

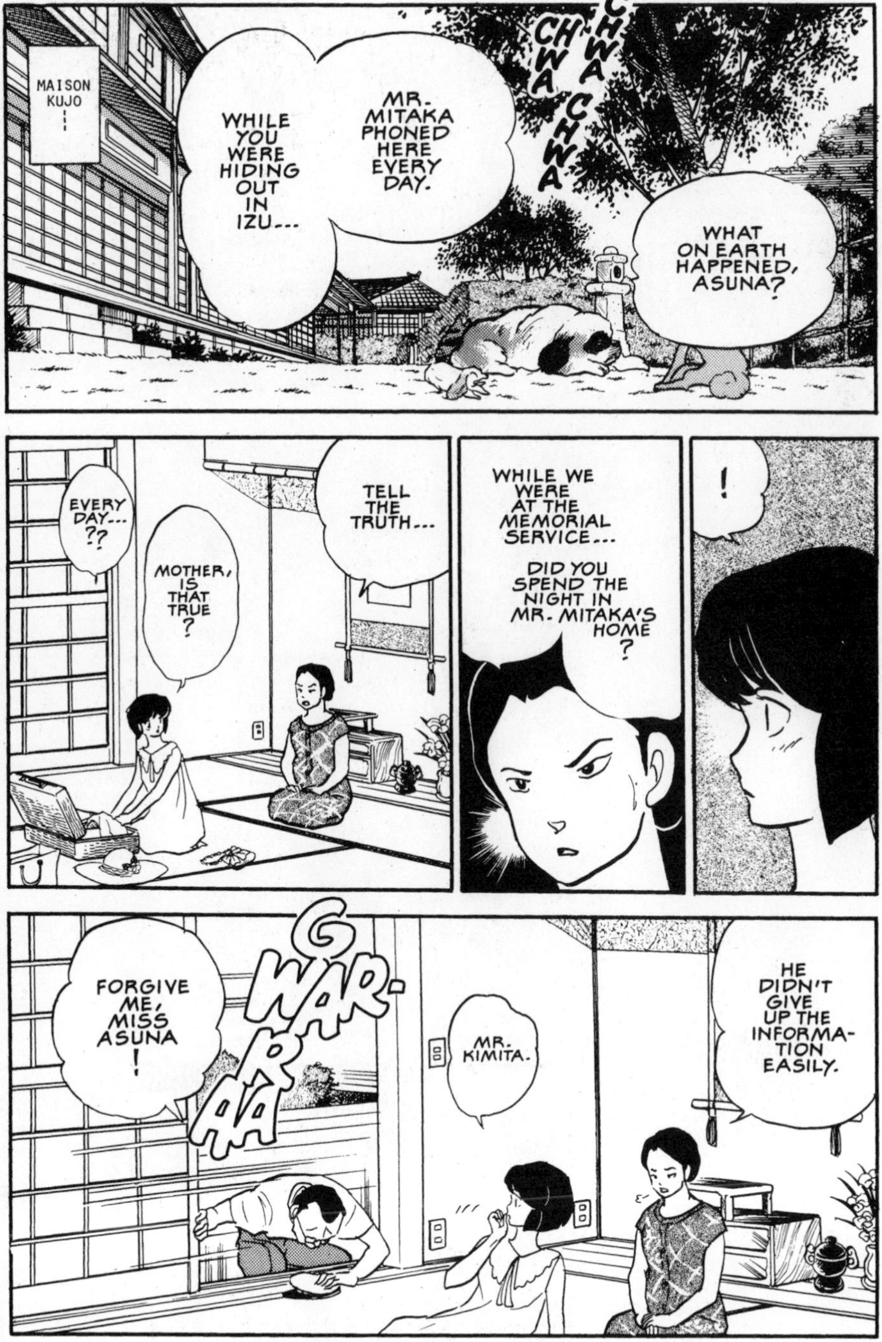
MAISON KUJO ...
WHILE YOU WERE HIDING OUT IN IZU...
MR. MITAKA PHONED HERE EVERY DAY.
CHWA CHWA CHWA CHWA
WHAT ON EARTH HAPPENED, ASUNA?
EVERY DAY...??
MOTHER, IS THAT TRUE?
TELL THE TRUTH...
WHILE WE WERE AT THE MEMORIAL SERVICE...
DID YOU SPEND THE NIGHT IN MR. MITAKA'S HOME?
!
FORGIVE ME, MISS ASUNA!
GWAR-RAA
MR. KIMITA.
HE DIDN'T GIVE UP THE INFORMATION EASILY.

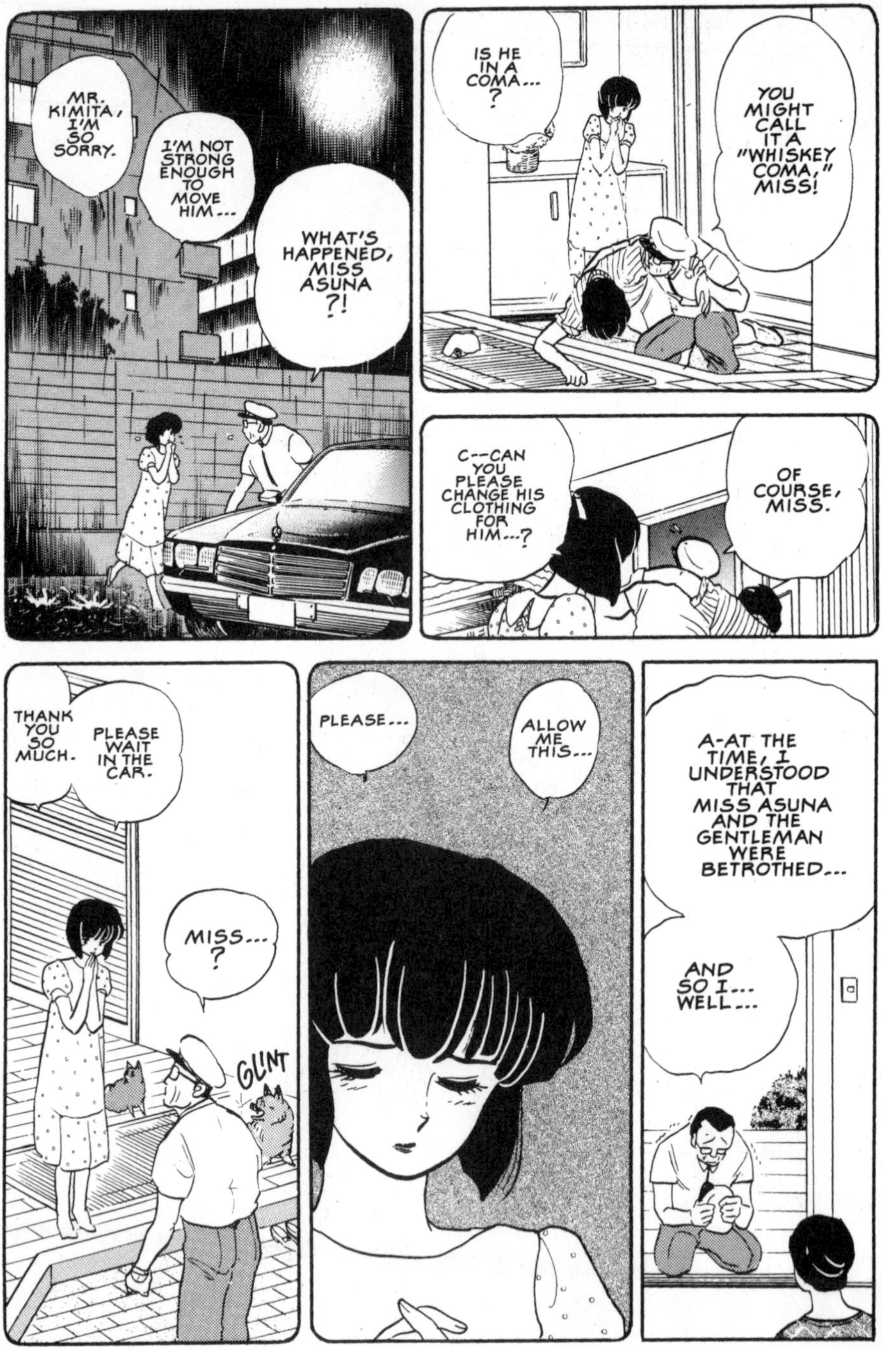
MR. KIMITA, I'M SO SORRY.
I'M NOT STRONG ENOUGH TO MOVE HIM...
WHAT'S HAPPENED, MISS ASUNA ?!
IS HE IN A COMA... ?
YOU MIGHT CALL IT A "WHISKEY COMA," MISS!
C--CAN YOU PLEASE CHANGE HIS CLOTHING FOR HIM...?
OF COURSE, MISS.
THANK YOU SO MUCH.
PLEASE WAIT IN THE CAR.
MISS... ?
GLINT
PLEASE...
ALLOW ME THIS...
A-AT THE TIME, I UNDERSTOOD THAT MISS ASUNA AND THE GENTLEMAN WERE BETROTHED...
AND SO I... WELL...

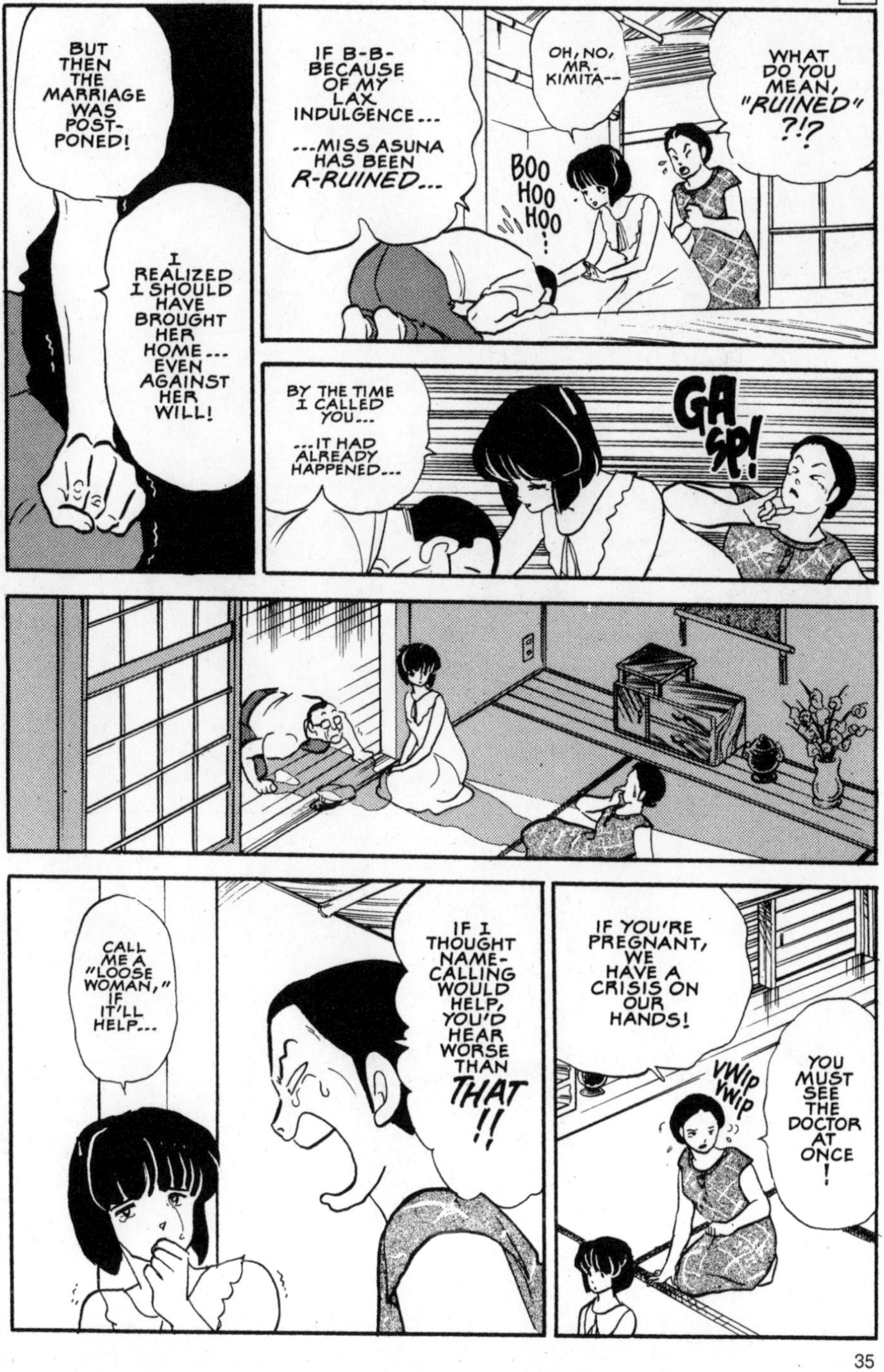
BUT THEN THE MARRIAGE WAS POST-PONED!
I REALIZED I SHOULD HAVE BROUGHT HER HOME... EVEN AGAINST HER WILL!
IF B-B-BECAUSE OF MY LAX INDULGENCE...
...MISS ASUNA HAS BEEN R-RUINED...
OH, NO, MR. KIMITA--
BOO HOO HOO
WHAT DO YOU MEAN, "RUINED" ?!?
BY THE TIME I CALLED YOU...
...IT HAD ALREADY HAPPENED...
GASP!
CALL ME A "LOOSE WOMAN," IF IT'LL HELP...
IF I THOUGHT NAME-CALLING WOULD HELP, YOU'D HEAR WORSE THAN THAT!!
IF YOU'RE PREGNANT, WE HAVE A CRISIS ON OUR HANDS!
VWIP VWIP
YOU MUST SEE THE DOCTOR AT ONCE!

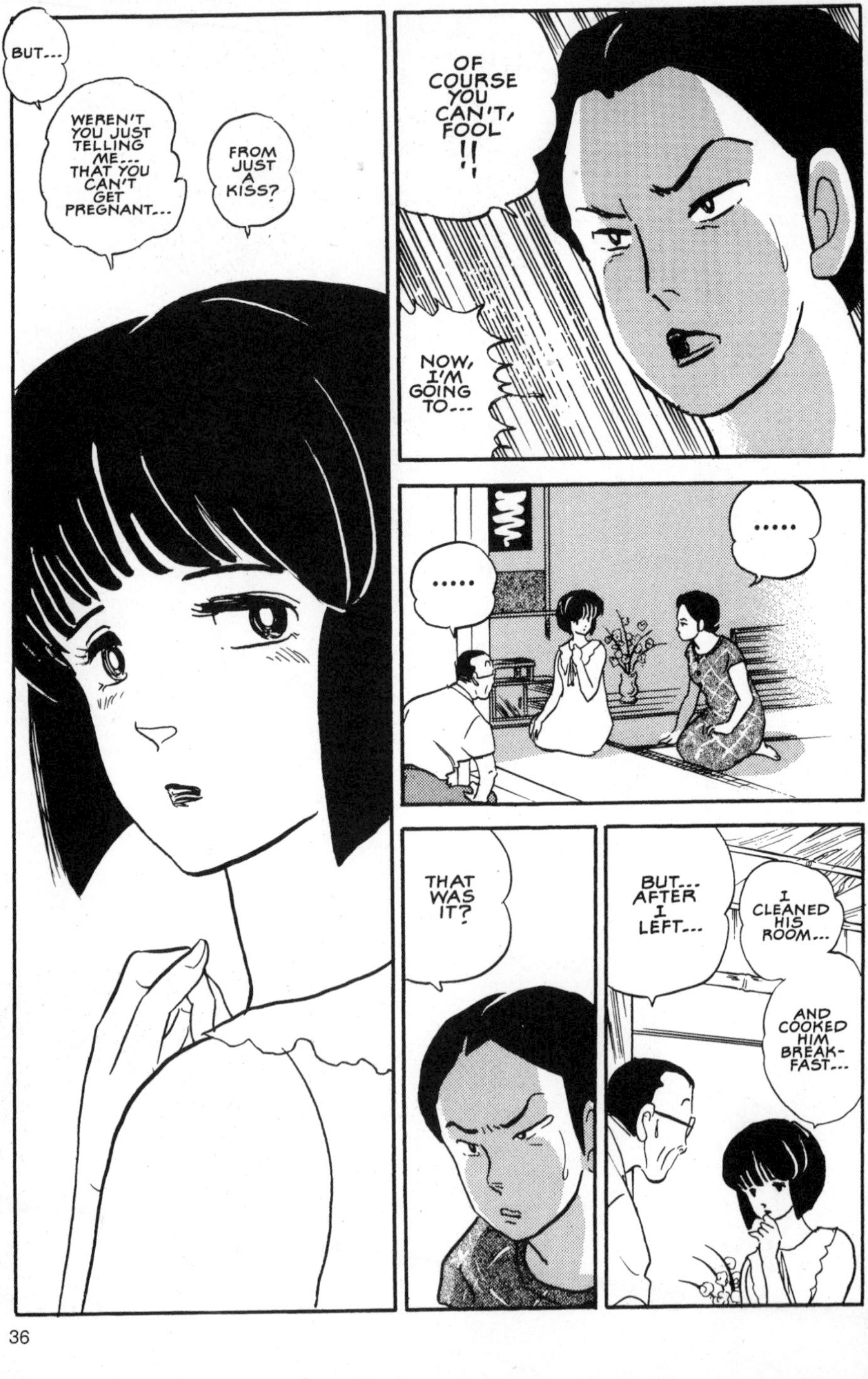
BUT...
WEREN'T YOU JUST TELLING ME... THAT YOU CAN'T GET PREGNANT...
FROM JUST A KISS?
OF COURSE YOU CAN'T, FOOL !!
NOW, I'M GOING TO...
......
......
THAT WAS IT?
BUT... AFTER I LEFT...
I CLEANED HIS ROOM...
AND COOKED HIM BREAK-FAST...

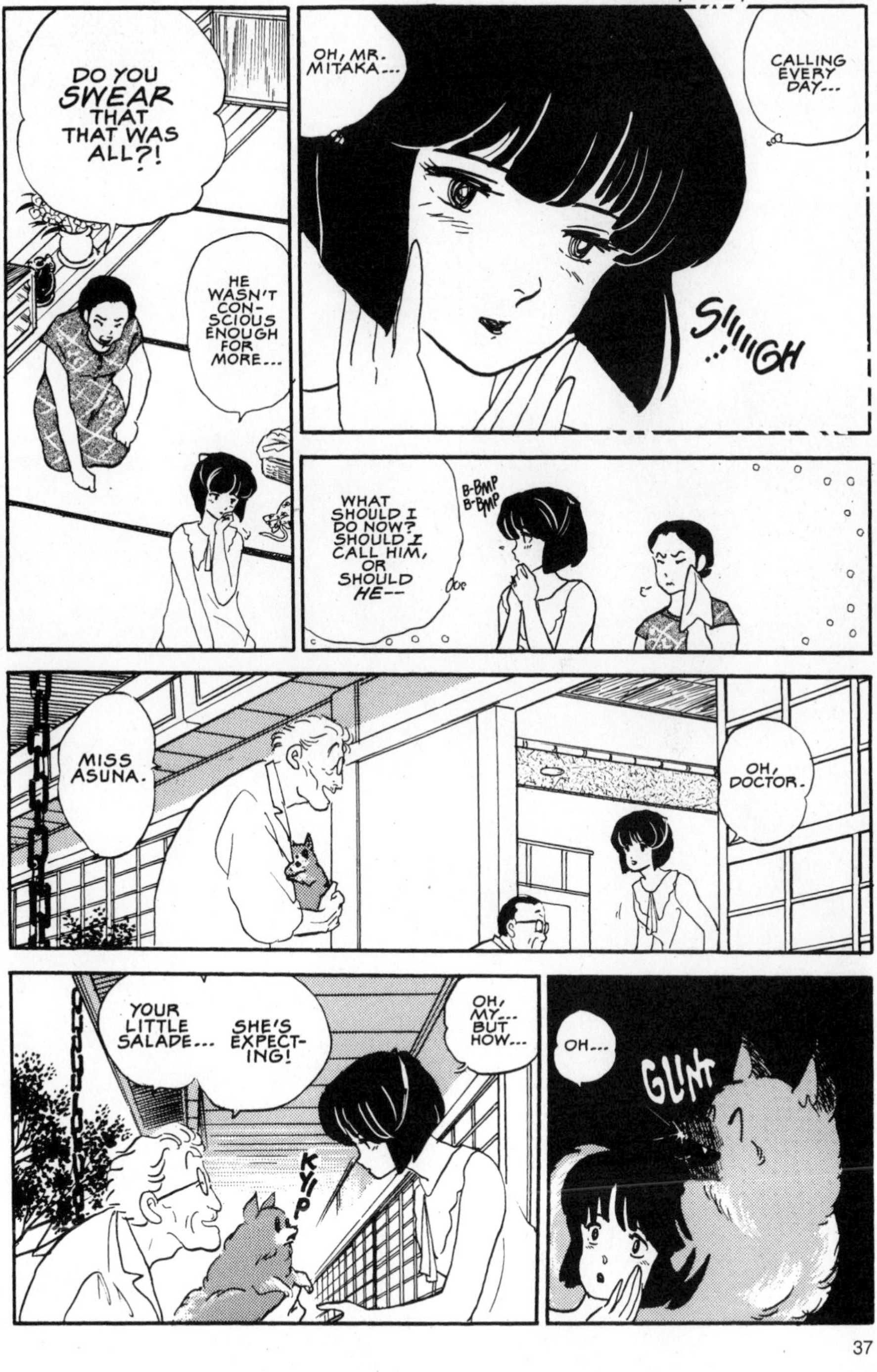
DO YOU SWEAR THAT THAT WAS ALL?!
HE WASN'T CON-SCIOUS ENOUGH FOR MORE...
OH, MR. MITAKA...
CALLING EVERY DAY...
SIIIIGH
WHAT SHOULD I DO NOW? SHOULD I CALL HIM, OR SHOULD HE--
B-BMP B-BMP
MISS ASUNA.
OH, DOCTOR.
YOUR LITTLE SALADE...
SHE'S EXPECT-ING!
KYIP
OH, MY... BUT HOW...
OH...
GLINT

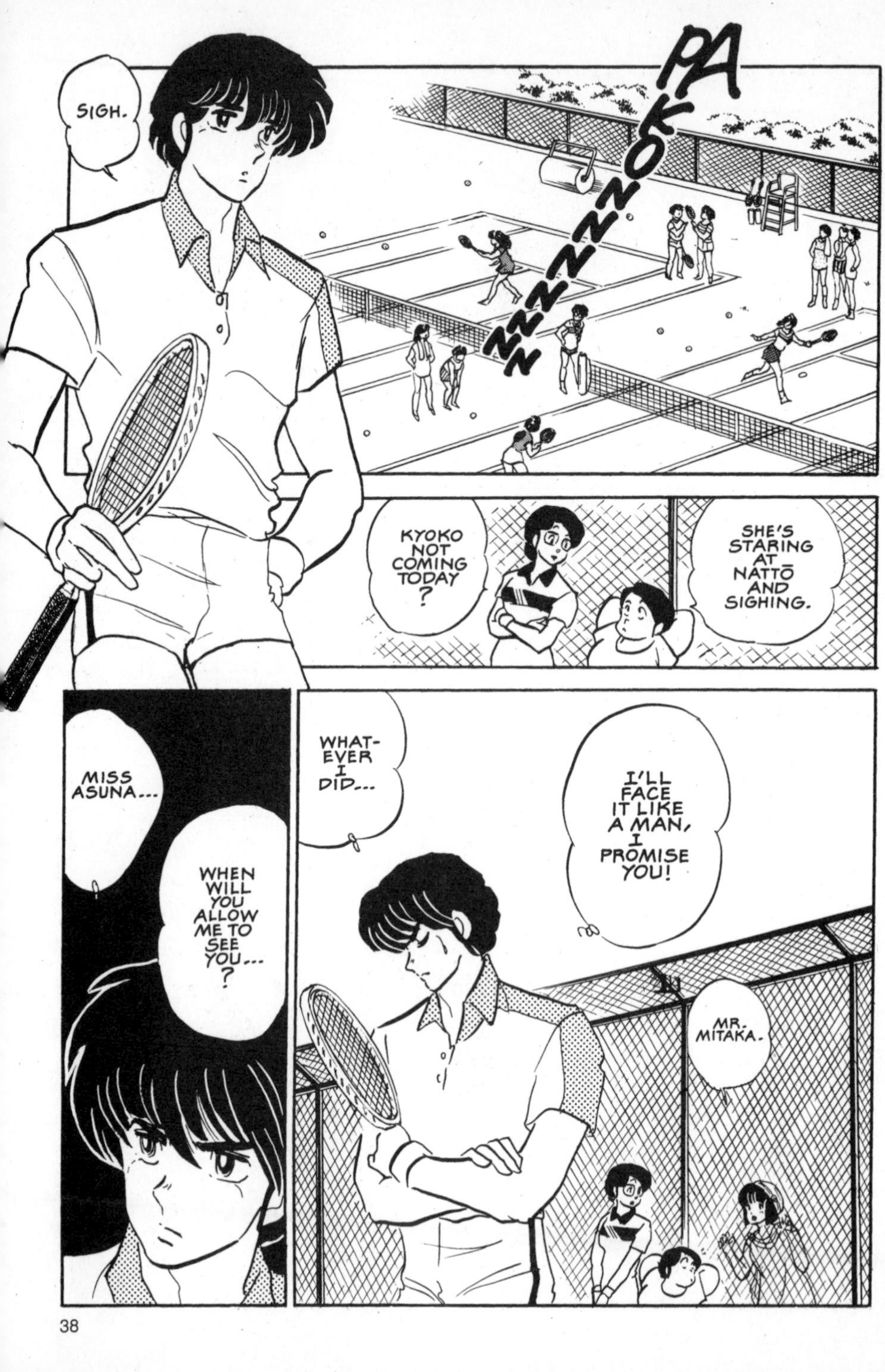
SIGH.
PAKONNNNNNNNN
KYOKO NOT COMING TODAY?
SHE'S STARING AT NATTŌ AND SIGHING.
MISS ASUNA...
WHEN WILL YOU ALLOW ME TO SEE YOU...?
WHAT-EVER I DID...
I'LL FACE IT LIKE A MAN, I PROMISE YOU!
MR. MITAKA.

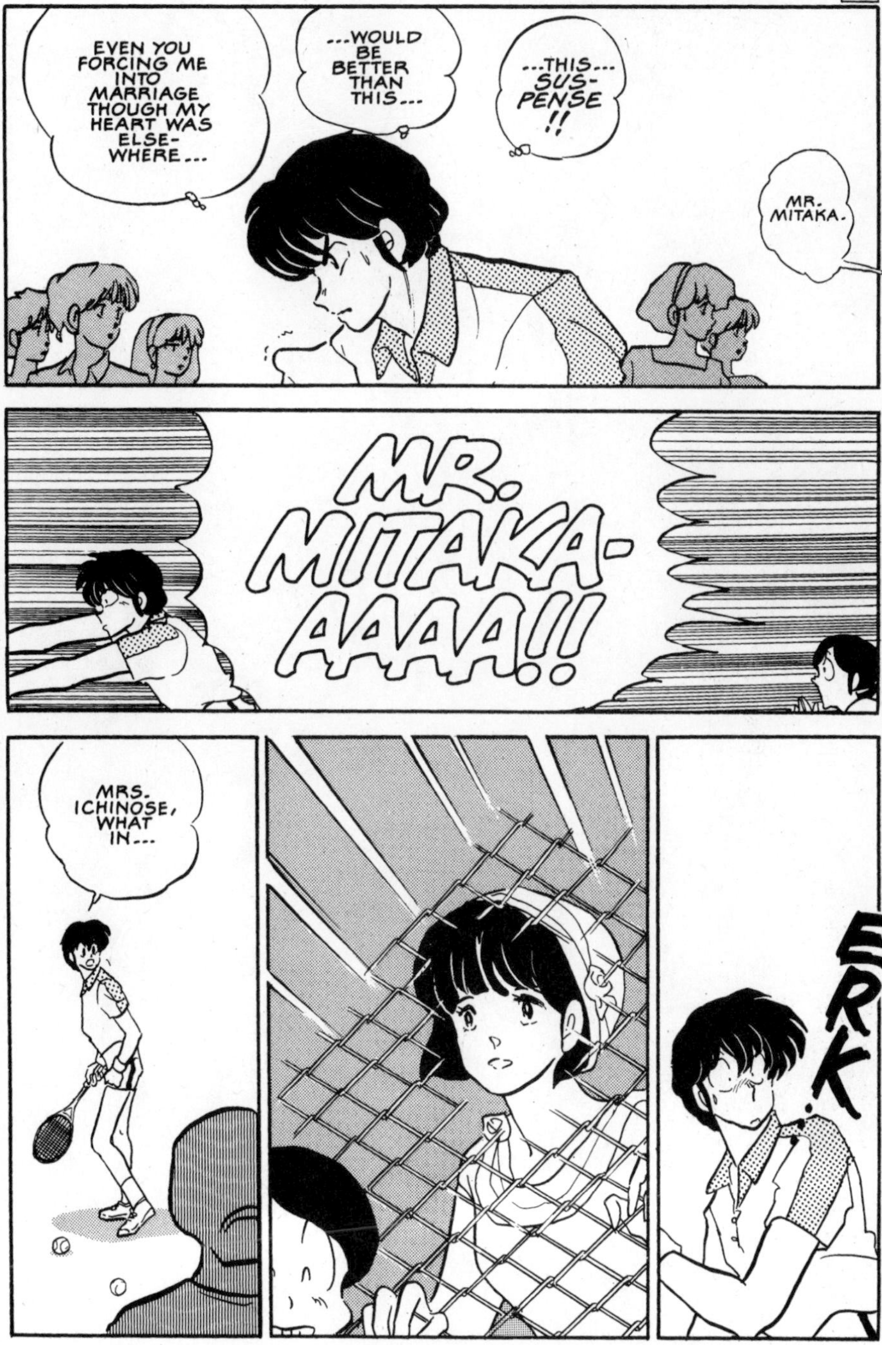
EVEN YOU FORCING ME INTO MARRIAGE THOUGH MY HEART WAS ELSE-WHERE...
...WOULD BE BETTER THAN THIS...
...THIS... SUS-PENSE !!
MR. MITAKA.
MR. MITAKA-AAAA!!
MRS. ICHINOSE, WHAT IN...
ERK

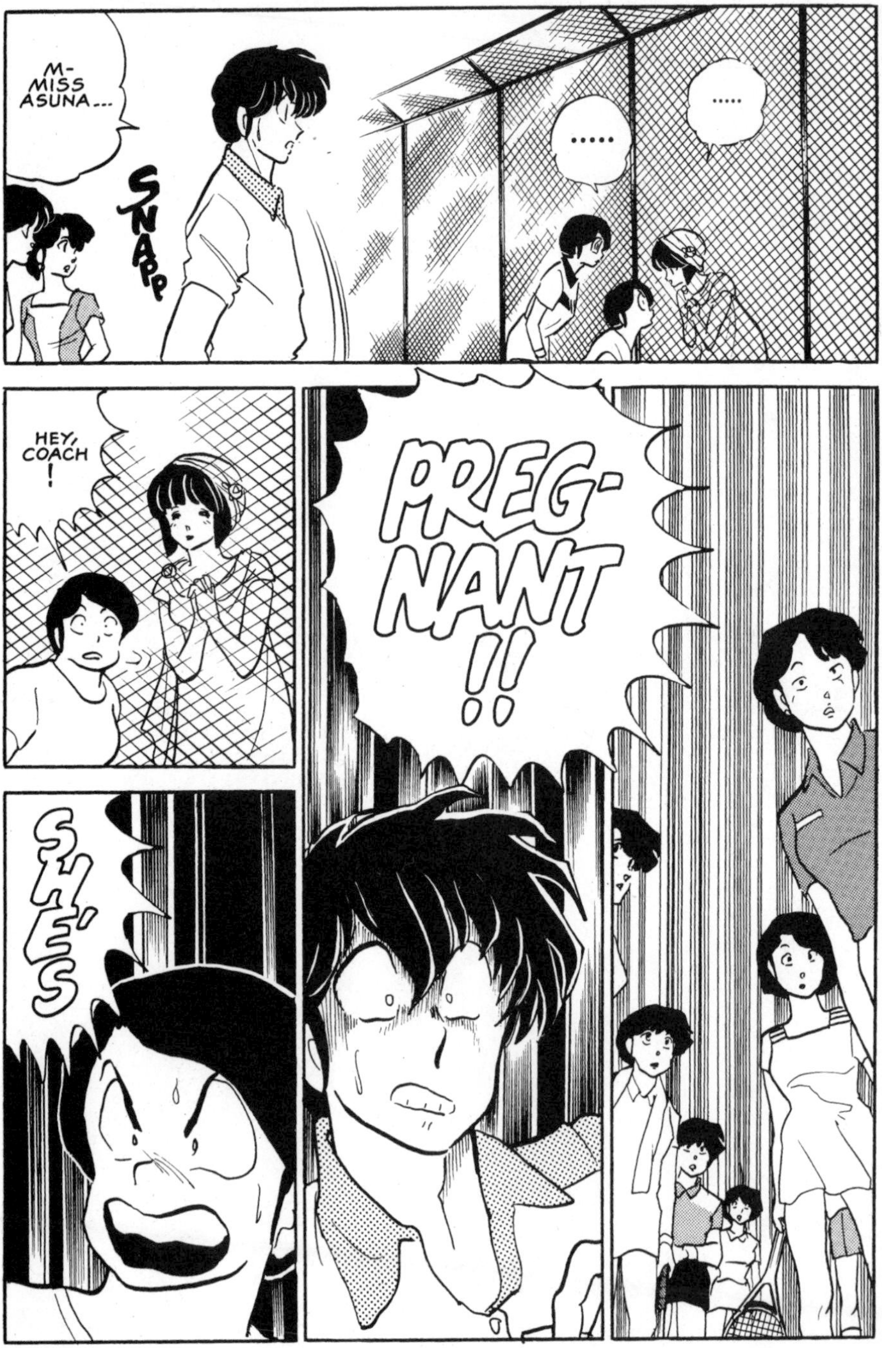
M-MISS ASUNA...
SNAPP
......
......
HEY, COACH!
SHE'S
PREG-NANT!!

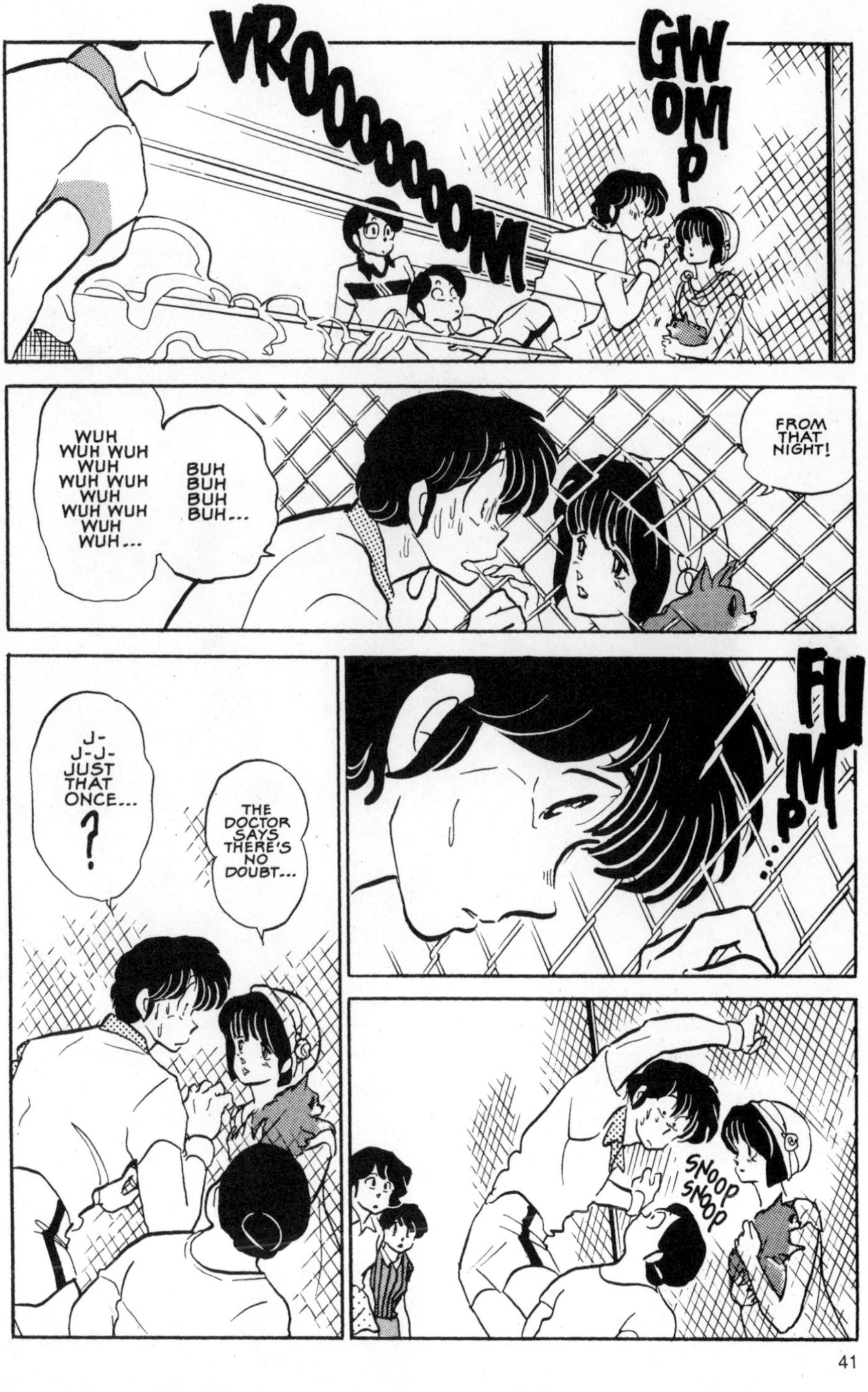
VROOOOOOOOOM
GWOMP
WUH WUH WUH WUH WUH WUH WUH WUH WUH WUH WUH... BUH BUH BUH BUH...
FROM THAT NIGHT!
J- J-J- JUST THAT ONCE... ?
THE DOCTOR SAYS THERE'S NO DOUBT...
FUMP
SNOOP SNOOP

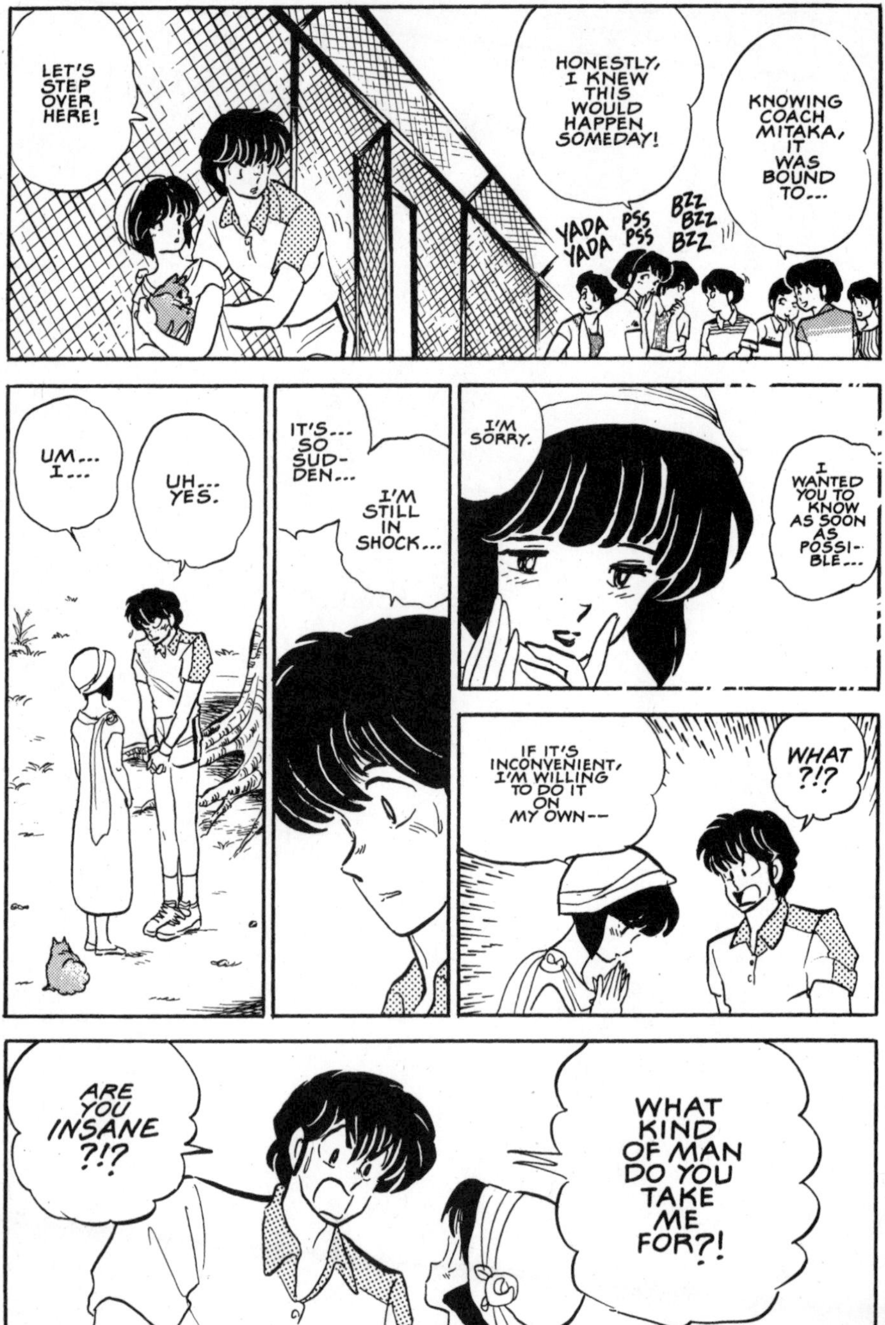

LET'S STEP OVER HERE!
HONESTLY, I KNEW THIS WOULD HAPPEN SOMEDAY!
YADA YADA
PSS PSS
BZZ BZZ BZZ
KNOWING COACH MITAKA, IT WAS BOUND TO...
UM... I...
UH... YES.
IT'S... SO SUD-DEN...
I'M STILL IN SHOCK...
I'M SORRY.
I WANTED YOU TO KNOW AS SOON AS POSSI-BLE...
IF IT'S INCONVENIENT, I'M WILLING TO DO IT ON MY OWN--
WHAT ?!?
ARE YOU INSANE ?!?
WHAT KIND OF MAN DO YOU TAKE ME FOR?!

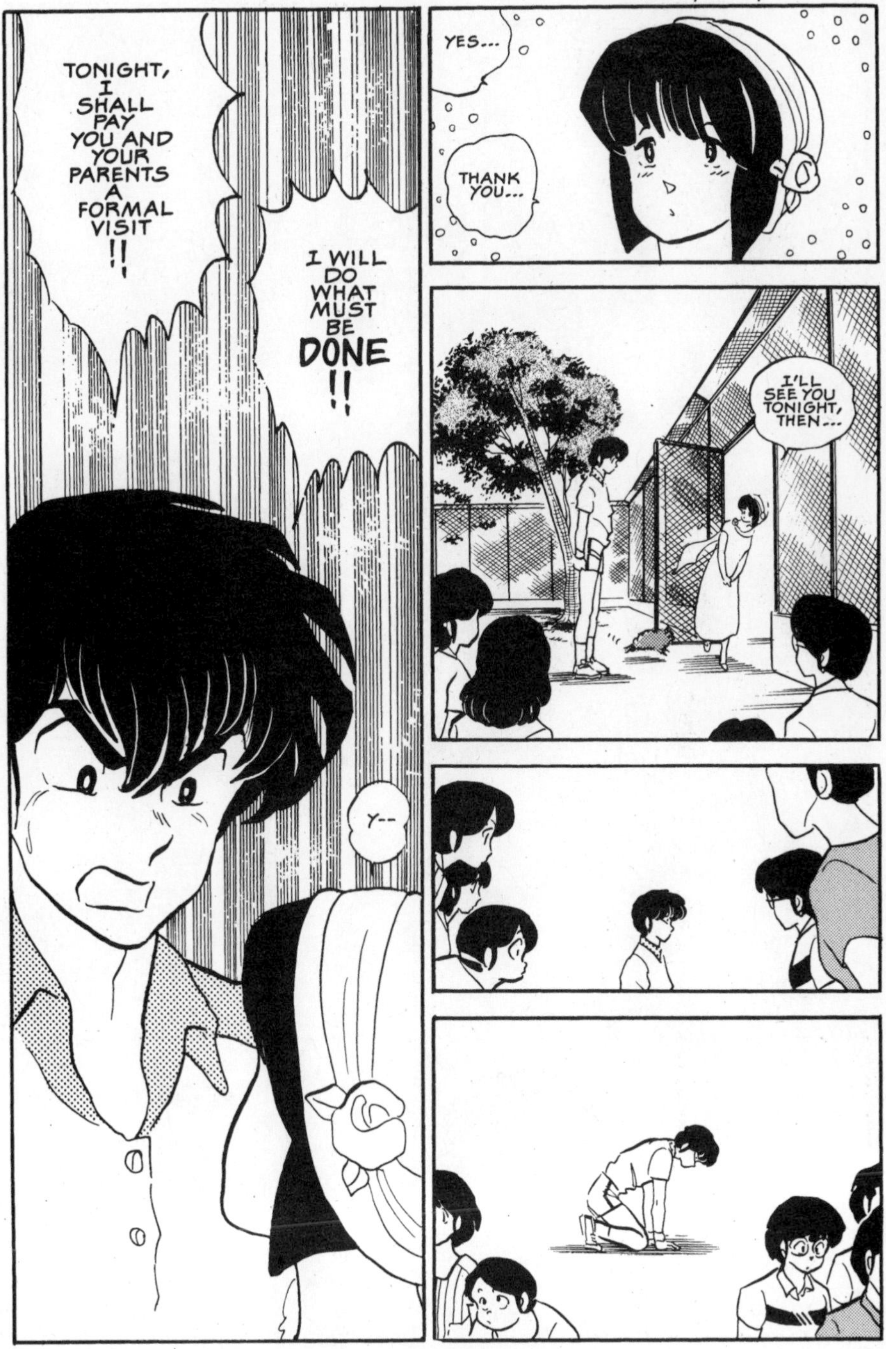
TONIGHT, I SHALL PAY YOU AND YOUR PARENTS A FORMAL VISIT !!
I WILL DO WHAT MUST BE DONE !!
Y--
YES...
THANK YOU...
I'LL SEE YOU TONIGHT, THEN...

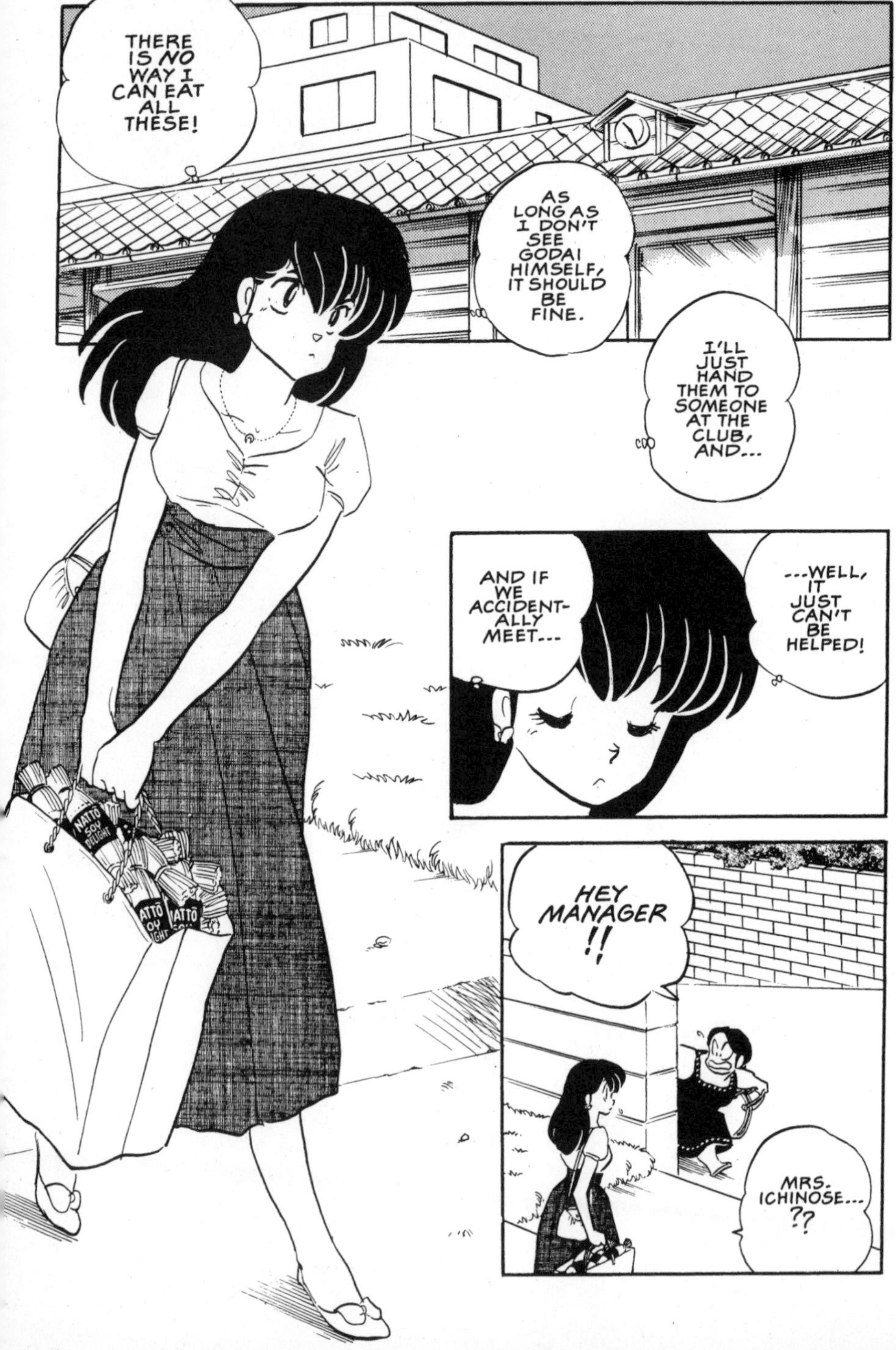
THERE IS NO WAY I CAN EAT ALL THESE!
AS LONG AS I DON'T SEE GODAI HIMSELF, IT SHOULD BE FINE.
I'LL JUST HAND THEM TO SOMEONE AT THE CLUB, AND...
NATTO SOY DELIGHT
AND IF WE ACCIDENT-ALLY MEET...
...WELL, IT JUST CAN'T BE HELPED!
HEY MANAGER !!
MRS. ICHINOSE... ??

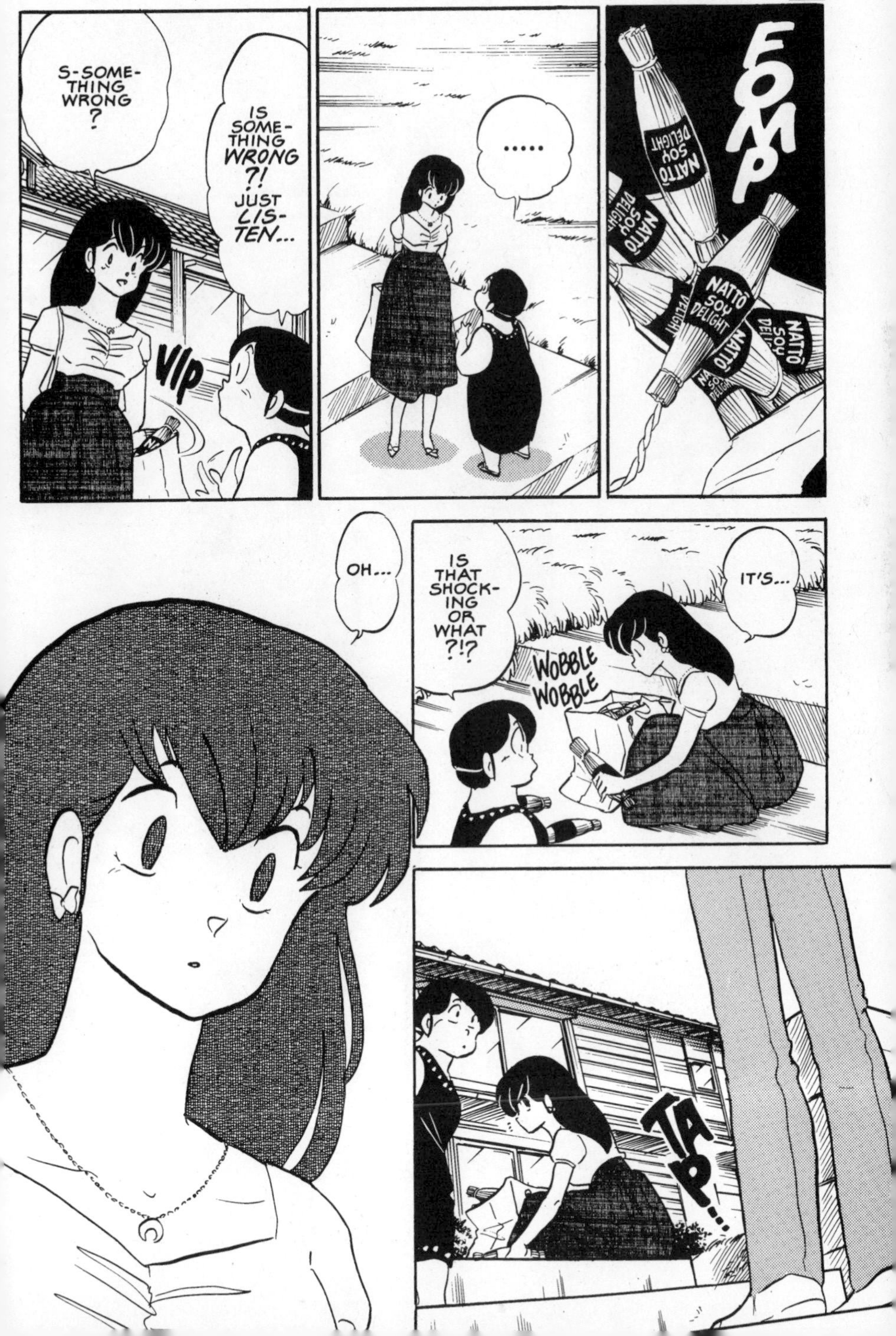
S-SOMETHING WRONG?
IS SOMETHING WRONG?! JUST LISTEN...
VIP
......
FOMP
NATTŌ SOY DELIGHT
OH...
IS THAT SHOCKING OR WHAT?!?
IT'S...
WOBBLE WOBBLE
TAP...

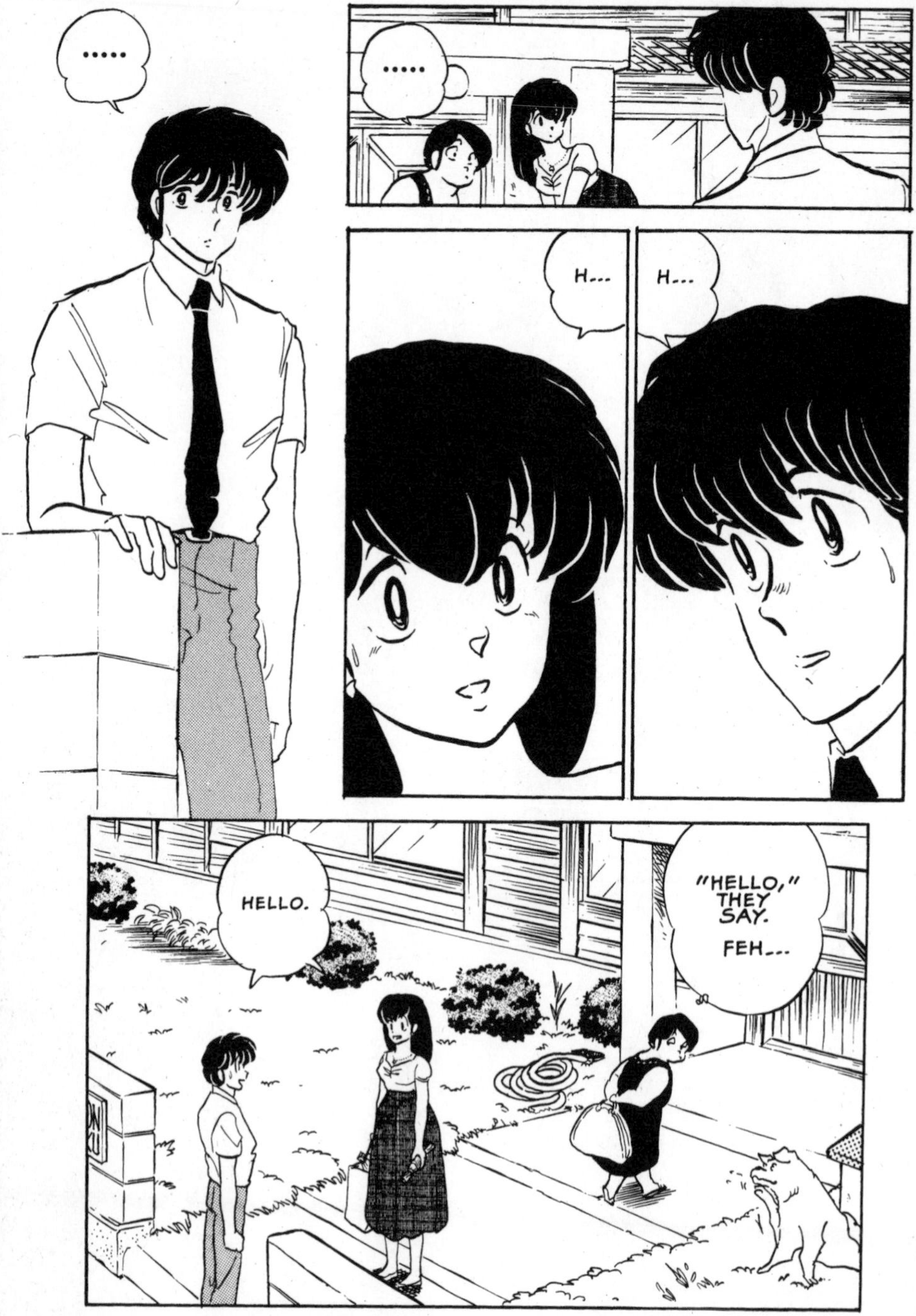
......
......
H...
H...
HELLO.
"HELLO," THEY SAY.
FEH...

PART THREE
THE HAPPINESS CURVE

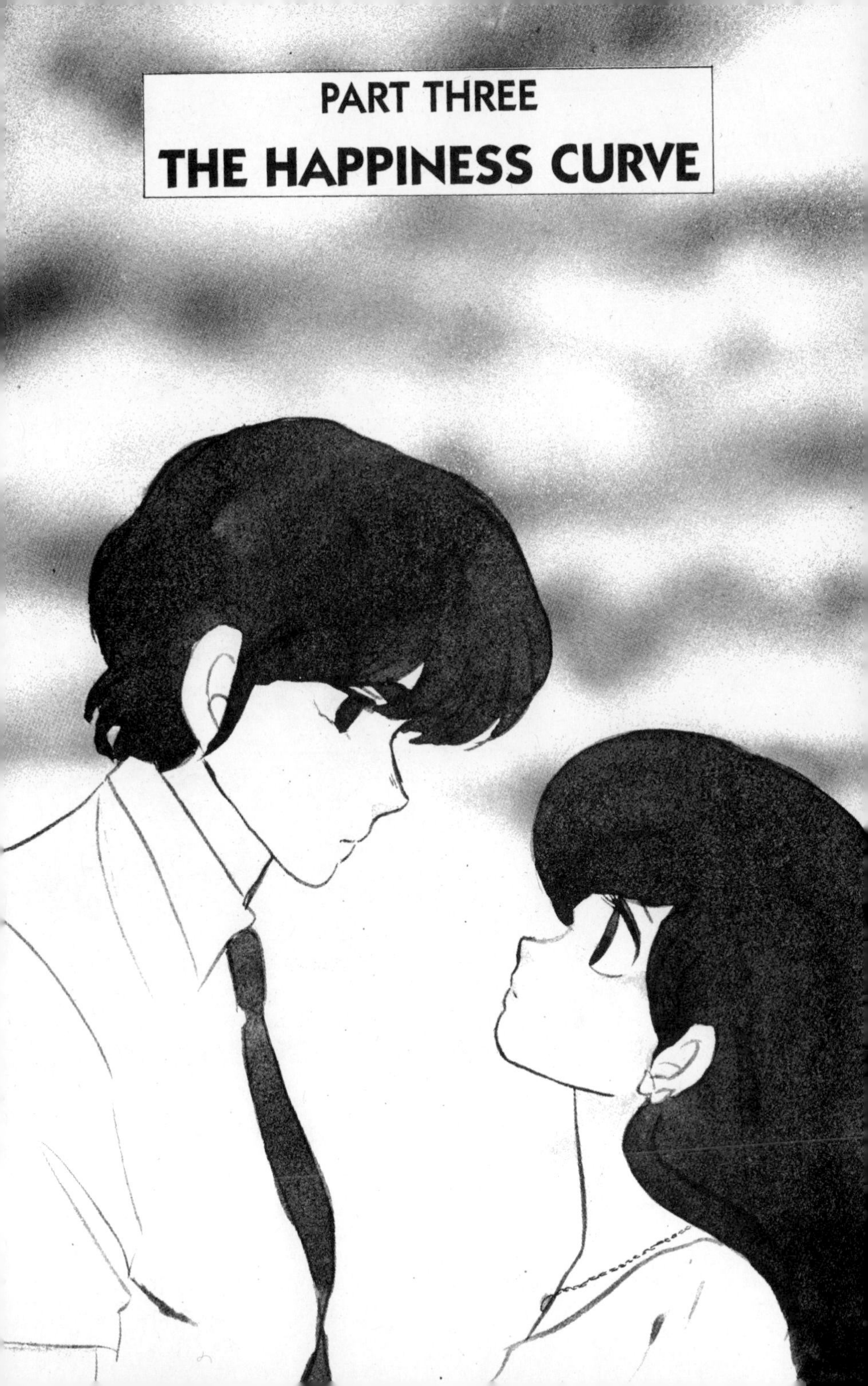

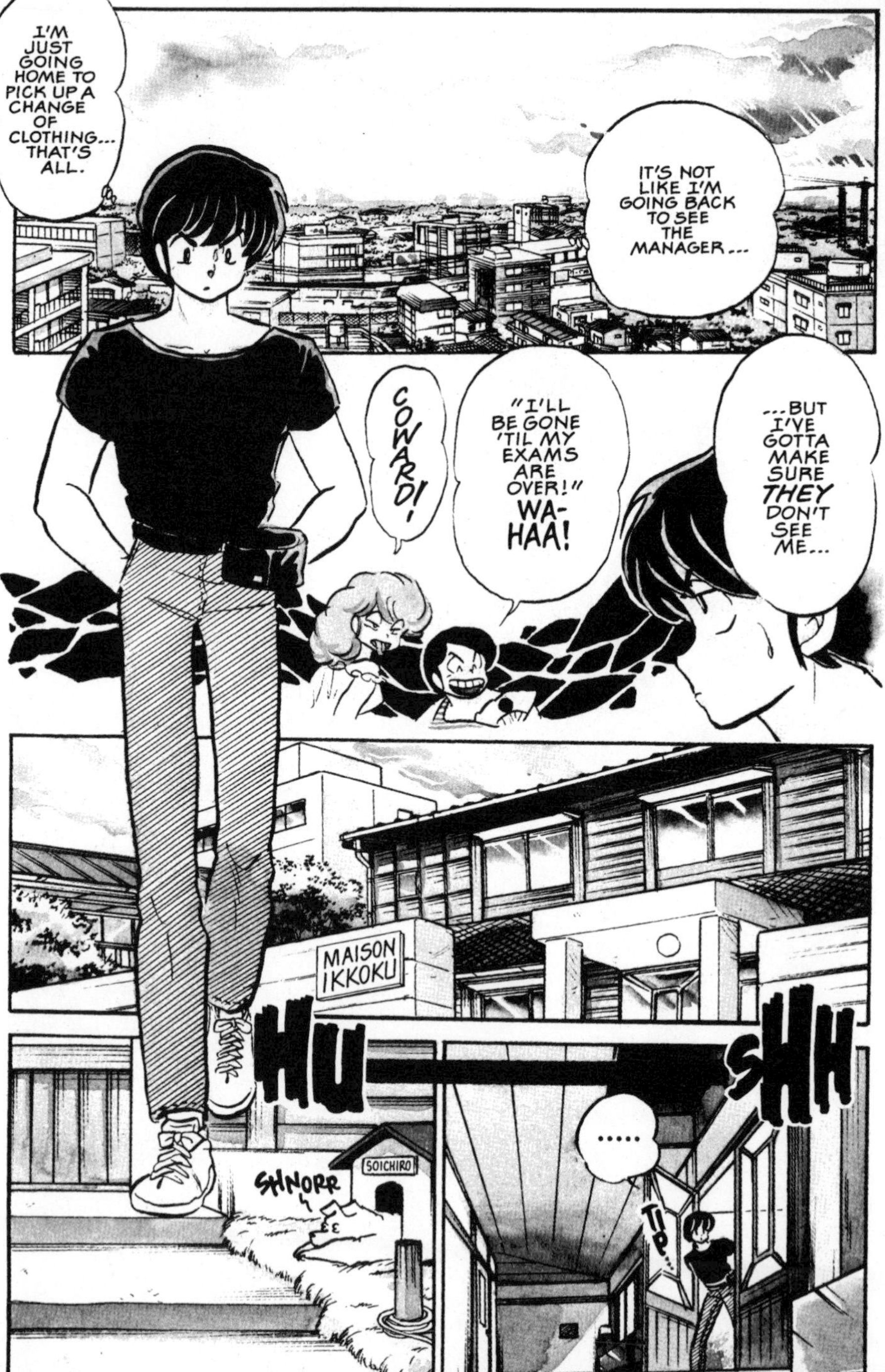
I'M JUST GOING HOME TO PICK UP A CHANGE OF CLOTHING... THAT'S ALL.
IT'S NOT LIKE I'M GOING BACK TO SEE THE MANAGER...
COWARD!
"I'LL BE GONE 'TIL MY EXAMS ARE OVER!" WA-HAA!
...BUT I'VE GOTTA MAKE SURE THEY DON'T SEE ME...
MAISON IKKOKU
HU
SHH
SOICHIRO
SHNORR
......
TIP...

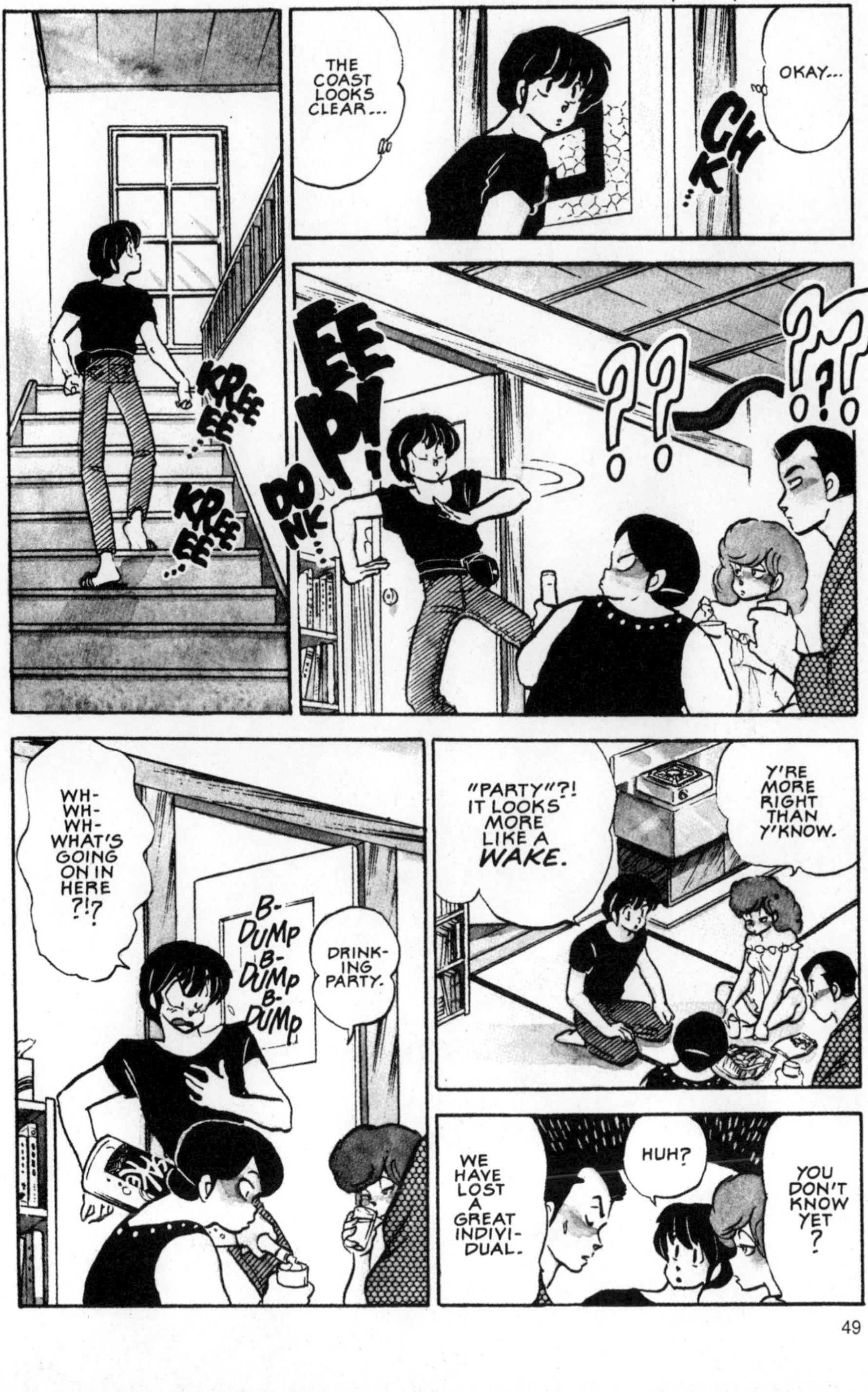
KREEEE...
KREEEE...
THE COAST LOOKS CLEAR...
CHK...
OKAY...
EEP!
DONK...
??? ???
WH-WH-WH-WHAT'S GOING ON IN HERE?!?
B-DUMP B-DUMP B-DUMP
DRINKING PARTY.
"PARTY"?! IT LOOKS MORE LIKE A WAKE.
Y'RE MORE RIGHT THAN Y'KNOW.
WE HAVE LOST A GREAT INDIVIDUAL.
HUH?
YOU DON'T KNOW YET?

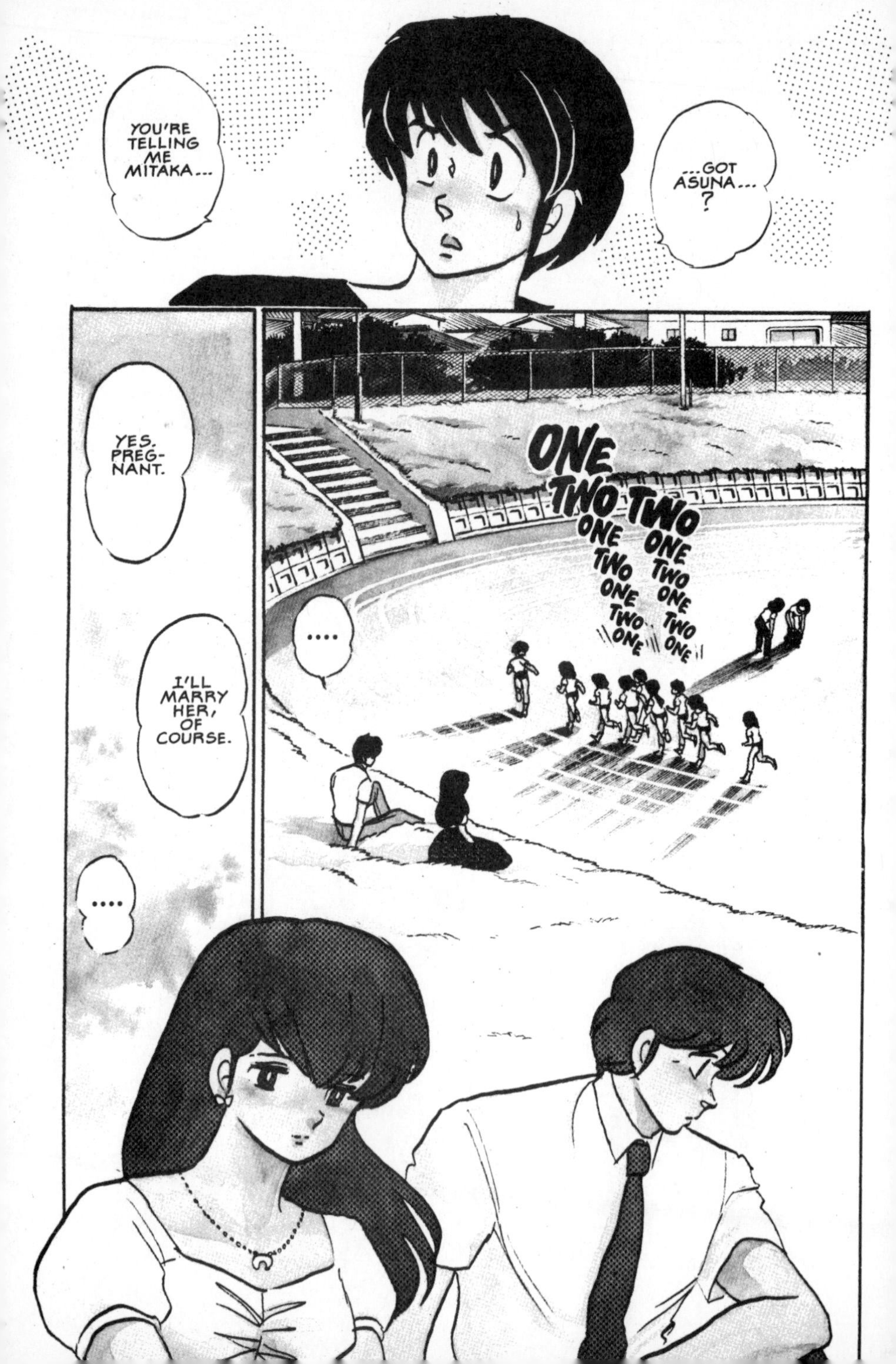
YOU'RE TELLING ME MITAKA...
...GOT ASUNA...?
YES. PREGNANT.
I'LL MARRY HER, OF COURSE.
....
ONE TWO TWO ONE ONE TWO TWO ONE ONE TWO TWO ONE ONE
....

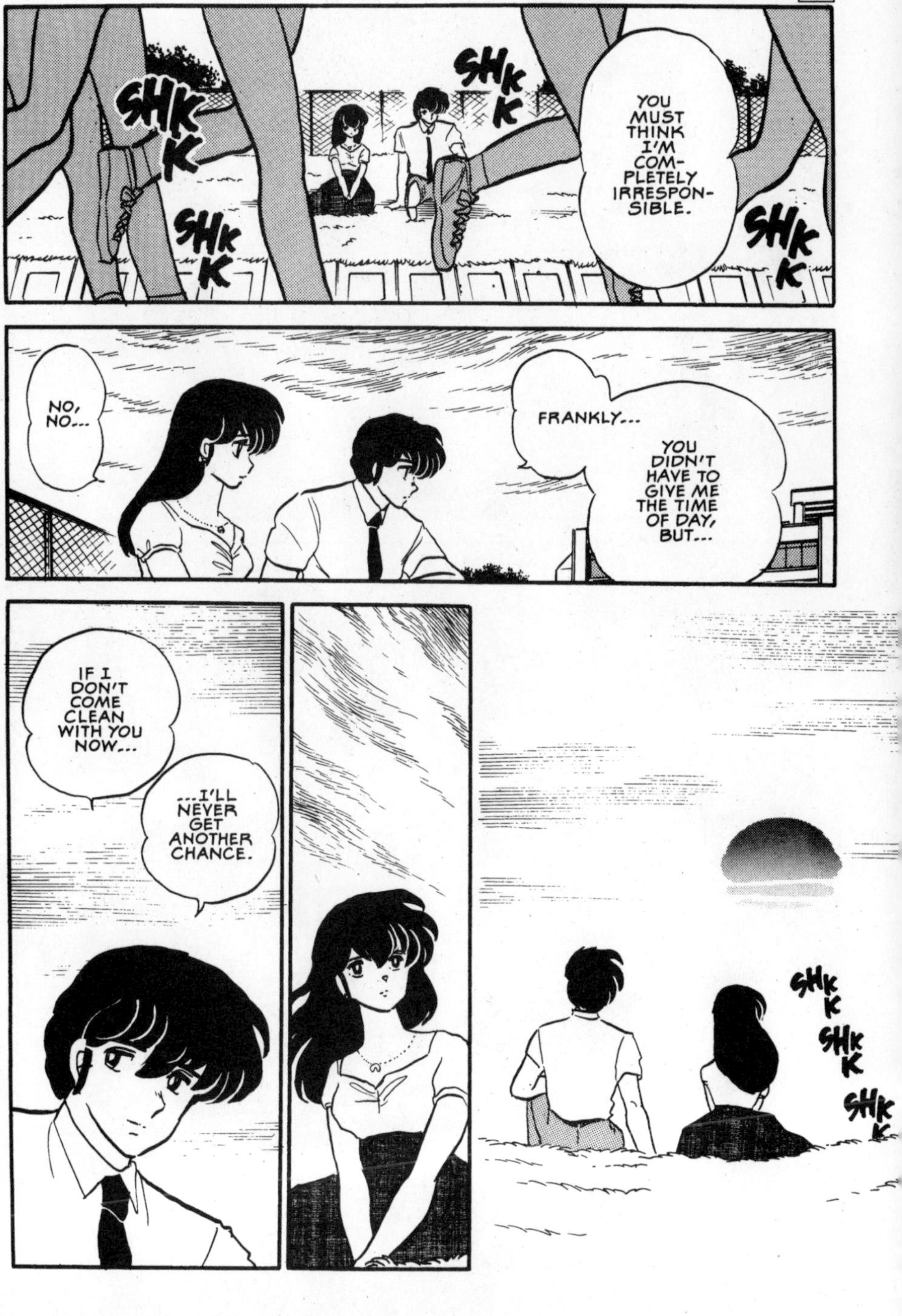
SHKK
SHKK
SHKK
YOU MUST THINK I'M COM-PLETELY IRRESPON-SIBLE.
SHKK
NO, NO...
FRANKLY...
YOU DIDN'T HAVE TO GIVE ME THE TIME OF DAY, BUT...
IF I DON'T COME CLEAN WITH YOU NOW...
...I'LL NEVER GET ANOTHER CHANCE.
SHKK
SHKK
SHKK

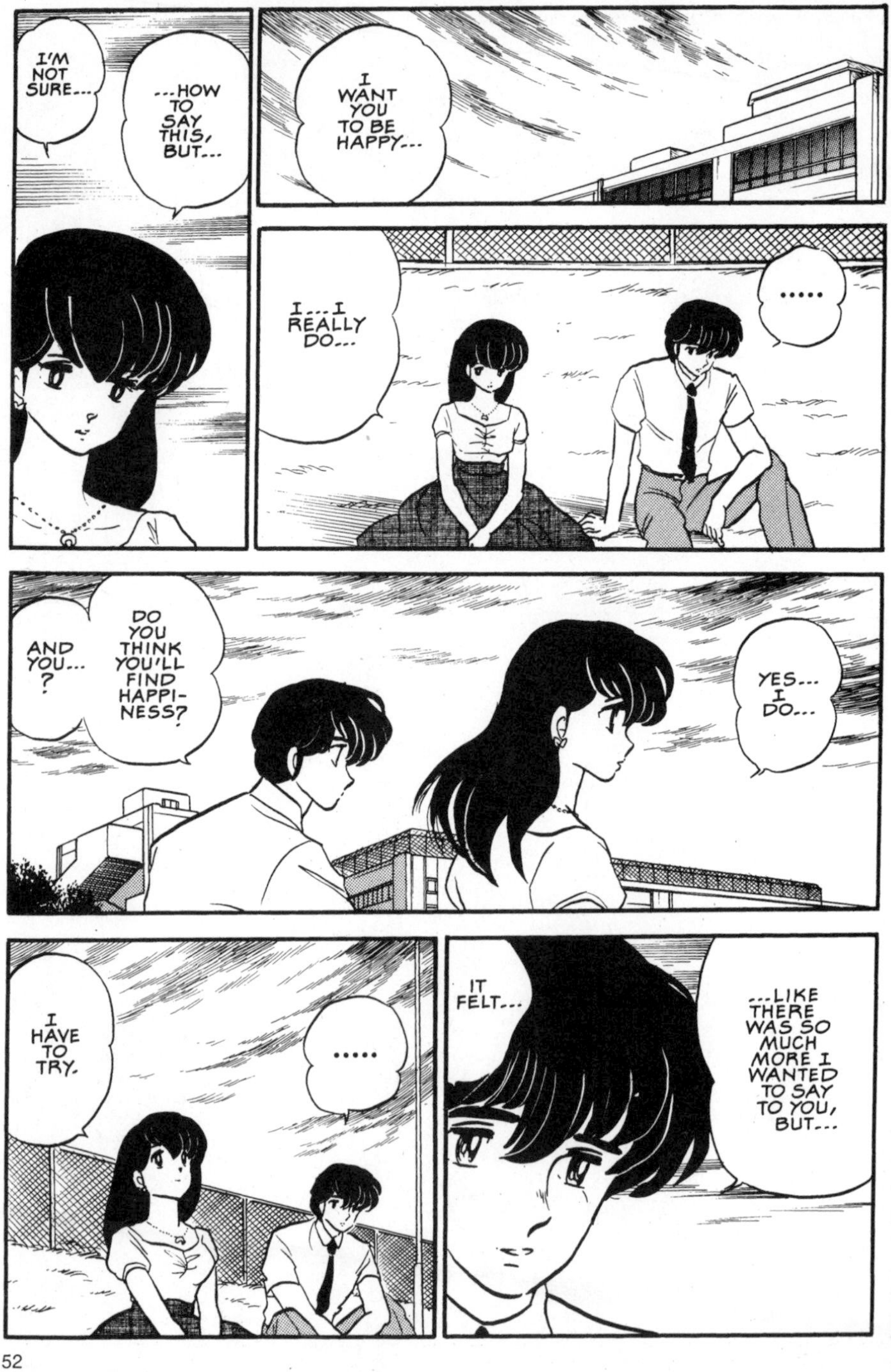

I'M NOT SURE...
...HOW TO SAY THIS, BUT...
I WANT YOU TO BE HAPPY...
I... I REALLY DO...
.....
AND YOU...?
DO YOU THINK YOU'LL FIND HAPPINESS?
YES... I DO...
I HAVE TO TRY.
.....
IT FELT...
...LIKE THERE WAS SO MUCH MORE I WANTED TO SAY TO YOU, BUT...

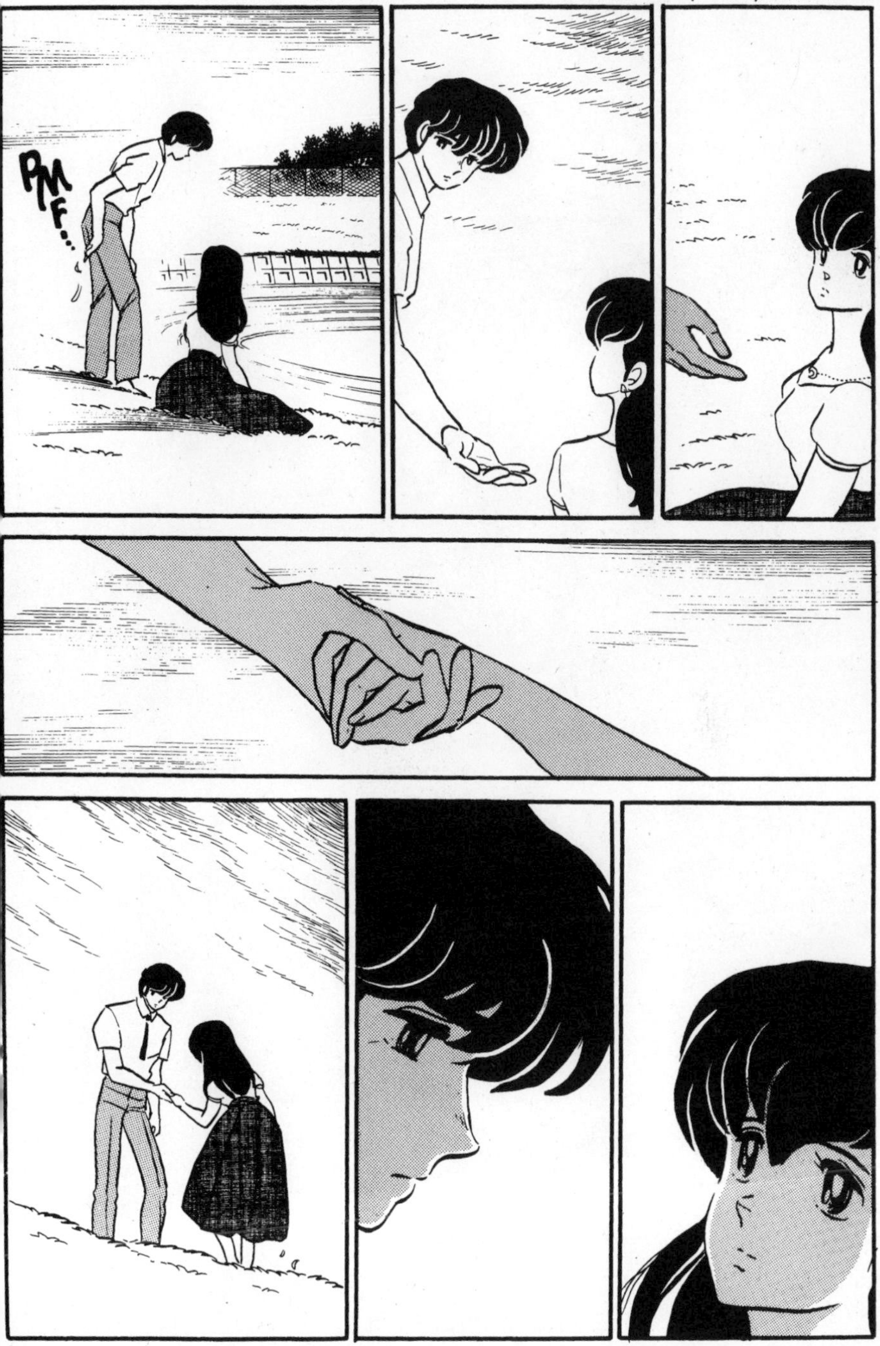
PMF...

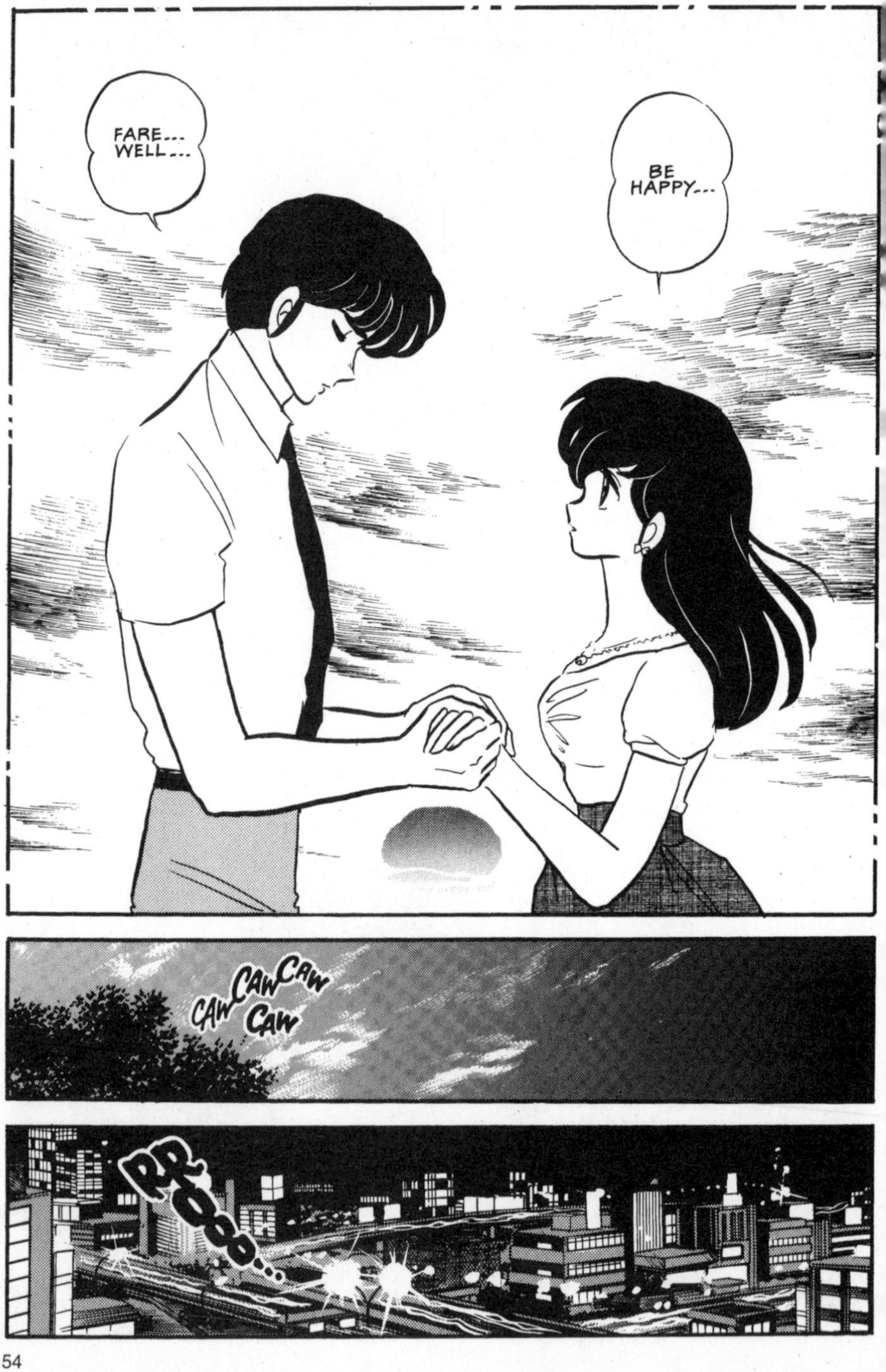
FARE... WELL...
BE HAPPY...
CAW CAW CAW CAW
RROOOO...

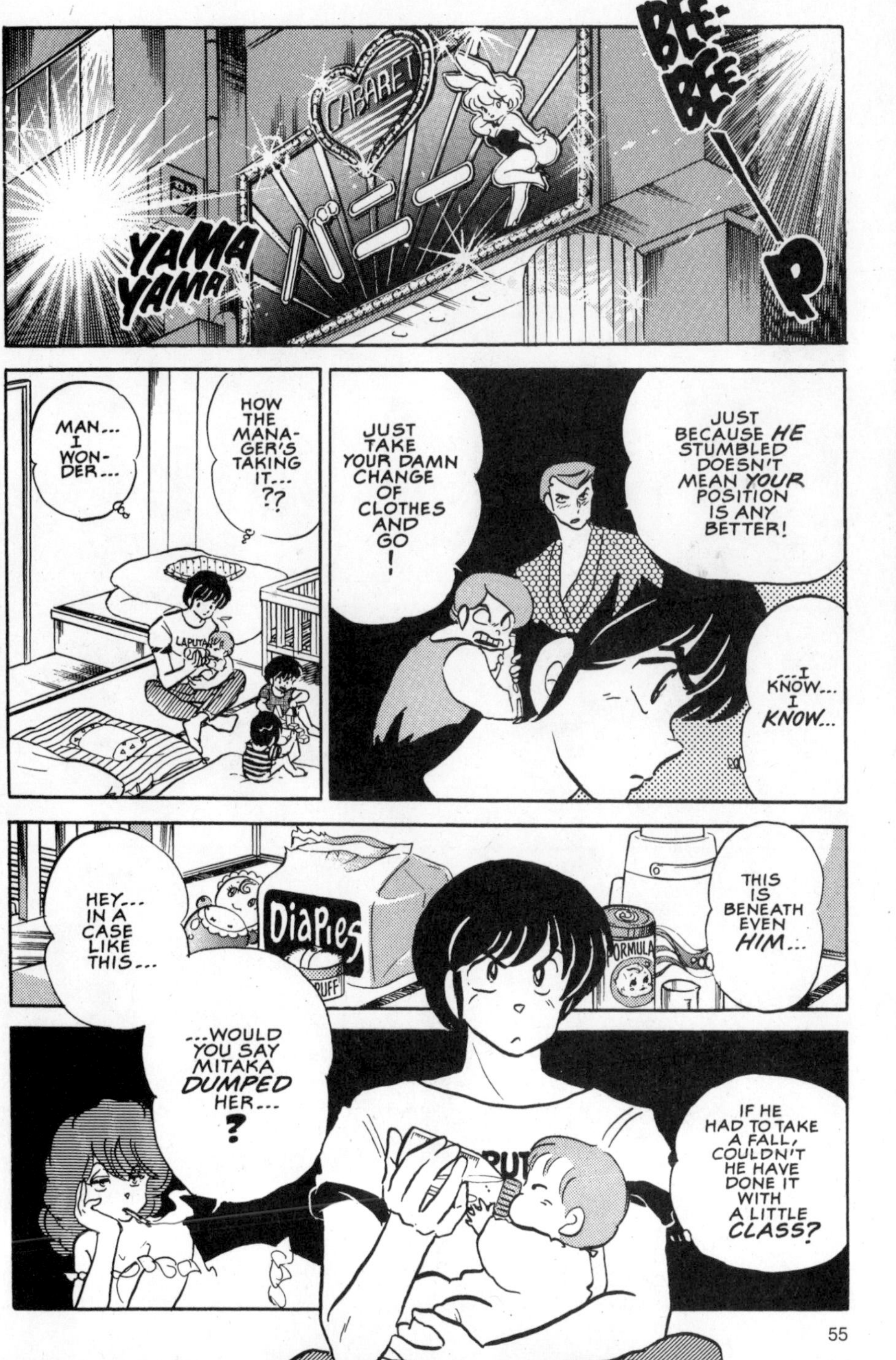
CABARET
YAMA YAMA
BEE-BEE
P
MAN... I WONDER...
HOW THE MANAGER'S TAKING IT...??
LAPUTA
JUST TAKE YOUR DAMN CHANGE OF CLOTHES AND GO!
JUST BECAUSE HE STUMBLED DOESN'T MEAN YOUR POSITION IS ANY BETTER!
...I KNOW... I KNOW...
HEY... IN A CASE LIKE THIS...
DiaPies
FORMULA
THIS IS BENEATH EVEN HIM...
...WOULD YOU SAY MITAKA DUMPED HER...?
IF HE HAD TO TAKE A FALL, COULDN'T HE HAVE DONE IT WITH A LITTLE CLASS?

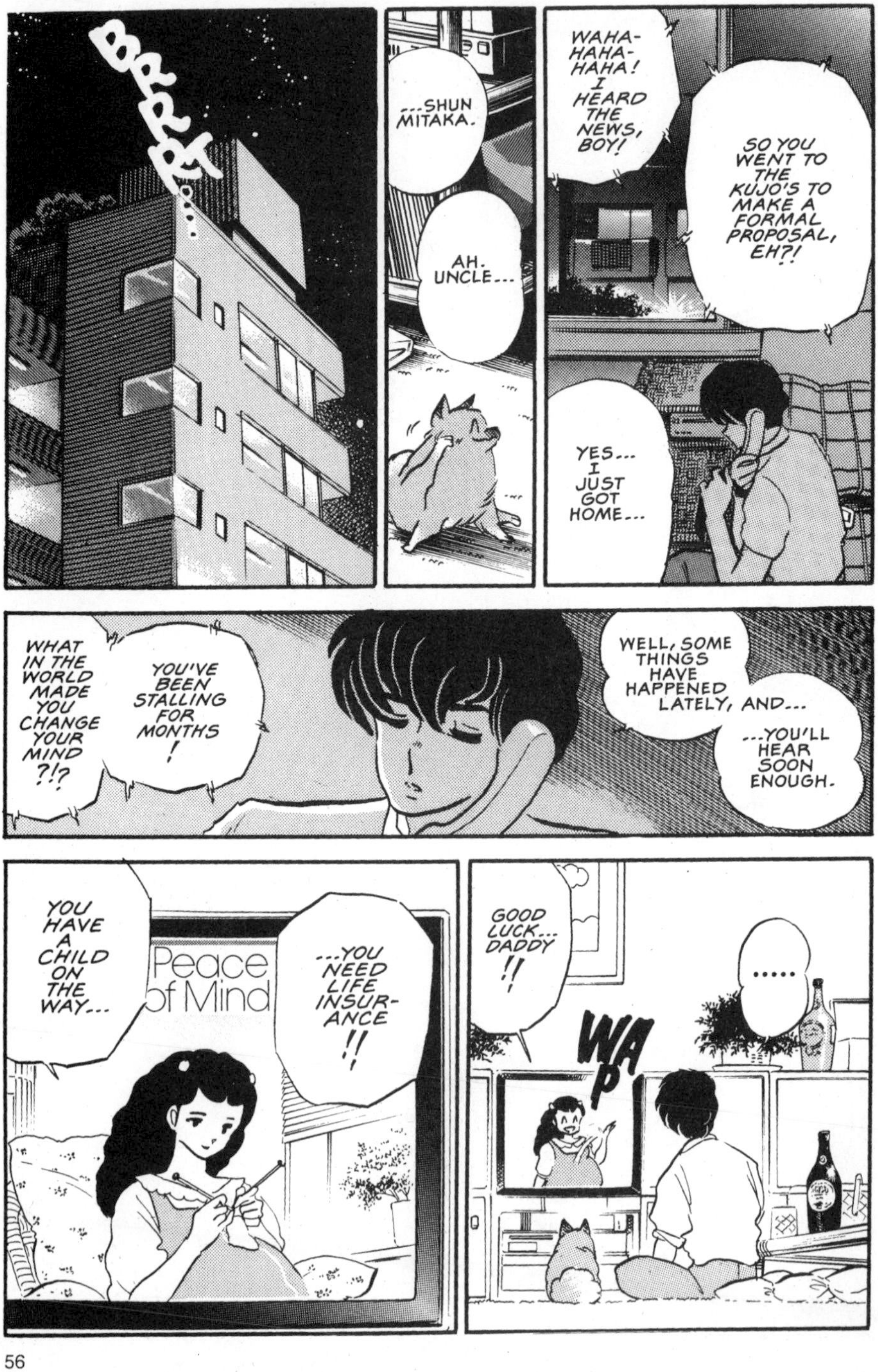
BRRRT...
...SHUN MITAKA.
AH. UNCLE...
WAHA-HAHA-HAHA! I HEARD THE NEWS, BOY!
SO YOU WENT TO THE KUJO'S TO MAKE A FORMAL PROPOSAL, EH?!
YES... I JUST GOT HOME...
WHAT IN THE WORLD MADE YOU CHANGE YOUR MIND?!?
YOU'VE BEEN STALLING FOR MONTHS!
WELL, SOME THINGS HAVE HAPPENED LATELY, AND...
...YOU'LL HEAR SOON ENOUGH.
YOU HAVE A CHILD ON THE WAY...
Peace of Mind
...YOU NEED LIFE INSURANCE!!
GOOD LUCK... DADDY!!
WAP
.....

"DADDY," HUH...??

IT STILL DOESN'T FEEL REAL...

HAF HAF HAF HAF

PLEASE GRANT ME YOUR DAUGHTER'S HAND IN MARRIAGE.

WHAT'S WRONG, ASUNA?

I'M HAPPY...

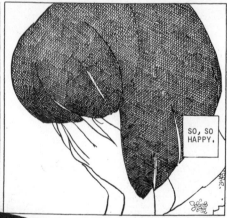

SO, SO HAPPY.

IT'S UP TO ME TO...

...MAKE SURE SHE STAYS THAT WAY.

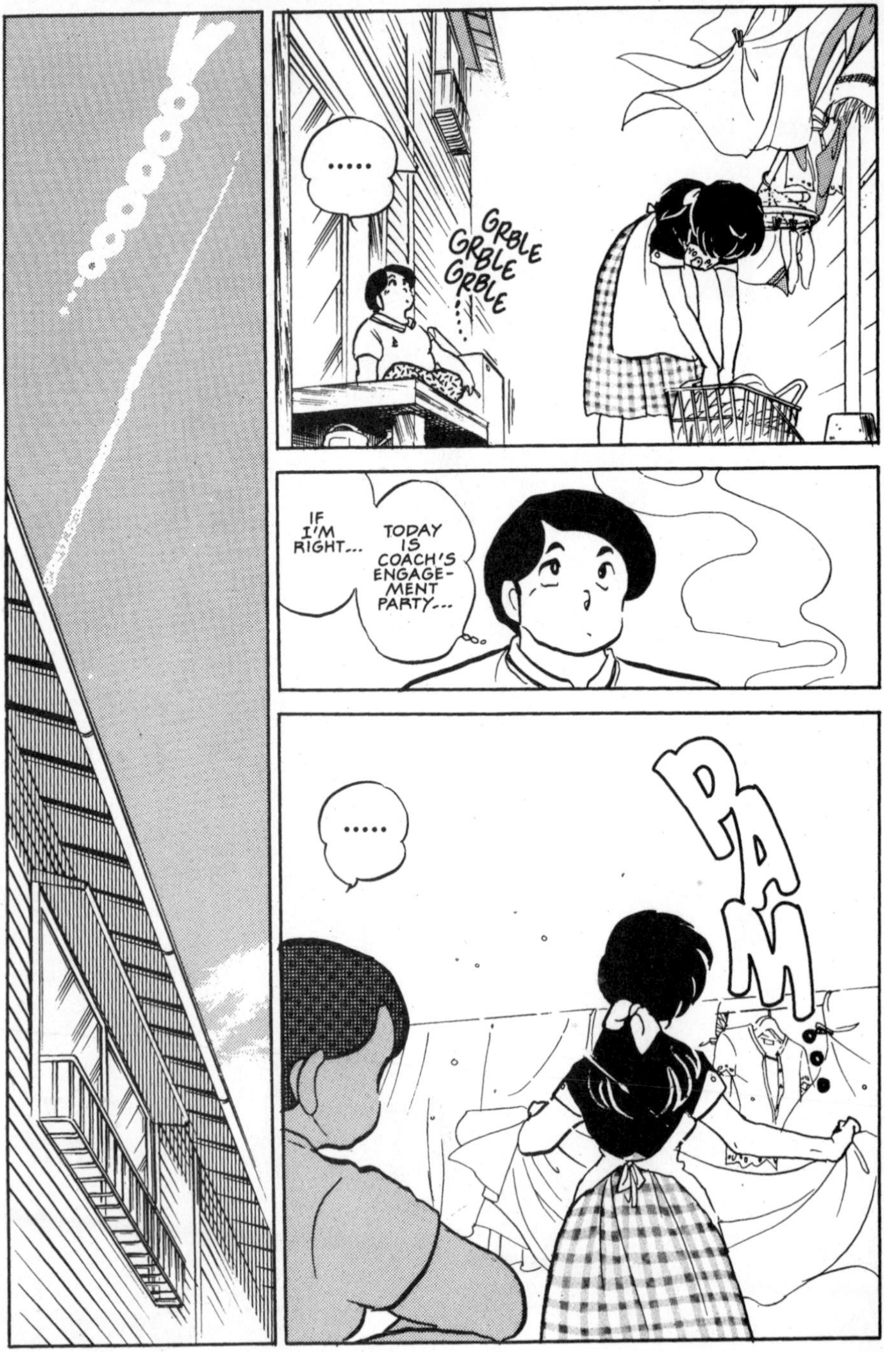
......
GRBLE GRBLE GRBLE
IF I'M RIGHT...
TODAY IS COACH'S ENGAGEMENT PARTY...
......
PAM

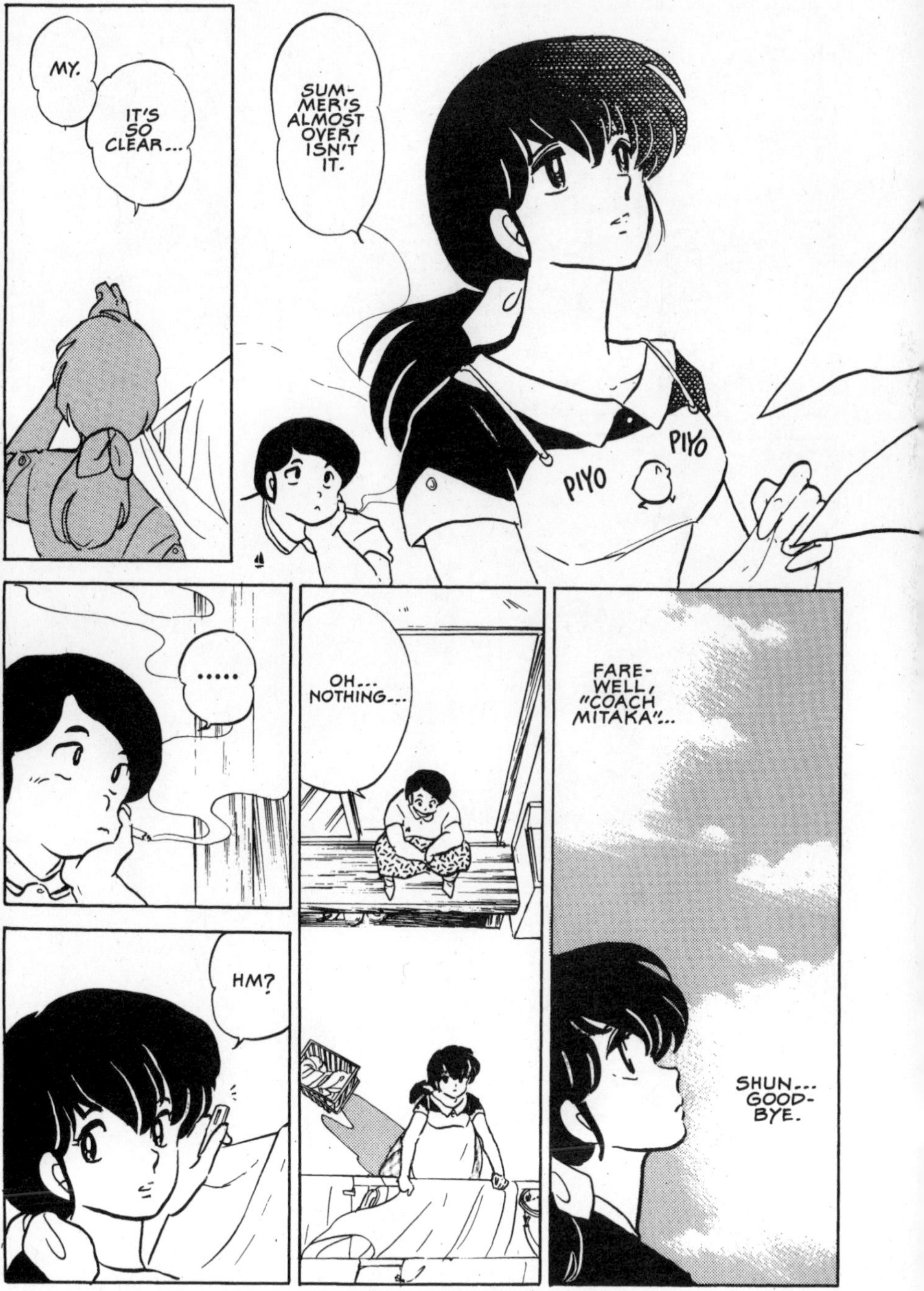
MY.
IT'S SO CLEAR...
SUMMER'S ALMOST OVER, ISN'T IT.
PIYO PIYO
.....
OH... NOTHING...
HM?
FAREWELL, "COACH MITAKA"...
SHUN... GOODBYE.

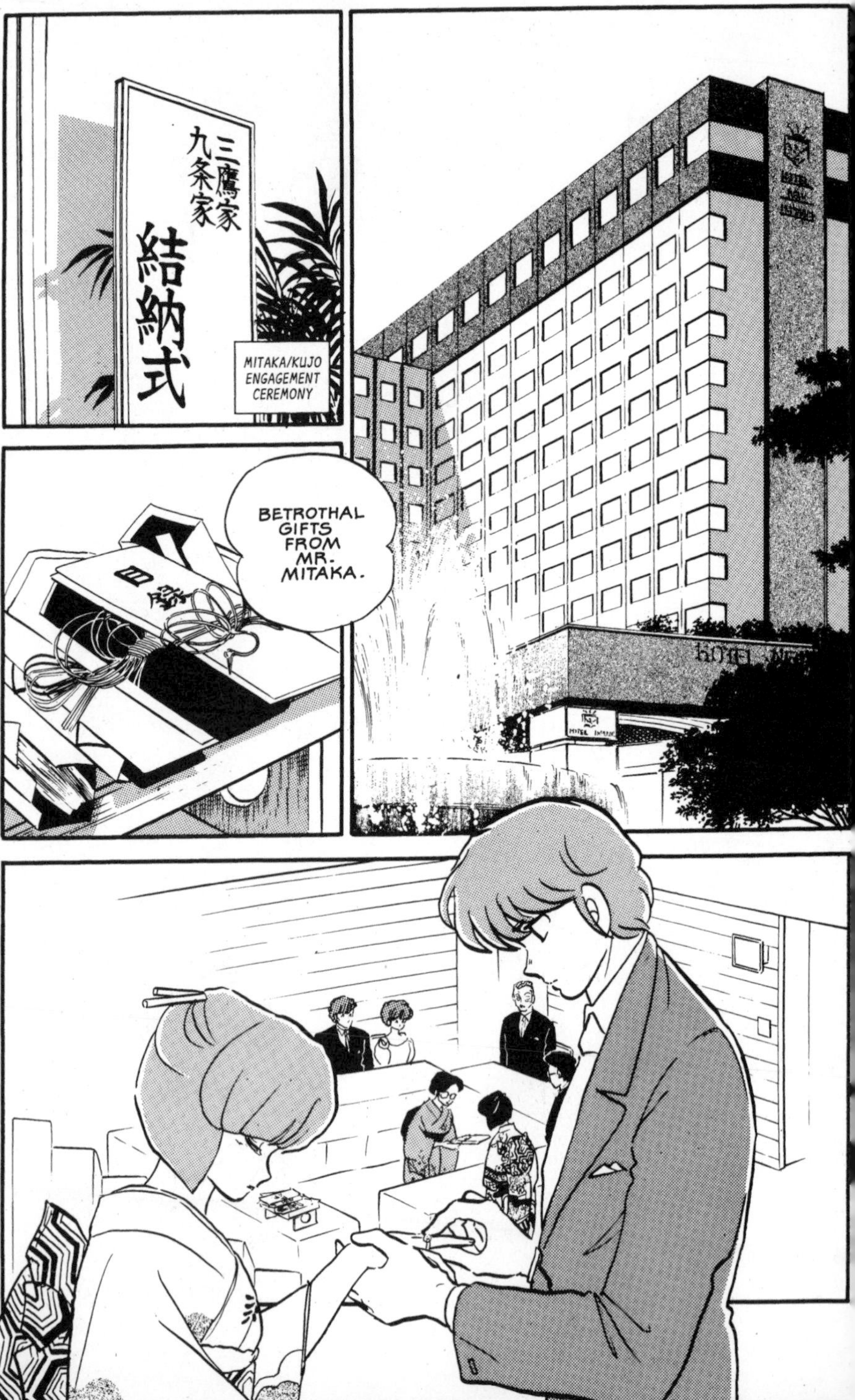
三鷹家
九条家
結納式
MITAKA/KUJO ENGAGEMENT CEREMONY
BETROTHAL GIFTS FROM MR. MITAKA.

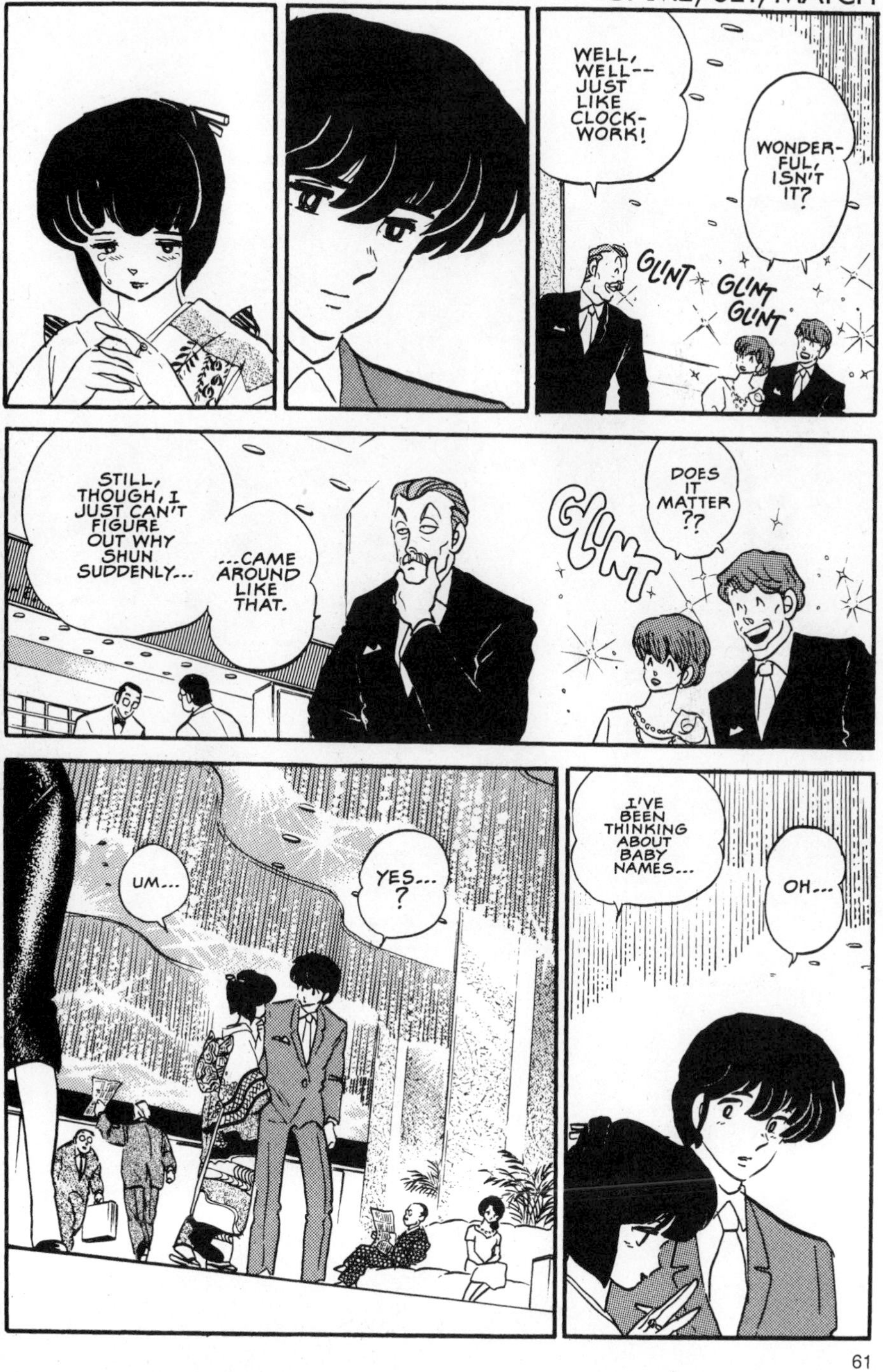

WELL, WELL-- JUST LIKE CLOCK-WORK!
WONDER-FUL, ISN'T IT?
GLINT
GLINT
GLINT
STILL, THOUGH, I JUST CAN'T FIGURE OUT WHY SHUN SUDDENLY...
...CAME AROUND LIKE THAT.
GLINT
DOES IT MATTER??
UM...
YES...?
I'VE BEEN THINKING ABOUT BABY NAMES...
OH...

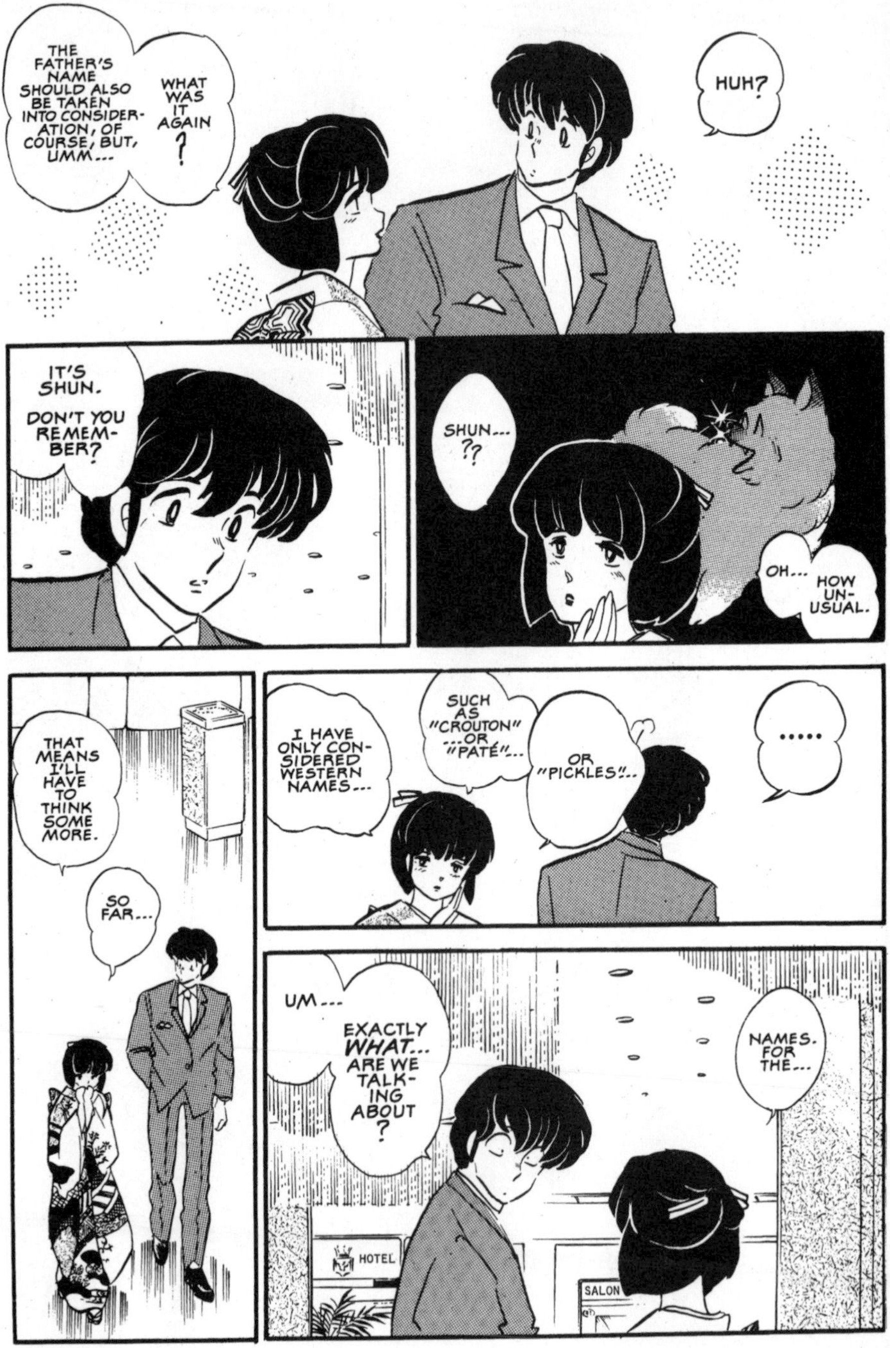
THE FATHER'S NAME SHOULD ALSO BE TAKEN INTO CONSIDER-ATION, OF COURSE, BUT, UMM...
WHAT WAS IT AGAIN ?
HUH?
IT'S SHUN.
DON'T YOU REMEM-BER?
SHUN... ??
OH... HOW UN-USUAL.
THAT MEANS I'LL HAVE TO THINK SOME MORE.
SO FAR...
I HAVE ONLY CON-SIDERED WESTERN NAMES...
SUCH AS "CROUTON" ...OR "PATÉ"...
OR "PICKLES"...
.....
UM...
EXACTLY WHAT... ARE WE TALK-ING ABOUT ?
NAMES. FOR THE...
HOTEL
SALON

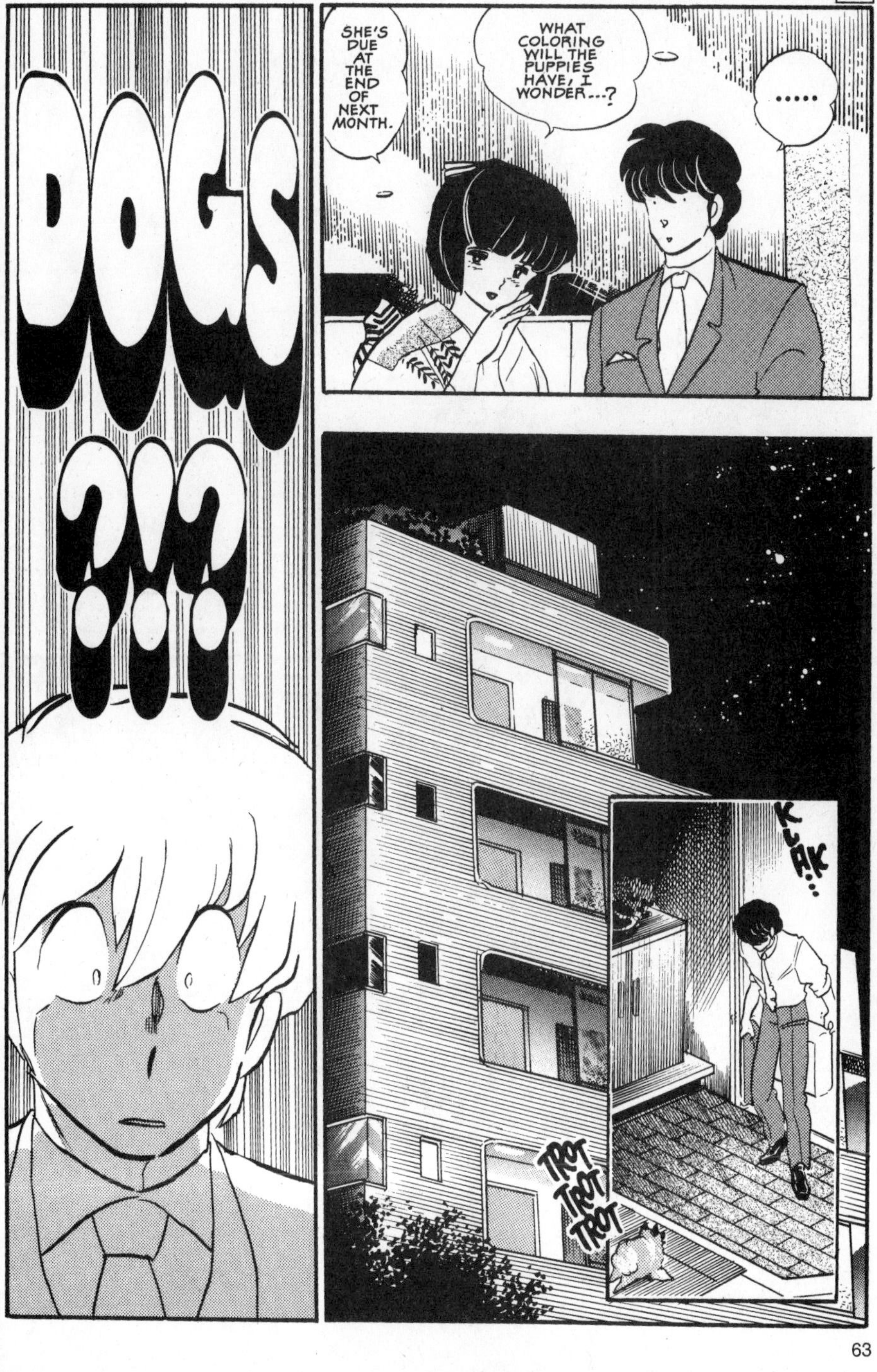
DOGS ?!?
SHE'S DUE AT THE END OF NEXT MONTH.
WHAT COLORING WILL THE PUPPIES HAVE, I WONDER...?
......
KLAK...
TROT TROT TROT

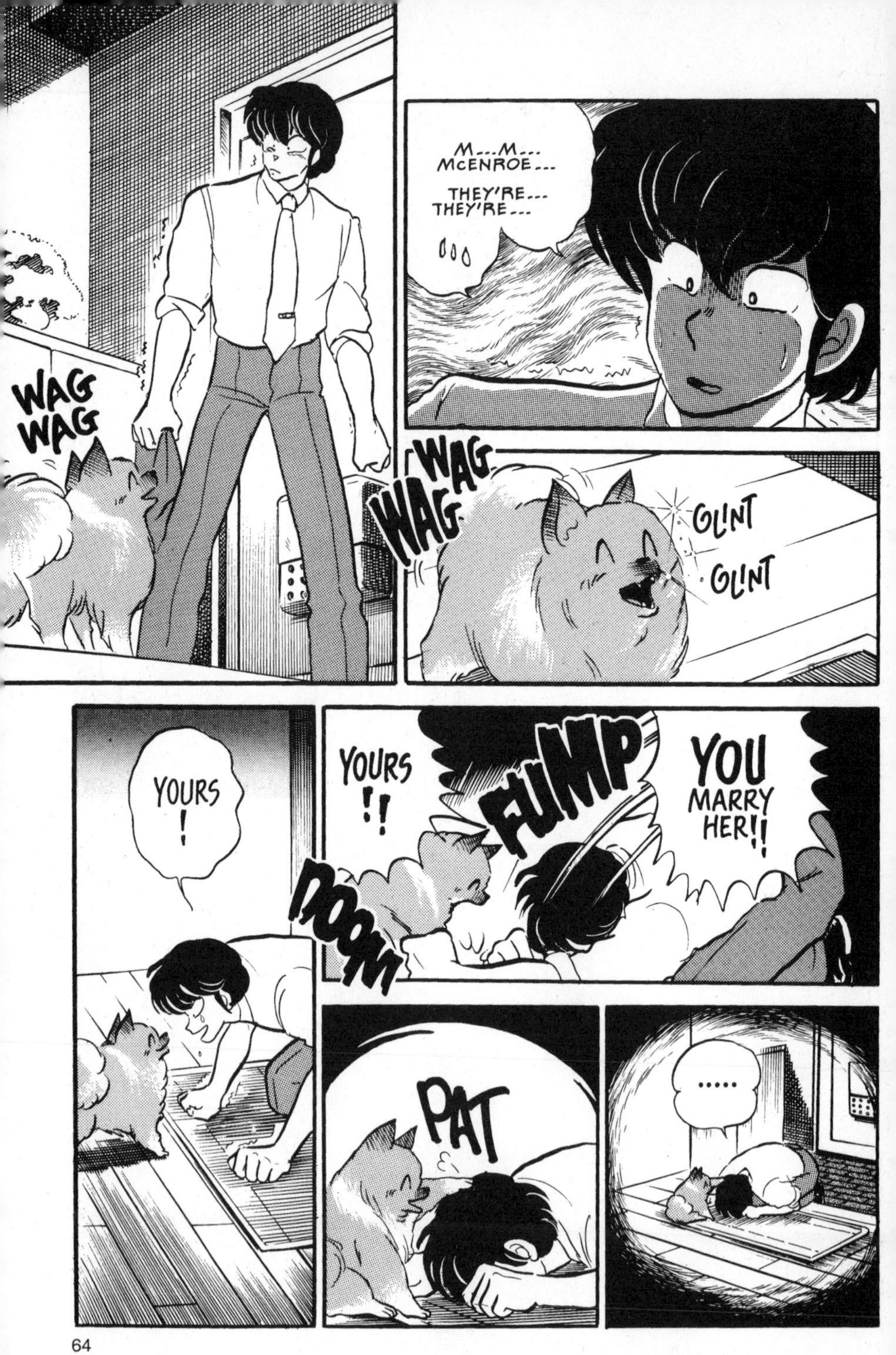
WAG WAG
M...M... McENROE...
THEY'RE... THEY'RE...
WAG WAG
GLINT
GLINT
YOURS !
YOURS !!
FUMP
YOU MARRY HER!!
DOOM
PAT
.....

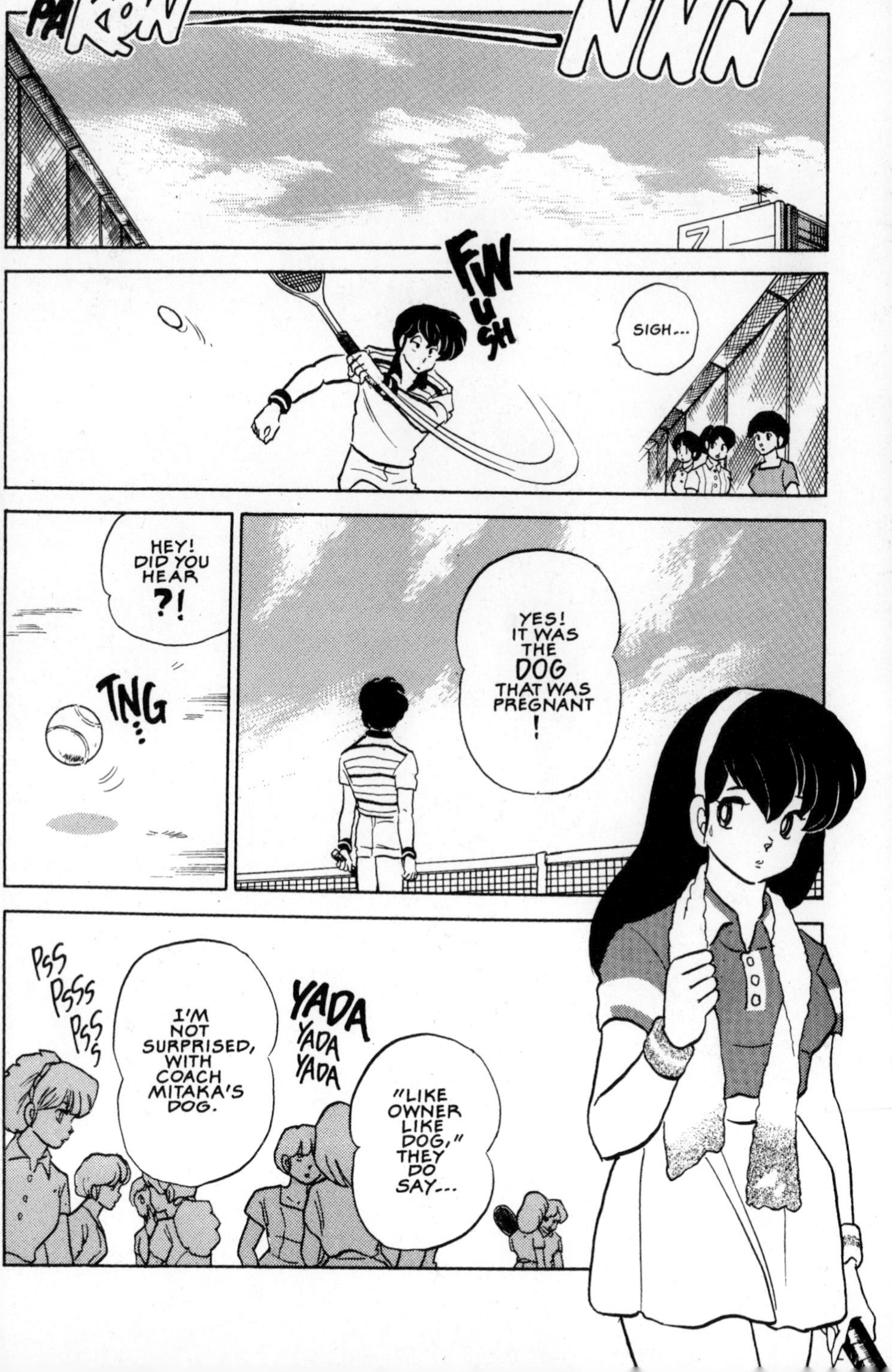
PAKON
NNN
FWUSH
SIGH...
HEY! DID YOU HEAR ?!
TNG...
YES! IT WAS THE DOG THAT WAS PREGNANT!
PSS PSSS PSSS
I'M NOT SURPRISED, WITH COACH MITAKA'S DOG.
YADA YADA YADA
"LIKE OWNER LIKE DOG," THEY DO SAY...

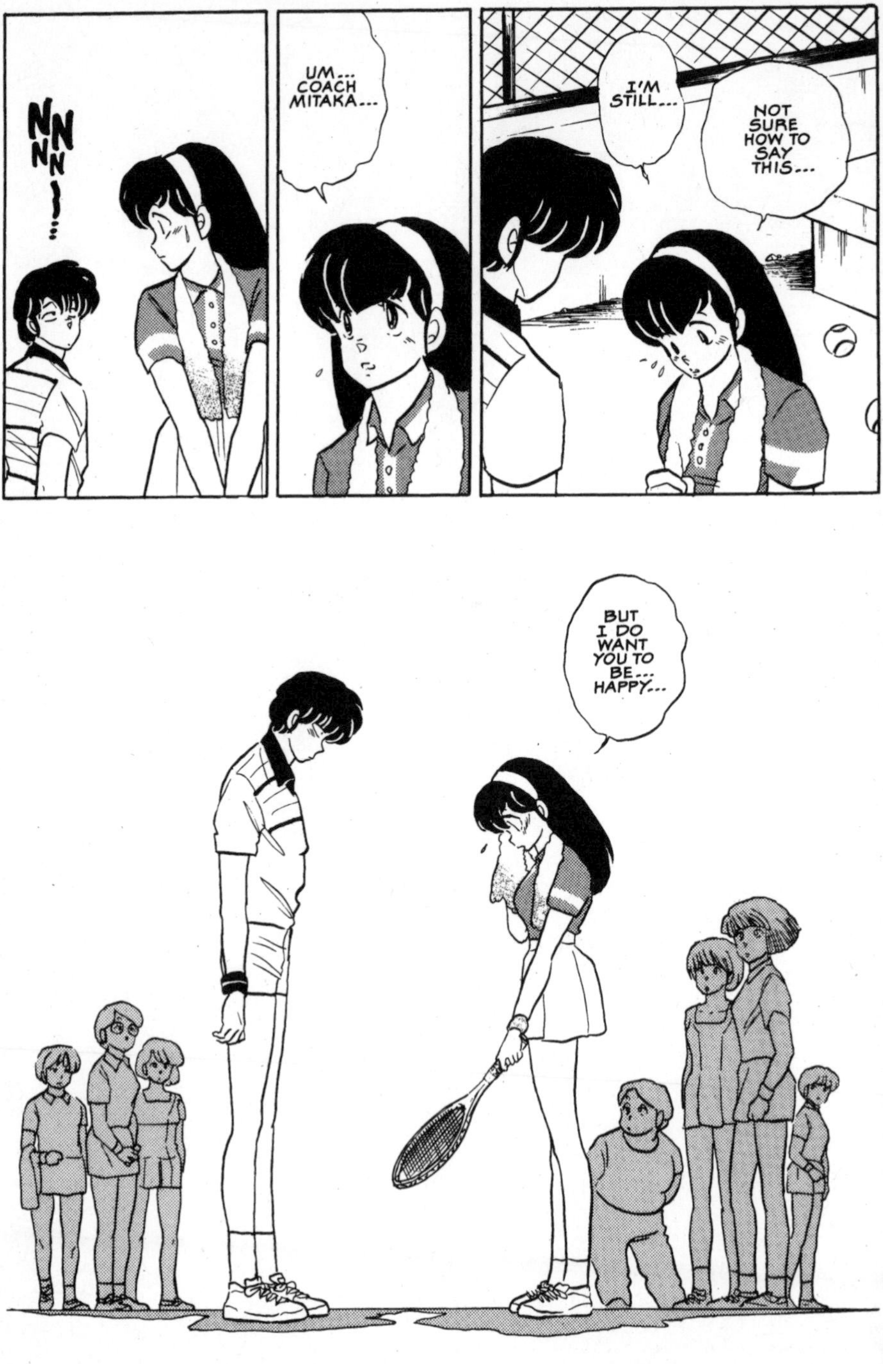
NNNN...
UM... COACH MITAKA...
I'M STILL...
NOT SURE HOW TO SAY THIS...
BUT I DO WANT YOU TO BE... HAPPY...

...CAN YOU BELIEVE IT? IT WAS THE *DOG*, NOT THE COACH.

B-BUT THAT MEANS--

GEEZ...

I ACTUALLY FEEL SORRY FOR HIM...

OF COURSE... AFTER THIS...

MITAKA ISN'T LIKELY TO FEEL SO...

COMMITTED.

HEY, DIRECTOR!

HUH?

CHNG

WHAT'S WRONG?

IT'S NOT SNACK TIME.

BUT WE'RE HUNGRY!

I GET IT...

YOUR MOM'S STILL ASLEEP, HUH?

WELL, CAN'T LET YOU STARVE.

BISTRO

CHIDA INC.

TEL LOCA

Home-Style Japanese CUISINE

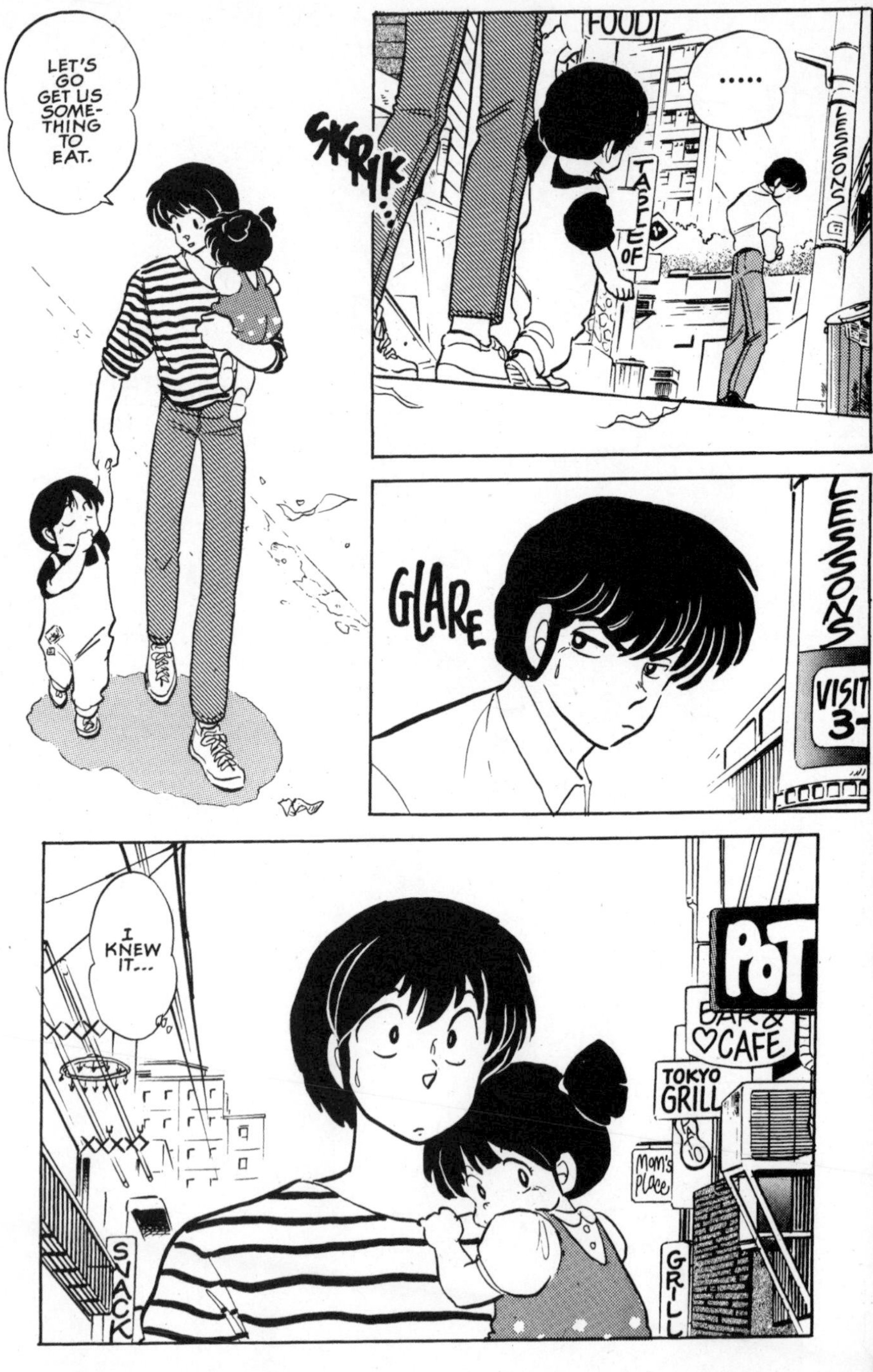
LET'S GO GET US SOME-THING TO EAT.
SKRIK!...
FOOD
TASTE OF
LESSONS
......
GLARE
LESSONS
VISIT 3-
I KNEW IT...
POT
BAR & ♡CAFE
TOKYO GRILL
Mom's Place
SNACK
GRILL

PART FOUR
ONE MORE ROUND

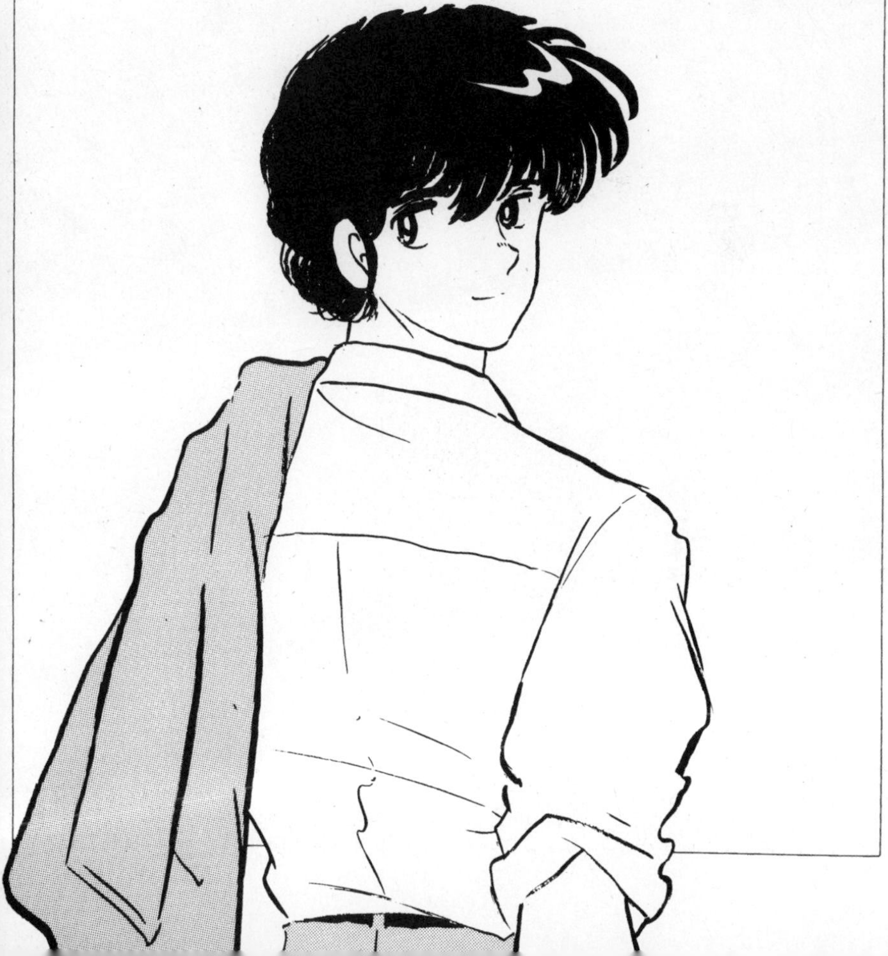

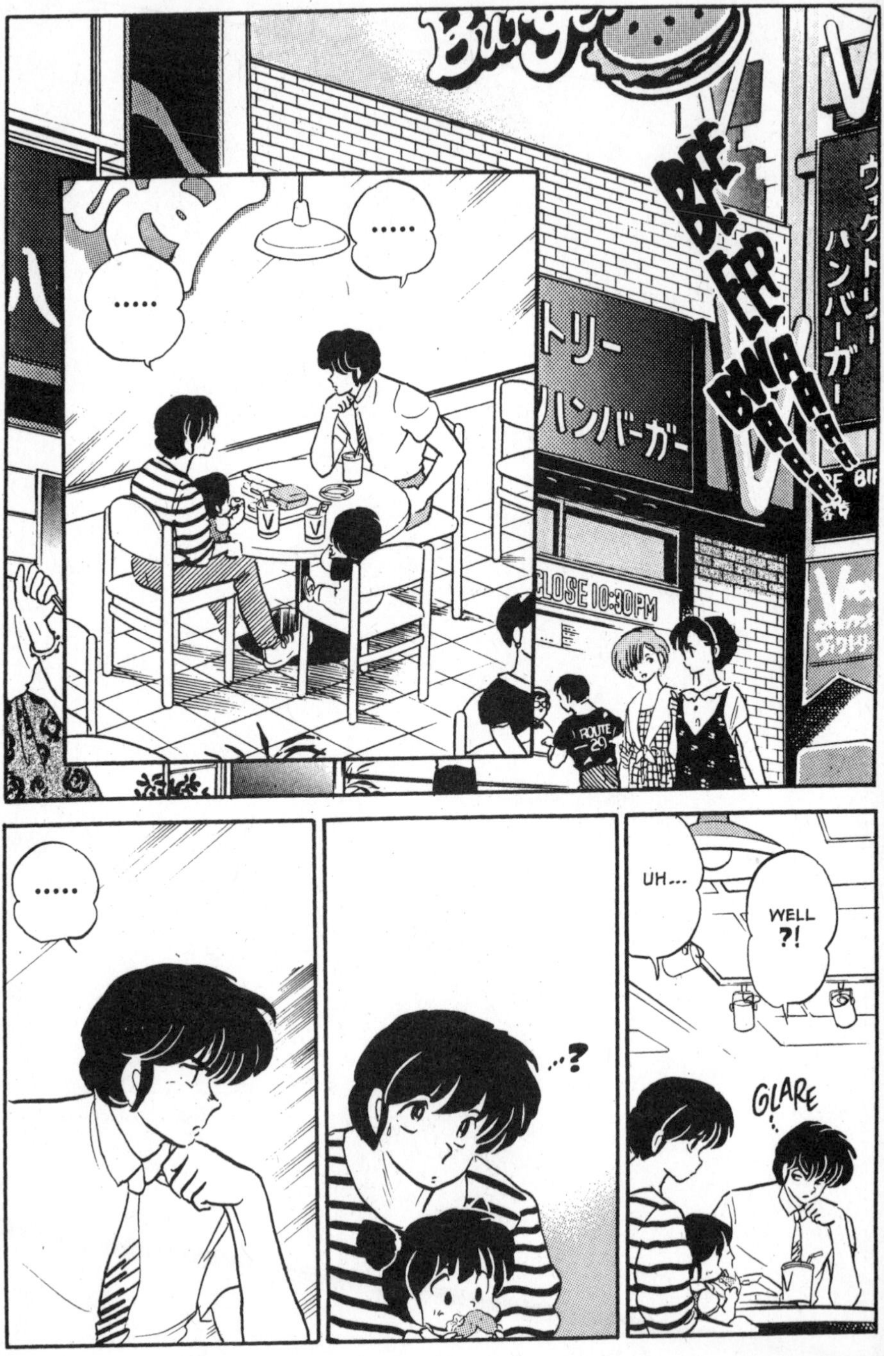
Burger
BEEP
ヴィクトリー ハンバーガー
トリー ハンバーガー
CLOSE 10:30PM
......
......
ROUTE 29
......
...?
UH...
WELL ?!
GLARE

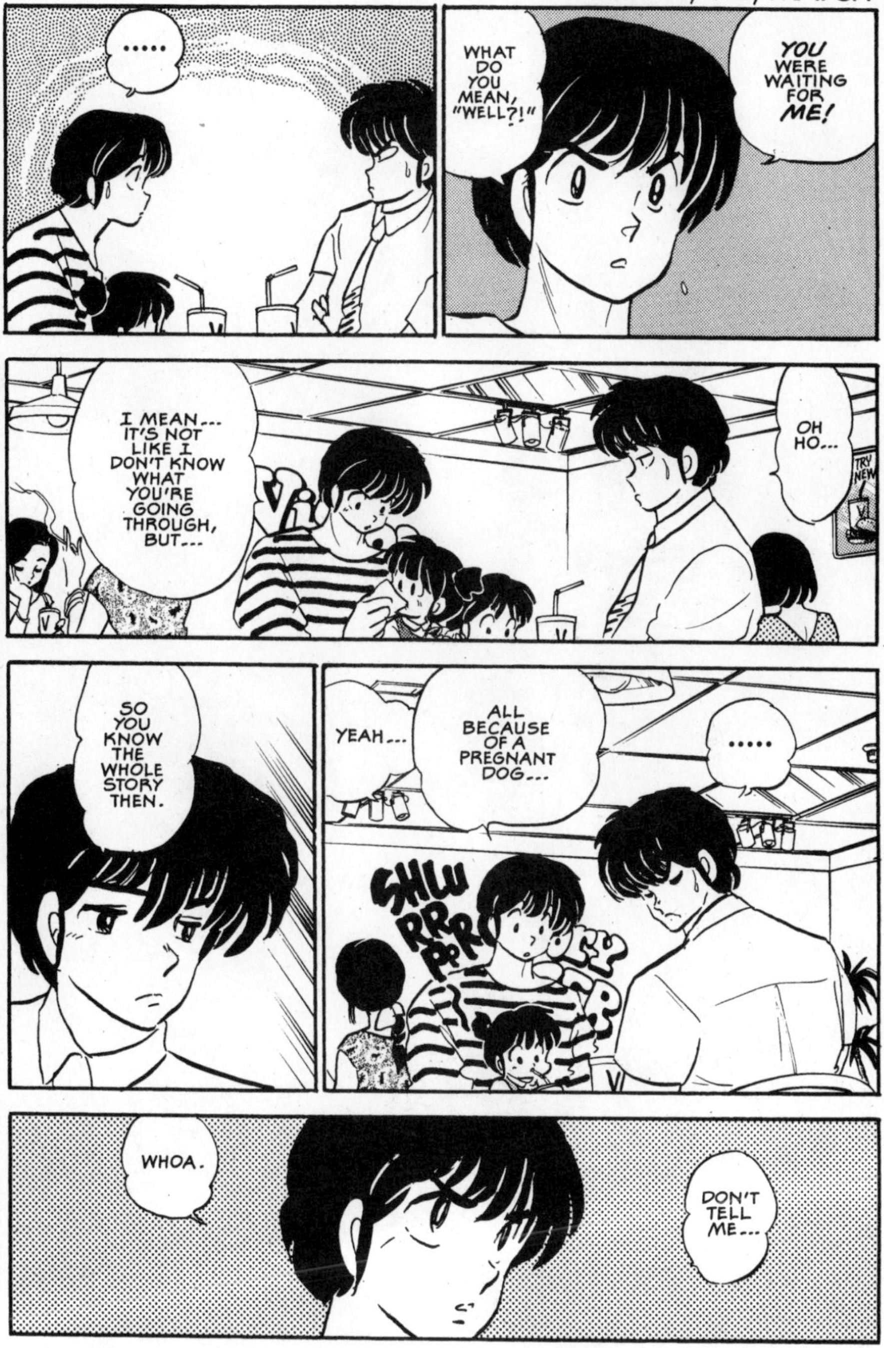
......
WHAT DO YOU MEAN, "WELL?!"
YOU WERE WAITING FOR ME!
I MEAN... IT'S NOT LIKE I DON'T KNOW WHAT YOU'RE GOING THROUGH, BUT...
OH HO...
SO YOU KNOW THE WHOLE STORY THEN.
YEAH...
ALL BECAUSE OF A PREGNANT DOG...
......
SHLURRRP
WHOA.
DON'T TELL ME...

...BECAUSE O' THAT MISUNDERSTANDING YOU'RE GONNA CANCEL THE—

I'LL DO NO SUCH THING!

GOOD.

HRRR

WHAT DOES *THAT* MEAN?!

I'M JUST THINK-ING...

HOW MISS KUJO WOULD FEEL.

OF COURSE NO ONE CARES HOW *I* FEEL!

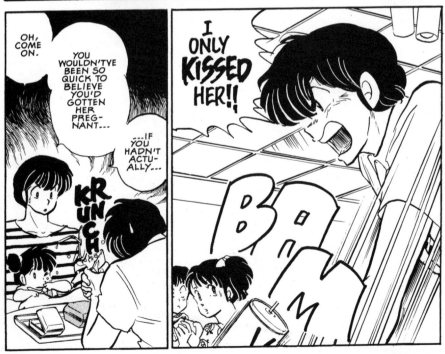

OH, COME ON.

YOU WOULDN'T'VE BEEN SO QUICK TO BELIEVE YOU'D GOTTEN HER PREG-NANT...

---IF YOU HADN'T ACTU-ALLY...

KR UN CH

I ONLY KISSED HER!!

BAM

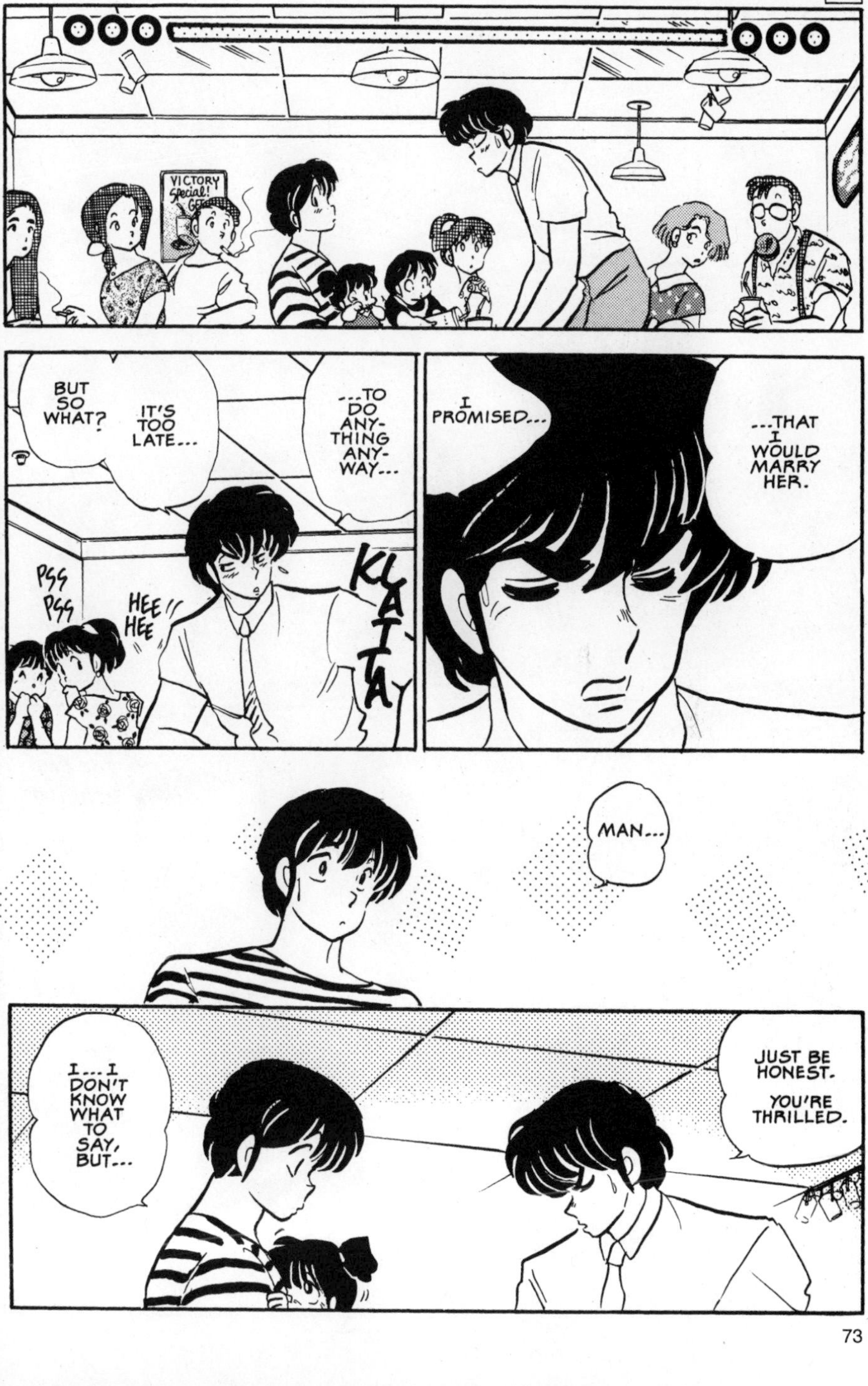
VICTORY Special!
BUT SO WHAT?
IT'S TOO LATE...
...TO DO ANYTHING ANYWAY...
PSS PSS
HEE HEE
KLATTA
I PROMISED...
...THAT I WOULD MARRY HER.
MAN...
I... I DON'T KNOW WHAT TO SAY, BUT...
JUST BE HONEST.
YOU'RE THRILLED.

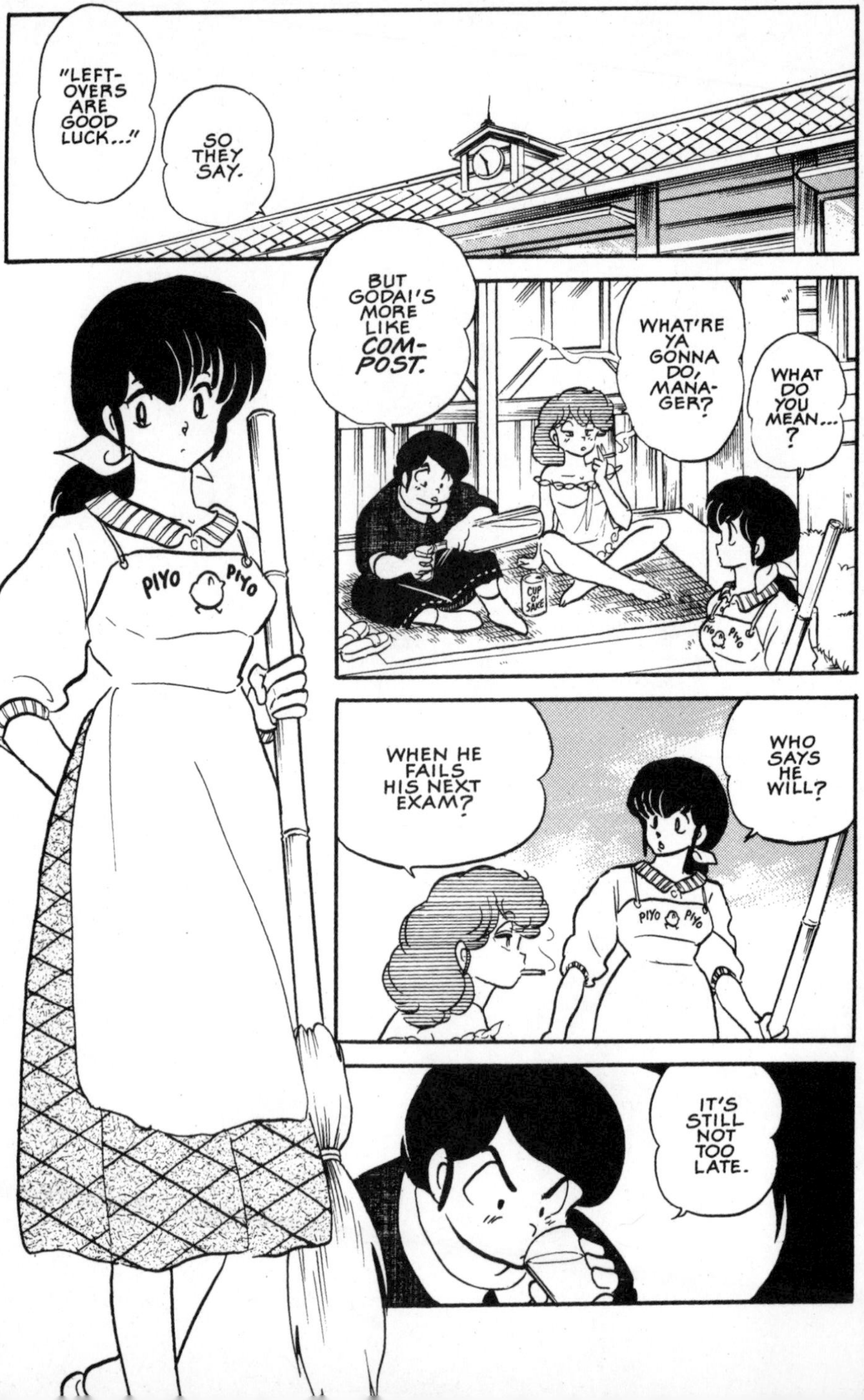
"LEFT-OVERS ARE GOOD LUCK..."
SO THEY SAY.
BUT GODAI'S MORE LIKE *COMPOST.*
WHAT'RE YA GONNA DO, MANAGER?
WHAT DO YOU MEAN...?
CUP O' SAKE
PIYO PIYO
WHEN HE FAILS HIS NEXT EXAM?
WHO SAYS HE WILL?
IT'S STILL NOT TOO LATE.

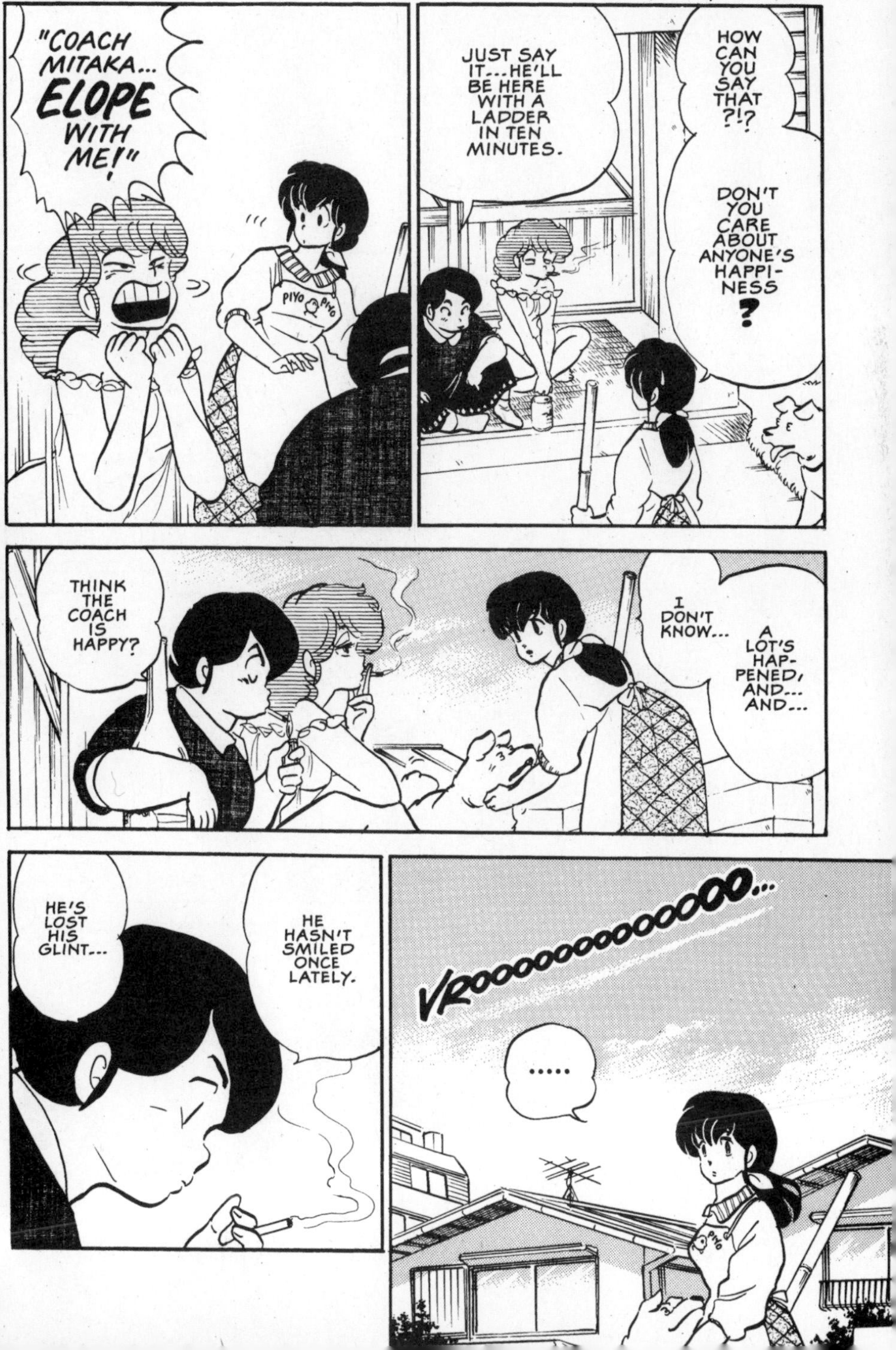
"COACH MITAKA... ELOPE WITH ME!"
JUST SAY IT...HE'LL BE HERE WITH A LADDER IN TEN MINUTES.
HOW CAN YOU SAY THAT?!?
DON'T YOU CARE ABOUT ANYONE'S HAPPI-NESS?
THINK THE COACH IS HAPPY?
I DON'T KNOW...
A LOT'S HAP-PENED, AND... AND...
HE'S LOST HIS GLINT...
HE HASN'T SMILED ONCE LATELY.
VROOOOOOOOOOOOOOOO...
.....

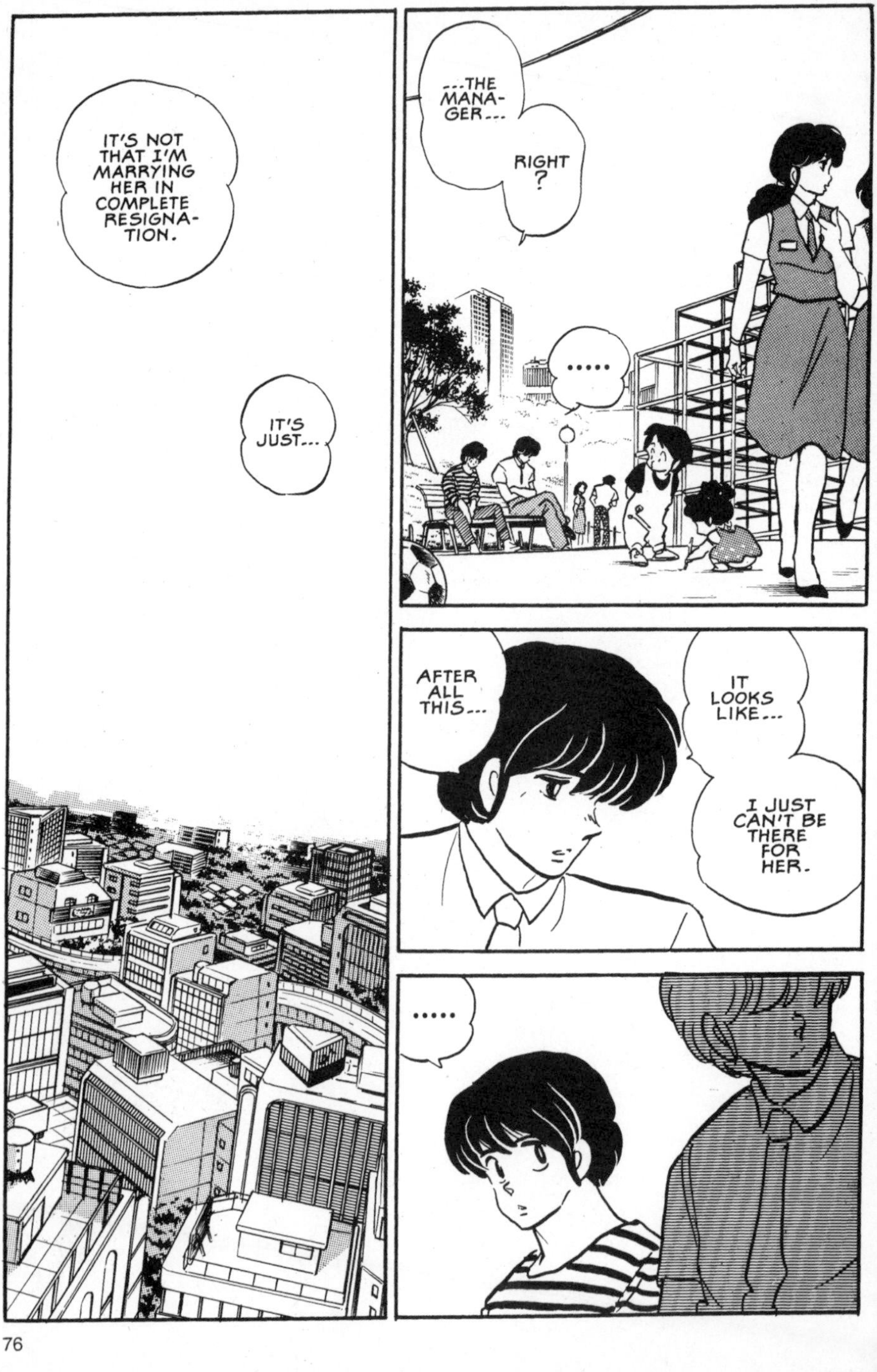
IT'S NOT THAT I'M MARRYING HER IN COMPLETE RESIGNATION.
IT'S JUST...
...THE MANAGER...
RIGHT?
.....
AFTER ALL THIS...
IT LOOKS LIKE...
I JUST CAN'T BE THERE FOR HER.
.....

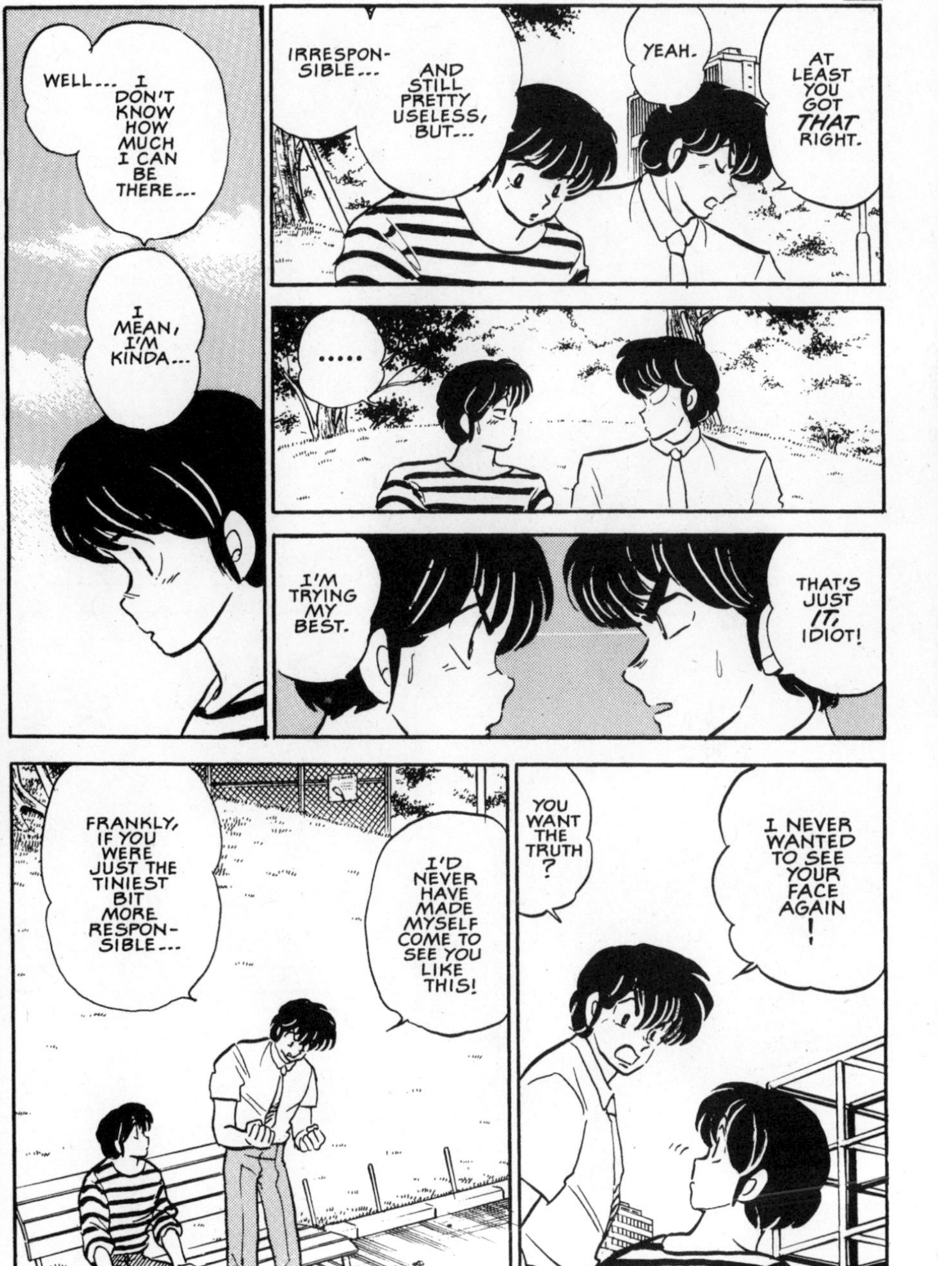
WELL... I DON'T KNOW HOW MUCH I CAN BE THERE...
I MEAN, I'M KINDA...
IRRESPON-SIBLE...
AND STILL PRETTY USELESS, BUT...
YEAH.
AT LEAST YOU GOT THAT RIGHT.
.....
I'M TRYING MY BEST.
THAT'S JUST IT, IDIOT!
FRANKLY, IF YOU WERE JUST THE TINIEST BIT MORE RESPON-SIBLE...
I'D NEVER HAVE MADE MYSELF COME TO SEE YOU LIKE THIS!
YOU WANT THE TRUTH?
I NEVER WANTED TO SEE YOUR FACE AGAIN!

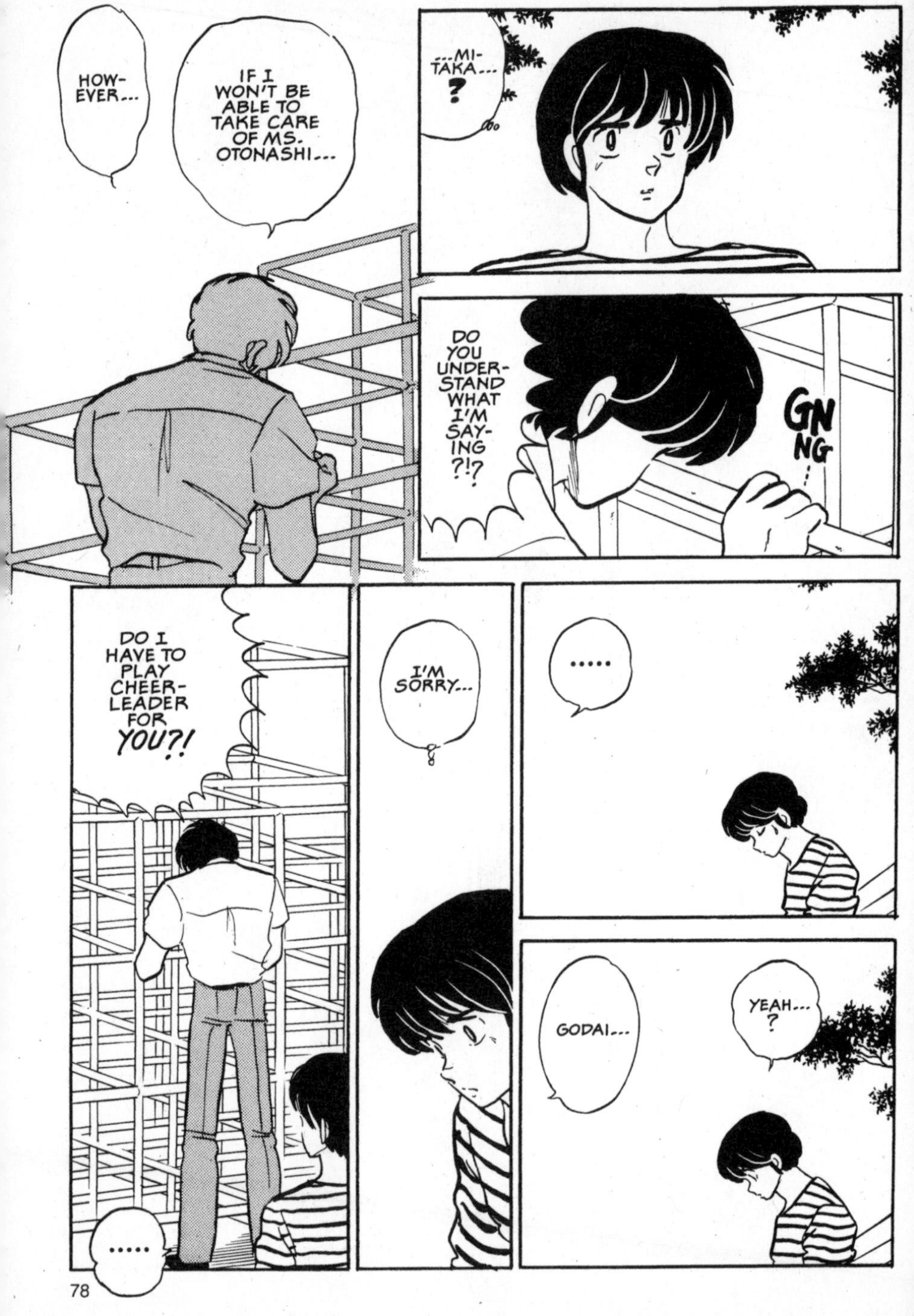
HOW-EVER...
IF I WON'T BE ABLE TO TAKE CARE OF MS. OTONASHI...
...MI-TAKA...?
DO YOU UNDER-STAND WHAT I'M SAY-ING?!?
GNNG
DO I HAVE TO PLAY CHEER-LEADER FOR YOU?!
.....
I'M SORRY...
.....
GODAI...
YEAH...?

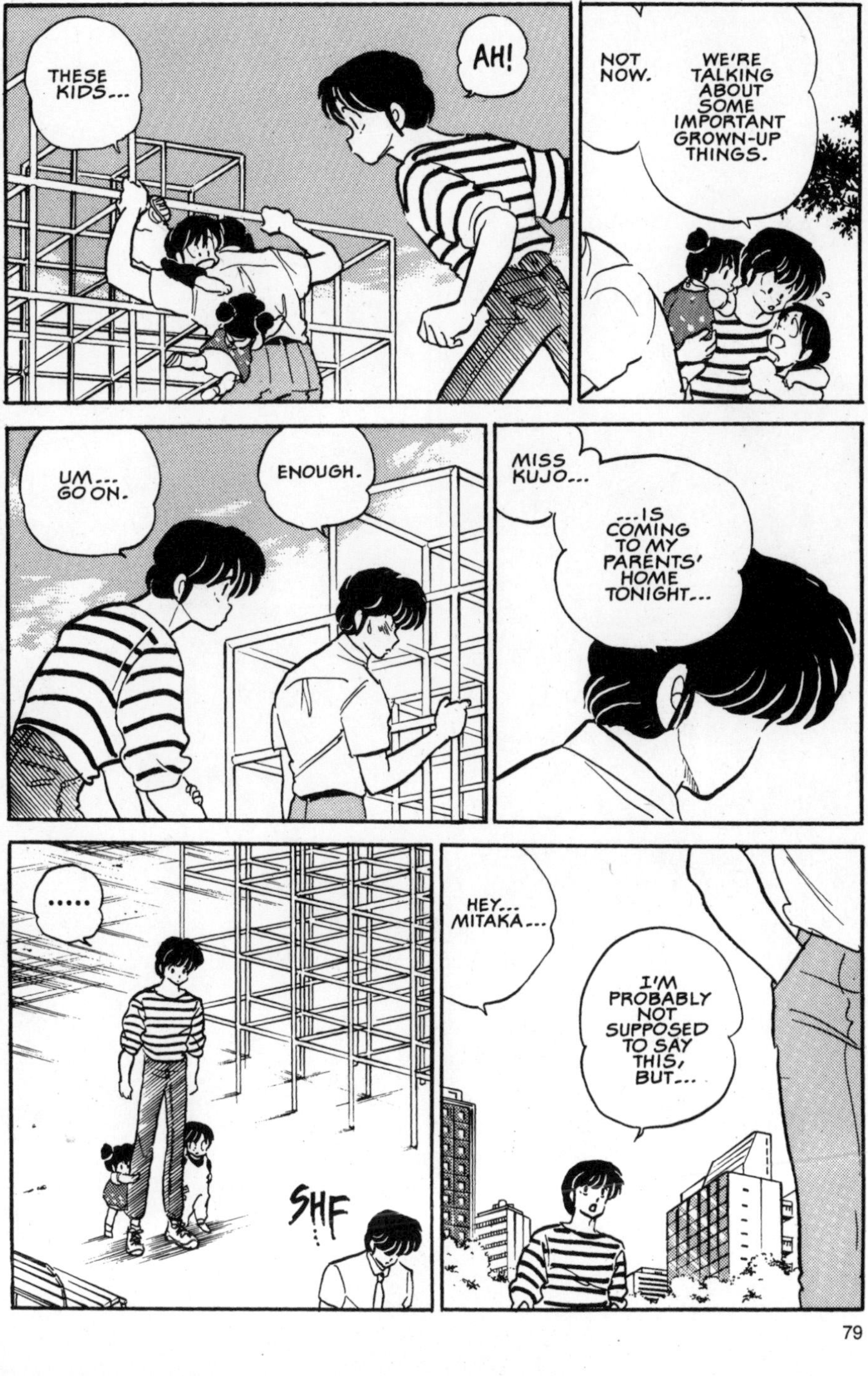
THESE KIDS...
AH!
NOT NOW.
WE'RE TALKING ABOUT SOME IMPORTANT GROWN-UP THINGS.
UM... GO ON.
ENOUGH.
MISS KUJO...
...IS COMING TO MY PARENTS' HOME TONIGHT...
......
SHF
HEY... MITAKA...
I'M PROBABLY NOT SUPPOSED TO SAY THIS, BUT...

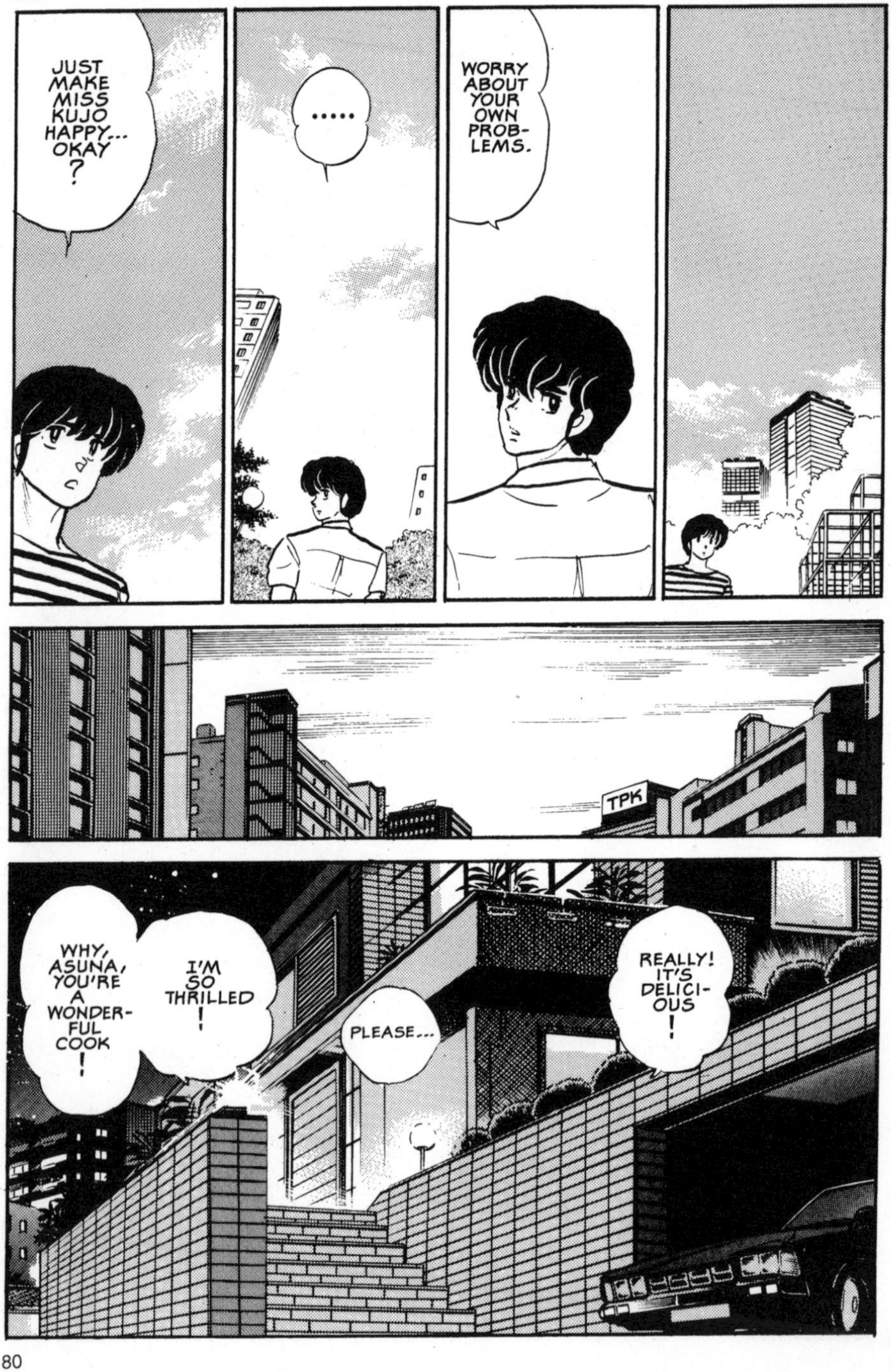
JUST MAKE MISS KUJO HAPPY... OKAY?
......
WORRY ABOUT YOUR OWN PROB-LEMS.
TPK
WHY, ASUNA, YOU'RE A WONDER-FUL COOK!
I'M SO THRILLED!
PLEASE...
REALLY! IT'S DELICI-OUS!

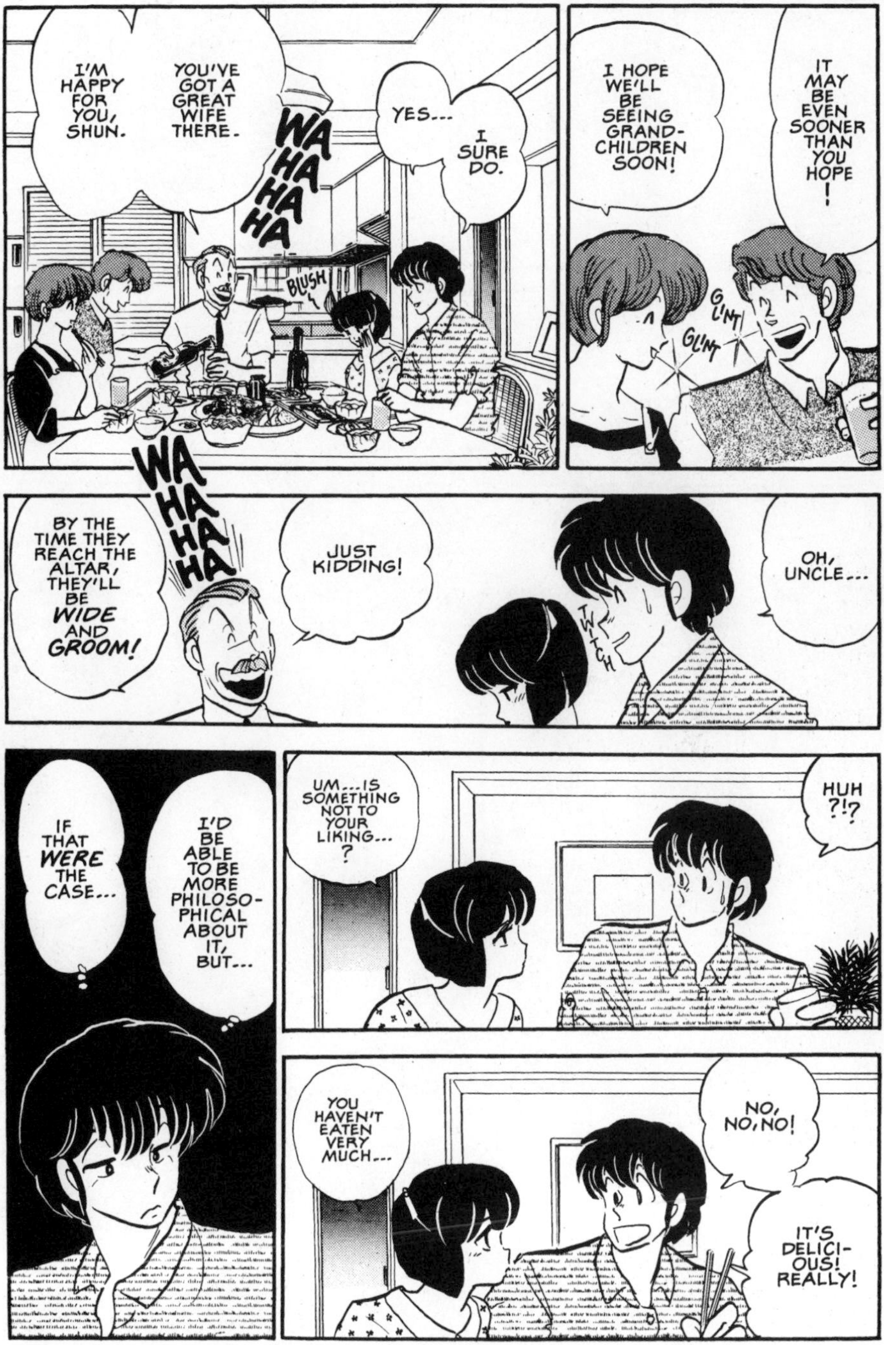
I'M HAPPY FOR YOU, SHUN.
YOU'VE GOT A GREAT WIFE THERE.
WAHAHAHA
BLUSH
YES...
I SURE DO.
I HOPE WE'LL BE SEEING GRANDCHILDREN SOON!
IT MAY BE EVEN SOONER THAN YOU HOPE!
GLINT
GLINT
WAHAHAHA
BY THE TIME THEY REACH THE ALTAR, THEY'LL BE WIDE AND GROOM!
JUST KIDDING!
TWITCH
OH, UNCLE...
IF THAT WERE THE CASE...
I'D BE ABLE TO BE MORE PHILOSOPHICAL ABOUT IT, BUT...
UM...IS SOMETHING NOT TO YOUR LIKING...?
HUH?!?
YOU HAVEN'T EATEN VERY MUCH...
NO, NO, NO!
IT'S DELICIOUS! REALLY!

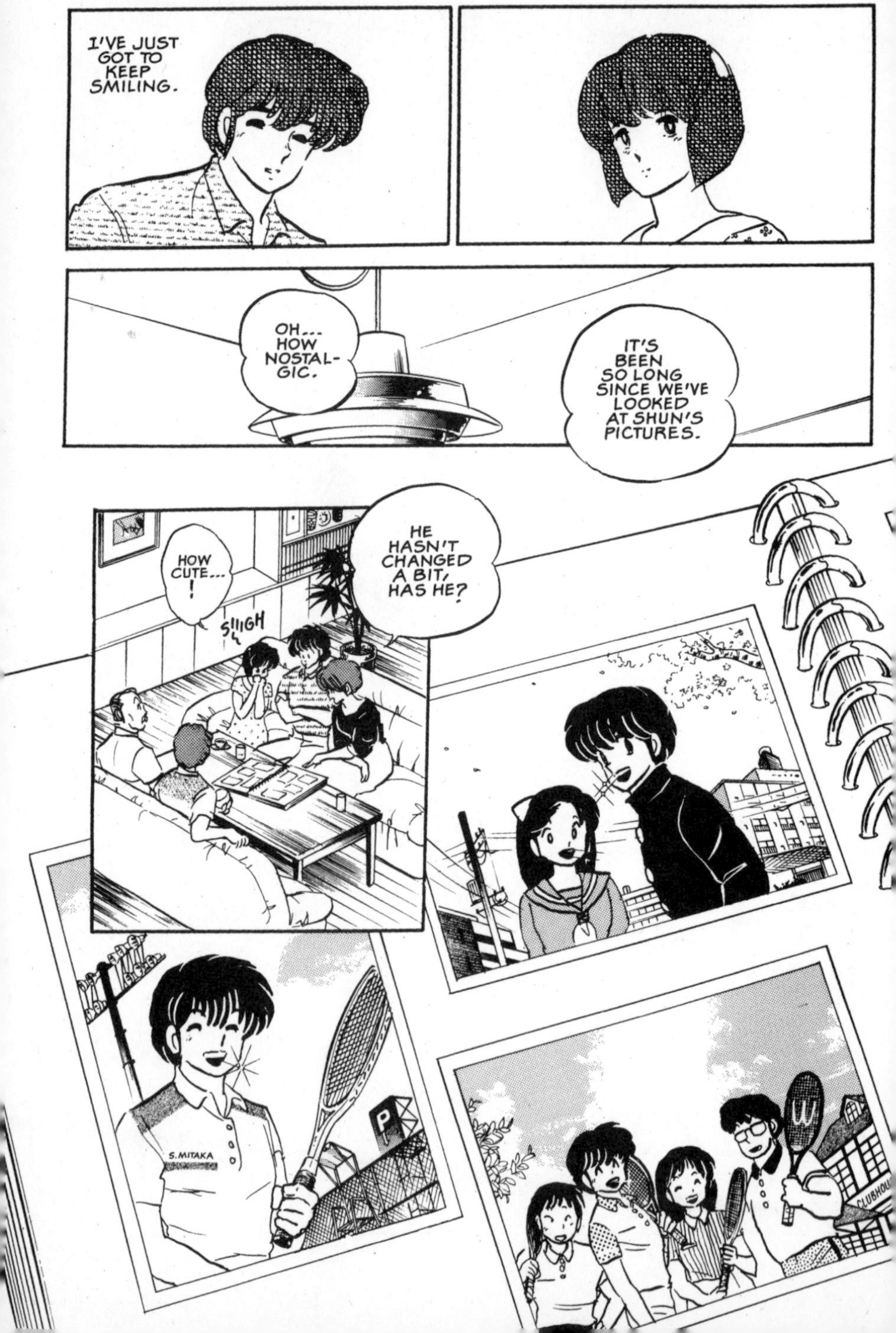
I'VE JUST GOT TO KEEP SMILING.
OH... HOW NOSTAL-GIC.
IT'S BEEN SO LONG SINCE WE'VE LOOKED AT SHUN'S PICTURES.
HOW CUTE...
!
SIIGH
HE HASN'T CHANGED A BIT, HAS HE?
S. MITAKA
P
CLUBHOU

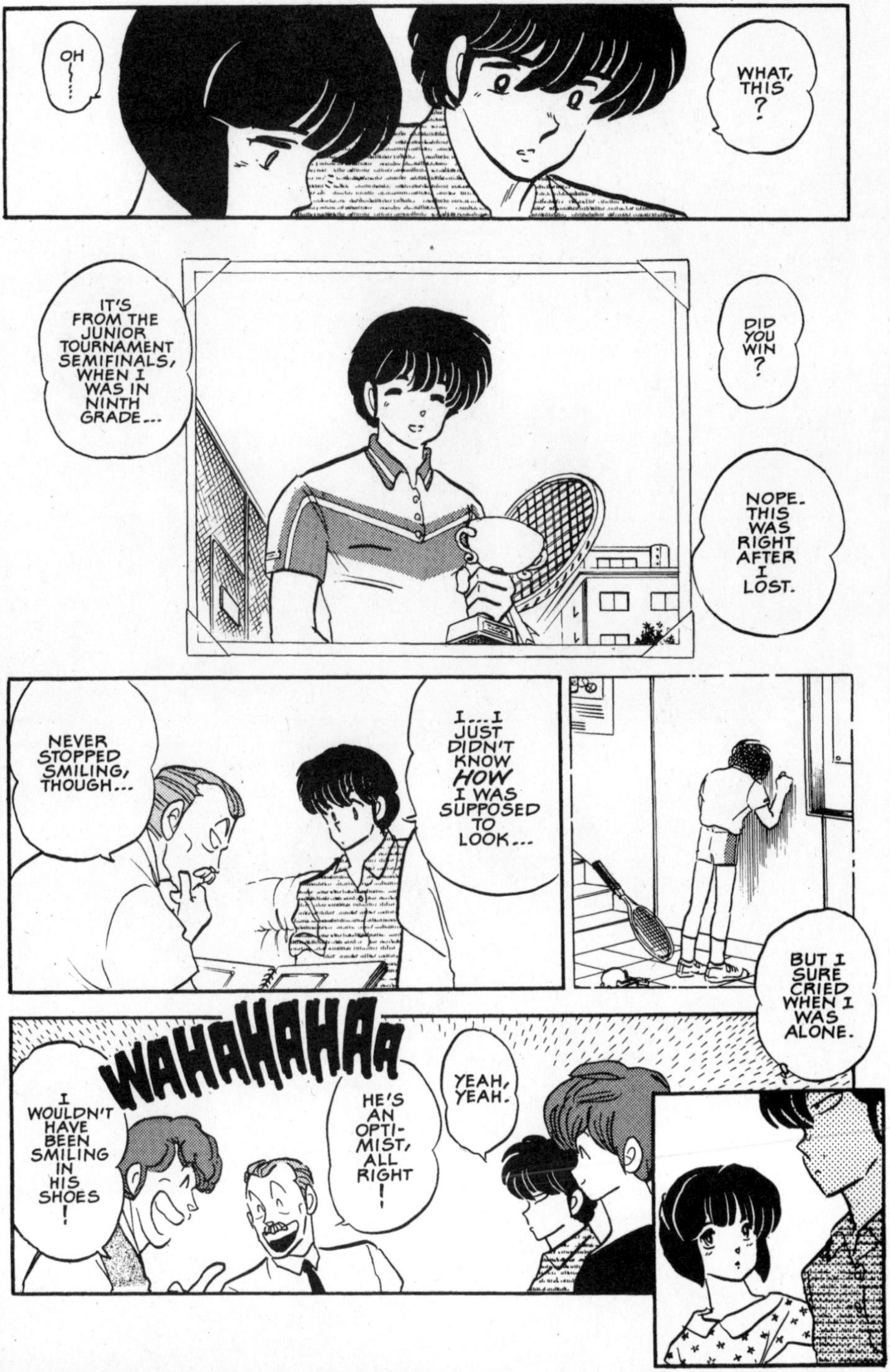
OH ...
WHAT, THIS?
IT'S FROM THE JUNIOR TOURNAMENT SEMIFINALS, WHEN I WAS IN NINTH GRADE...
DID YOU WIN?
NOPE. THIS WAS RIGHT AFTER I LOST.
NEVER STOPPED SMILING, THOUGH...
I... I JUST DIDN'T KNOW HOW I WAS SUPPOSED TO LOOK...
BUT I SURE CRIED WHEN I WAS ALONE.
WAHAHAHAA
I WOULDN'T HAVE BEEN SMILING IN HIS SHOES!
HE'S AN OPTI-MIST, ALL RIGHT!
YEAH, YEAH.

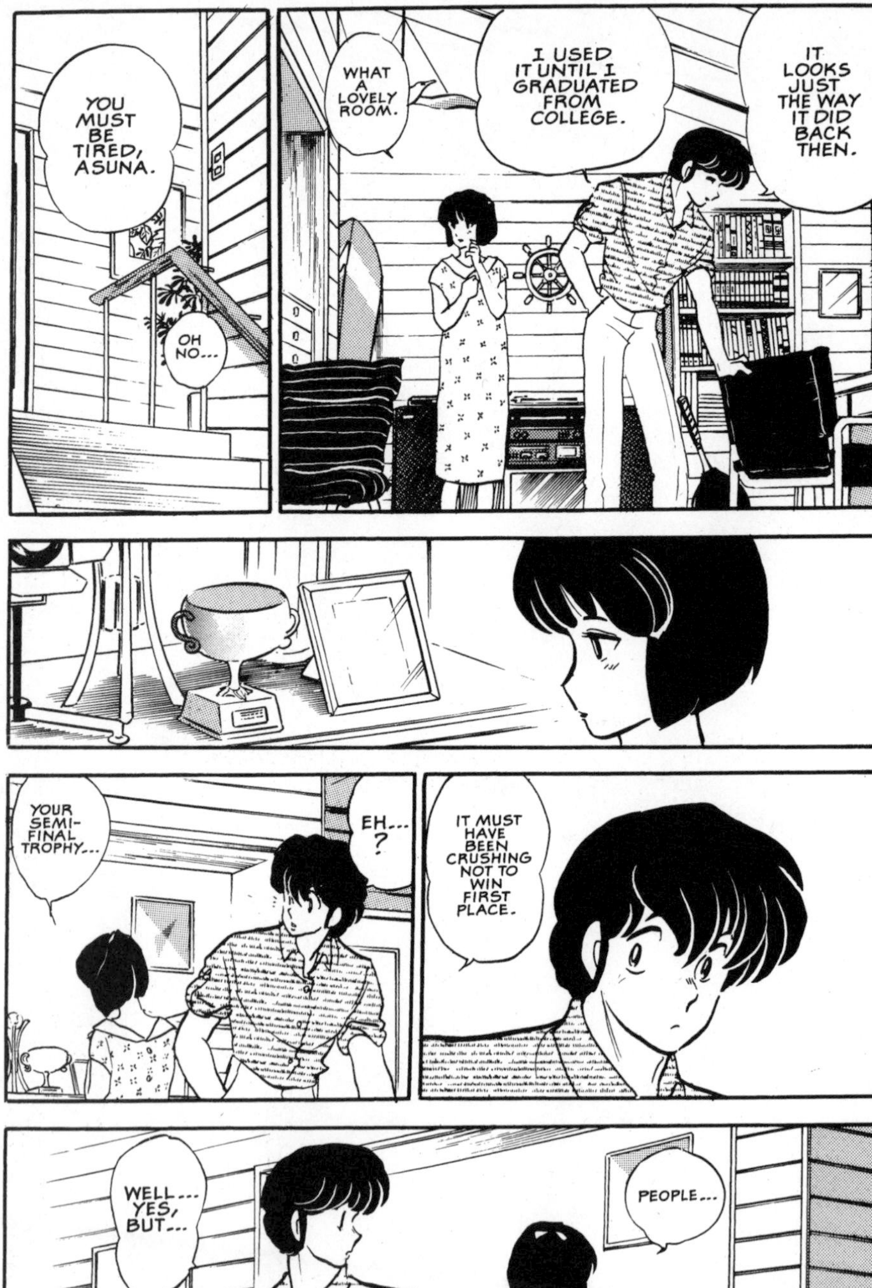
YOU MUST BE TIRED, ASUNA.
OH NO...
WHAT A LOVELY ROOM.
I USED IT UNTIL I GRADUATED FROM COLLEGE.
IT LOOKS JUST THE WAY IT DID BACK THEN.
YOUR SEMI-FINAL TROPHY...
EH...?
IT MUST HAVE BEEN CRUSHING NOT TO WIN FIRST PLACE.
WELL... YES, BUT...
PEOPLE...

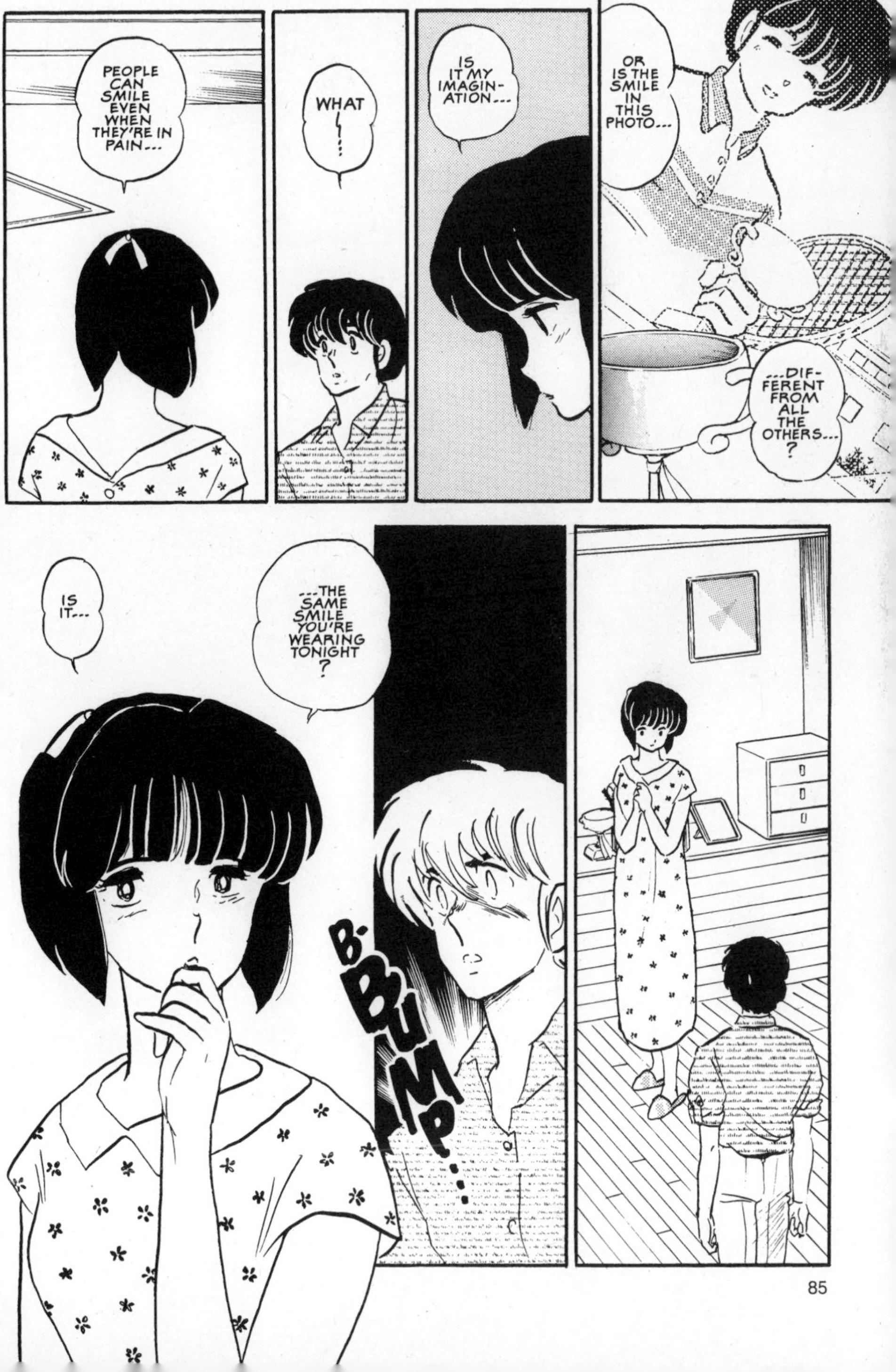
PEOPLE CAN SMILE EVEN WHEN THEY'RE IN PAIN...
WHAT!?
IS IT MY IMAGINATION...
OR IS THE SMILE IN THIS PHOTO...
...DIFFERENT FROM ALL THE OTHERS...?
IS IT...
...THE SAME SMILE YOU'RE WEARING TONIGHT?
B-BUMP...

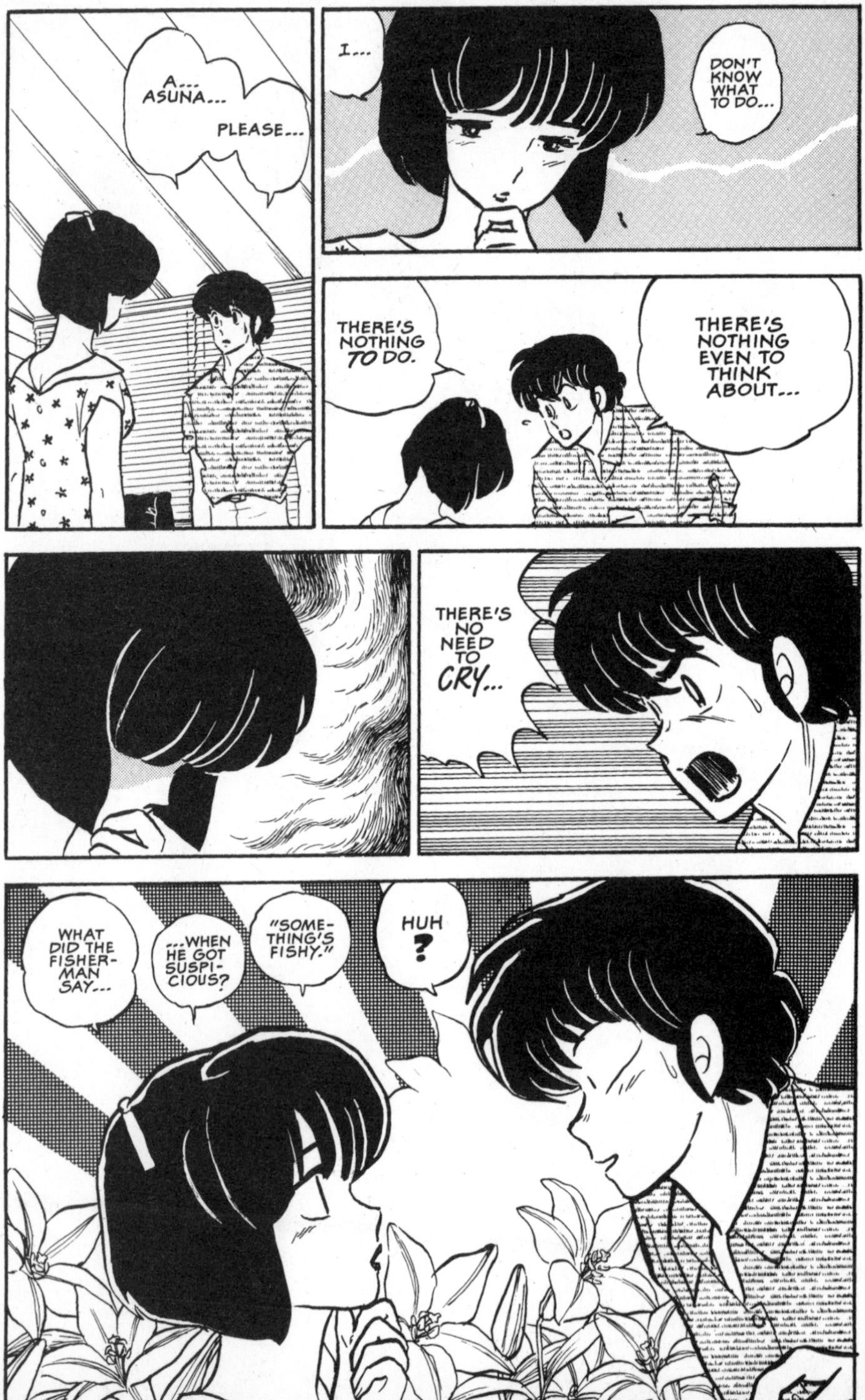
A... ASUNA...
PLEASE...
I...
DON'T KNOW WHAT TO DO...
THERE'S NOTHING TO DO.
THERE'S NOTHING EVEN TO THINK ABOUT...
THERE'S NO NEED TO CRY...
WHAT DID THE FISHERMAN SAY...
...WHEN HE GOT SUSPICIOUS?
"SOMETHING'S FISHY."
HUH?

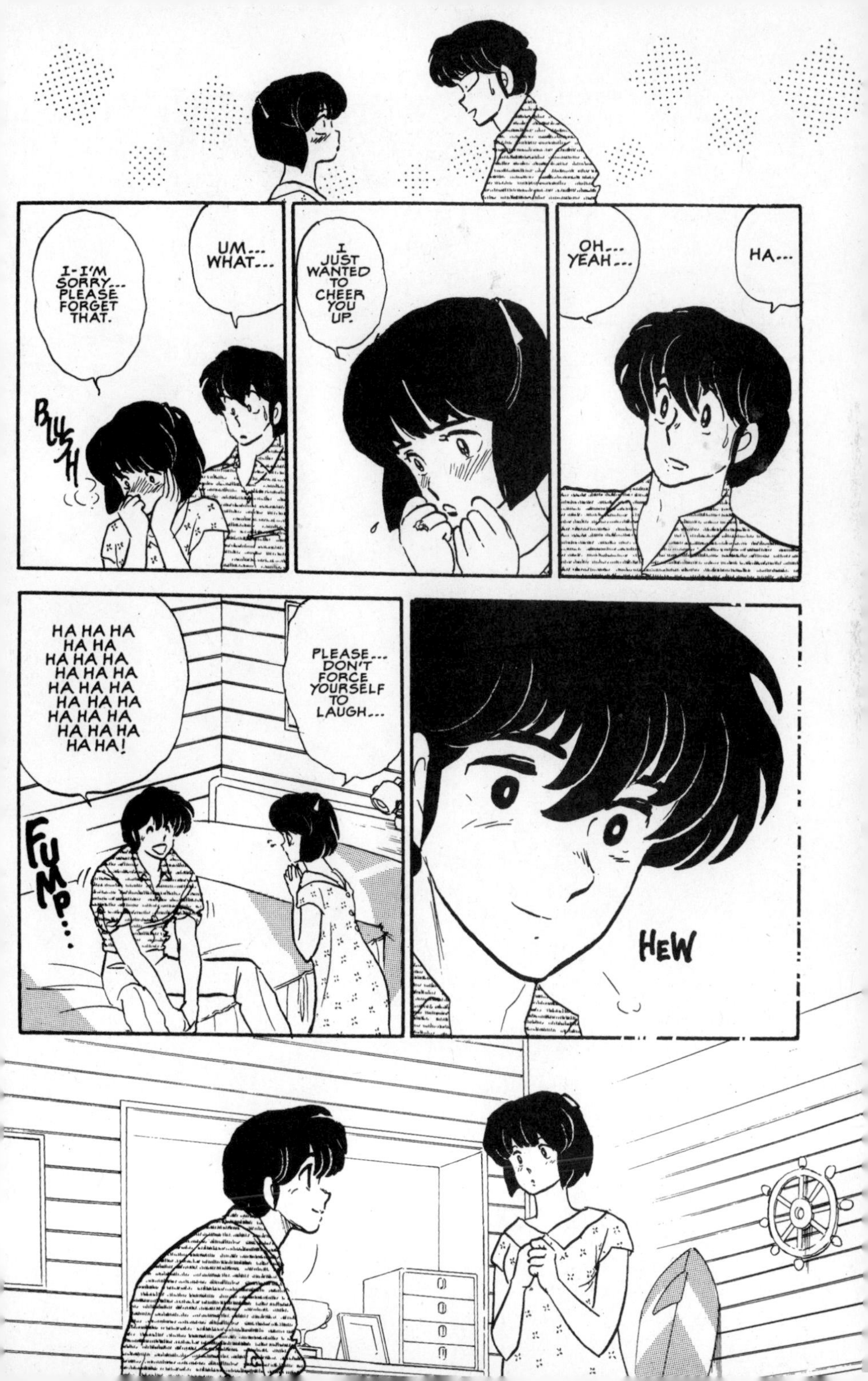
UM... WHAT...
I-I'M SORRY... PLEASE FORGET THAT.
BLUSH
I JUST WANTED TO CHEER YOU UP.
HA...
OH... YEAH...
HA HA HA HA HA HA HA HA HA HA HA HA HA HA HA HA HA HA HA HA HA HA HA HA HA HA!
PLEASE... DON'T FORCE YOURSELF TO LAUGH...
FUMP...
HEW

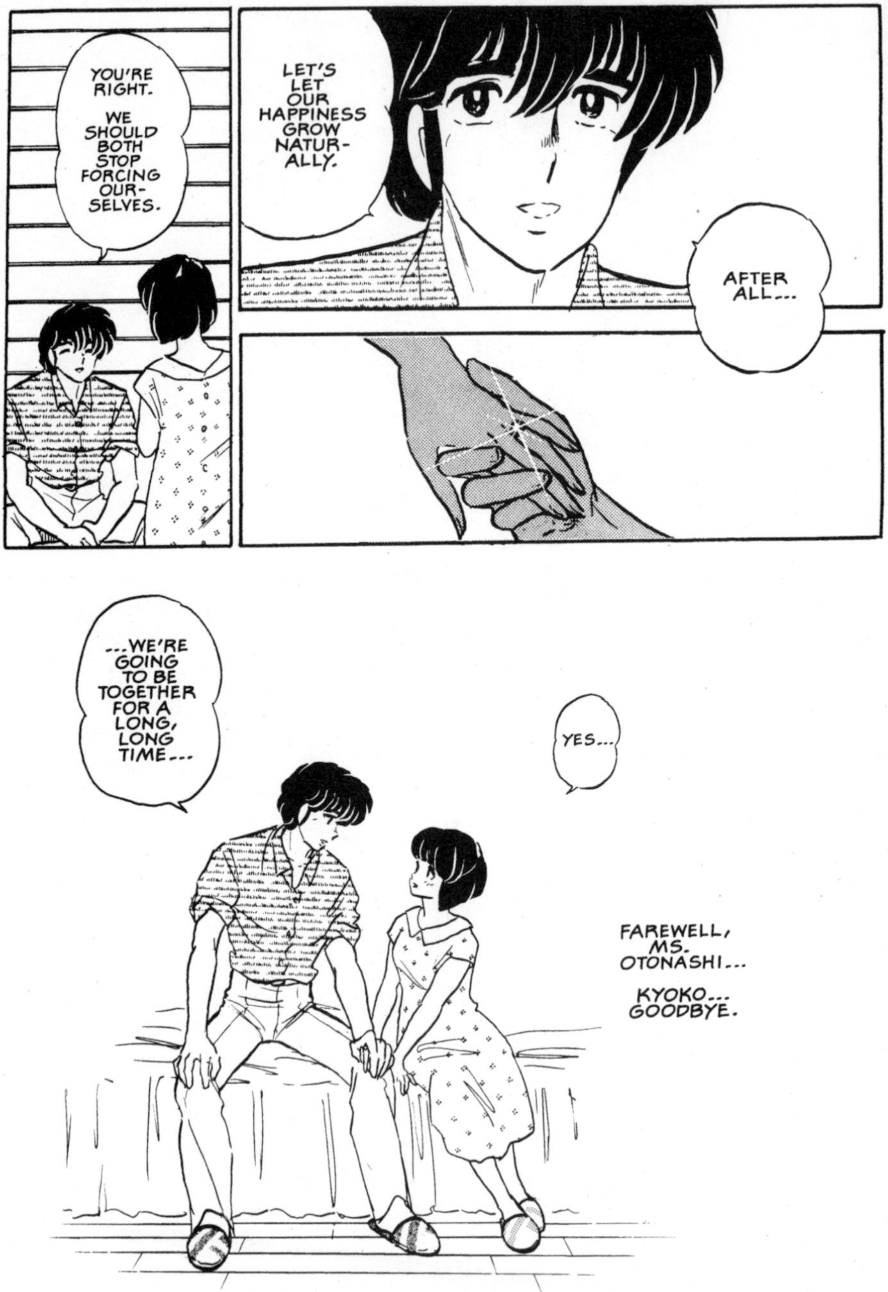
YOU'RE RIGHT. WE SHOULD BOTH STOP FORCING OUR-SELVES.
LET'S LET OUR HAPPINESS GROW NATUR-ALLY.
AFTER ALL...
...WE'RE GOING TO BE TOGETHER FOR A LONG, LONG TIME...
YES...
FAREWELL, MS. OTONASHI...
KYOKO... GOODBYE.

PART FIVE
TWISTS UPON TWISTS

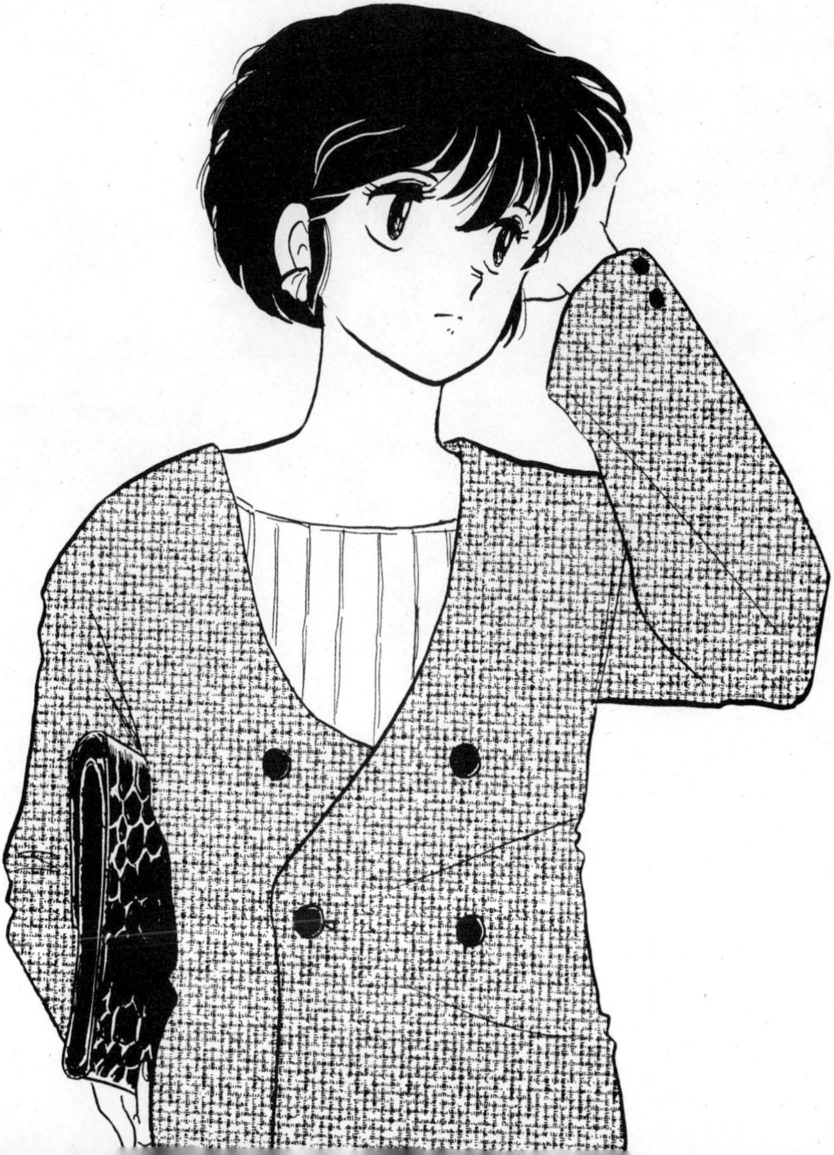

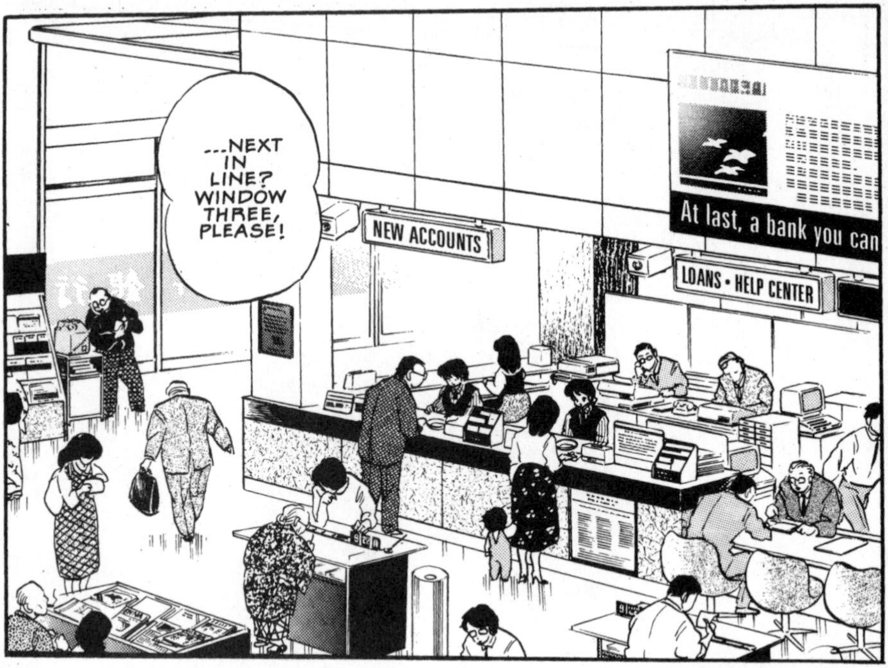
At last, a bank you can
...NEXT IN LINE? WINDOW THREE, PLEASE!
NEW ACCOUNTS
LOANS • HELP CENTER

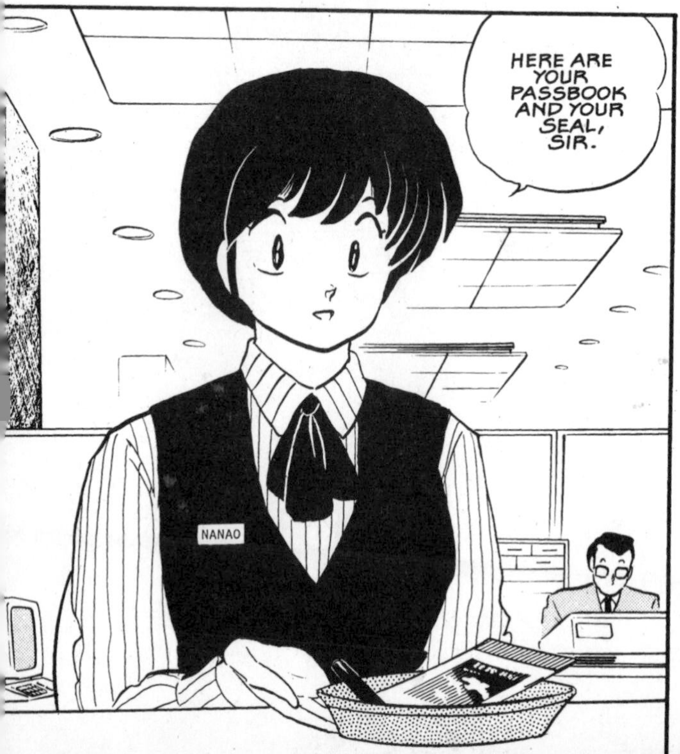
HERE ARE YOUR PASSBOOK AND YOUR SEAL, SIR.
NANAO

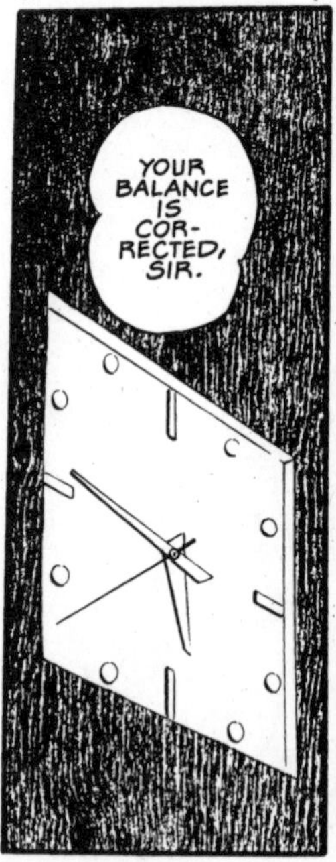
YOUR BALANCE IS COR-RECTED, SIR.

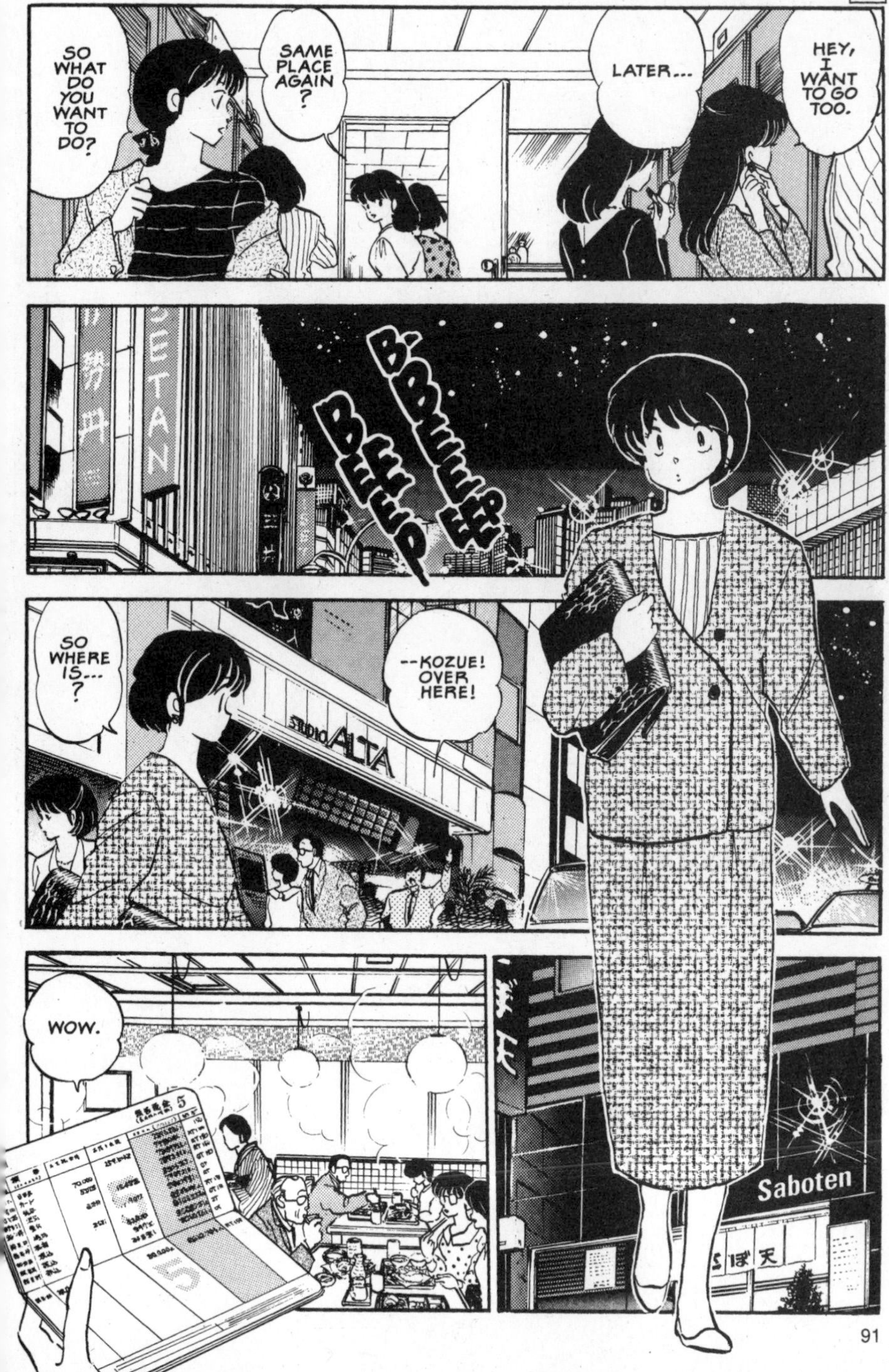
SO WHAT DO YOU WANT TO DO?
SAME PLACE AGAIN?
LATER...
HEY, I WANT TO GO TOO.
SETAN
B-BEEEEP
BEEEP
SO WHERE IS...?
STUDIO ALTA
--KOZUE! OVER HERE!
WOW.
Saboten

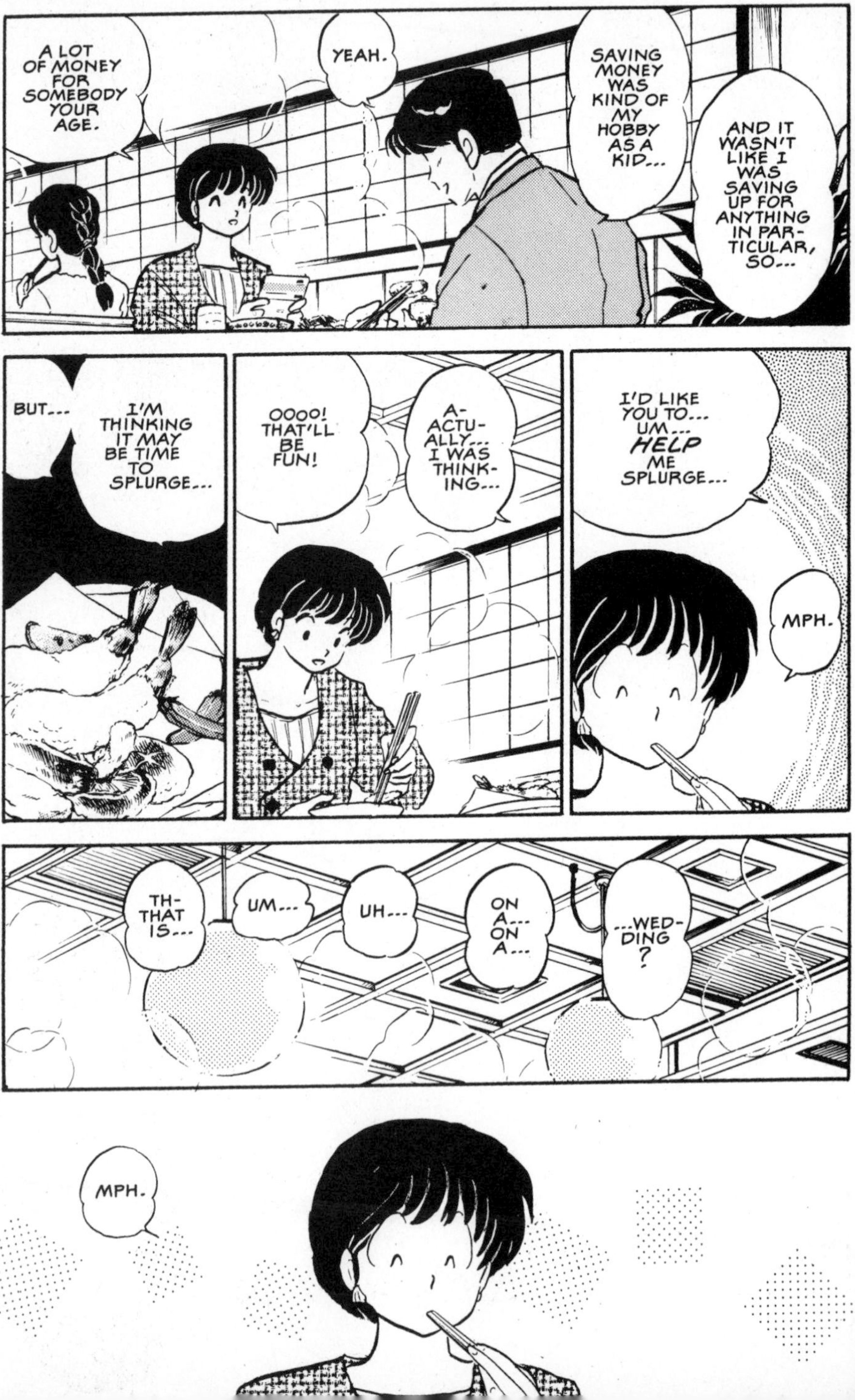

A LOT OF MONEY FOR SOMEBODY YOUR AGE.
YEAH.
SAVING MONEY WAS KIND OF MY HOBBY AS A KID...
AND IT WASN'T LIKE I WAS SAVING UP FOR ANYTHING IN PAR-TICULAR, SO...
BUT...
I'M THINKING IT MAY BE TIME TO SPLURGE...
OOOO! THAT'LL BE FUN!
A-ACTU-ALLY... I WAS THINK-ING...
I'D LIKE YOU TO... UM... HELP ME SPLURGE...
MPH.
TH-THAT IS...
UM...
UH...
ON A... ON A...
...WED-DING?
MPH.

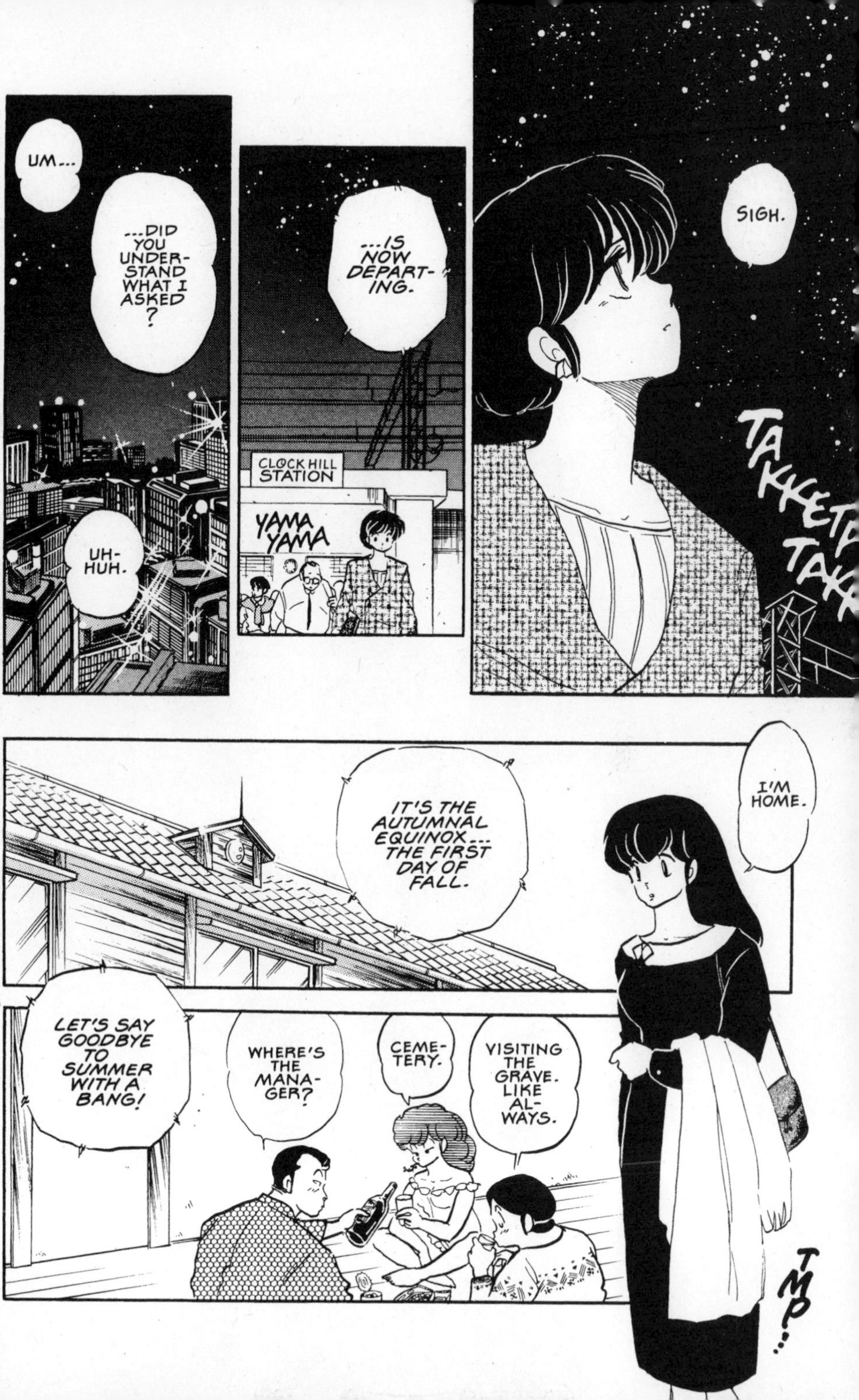
UM...
...DID YOU UNDERSTAND WHAT I ASKED?
UH-HUH.
...IS NOW DEPARTING.
CLOCK HILL STATION
YAMA YAMA
SIGH.
IT'S THE AUTUMNAL EQUINOX... THE FIRST DAY OF FALL.
I'M HOME.
LET'S SAY GOODBYE TO SUMMER WITH A BANG!
WHERE'S THE MANAGER?
CEMETERY.
VISITING THE GRAVE. LIKE ALWAYS.
TMP...

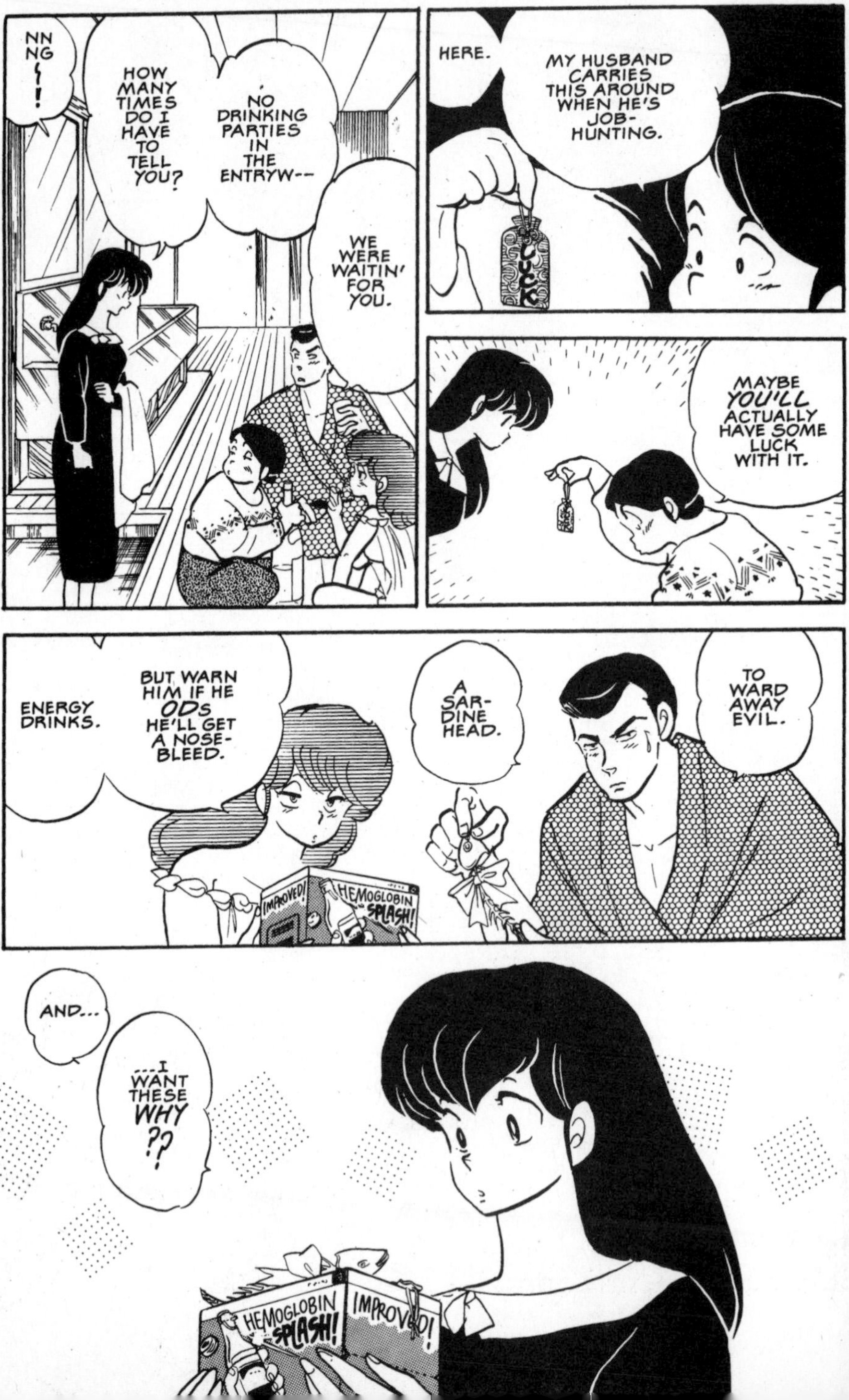
NNNG!!
HOW MANY TIMES DO I HAVE TO TELL YOU?
NO DRINKING PARTIES IN THE ENTRYW--
WE WERE WAITIN' FOR YOU.
HERE.
MY HUSBAND CARRIES THIS AROUND WHEN HE'S JOB-HUNTING.
LUCK
MAYBE YOU'LL ACTUALLY HAVE SOME LUCK WITH IT.
ENERGY DRINKS.
BUT WARN HIM IF HE ODs HE'LL GET A NOSE-BLEED.
IMPROVED!
HEMOGLOBIN SPLASH!
A SARDINE HEAD.
TO WARD AWAY EVIL.
AND...
...I WANT THESE WHY??
HEMOGLOBIN SPLASH!
IMPROVED!

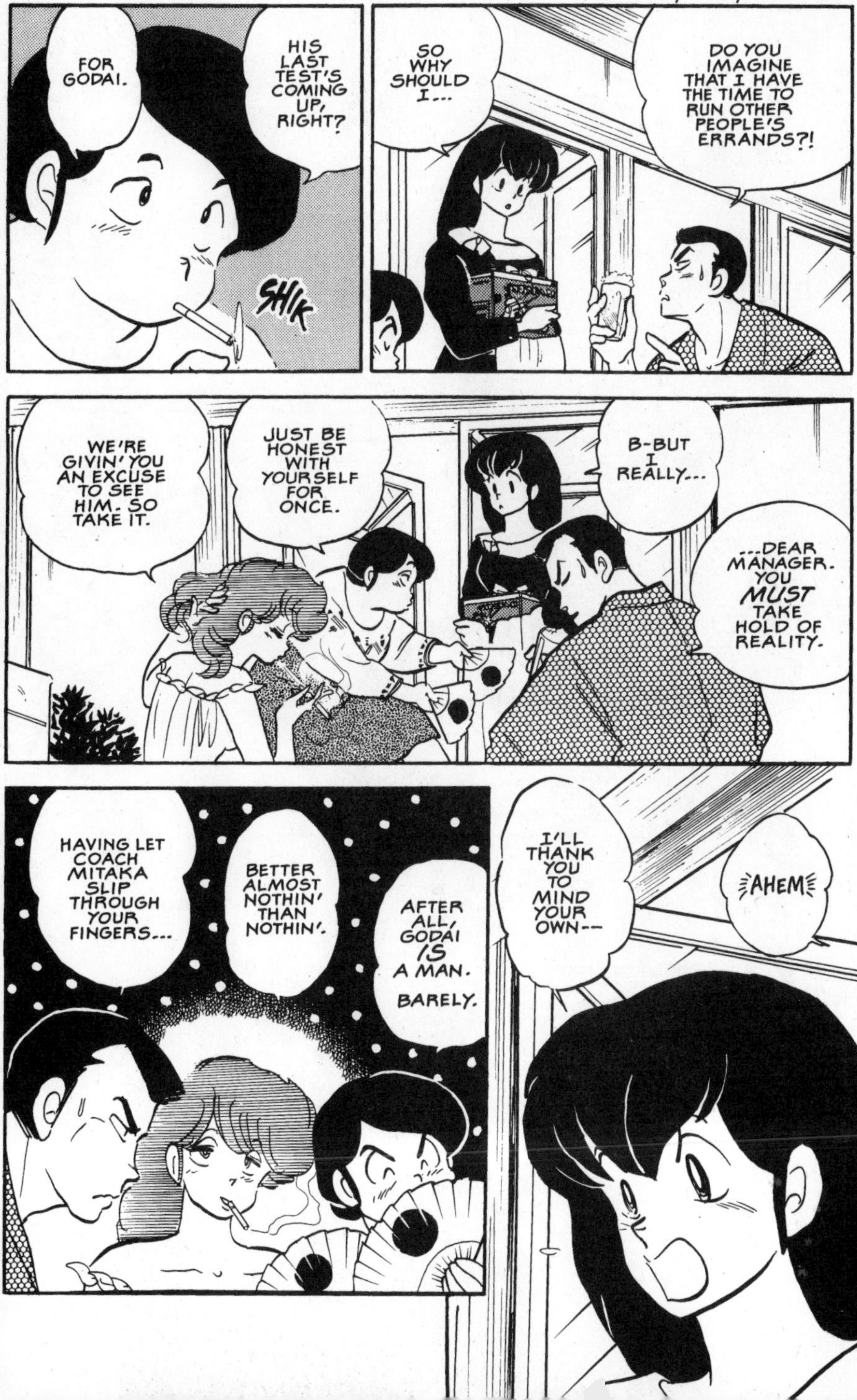
FOR GODAI.
HIS LAST TEST'S COMING UP, RIGHT?
SHIK
SO WHY SHOULD I...
DO YOU IMAGINE THAT I HAVE THE TIME TO RUN OTHER PEOPLE'S ERRANDS?!
WE'RE GIVIN' YOU AN EXCUSE TO SEE HIM. SO TAKE IT.
JUST BE HONEST WITH YOURSELF FOR ONCE.
B-BUT I REALLY...
...DEAR MANAGER. YOU MUST TAKE HOLD OF REALITY.
HAVING LET COACH MITAKA SLIP THROUGH YOUR FINGERS...
BETTER ALMOST NOTHIN' THAN NOTHIN'.
AFTER ALL, GODAI IS A MAN.
BARELY.
I'LL THANK YOU TO MIND YOUR OWN--
AHEM

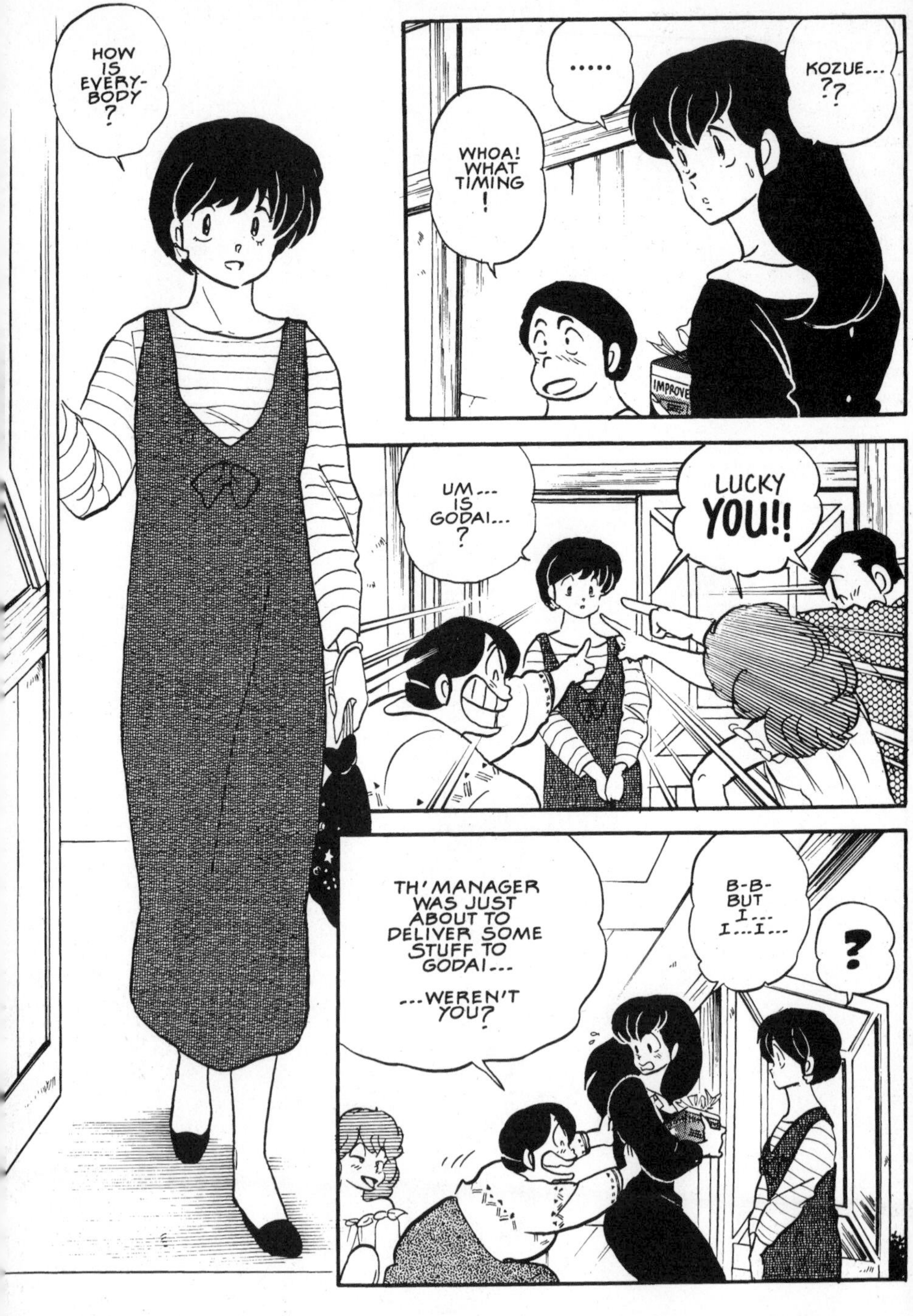
HOW IS EVERY-BODY?
.....
KOZUE...??
WHOA! WHAT TIMING!
IMPROVE
UM... IS GODAI...?
LUCKY YOU!!
TH' MANAGER WAS JUST ABOUT TO DELIVER SOME STUFF TO GODAI...
...WEREN'T YOU?
B-B-BUT I... I...I...
?

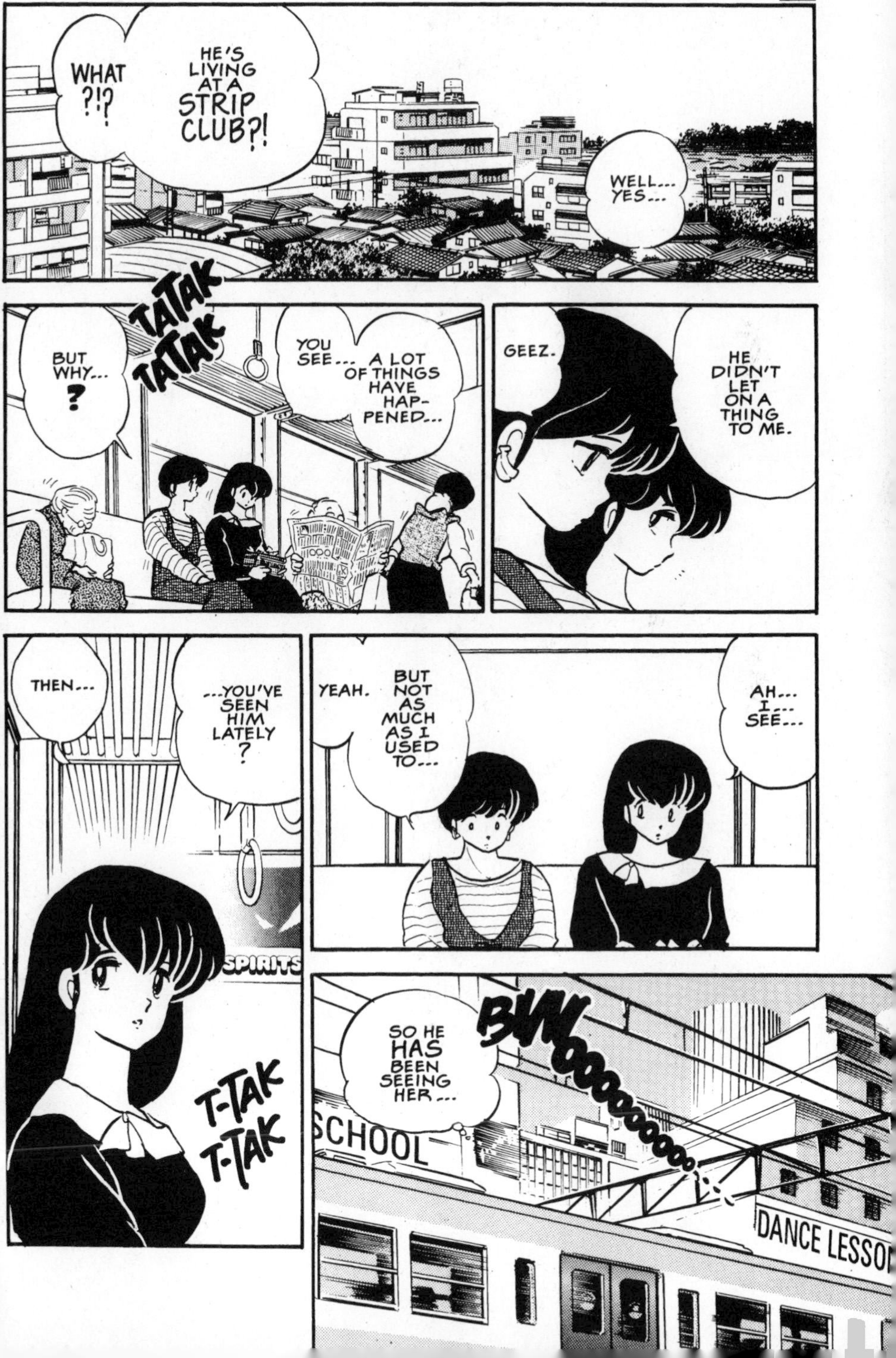
WHAT ?!?
HE'S LIVING AT A STRIP CLUB?!
WELL... YES...
BUT WHY... ?
TATAK TATAK
YOU SEE... A LOT OF THINGS HAVE HAP-PENED...
GEEZ.
HE DIDN'T LET ON A THING TO ME.
THEN...
...YOU'VE SEEN HIM LATELY ?
YEAH.
BUT NOT AS MUCH AS I USED TO...
AH... I... SEE...
SPIRITS
T-TAK T-TAK
SO HE HAS BEEN SEEING HER...
BWWOOOOOOOOOOOO
SCHOOL
DANCE LESSO

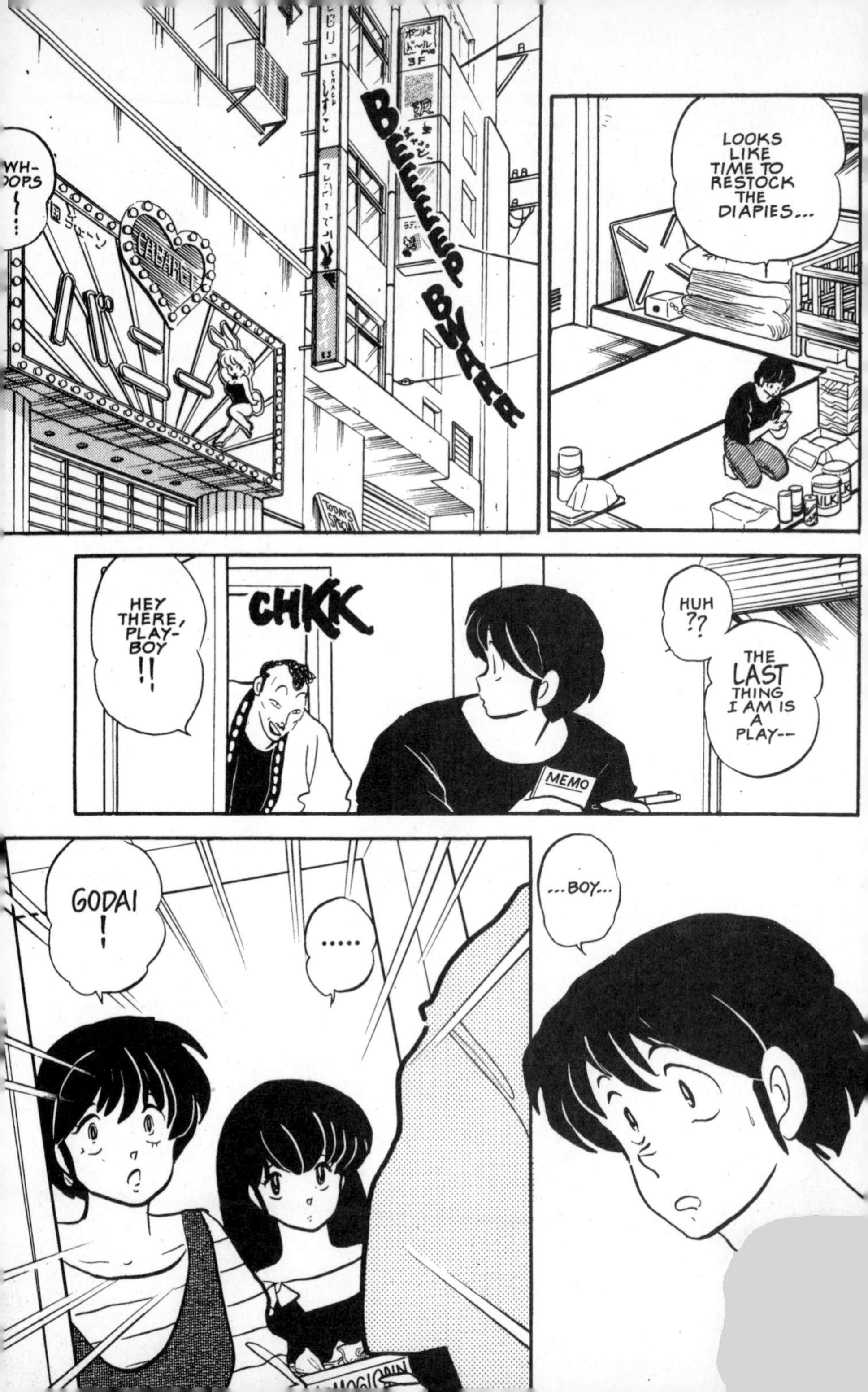

WH-OOPS~!...
BEEEEEP BWAAA
LOOKS LIKE TIME TO RESTOCK THE DIAPIES...
MILK
HEY THERE, PLAY-BOY!!
CHKK
HUH??
THE LAST THING I AM IS A PLAY--
MEMO
GODAI!
......
...BOY...

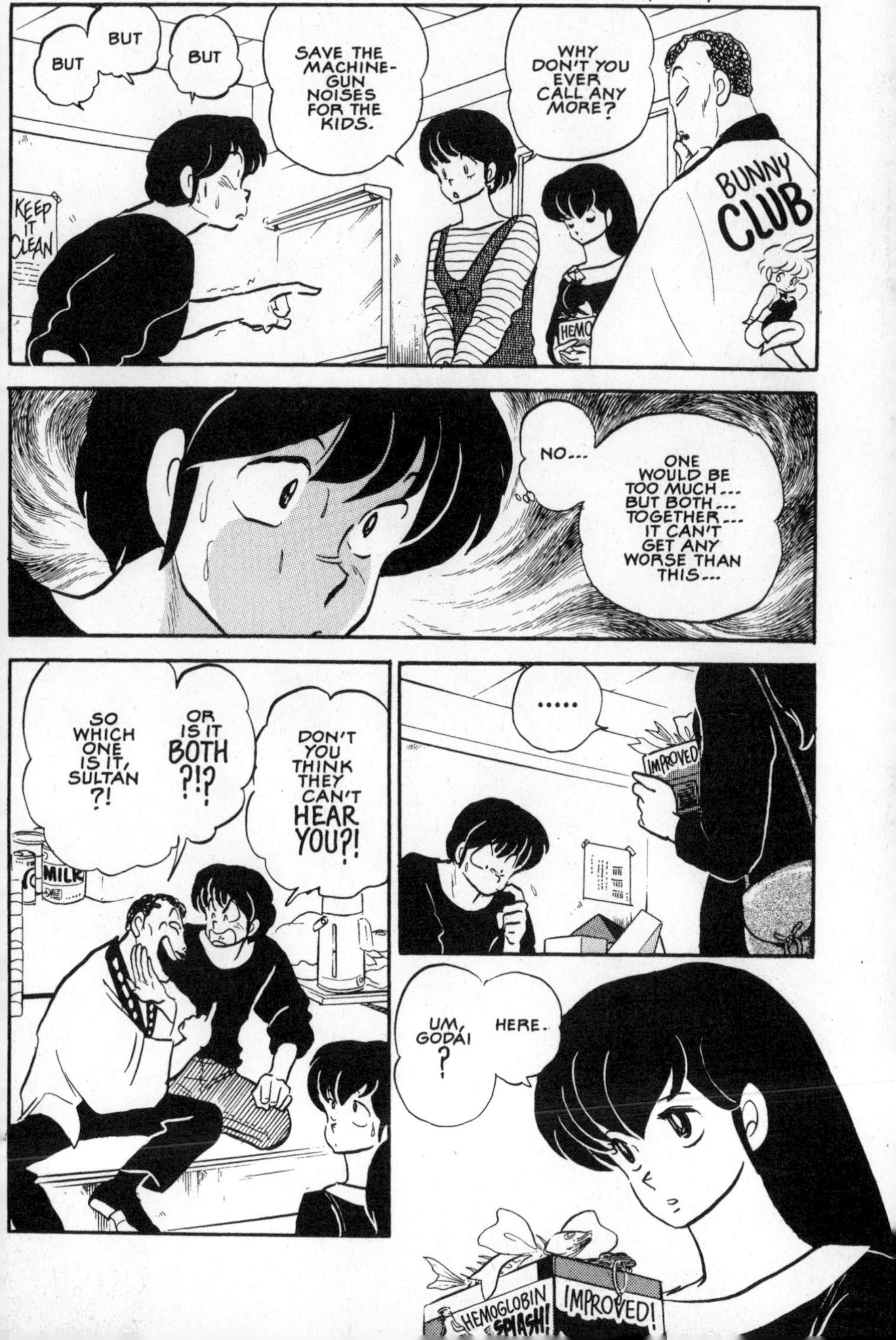
BUT
BUT
BUT
SAVE THE MACHINE-GUN NOISES FOR THE KIDS.
WHY DON'T YOU EVER CALL ANY MORE?
KEEP IT CLEAN
BUNNY CLUB
HEMO
NO...
ONE WOULD BE TOO MUCH... BUT BOTH... TOGETHER... IT CAN'T GET ANY WORSE THAN THIS...
SO WHICH ONE IS IT, SULTAN ?!
OR IS IT BOTH ?!?
DON'T YOU THINK THEY CAN'T HEAR YOU?!
MILK
.....
IMPROVED
UM, GODAI ?
HERE.
HEMOGLOBIN SPLASH!
IMPROVED!

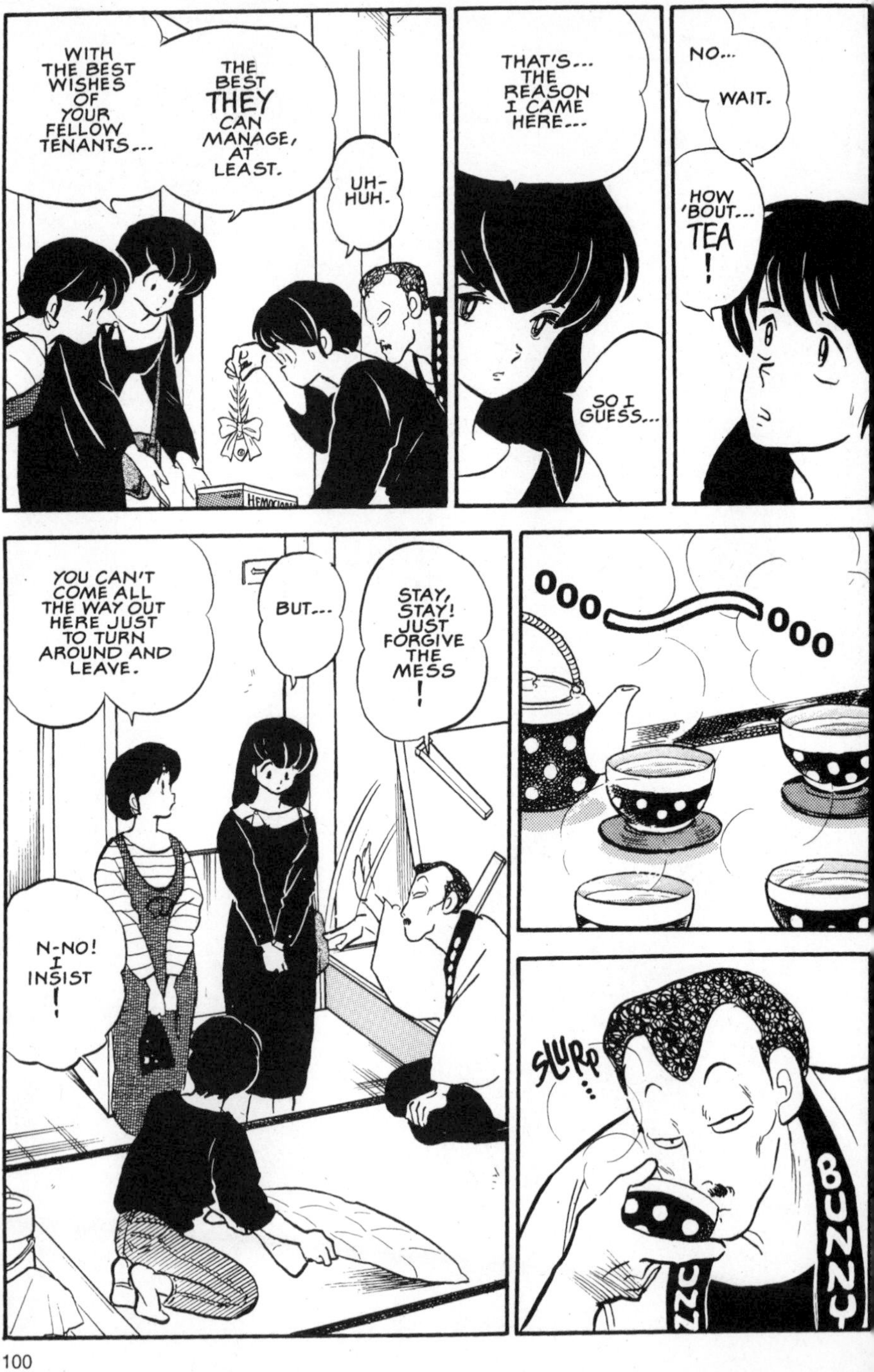
WITH THE BEST WISHES OF YOUR FELLOW TENANTS...
THE BEST THEY CAN MANAGE, AT LEAST.
UH-HUH.
THAT'S... THE REASON I CAME HERE...
SO I GUESS...
NO...
WAIT.
HOW 'BOUT... TEA!
YOU CAN'T COME ALL THE WAY OUT HERE JUST TO TURN AROUND AND LEAVE.
BUT...
STAY, STAY! JUST FORGIVE THE MESS!
N-NO! I INSIST!
OOO~OOO
SLURP...
BUNNY

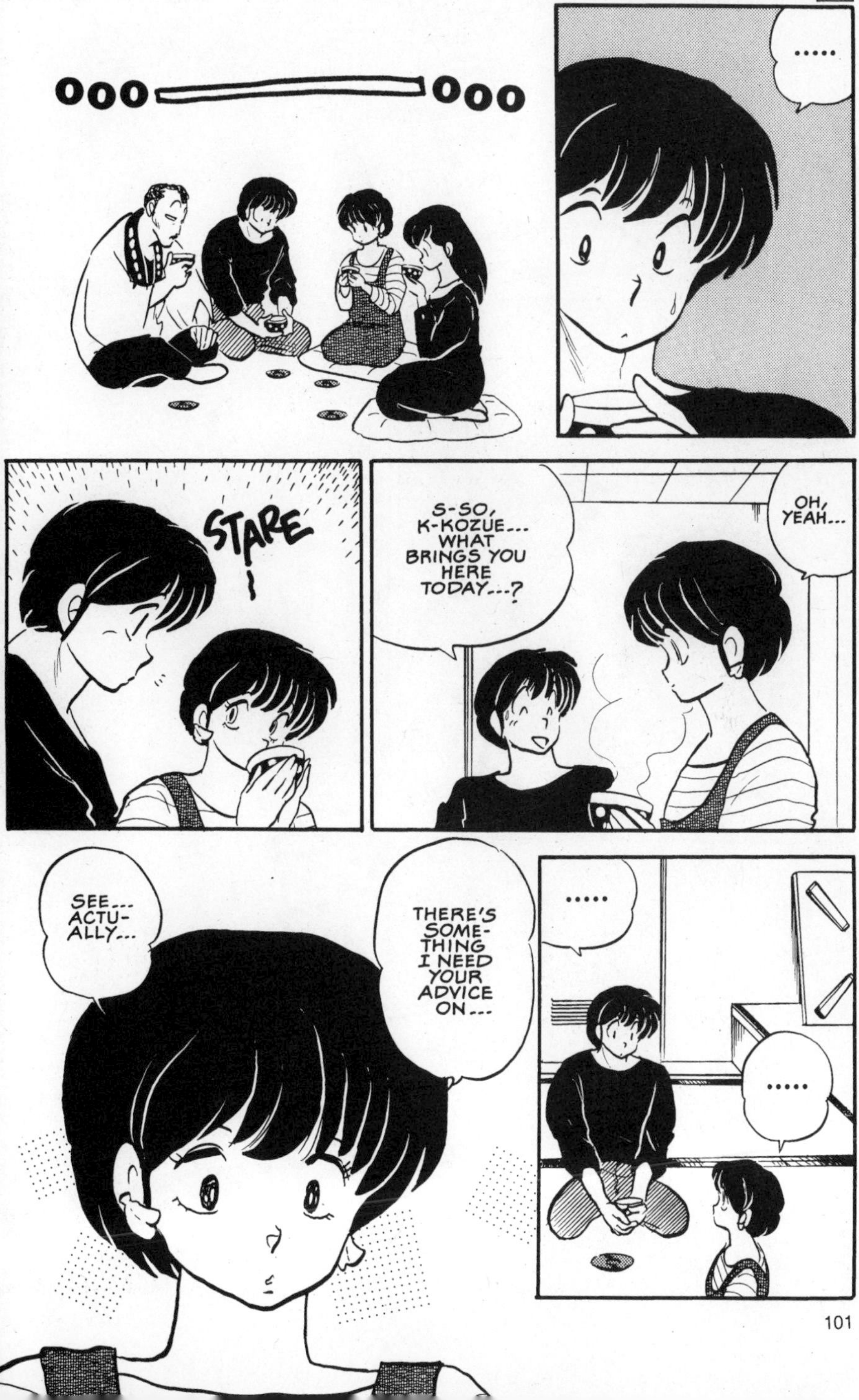
OOO——OOO
.....
STARE
S-SO, K-KOZUE... WHAT BRINGS YOU HERE TODAY...?
OH, YEAH...
SEE... ACTU-ALLY...
THERE'S SOME-THING I NEED YOUR ADVICE ON...
.....
.....

TAKE THE HINT.

YOU TWO GO TO A COFFEE SHOP OR SOMEPLACE.

RIGHT.

BUT...

BUZZ

NO, PLEASE GO.

I SHOULD BE GETTING HOME ANYWAY.

YAH...

I HOPE YOU DON'T MIND, MS. OTONASHI.

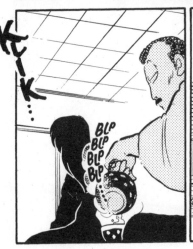

KIK...

BLP BLP BLP BLP

OH... PLEASE... REALLY...

THE LUNCHES...

102

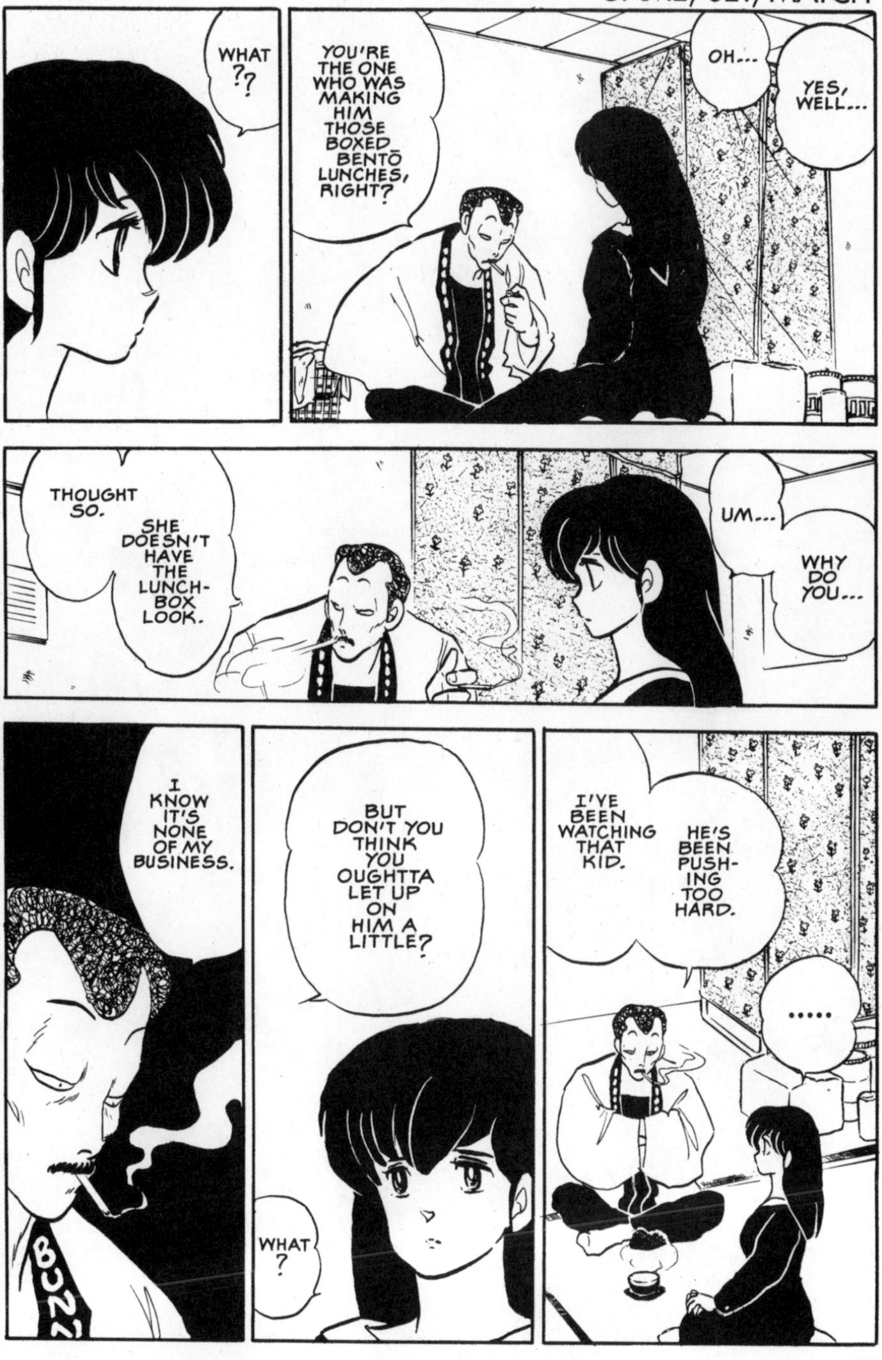
WHAT ??
YOU'RE THE ONE WHO WAS MAKING HIM THOSE BOXED BENTŌ LUNCHES, RIGHT?
OH...
YES, WELL...
THOUGHT SO.
SHE DOESN'T HAVE THE LUNCH-BOX LOOK.
UM...
WHY DO YOU...
I KNOW IT'S NONE OF MY BUSINESS.
BUT DON'T YOU THINK YOU OUGHTTA LET UP ON HIM A LITTLE?
WHAT ?
I'VE BEEN WATCHING THAT KID.
HE'S BEEN PUSH-ING TOO HARD.
.....

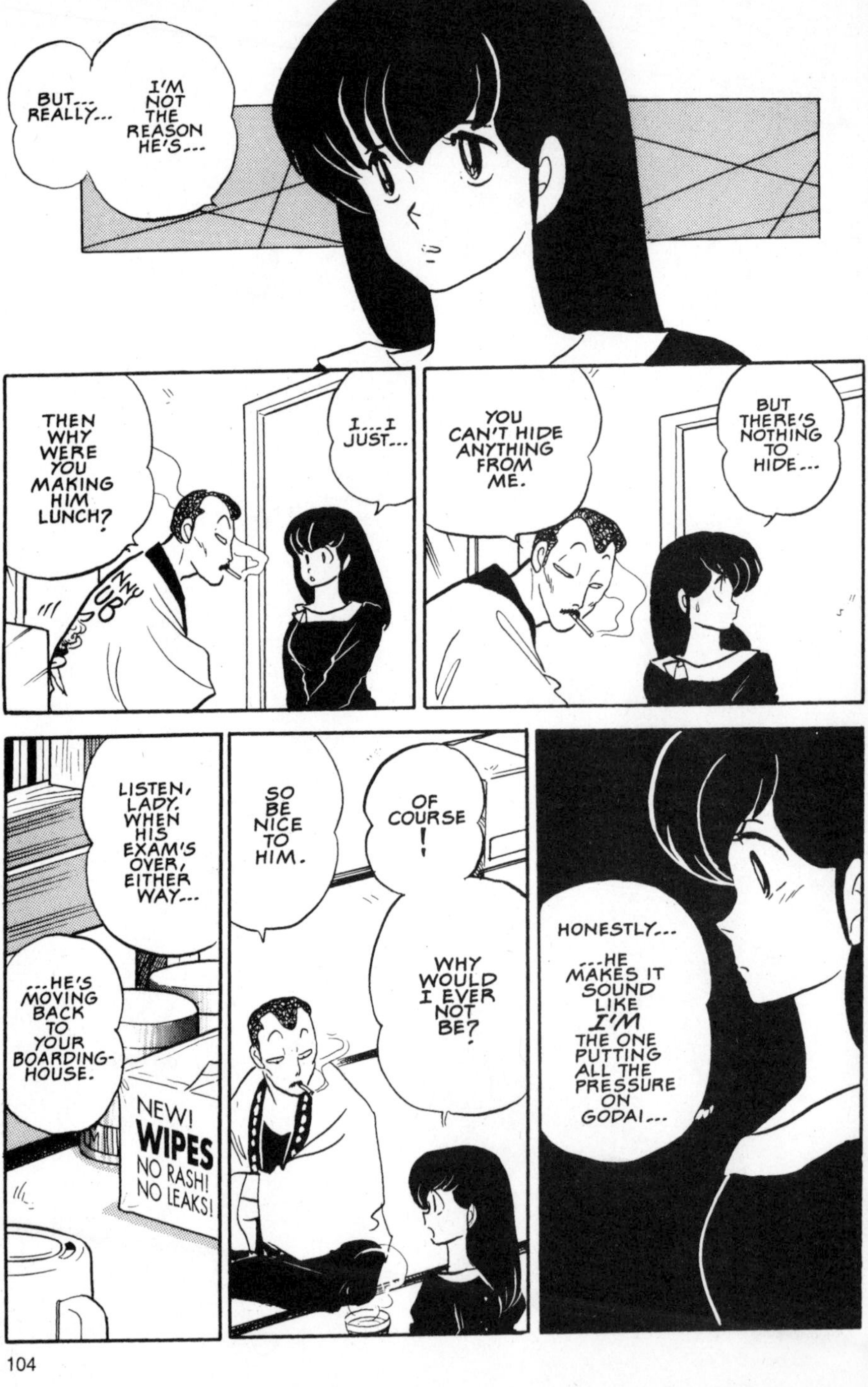
BUT... REALLY...
I'M NOT THE REASON HE'S...
THEN WHY WERE *YOU* MAKING HIM LUNCH?
I... I JUST...
YOU CAN'T HIDE ANYTHING FROM ME.
BUT THERE'S NOTHING TO HIDE...
LISTEN, LADY. WHEN HIS EXAM'S OVER, EITHER WAY...
...HE'S MOVING BACK TO YOUR BOARDING-HOUSE.
NEW! WIPES NO RASH! NO LEAKS!
SO BE NICE TO HIM.
OF COURSE!
WHY WOULD I EVER NOT BE?
HONESTLY...
...HE MAKES IT SOUND LIKE *I'M* THE ONE PUTTING ALL THE PRESSURE ON GODAI...

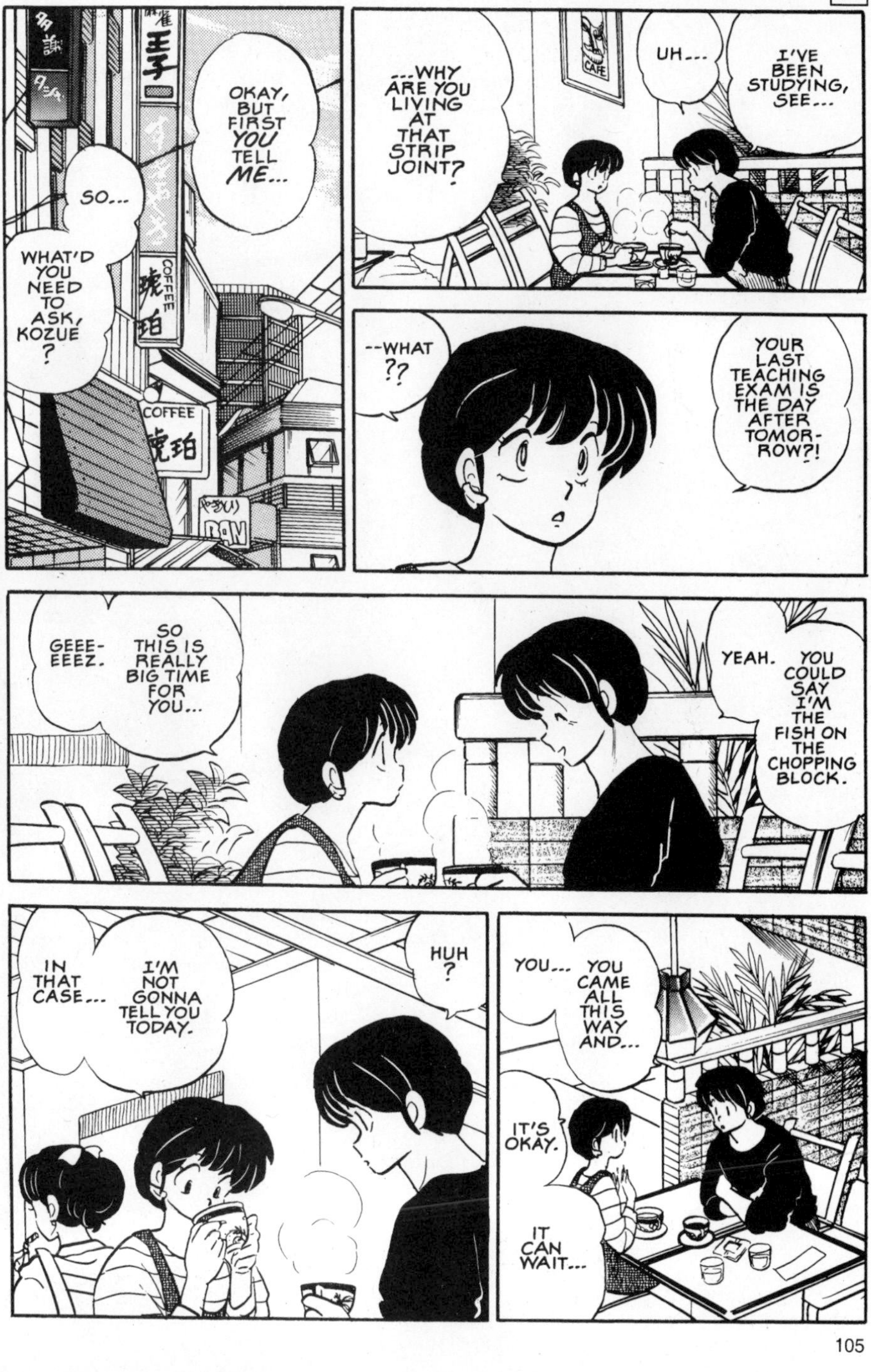
SO...
WHAT'D YOU NEED TO ASK, KOZUE?
OKAY, BUT FIRST YOU TELL ME...
...WHY ARE YOU LIVING AT THAT STRIP JOINT?
UH...
I'VE BEEN STUDYING, SEE...
--WHAT ??
YOUR LAST TEACHING EXAM IS THE DAY AFTER TOMOR-ROW?!
GEEE-EEEZ.
SO THIS IS REALLY BIG TIME FOR YOU...
YEAH.
YOU COULD SAY I'M THE FISH ON THE CHOPPING BLOCK.
IN THAT CASE...
I'M NOT GONNA TELL YOU TODAY.
HUH?
YOU...
YOU CAME ALL THIS WAY AND...
IT'S OKAY.
IT CAN WAIT...

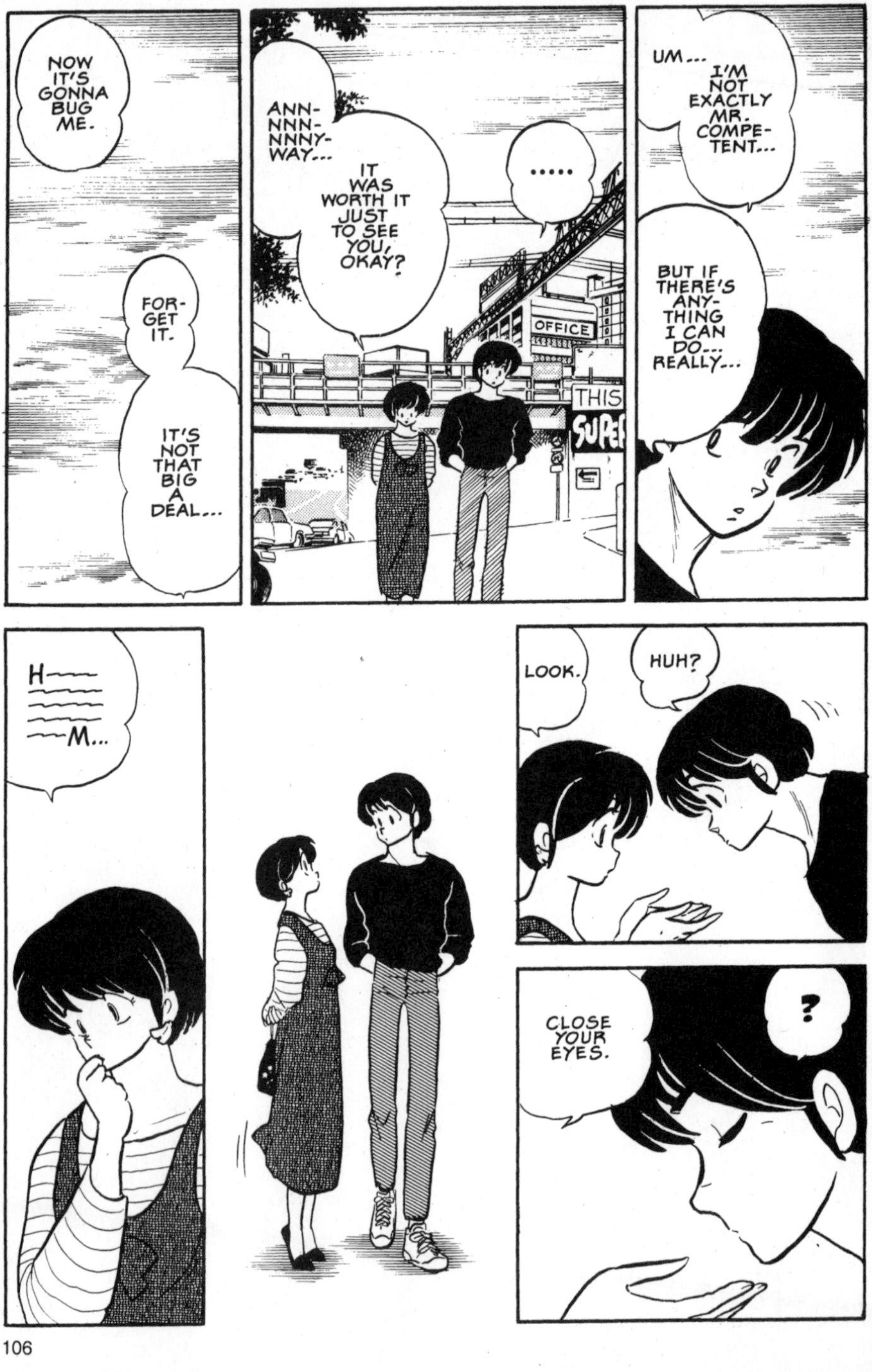
NOW IT'S GONNA BUG ME.
FOR-GET IT.
IT'S NOT THAT BIG A DEAL...
ANN-NNN-NNNY-WAY...
IT WAS WORTH IT JUST TO SEE YOU, OKAY?
......
OFFICE
THIS
SUPE
UM...
I'M NOT EXACTLY MR. COMPE-TENT...
BUT IF THERE'S ANY-THING I CAN DO... REALLY...
H——————M...
LOOK.
HUH?
CLOSE YOUR EYES.
?

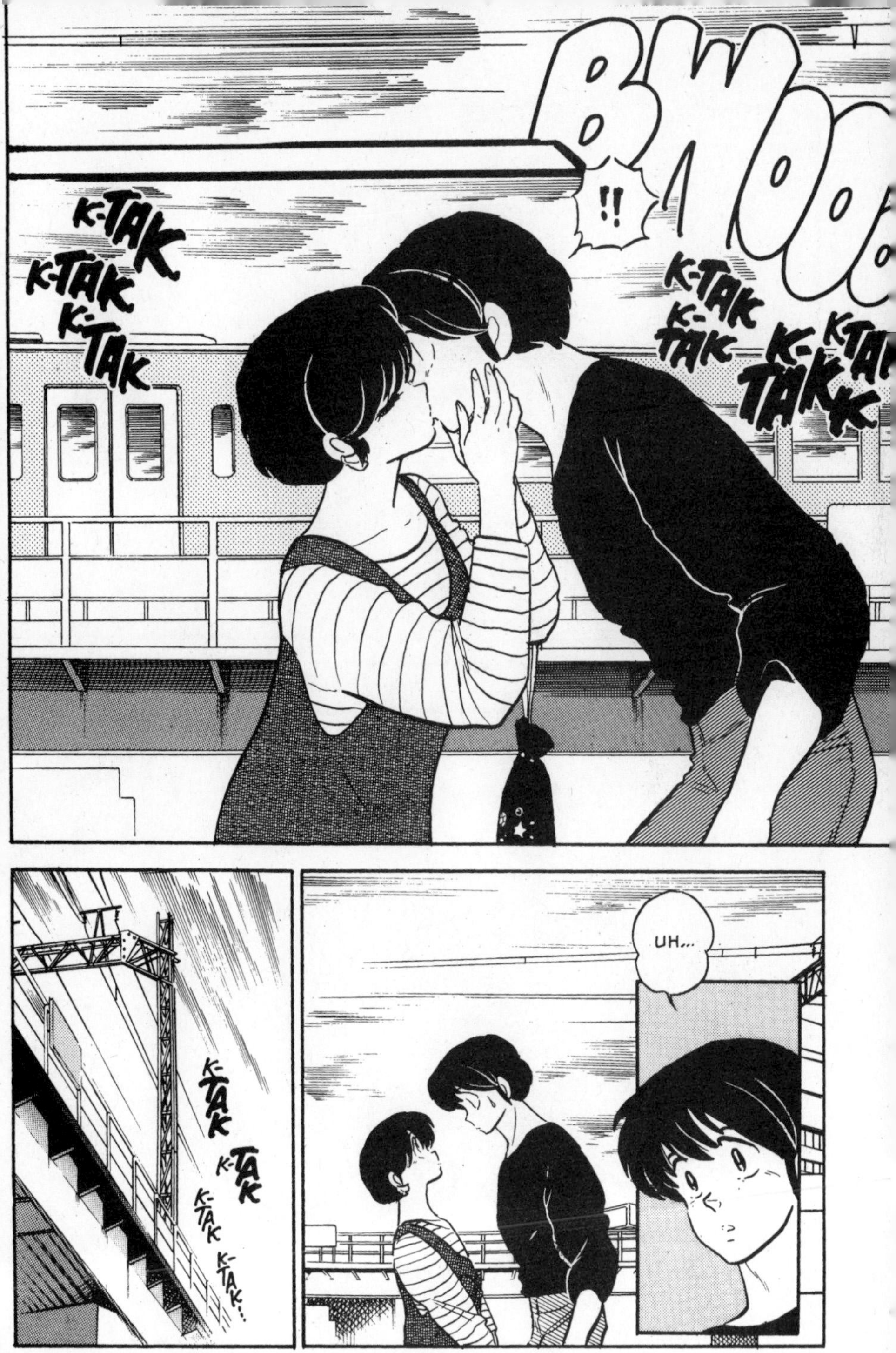
BWOOO...
K-TAK K-TAK K-TAK
!!
K-TAK K-TAK
K-TAK K-TAKK
K-TAK
K-TAK K-TAK K-TAK K-TAK...
UH...

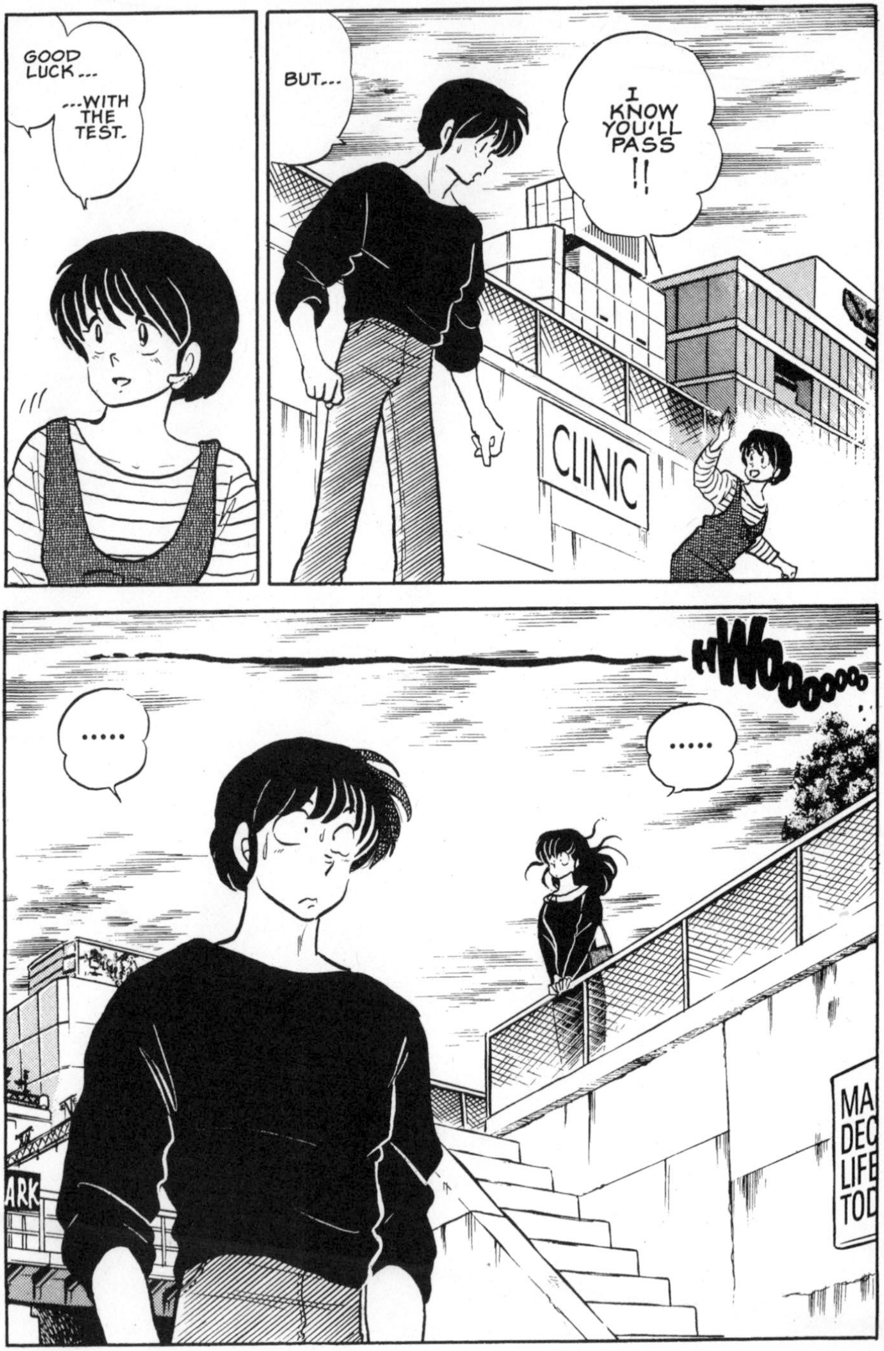
GOOD LUCK...
...WITH THE TEST.
BUT...
I KNOW YOU'LL PASS !!
CLINIC
HWOOOOOOO
......
......
MA DEC LIFE TOD
ARK

HAH
HAH
HAH

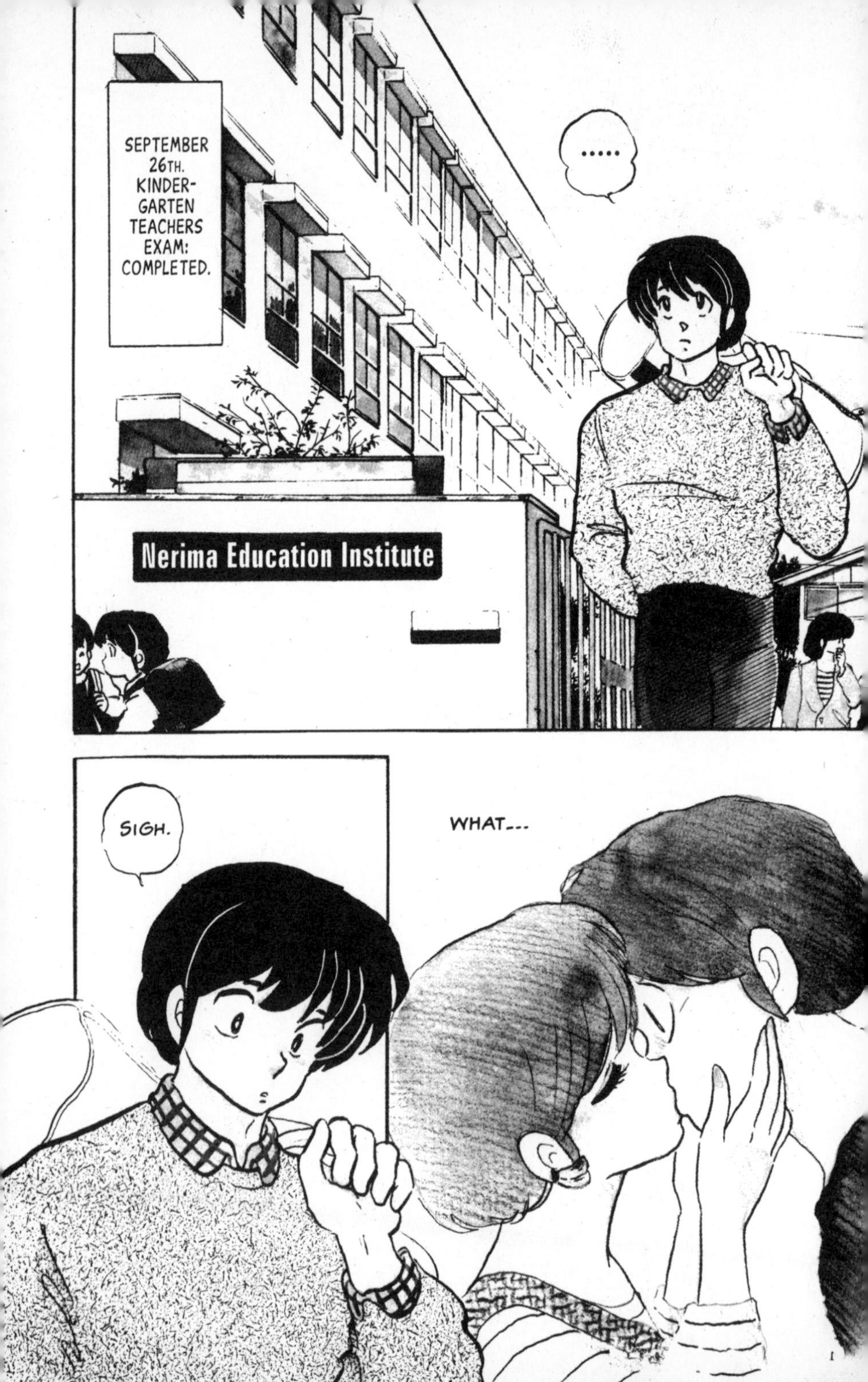

SEPTEMBER 26TH. KINDER-GARTEN TEACHERS EXAM: COMPLETED.
......
Nerima Education Institute
SIGH.
WHAT---

PART SIX
CAN'T YOU UNDERSTAND

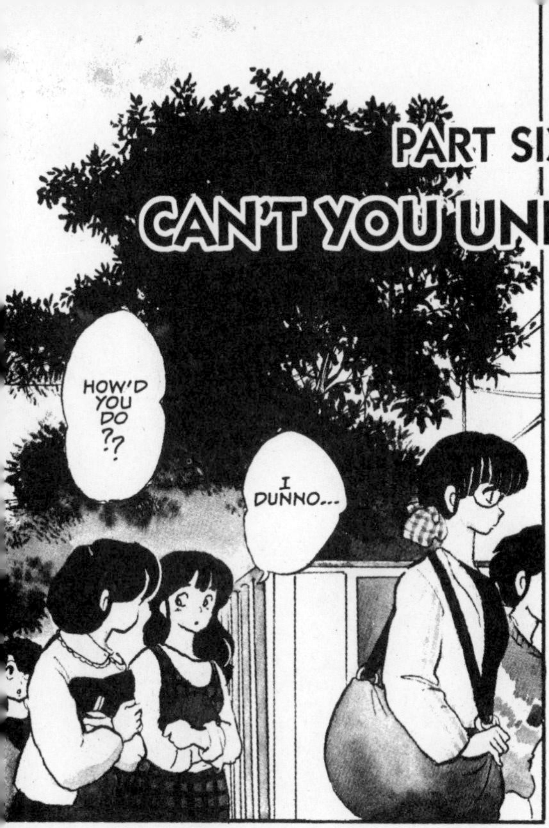
HOW'D YOU DO ??
I DUNNO...

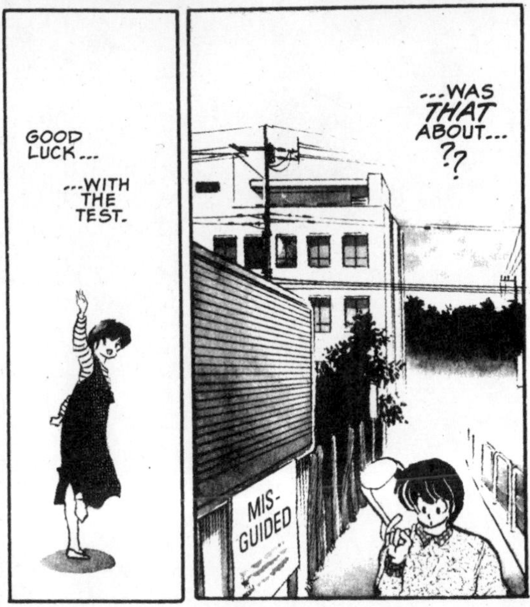
GOOD LUCK...
...WITH THE TEST.
...WAS THAT ABOUT...??
MIS-GUIDED

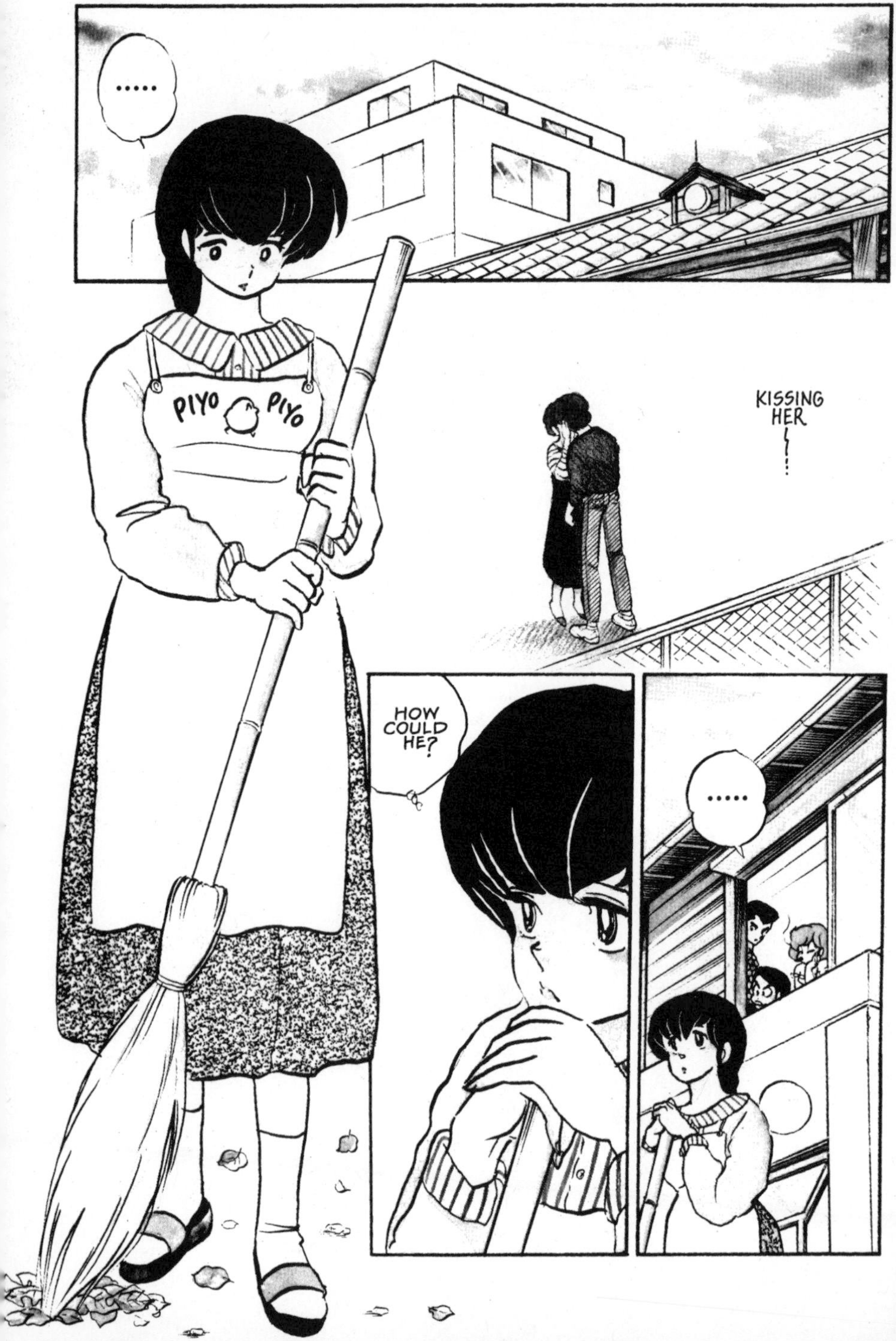
.....
KISSING HER...!
HOW COULD HE?
.....
PIYO PIYO

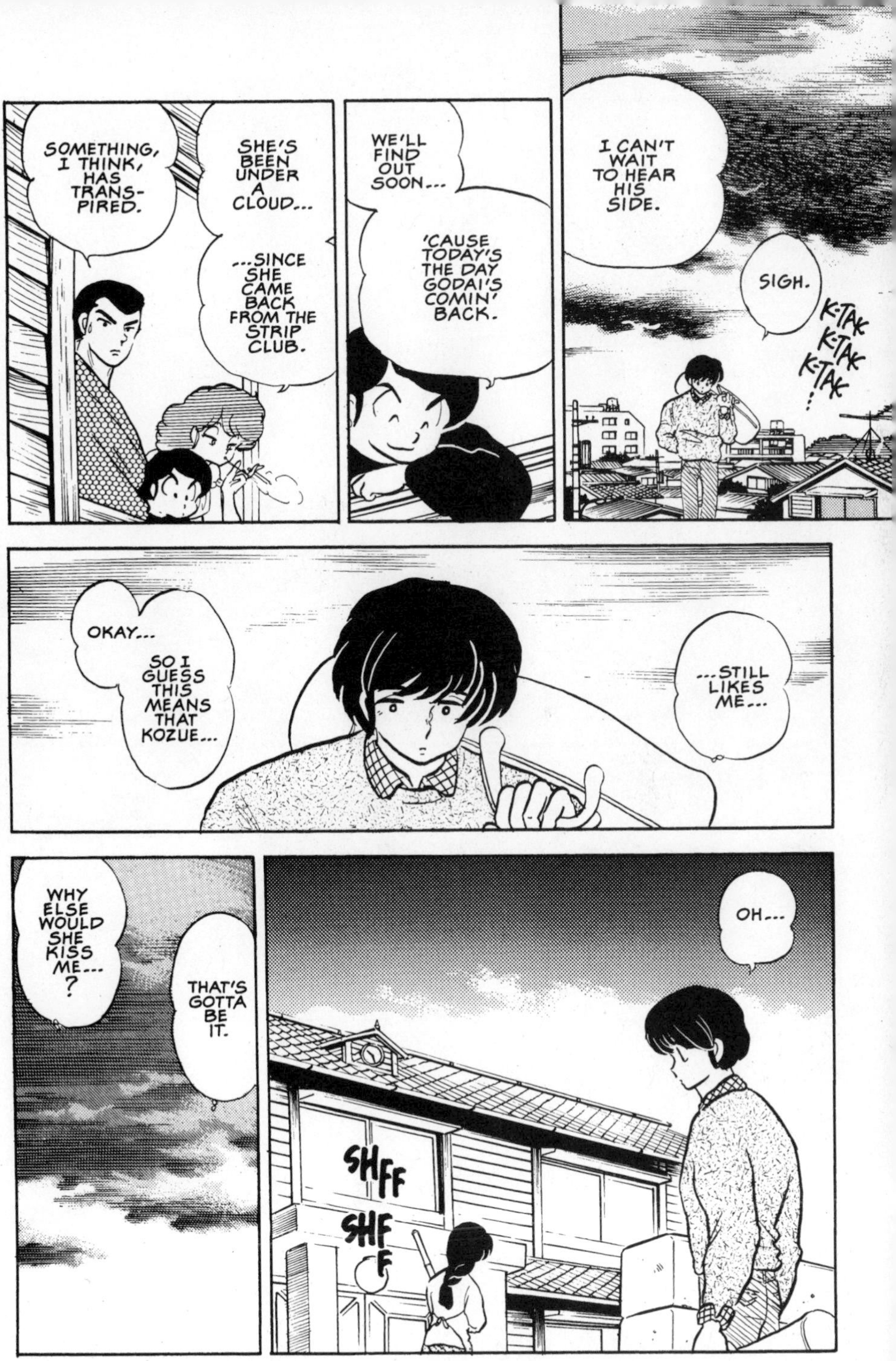
SOMETHING, I THINK, HAS TRANSPIRED.
SHE'S BEEN UNDER A CLOUD...
...SINCE SHE CAME BACK FROM THE STRIP CLUB.
WE'LL FIND OUT SOON...
'CAUSE TODAY'S THE DAY GODAI'S COMIN' BACK.
I CAN'T WAIT TO HEAR HIS SIDE.
SIGH.
K-TAK K-TAK K-TAK
OKAY...
SO I GUESS THIS MEANS THAT KOZUE...
...STILL LIKES ME...
WHY ELSE WOULD SHE KISS ME...?
THAT'S GOTTA BE IT.
OH...
SHFF
SHFF

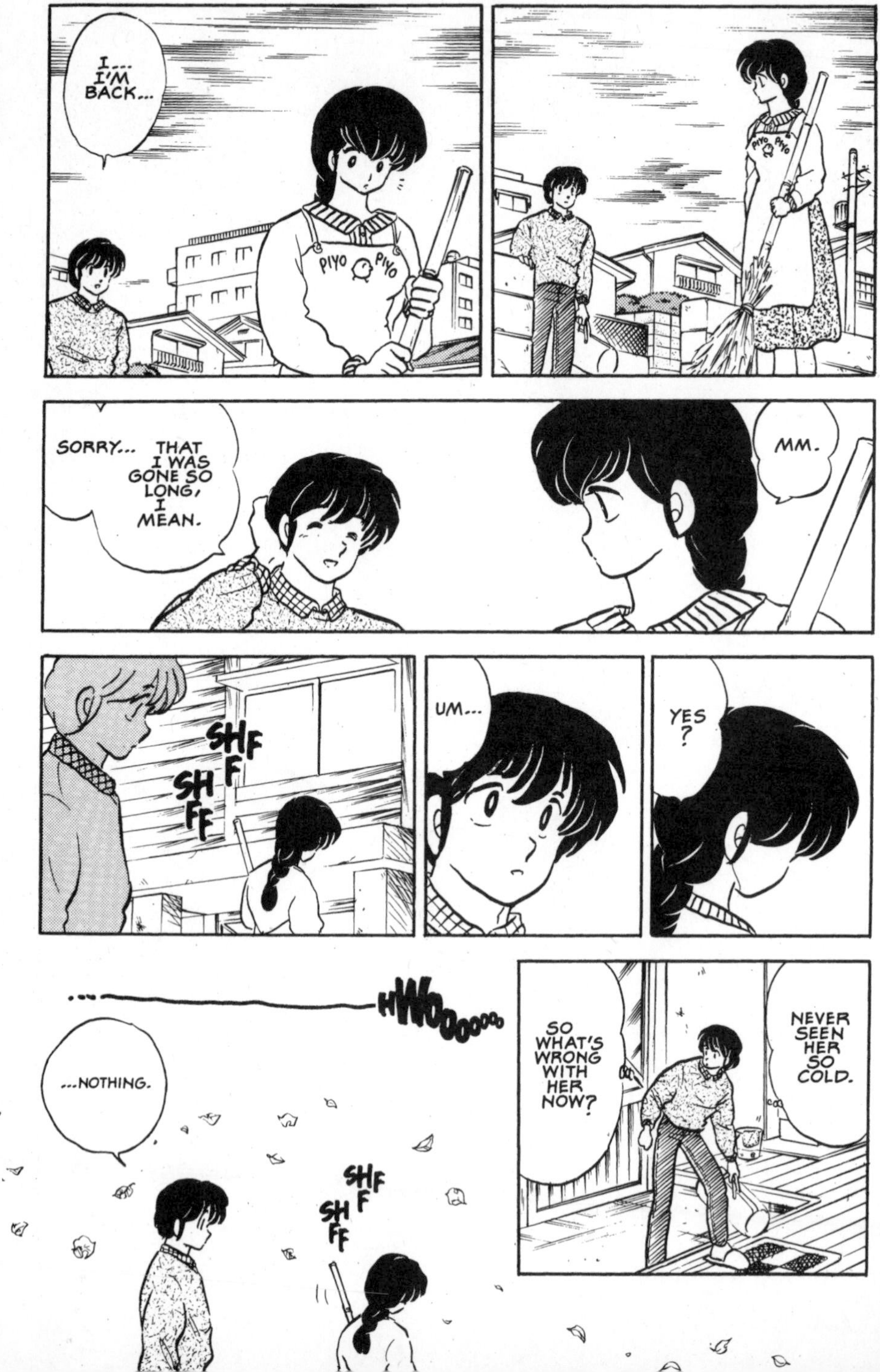
I... I'M BACK...
PIYO PIYO
PIYO PIYO
SORRY... THAT I WAS GONE SO LONG, I MEAN.
MM.
SHF F
SH FF
UM...
YES?
...NOTHING.
...HWOOOOOO
SHF F
SH FF
SO WHAT'S WRONG WITH HER NOW?
NEVER SEEN HER SO COLD.

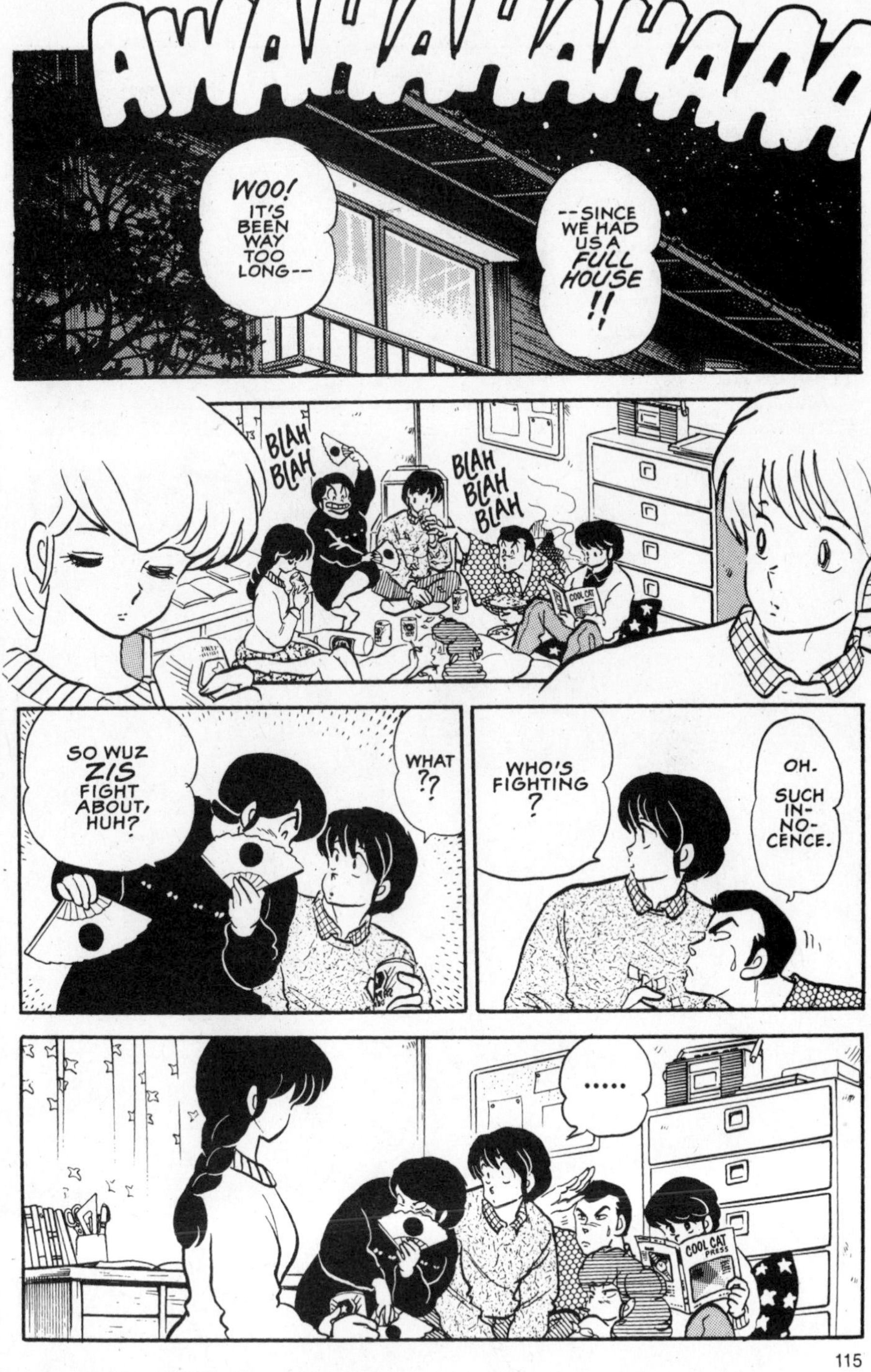
AWAHAHAHAAA
WOO! IT'S BEEN WAY TOO LONG--
--SINCE WE HAD US A FULL HOUSE !!
BLAH BLAH
BLAH BLAH BLAH
COOL CAT
SO WUZ ZIS FIGHT ABOUT, HUH?
WHAT ??
WHO'S FIGHTING ?
OH. SUCH IN-NO-CENCE.
......
COOL CAT PRESS

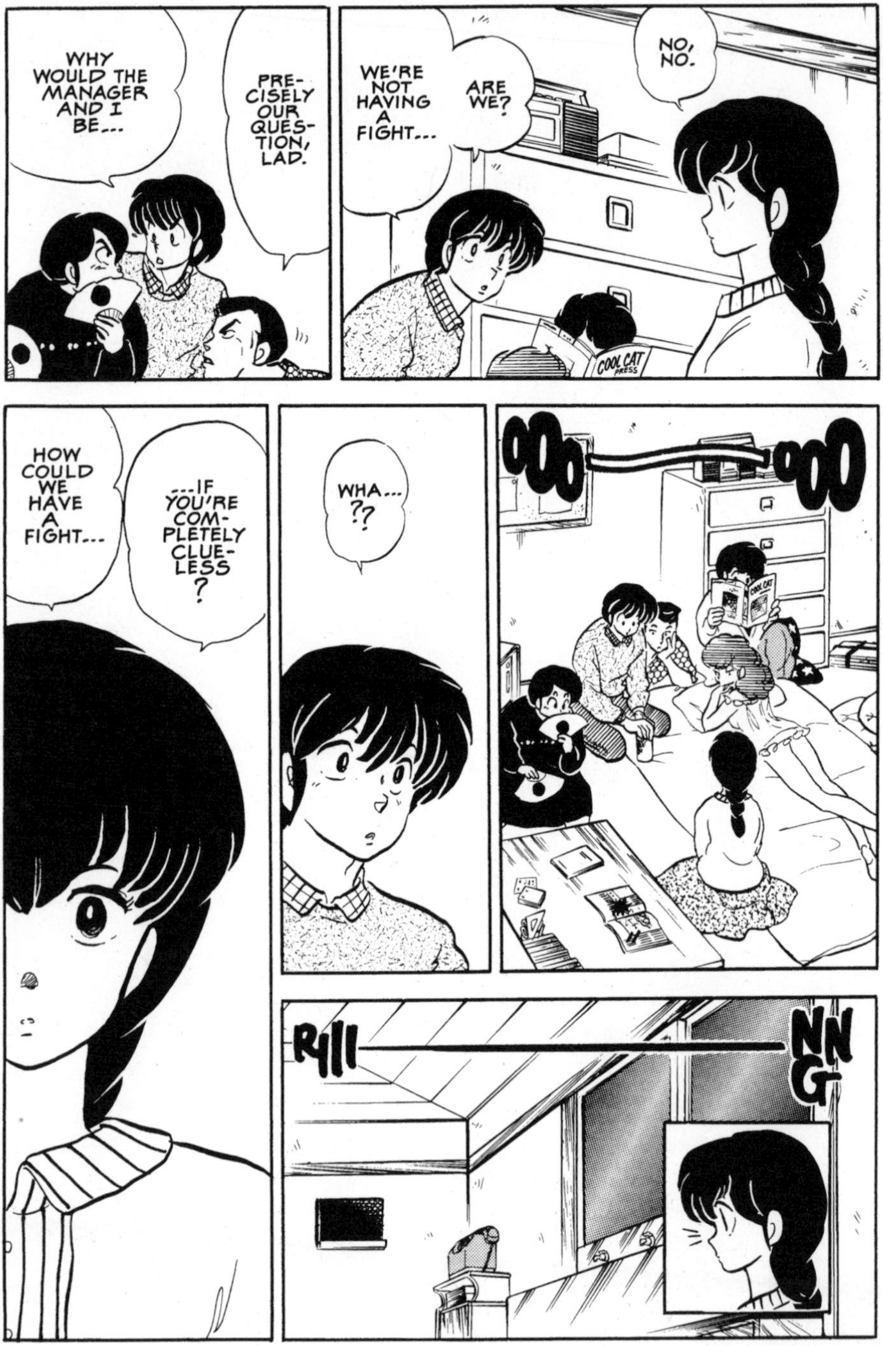
WHY WOULD THE MANAGER AND I BE...
PRE-CISELY OUR QUES-TION, LAD.
WE'RE NOT HAVING A FIGHT...
ARE WE?
NO, NO.
COOL CAT PRESS
HOW COULD WE HAVE A FIGHT...
...IF YOU'RE COM-PLETELY CLUE-LESS?
WHA...??
OOO—OOO
COOL CAT
RIII—NNG

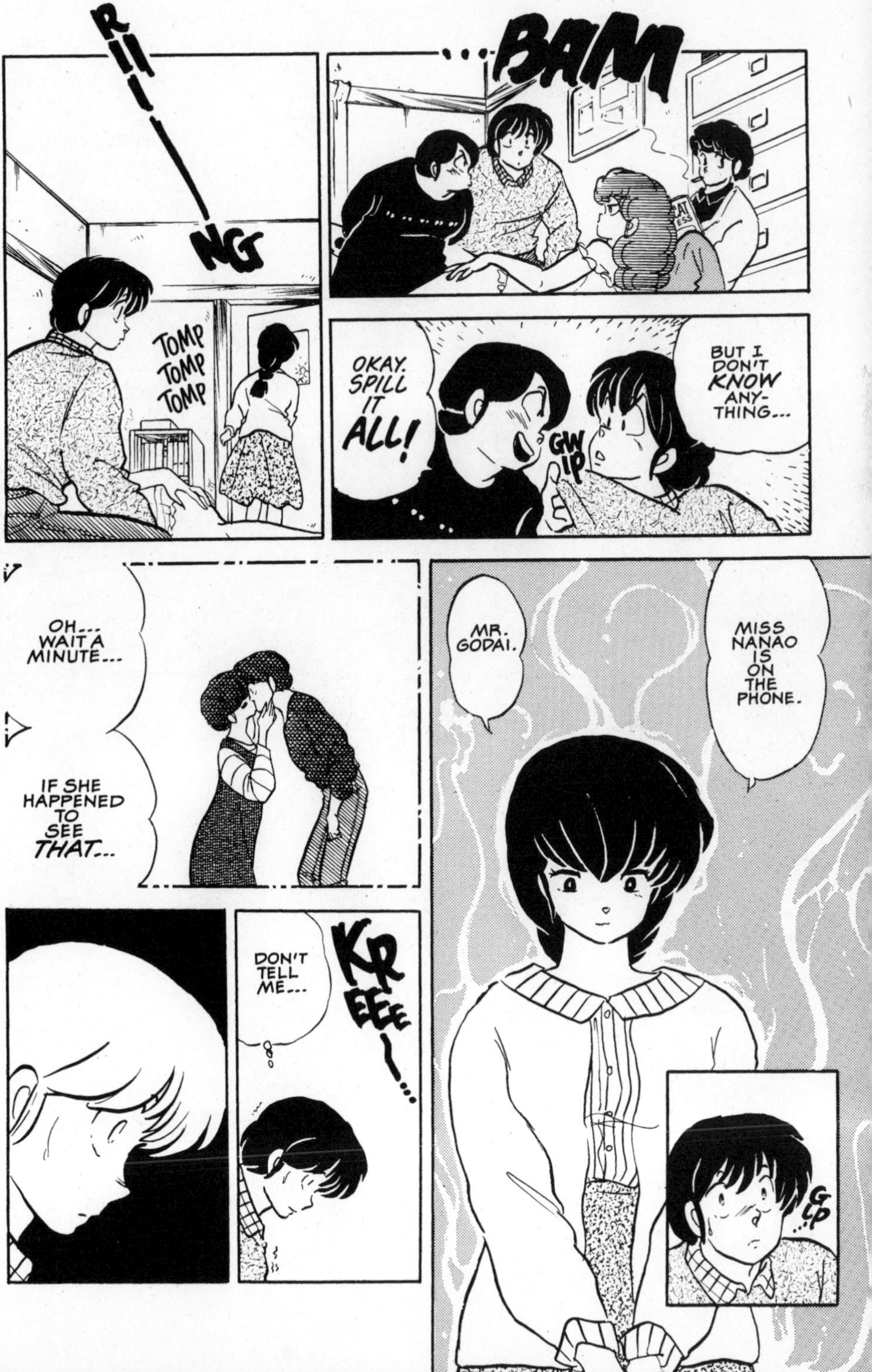
RIIIII—NG
TOMP TOMP TOMP
...BAM
OKAY. SPILL IT ALL!
GWLP
BUT I DON'T KNOW ANYTHING...
OH... WAIT A MINUTE...
IF SHE HAPPENED TO SEE THAT...
MR. GODAI.
MISS NANAO IS ON THE PHONE.
DON'T TELL ME...
KREEEE—...
GLP...

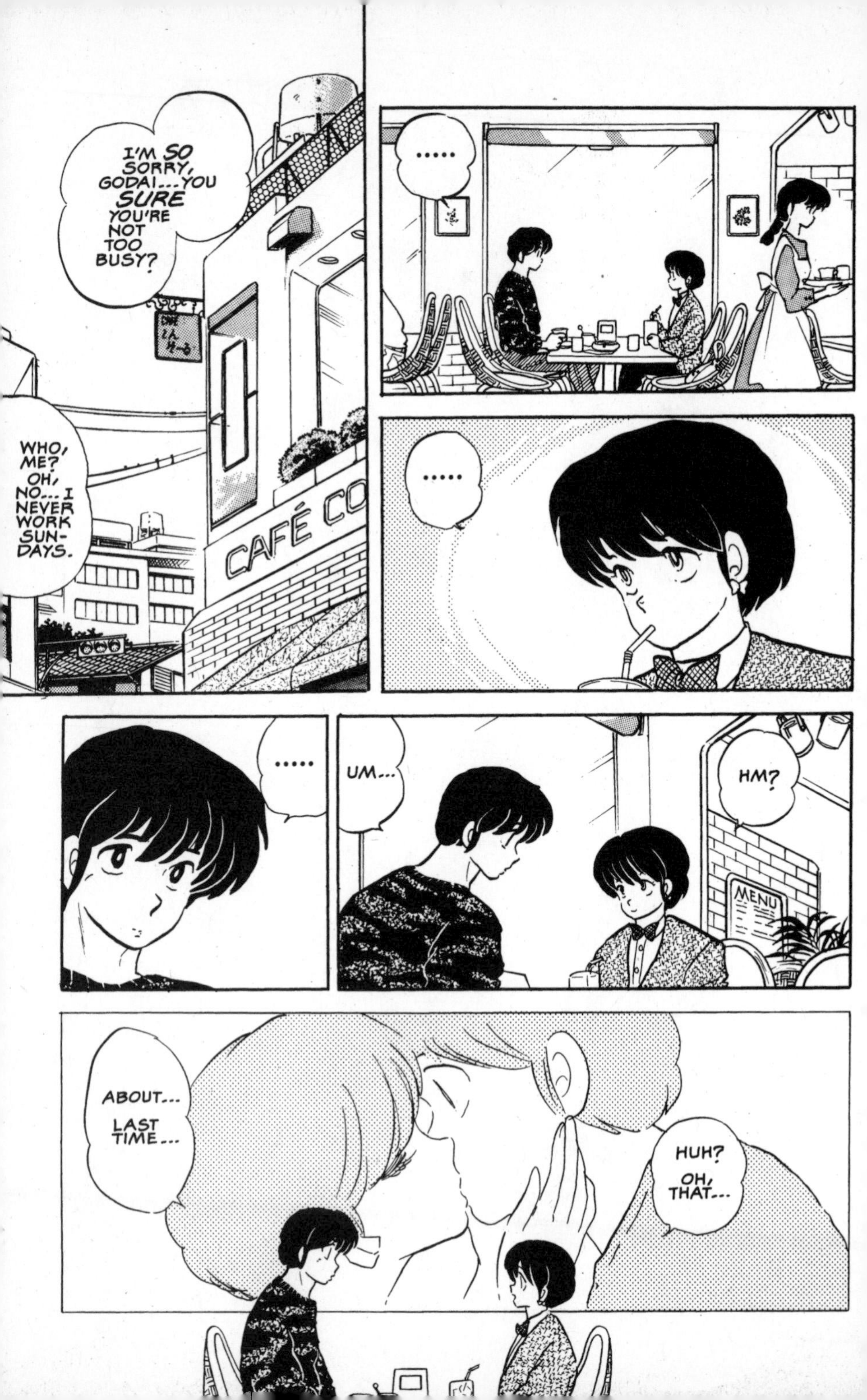
I'M SO SORRY, GODAI... YOU SURE YOU'RE NOT TOO BUSY?
WHO, ME? OH, NO... I NEVER WORK SUNDAYS.
CAFÉ CO
......
......
......
UM...
HM?
MENU
ABOUT... LAST TIME...
HUH? OH, THAT...

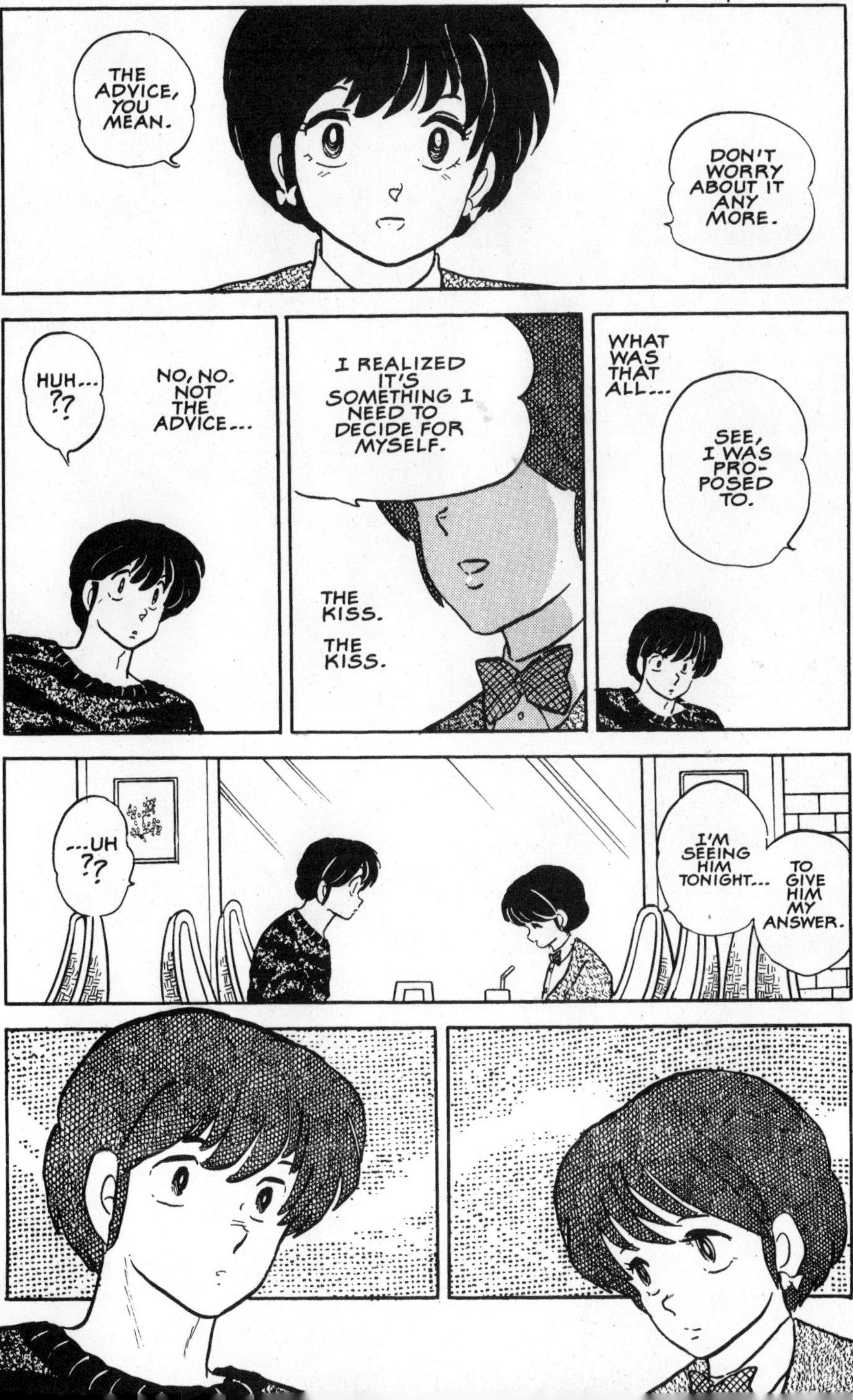
THE ADVICE, YOU MEAN.
DON'T WORRY ABOUT IT ANY MORE.
HUH... ??
NO, NO. NOT THE ADVICE...
I REALIZED IT'S SOMETHING I NEED TO DECIDE FOR MYSELF.
THE KISS.
THE KISS.
WHAT WAS THAT ALL...
SEE, I WAS PRO-POSED TO.
...UH ??
I'M SEEING HIM TONIGHT...
TO GIVE HIM MY ANSWER.

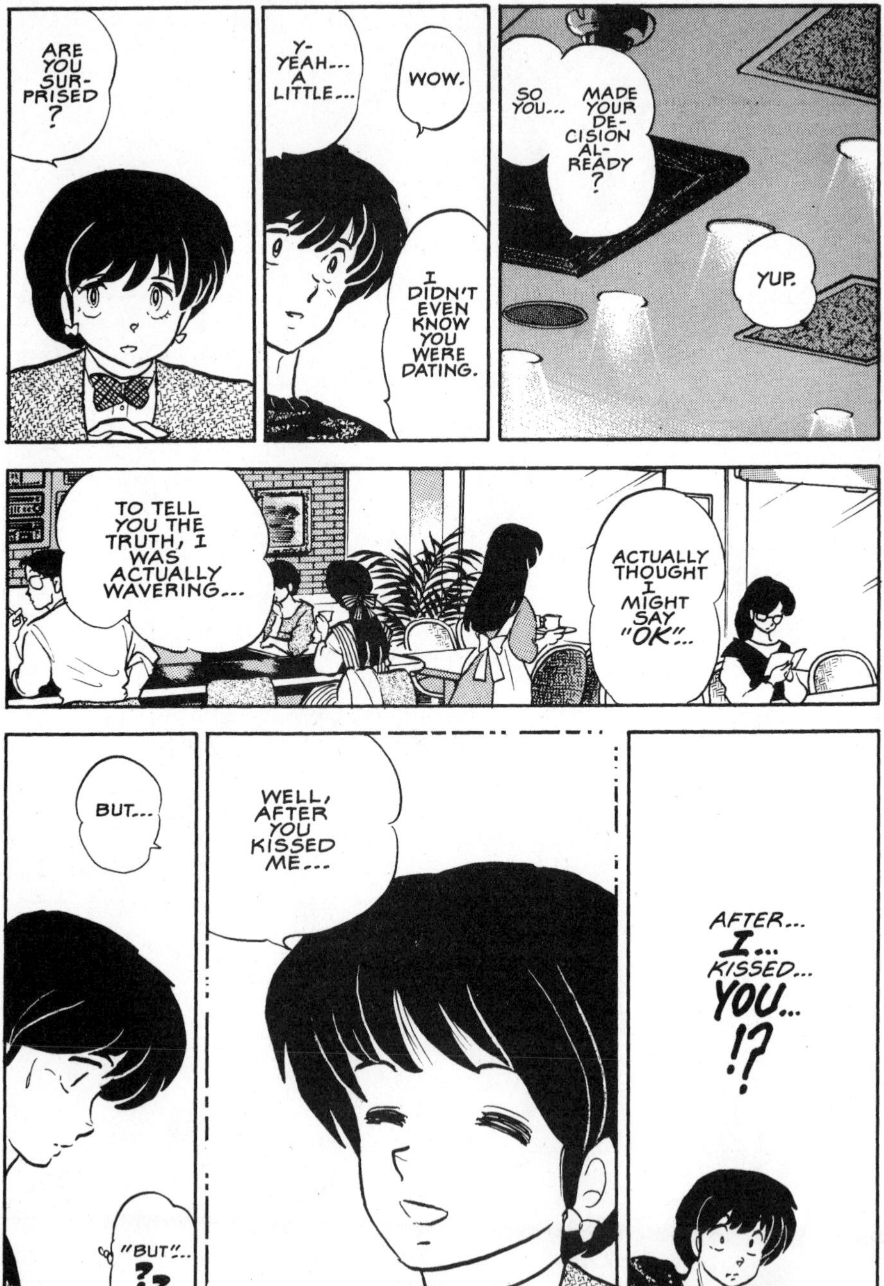

ARE YOU SUR-PRISED?
Y-YEAH... A LITTLE...
WOW.
I DIDN'T EVEN KNOW YOU WERE DATING.
SO YOU... MADE YOUR DE-CISION AL-READY?
YUP.
TO TELL YOU THE TRUTH, I WAS ACTUALLY WAVERING...
ACTUALLY THOUGHT I MIGHT SAY "OK"...
BUT...
"BUT"...??
WELL, AFTER YOU KISSED ME...
AFTER... I... KISSED... YOU...!?

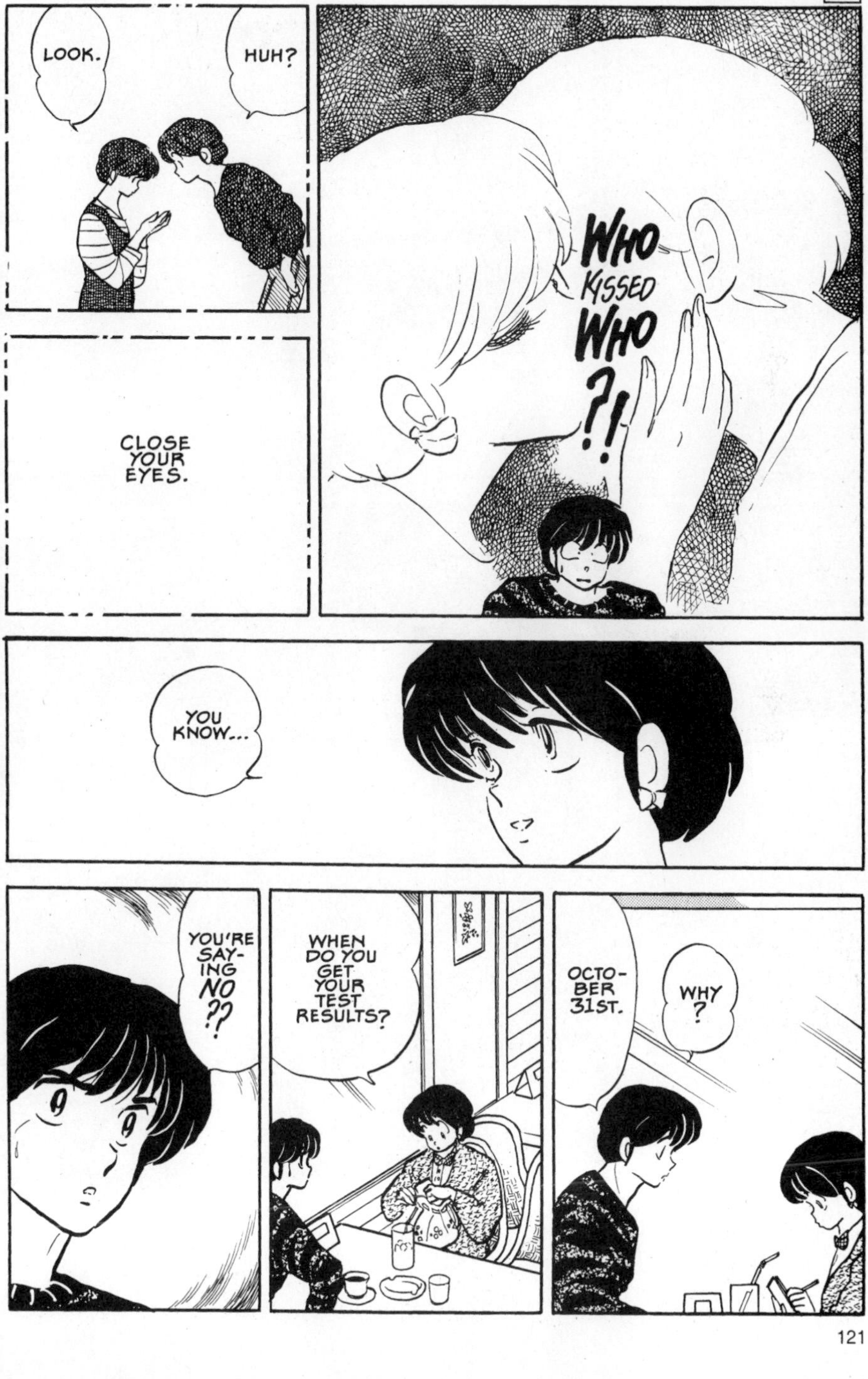
LOOK.
HUH?
CLOSE YOUR EYES.
WHO KISSED WHO ?!
YOU KNOW...
YOU'RE SAYING NO ??
WHEN DO YOU GET YOUR TEST RESULTS?
OCTOBER 31ST.
WHY ?

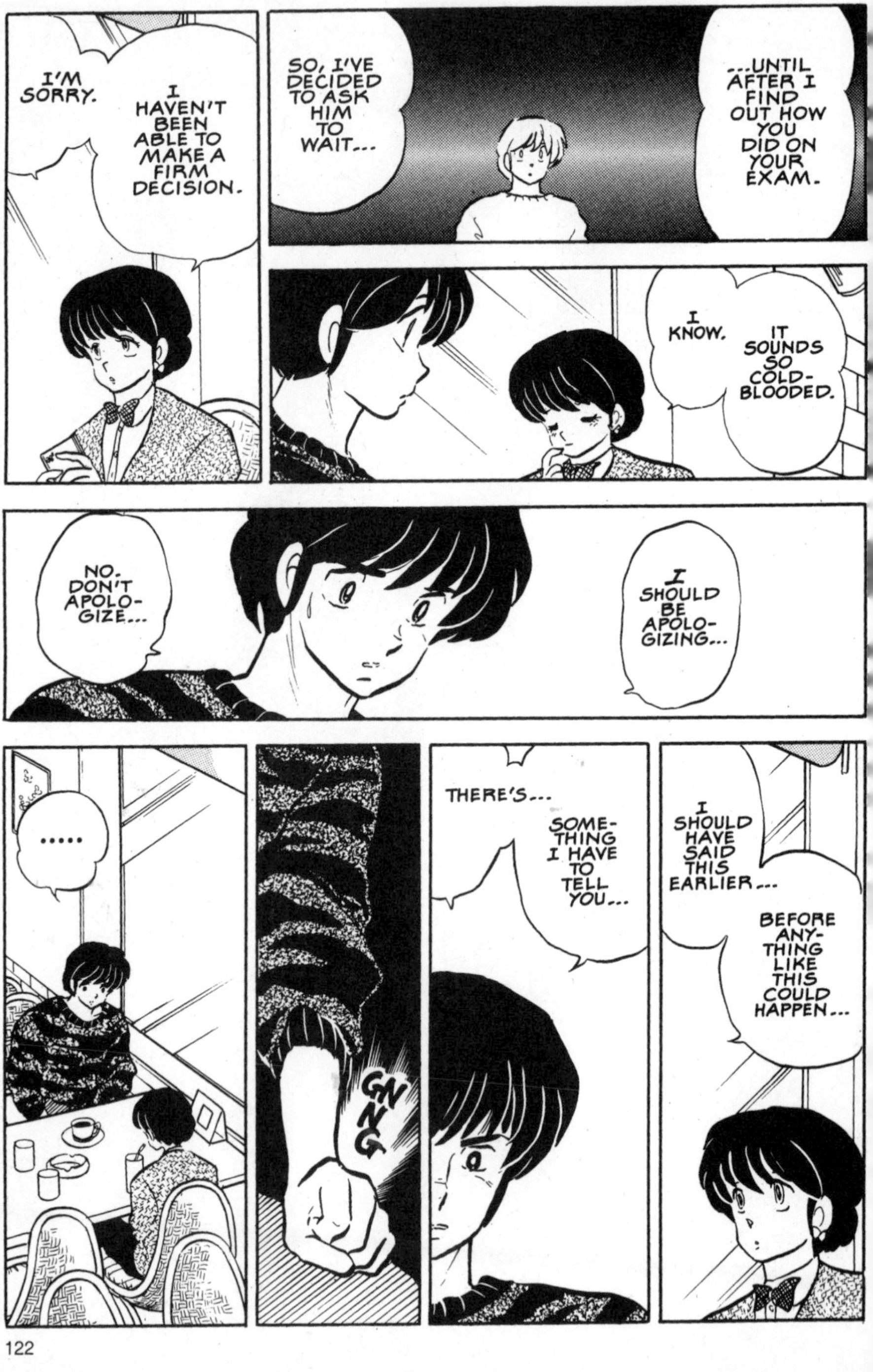
I'M SORRY.
I HAVEN'T BEEN ABLE TO MAKE A FIRM DECISION.
SO, I'VE DECIDED TO ASK HIM TO WAIT...
...UNTIL AFTER I FIND OUT HOW YOU DID ON YOUR EXAM.
I KNOW.
IT SOUNDS SO COLD-BLOODED.
NO. DON'T APOLOGIZE...
I SHOULD BE APOLOGIZING...
.....
GNNG
THERE'S...
SOMETHING I HAVE TO TELL YOU...
I SHOULD HAVE SAID THIS EARLIER...
BEFORE ANYTHING LIKE THIS COULD HAPPEN...

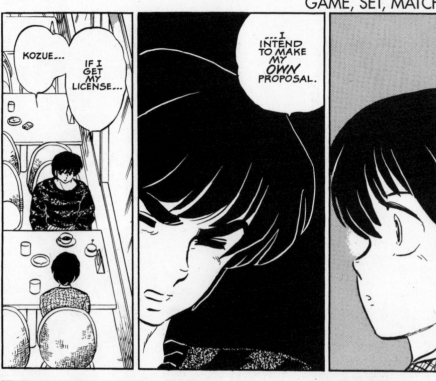

KOZUE... IF I GET MY LICENSE...

...I INTEND TO MAKE MY *OWN* PROPOSAL.

SO... YOUR REPLY TO THIS OTHER GUY...

...SHOULDN'T DEPEND ON ME...

•••••

•••••

123

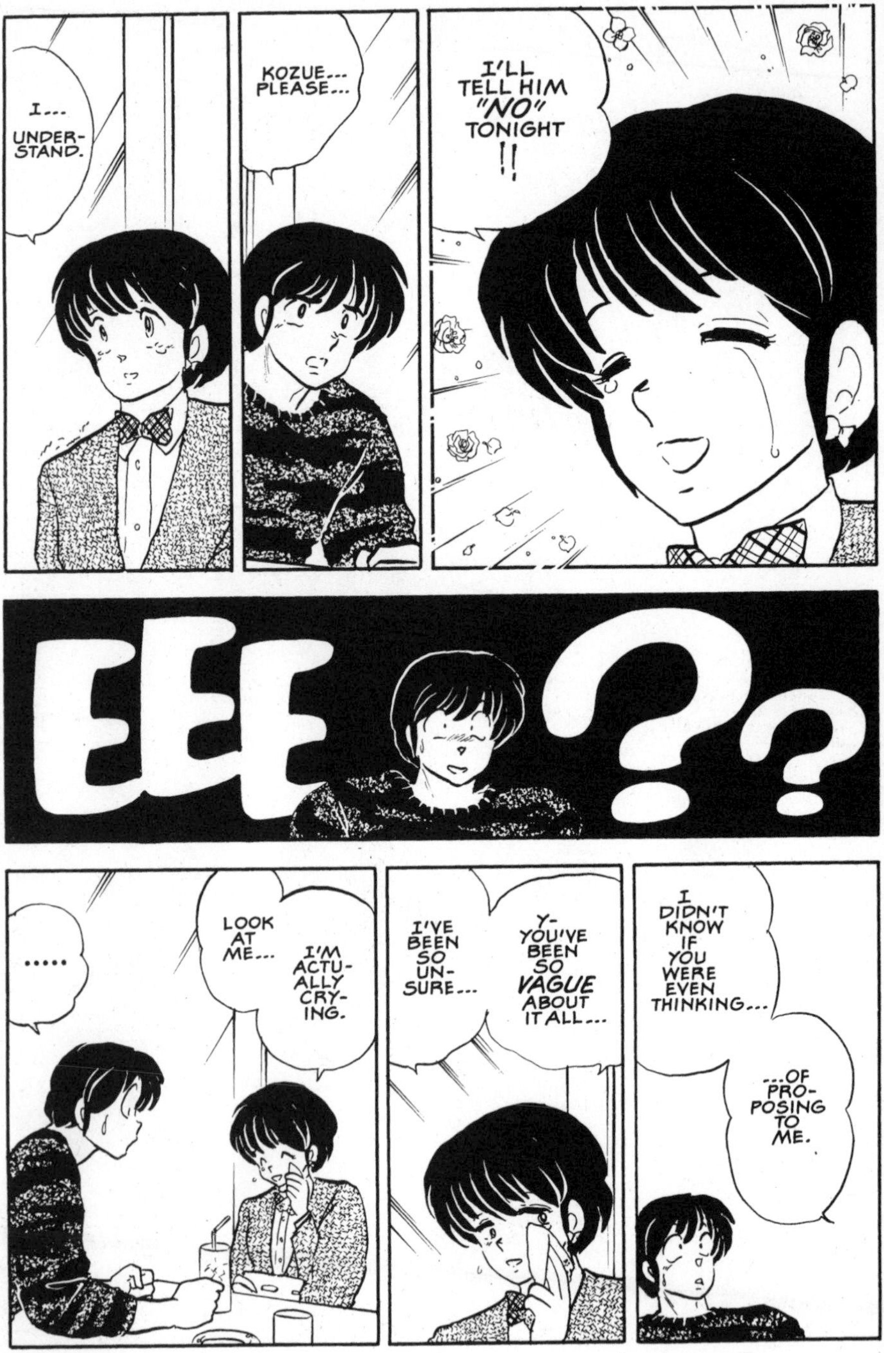

I... UNDERSTAND.
KOZUE... PLEASE...
I'LL TELL HIM "NO" TONIGHT !!
EEE ???
......
LOOK AT ME...
I'M ACTUALLY CRYING.
I'VE BEEN SO UNSURE...
Y-YOU'VE BEEN SO VAGUE ABOUT IT ALL...
I DIDN'T KNOW IF YOU WERE EVEN THINKING...
...OF PROPOSING TO ME.

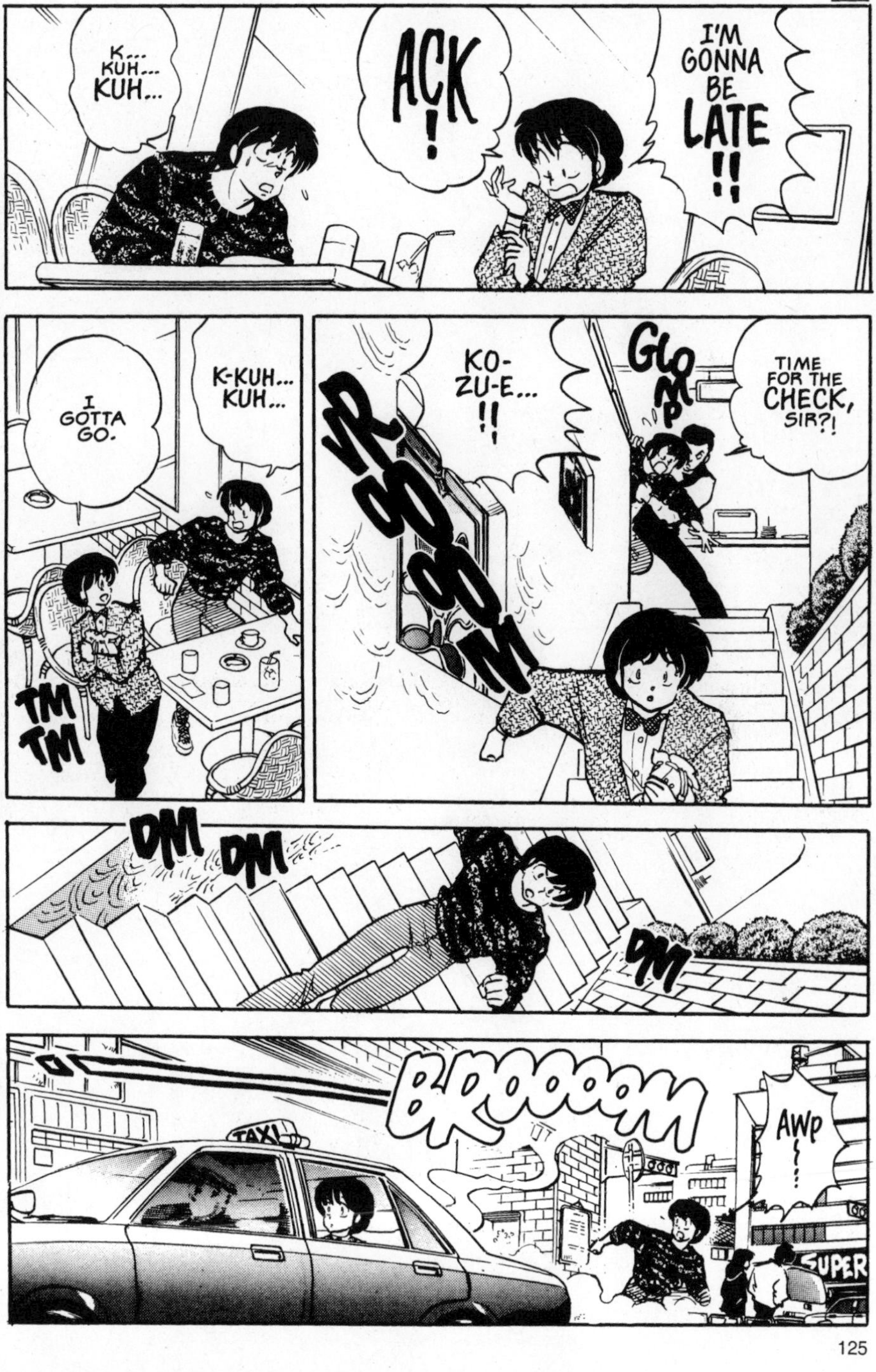
K... KUH... KUH...
ACK!
I'M GONNA BE LATE!!
I GOTTA GO.
K-KUH... KUH...
TM TM
KO-ZU-E...!!
SHOOOM
GLOMP
TIME FOR THE CHECK, SIR?!
DM DM
DM
TAXI
BROOOOM
AWP...
SUPER

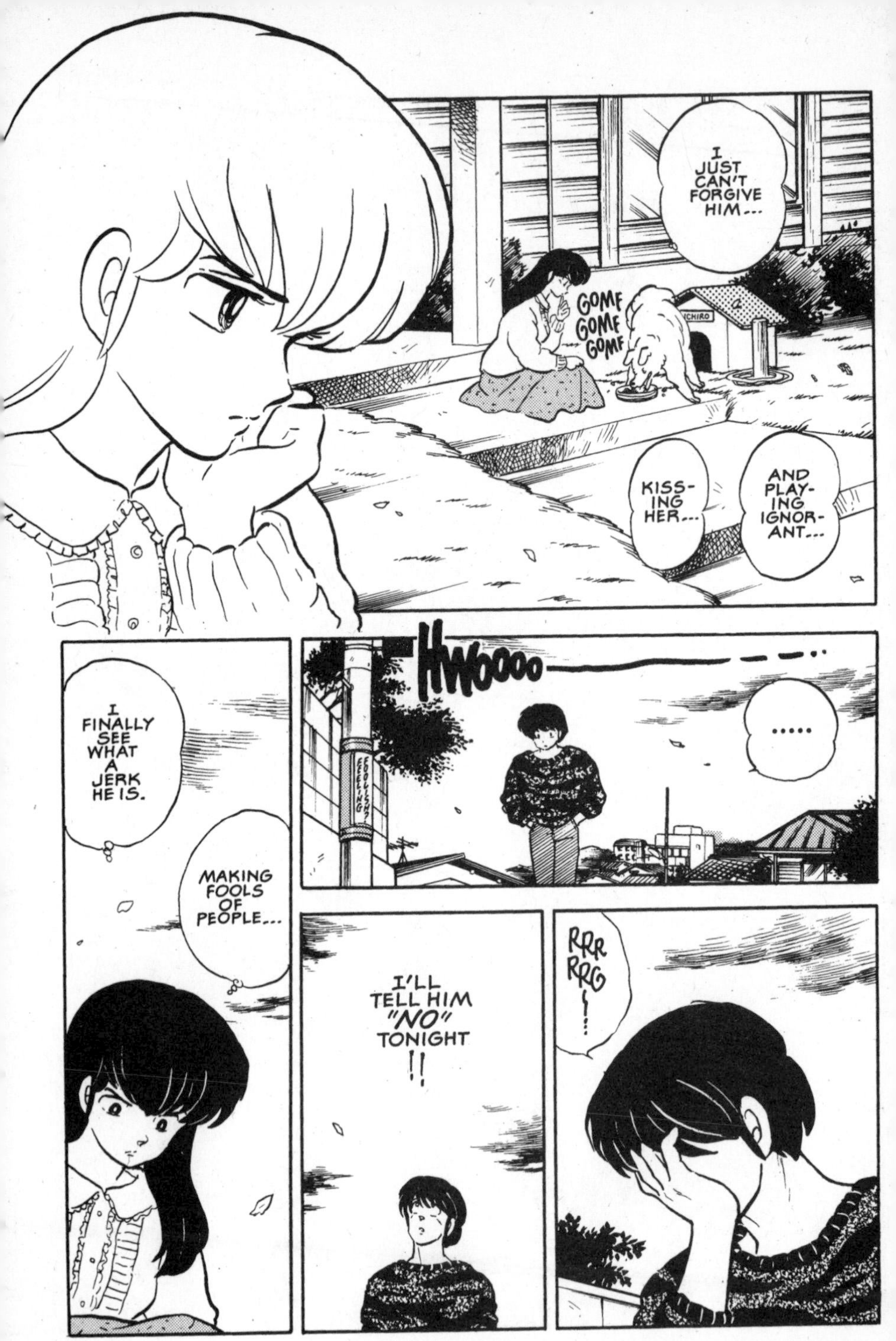
I JUST CAN'T FORGIVE HIM...
GOMF GOMF GOMF
KISS-ING HER...
AND PLAY-ING IGNOR-ANT...
I FINALLY SEE WHAT A JERK HE IS.
MAKING FOOLS OF PEOPLE...
HWOOOO
.....
I'LL TELL HIM "NO" TONIGHT !!
RRRRRG...!!

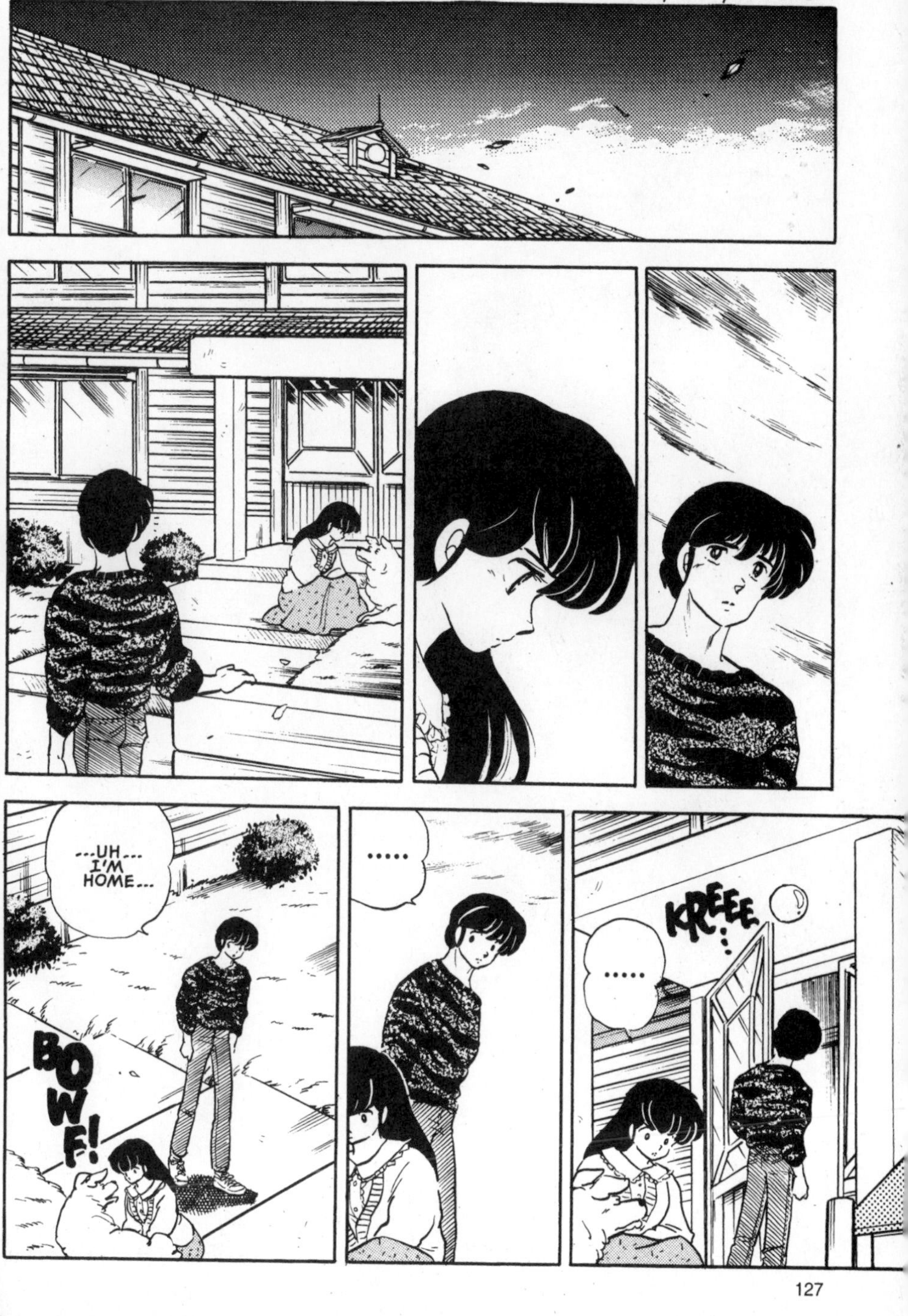
...UH... I'M HOME...
BOWF!
.....
.....
KREEEE...

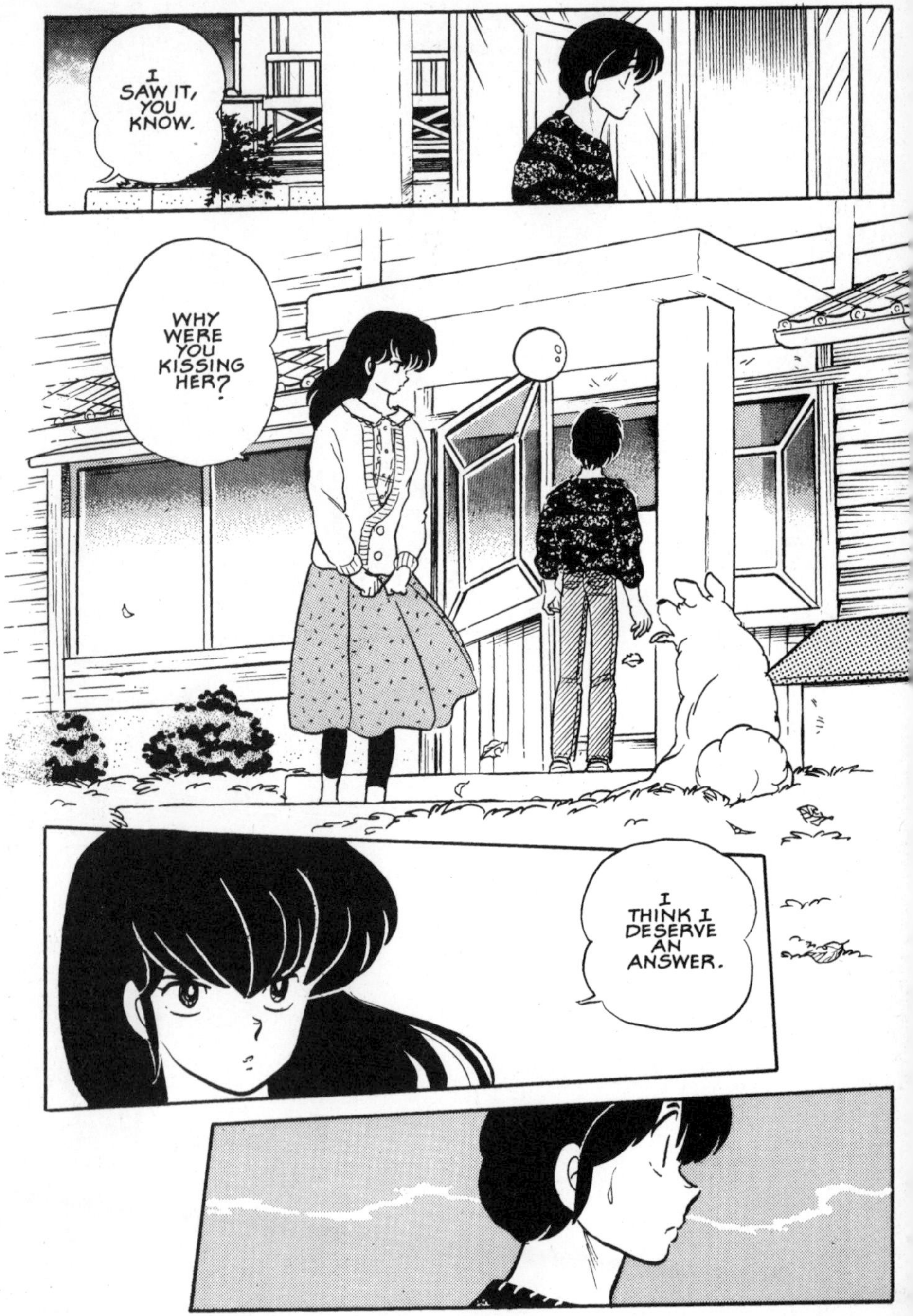
I SAW IT, YOU KNOW.
WHY WERE YOU KISSING HER?
I THINK I DESERVE AN ANSWER.

PART SEVEN
TURNABOUT

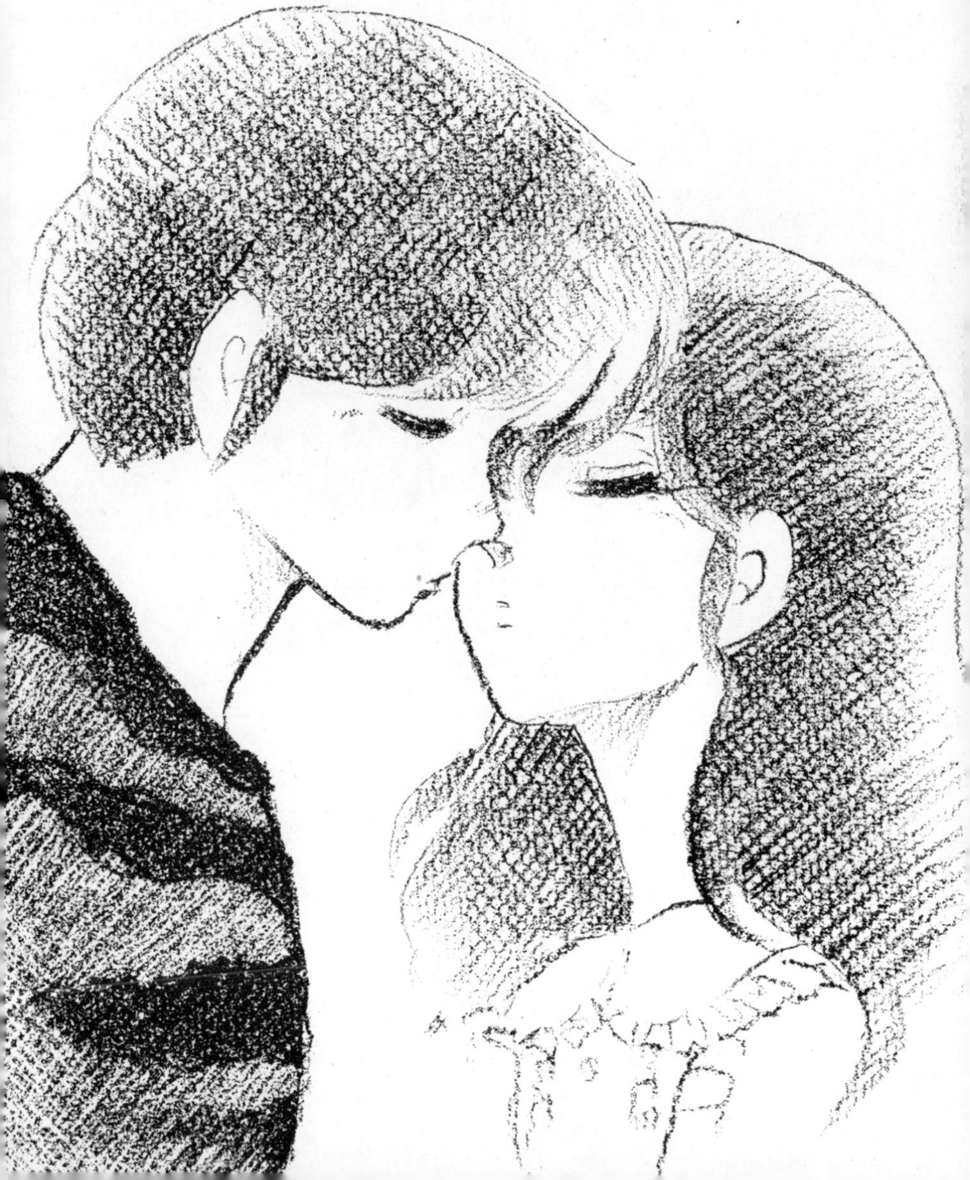

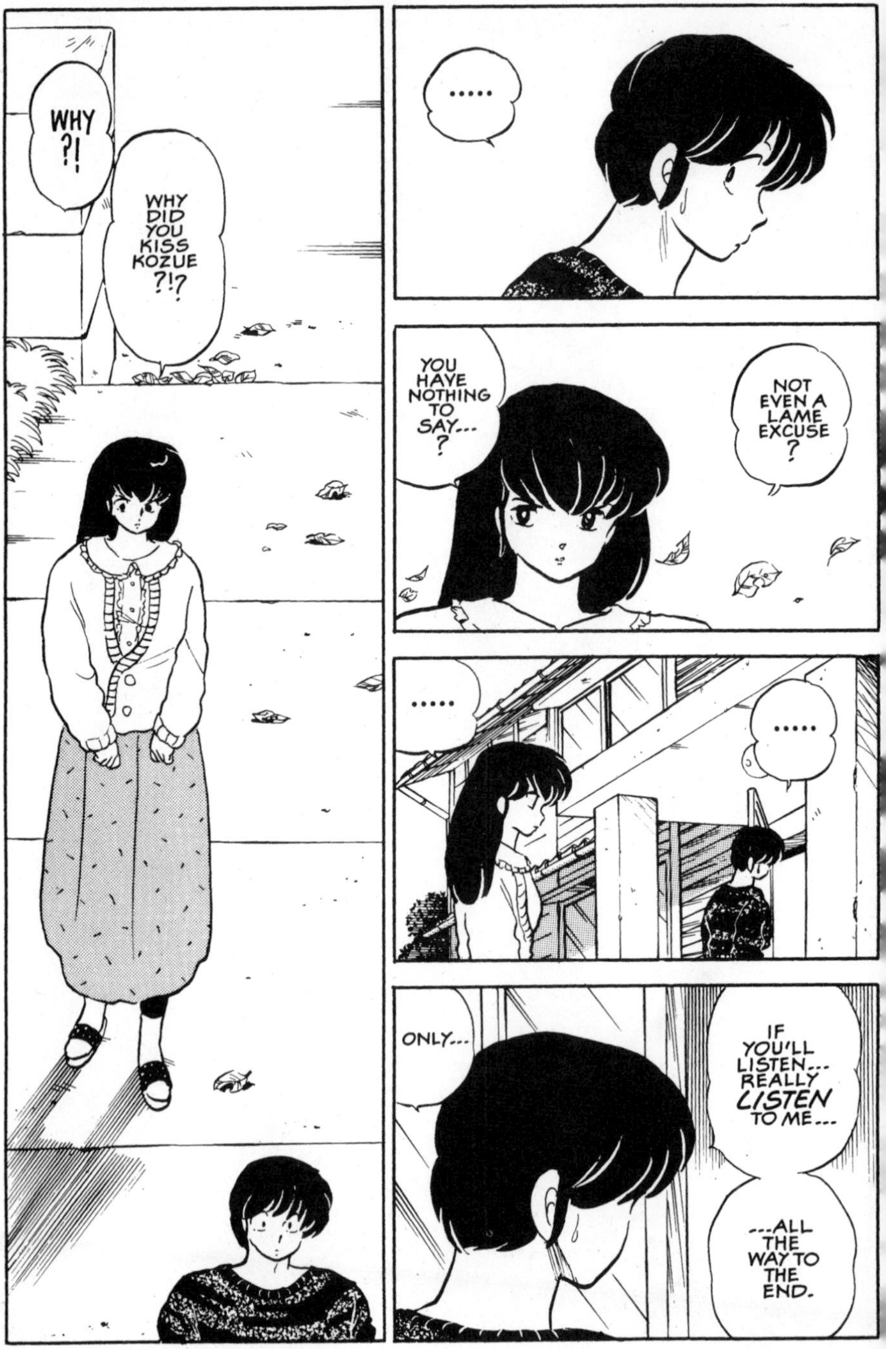
WHY ?!
WHY DID YOU KISS KOZUE ?!?
......
YOU HAVE NOTHING TO SAY... ?
NOT EVEN A LAME EXCUSE ?
.....
.....
ONLY...
IF YOU'LL LISTEN... REALLY LISTEN TO ME...
...ALL THE WAY TO THE END.

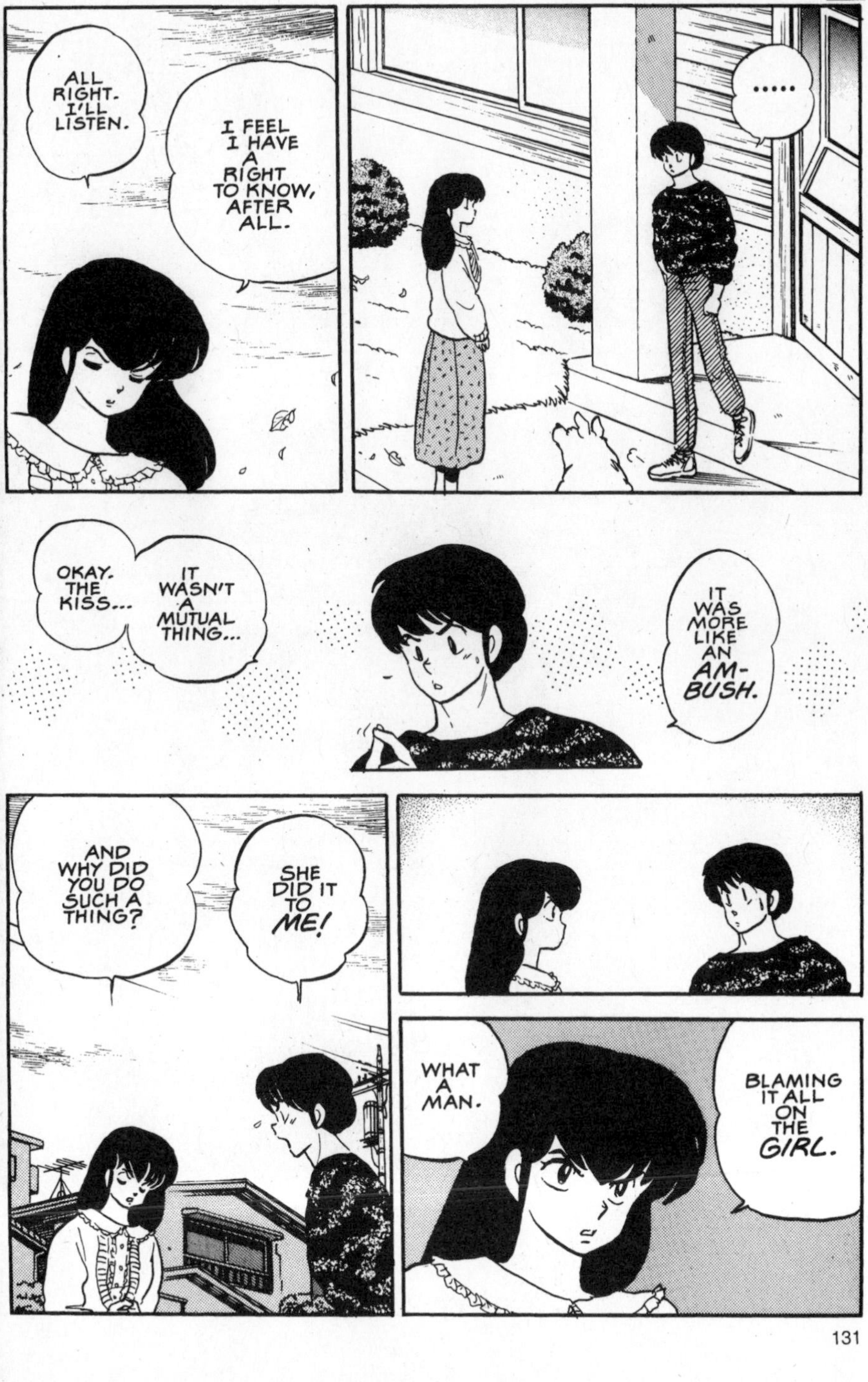
ALL RIGHT. I'LL LISTEN.
I FEEL I HAVE A RIGHT TO KNOW, AFTER ALL.
.....
OKAY. THE KISS...
IT WASN'T A MUTUAL THING...
IT WAS MORE LIKE AN AM-BUSH.
AND WHY DID YOU DO SUCH A THING?
SHE DID IT TO ME!
WHAT A MAN.
BLAMING IT ALL ON THE GIRL.

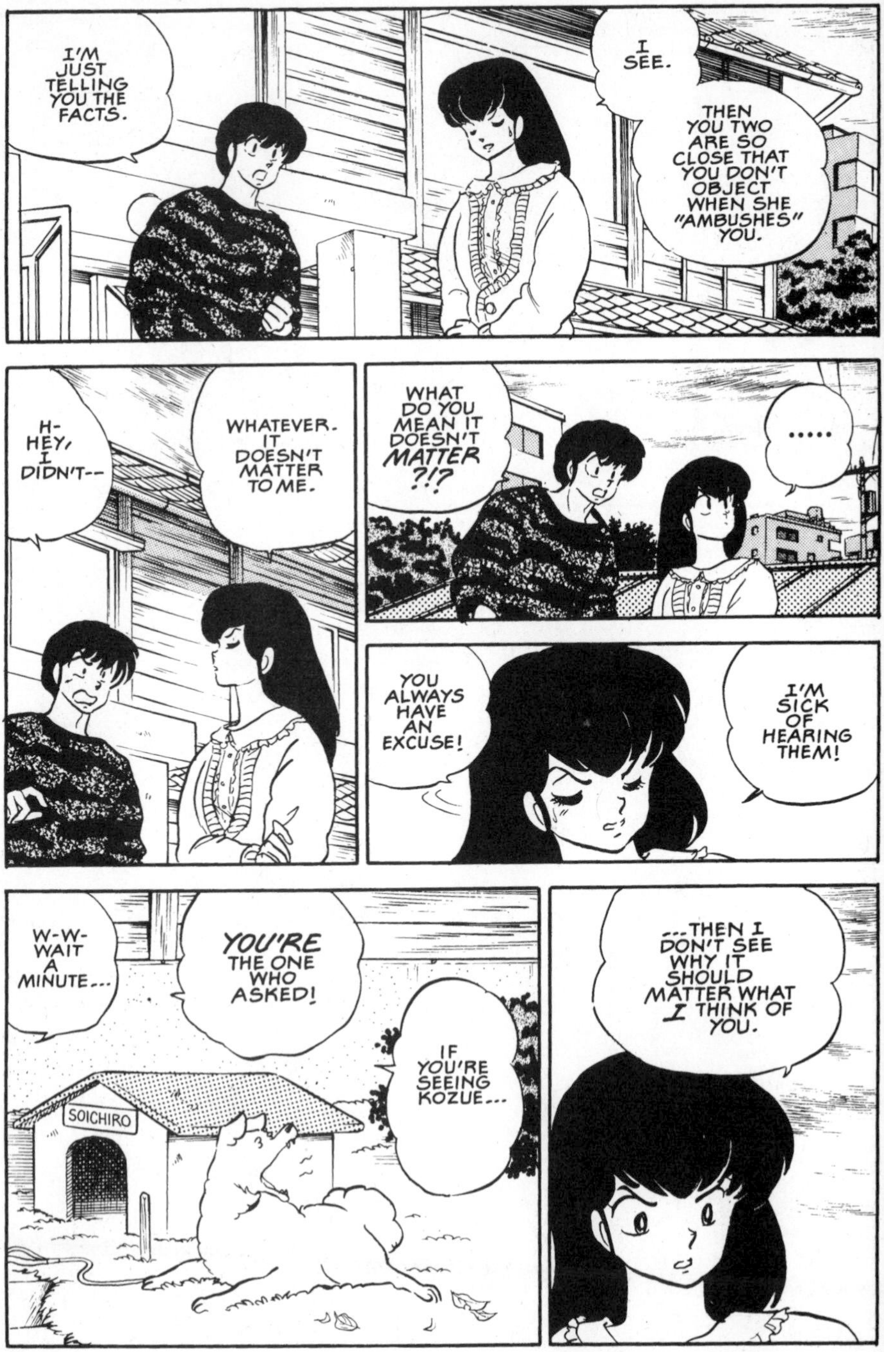
I'M JUST TELLING YOU THE FACTS.
I SEE.
THEN YOU TWO ARE SO CLOSE THAT YOU DON'T OBJECT WHEN SHE "AMBUSHES" YOU.
H-HEY, I DIDN'T--
WHATEVER. IT DOESN'T MATTER TO ME.
WHAT DO YOU MEAN IT DOESN'T *MATTER* ?!?
.....
YOU ALWAYS HAVE AN EXCUSE!
I'M SICK OF HEARING THEM!
W-W-WAIT A MINUTE...
YOU'RE THE ONE WHO ASKED!
SOICHIRO
IF YOU'RE SEEING KOZUE...
...THEN I DON'T SEE WHY IT SHOULD MATTER WHAT *I* THINK OF YOU.

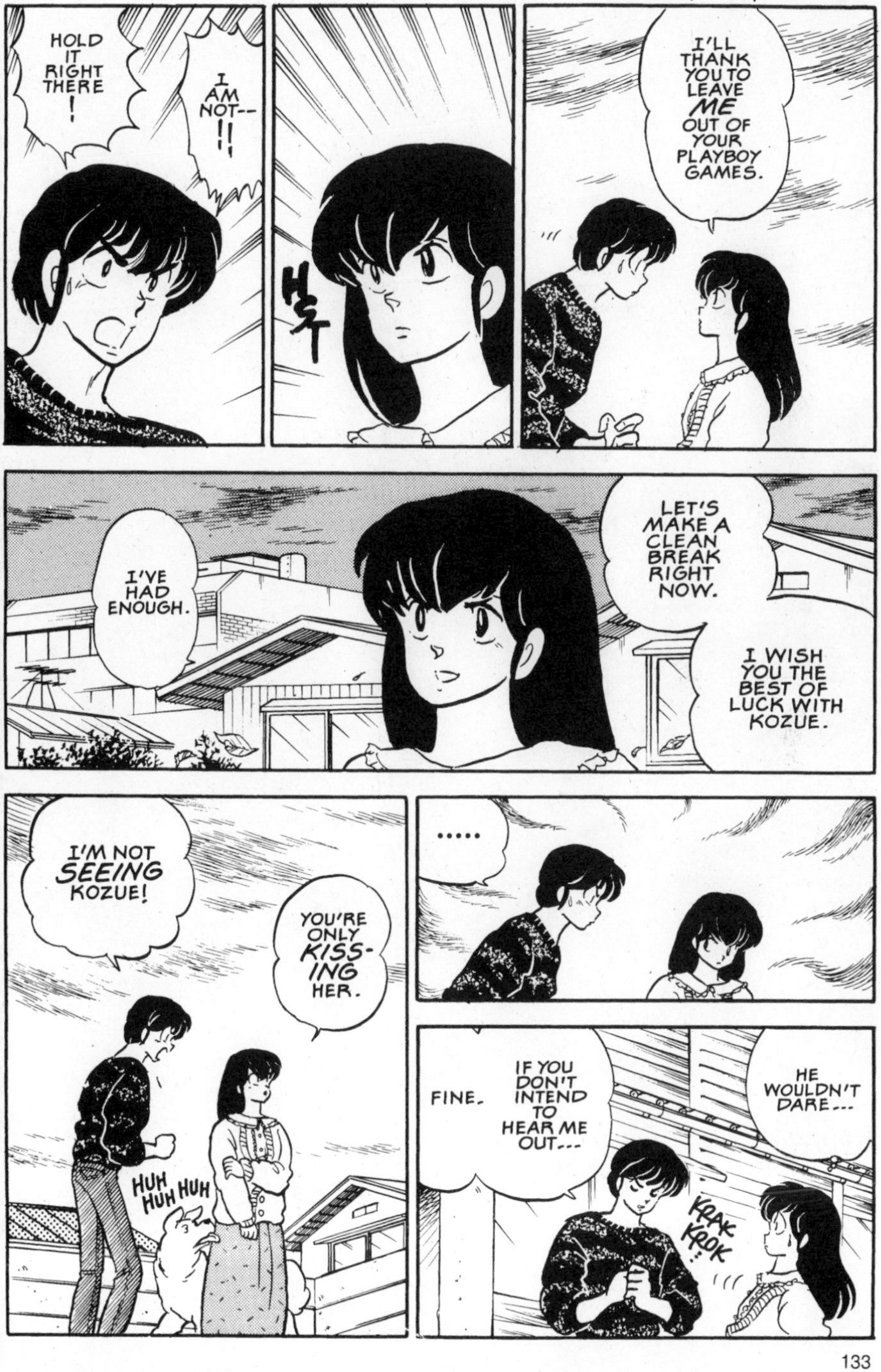
HOLD IT RIGHT THERE!
I AM NOT--!!
HST
I'LL THANK YOU TO LEAVE ME OUT OF YOUR PLAYBOY GAMES.
I'VE HAD ENOUGH.
LET'S MAKE A CLEAN BREAK RIGHT NOW.
I WISH YOU THE BEST OF LUCK WITH KOZUE.
I'M NOT SEEING KOZUE!
YOU'RE ONLY KISSING HER.
HUH HUH HUH
.....
FINE.
IF YOU DON'T INTEND TO HEAR ME OUT...
HE WOULDN'T DARE...
KRAK KROK

C'MON, MANA-GER... ...PEER BE-TWEEN MY HANDS.

?

...WHAT IS THIS?

JUST LOOK, WILL YOU?

OKAY. NOW CLOSE YOUR EYES.

SOICHIR

.....

AHEM.

YOUR EYES...?

WHY?

HMM

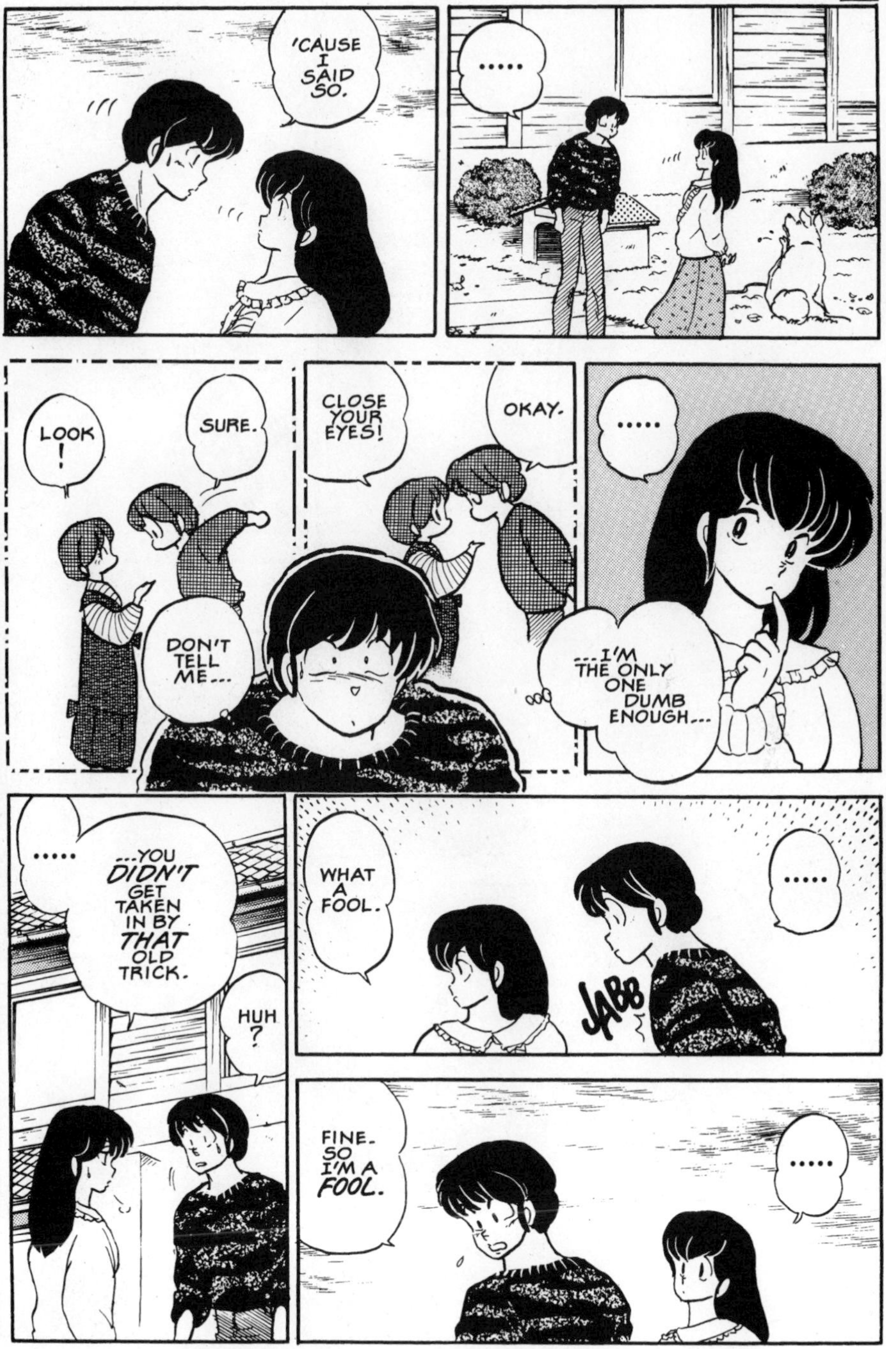
'CAUSE I SAID SO.
.....
LOOK!
SURE.
CLOSE YOUR EYES!
OKAY.
DON'T TELL ME...
.....
...I'M THE ONLY ONE DUMB ENOUGH...
.....
...YOU DIDN'T GET TAKEN IN BY THAT OLD TRICK.
HUH?
WHAT A FOOL.
.....
JABB
FINE. SO I'M A FOOL.
.....

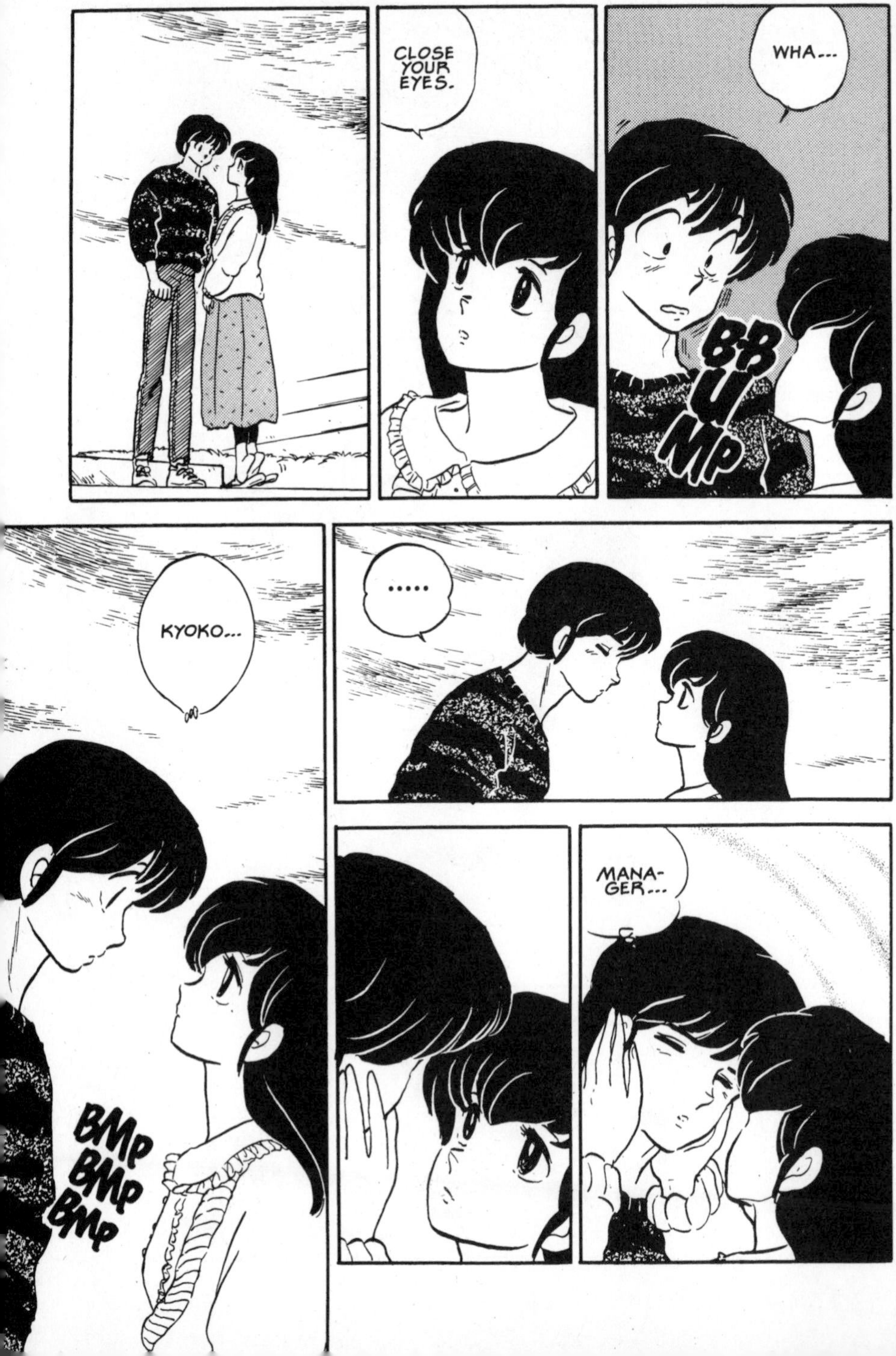
CLOSE YOUR EYES.
WHA...
BBUMP
KYOKO...
......
BMP BMP BMP
MANA-GER...

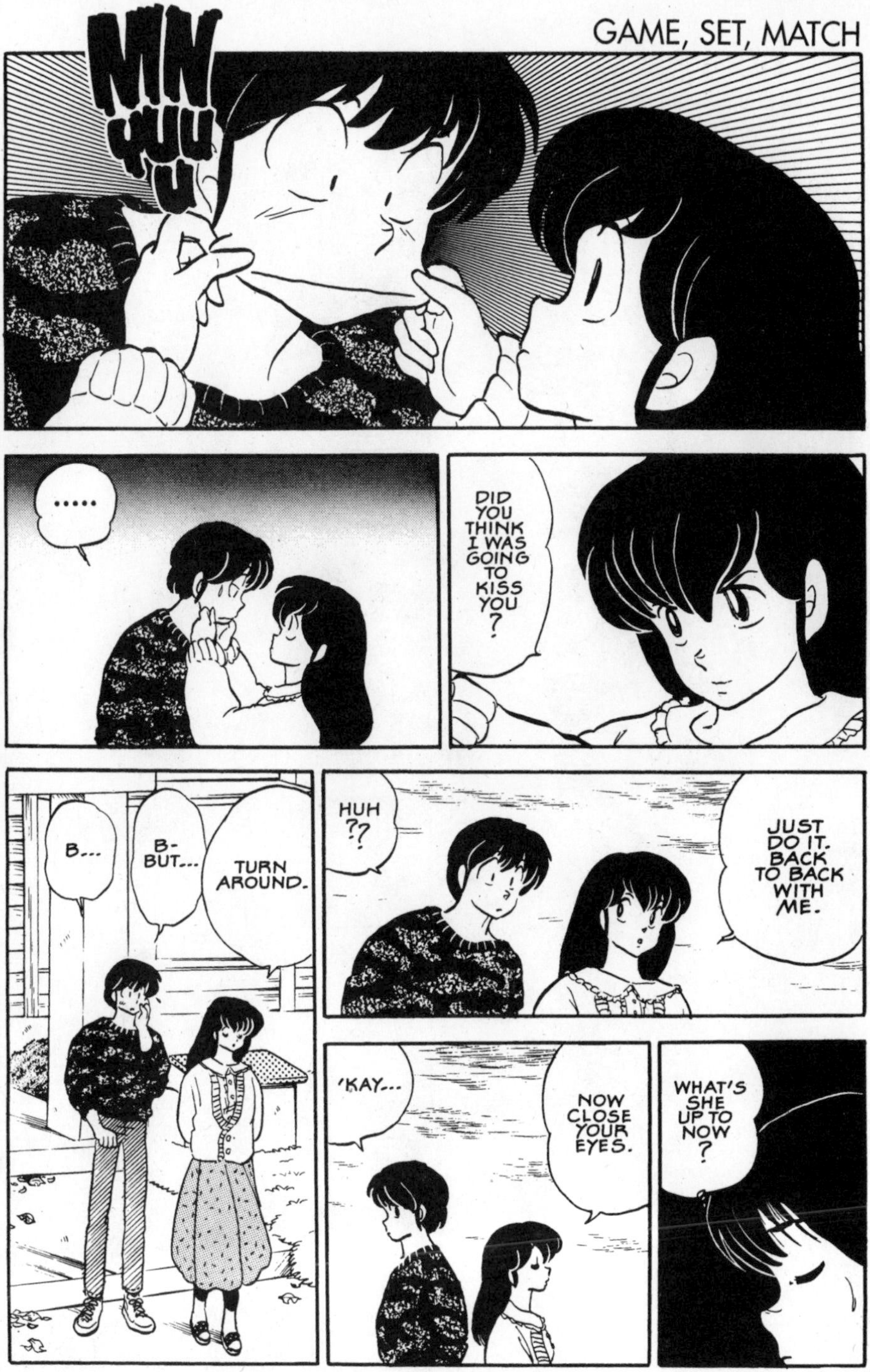
MNYUUU
......
DID YOU THINK I WAS GOING TO KISS YOU?
B...
B-BUT...
TURN AROUND.
HUH??
JUST DO IT. BACK TO BACK WITH ME.
'KAY...
NOW CLOSE YOUR EYES.
WHAT'S SHE UP TO NOW?

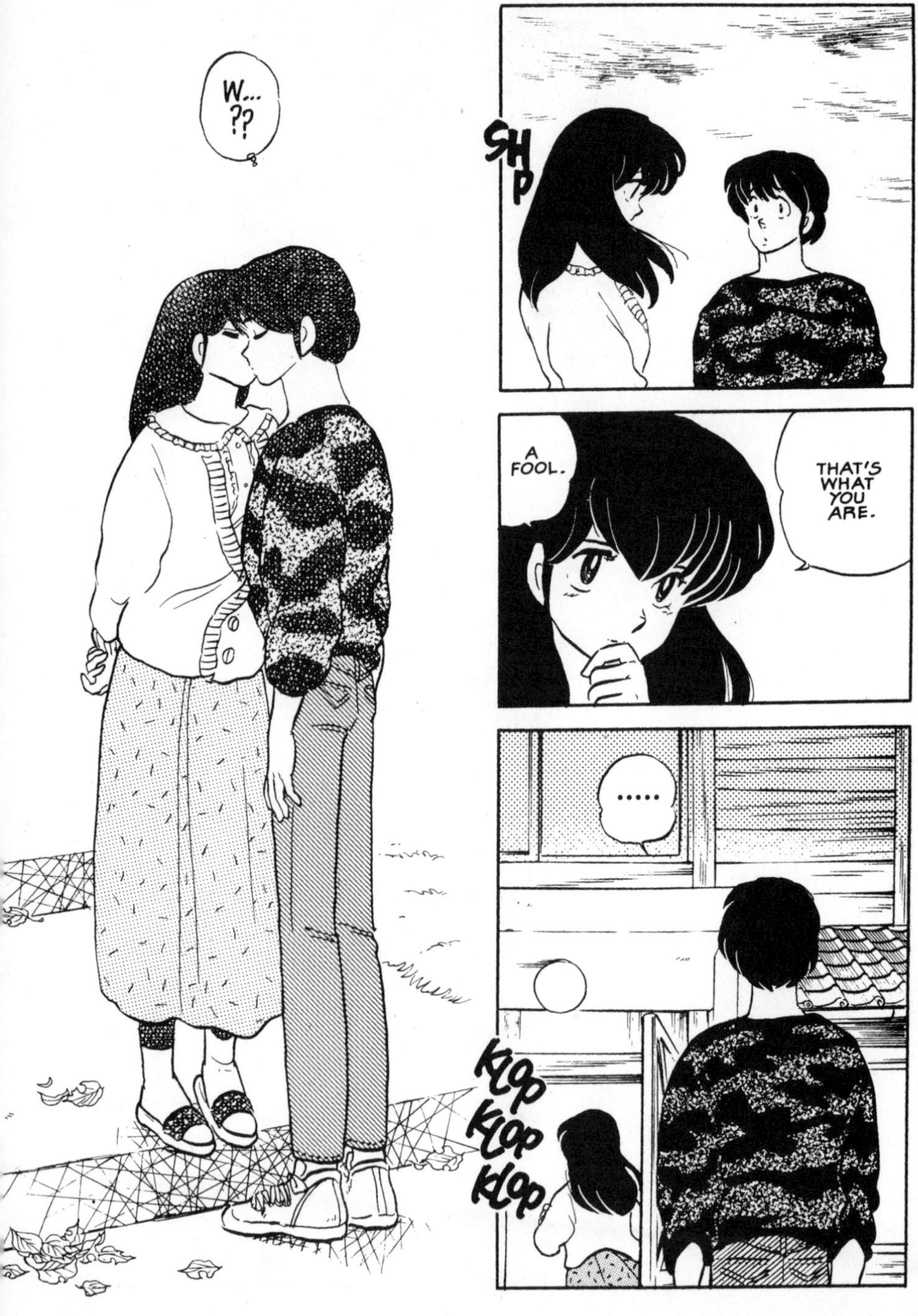
W... ??
SHP
A FOOL.
THAT'S WHAT YOU ARE.
......
KLOP KLOP KLOP

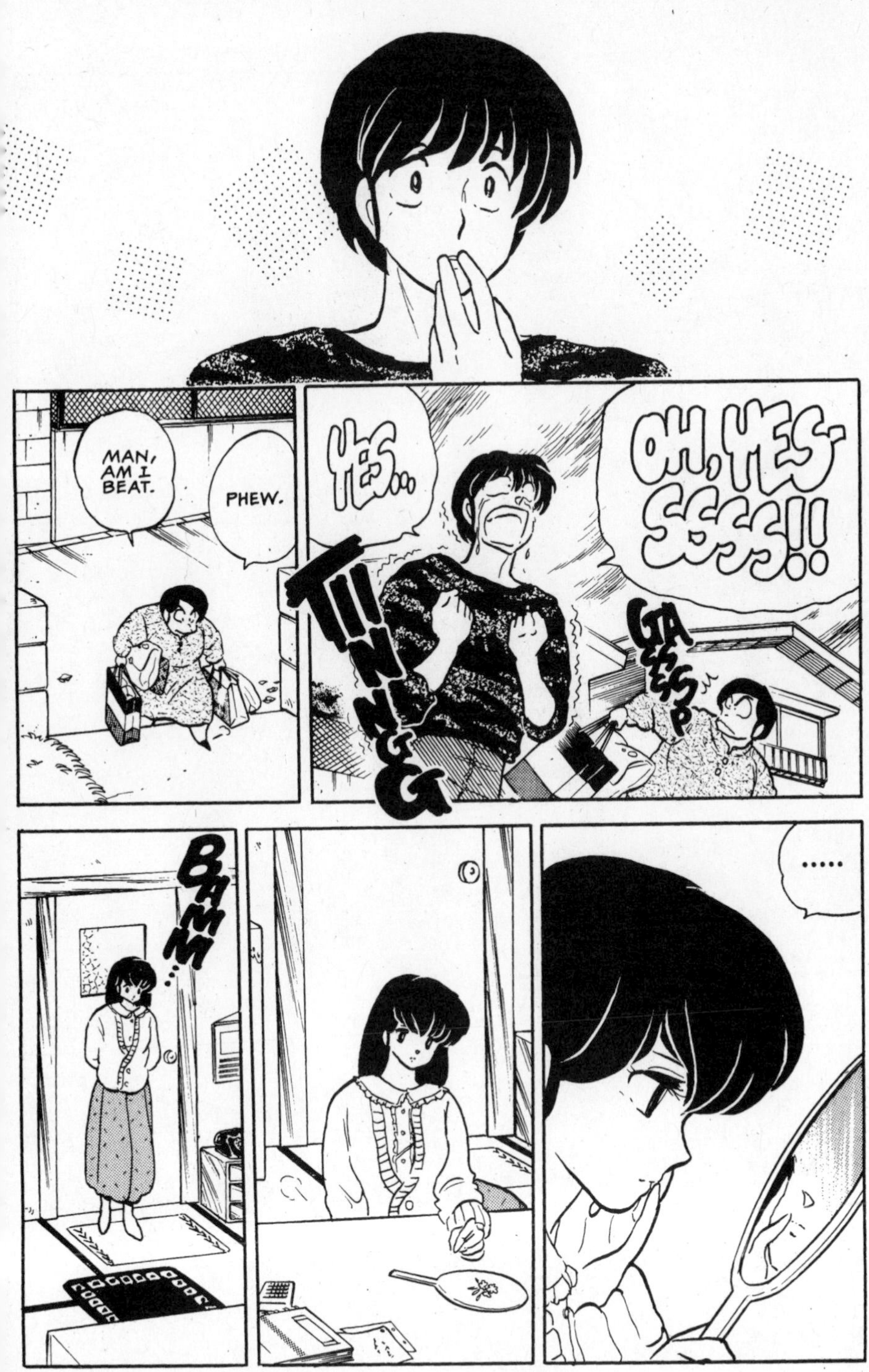
MAN, AM I BEAT.
PHEW.
YES...
OH, YES-SSSS!!
TIIINNNGGG
GAAASP
BAMM...
.....

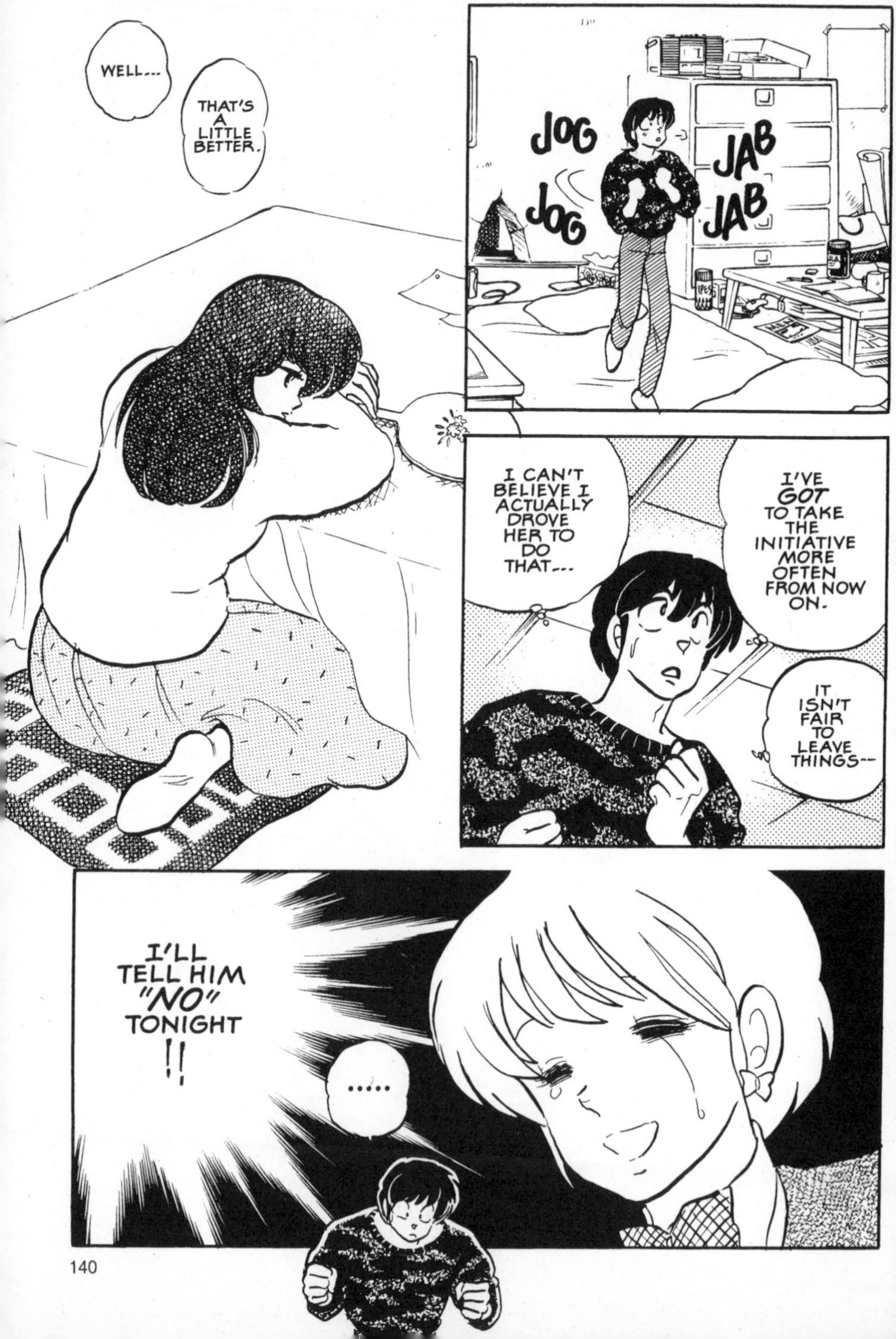
WELL...
THAT'S A LITTLE BETTER.
JOG JOG
JAB JAB
I CAN'T BELIEVE I ACTUALLY DROVE HER TO DO THAT...
I'VE *GOT* TO TAKE THE INITIATIVE MORE OFTEN FROM NOW ON.
IT ISN'T FAIR TO LEAVE THINGS--
I'LL TELL HIM *"NO"* TONIGHT !!
......

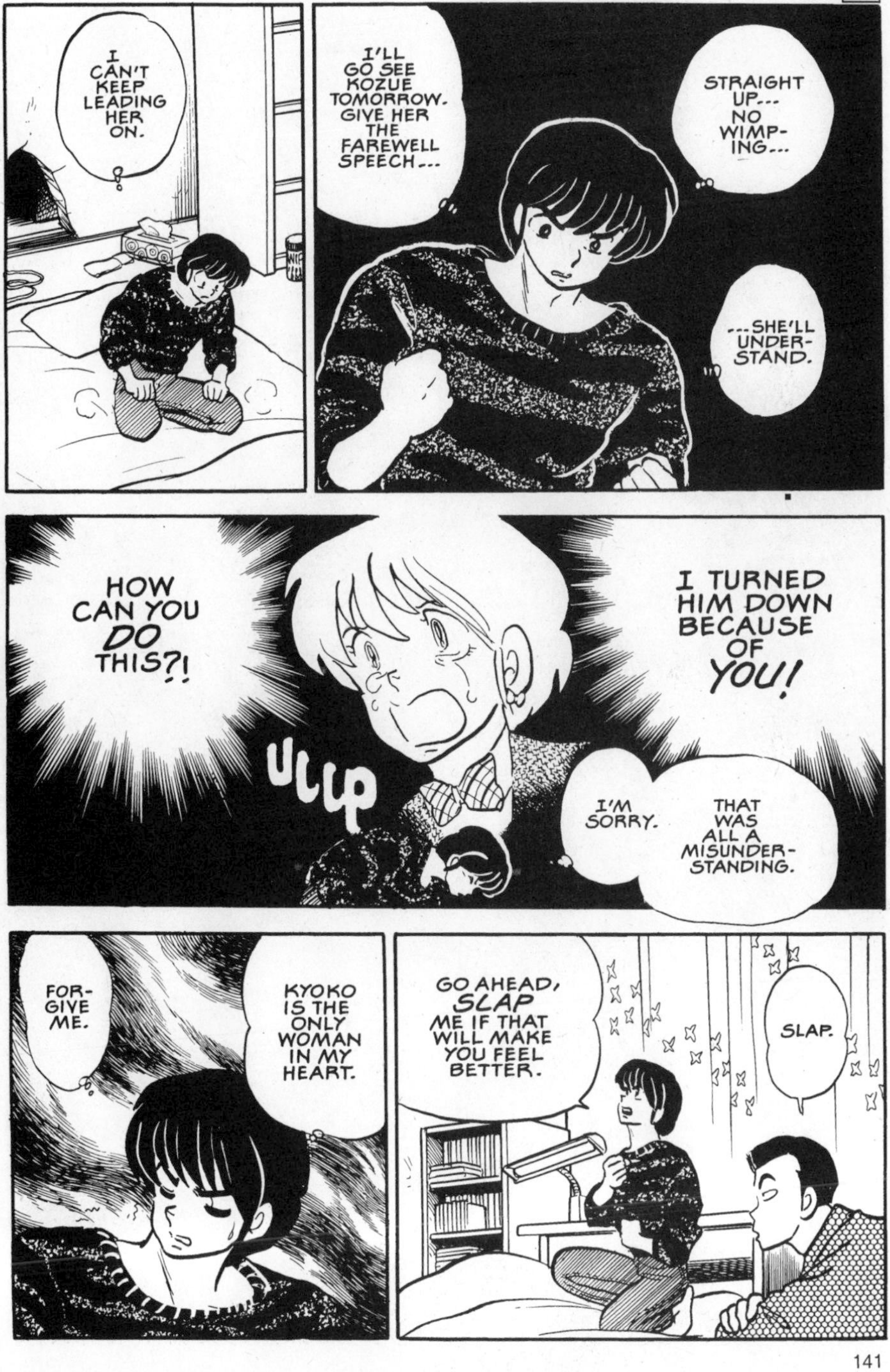
I CAN'T KEEP LEADING HER ON.
I'LL GO SEE KOZUE TOMORROW. GIVE HER THE FAREWELL SPEECH...
STRAIGHT UP... NO WIMP-ING...
...SHE'LL UNDER-STAND.
HOW CAN YOU DO THIS?!
I TURNED HIM DOWN BECAUSE OF YOU!
ULLP
I'M SORRY.
THAT WAS ALL A MISUNDER-STANDING.
FOR-GIVE ME.
KYOKO IS THE ONLY WOMAN IN MY HEART.
GO AHEAD, SLAP ME IF THAT WILL MAKE YOU FEEL BETTER.
SLAP.

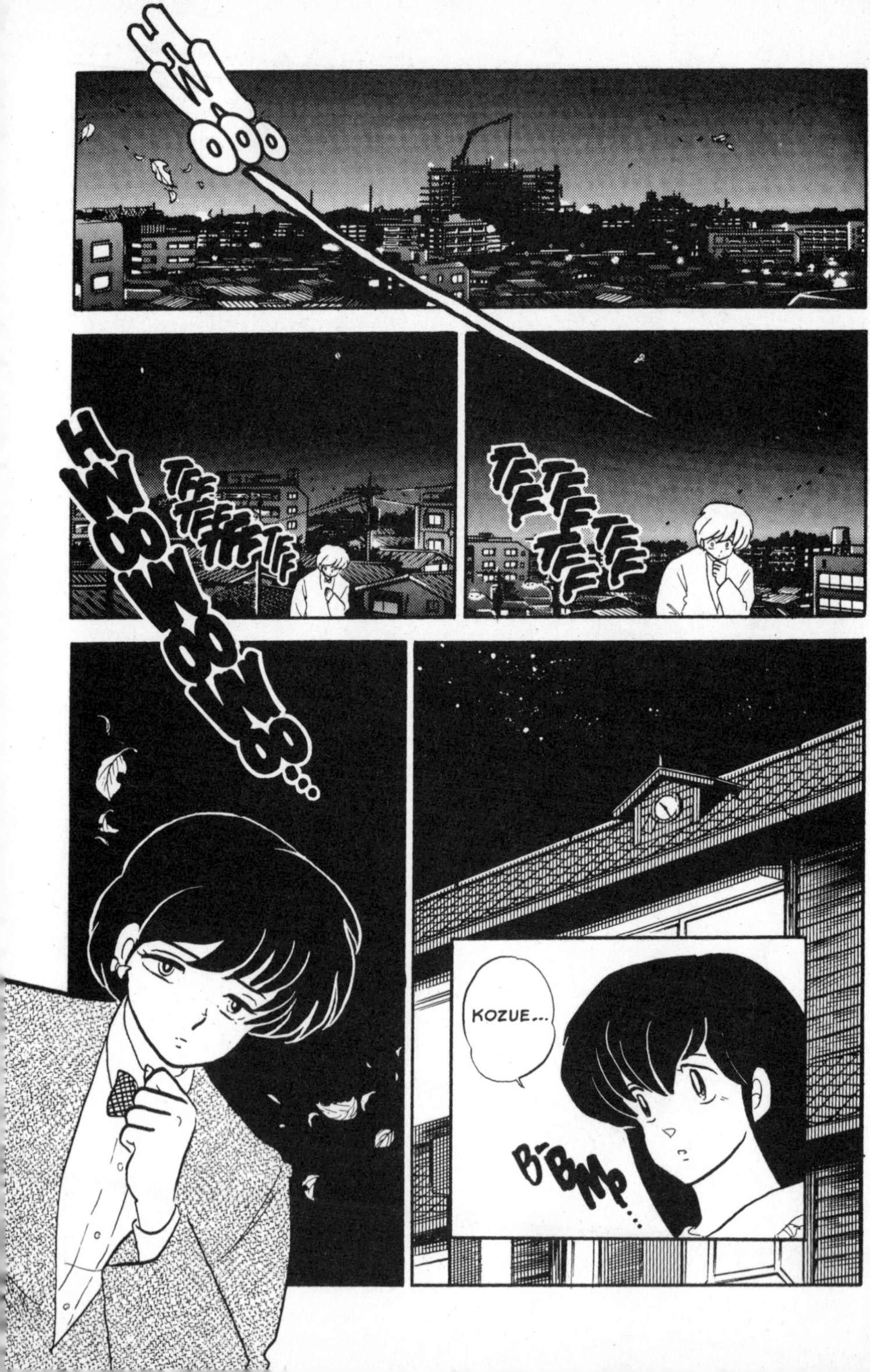
FWOOO
HWOOWOOWOO...
KOZUE...
B-BMP...

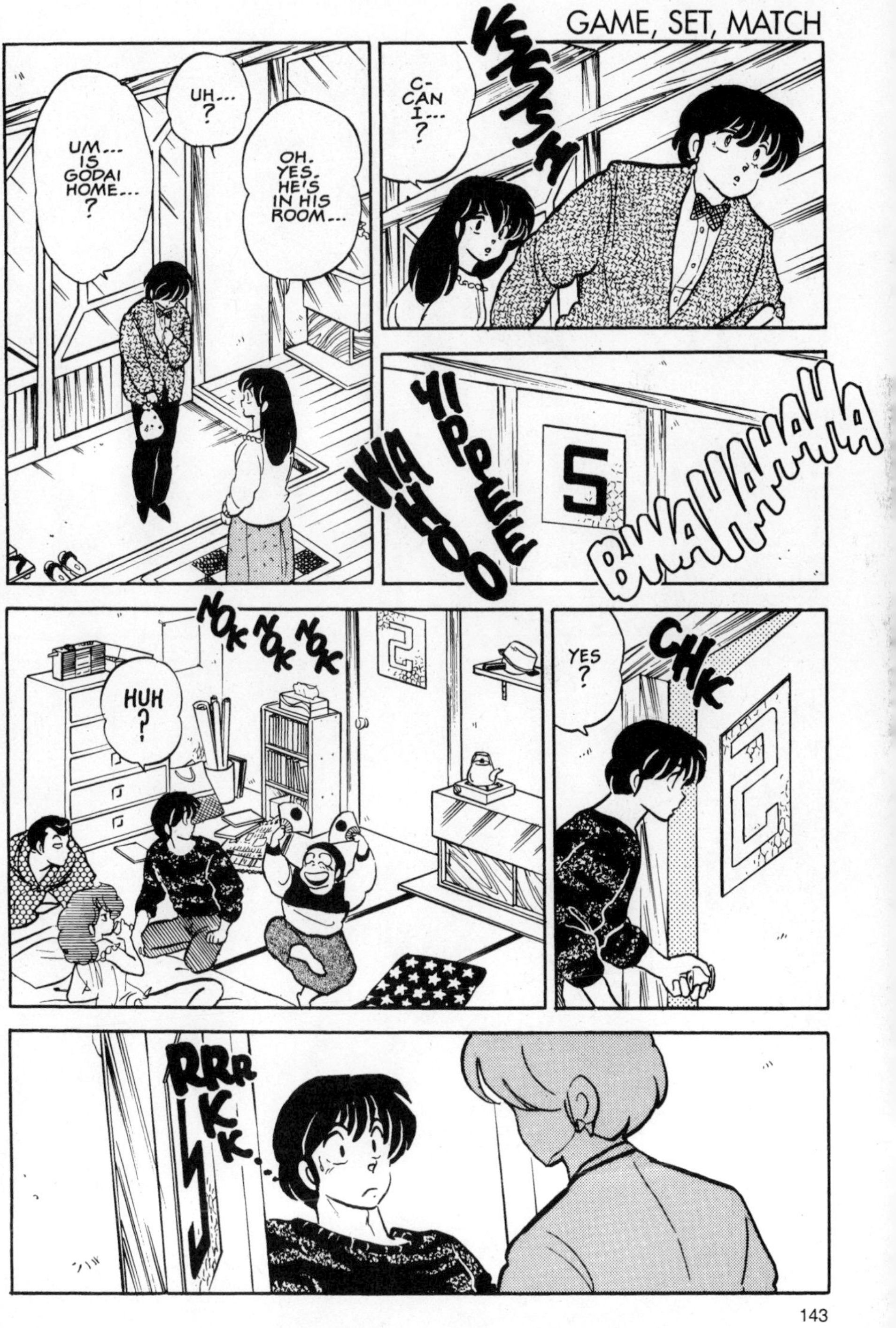
UM... IS GODAI HOME...?
UH...?
OH. YES. HE'S IN HIS ROOM...
C-CAN I...?
YIPPEEE
WAHOOO
5
BWAHAHAHAHA
NOK NOK NOK
HUH?
YES?
CHK
RRRKK...

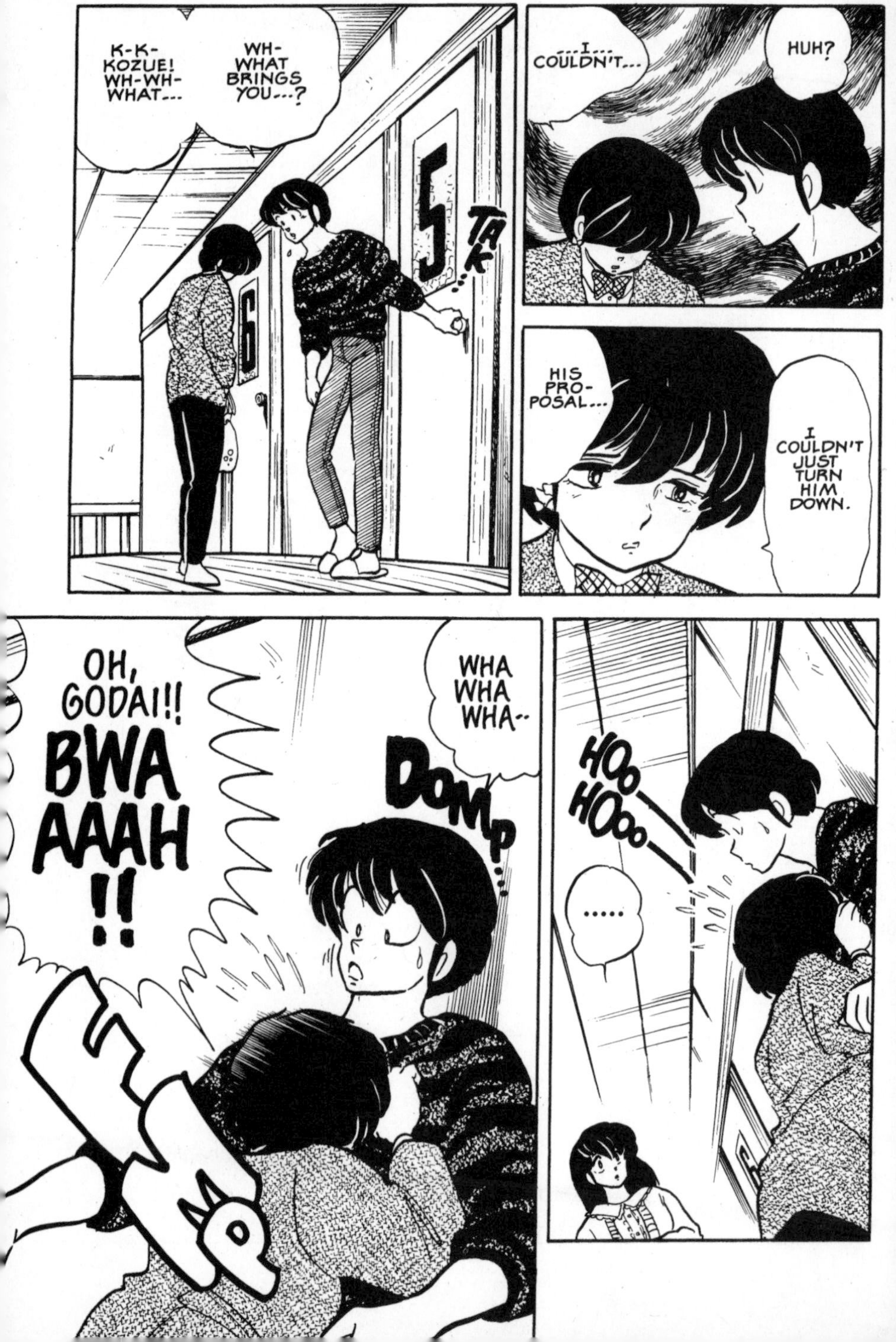
K-K-KOZUE! WH-WH-WHAT...
WH-WHAT BRINGS YOU...?
TAK
...I... COULDN'T...
HUH?
HIS PRO-POSAL...
I COULDN'T JUST TURN HIM DOWN.
OH, GODAI!! BWA AAAH !!
WHA WHA WHA..
DOMP...
HOO HOOO
......

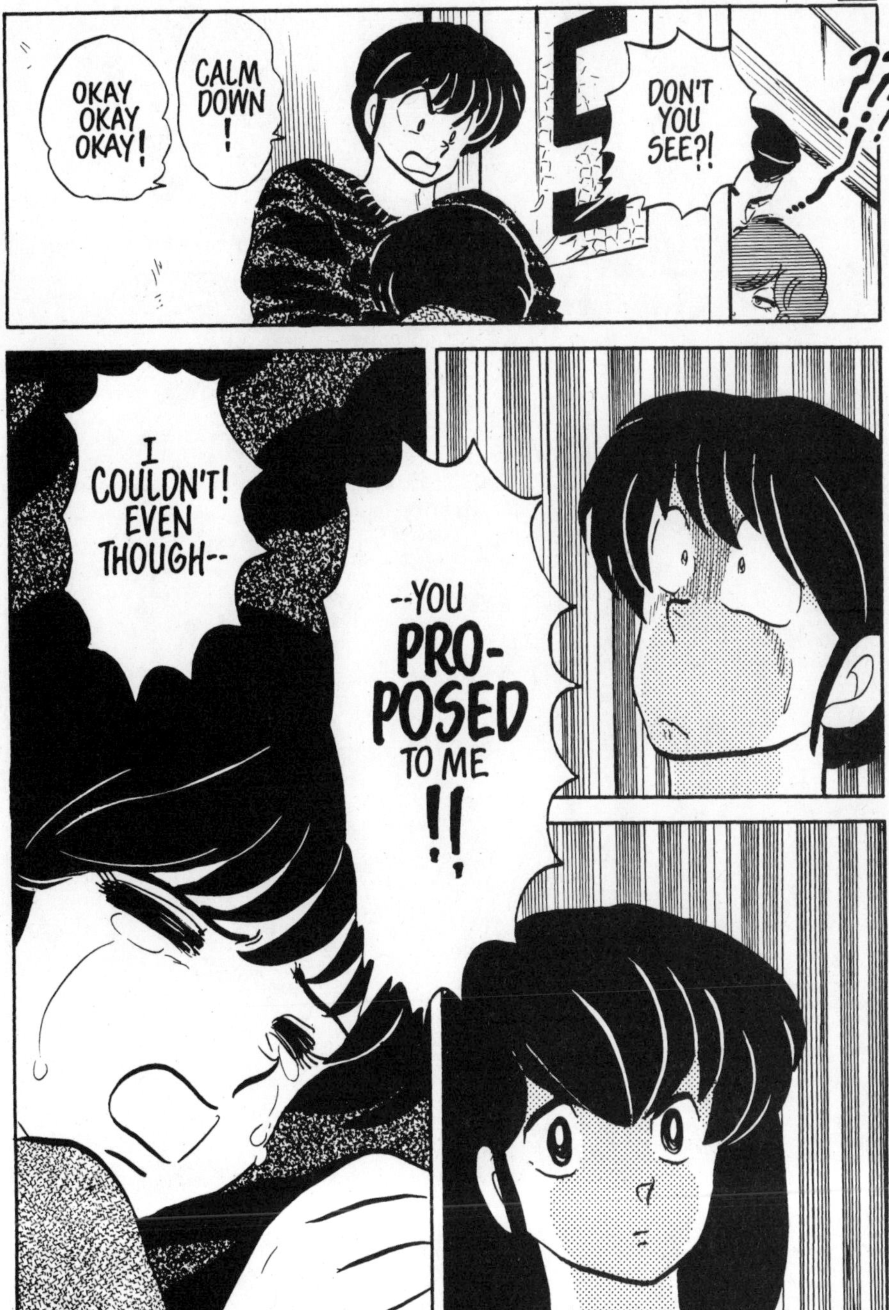
OKAY OKAY OKAY!
CALM DOWN!
DON'T YOU SEE?!
???
I COULDN'T! EVEN THOUGH--
--YOU PROPOSED TO ME!!

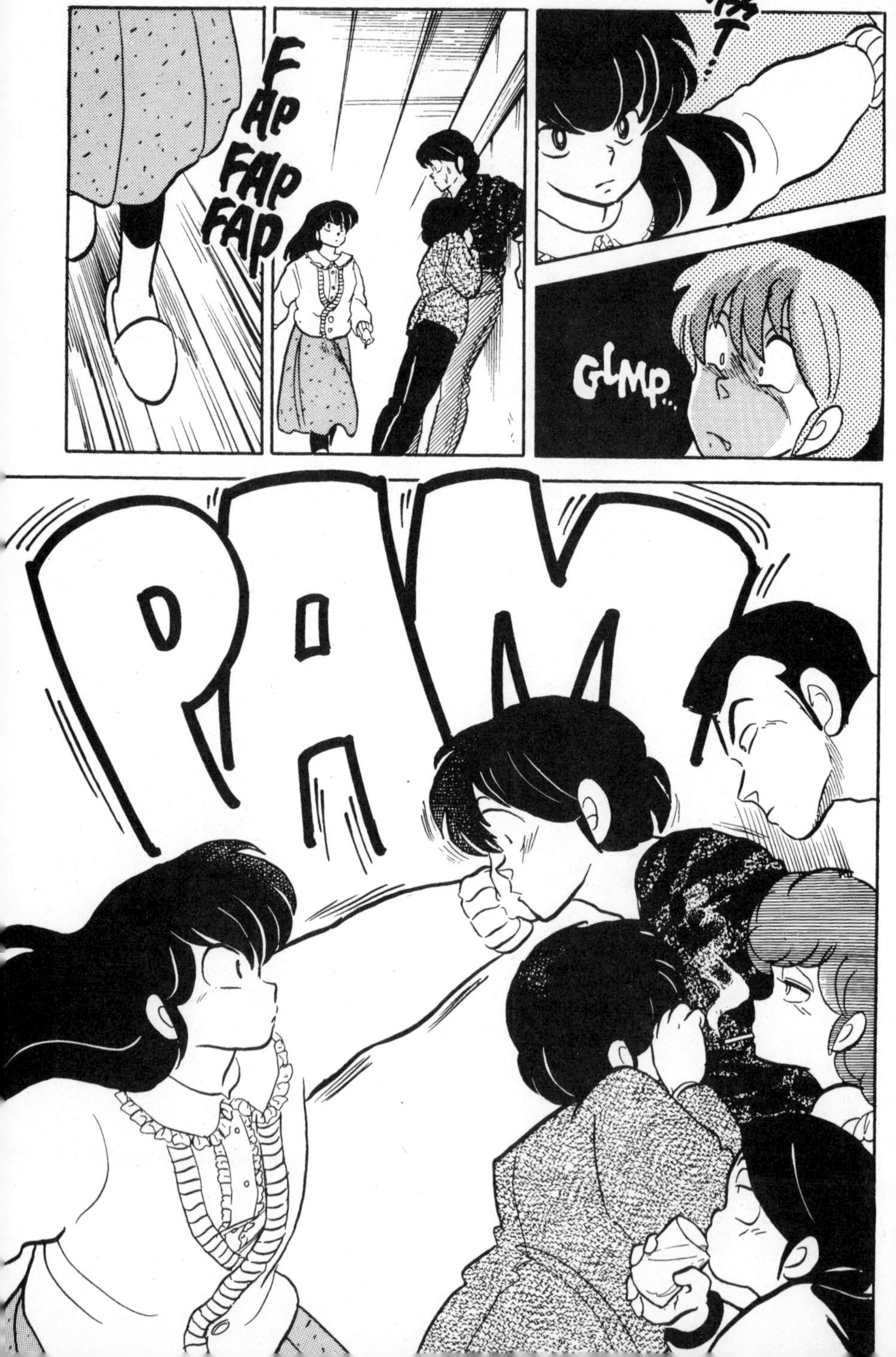
FAP FAP FAP
HSST!...
GLMP...
PAM

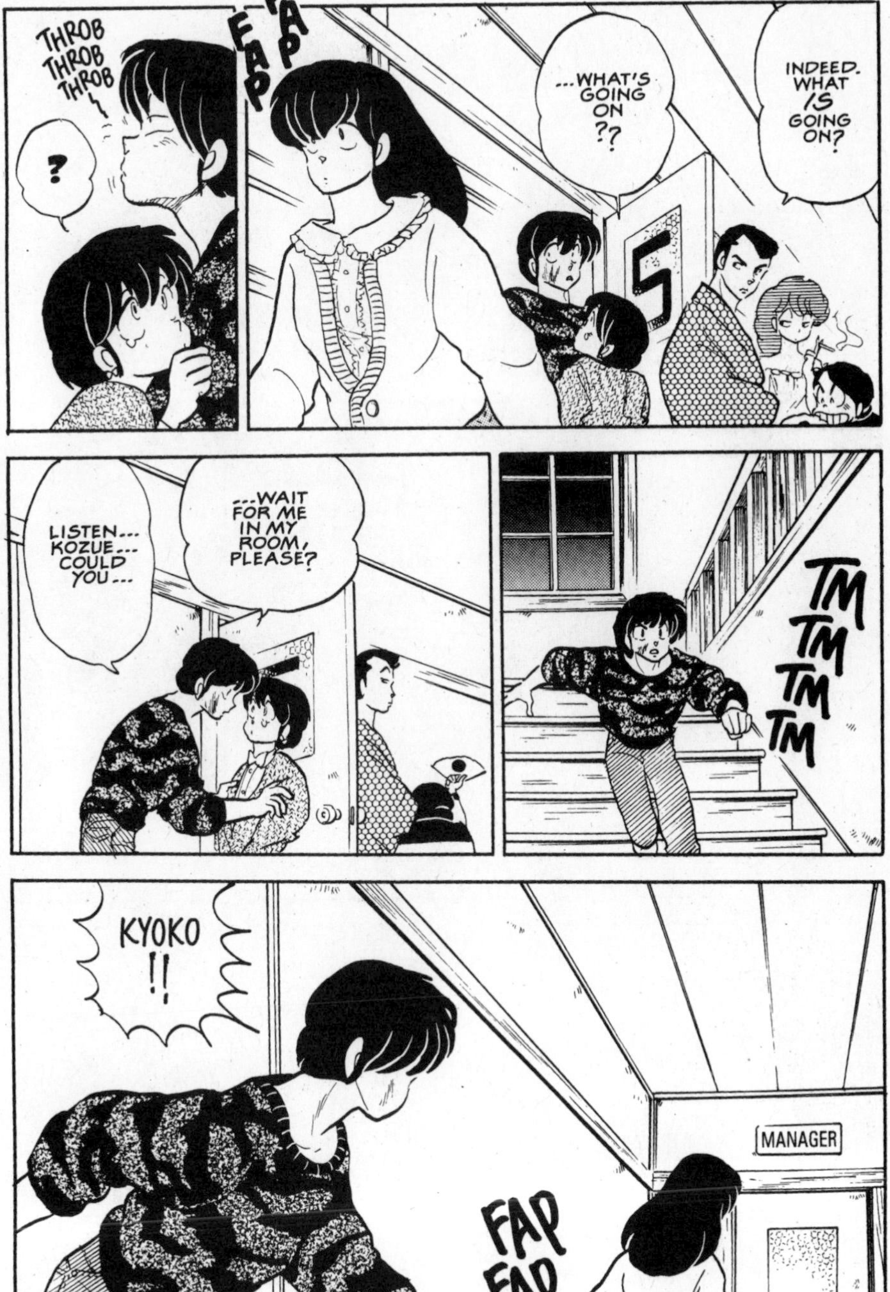
THROB THROB THROB
?
FAP FAP
...WHAT'S GOING ON ??
INDEED. WHAT IS GOING ON?
5
LISTEN... KOZUE... COULD YOU...
...WAIT FOR ME IN MY ROOM, PLEASE?
TM TM TM TM
KYOKO !!
MANAGER
FAP FAP

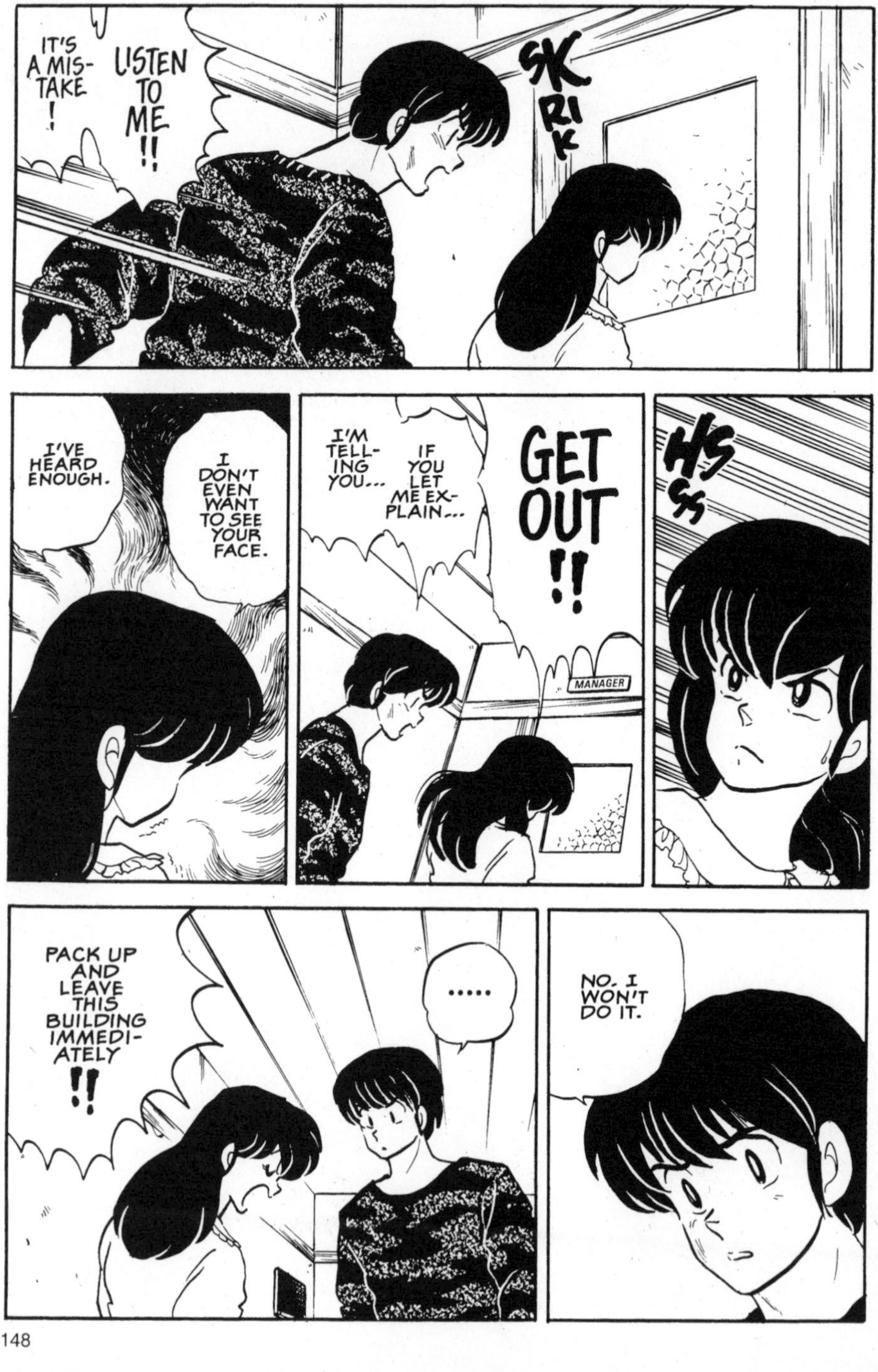
IT'S A MIS-TAKE!
LISTEN TO ME!!
SKRIK
I'VE HEARD ENOUGH.
I DON'T EVEN WANT TO SEE YOUR FACE.
I'M TELLING YOU...
IF YOU LET ME EX-PLAIN...
GET OUT!!
MANAGER
HISSS
PACK UP AND LEAVE THIS BUILDING IMMEDI-ATELY!!
.....
NO. I WON'T DO IT.

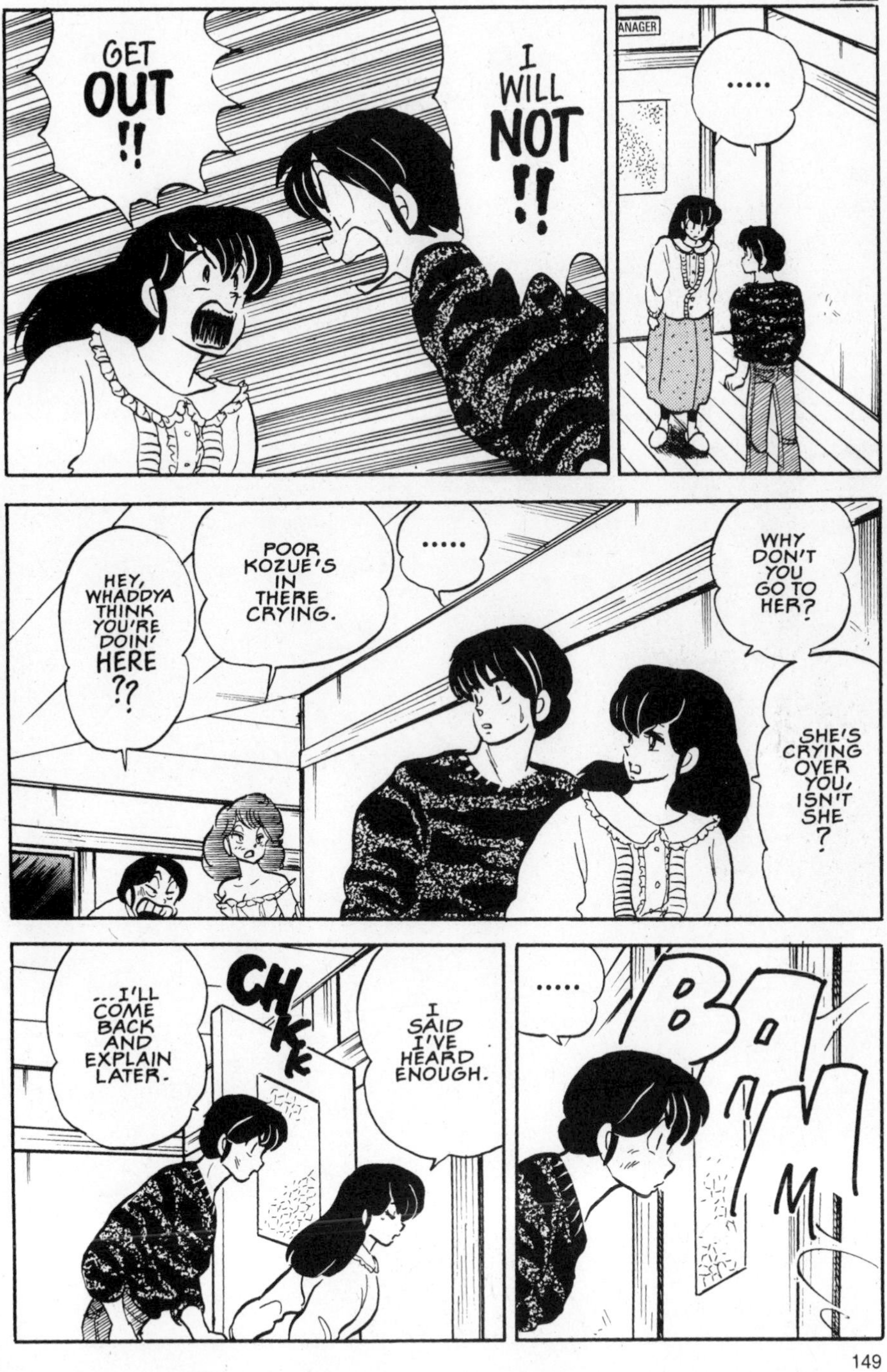
GET OUT !!
I WILL NOT !!
ANAGER
.....
HEY, WHADDYA THINK YOU'RE DOIN' HERE ??
POOR KOZUE'S IN THERE CRYING.
.....
WHY DON'T YOU GO TO HER?
SHE'S CRYING OVER YOU, ISN'T SHE ?
...I'LL COME BACK AND EXPLAIN LATER.
CHKKK
I SAID I'VE HEARD ENOUGH.
.....
BAM

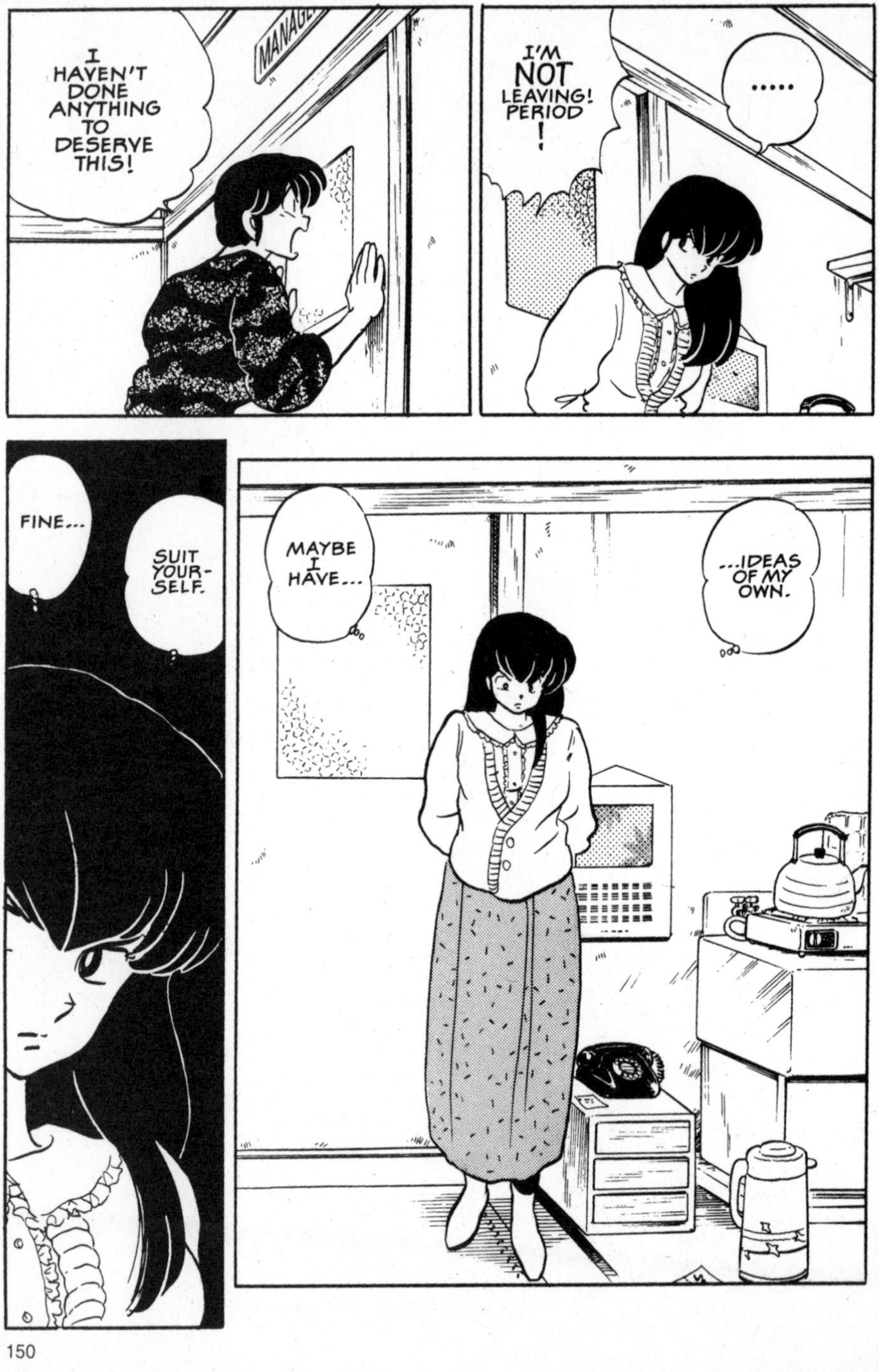
I HAVEN'T DONE ANYTHING TO DESERVE THIS!
MANAG
I'M NOT LEAVING! PERIOD!
.....
FINE...
SUIT YOURSELF.
MAYBE I HAVE...
...IDEAS OF MY OWN.

PART EIGHT
THE FIRST MOVE

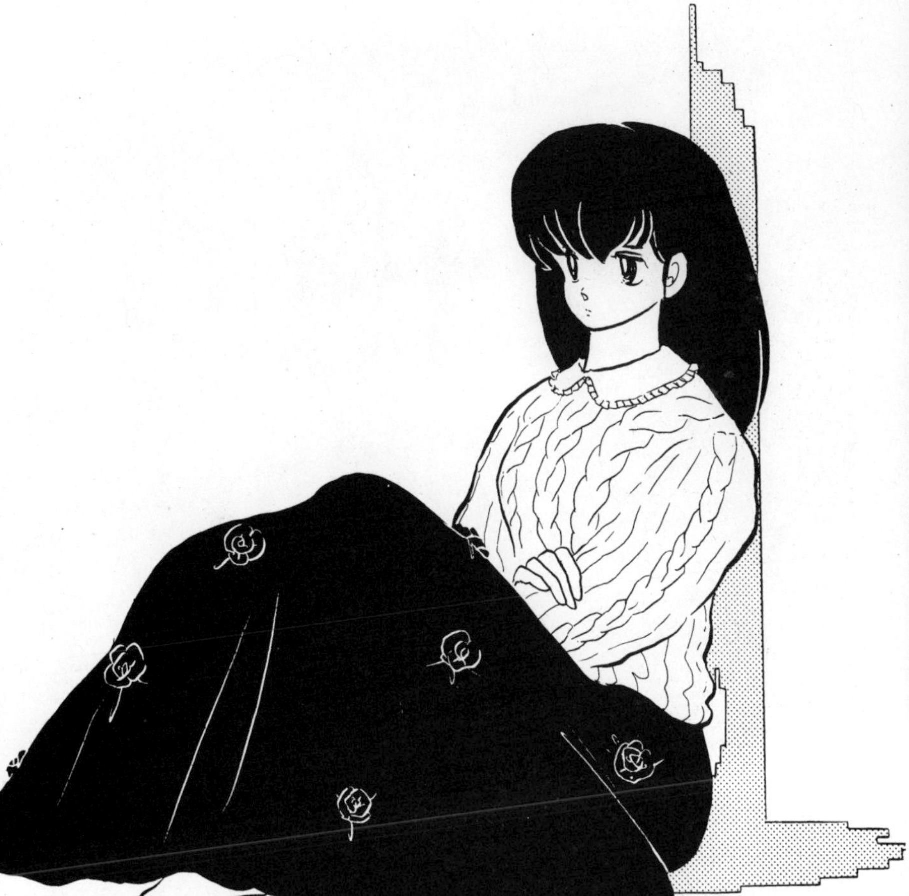

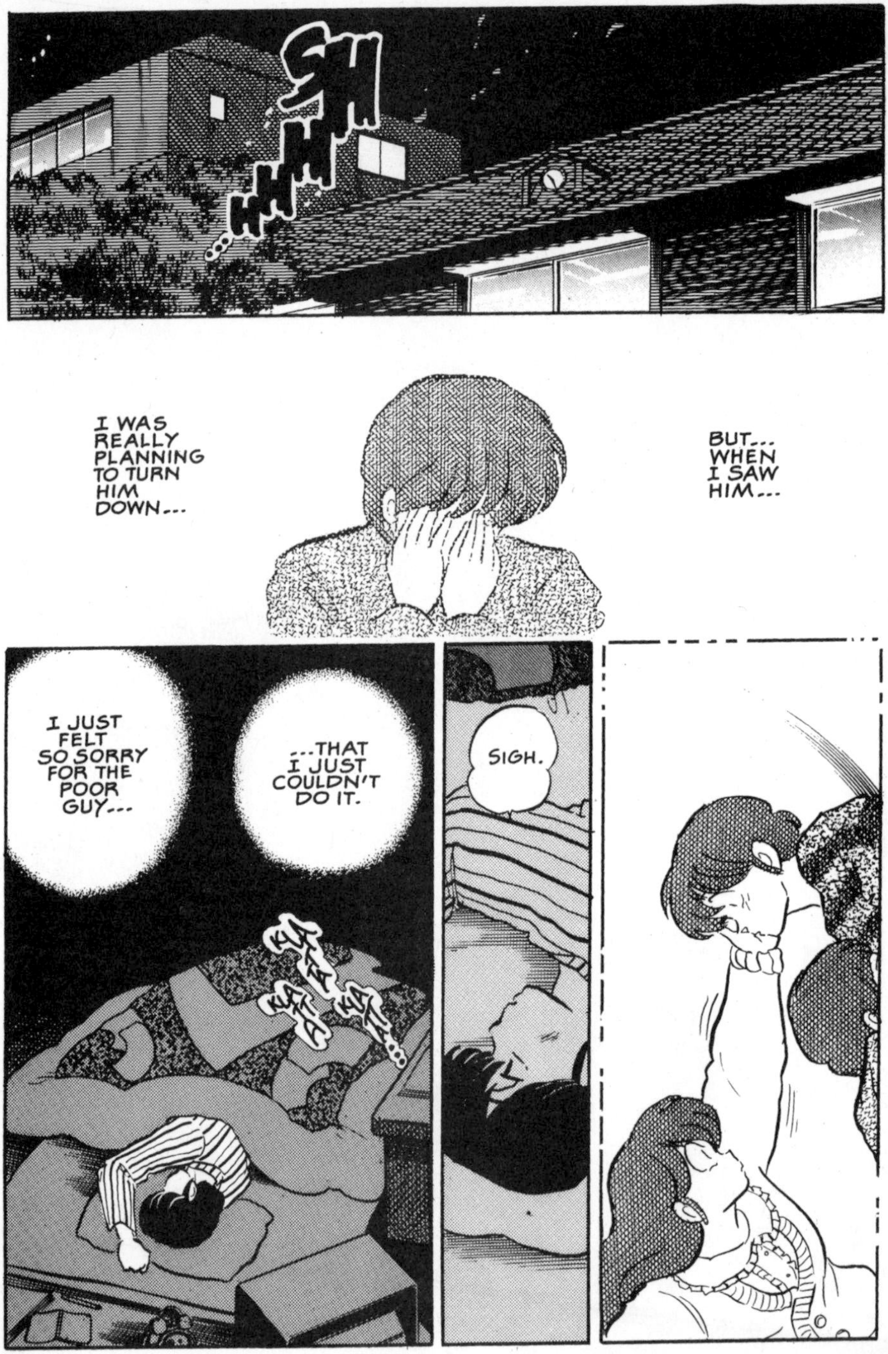
SHHHHH...
I WAS REALLY PLANNING TO TURN HIM DOWN...
BUT... WHEN I SAW HIM...
I JUST FELT SO SORRY FOR THE POOR GUY...
...THAT I JUST COULDN'T DO IT.
KYATTA KYATTA KYATTA...
SIGH.

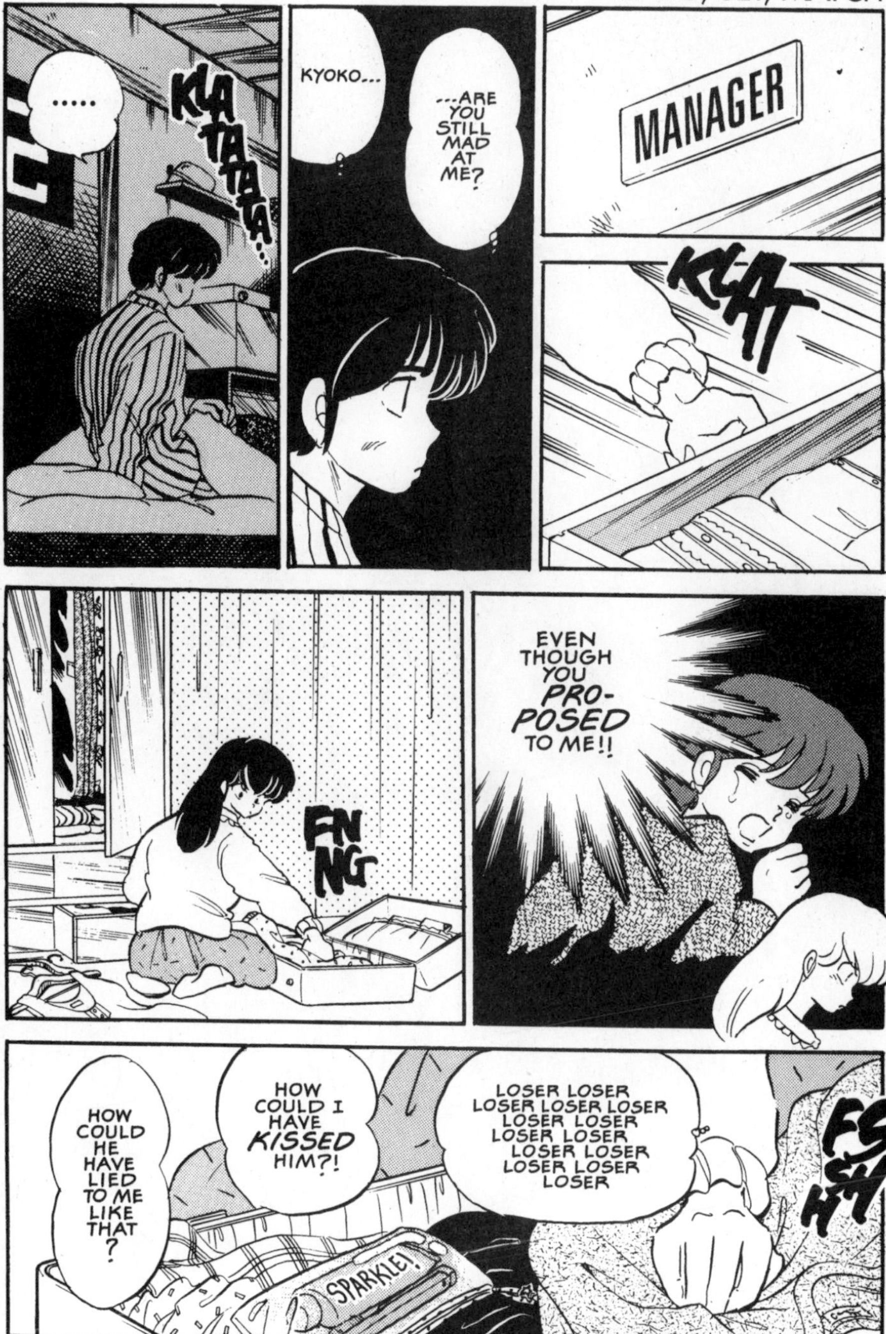

......
KLATATATATA...
KYOKO...
...ARE YOU STILL MAD AT ME?
MANAGER
KLAT
FNNG
EVEN THOUGH YOU PRO-POSED TO ME!!
HRRRRR
HOW COULD HE HAVE LIED TO ME LIKE THAT?
HOW COULD I HAVE KISSED HIM?!
LOSER LOSER LOSER LOSER LOSER LOSER LOSER LOSER LOSER LOSER LOSER LOSER LOSER LOSER
SPARKLE!
FSSHH

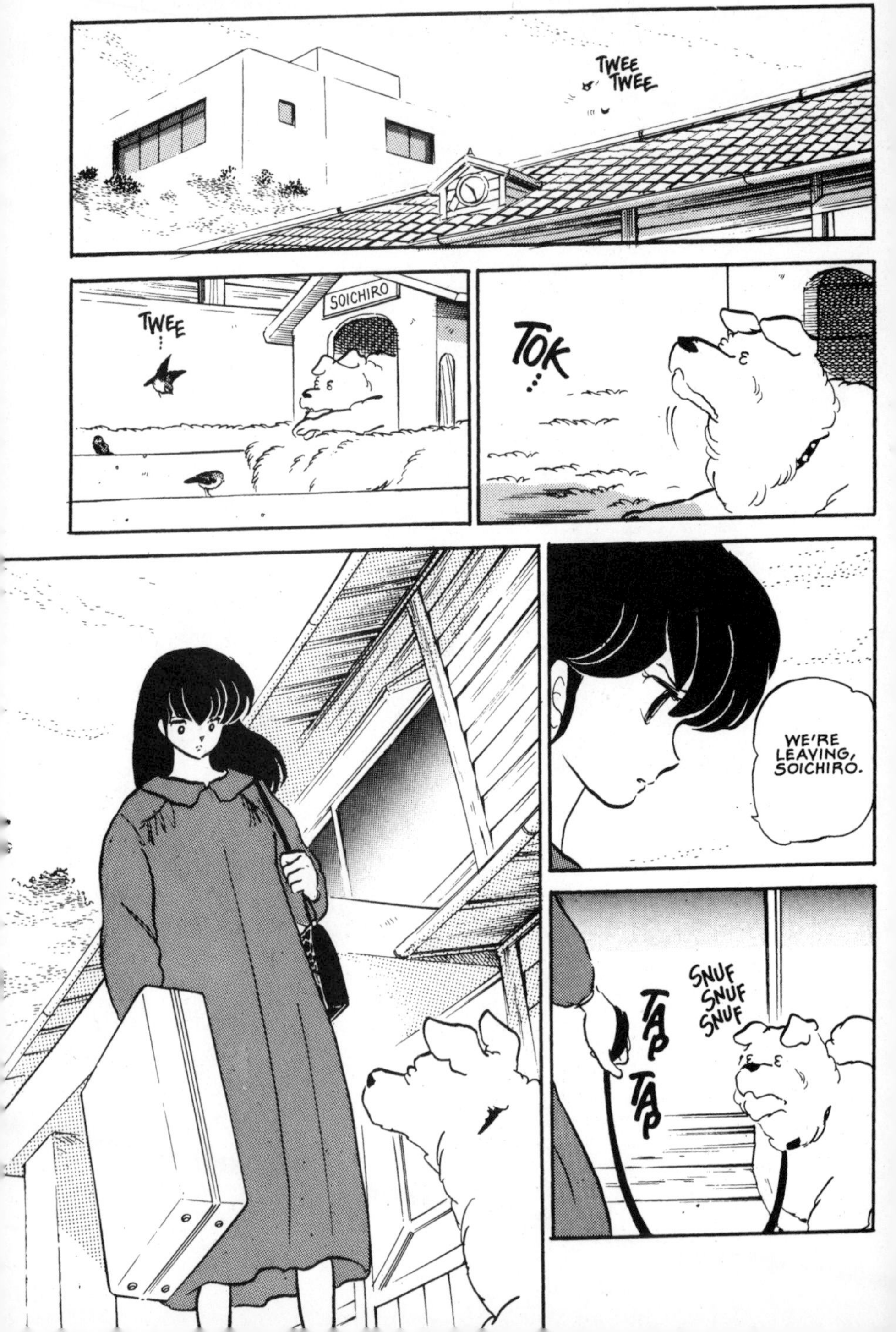
TWEE TWEE
SOICHIRO
TWEE
TOK
WE'RE LEAVING, SOICHIRO.
SNUF SNUF SNUF
TAP TAP

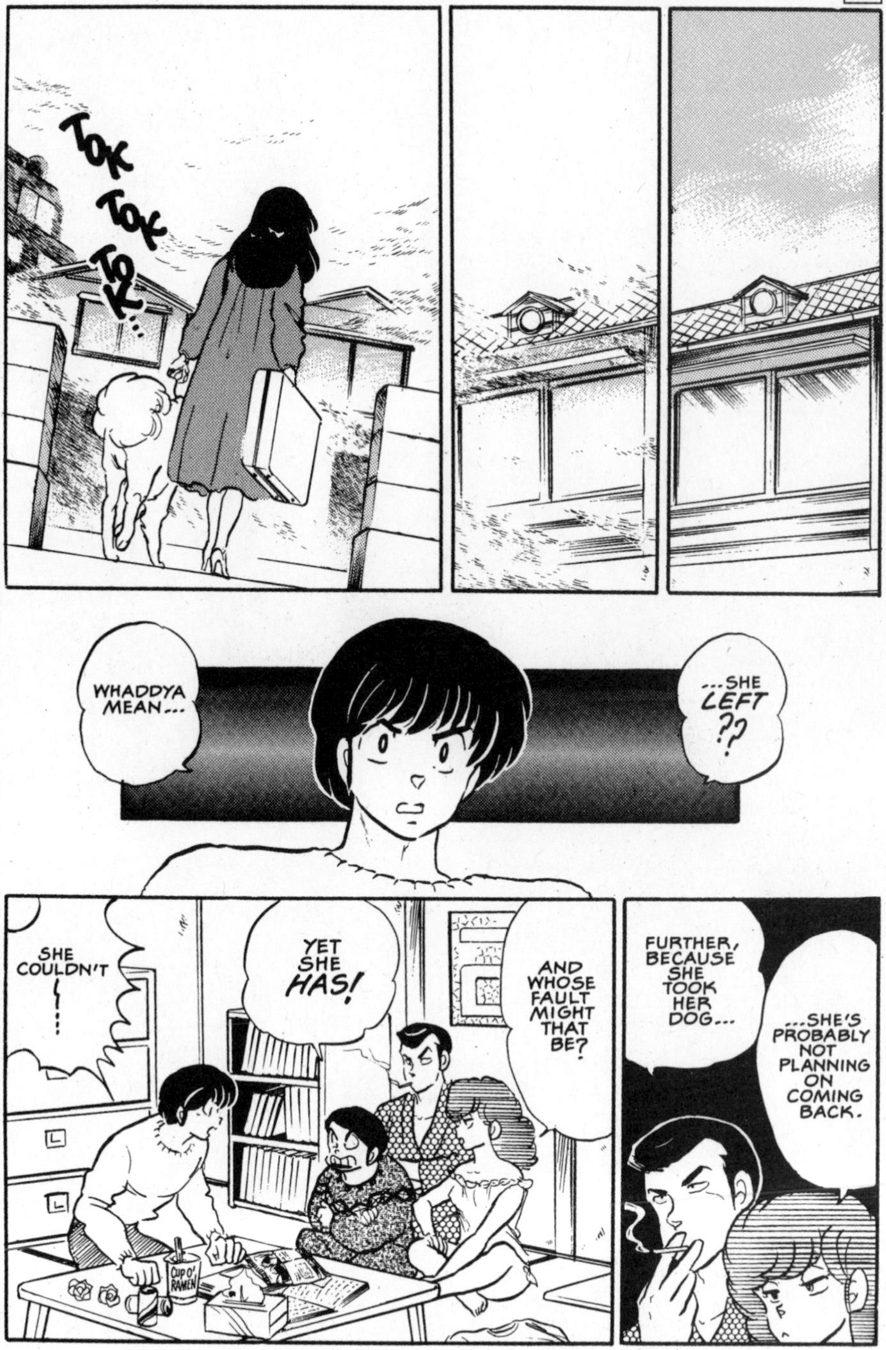
TOK TOK TOK...
WHADDYA MEAN...
...SHE LEFT ??
SHE COULDN'T ...!
YET SHE HAS!
AND WHOSE FAULT MIGHT THAT BE?
CUP O' RAMEN
FURTHER, BECAUSE SHE TOOK HER DOG...
...SHE'S PROBABLY NOT PLANNING ON COMING BACK.

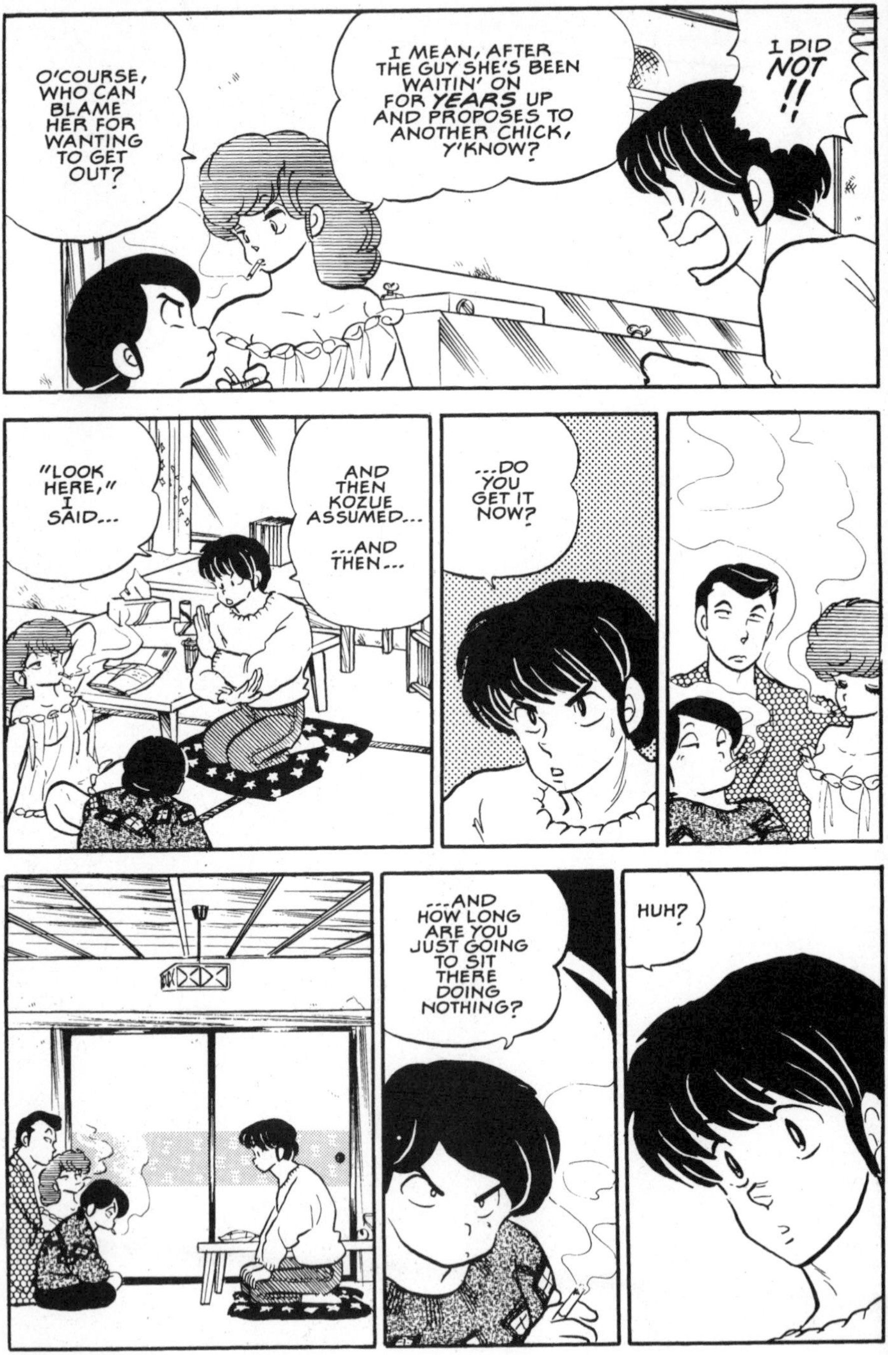
O'COURSE, WHO CAN BLAME HER FOR WANTING TO GET OUT?
I MEAN, AFTER THE GUY SHE'S BEEN WAITIN' ON FOR YEARS UP AND PROPOSES TO ANOTHER CHICK, Y'KNOW?
I DID NOT !!
"LOOK HERE," I SAID...
AND THEN KOZUE ASSUMED...
...AND THEN...
...DO YOU GET IT NOW?
...AND HOW LONG ARE YOU JUST GOING TO SIT THERE DOING NOTHING?
HUH?

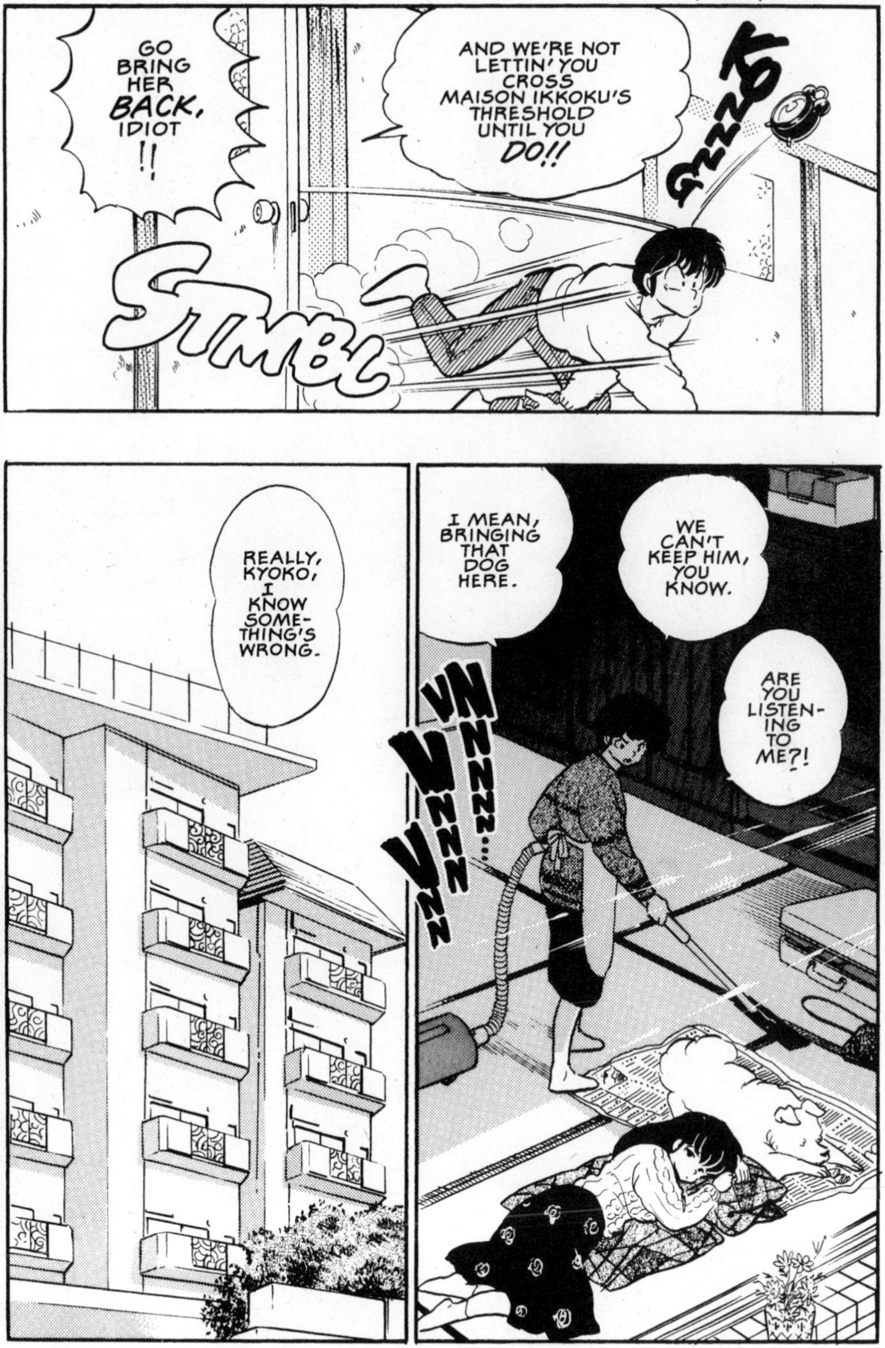
GO BRING HER BACK, IDIOT !!
AND WE'RE NOT LETTIN' YOU CROSS MAISON IKKOKU'S THRESHOLD UNTIL YOU DO!!
GRZZT
STMBL
REALLY, KYOKO, I KNOW SOMETHING'S WRONG.
I MEAN, BRINGING THAT DOG HERE.
WE CAN'T KEEP HIM, YOU KNOW.
ARE YOU LISTENING TO ME?!
VNNNNN...
VNNNN
VNN

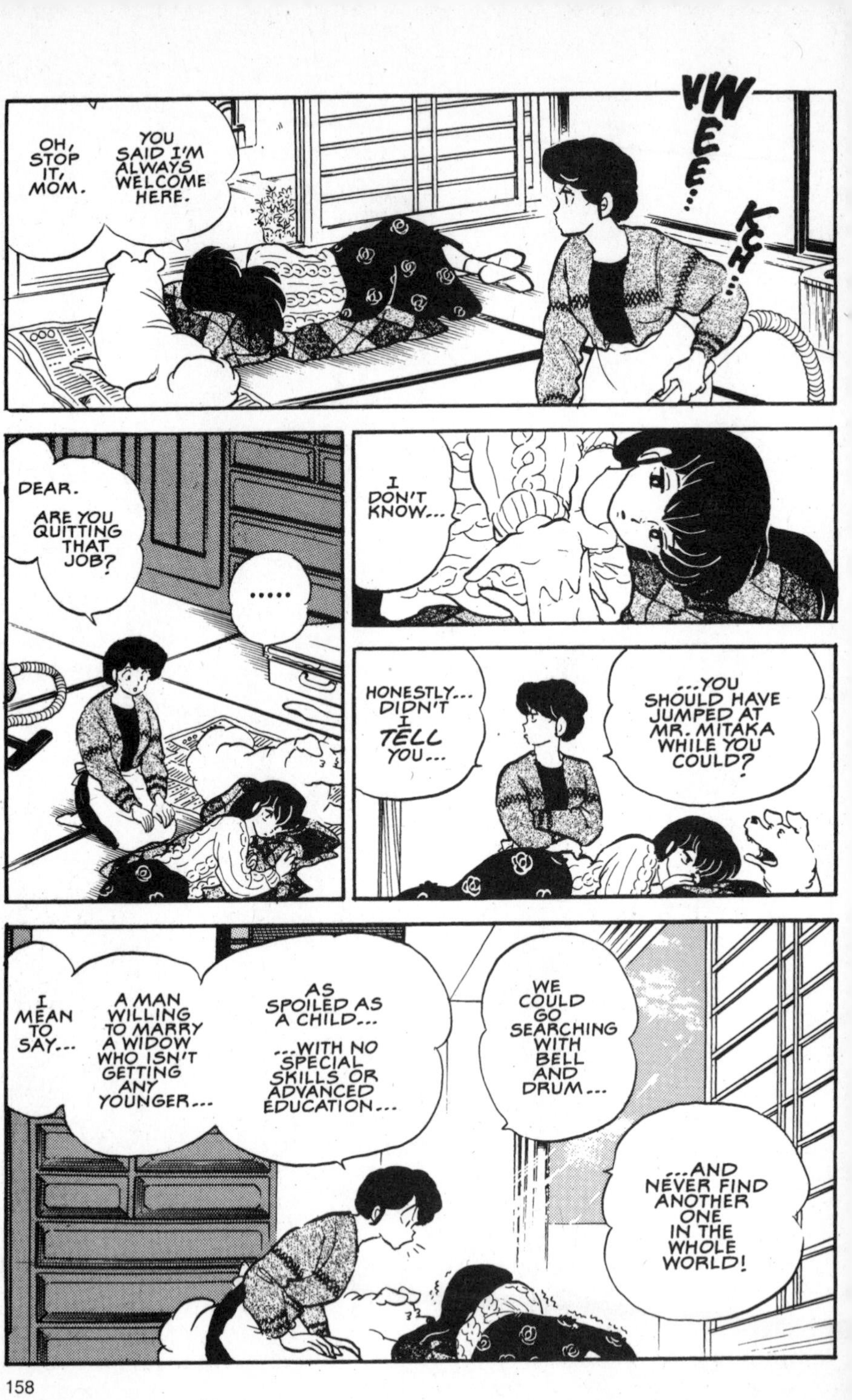
OH, STOP IT, MOM.
YOU SAID I'M ALWAYS WELCOME HERE.
VWEEE...
KCH...
DEAR.
ARE YOU QUITTING THAT JOB?
.....
I DON'T KNOW...
HONESTLY... DIDN'T I TELL YOU...
...YOU SHOULD HAVE JUMPED AT MR. MITAKA WHILE YOU COULD?
I MEAN TO SAY...
A MAN WILLING TO MARRY A WIDOW WHO ISN'T GETTING ANY YOUNGER...
AS SPOILED AS A CHILD...
...WITH NO SPECIAL SKILLS OR ADVANCED EDUCATION...
WE COULD GO SEARCHING WITH BELL AND DRUM...
...AND NEVER FIND ANOTHER ONE IN THE WHOLE WORLD!

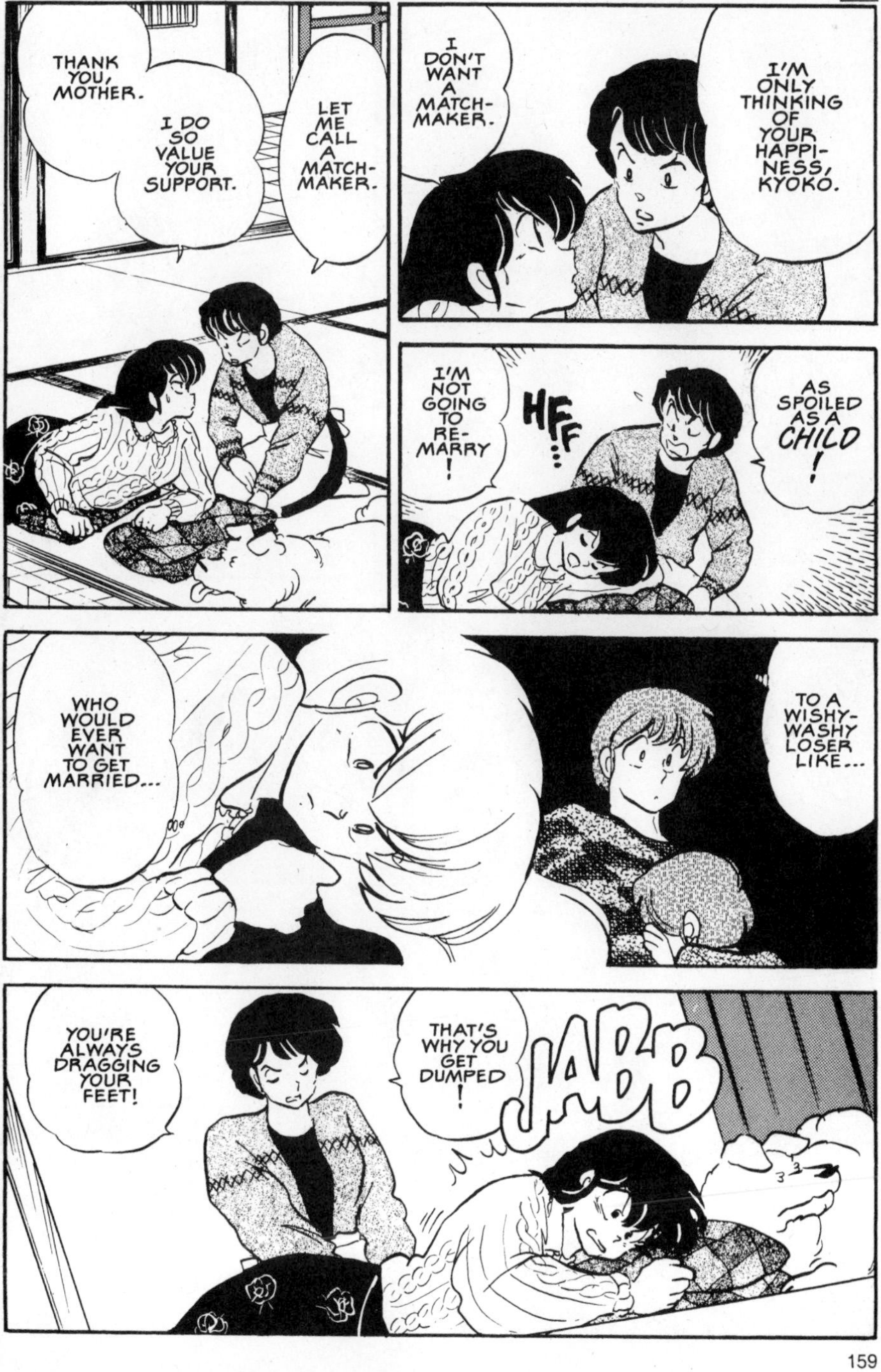
THANK YOU, MOTHER.
I DO SO VALUE YOUR SUPPORT.
LET ME CALL A MATCH-MAKER.
I DON'T WANT A MATCH-MAKER.
I'M ONLY THINKING OF YOUR HAPPI-NESS, KYOKO.
I'M NOT GOING TO RE-MARRY!
HFF
AS SPOILED AS A CHILD!
WHO WOULD EVER WANT TO GET MARRIED...
TO A WISHY-WASHY LOSER LIKE...
YOU'RE ALWAYS DRAGGING YOUR FEET!
THAT'S WHY YOU GET DUMPED!
JABB

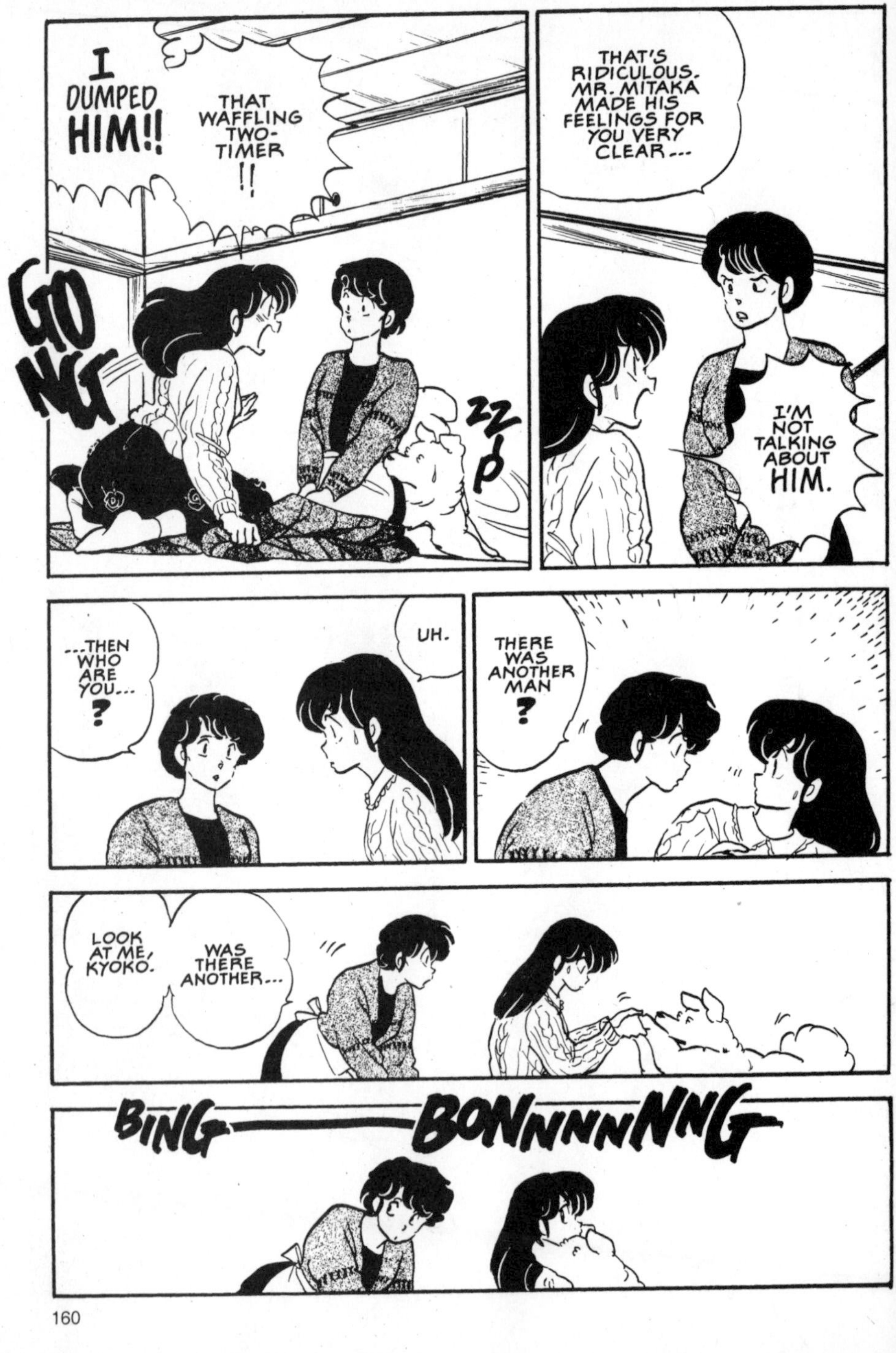
I DUMPED HIM!!
THAT WAFFLING TWO-TIMER !!
GONG
ZZZIP
THAT'S RIDICULOUS. MR. MITAKA MADE HIS FEELINGS FOR YOU VERY CLEAR...
I'M NOT TALKING ABOUT HIM.
...THEN WHO ARE YOU...?
UH.
THERE WAS ANOTHER MAN?
LOOK AT ME, KYOKO.
WAS THERE ANOTHER...
BING—BONNNNNNG

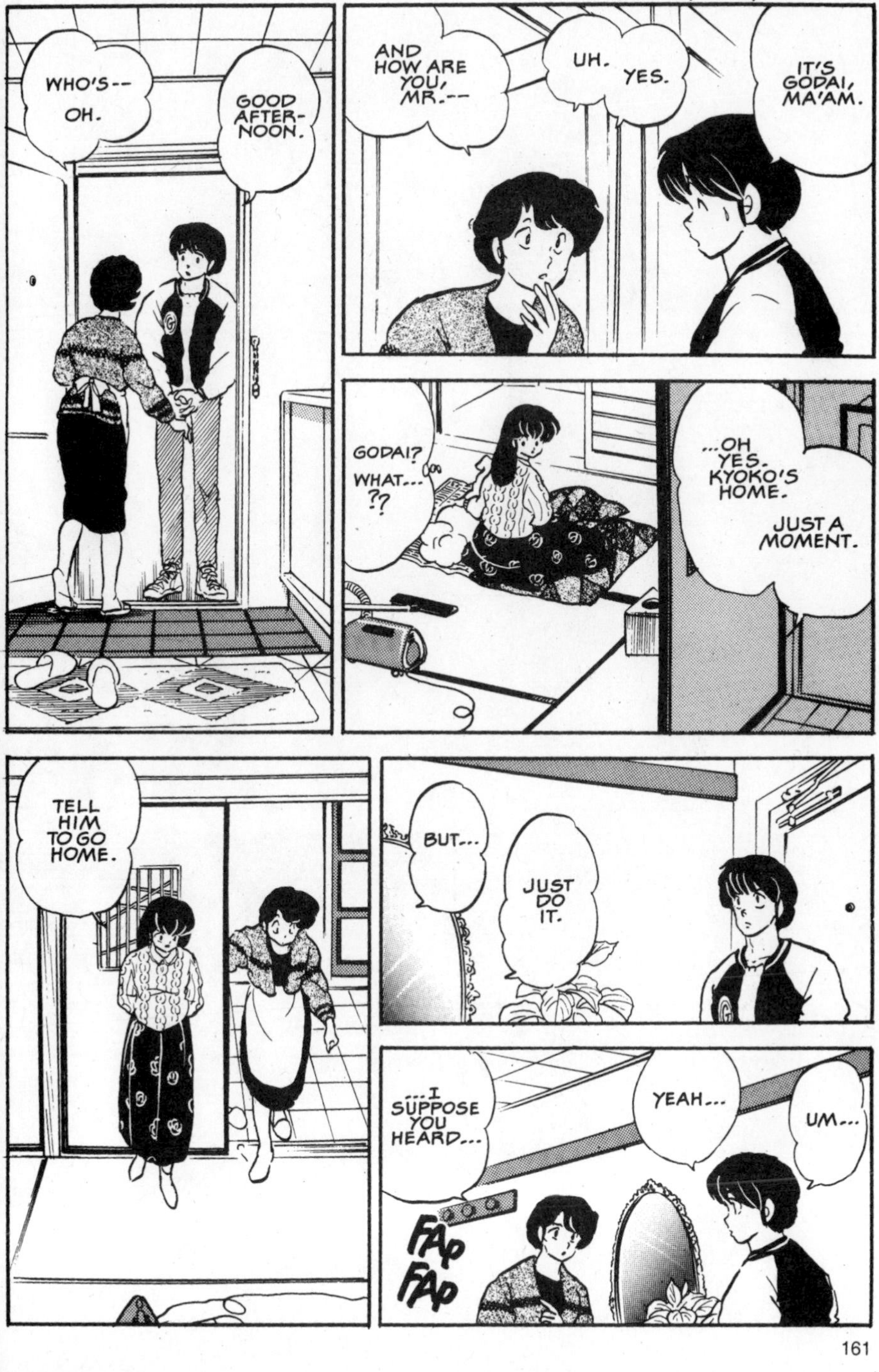
WHO'S-- OH.
GOOD AFTERNOON.
AND HOW ARE YOU, MR.--
UH. YES.
IT'S GODAI, MA'AM.
GODAI? WHAT... ??
...OH YES. KYOKO'S HOME.
JUST A MOMENT.
TELL HIM TO GO HOME.
BUT...
JUST DO IT.
...I SUPPOSE YOU HEARD...
YEAH...
UM...
FAP FAP

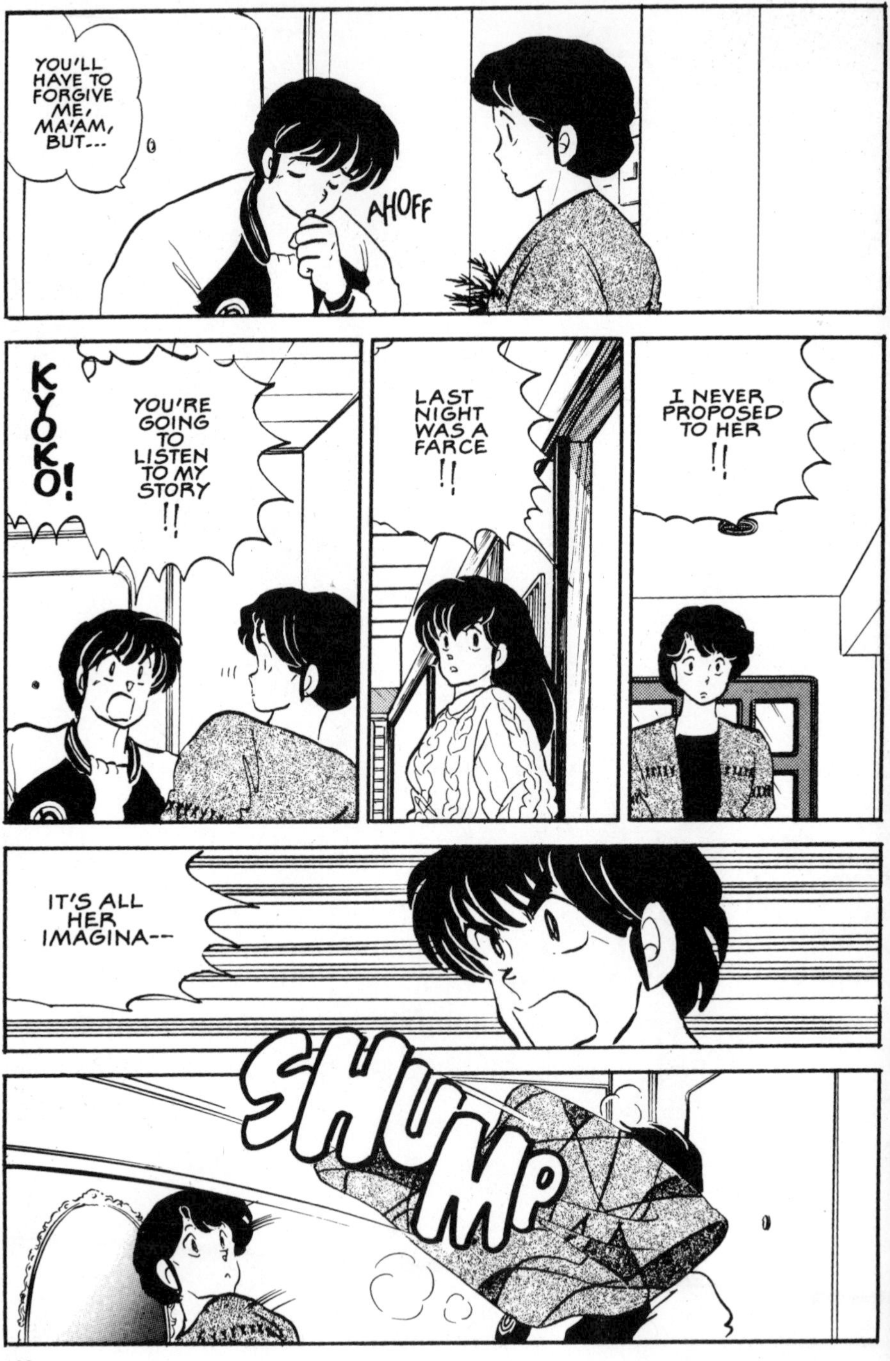

YOU'LL HAVE TO FORGIVE ME, MA'AM, BUT...
AHOFF
KYOKO!
YOU'RE GOING TO LISTEN TO MY STORY !!
LAST NIGHT WAS A FARCE !!
I NEVER PROPOSED TO HER !!
IT'S ALL HER IMAGINA--
SHUMP

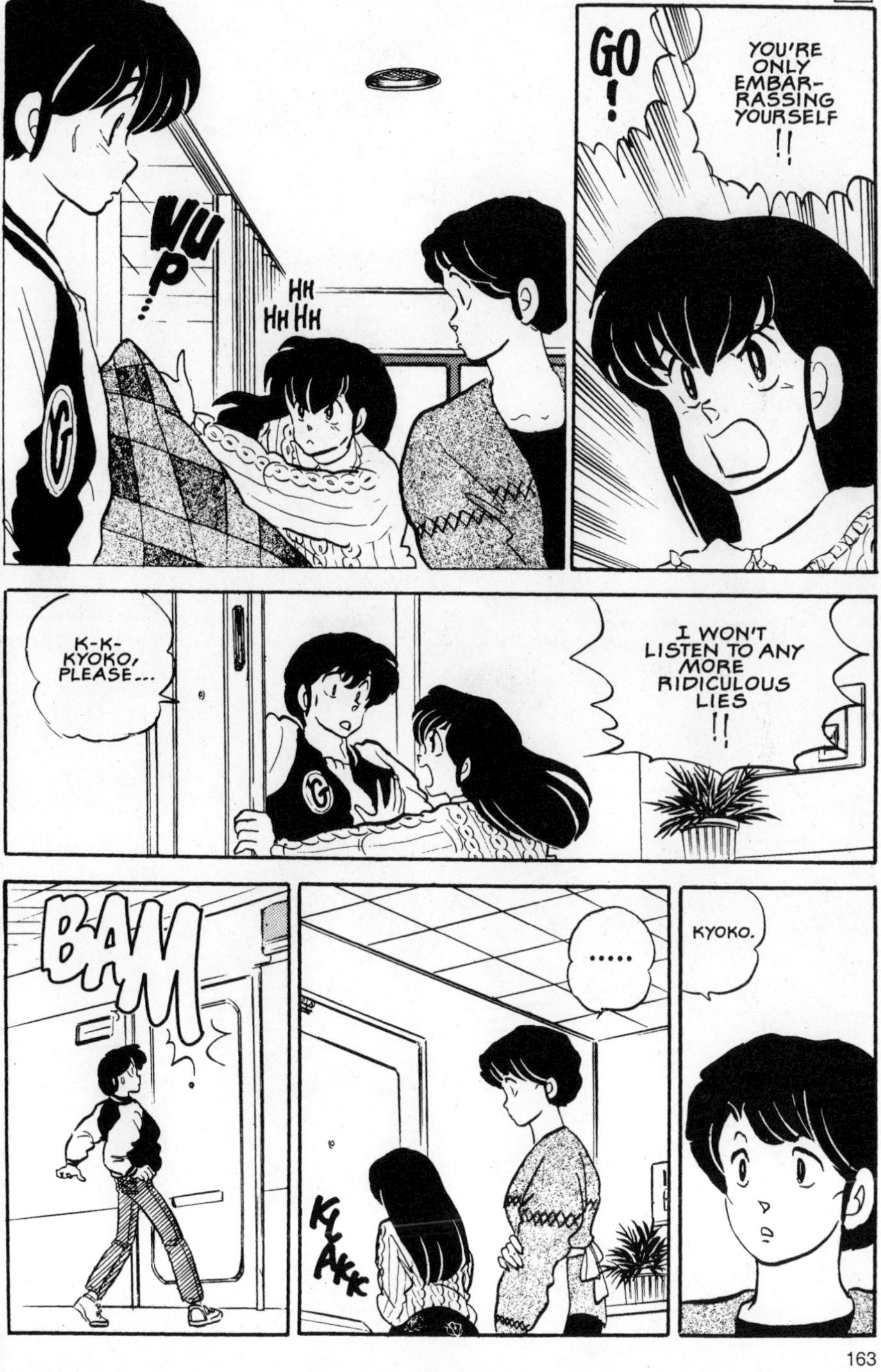
WUP...
HH HH HH
GO!
YOU'RE ONLY EMBARRASSING YOURSELF!!
K-K-KYOKO, PLEASE...
I WON'T LISTEN TO ANY MORE RIDICULOUS LIES!!
BAM
.....
KLAKK
KYOKO.

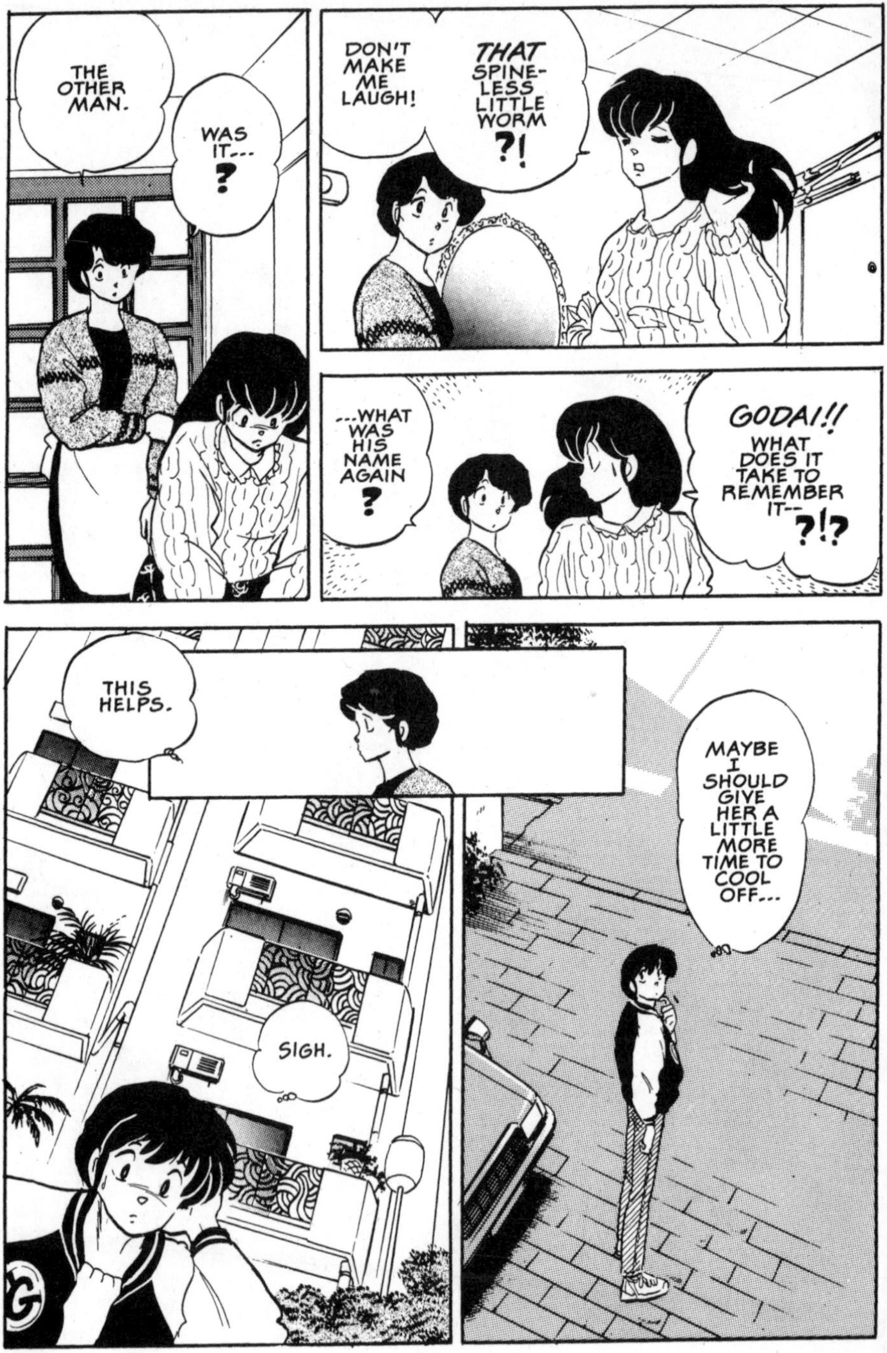
THE OTHER MAN.
WAS IT...?
DON'T MAKE ME LAUGH!
THAT SPINELESS LITTLE WORM?!
...WHAT WAS HIS NAME AGAIN?
GODAI!! WHAT DOES IT TAKE TO REMEMBER IT--?!?
THIS HELPS.
SIGH.
MAYBE I SHOULD GIVE HER A LITTLE MORE TIME TO COOL OFF...

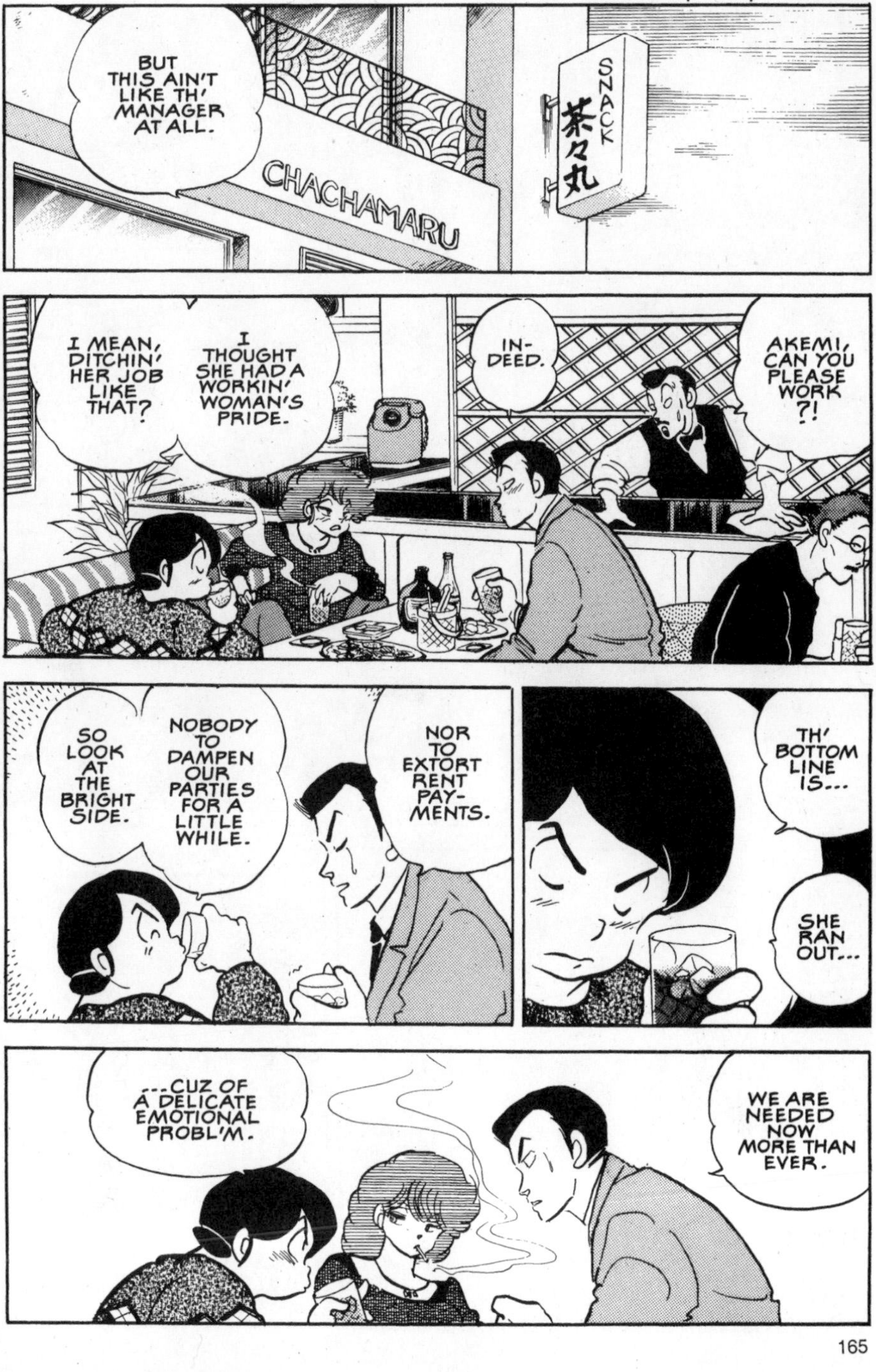
BUT THIS AIN'T LIKE TH' MANAGER AT ALL.
CHACHAMARU
SNACK
茶々丸
I MEAN, DITCHIN' HER JOB LIKE THAT?
I THOUGHT SHE HAD A WORKIN' WOMAN'S PRIDE.
IN-DEED.
AKEMI, CAN YOU PLEASE WORK ?!
SO LOOK AT THE BRIGHT SIDE.
NOBODY TO DAMPEN OUR PARTIES FOR A LITTLE WHILE.
NOR TO EXTORT RENT PAY-MENTS.
TH' BOTTOM LINE IS...
SHE RAN OUT...
...CUZ OF A DELICATE EMOTIONAL PROBL'M.
WE ARE NEEDED NOW MORE THAN EVER.

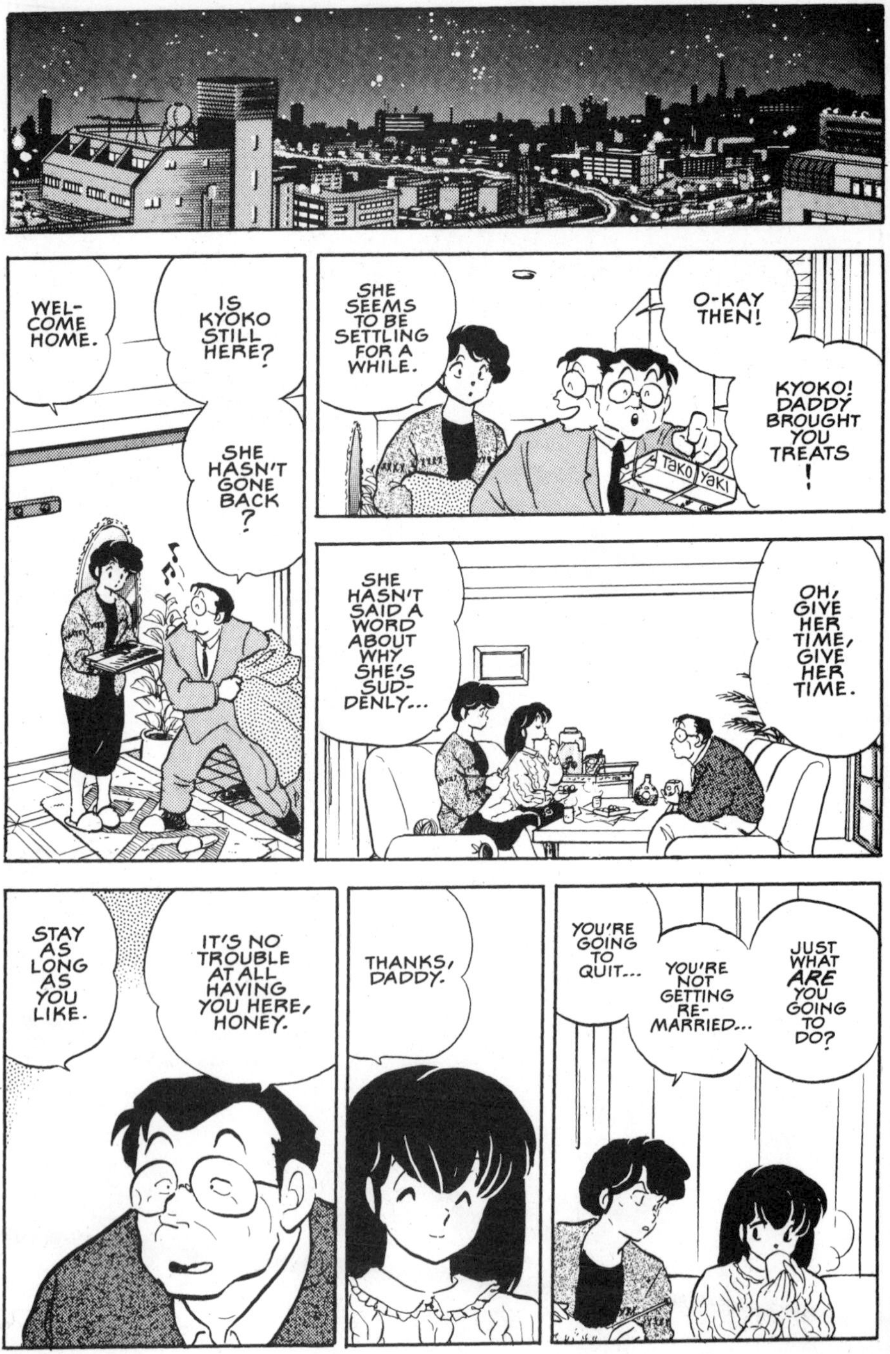
WEL-COME HOME.
IS KYOKO STILL HERE?
SHE HASN'T GONE BACK?
SHE SEEMS TO BE SETTLING FOR A WHILE.
O-KAY THEN!
KYOKO! DADDY BROUGHT YOU TREATS!
TAKO YAKI
SHE HASN'T SAID A WORD ABOUT WHY SHE'S SUD-DENLY...
OH, GIVE HER TIME, GIVE HER TIME.
STAY AS LONG AS YOU LIKE.
IT'S NO TROUBLE AT ALL HAVING YOU HERE, HONEY.
THANKS, DADDY.
YOU'RE GOING TO QUIT...
YOU'RE NOT GETTING RE-MARRIED...
JUST WHAT ARE YOU GOING TO DO?

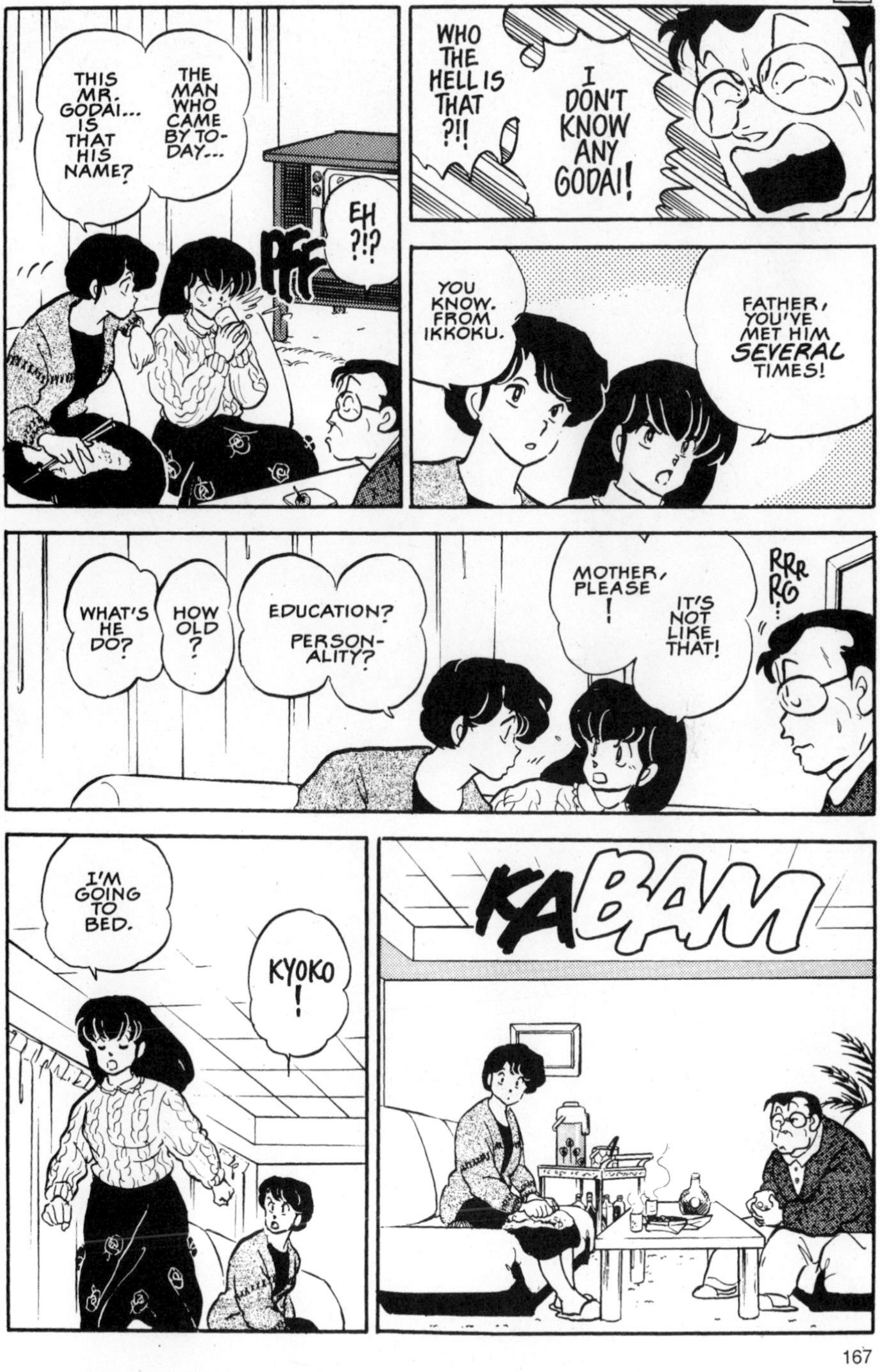
THIS MR. GODAI... IS THAT HIS NAME?
THE MAN WHO CAME BY TO-DAY...
PFF
EH ?!?
WHO THE HELL IS THAT ?!!
I DON'T KNOW ANY GODAI!
YOU KNOW. FROM IKKOKU.
FATHER, YOU'VE MET HIM SEVERAL TIMES!
WHAT'S HE DO?
HOW OLD ?
EDUCATION? PERSON-ALITY?
MOTHER, PLEASE !
IT'S NOT LIKE THAT!
RRRRG...
I'M GOING TO BED.
KYOKO !
KABAM

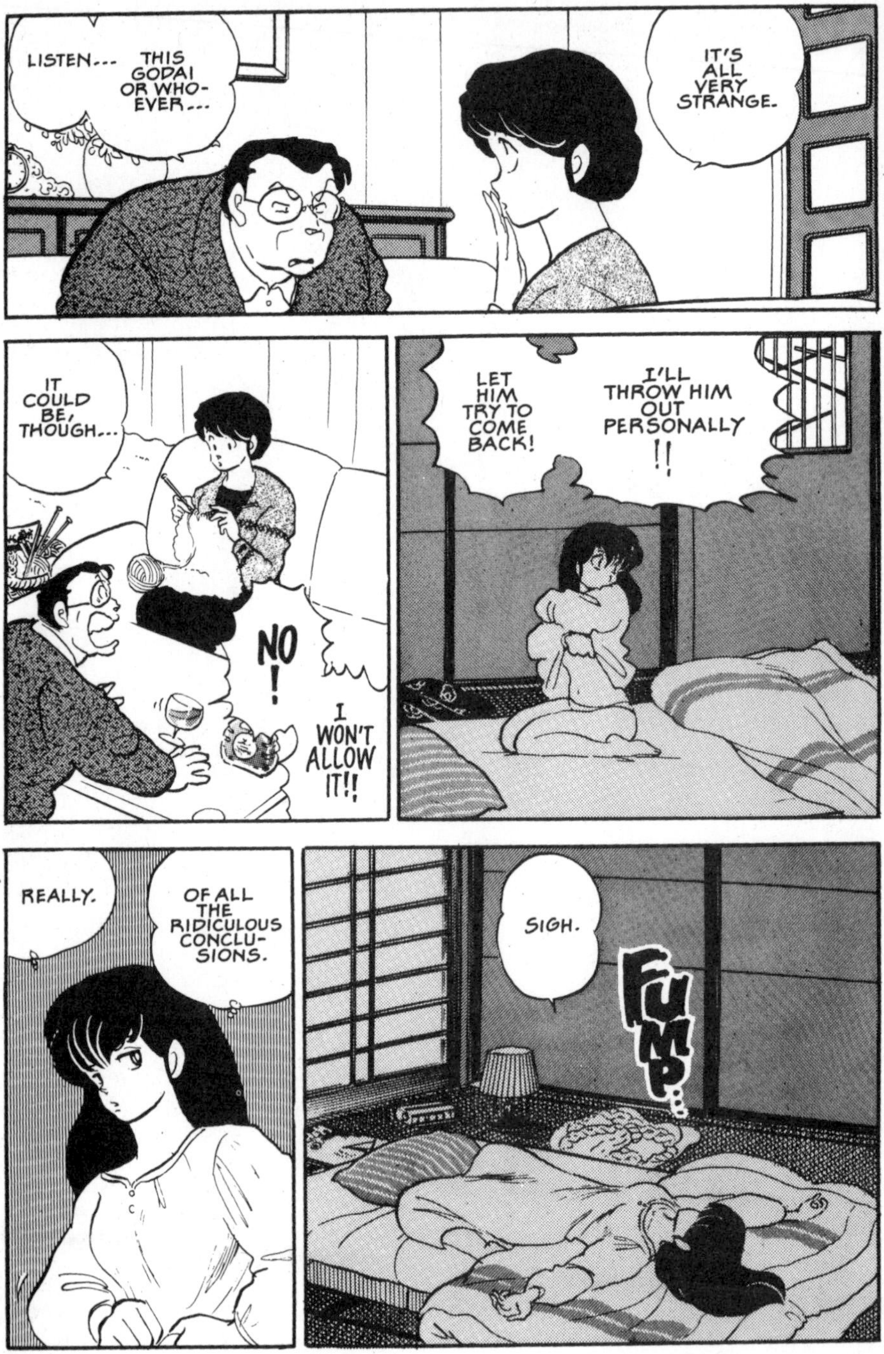
LISTEN... THIS GODAI OR WHO-EVER...
IT'S ALL VERY STRANGE.
IT COULD BE, THOUGH...
NO! I WON'T ALLOW IT!!
LET HIM TRY TO COME BACK!
I'LL THROW HIM OUT PERSONALLY!!
REALLY.
OF ALL THE RIDICULOUS CONCLUSIONS.
SIGH.
FUMP...

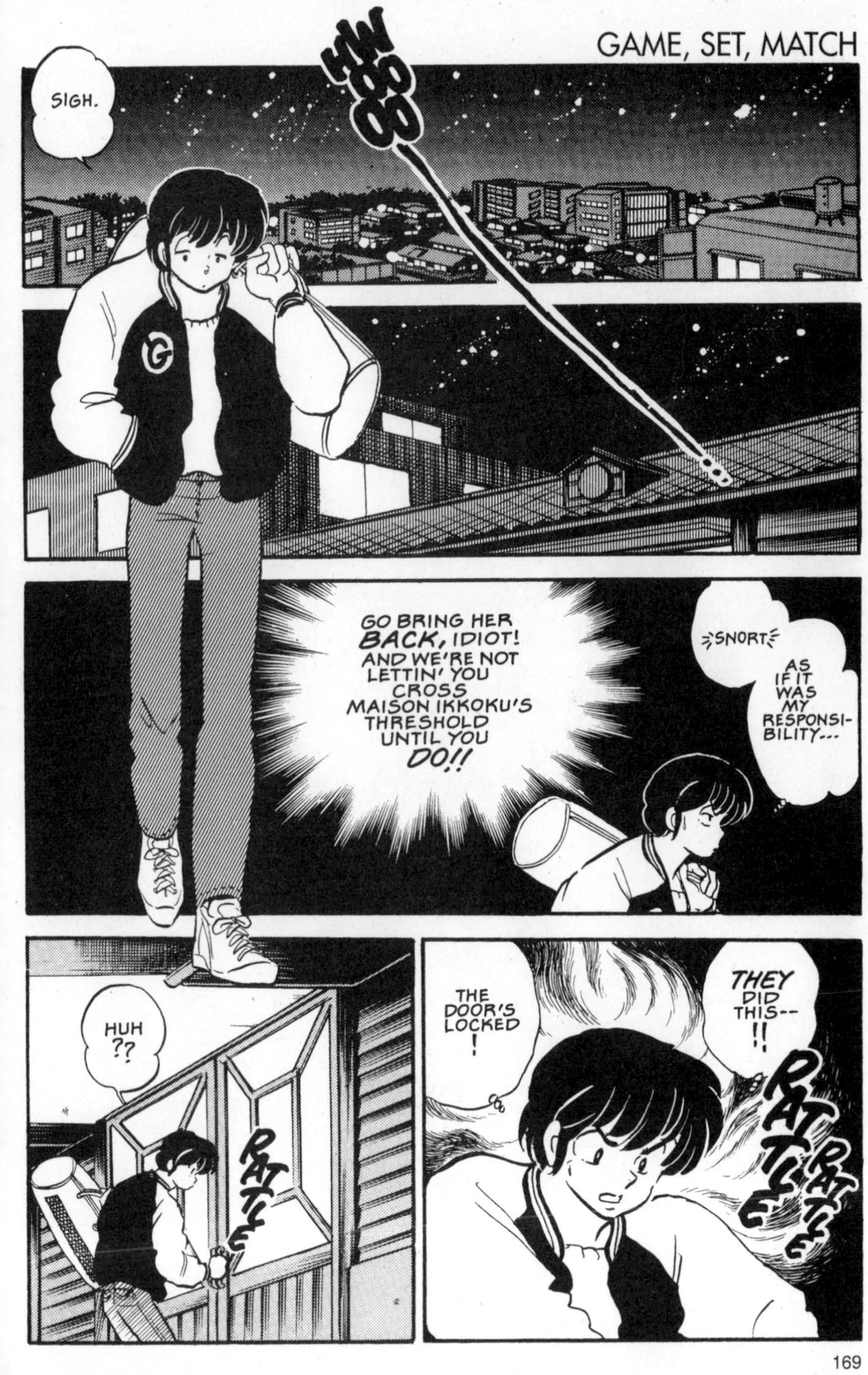
SIGH.
HWOOOO
GO BRING HER BACK, IDIOT! AND WE'RE NOT LETTIN' YOU CROSS MAISON IKKOKU'S THRESHOLD UNTIL YOU DO!!
SNORT
AS IF IT WAS MY RESPONSIBILITY...
HUH ??
RATTLE
THE DOOR'S LOCKED !
THEY DID THIS-- !!
RATTLE RATTLE

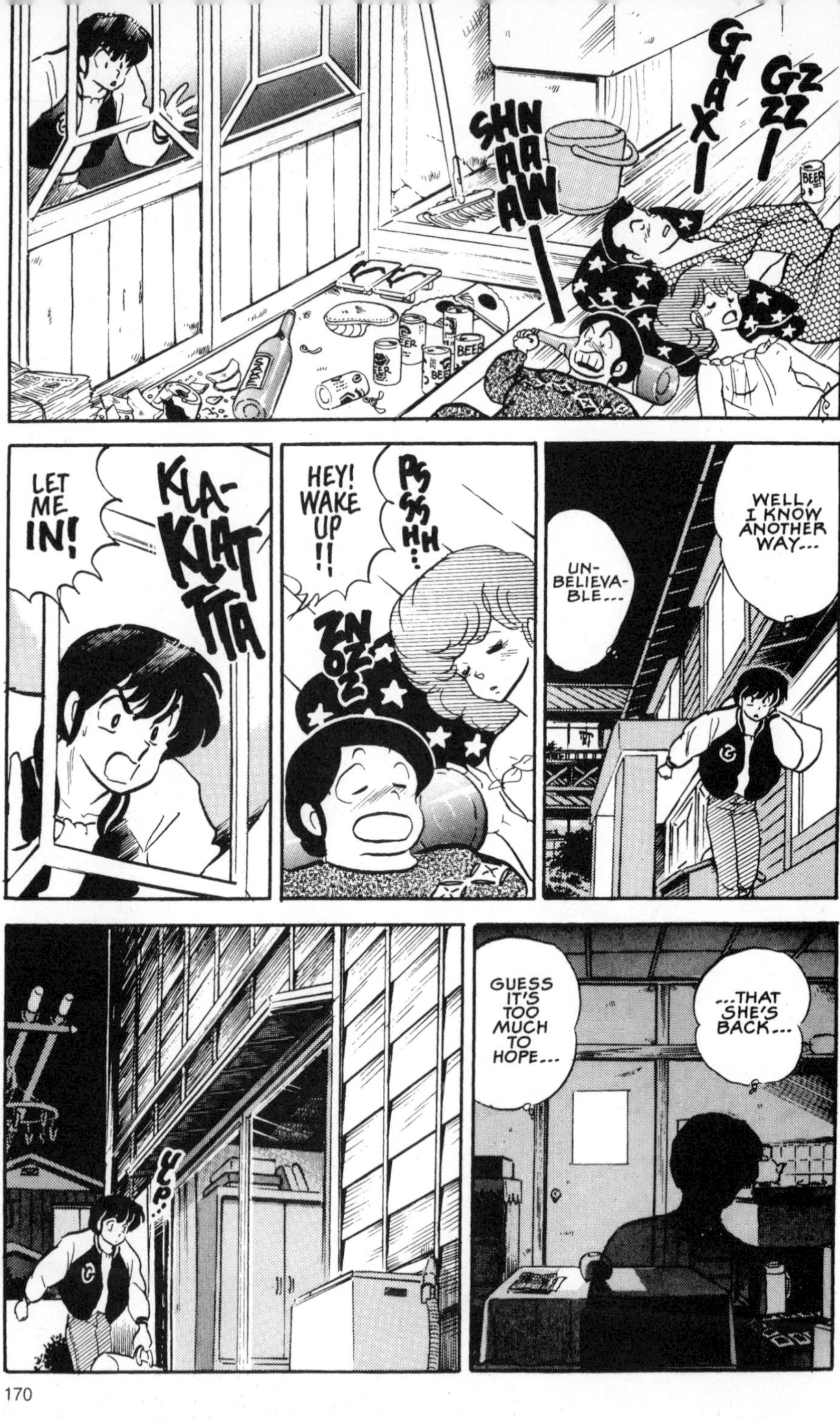
SHNAAAW—
GNAX—
GZZZ—
BEER
LET ME IN!
KLA-KLATTTA
HEY! WAKE UP!!
PSSSHH...
ZNOZZ
UN-BELIEVABLE...
WELL, I KNOW ANOTHER WAY...
UP...
GUESS IT'S TOO MUCH TO HOPE...
...THAT SHE'S BACK...

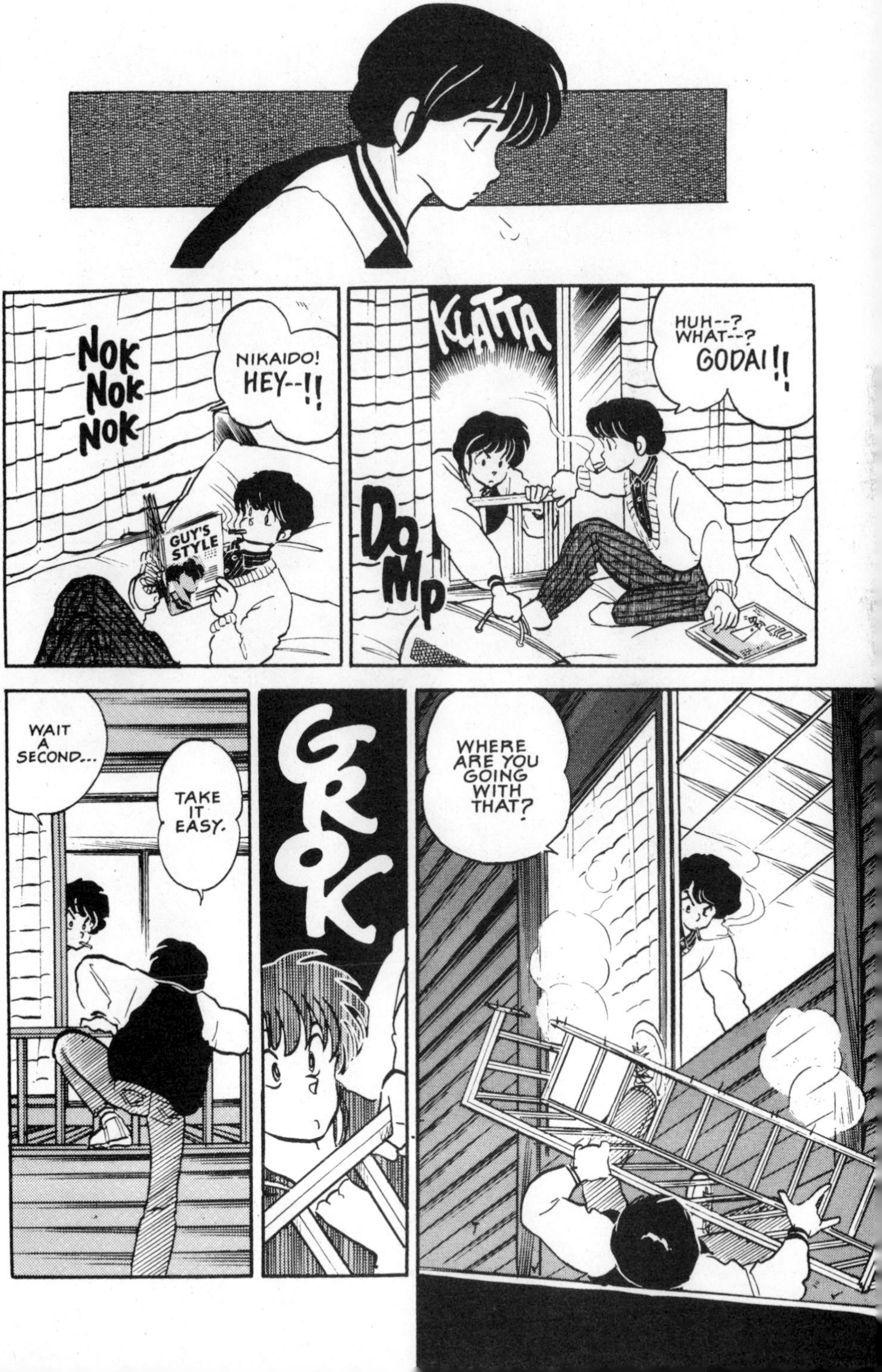
NOK NOK NOK
NIKAIDO! HEY--!!
GUY'S STYLE
KLATTA
DOMP
HUH--? WHAT--? GODAI!!
WAIT A SECOND...
TAKE IT EASY.
GROK
WHERE ARE YOU GOING WITH THAT?

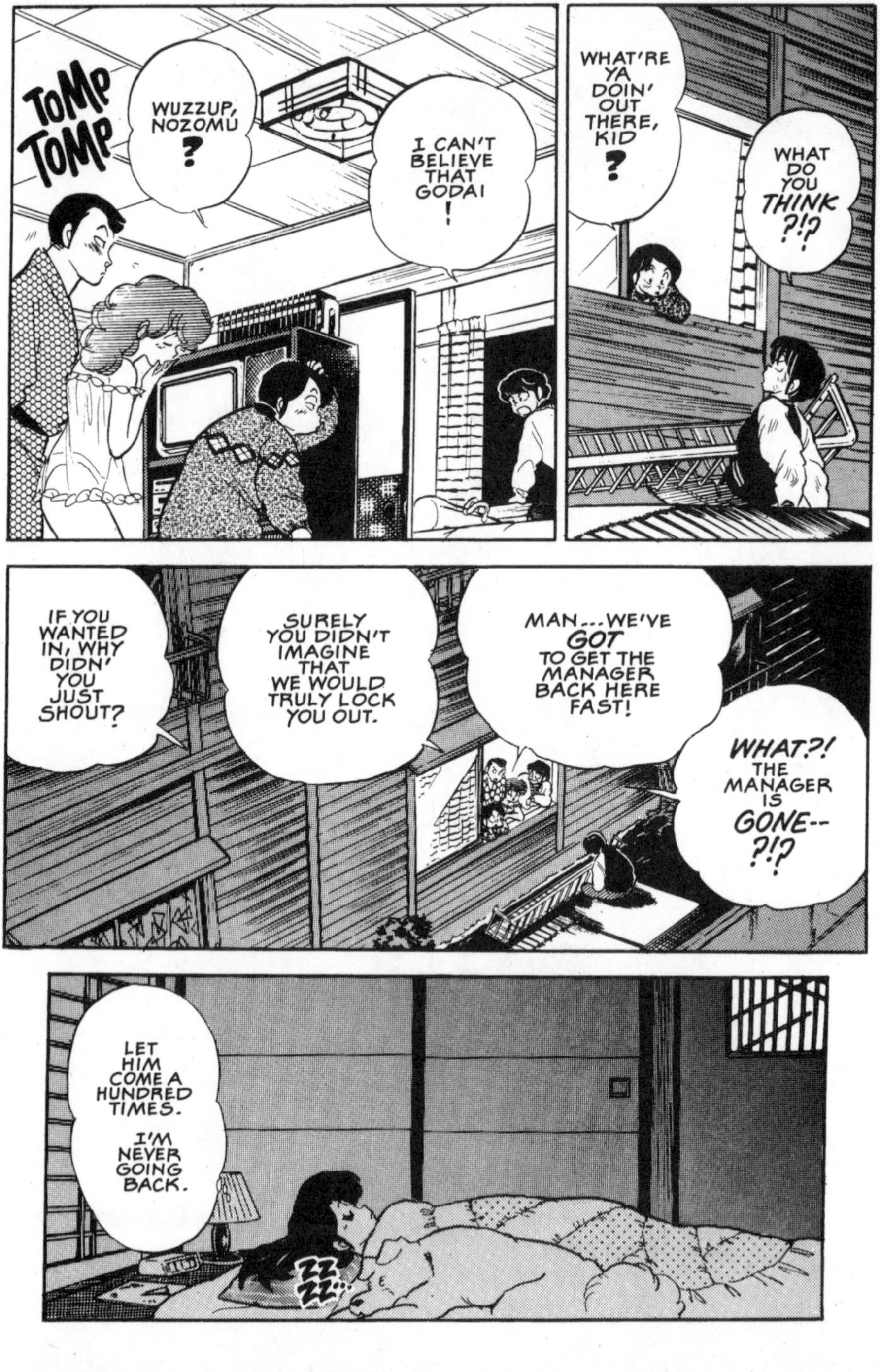
TOMP TOMP
WUZZUP, NOZOMU ?
I CAN'T BELIEVE THAT GODAI !
WHAT'RE YA DOIN' OUT THERE, KID ?
WHAT DO YOU THINK ?!?
IF YOU WANTED IN, WHY DIDN' YOU JUST SHOUT?
SURELY YOU DIDN'T IMAGINE THAT WE WOULD TRULY LOCK YOU OUT.
MAN...WE'VE GOT TO GET THE MANAGER BACK HERE FAST!
WHAT?! THE MANAGER IS GONE-- ?!?
LET HIM COME A HUNDRED TIMES.
I'M NEVER GOING BACK.
ZZZZZ...

PART NINE

SUDDENLY KYOKO

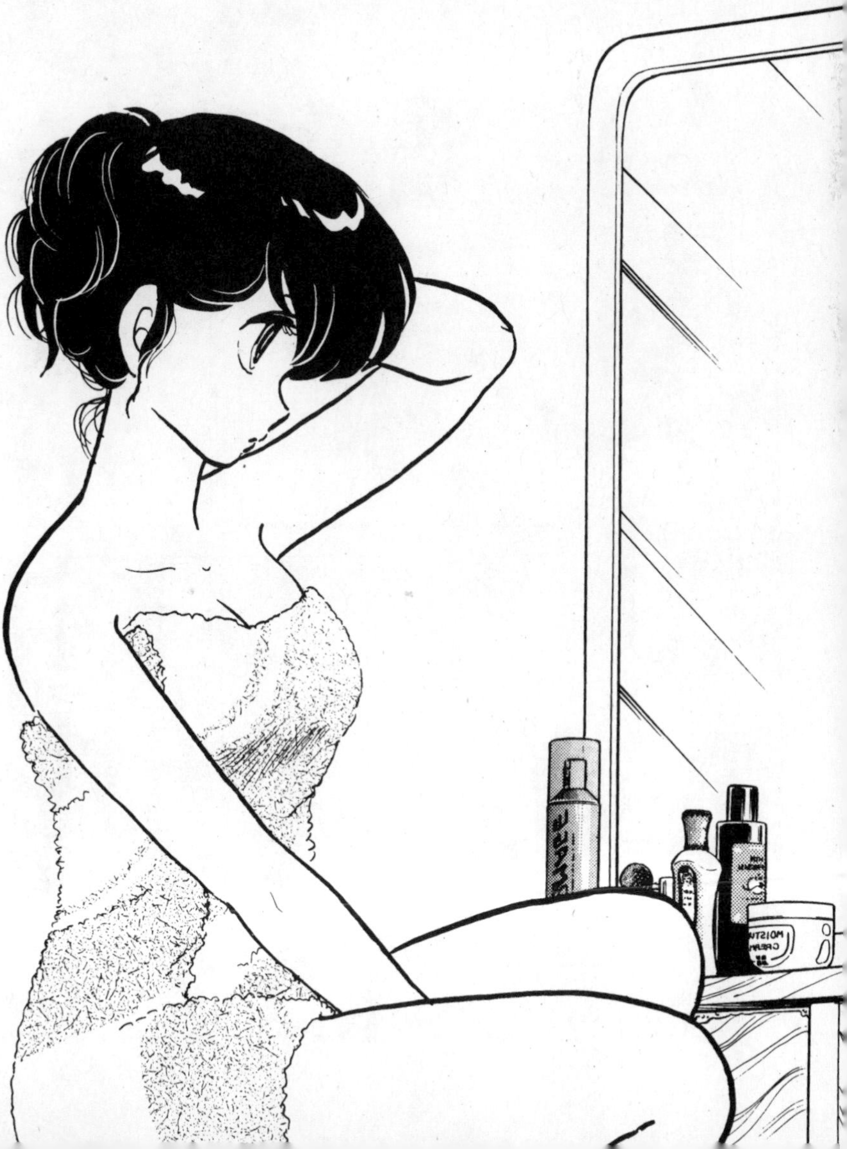

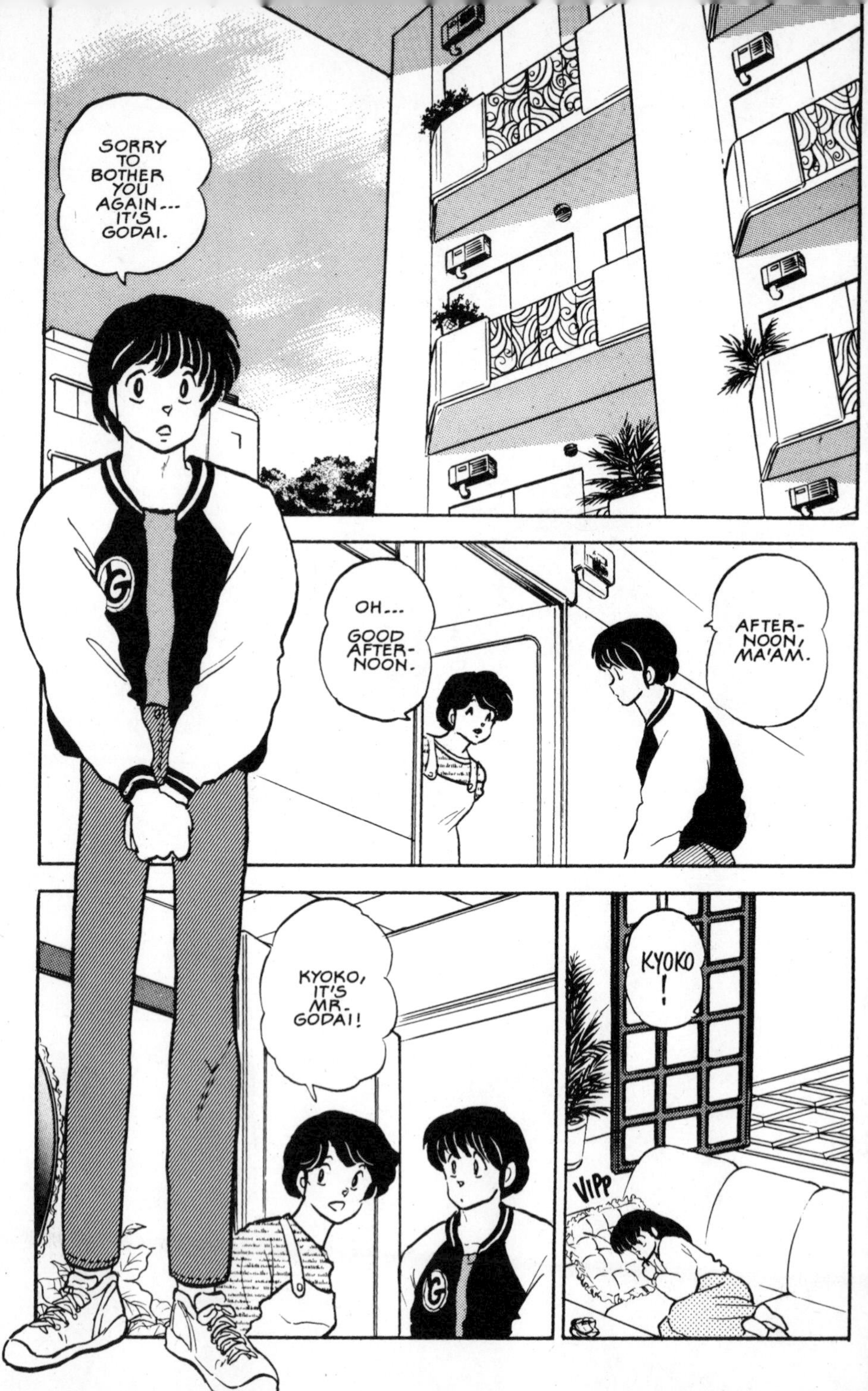
SORRY TO BOTHER YOU AGAIN... IT'S GODAI.
OH... GOOD AFTER-NOON.
AFTER-NOON, MA'AM.
KYOKO, IT'S MR. GODAI!
KYOKO!
VIPP

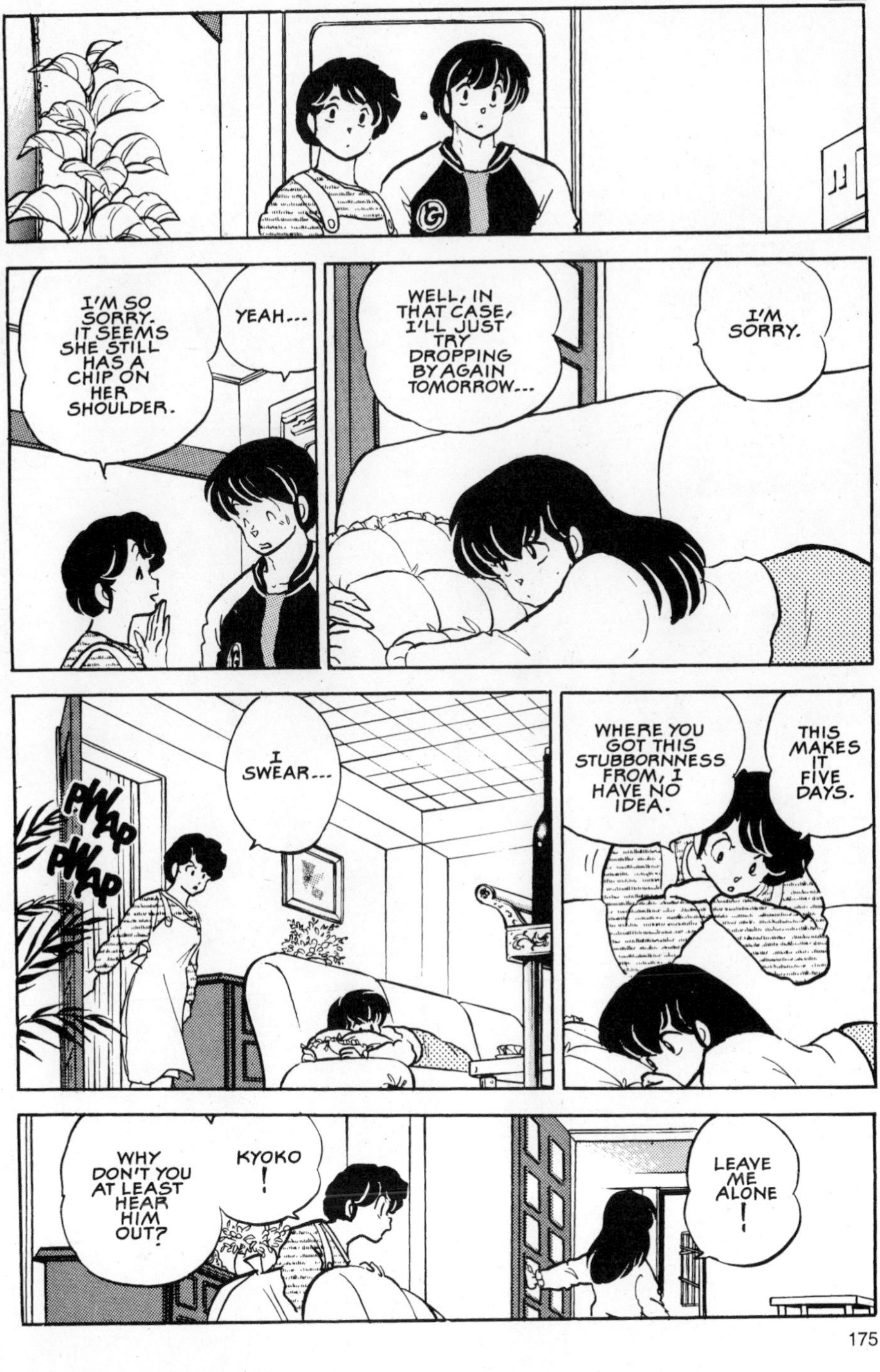
I'M SO SORRY. IT SEEMS SHE STILL HAS A CHIP ON HER SHOULDER.
YEAH...
WELL, IN THAT CASE, I'LL JUST TRY DROPPING BY AGAIN TOMORROW...
I'M SORRY.
PWAP PWAP
I SWEAR...
WHERE YOU GOT THIS STUBBORNNESS FROM, I HAVE NO IDEA.
THIS MAKES IT FIVE DAYS.
WHY DON'T YOU AT LEAST HEAR HIM OUT?
KYOKO!
LEAVE ME ALONE!

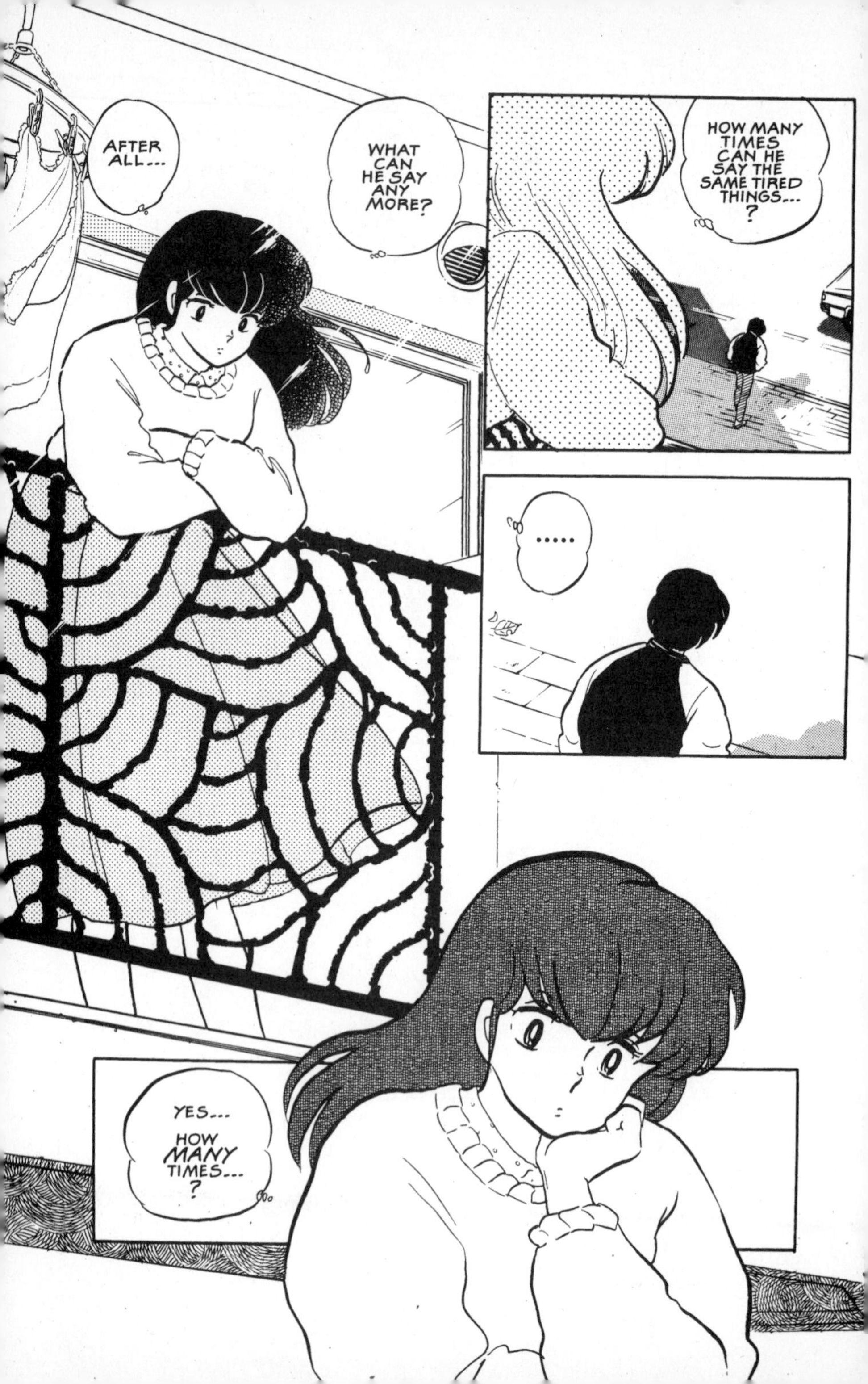
AFTER ALL...
WHAT CAN HE SAY ANY MORE?
HOW MANY TIMES CAN HE SAY THE SAME TIRED THINGS...?
......
YES... HOW MANY TIMES...?

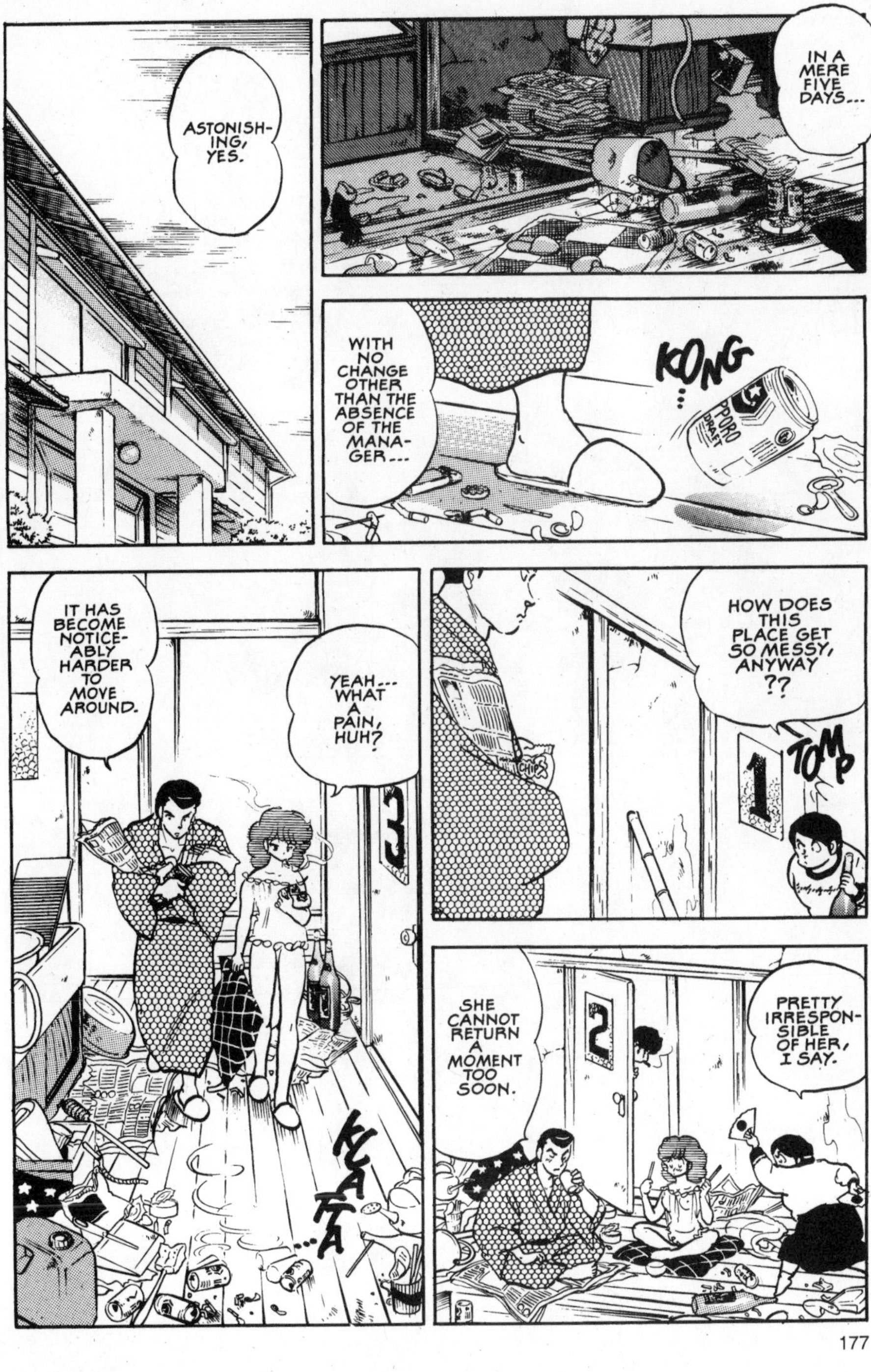

ASTONISHING, YES.
IN A MERE FIVE DAYS...
WITH NO CHANGE OTHER THAN THE ABSENCE OF THE MANAGER...
KONG
PPORO DRAFT
IT HAS BECOME NOTICEABLY HARDER TO MOVE AROUND.
YEAH... WHAT A PAIN, HUH?
KLATTA
HOW DOES THIS PLACE GET SO MESSY, ANYWAY??
CHIPS
TOMP
SHE CANNOT RETURN A MOMENT TOO SOON.
PRETTY IRRESPONSIBLE OF HER, I SAY.

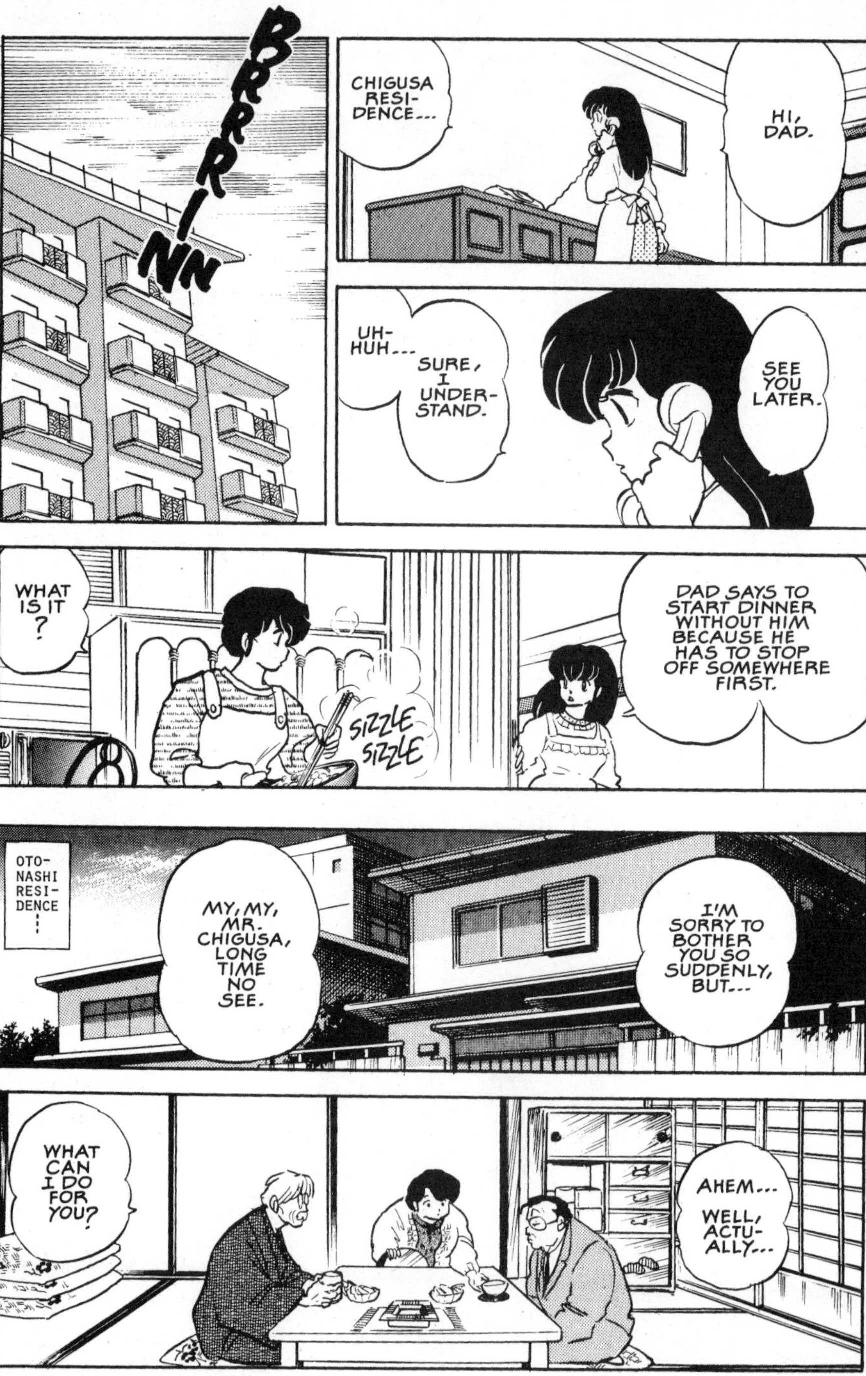
BRRRIINN
CHIGUSA RESI-DENCE...
HI, DAD.
UH-HUH...
SURE, I UNDER-STAND.
SEE YOU LATER.
WHAT IS IT?
SIZZLE SIZZLE
DAD SAYS TO START DINNER WITHOUT HIM BECAUSE HE HAS TO STOP OFF SOMEWHERE FIRST.
OTO-NASHI RESI-DENCE...
MY, MY, MR. CHIGUSA, LONG TIME NO SEE.
I'M SORRY TO BOTHER YOU SO SUDDENLY, BUT...
WHAT CAN I DO FOR YOU?
AHEM...
WELL, ACTU-ALLY...

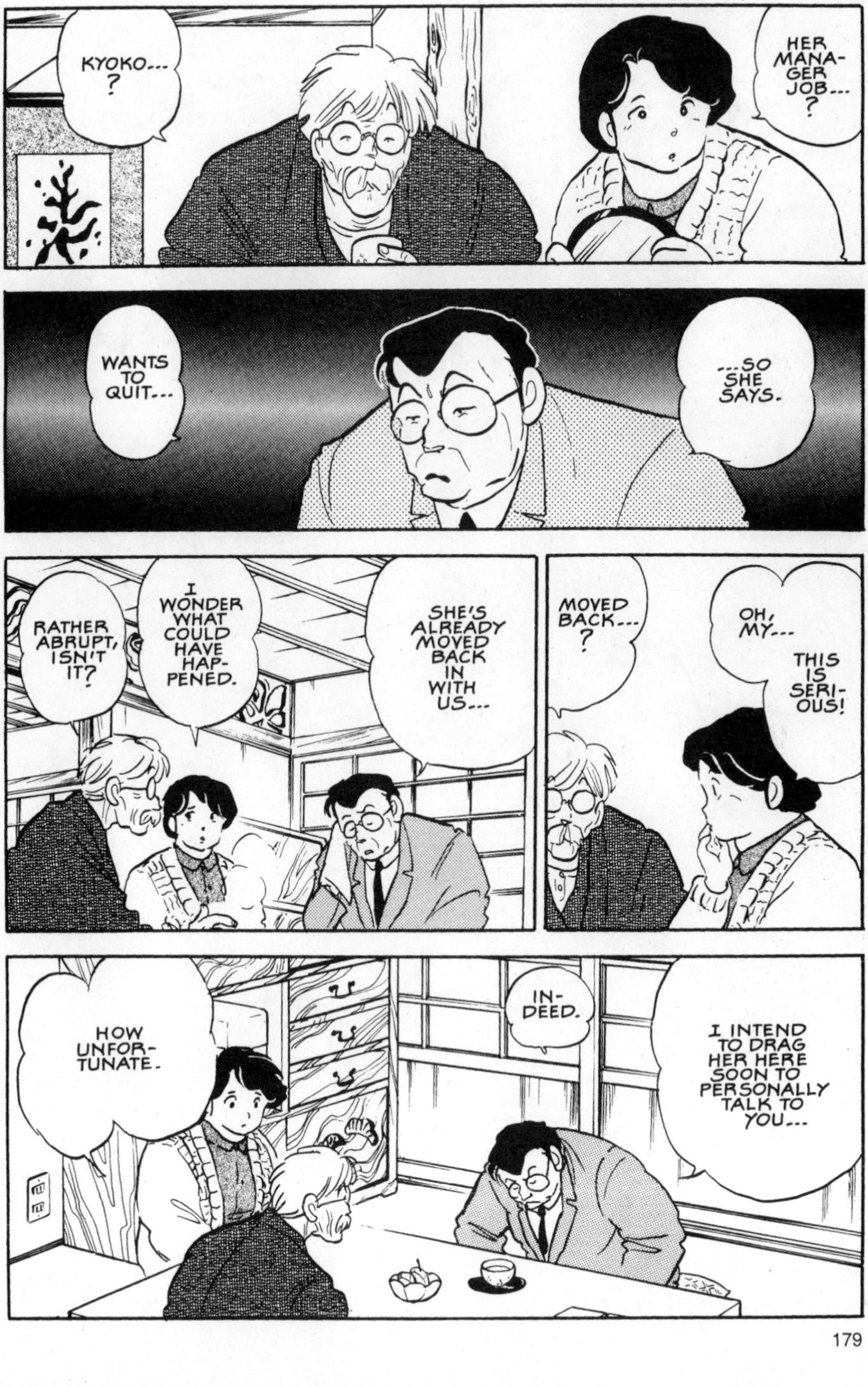
KYOKO...?
HER MANAGER JOB...?
WANTS TO QUIT...
...SO SHE SAYS.
RATHER ABRUPT, ISN'T IT?
I WONDER WHAT COULD HAVE HAPPENED.
SHE'S ALREADY MOVED BACK IN WITH US...
MOVED BACK...?
OH, MY...
THIS IS SERIOUS!
HOW UNFORTUNATE.
INDEED.
I INTEND TO DRAG HER HERE SOON TO PERSONALLY TALK TO YOU...

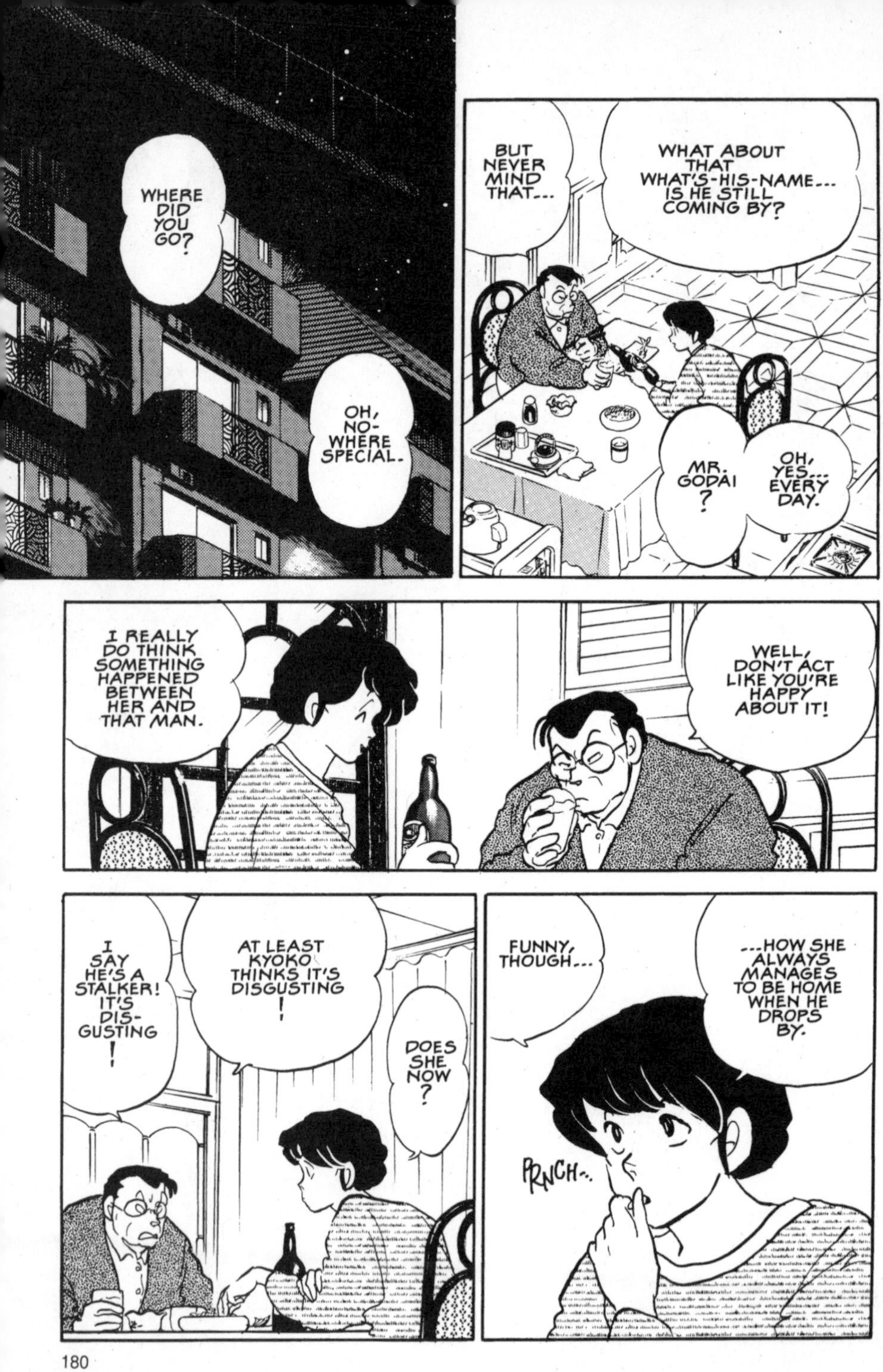
WHERE DID YOU GO?
OH, NO-WHERE SPECIAL.
BUT NEVER MIND THAT...
WHAT ABOUT THAT WHAT'S-HIS-NAME... IS HE STILL COMING BY?
MR. GODAI?
OH, YES... EVERY DAY.
I REALLY DO THINK SOMETHING HAPPENED BETWEEN HER AND THAT MAN.
WELL, DON'T ACT LIKE YOU'RE HAPPY ABOUT IT!
I SAY HE'S A STALKER! IT'S DIS-GUSTING!
AT LEAST KYOKO THINKS IT'S DISGUSTING!
DOES SHE NOW?
FUNNY, THOUGH...
...HOW SHE ALWAYS MANAGES TO BE HOME WHEN HE DROPS BY.
PRNCH...

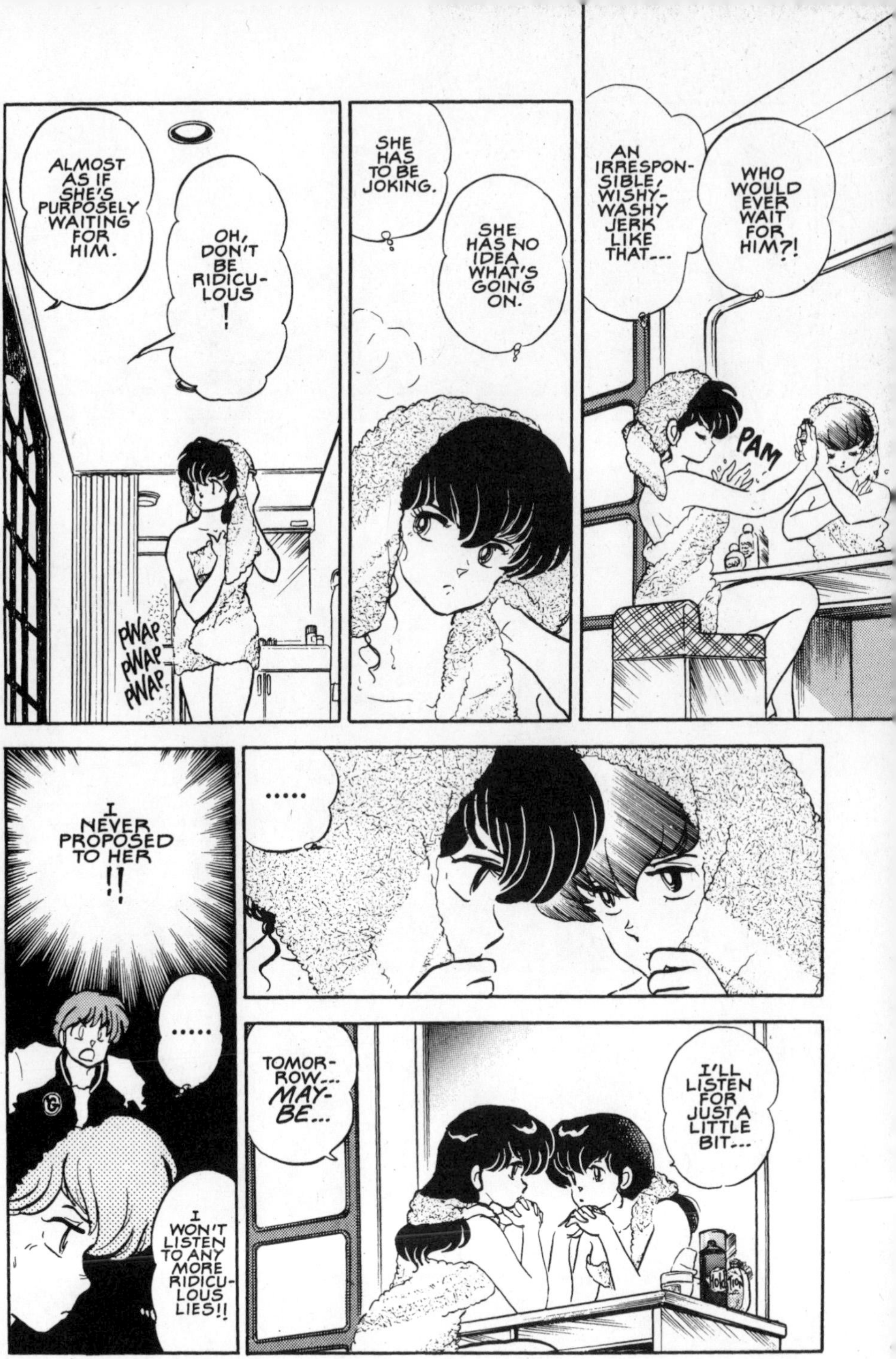
ALMOST AS IF SHE'S PURPOSELY WAITING FOR HIM.
OH, DON'T BE RIDICULOUS!
PWAP PWAP PWAP
SHE HAS TO BE JOKING.
SHE HAS NO IDEA WHAT'S GOING ON.
AN IRRESPONSIBLE, WISHY-WASHY JERK LIKE THAT...
WHO WOULD EVER WAIT FOR HIM?!
PAM
I NEVER PROPOSED TO HER!!
.....
I WON'T LISTEN TO ANY MORE RIDICULOUS LIES!!
.....
TOMORROW... MAYBE...
I'LL LISTEN FOR JUST A LITTLE BIT...

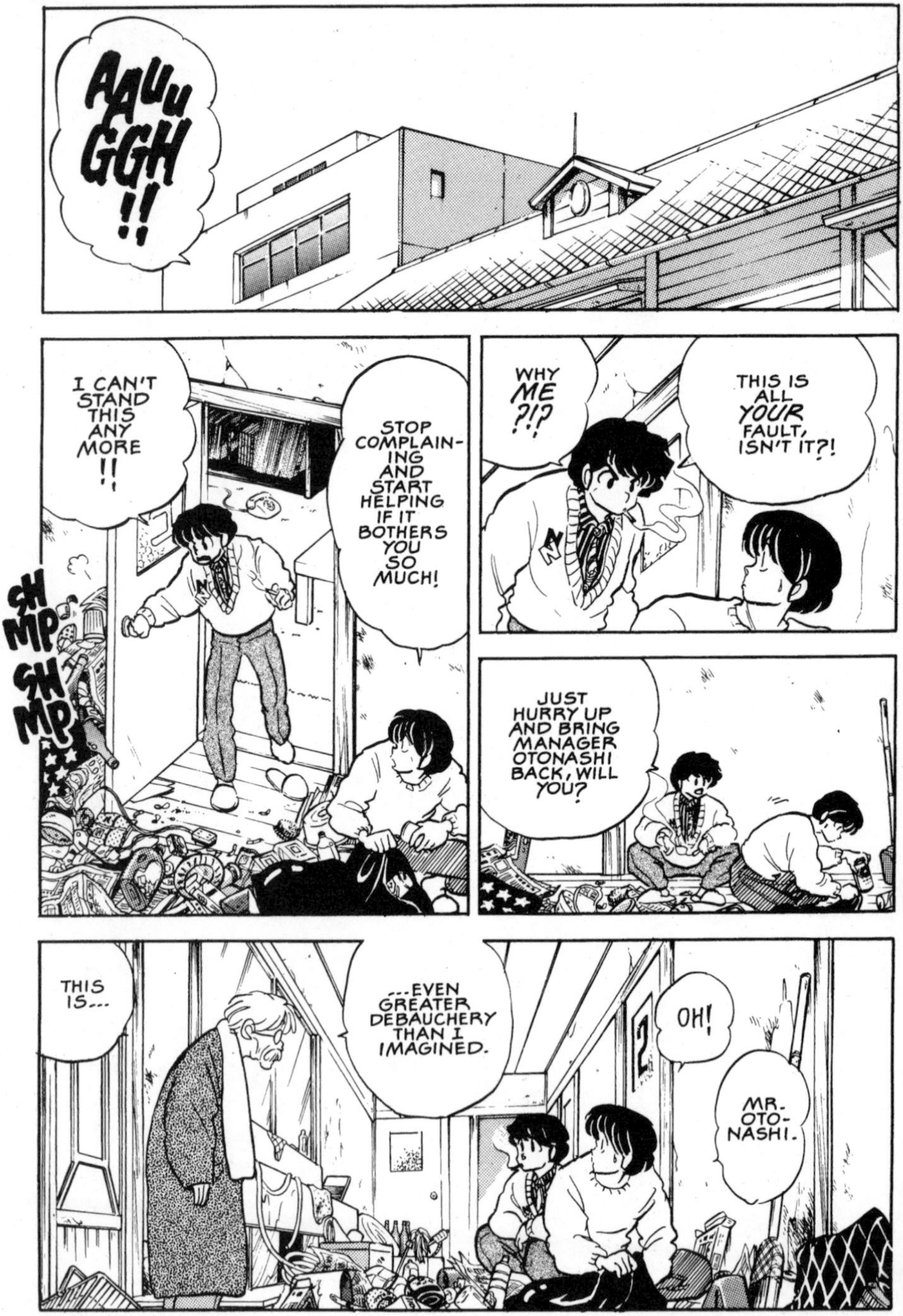
AAUU GGH!!
I CAN'T STAND THIS ANY MORE!!
STOP COMPLAINING AND START HELPING IF IT BOTHERS YOU SO MUCH!
SHMP SHMP
WHY ME?!?
THIS IS ALL YOUR FAULT, ISN'T IT?!
JUST HURRY UP AND BRING MANAGER OTONASHI BACK, WILL YOU?
THIS IS...
...EVEN GREATER DEBAUCHERY THAN I IMAGINED.
OH!
MR. OTONASHI.

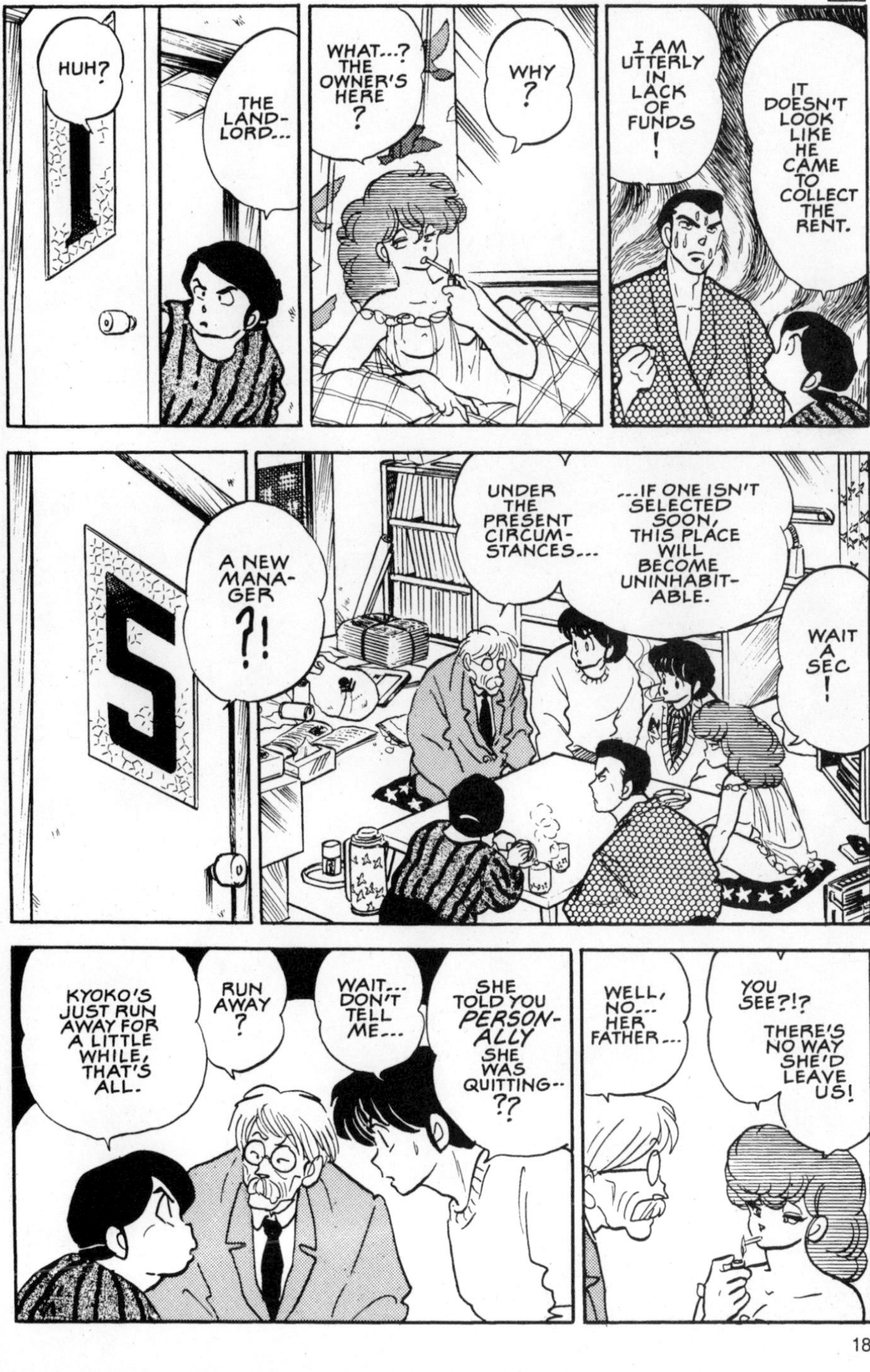
HUH?
THE LANDLORD...
WHAT...? THE OWNER'S HERE?
WHY?
I AM UTTERLY IN LACK OF FUNDS!
IT DOESN'T LOOK LIKE HE CAME TO COLLECT THE RENT.
A NEW MANAGER?!
UNDER THE PRESENT CIRCUMSTANCES...
...IF ONE ISN'T SELECTED SOON, THIS PLACE WILL BECOME UNINHABITABLE.
WAIT A SEC!
KYOKO'S JUST RUN AWAY FOR A LITTLE WHILE, THAT'S ALL.
RUN AWAY?
WAIT... DON'T TELL ME...
SHE TOLD YOU PERSONALLY SHE WAS QUITTING..??
WELL, NO... HER FATHER...
YOU SEE?!?
THERE'S NO WAY SHE'D LEAVE US!

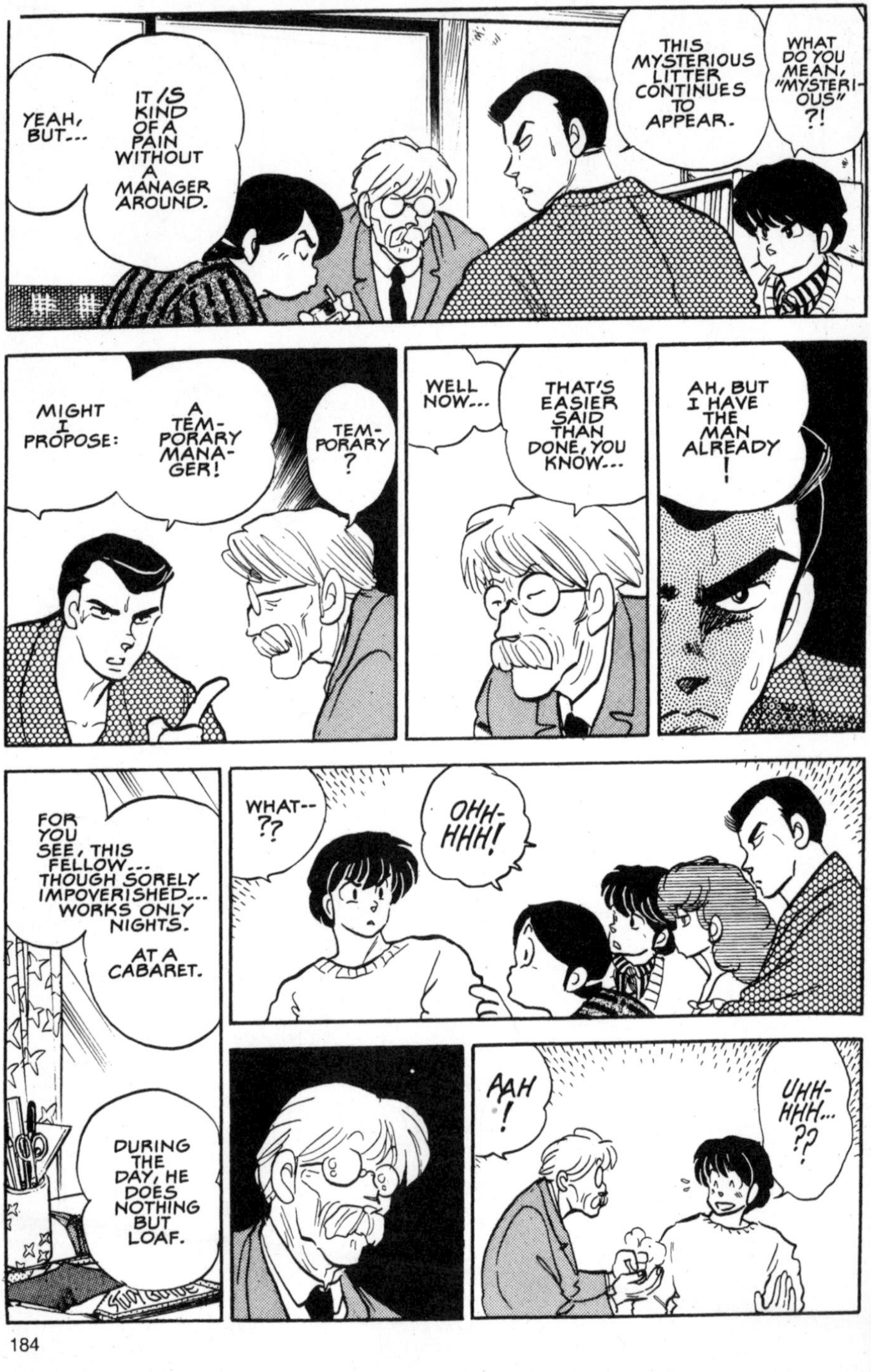
YEAH, BUT...
IT IS KIND OF A PAIN WITHOUT A MANAGER AROUND.
THIS MYSTERIOUS LITTER CONTINUES TO APPEAR.
WHAT DO YOU MEAN, "MYSTERIOUS"?!
MIGHT I PROPOSE:
A TEMPORARY MANAGER!
TEMPORARY?
WELL NOW...
THAT'S EASIER SAID THAN DONE, YOU KNOW...
AH, BUT I HAVE THE MAN ALREADY!
FOR YOU SEE, THIS FELLOW... THOUGH SORELY IMPOVERISHED... WORKS ONLY NIGHTS.
AT A CABARET.
DURING THE DAY, HE DOES NOTHING BUT LOAF.
STUDY GUIDE
WHAT--??
OHHHHH!
AAH!
UHHHHH...??

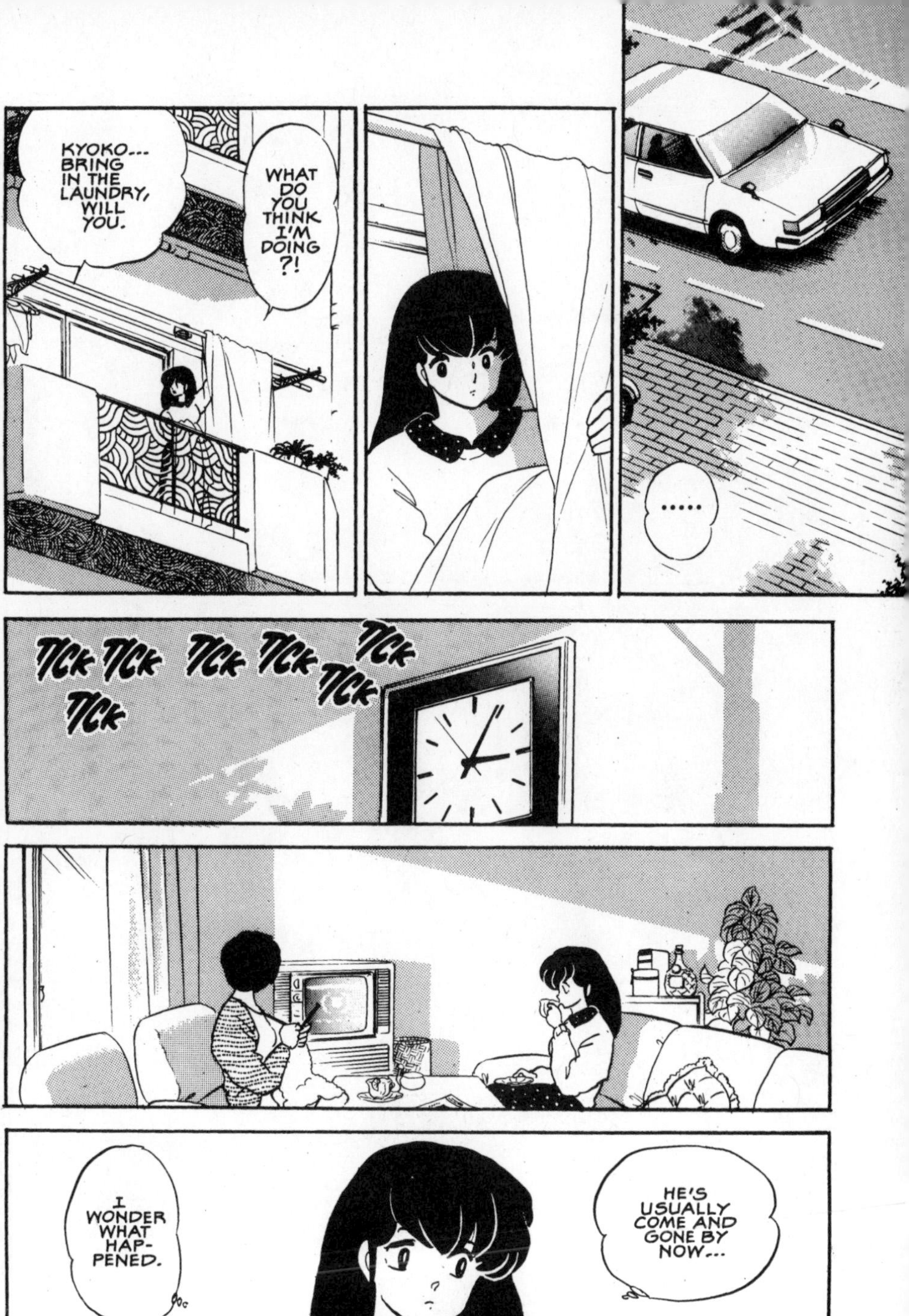
KYOKO... BRING IN THE LAUNDRY, WILL YOU.
WHAT DO YOU THINK I'M DOING ?!
......
TICK TICK TICK TICK TICK TICK TICK
I WONDER WHAT HAP-PENED.
HE'S USUALLY COME AND GONE BY NOW...

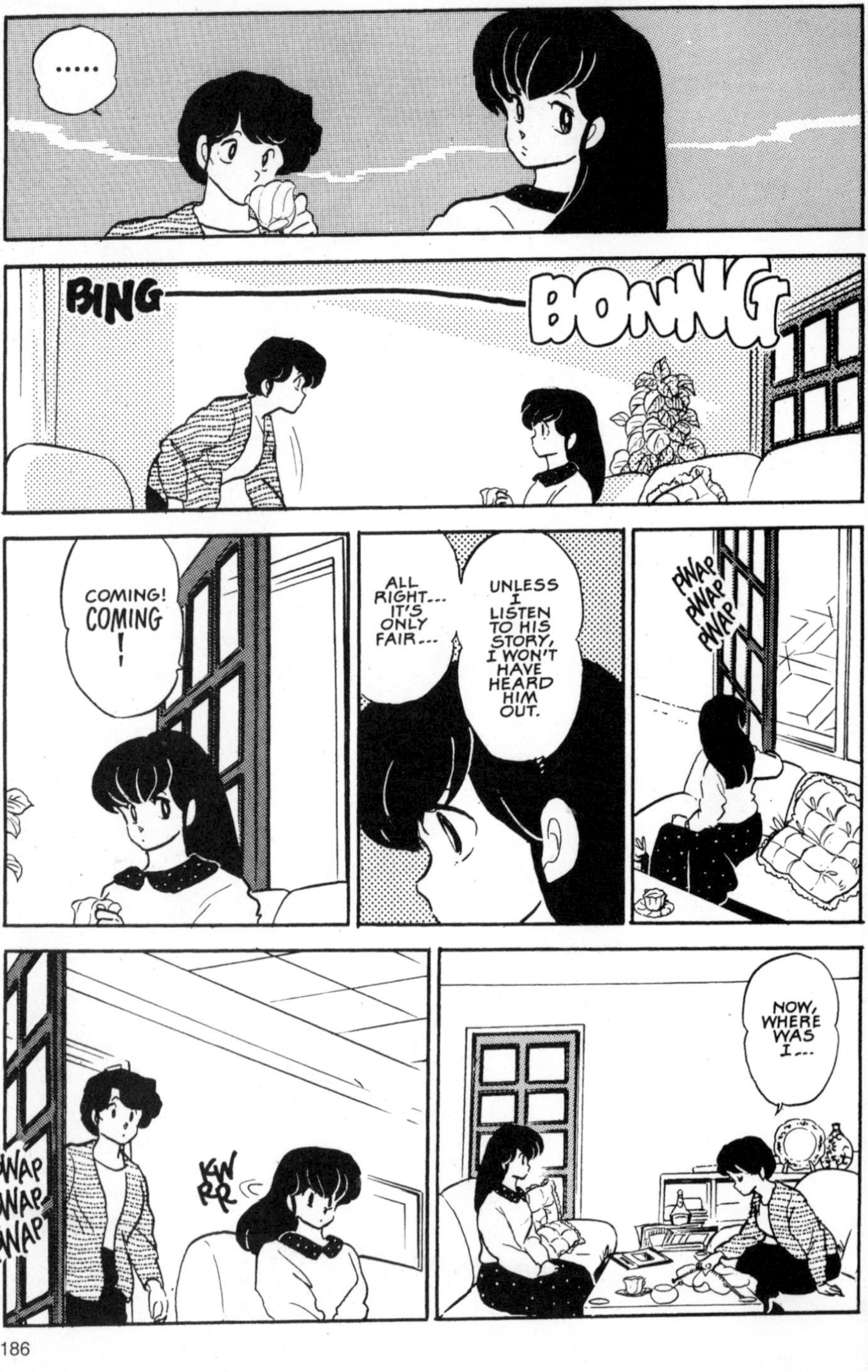

......
BING
BONNG
COMING! COMING!
ALL RIGHT... IT'S ONLY FAIR...
UNLESS I LISTEN TO HIS STORY, I WON'T HAVE HEARD HIM OUT.
PWAP PWAP PWAP
PWAP PWAP PWAP
KWRR
NOW, WHERE WAS I...

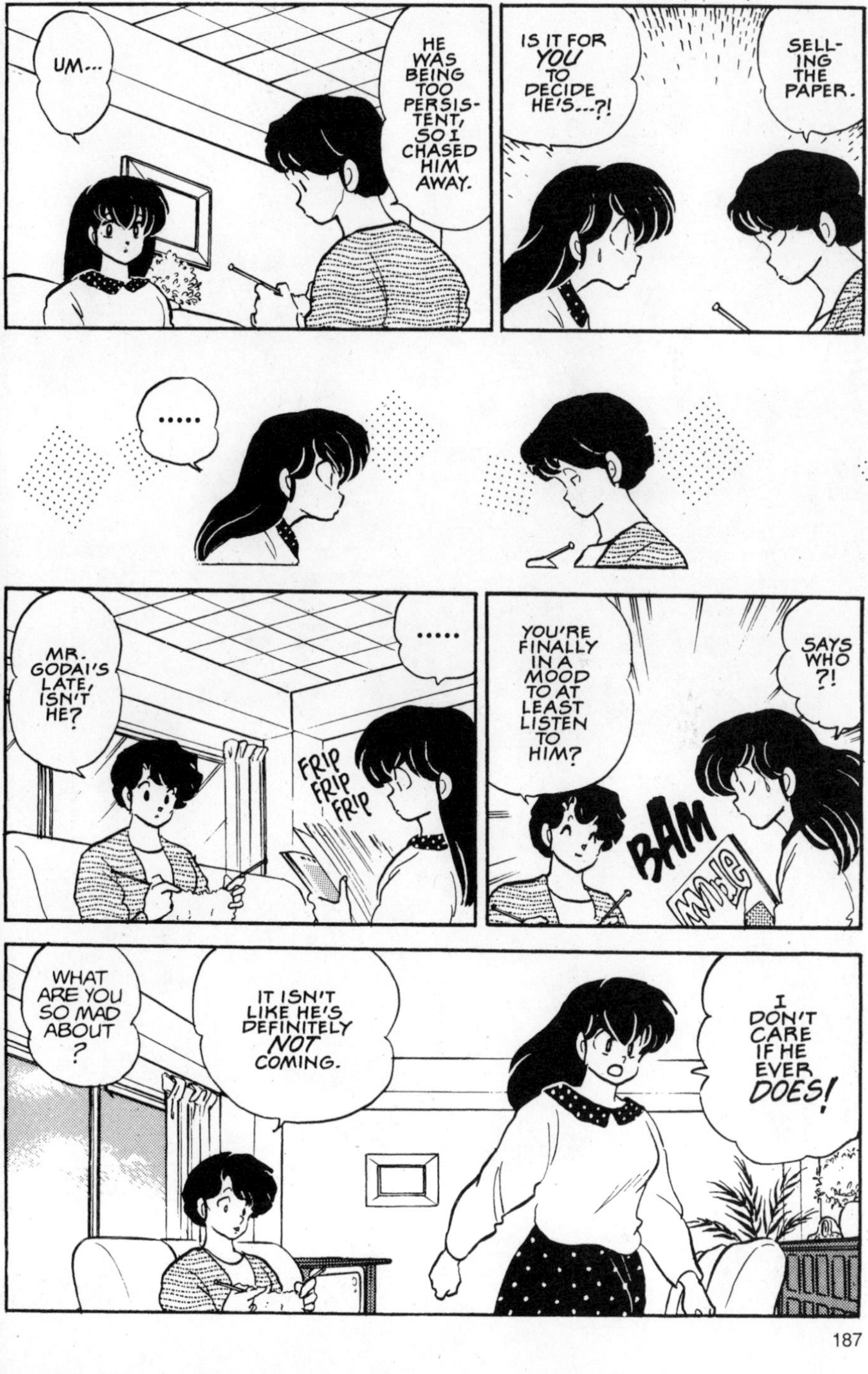
UM...
HE WAS BEING TOO PERSIS-TENT, SO I CHASED HIM AWAY.
IS IT FOR YOU TO DECIDE HE'S...?!
SELL-ING THE PAPER.
.....
MR. GODAI'S LATE, ISN'T HE?
.....
FRIP FRIP FRIP
YOU'RE FINALLY IN A MOOD TO AT LEAST LISTEN TO HIM?
SAYS WHO ?!
BAM
WHAT ARE YOU SO MAD ABOUT ?
IT ISN'T LIKE HE'S DEFINITELY NOT COMING.
I DON'T CARE IF HE EVER DOES!

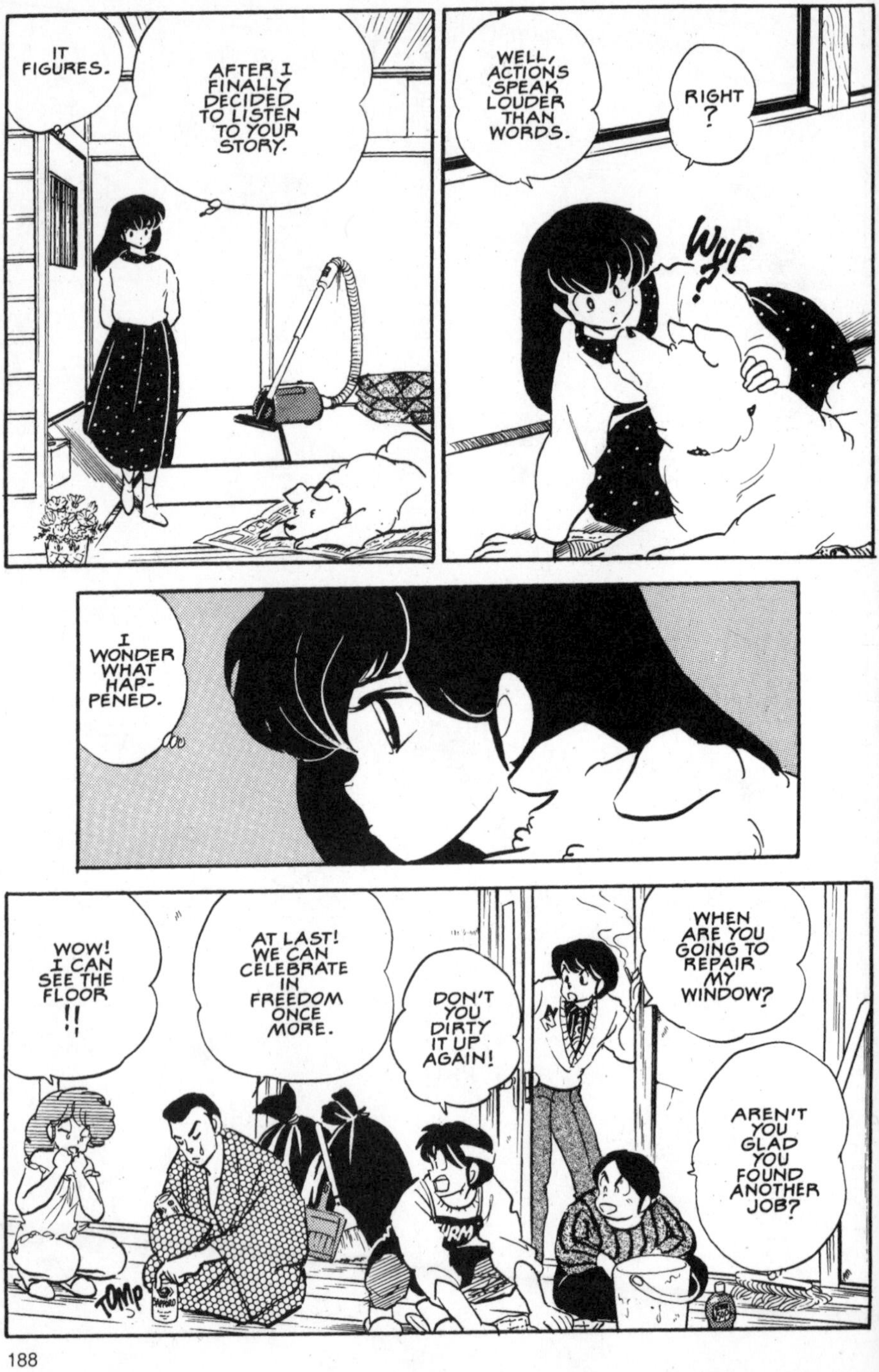
IT FIGURES.
AFTER I FINALLY DECIDED TO LISTEN TO YOUR STORY.
WELL, ACTIONS SPEAK LOUDER THAN WORDS.
RIGHT?
WUF?
I WONDER WHAT HAP-PENED.
WOW! I CAN SEE THE FLOOR!!
AT LAST! WE CAN CELEBRATE IN FREEDOM ONCE MORE.
DON'T YOU DIRTY IT UP AGAIN!
WHEN ARE YOU GOING TO REPAIR MY WINDOW?
AREN'T YOU GLAD YOU FOUND ANOTHER JOB?
TOMP

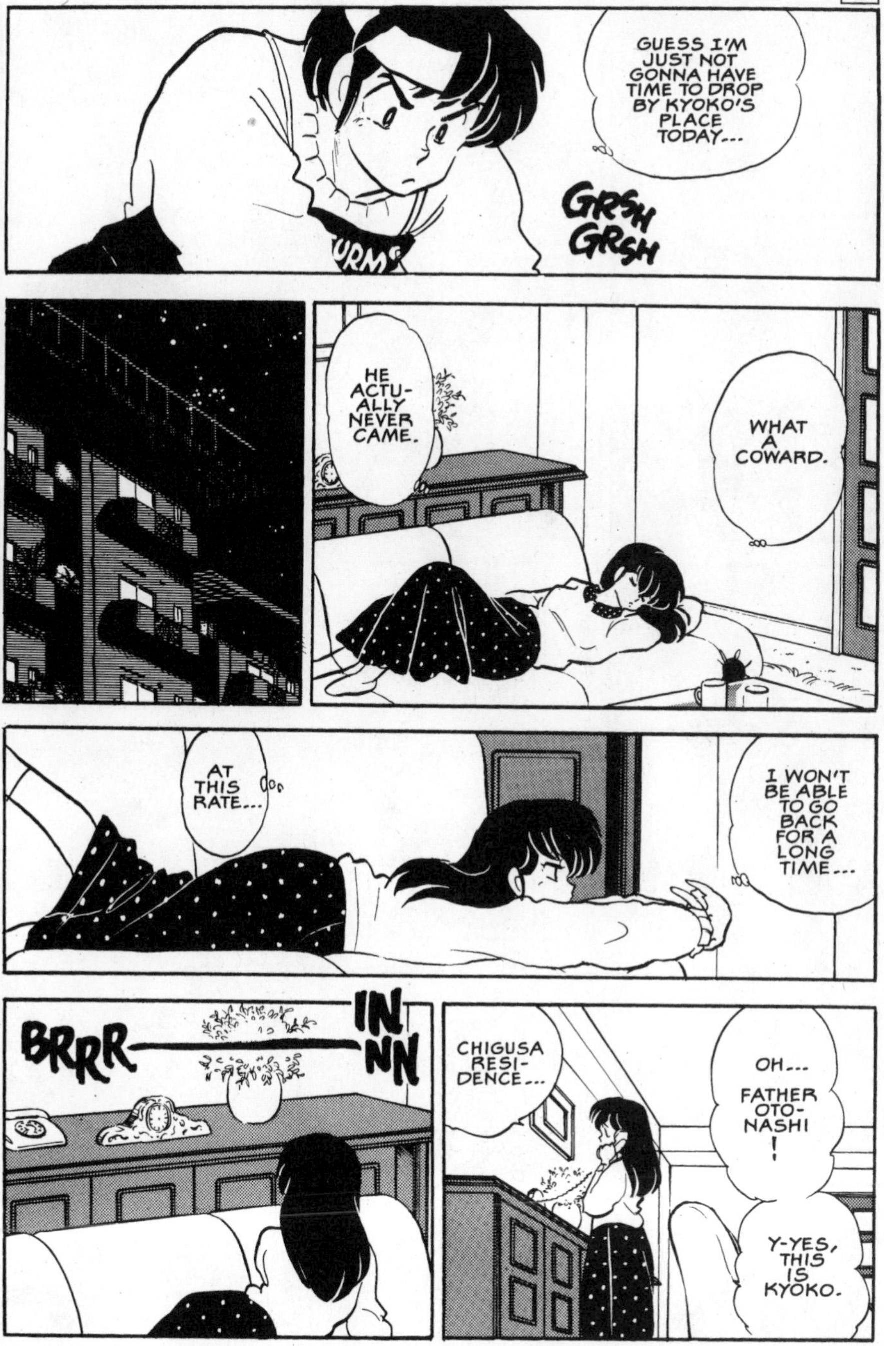
GUESS I'M JUST NOT GONNA HAVE TIME TO DROP BY KYOKO'S PLACE TODAY...
GRSH GRSH
HE ACTU-ALLY NEVER CAME.
WHAT A COWARD.
AT THIS RATE...
I WON'T BE ABLE TO GO BACK FOR A LONG TIME...
BRRR——————INNN
CHIGUSA RESI-DENCE...
OH... FATHER OTO-NASHI!
Y-YES, THIS IS KYOKO.

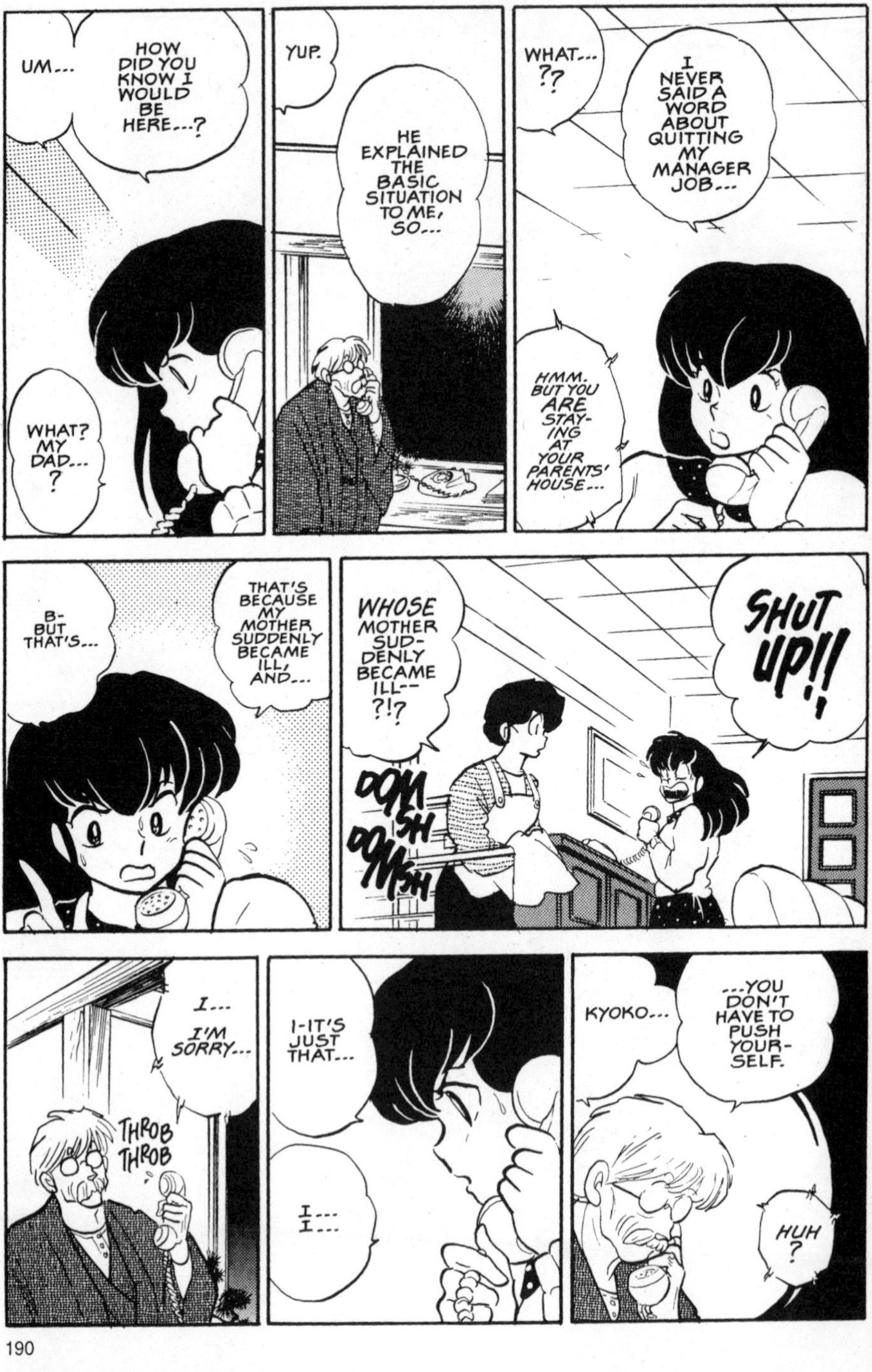
UM...
HOW DID YOU KNOW I WOULD BE HERE...?
WHAT? MY DAD...?
YUP.
HE EXPLAINED THE BASIC SITUATION TO ME, SO...
WHAT...??
I NEVER SAID A WORD ABOUT QUITTING MY MANAGER JOB...
HMM. BUT YOU ARE STAYING AT YOUR PARENTS' HOUSE...
B-BUT THAT'S...
THAT'S BECAUSE MY MOTHER SUDDENLY BECAME ILL, AND...
WHOSE MOTHER SUDDENLY BECAME ILL--?!?
DOMSH DOMSH
SHUT UP!!
I... I'M SORRY...
THROB THROB
I-IT'S JUST THAT...
I... I...
KYOKO...
...YOU DON'T HAVE TO PUSH YOURSELF.
HUH?

IN FACT, I APPRECIATE HOW YOU PERSEVERED AT THAT PLACE FOR THIS LONG.

IN ANY CASE, I'VE HIRED A NEW MANAGER FOR NOW, SO...

WHAT??

NOW, NOW, IT'S ONLY TEMPORARY...

WH-WHAT THE HELL...?!

A NEW MANAGER?!?

KYOKO? ARE YOU STILL THERE?

Y-YES...

AS I WAS SAY-ING...

YOU DON'T HAVE TO WORRY ABOUT MAISON IKKOKU...

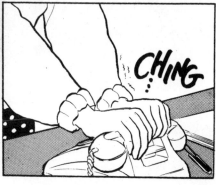

CHING

191

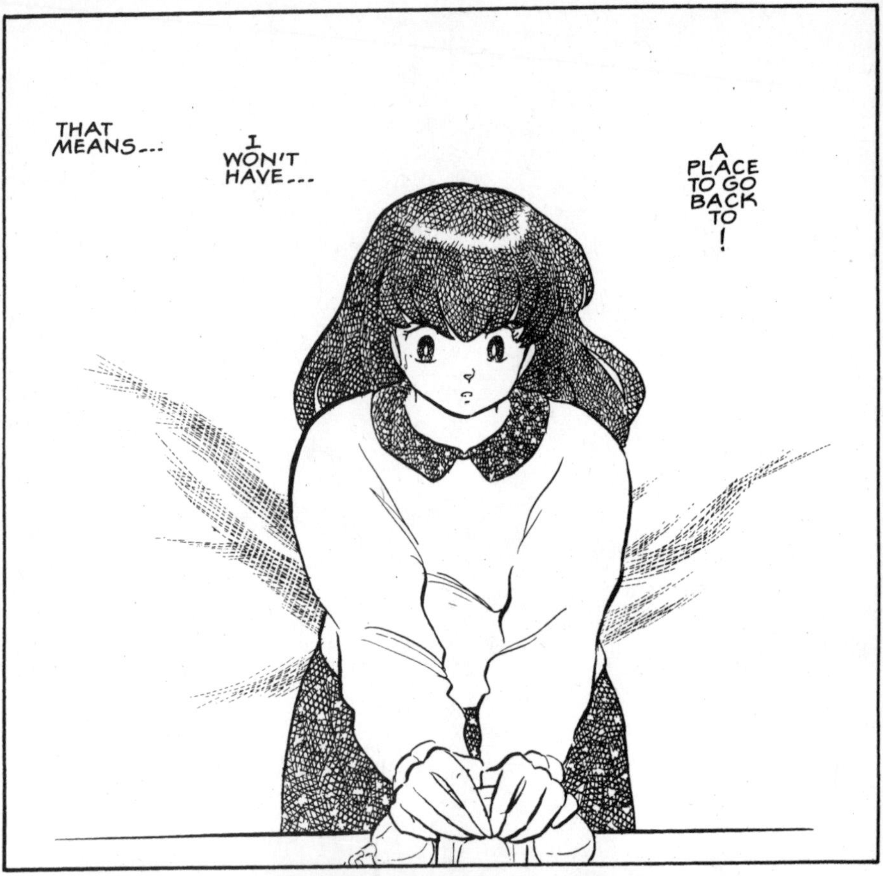
THAT MEANS...
I WON'T HAVE...
A PLACE TO GO BACK TO!
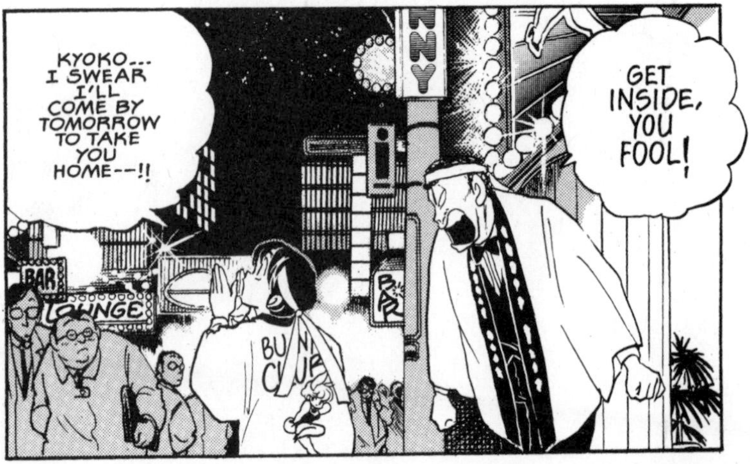
KYOKO... I SWEAR I'LL COME BY TOMORROW TO TAKE YOU HOME--!!
GET INSIDE, YOU FOOL!
BAR
LOUNGE

PART TEN
SHAME!

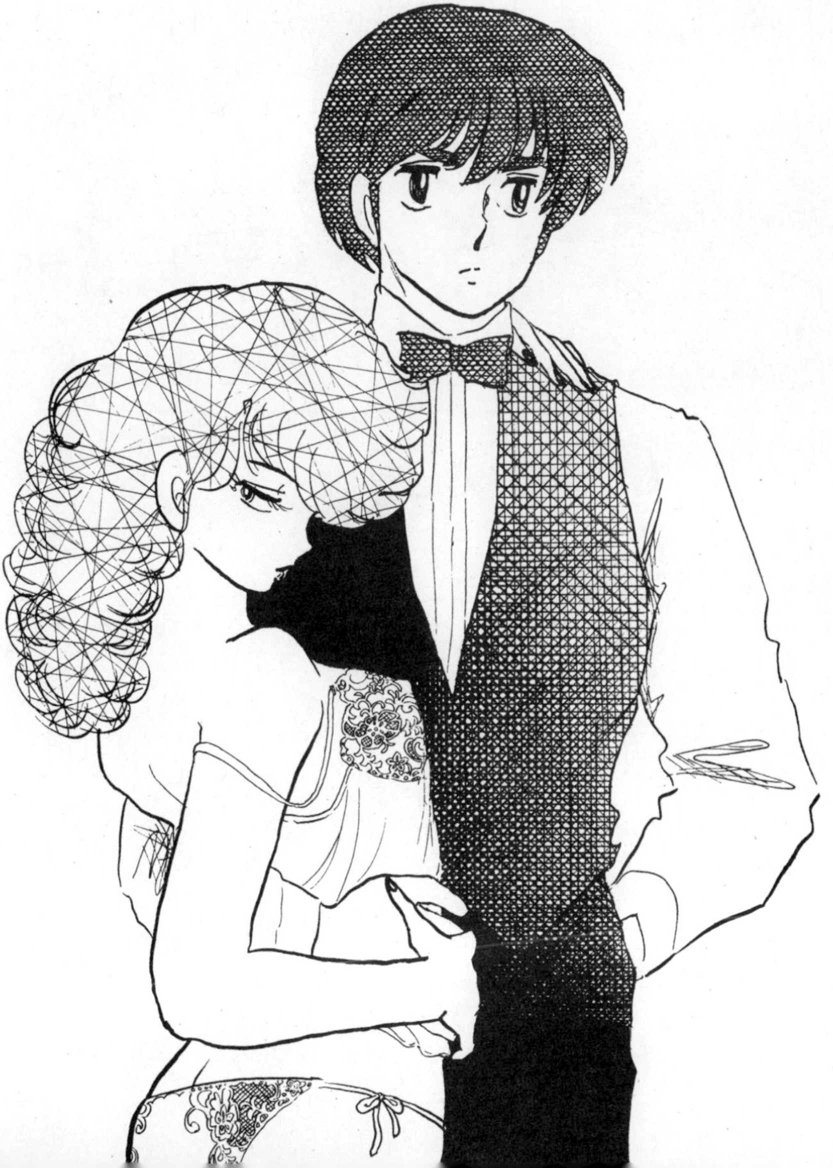

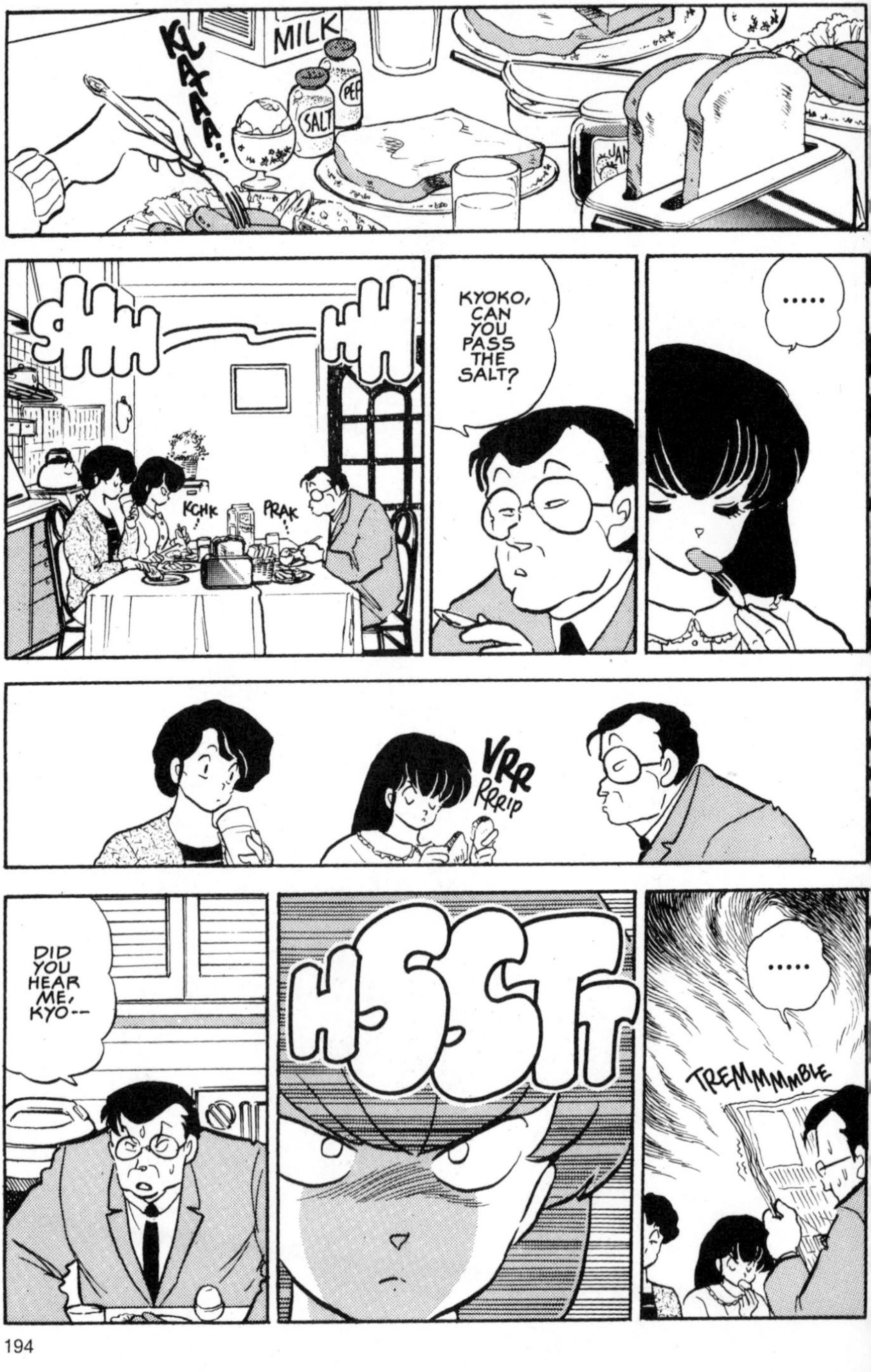
MILK
SALT
PEP
JAM
KLATAA...
SHHHHHH
KCHK
PRAK
KYOKO, CAN YOU PASS THE SALT?
......
VRR RRRIP
DID YOU HEAR ME, KYO--
HSST
......
TREMMMMMBLE

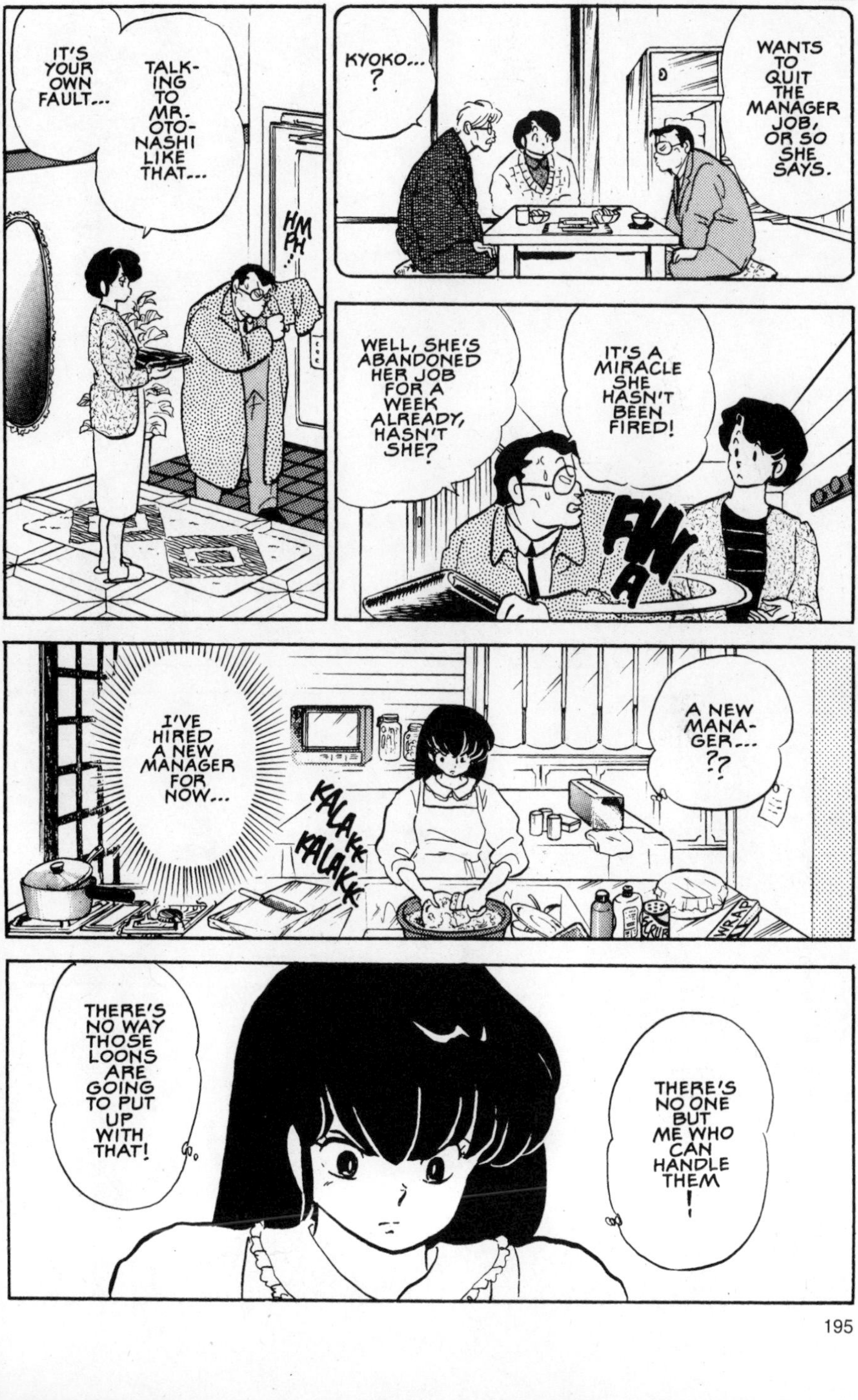
IT'S YOUR OWN FAULT... TALKING TO MR. OTONASHI LIKE THAT...
HMPH
KYOKO... ?
WANTS TO QUIT THE MANAGER JOB, OR SO SHE SAYS.
WELL, SHE'S ABANDONED HER JOB FOR A WEEK ALREADY, HASN'T SHE?
IT'S A MIRACLE SHE HASN'T BEEN FIRED!
FWA
I'VE HIRED A NEW MANAGER FOR NOW...
KALAKK KALAKK
A NEW MANAGER... ??
WRAP
THERE'S NO WAY THOSE LOONS ARE GOING TO PUT UP WITH THAT!
THERE'S NO ONE BUT ME WHO CAN HANDLE THEM!

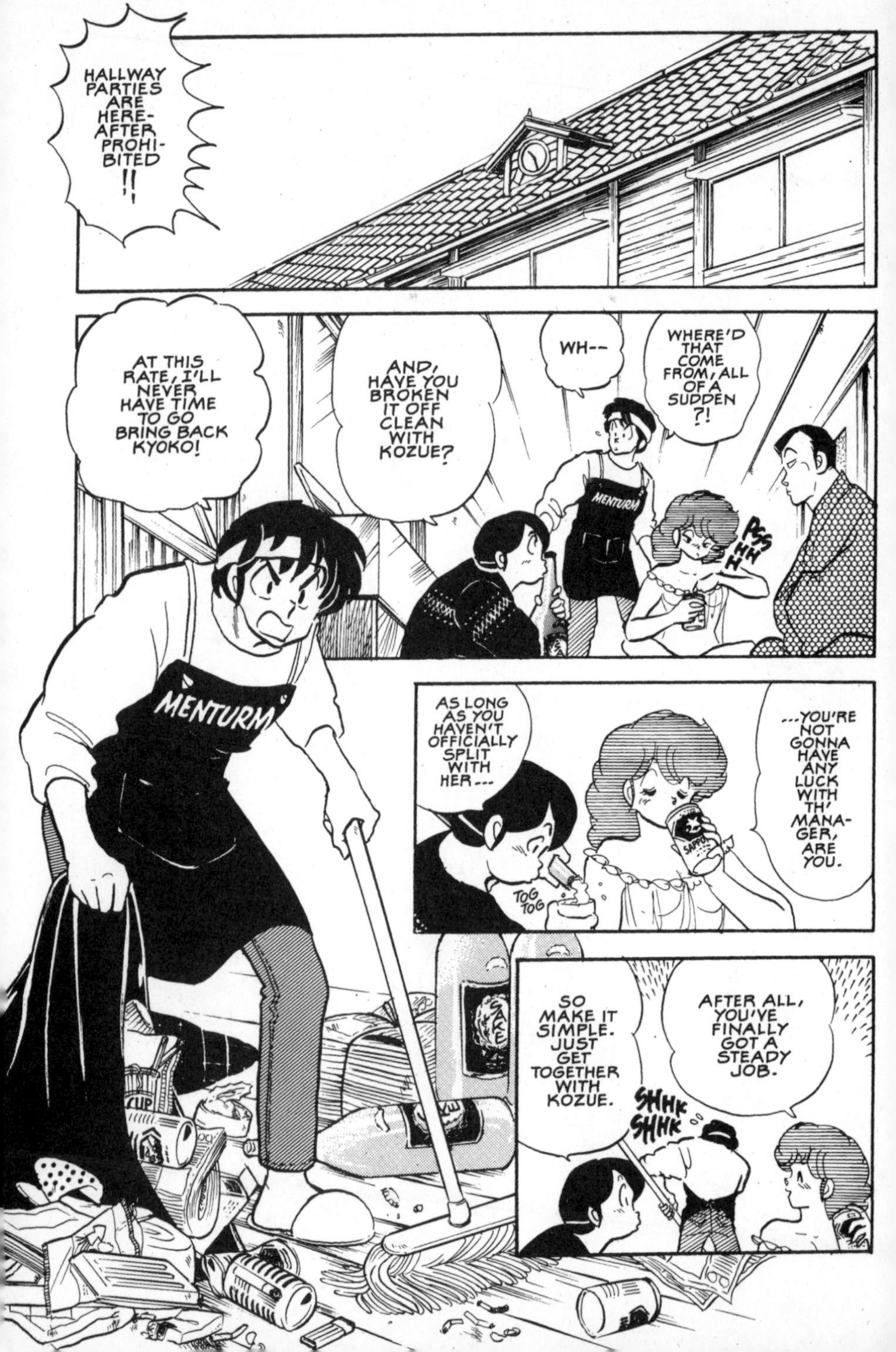
HALLWAY PARTIES ARE HERE-AFTER PROHIBITED !!
AT THIS RATE, I'LL NEVER HAVE TIME TO GO BRING BACK KYOKO!
AND, HAVE YOU BROKEN IT OFF CLEAN WITH KOZUE?
WH--
WHERE'D THAT COME FROM, ALL OF A SUDDEN ?!
MENTURM
PSSHH
MENTURM
AS LONG AS YOU HAVEN'T OFFICIALLY SPLIT WITH HER...
...YOU'RE NOT GONNA HAVE ANY LUCK WITH TH' MANAGER, ARE YOU.
TOG TOG
SAKE
SO MAKE IT SIMPLE. JUST GET TOGETHER WITH KOZUE.
AFTER ALL, YOU'VE FINALLY GOT A STEADY JOB.
SHHK SHHK

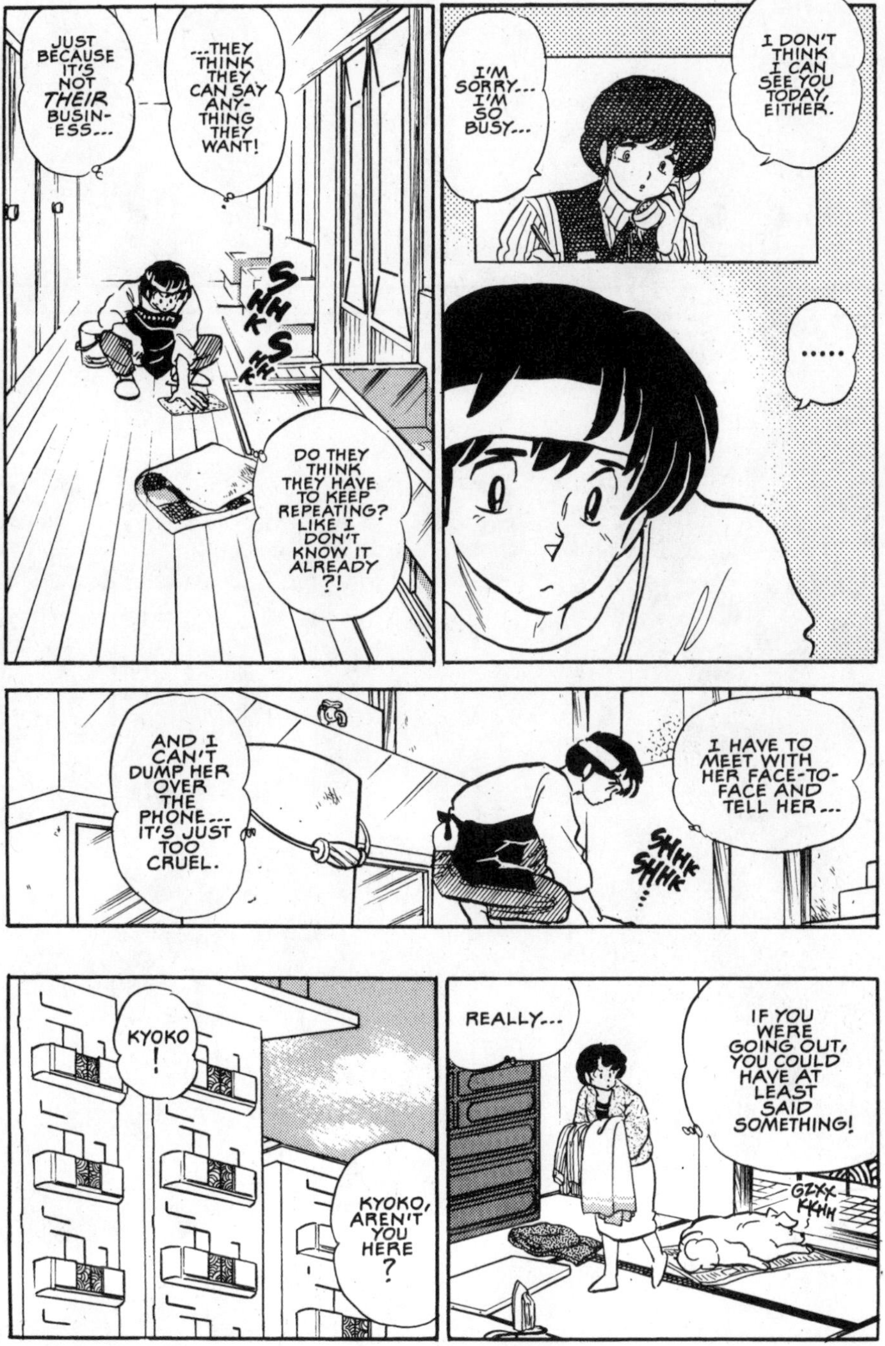

JUST BECAUSE IT'S NOT THEIR BUSINESS...
...THEY THINK THEY CAN SAY ANYTHING THEY WANT!
SHHK SHHK
DO THEY THINK THEY HAVE TO KEEP REPEATING? LIKE I DON'T KNOW IT ALREADY?!
I'M SORRY... I'M SO BUSY...
I DON'T THINK I CAN SEE YOU TODAY, EITHER.
......
AND I CAN'T DUMP HER OVER THE PHONE... IT'S JUST TOO CRUEL.
I HAVE TO MEET WITH HER FACE-TO-FACE AND TELL HER...
SHHK SHHK...
KYOKO!
KYOKO, AREN'T YOU HERE?
REALLY...
IF YOU WERE GOING OUT, YOU COULD HAVE AT LEAST SAID SOMETHING!
GZXXKKHH

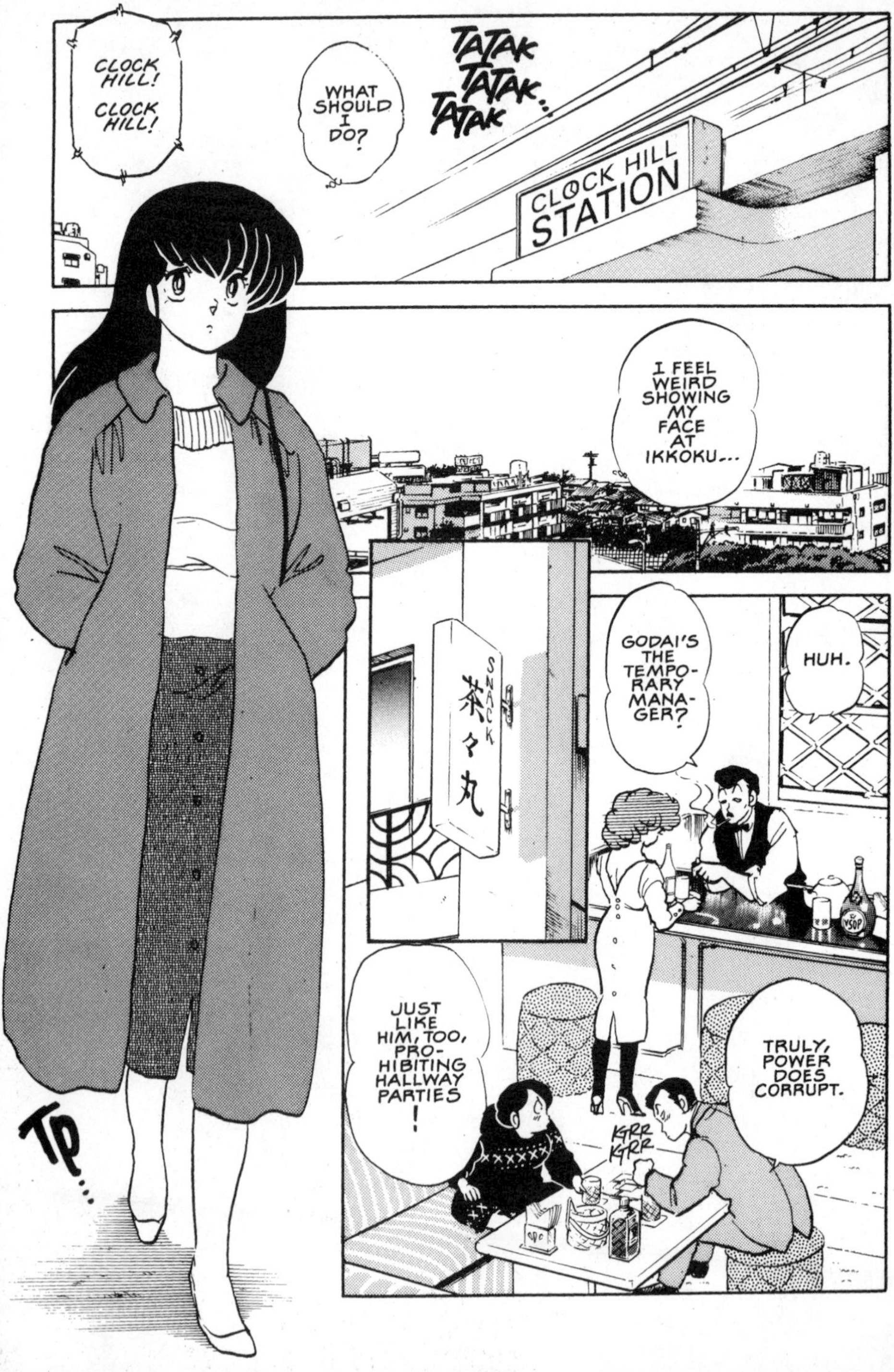

CLOCK HILL! CLOCK HILL!
WHAT SHOULD I DO?
TATAK TATAK TATAK...
CLOCK HILL STATION
TP...
I FEEL WEIRD SHOWING MY FACE AT IKKOKU...
SNACK 茶々丸
GODAI'S THE TEMPORARY MANAGER?
HUH.
JUST LIKE HIM, TOO, PROHIBITING HALLWAY PARTIES!
KGRR KGRR
TRULY, POWER DOES CORRUPT.

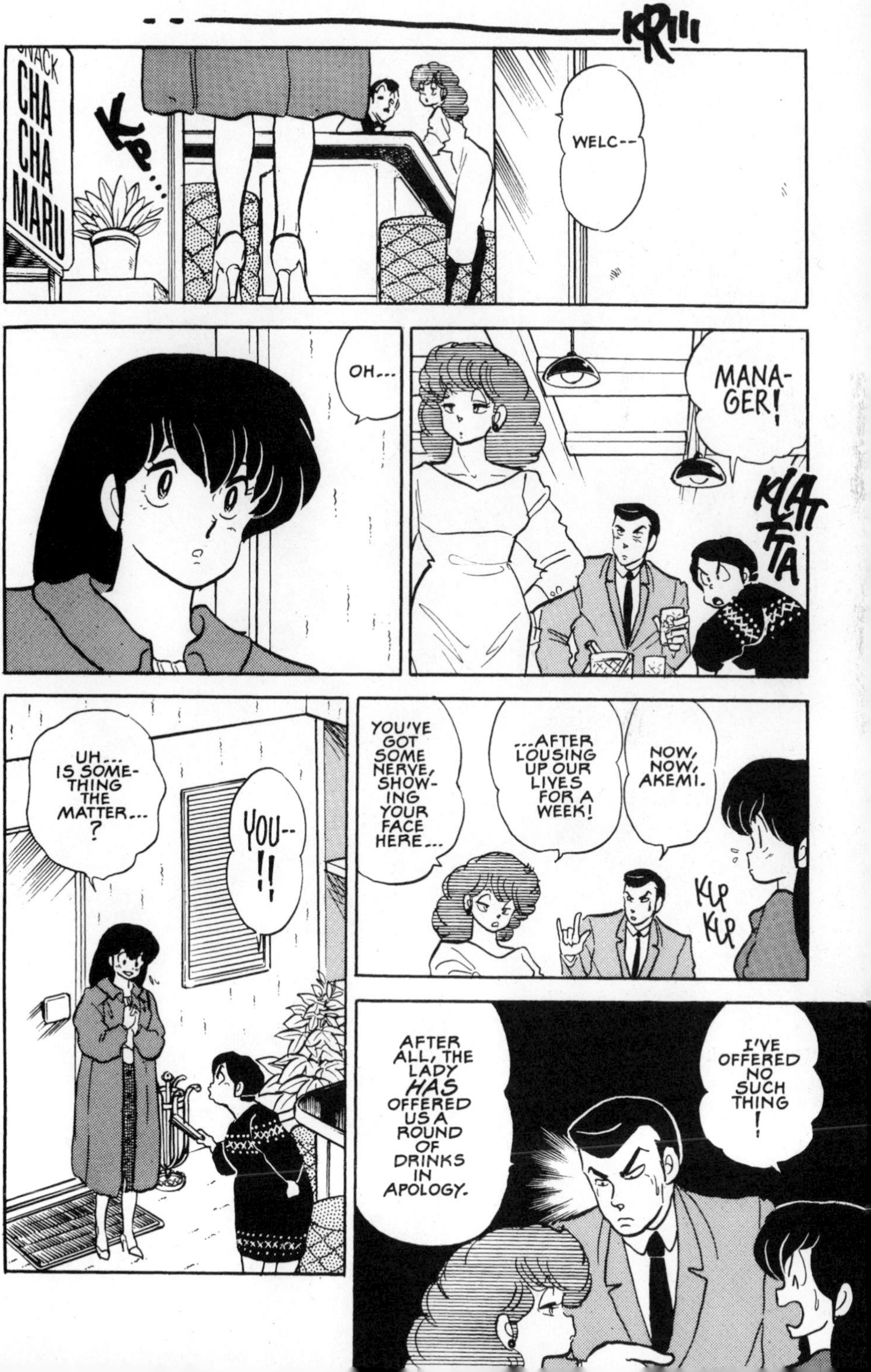
KRIII
SNACK CHA CHA MARU
KLP...
WELC--
OH...
MANA-GER!
KLATTA
UH... IS SOME-THING THE MATTER...?
YOU--!!
YOU'VE GOT SOME NERVE, SHOW-ING YOUR FACE HERE...
...AFTER LOUSING UP OUR LIVES FOR A WEEK!
NOW, NOW, AKEMI.
KLP KLP
AFTER ALL, THE LADY HAS OFFERED US A ROUND OF DRINKS IN APOLOGY.
I'VE OFFERED NO SUCH THING!

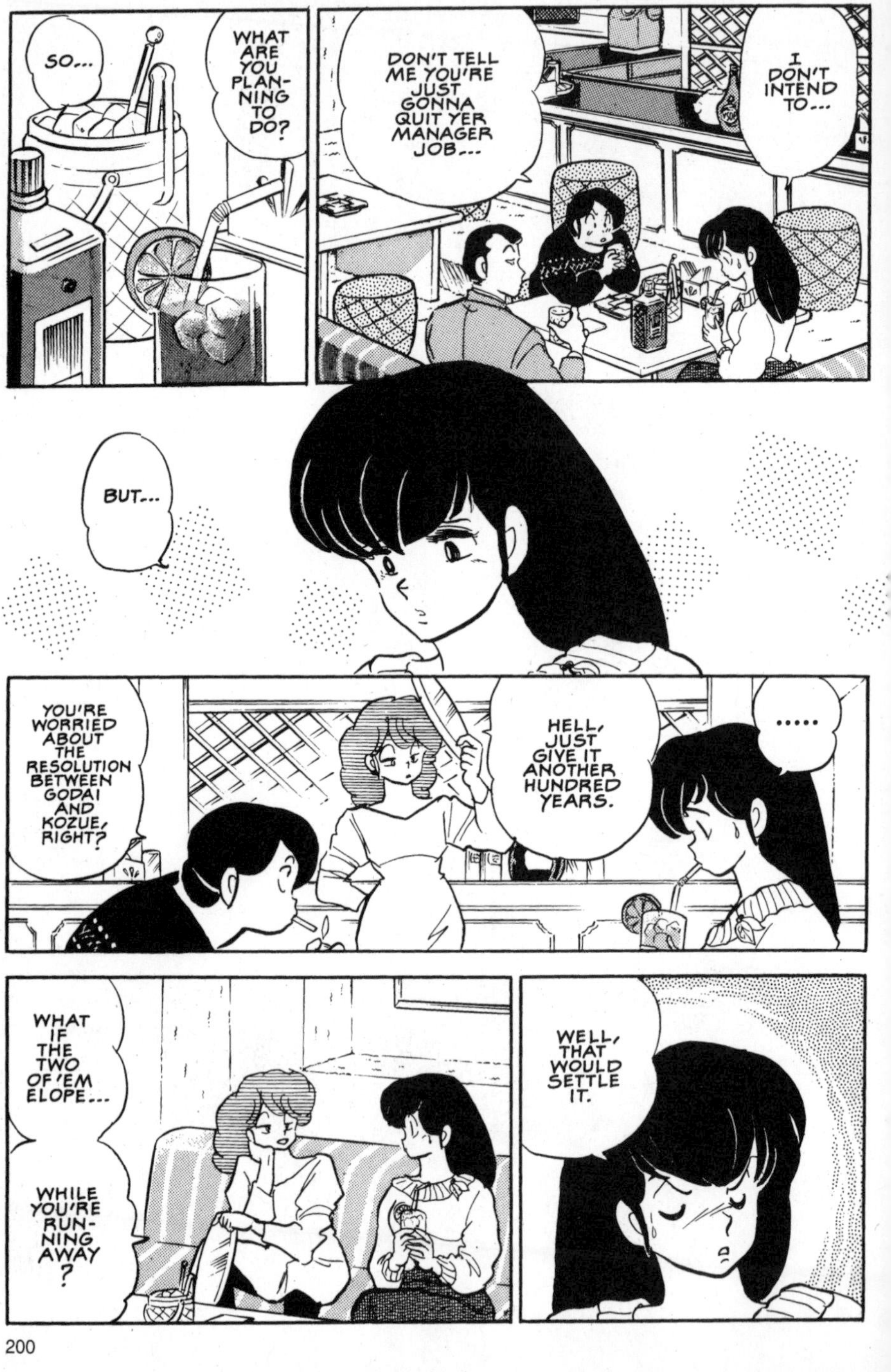
SO...
WHAT ARE YOU PLANNING TO DO?
DON'T TELL ME YOU'RE JUST GONNA QUIT YER MANAGER JOB...
I DON'T INTEND TO...
BUT...
YOU'RE WORRIED ABOUT THE RESOLUTION BETWEEN GODAI AND KOZUE, RIGHT?
HELL, JUST GIVE IT ANOTHER HUNDRED YEARS.
.....
WHAT IF THE TWO OF 'EM ELOPE...
WHILE YOU'RE RUNNING AWAY?
WELL, THAT WOULD SETTLE IT.

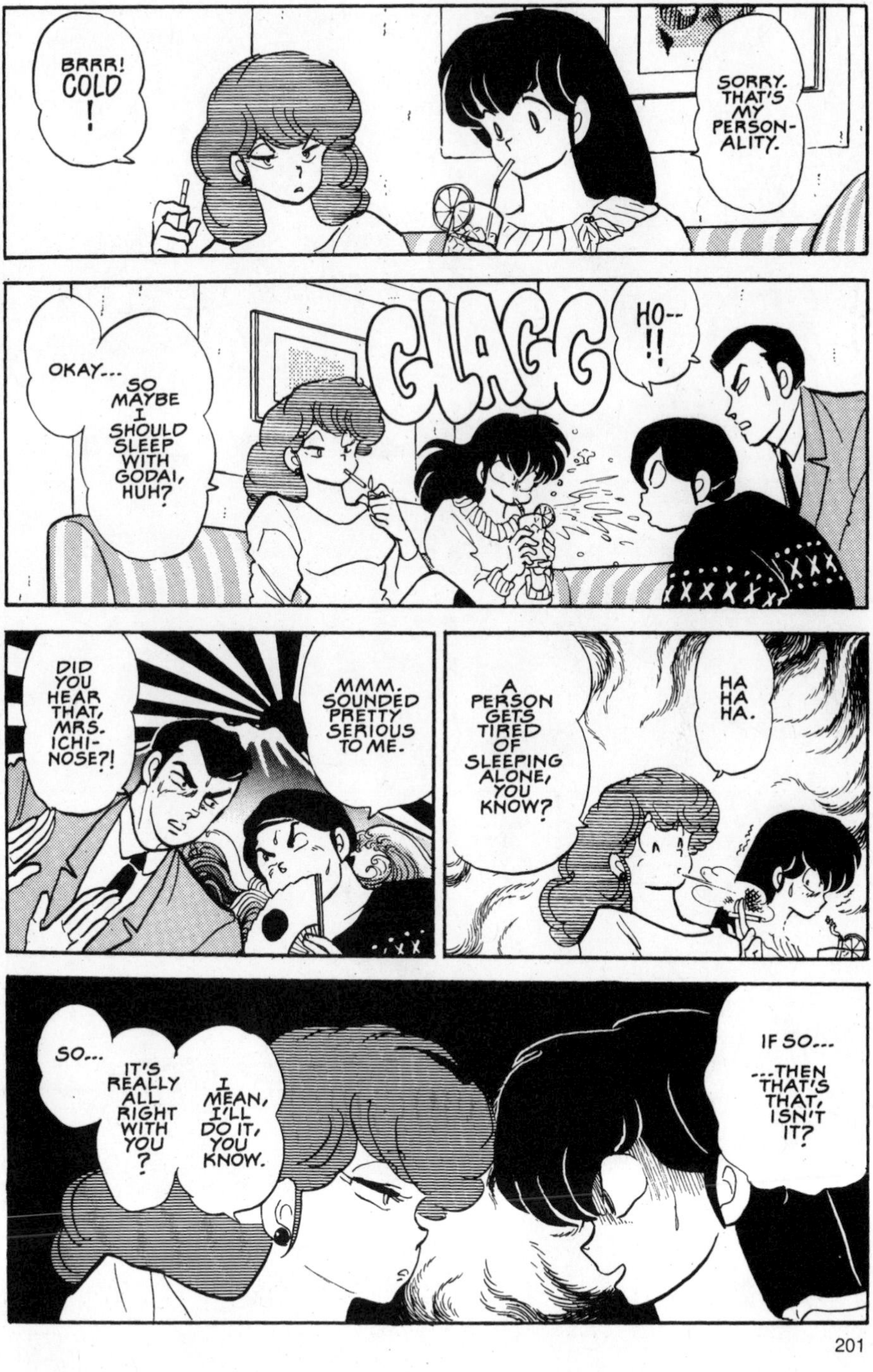
BRRR! COLD!
SORRY. THAT'S MY PERSONALITY.
OKAY... SO MAYBE I SHOULD SLEEP WITH GODAI, HUH?
GLAGG
HO--!!
DID YOU HEAR THAT, MRS. ICHINOSE?!
MMM. SOUNDED PRETTY SERIOUS TO ME.
A PERSON GETS TIRED OF SLEEPING ALONE, YOU KNOW?
HA HA HA.
SO... IT'S REALLY ALL RIGHT WITH YOU?
I MEAN, I'LL DO IT, YOU KNOW.
IF SO...
...THEN THAT'S THAT, ISN'T IT?

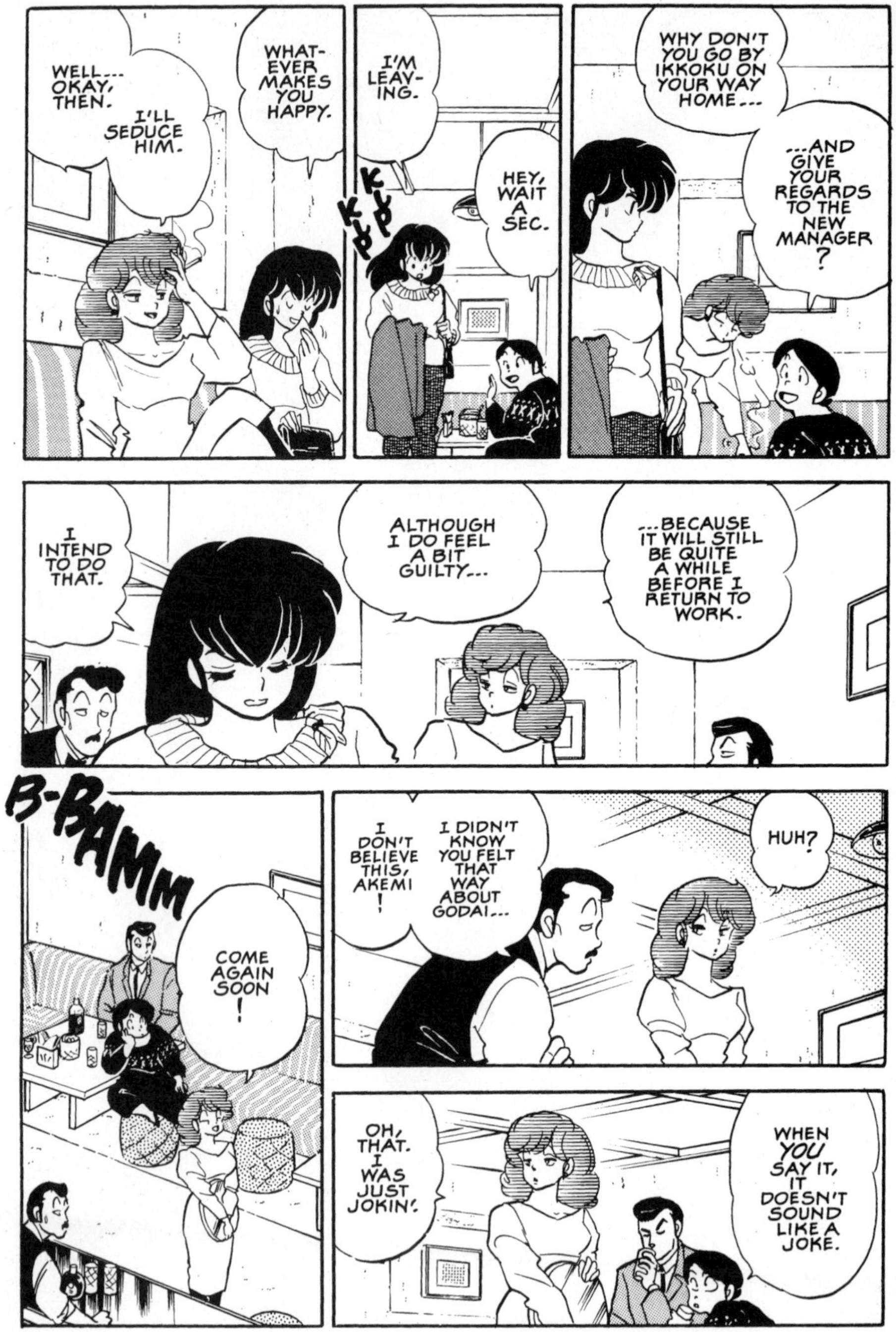

WELL... OKAY, THEN.
I'LL SEDUCE HIM.
WHAT-EVER MAKES YOU HAPPY.
I'M LEAV-ING.
KIP KIP
HEY, WAIT A SEC.
WHY DON'T YOU GO BY IKKOKU ON YOUR WAY HOME...
...AND GIVE YOUR REGARDS TO THE NEW MANAGER?
I INTEND TO DO THAT.
ALTHOUGH I DO FEEL A BIT GUILTY...
...BECAUSE IT WILL STILL BE QUITE A WHILE BEFORE I RETURN TO WORK.
B-BAMM
COME AGAIN SOON!
I DON'T BELIEVE THIS, AKEMI!
I DIDN'T KNOW YOU FELT THAT WAY ABOUT GODAI...
HUH?
OH, THAT. I WAS JUST JOKIN'.
WHEN YOU SAY IT, IT DOESN'T SOUND LIKE A JOKE.

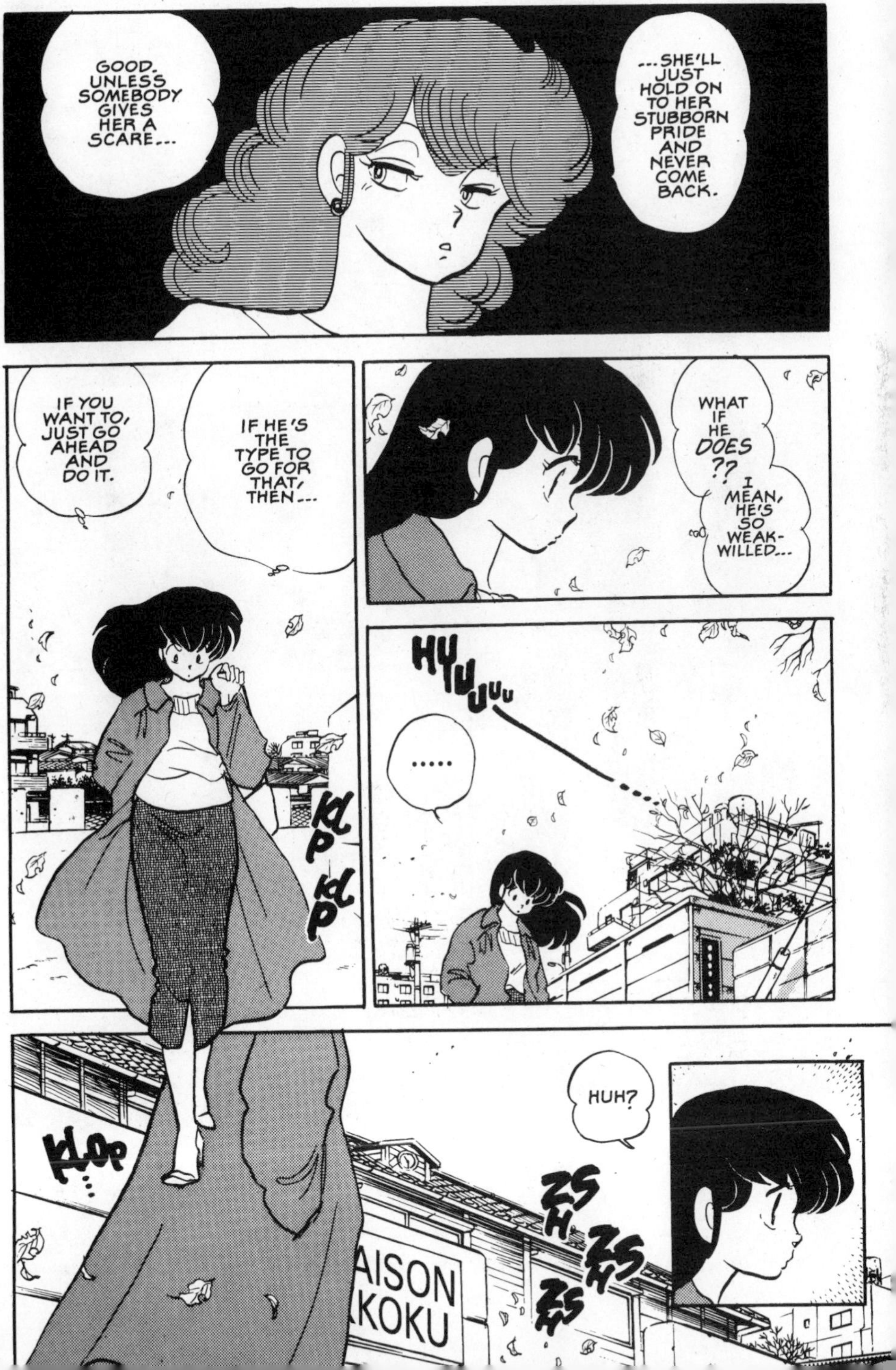
GOOD. UNLESS SOMEBODY GIVES HER A SCARE...
...SHE'LL JUST HOLD ON TO HER STUBBORN PRIDE AND NEVER COME BACK.
IF YOU WANT TO, JUST GO AHEAD AND DO IT.
IF HE'S THE TYPE TO GO FOR THAT, THEN...
WHAT IF HE DOES??
I MEAN, HE'S SO WEAK-WILLED...
KLP
KLP
HYUUUUU
......
KLOP...
HUH?
MAISON IKKOKU
ZSH
ZSH
ZS

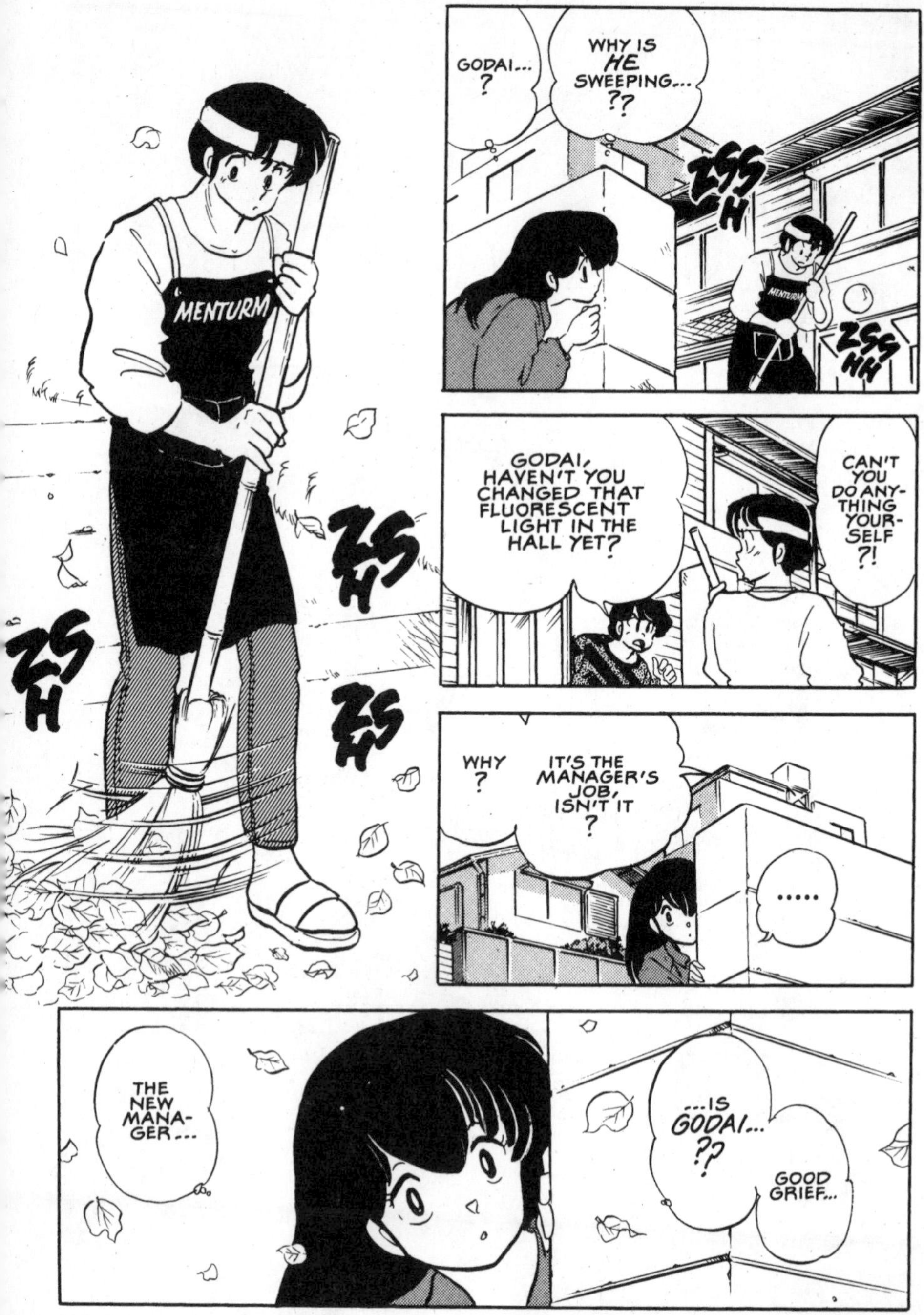
MENTURM
ZSSH
ZSSH
ZSSH
GODAI...?
WHY IS HE SWEEPING...??
ZSSH
MENTURM
ZSSH
GODAI, HAVEN'T YOU CHANGED THAT FLUORESCENT LIGHT IN THE HALL YET?
CAN'T YOU DO ANYTHING YOURSELF?!
WHY?
IT'S THE MANAGER'S JOB, ISN'T IT?
.....
THE NEW MANAGER...
...IS GODAI...??
GOOD GRIEF...

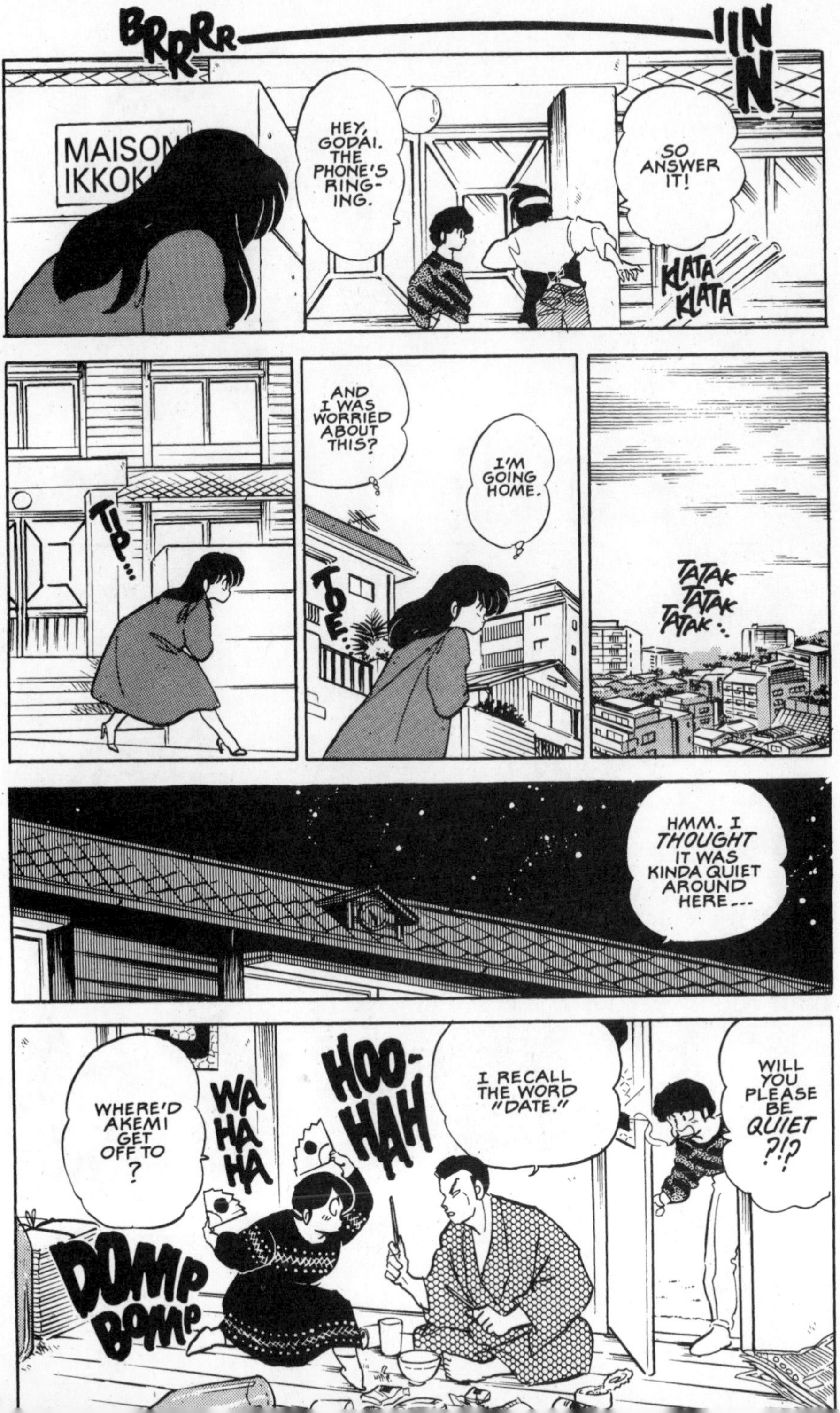
BRRRRR———IINN
MAISON IKKOKU
HEY, GODAI. THE PHONE'S RING-ING.
SO ANSWER IT!
KLATA KLATA
TIP...
AND I WAS WORRIED ABOUT THIS?
TOE...
I'M GOING HOME.
TATAK TATAK TATAK...
HMM. I THOUGHT IT WAS KINDA QUIET AROUND HERE...
WHERE'D AKEMI GET OFF TO?
WA HA HA HA
HOO-HAH
I RECALL THE WORD "DATE."
WILL YOU PLEASE BE QUIET ?!?
DOMP BOMP

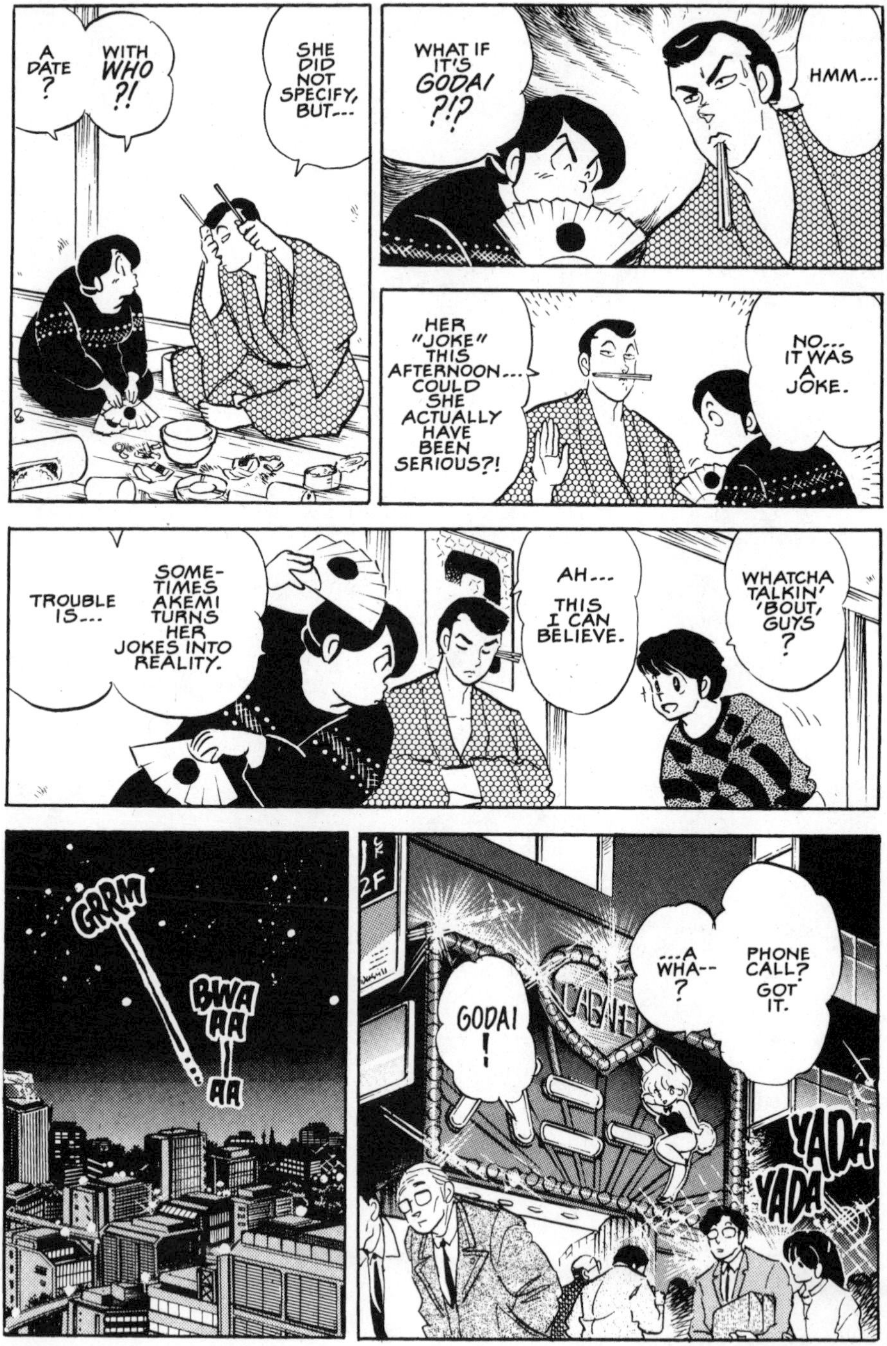
A DATE?
WITH WHO?!
SHE DID NOT SPECIFY, BUT...
WHAT IF IT'S GODAI?!?
HMM...
HER "JOKE" THIS AFTERNOON... COULD SHE ACTUALLY HAVE BEEN SERIOUS?!
NO... IT WAS A JOKE.
TROUBLE IS...
SOMETIMES AKEMI TURNS HER JOKES INTO REALITY.
AH...
THIS I CAN BELIEVE.
WHATCHA TALKIN' 'BOUT, GUYS?
GRRM
BWAAA--AA
2F
GODAI!
...A WHA--?
PHONE CALL? GOT IT.
YADA YADA

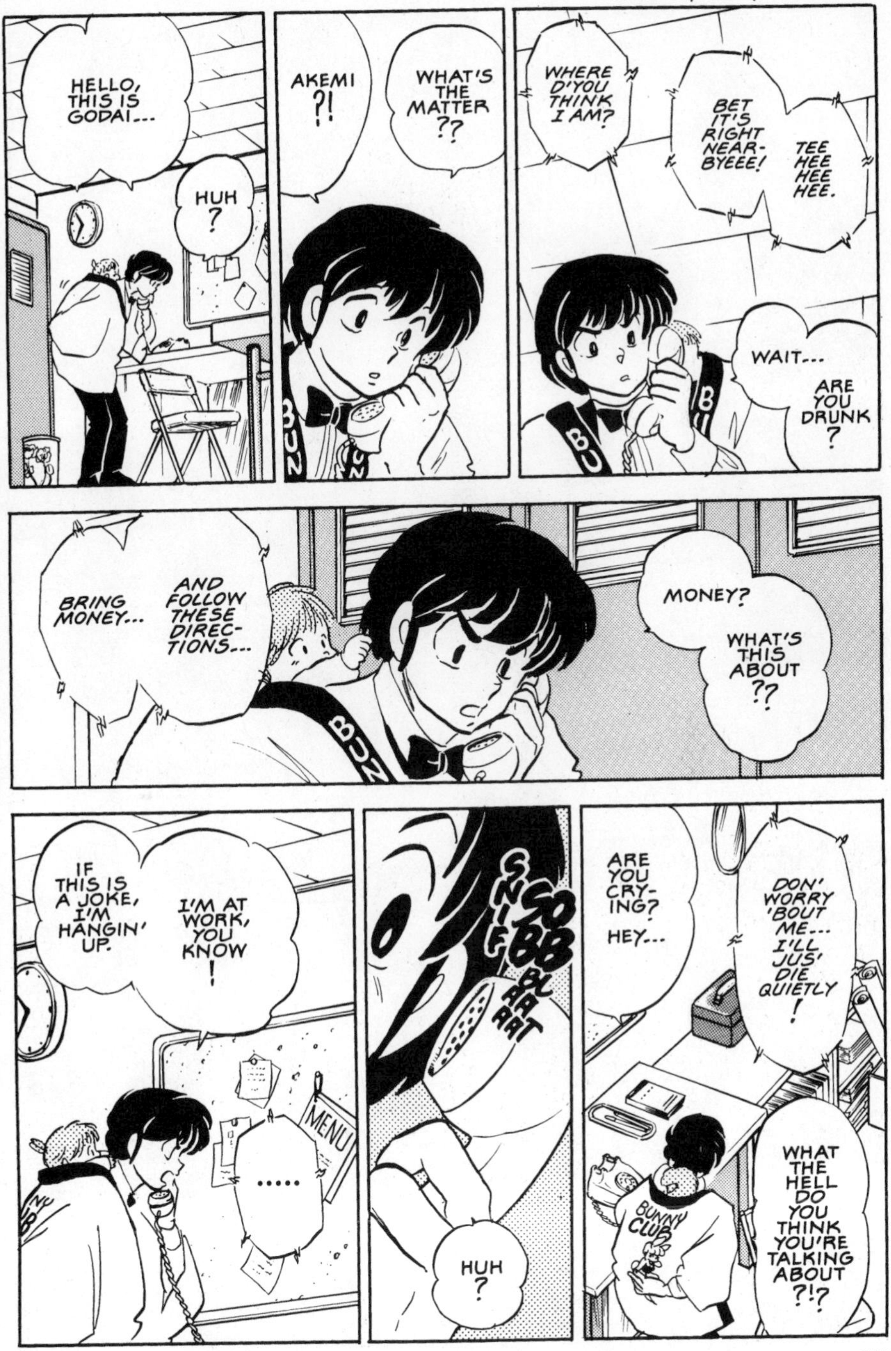
HELLO, THIS IS GODAI...
HUH?
AKEMI ?!
WHAT'S THE MATTER ??
WHERE D'YOU THINK I AM?
BET IT'S RIGHT NEAR-BYEEE!
TEE HEE HEE HEE.
WAIT... ARE YOU DRUNK?
BRING MONEY...
AND FOLLOW THESE DIRECTIONS...
MONEY? WHAT'S THIS ABOUT ??
IF THIS IS A JOKE, I'M HANGIN' UP.
I'M AT WORK, YOU KNOW!
.....
SNIF
SOBB
BLAAAT
HUH?
ARE YOU CRY-ING? HEY...
DON' WORRY 'BOUT ME... I'LL JUS' DIE QUIETLY!
WHAT THE HELL DO YOU THINK YOU'RE TALKING ABOUT ?!?

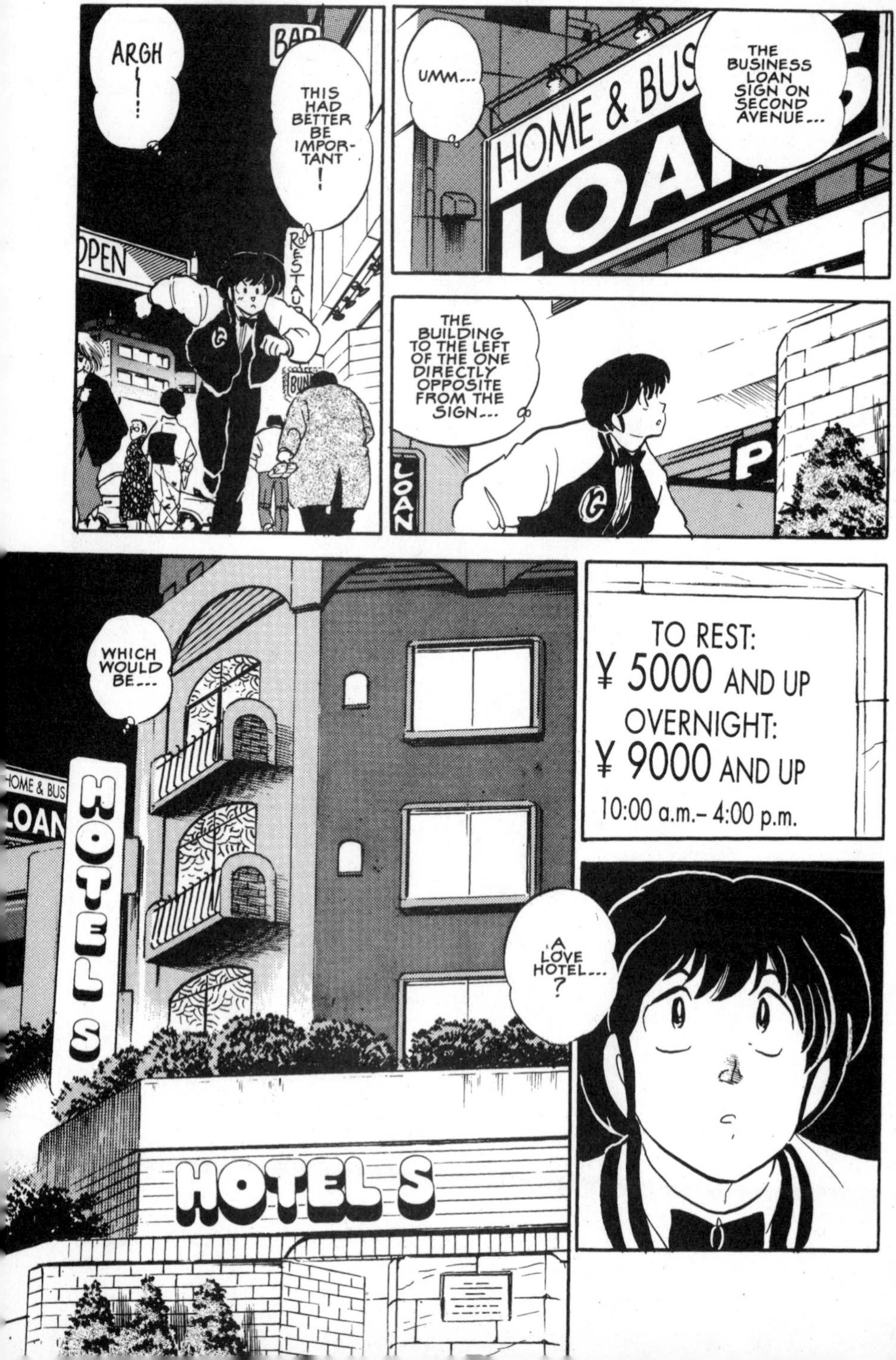
BAR
ARGH !!!
THIS HAD BETTER BE IMPORTANT !
OPEN
RESTAU
UMM...
HOME & BUS
LOAN
THE BUSINESS LOAN SIGN ON SECOND AVENUE...
THE BUILDING TO THE LEFT OF THE ONE DIRECTLY OPPOSITE FROM THE SIGN...
LOAN
P
WHICH WOULD BE...
HOME & BUS
LOAN
HOTEL S
HOTEL S
TO REST:
¥ 5000 AND UP
OVERNIGHT:
¥ 9000 AND UP
10:00 a.m.– 4:00 p.m.
A LOVE HOTEL...?

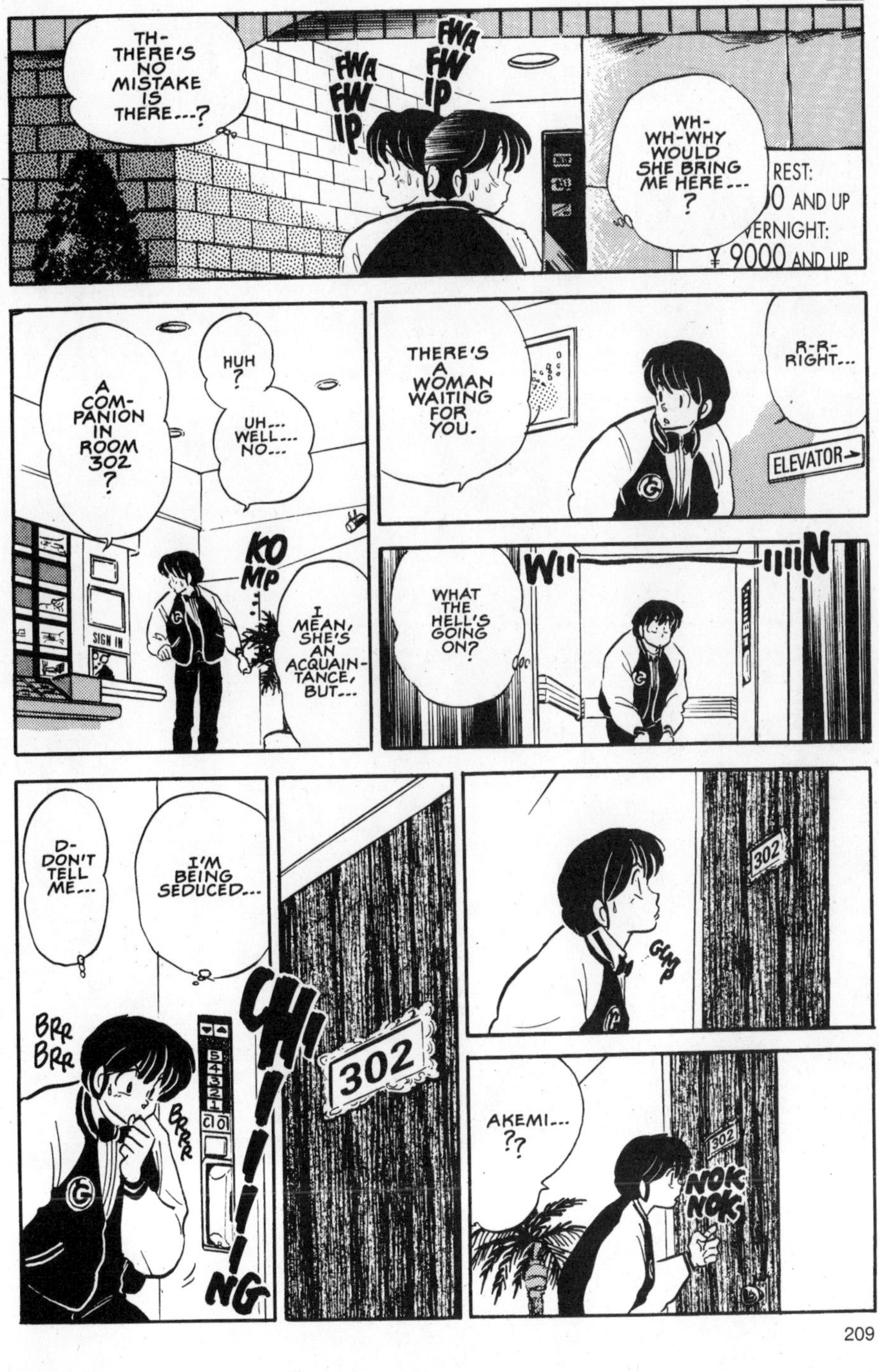
TH-THERE'S NO MISTAKE IS THERE...?
FWA FWIP
FWA FWIP
WH-WH-WHY WOULD SHE BRING ME HERE...?
REST:
0 AND UP
VERNIGHT:
¥ 9000 AND UP
A COMPANION IN ROOM 302?
HUH?
UH... WELL... NO...
SIGN IN
KOMP
I MEAN, SHE'S AN ACQUAINTANCE, BUT...
THERE'S A WOMAN WAITING FOR YOU.
R-R-RIGHT...
ELEVATOR
WII N
WHAT THE HELL'S GOING ON?
D-DON'T TELL ME...
I'M BEING SEDUCED...
BRR BRR
BRRR
302
CHI I I I I I NG
302
GLMP
AKEMI...??
302
NOK NOK

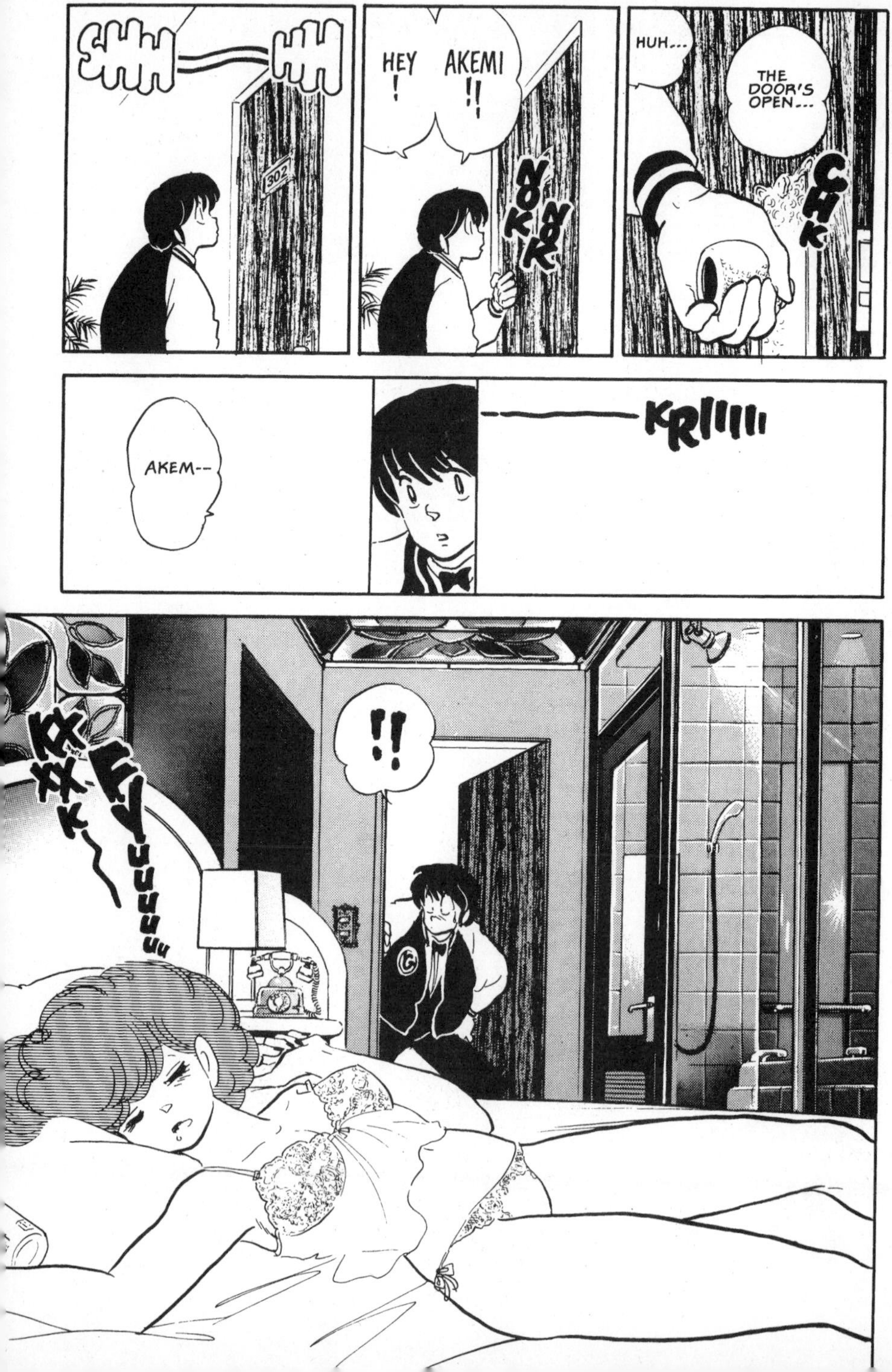
SHHH—HHH
HEY! AKEMI!!
NOK NOK
HUH...
THE DOOR'S OPEN...
CHK
AKEM--
KRIIIII
!!
FYUUUUUU
KKKK~

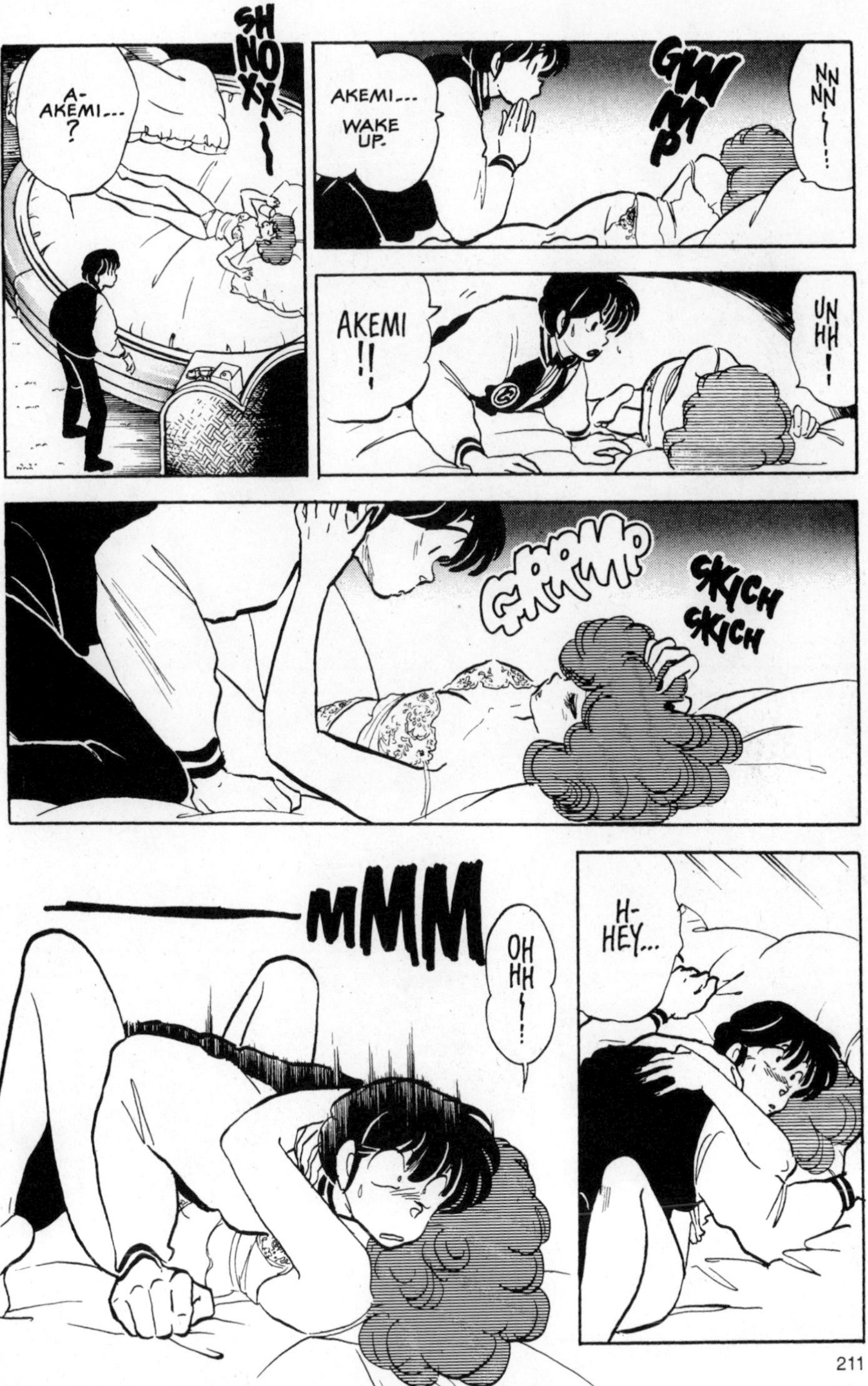

SHNOXX~
A-AKEMI...?
AKEMI... WAKE UP.
GWMP
NNNNN~...
AKEMI!!
UNHH!
GRROMP
SKICH SKICH
MMM
OHHH~!
H-HEY...

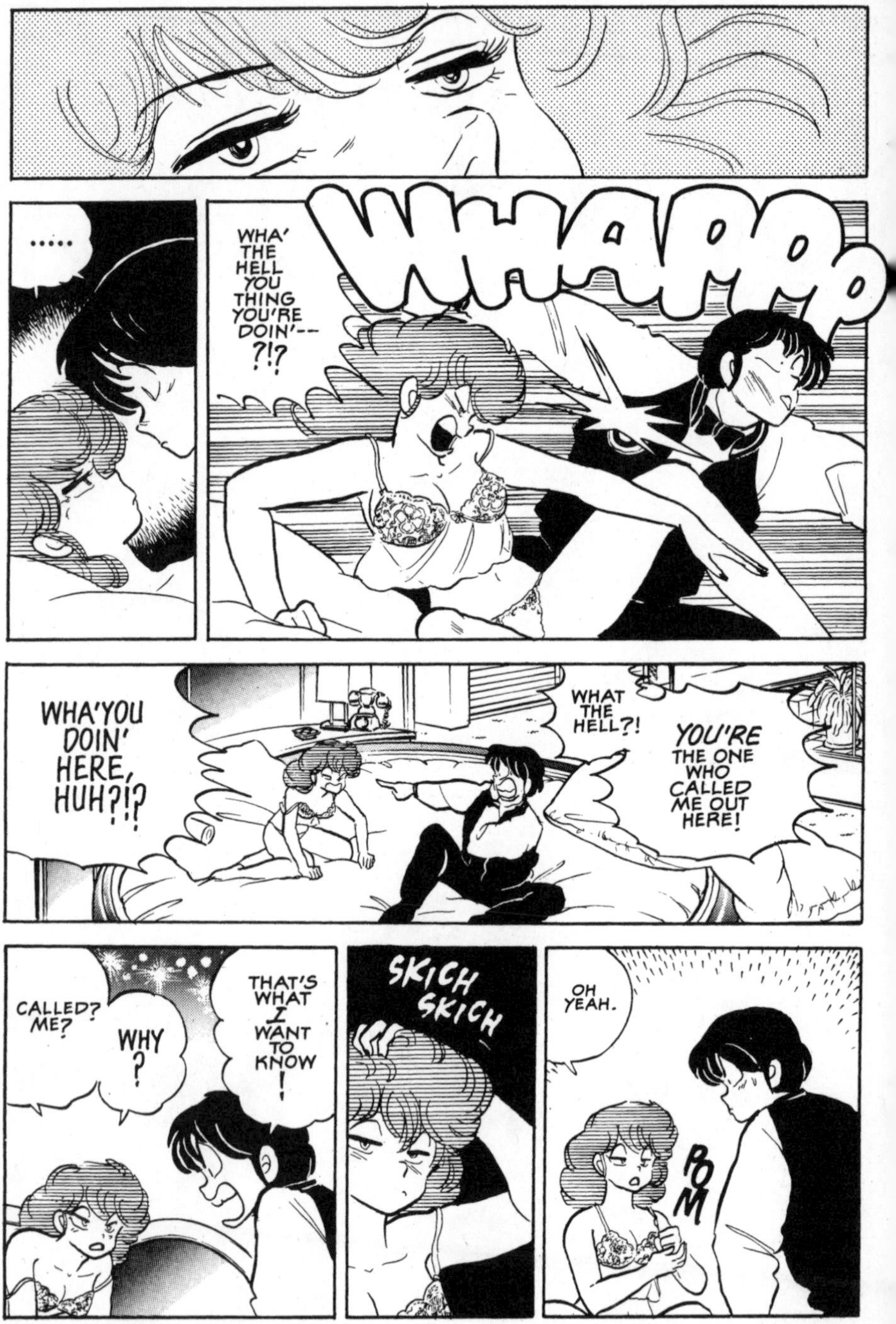
......
WHA' THE HELL YOU THING YOU'RE DOIN'-- ?!?
WHAPP
WHA'YOU DOIN' HERE, HUH?!?
WHAT THE HELL?!
YOU'RE THE ONE WHO CALLED ME OUT HERE!
CALLED? ME?
WHY ?
THAT'S WHAT I WANT TO KNOW !
SKICH SKICH
OH YEAH.
POM

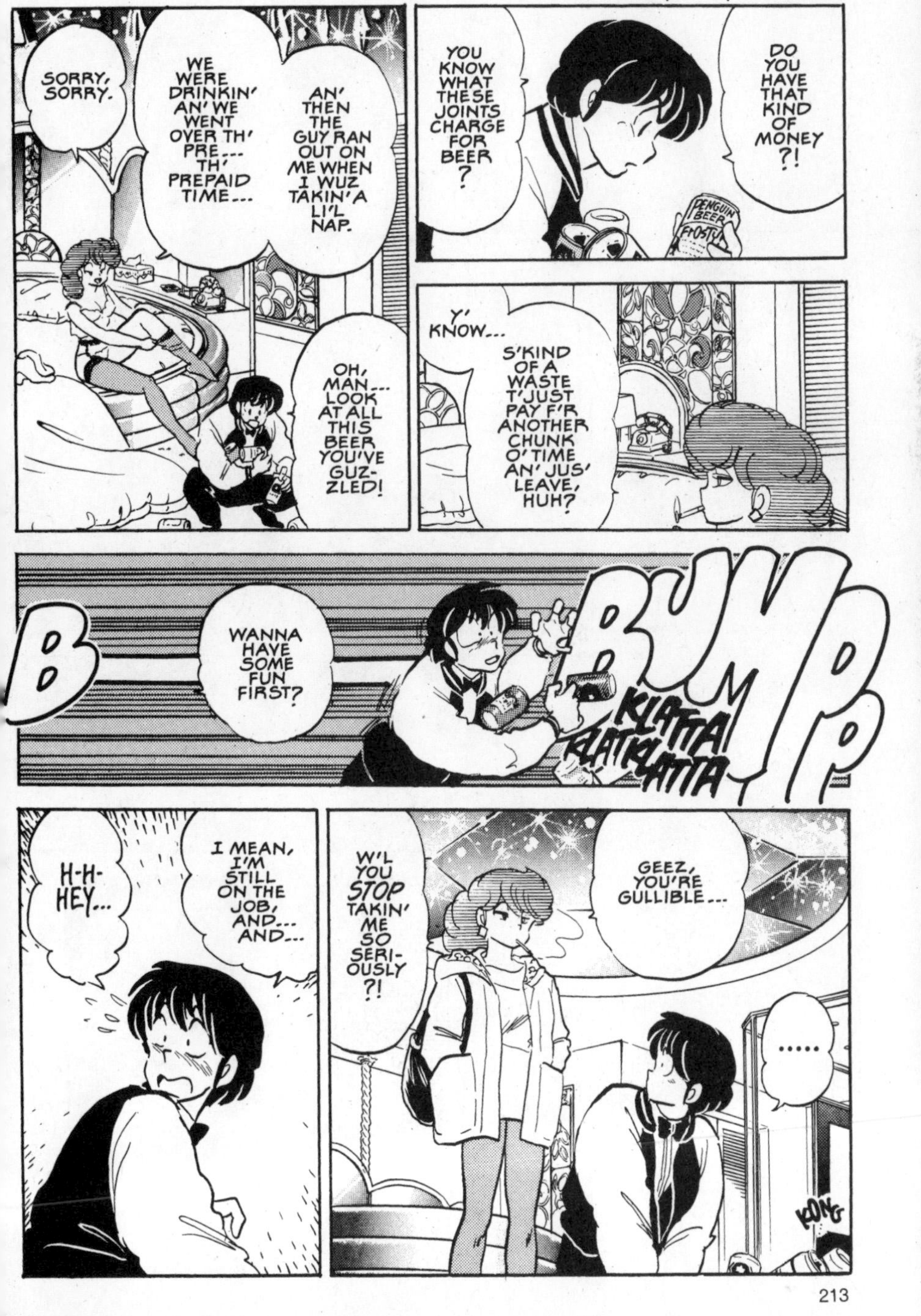
SORRY, SORRY.
WE WERE DRINKIN' AN' WE WENT OVER TH' PRE--- TH' PREPAID TIME---
AN' THEN THE GUY RAN OUT ON ME WHEN I WUZ TAKIN' A LI'L NAP.
OH, MAN--- LOOK AT ALL THIS BEER YOU'VE GUZZLED!
YOU KNOW WHAT THESE JOINTS CHARGE FOR BEER?
DO YOU HAVE THAT KIND OF MONEY?!
PENGUIN BEER FROSTY
Y' KNOW---
S'KIND OF A WASTE T'JUST PAY F'R ANOTHER CHUNK O'TIME AN' JUS' LEAVE, HUH?
WANNA HAVE SOME FUN FIRST?
BUMP
KLATTA KLATKLATTA
H-H-HEY...
I MEAN, I'M STILL ON THE JOB, AND--- AND---
W'L YOU STOP TAKIN' ME SO SERIOUSLY?!
GEEZ, YOU'RE GULLIBLE---
......
KONG

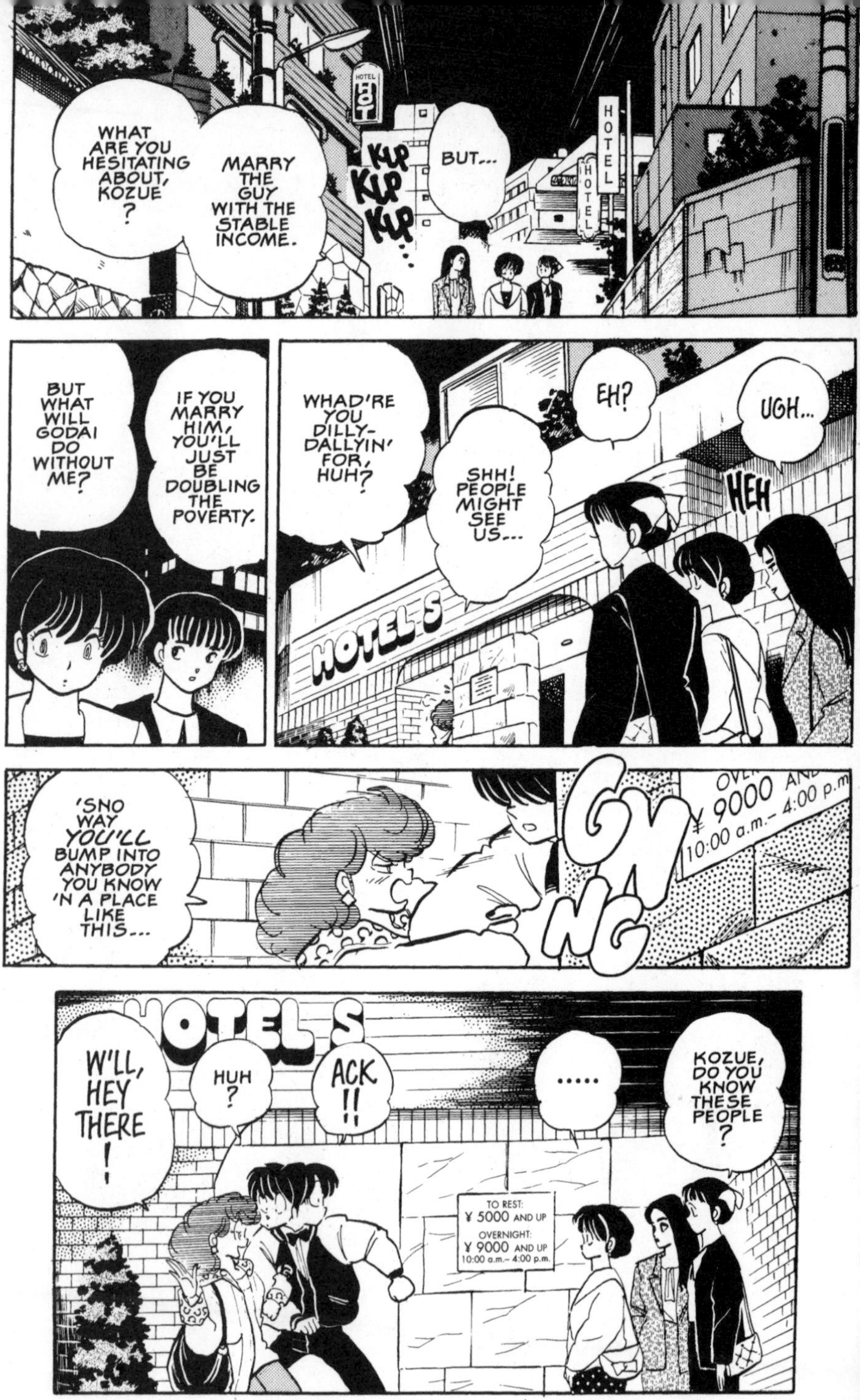
HOTEL
WHAT ARE YOU HESITATING ABOUT, KOZUE?
MARRY THE GUY WITH THE STABLE INCOME.
KLIP KLIP KLIP
BUT...
HOTEL
HOTEL
BUT WHAT WILL GODAI DO WITHOUT ME?
IF YOU MARRY HIM, YOU'LL JUST BE DOUBLING THE POVERTY.
WHAD'RE YOU DILLY-DALLYIN' FOR, HUH?
SHH! PEOPLE MIGHT SEE US...
EH?
UGH...
HEH
HOTEL S
'SNO WAY YOU'LL BUMP INTO ANYBODY YOU KNOW 'N A PLACE LIKE THIS...
GNNG
¥ 9000
10:00 a.m.– 4:00 p.m
HOTEL S
W'LL, HEY THERE!
HUH?
ACK!!
.....
KOZUE, DO YOU KNOW THESE PEOPLE?
TO REST:
¥ 5000 AND UP
OVERNIGHT:
¥ 9000 AND UP
10:00 a.m.– 4:00 p.m.

PART ELEVEN
HOTEL INCIDENT

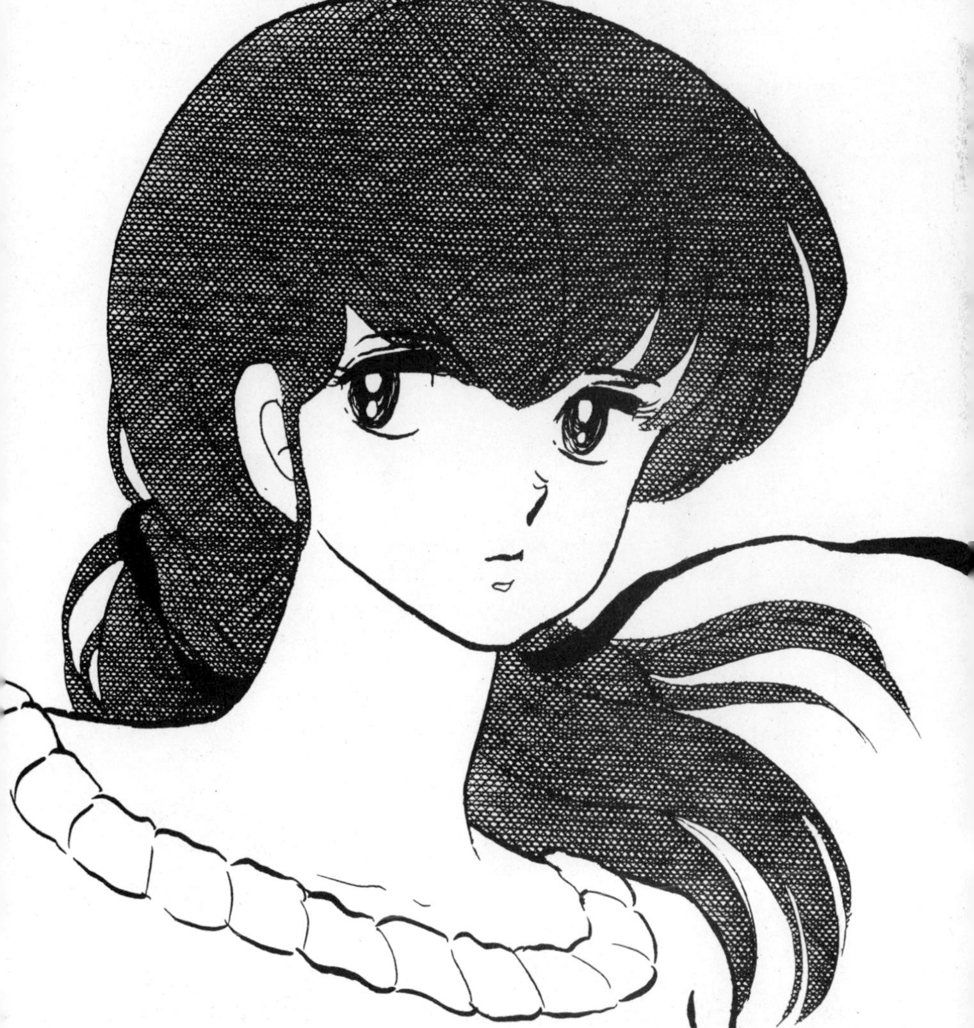

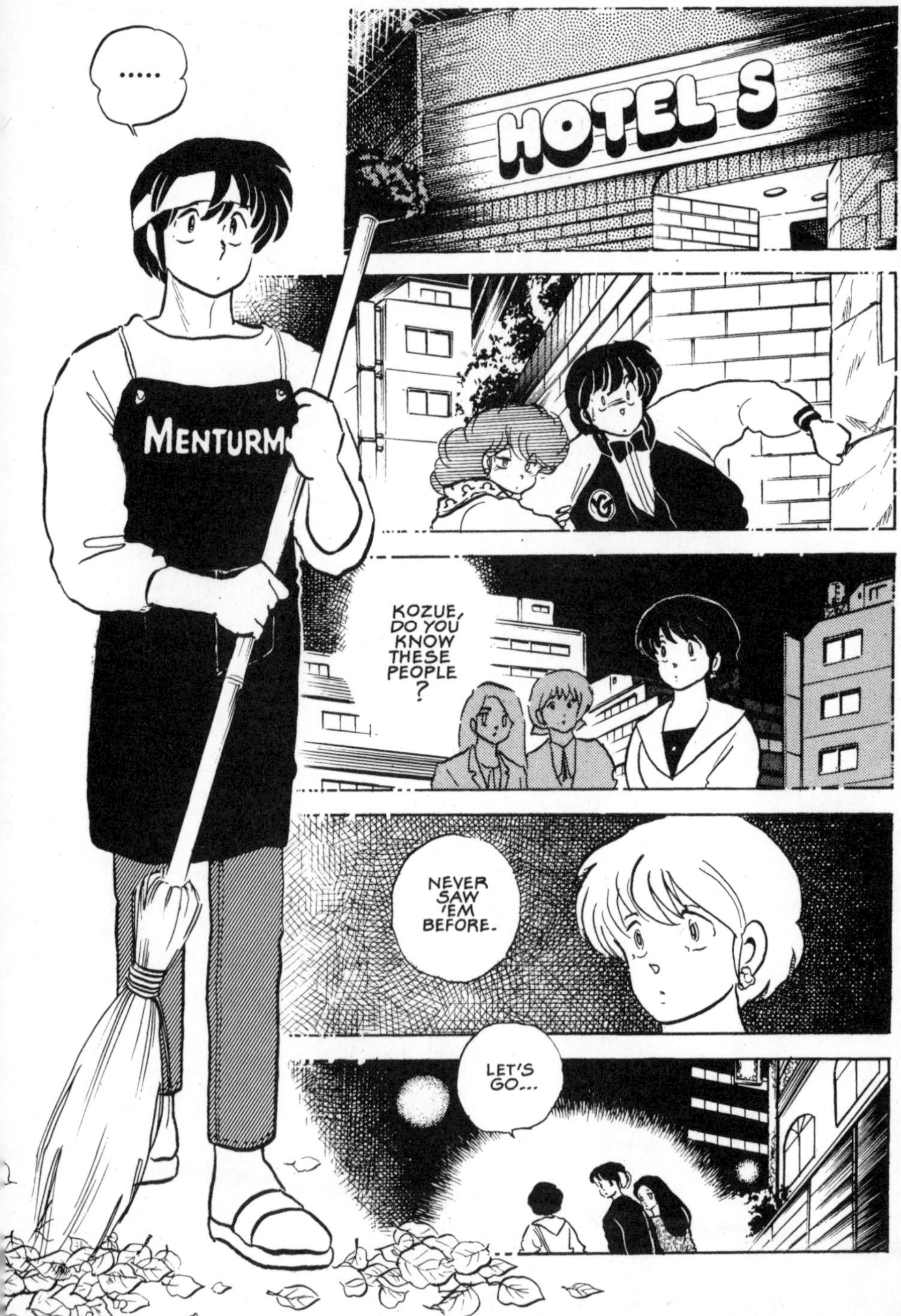
......
HOTEL S
MENTURM
KOZUE, DO YOU KNOW THESE PEOPLE ?
NEVER SAW 'EM BEFORE.
LET'S GO...

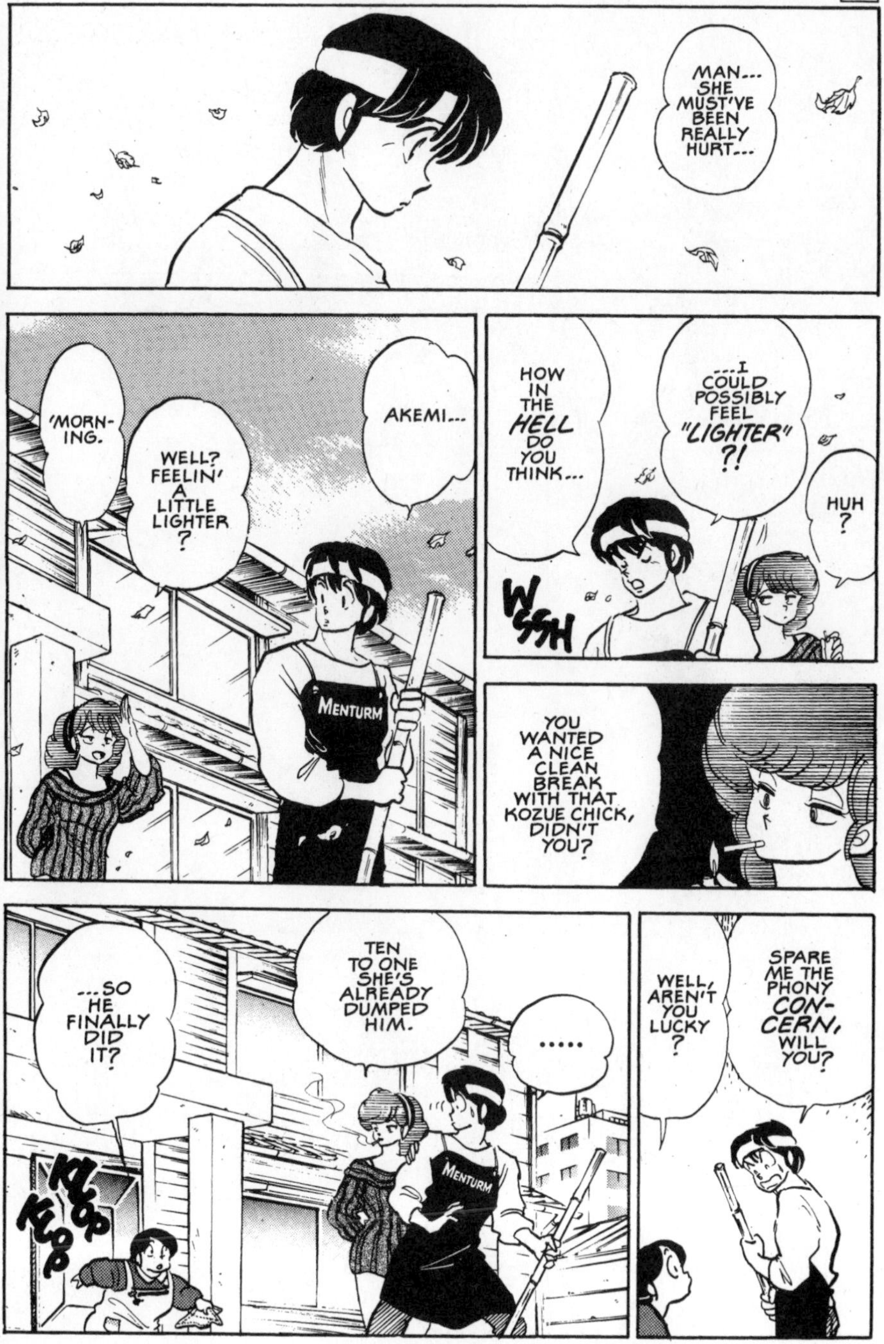
MAN... SHE MUST'VE BEEN REALLY HURT...
'MORN-ING.
WELL? FEELIN' A LITTLE LIGHTER?
AKEMI...
HOW IN THE HELL DO YOU THINK...
...I COULD POSSIBLY FEEL "LIGHTER"?!
HUH?
WSSH
YOU WANTED A NICE CLEAN BREAK WITH THAT KOZUE CHICK, DIDN'T YOU?
MENTURM
...SO HE FINALLY DID IT?
KLOP KLOP
TEN TO ONE SHE'S ALREADY DUMPED HIM.
.....
MENTURM
WELL, AREN'T YOU LUCKY?
SPARE ME THE PHONY CON-CERN, WILL YOU?

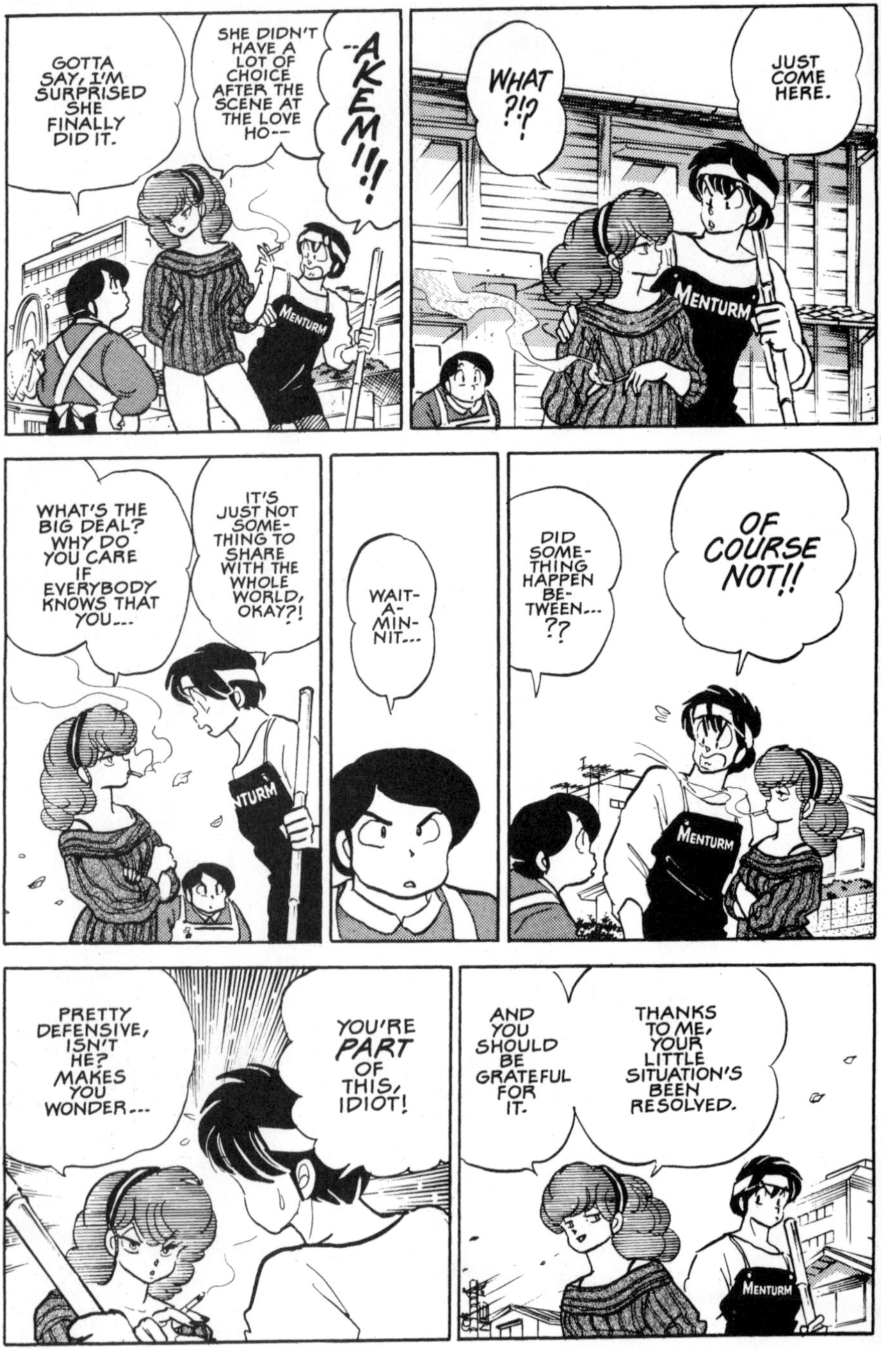

GOTTA SAY, I'M SURPRISED SHE FINALLY DID IT.
SHE DIDN'T HAVE A LOT OF CHOICE AFTER THE SCENE AT THE LOVE HO--
--AKEMI!!!
MENTURM
WHAT ?!?
JUST COME HERE.
MENTURM
WHAT'S THE BIG DEAL? WHY DO YOU CARE IF EVERYBODY KNOWS THAT YOU...
IT'S JUST NOT SOMETHING TO SHARE WITH THE WHOLE WORLD, OKAY?!
NTURM
WAIT-A-MIN-NIT...
DID SOMETHING HAPPEN BETWEEN...??
OF COURSE NOT!!
MENTURM
PRETTY DEFENSIVE, ISN'T HE? MAKES YOU WONDER...
YOU'RE *PART* OF THIS, IDIOT!
THANKS TO ME, YOUR LITTLE SITUATION'S BEEN RESOLVED.
AND YOU SHOULD BE GRATEFUL FOR IT.
MENTURM

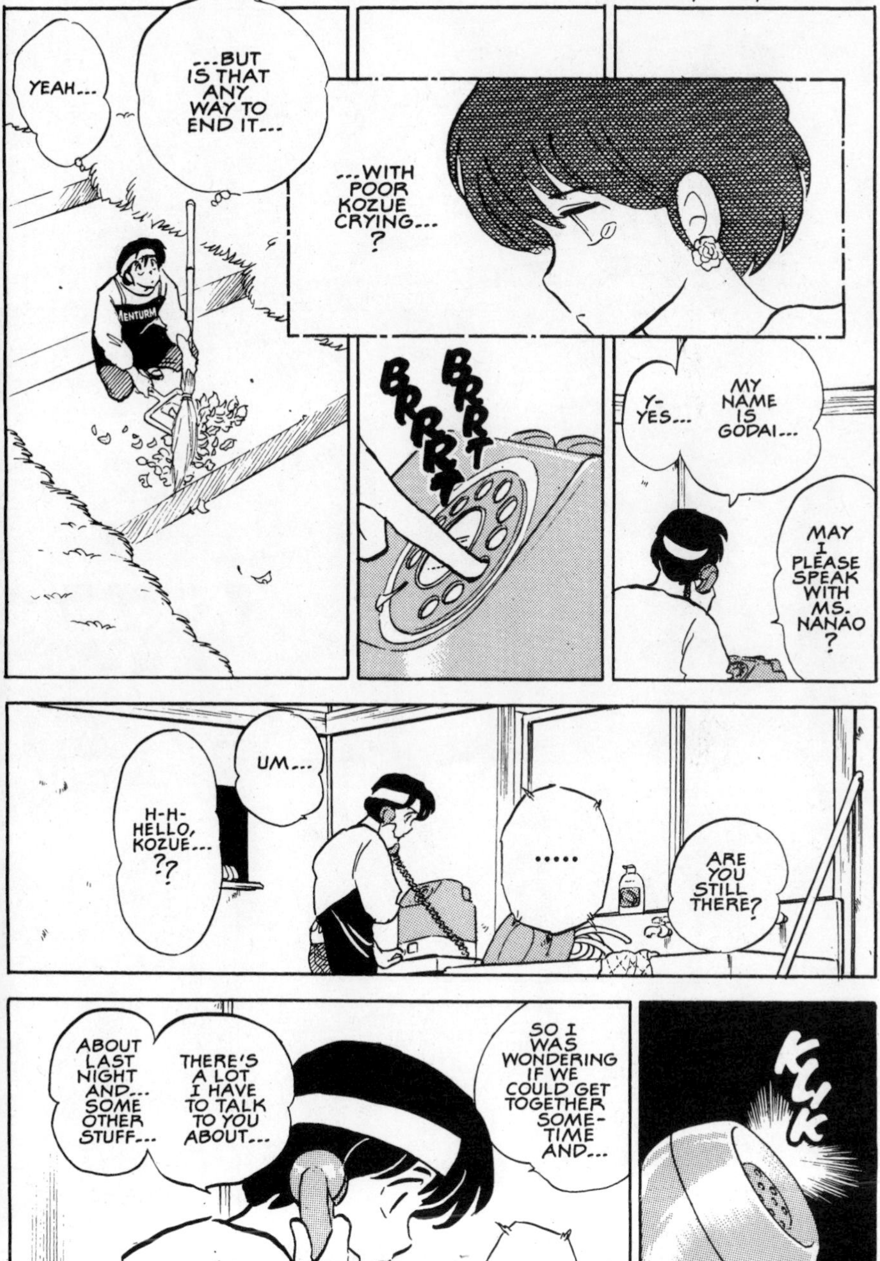
YEAH...
...BUT IS THAT ANY WAY TO END IT...
...WITH POOR KOZUE CRYING...?
BRRRT
BRRRT
Y-YES...
MY NAME IS GODAI...
MAY I PLEASE SPEAK WITH MS. NANAO?
H-H-HELLO, KOZUE...??
UM...
.....
ARE YOU STILL THERE?
ABOUT LAST NIGHT AND... SOME OTHER STUFF...
THERE'S A LOT I HAVE TO TALK TO YOU ABOUT...
SO I WAS WONDERING IF WE COULD GET TOGETHER SOME-TIME AND...
.....
KLIK

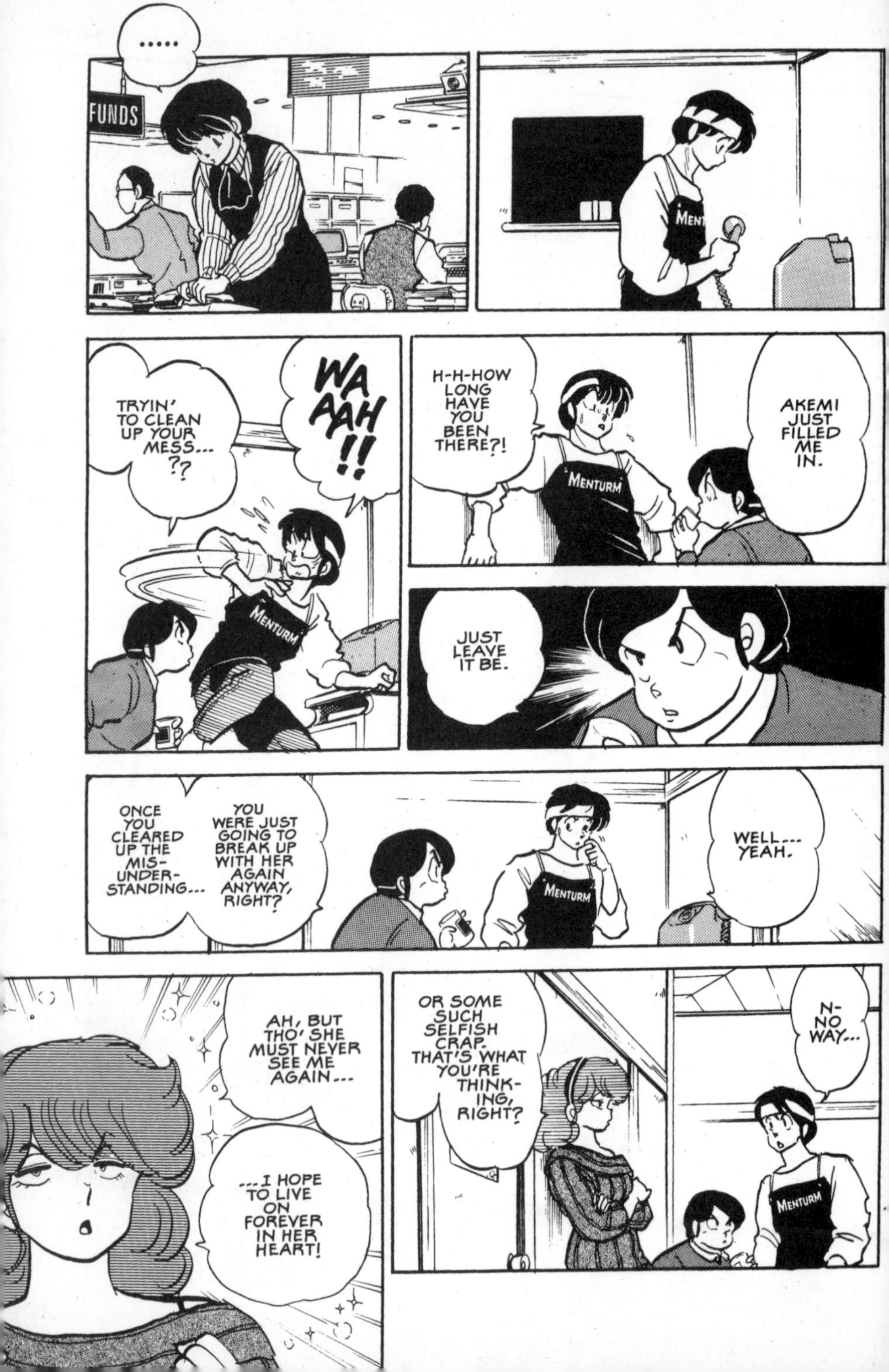
......
FUNDS
MENTURM
TRYIN' TO CLEAN UP YOUR MESS...??
WA AAH!!
H-H-HOW LONG HAVE YOU BEEN THERE?!
AKEMI JUST FILLED ME IN.
JUST LEAVE IT BE.
ONCE YOU CLEARED UP THE MIS-UNDER-STANDING...
YOU WERE JUST GOING TO BREAK UP WITH HER AGAIN ANYWAY, RIGHT?
WELL... YEAH.
AH, BUT THO' SHE MUST NEVER SEE ME AGAIN...
...I HOPE TO LIVE ON FOREVER IN HER HEART!
OR SOME SUCH SELFISH CRAP. THAT'S WHAT YOU'RE THINK-ING, RIGHT?
N-NO WAY...

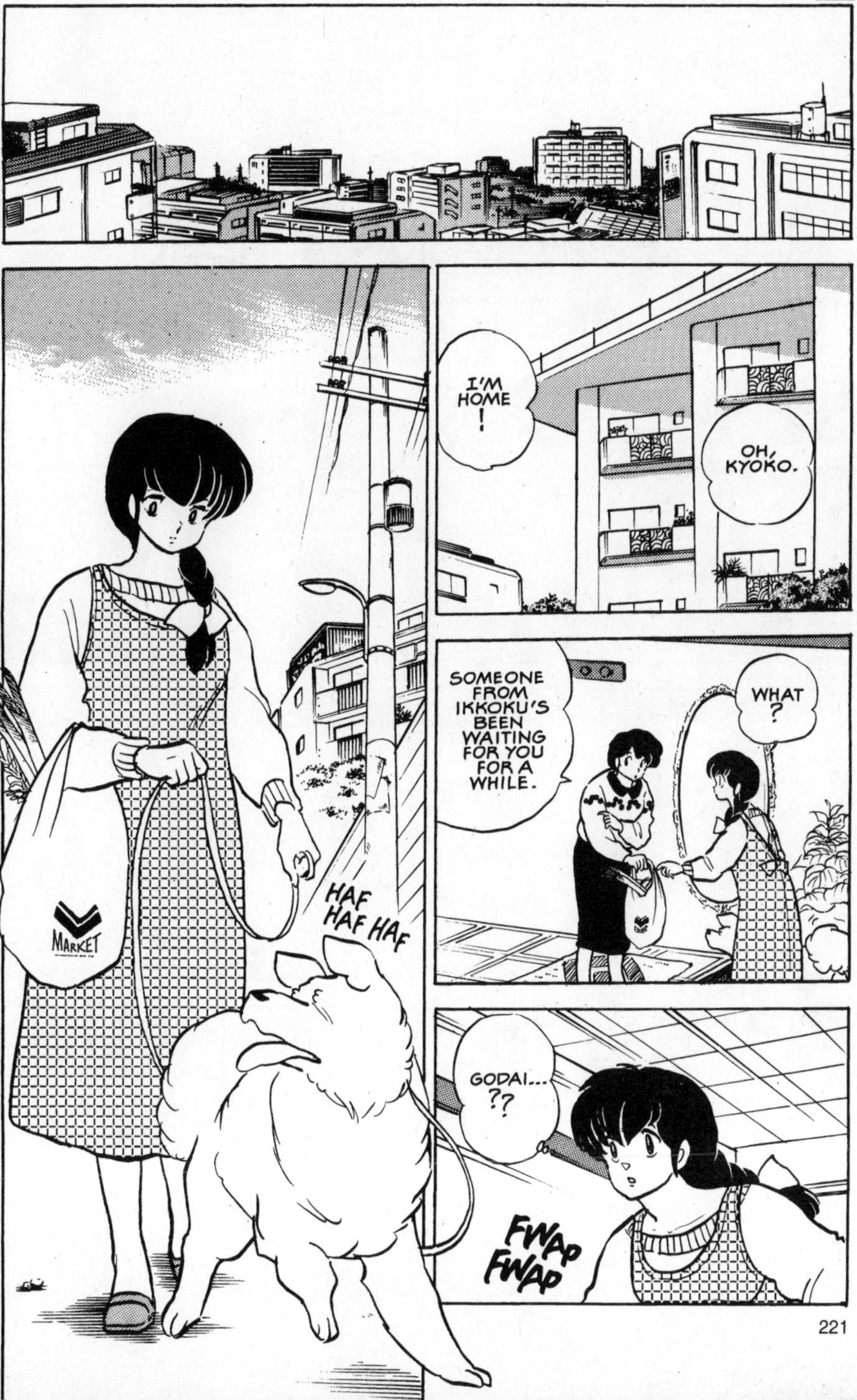
MARKET
HAF HAF HAF
I'M HOME !
OH, KYOKO.
SOMEONE FROM IKKOKU'S BEEN WAITING FOR YOU FOR A WHILE.
WHAT ?
GODAI... ??
FWAP FWAP

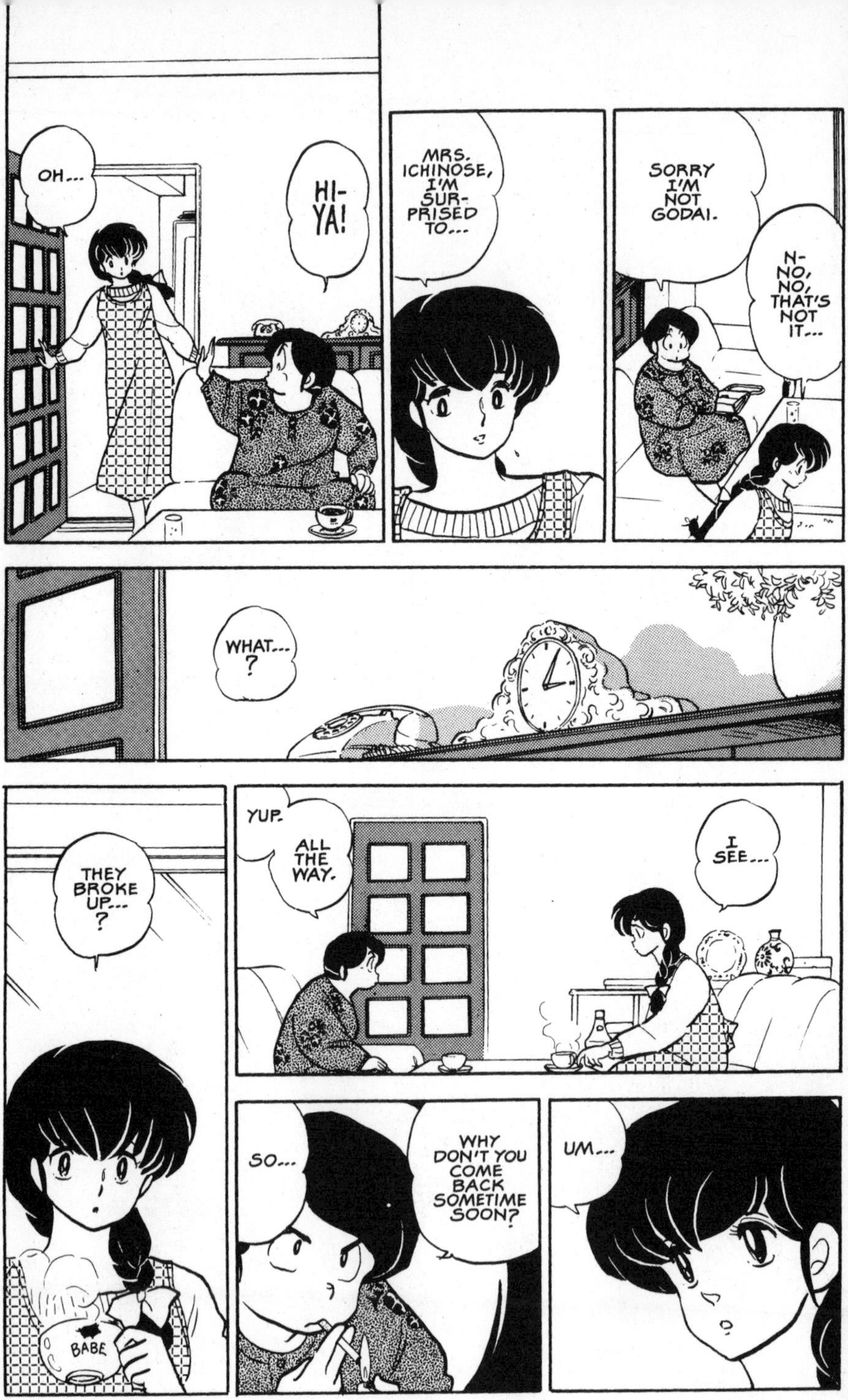
OH...
HI-YA!
MRS. ICHINOSE, I'M SUR-PRISED TO...
SORRY I'M NOT GODAI.
N-NO, NO, THAT'S NOT IT...
WHAT...?
THEY BROKE UP...?
BABE
YUP.
ALL THE WAY.
I SEE...
SO...
WHY DON'T YOU COME BACK SOMETIME SOON?
UM...

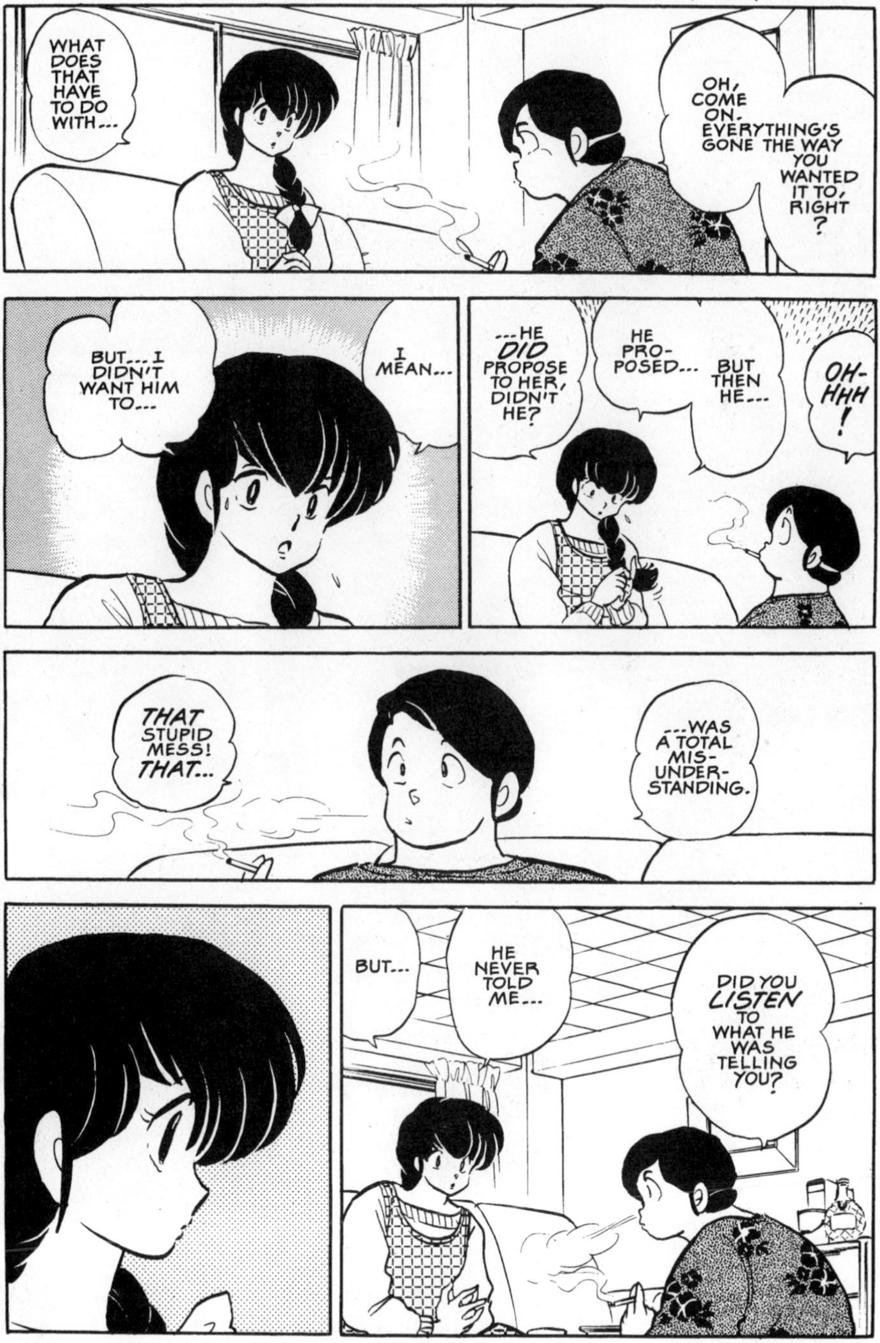
WHAT DOES THAT HAVE TO DO WITH...
OH, COME ON. EVERYTHING'S GONE THE WAY YOU WANTED IT TO, RIGHT?
BUT... I DIDN'T WANT HIM TO...
I MEAN...
...HE *DID* PROPOSE TO HER, DIDN'T HE?
HE PRO-POSED...
BUT THEN HE...
OH-HHH!
THAT STUPID MESS! *THAT*...
...WAS A TOTAL MIS-UNDER-STANDING.
BUT...
HE NEVER TOLD ME...
DID YOU *LISTEN* TO WHAT HE WAS TELLING *YOU*?

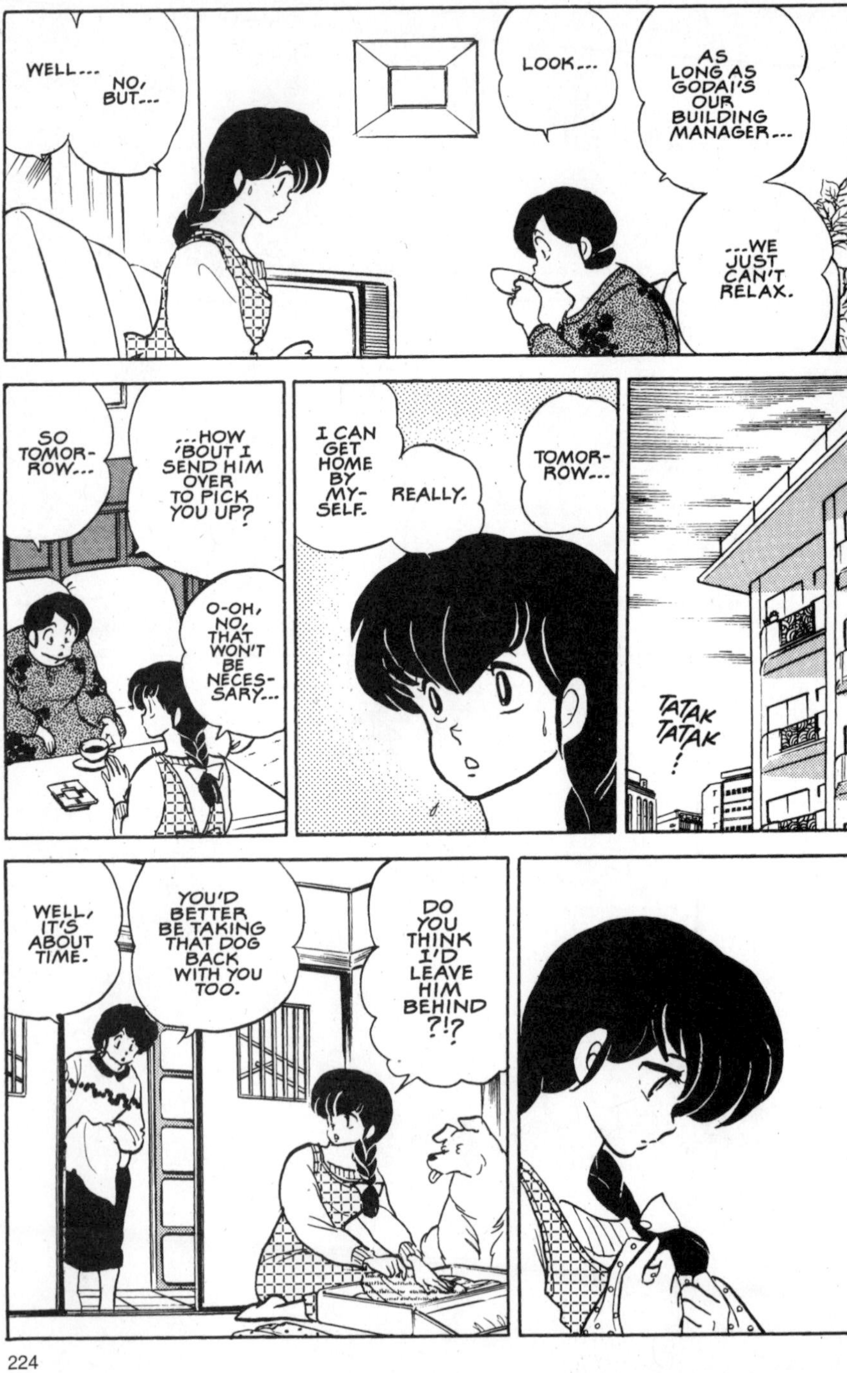
WELL... NO, BUT...
LOOK...
AS LONG AS GODAI'S OUR BUILDING MANAGER...
...WE JUST CAN'T RELAX.
SO TOMOR-ROW...
...HOW 'BOUT I SEND HIM OVER TO PICK YOU UP?
O-OH, NO, THAT WON'T BE NECES-SARY...
I CAN GET HOME BY MY-SELF.
REALLY.
TOMOR-ROW...
TATAK TATAK
WELL, IT'S ABOUT TIME.
YOU'D BETTER BE TAKING THAT DOG BACK WITH YOU TOO.
DO YOU THINK I'D LEAVE HIM BEHIND ?!?

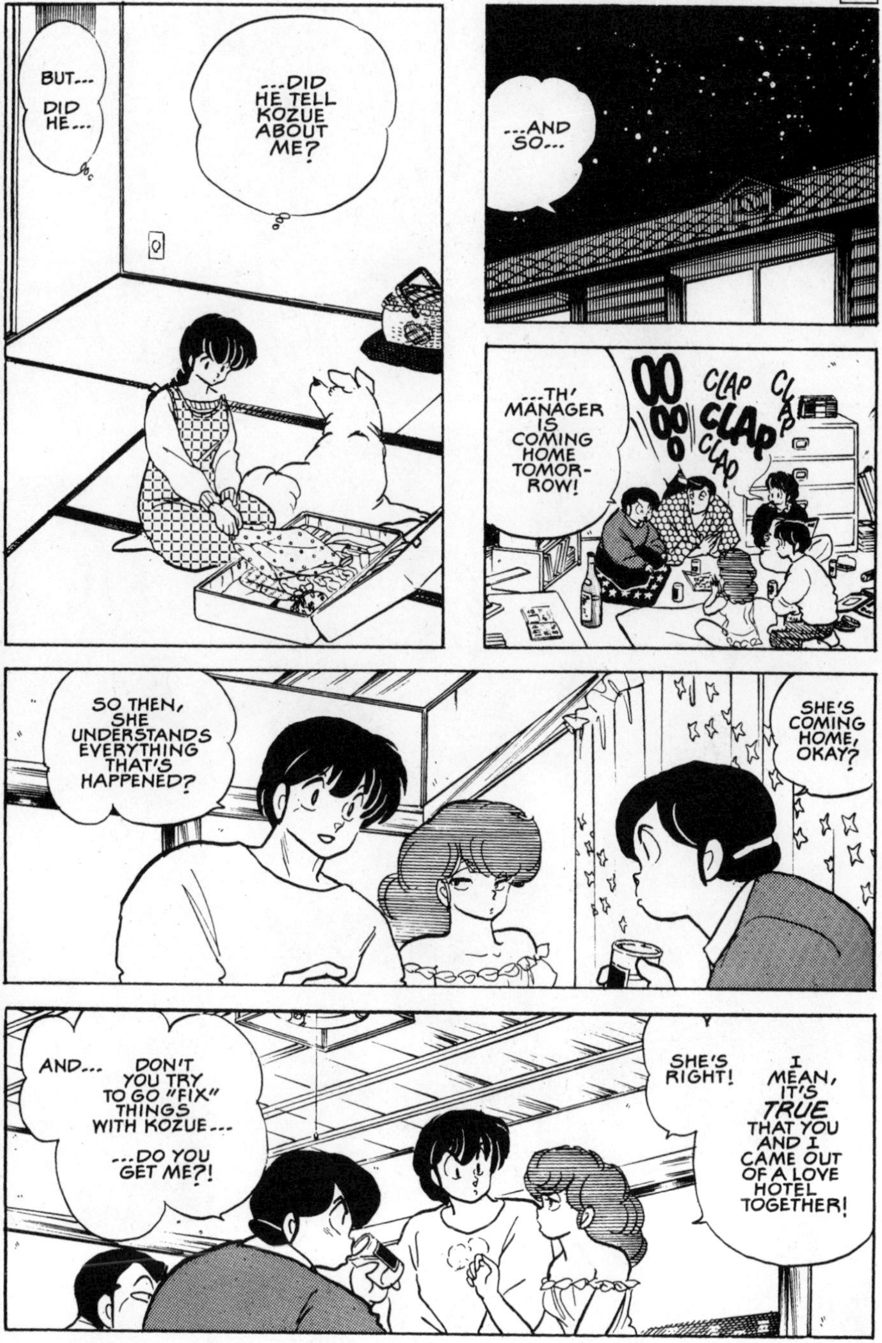
BUT... DID HE...
...DID HE TELL KOZUE ABOUT ME?
...AND SO...
...TH' MANAGER IS COMING HOME TOMORROW!
OOOOO
CLAP CLAP CLAP CLAP CLAP
SO THEN, SHE UNDERSTANDS EVERYTHING THAT'S HAPPENED?
SHE'S COMING HOME, OKAY?
AND... DON'T YOU TRY TO GO "FIX" THINGS WITH KOZUE...
...DO YOU GET ME?!
SHE'S RIGHT!
I MEAN, IT'S *TRUE* THAT YOU AND I CAME OUT OF A LOVE HOTEL TOGETHER!

MR. GODAI, YOU DISAPPOINT ME!

WE CAME OUT TOGETHER!

WE ONLY CAME OUT!

AND HOW DOES ONE "COME OUT" WITHOUT GOING IN?

WE DIDN'T DO ANYTHING!

.....

WHEN I WOKE UP, YOU WERE ON TOP OF ME...

HOW DO I KNOW YOU DIDN'T DO ANYTHING?

WHY WOULD I...?!?

IF YOU'VE GOT NOTHING TO HIDE...

...LOOK ME STRAIGHT IN THE EYE.

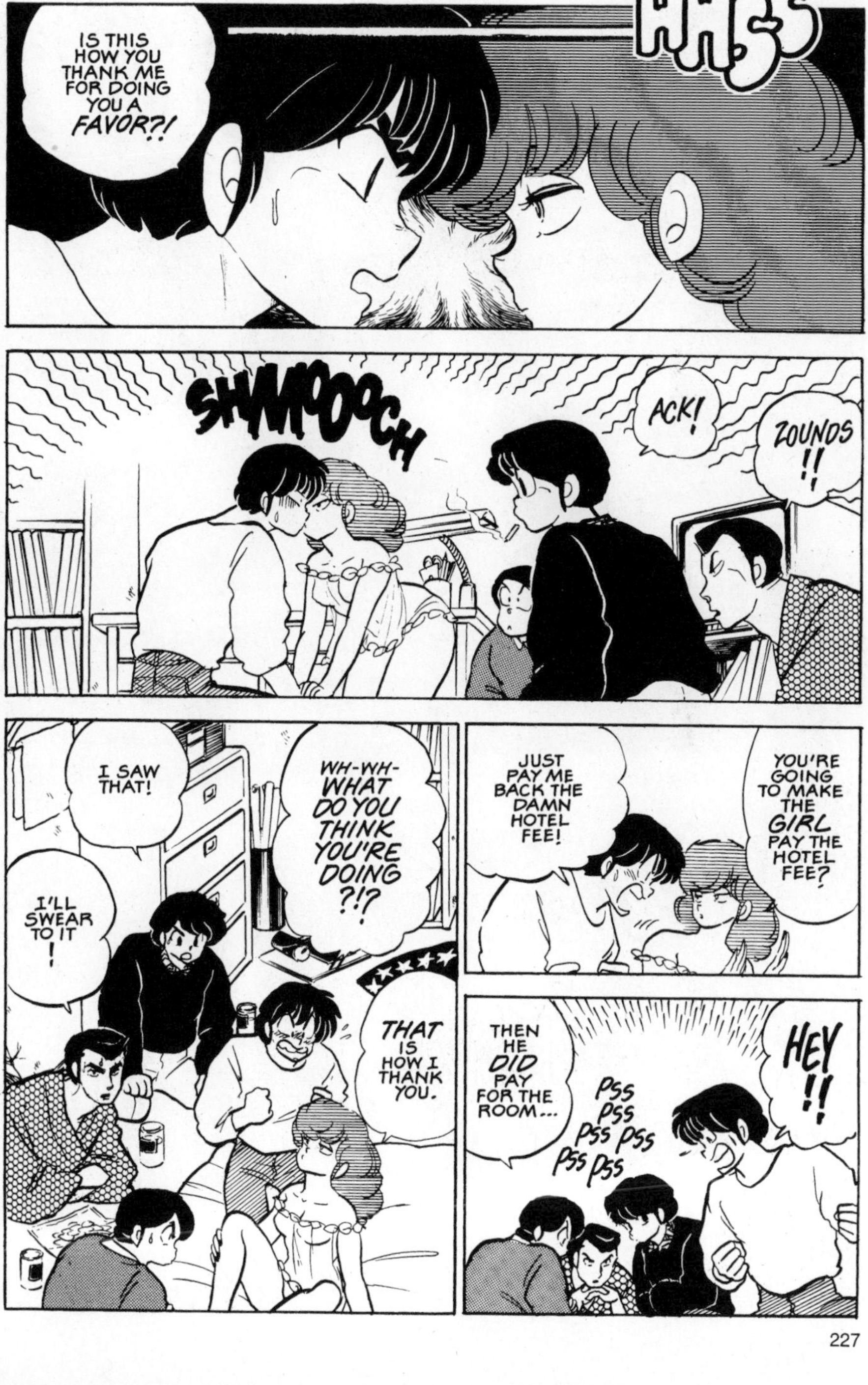
IS THIS HOW YOU THANK ME FOR DOING YOU A FAVOR?!
HHS-S
SHMOOOCH
ACK!
ZOUNDS !!
I SAW THAT!
I'LL SWEAR TO IT!
WH-WH-WHAT DO YOU THINK YOU'RE DOING ?!?
THAT IS HOW I THANK YOU.
JUST PAY ME BACK THE DAMN HOTEL FEE!
YOU'RE GOING TO MAKE THE GIRL PAY THE HOTEL FEE?
THEN HE DID PAY FOR THE ROOM...
PSS PSS PSS PSS PSS PSS
HEY !!

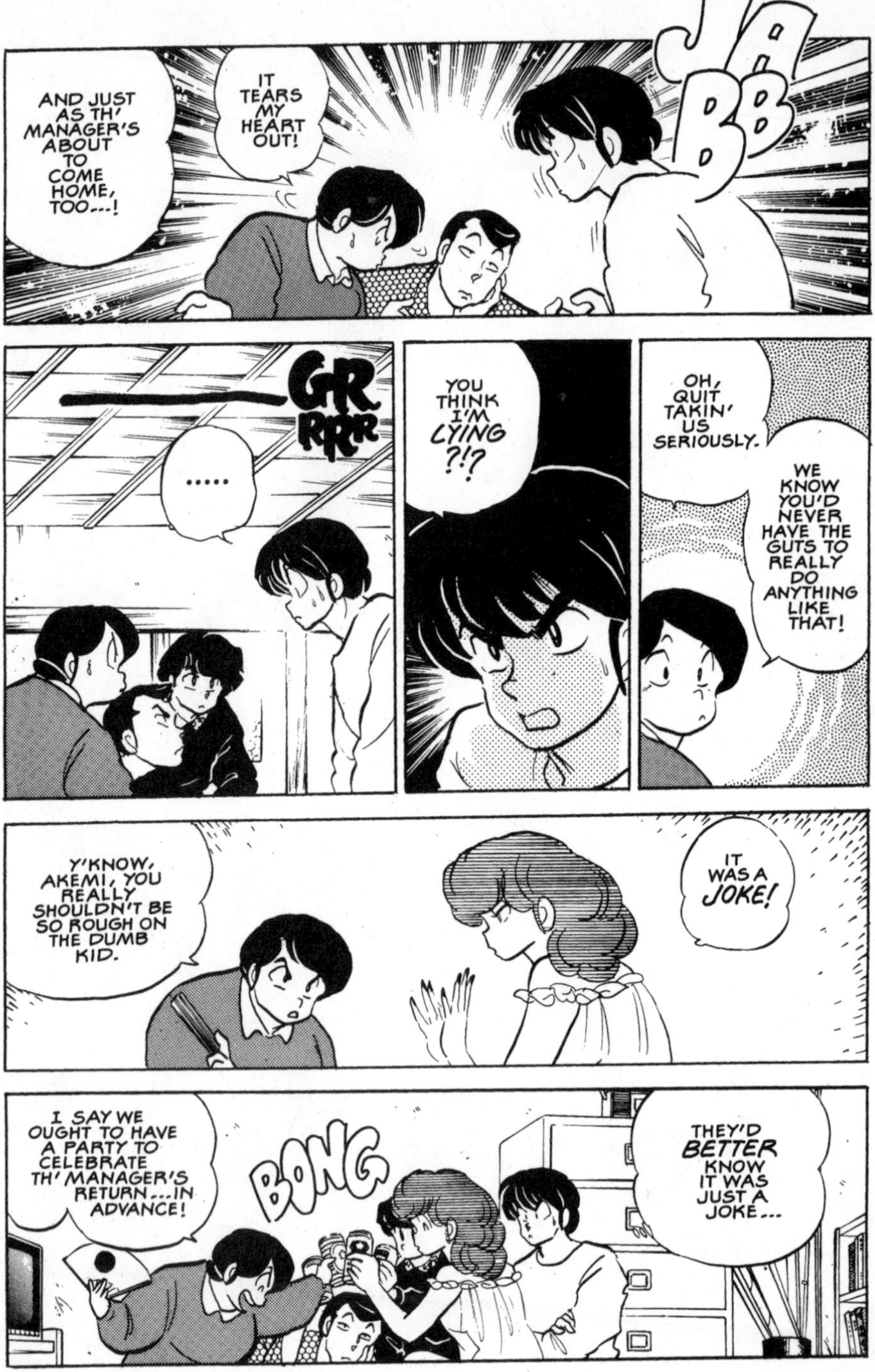
AND JUST AS TH' MANAGER'S ABOUT TO COME HOME, TOO...!
IT TEARS MY HEART OUT!
JABBB
.....
GRRRR
YOU THINK I'M LYING ?!?
OH, QUIT TAKIN' US SERIOUSLY.
WE KNOW YOU'D NEVER HAVE THE GUTS TO REALLY DO ANYTHING LIKE THAT!
Y'KNOW, AKEMI, YOU REALLY SHOULDN'T BE SO ROUGH ON THE DUMB KID.
IT WAS A JOKE!
I SAY WE OUGHT TO HAVE A PARTY TO CELEBRATE TH' MANAGER'S RETURN...IN ADVANCE!
BONG
THEY'D BETTER KNOW IT WAS JUST A JOKE...

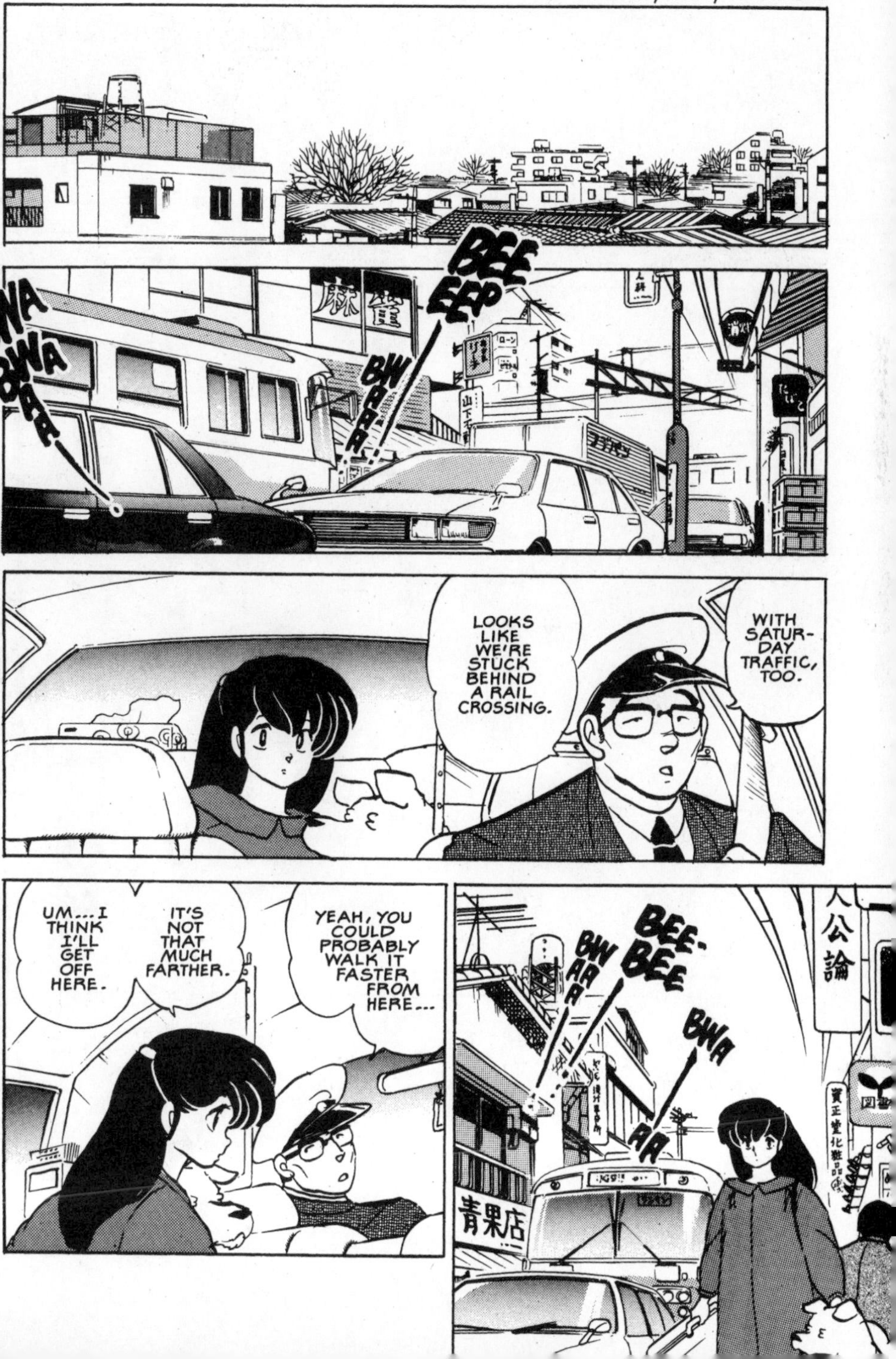
BEE EEP
BWAAAA!
LOOKS LIKE WE'RE STUCK BEHIND A RAIL CROSSING.
WITH SATURDAY TRAFFIC, TOO.
UM... I THINK I'LL GET OFF HERE.
IT'S NOT THAT MUCH FARTHER.
YEAH, YOU COULD PROBABLY WALK IT FASTER FROM HERE...
BEE-BEE
BWAAA
BWA
AA
青果店

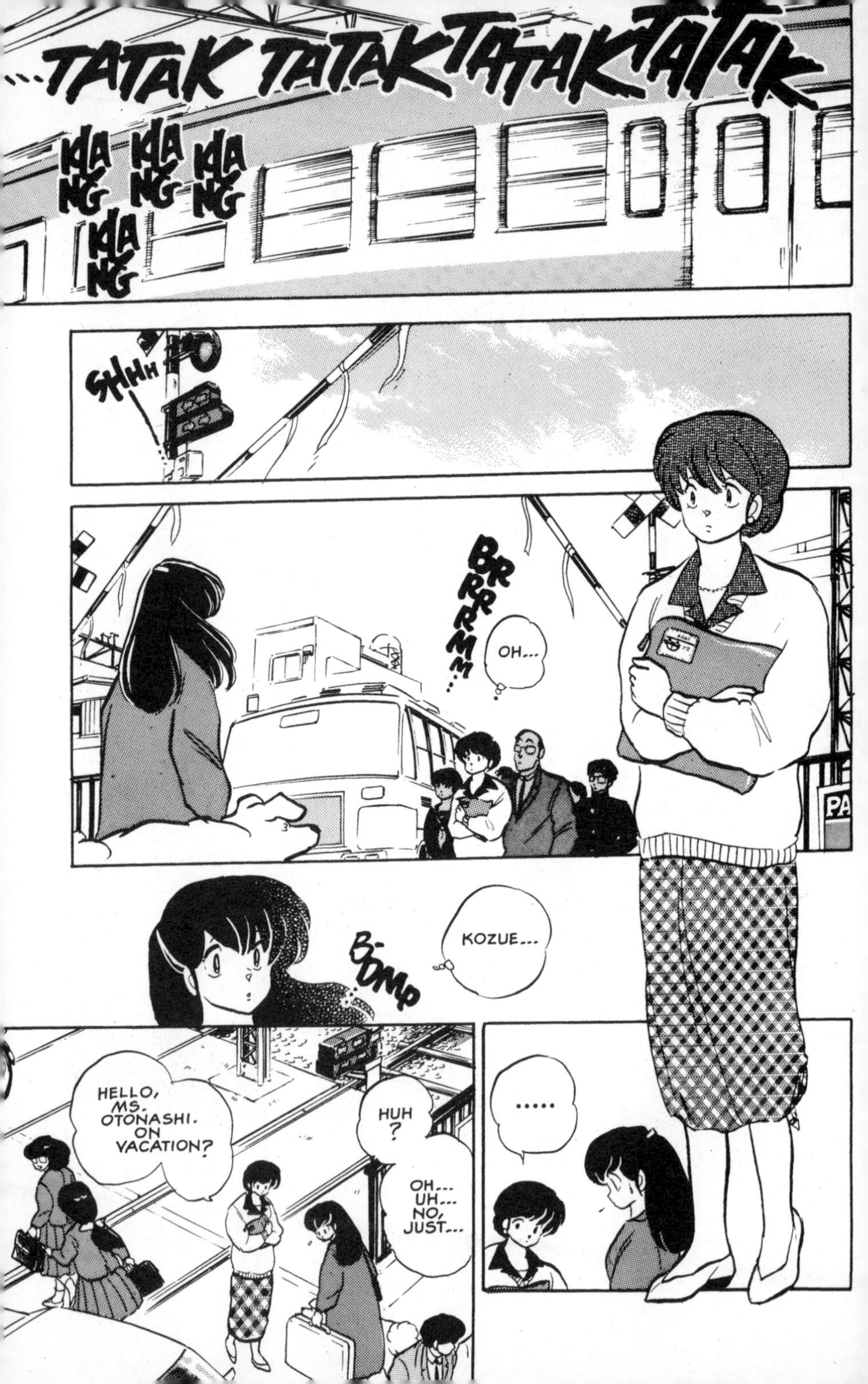
TATAK TATAK TATAK TATAK
KLANG KLANG KLANG KLANG
SHHH
BRRRRMM...
OH...
KOZUE...
B-DMP
HELLO, MS. OTONASHI. ON VACATION?
HUH?
OH... UH... NO, JUST...
.....

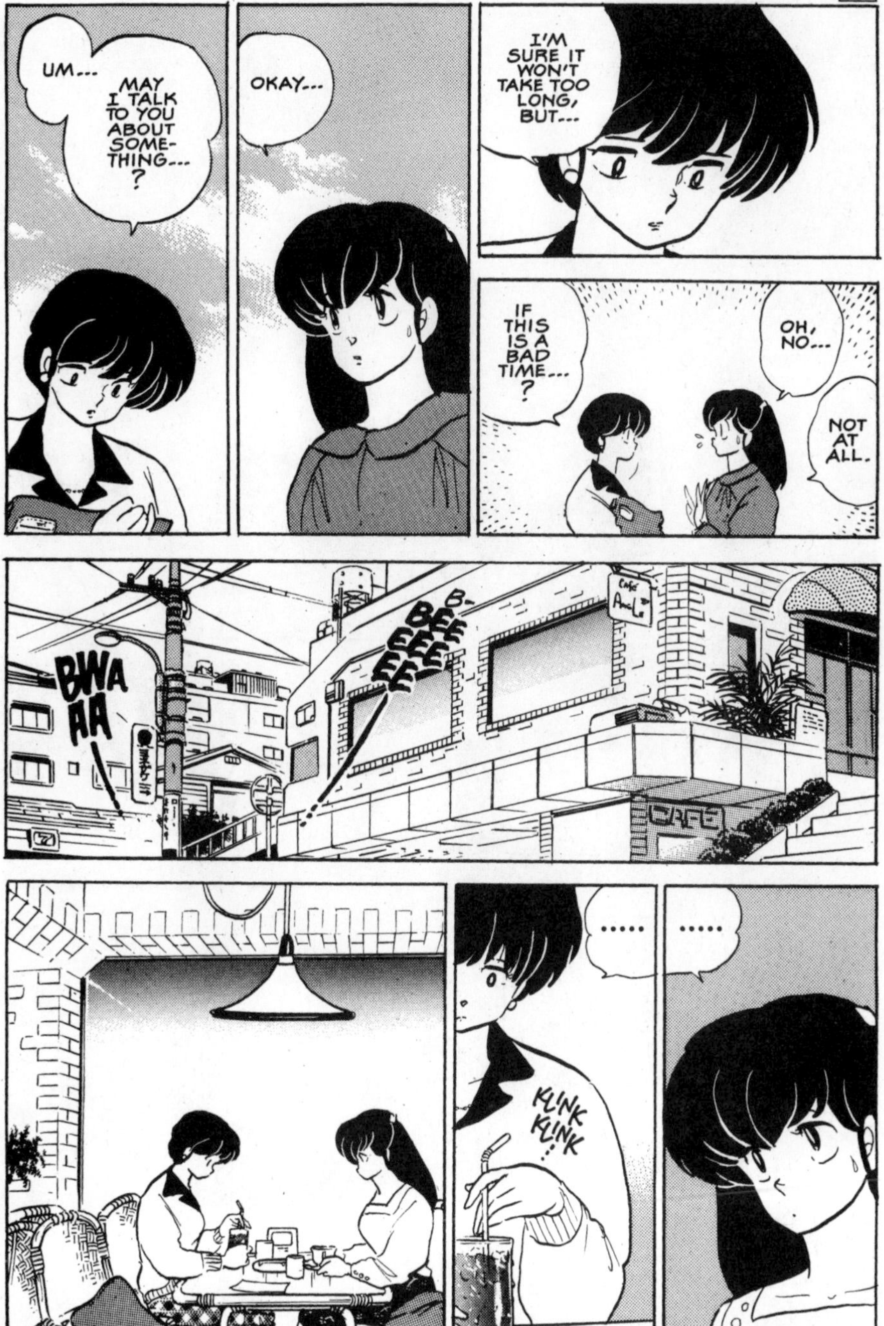
UM... MAY I TALK TO YOU ABOUT SOME- THING... ?
OKAY...
I'M SURE IT WON'T TAKE TOO LONG, BUT...
IF THIS IS A BAD TIME... ?
OH, NO...
NOT AT ALL.
BWAAA
B- BEEEEEEEE
CAFE
......
......
KLINK KLINK

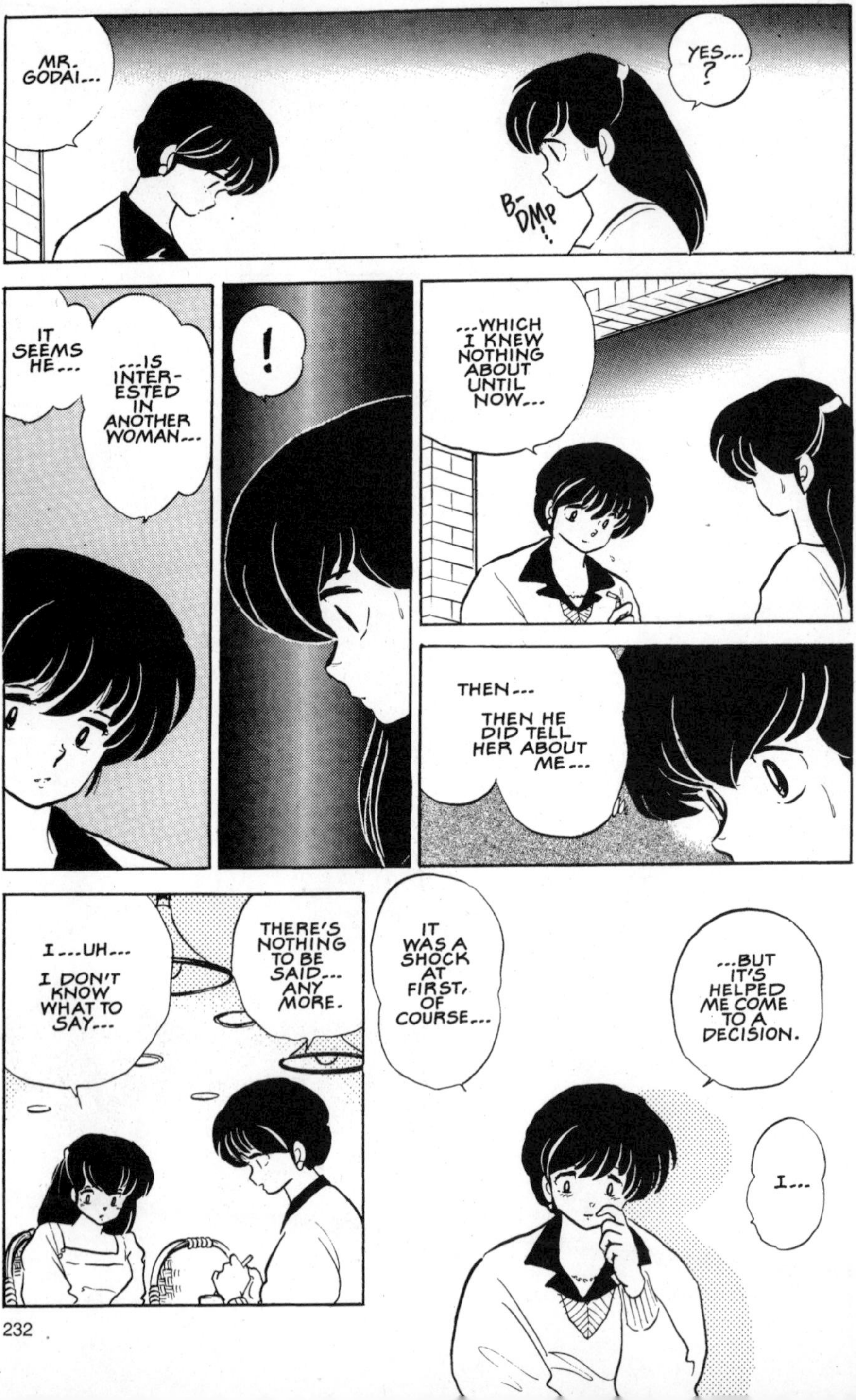
MR. GODAI...
YES... ?
B-DMP...
IT SEEMS HE...
...IS INTERESTED IN ANOTHER WOMAN...
!
...WHICH I KNEW NOTHING ABOUT UNTIL NOW...
THEN...
THEN HE DID TELL HER ABOUT ME...
I...UH...
I DON'T KNOW WHAT TO SAY...
THERE'S NOTHING TO BE SAID... ANY MORE.
IT WAS A SHOCK AT FIRST, OF COURSE...
...BUT IT'S HELPED ME COME TO A DECISION.
I...

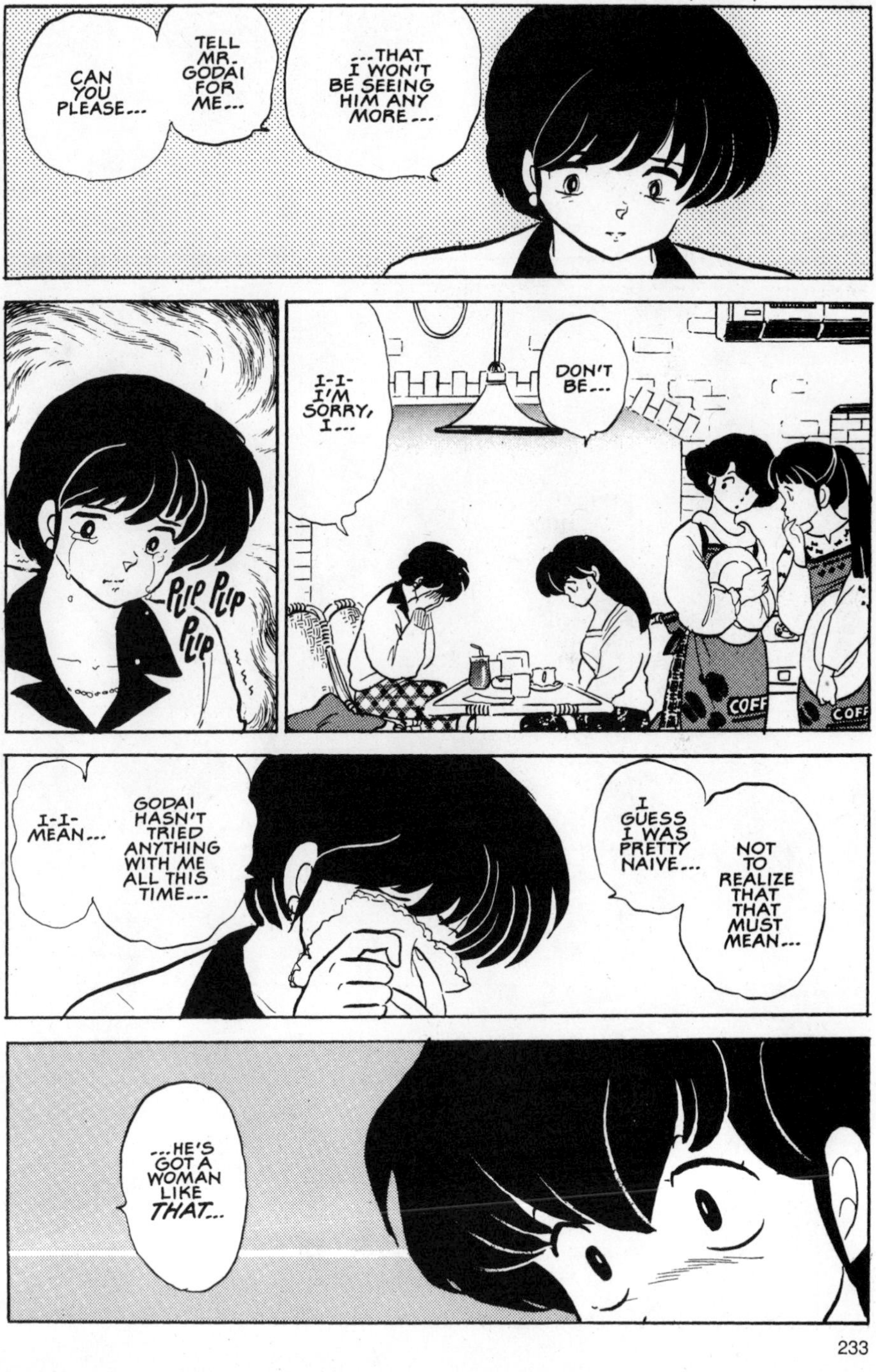
CAN YOU PLEASE...
TELL MR. GODAI FOR ME...
...THAT I WON'T BE SEEING HIM ANY MORE...
PLIP PLIP PLIP
I-I-I'M SORRY, I...
DON'T BE...
COFF
COFF
I-I-MEAN...
GODAI HASN'T TRIED ANYTHING WITH ME ALL THIS TIME...
I GUESS I WAS PRETTY NAIVE...
NOT TO REALIZE THAT THAT MUST MEAN...
...HE'S GOT A WOMAN LIKE *THAT*...

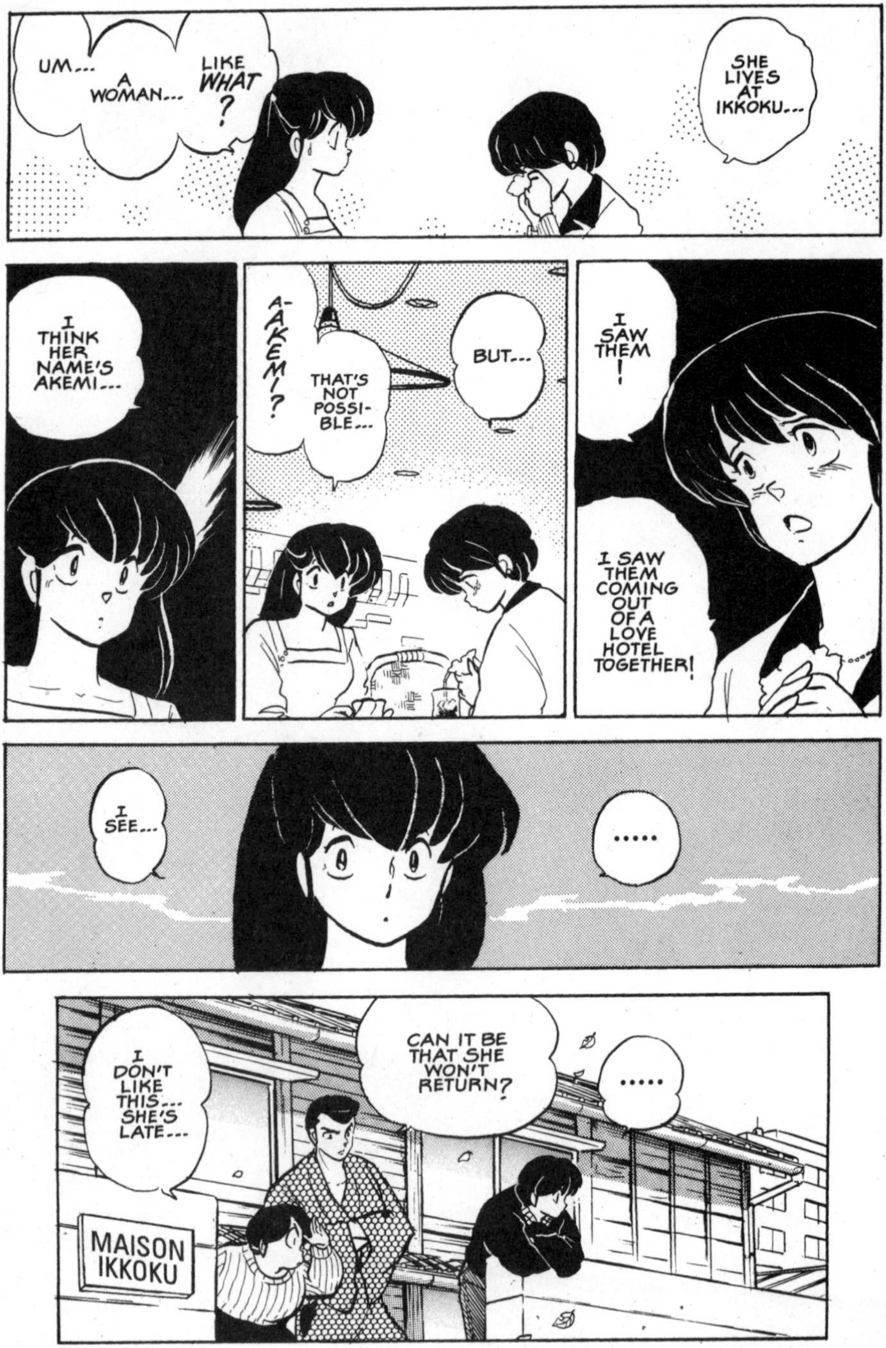
UM... A WOMAN... LIKE WHAT?
SHE LIVES AT IKKOKU...
I THINK HER NAME'S AKEMI...
A-AKEMI?
THAT'S NOT POSSIBLE...
BUT...
I SAW THEM!
I SAW THEM COMING OUT OF A LOVE HOTEL TOGETHER!
I SEE...
......
I DON'T LIKE THIS... SHE'S LATE...
CAN IT BE THAT SHE WON'T RETURN?
......
MAISON IKKOKU

PART TWELVE

THE MOST IMPORTANT DETAIL

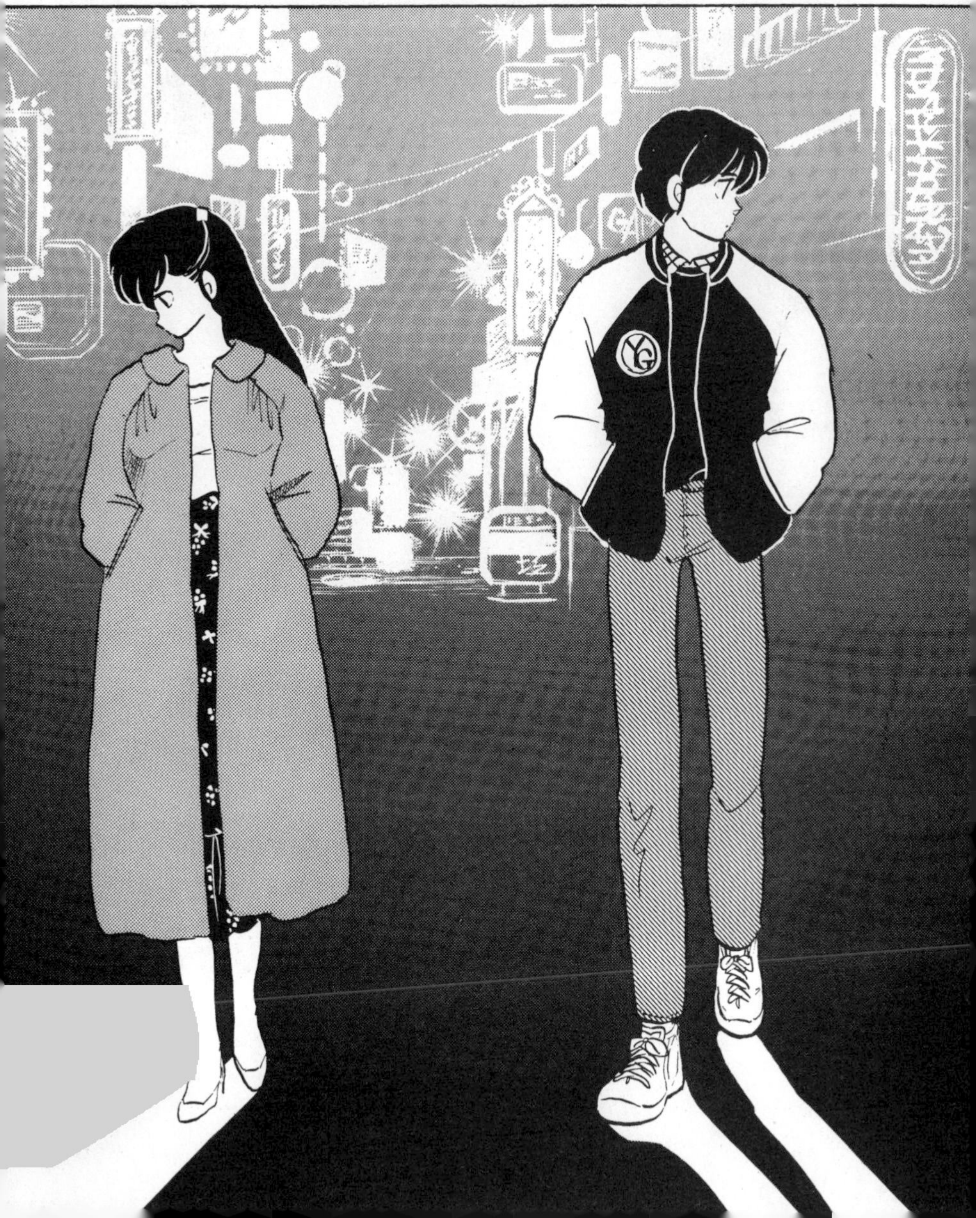

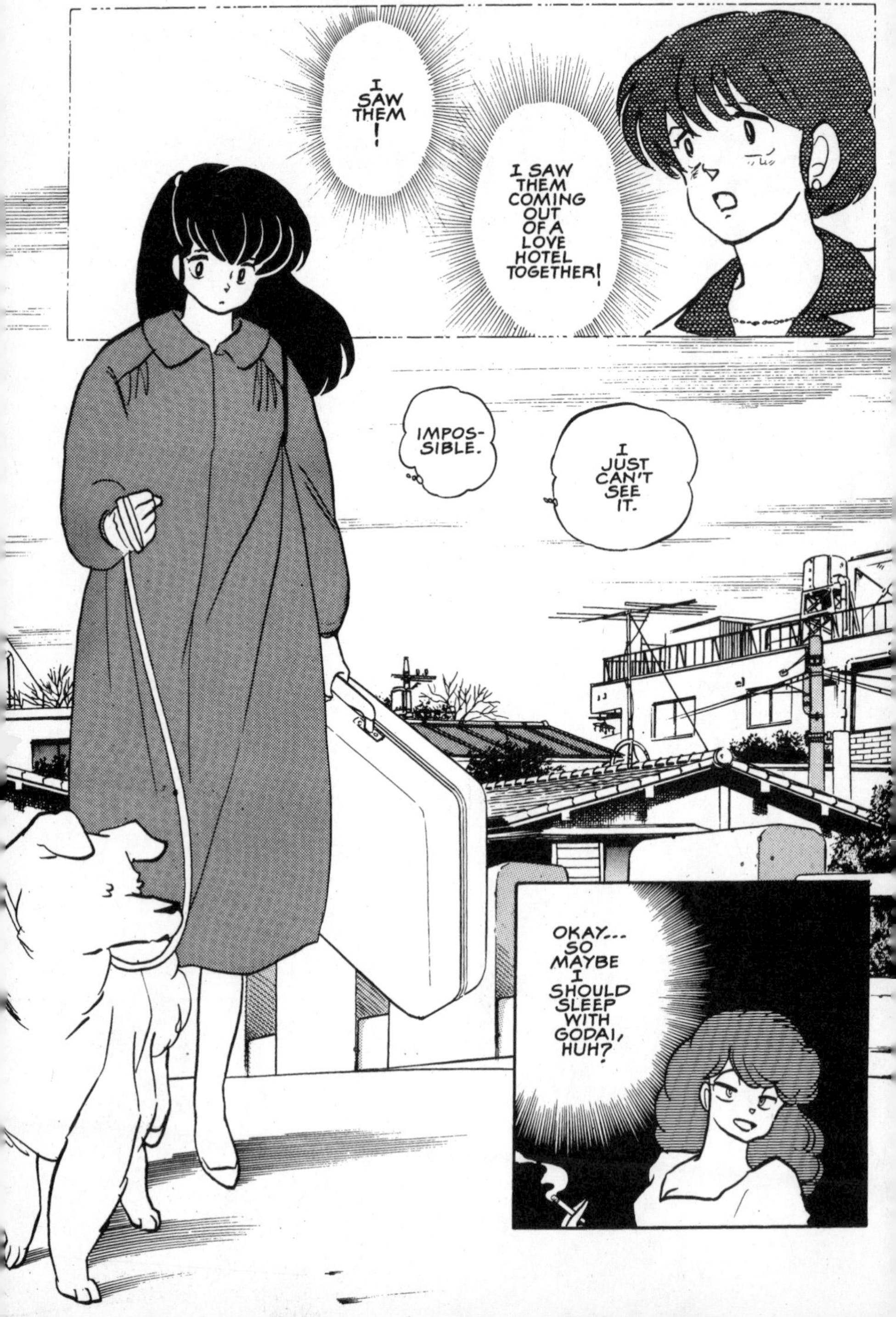
I SAW THEM!
I SAW THEM COMING OUT OF A LOVE HOTEL TOGETHER!
IMPOSSIBLE.
I JUST CAN'T SEE IT.
OKAY... SO MAYBE I SHOULD SLEEP WITH GODAI, HUH?

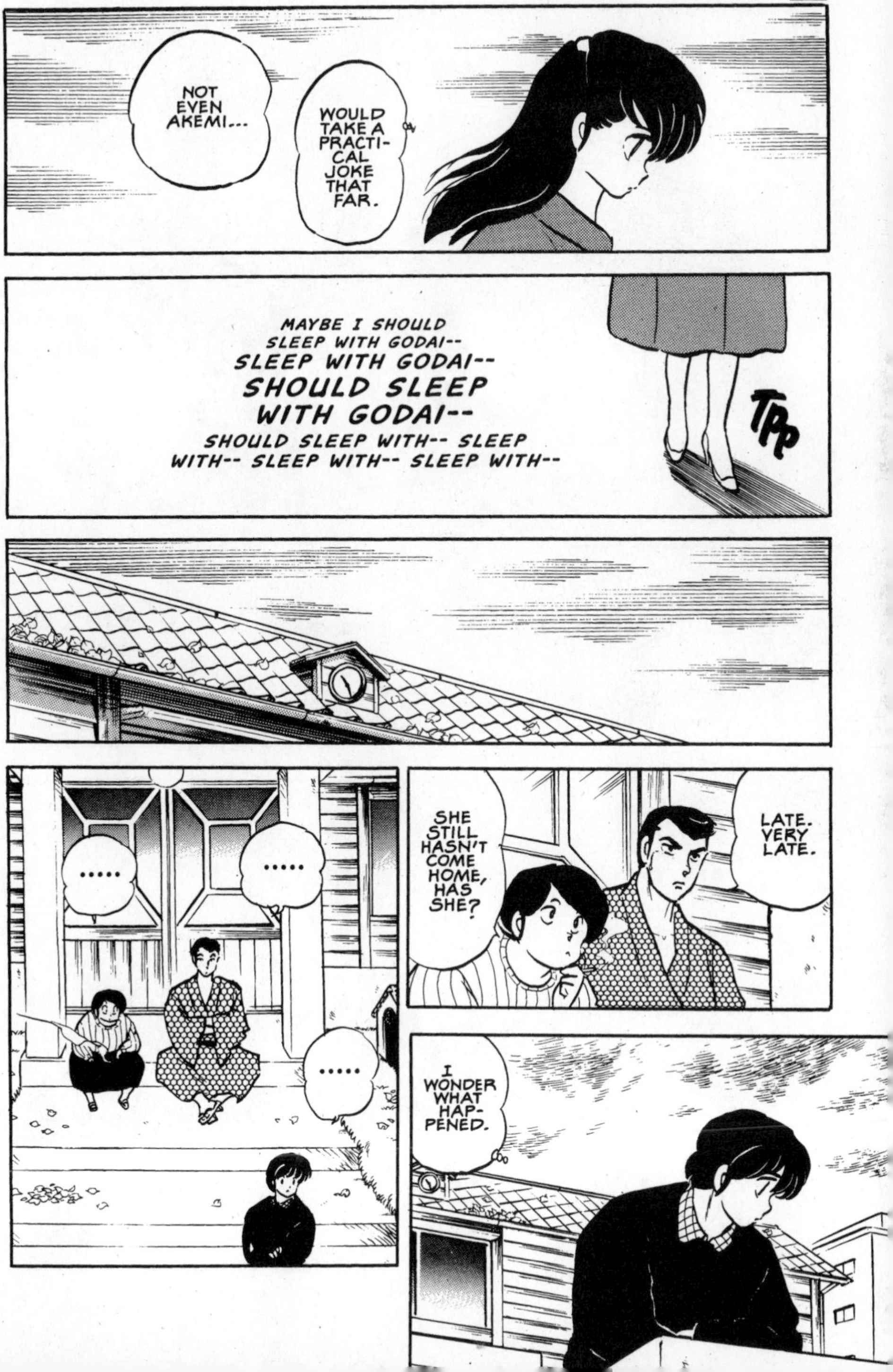
NOT EVEN AKEMI...
WOULD TAKE A PRACTICAL JOKE THAT FAR.
MAYBE I SHOULD SLEEP WITH GODAI-- SLEEP WITH GODAI-- SHOULD SLEEP WITH GODAI-- SHOULD SLEEP WITH-- SLEEP WITH-- SLEEP WITH-- SLEEP WITH--
TPP
......
.....
......
SHE STILL HASN'T COME HOME, HAS SHE?
LATE. VERY LATE.
I WONDER WHAT HAPPENED.

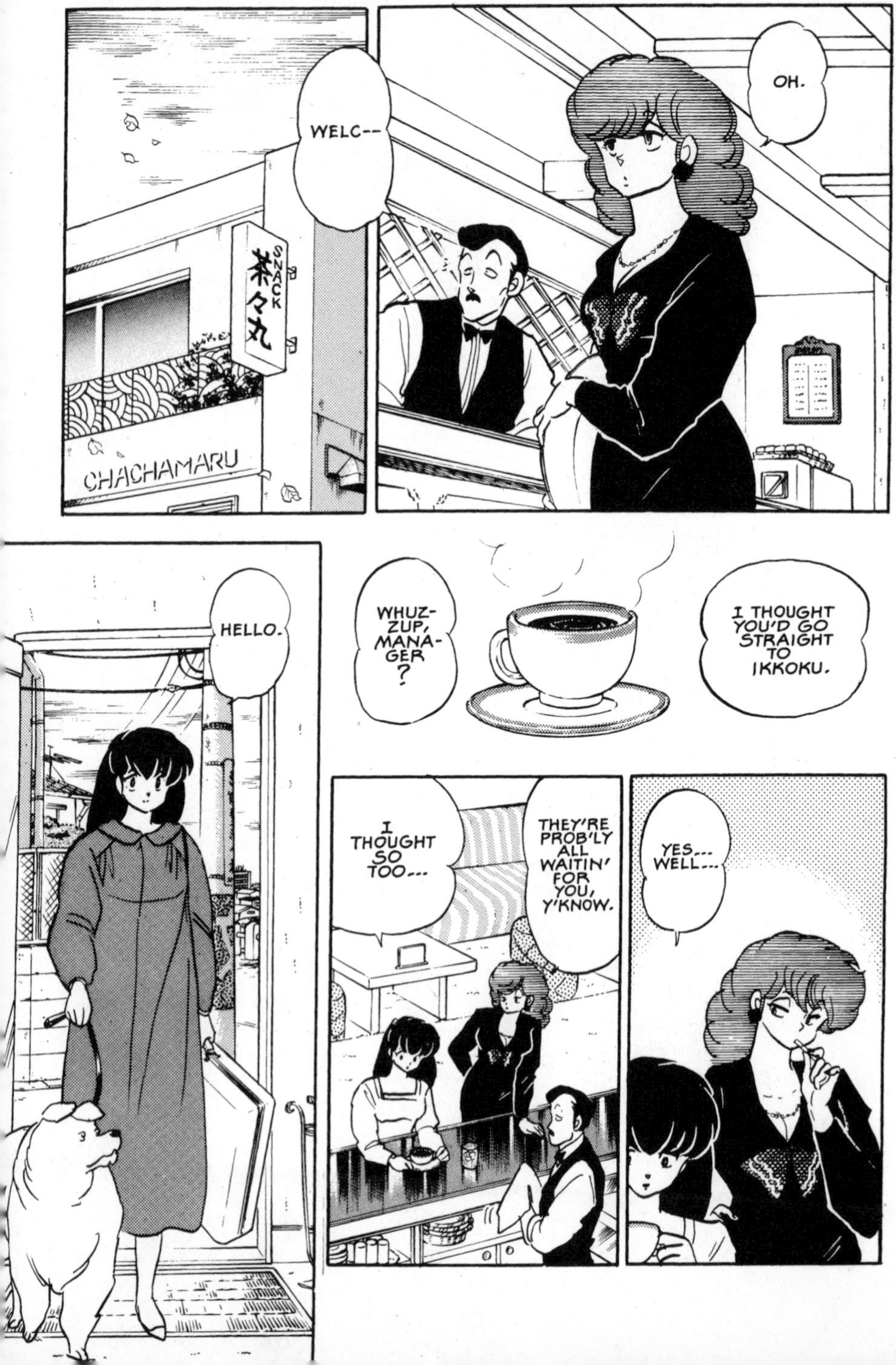
WELC--
SNACK 茶々丸
CHACHAMARU
OH.
HELLO.
WHUZ-ZUP, MANAGER?
I THOUGHT YOU'D GO STRAIGHT TO IKKOKU.
I THOUGHT SO TOO...
THEY'RE PROB'LY ALL WAITIN' FOR YOU, Y'KNOW.
YES... WELL...

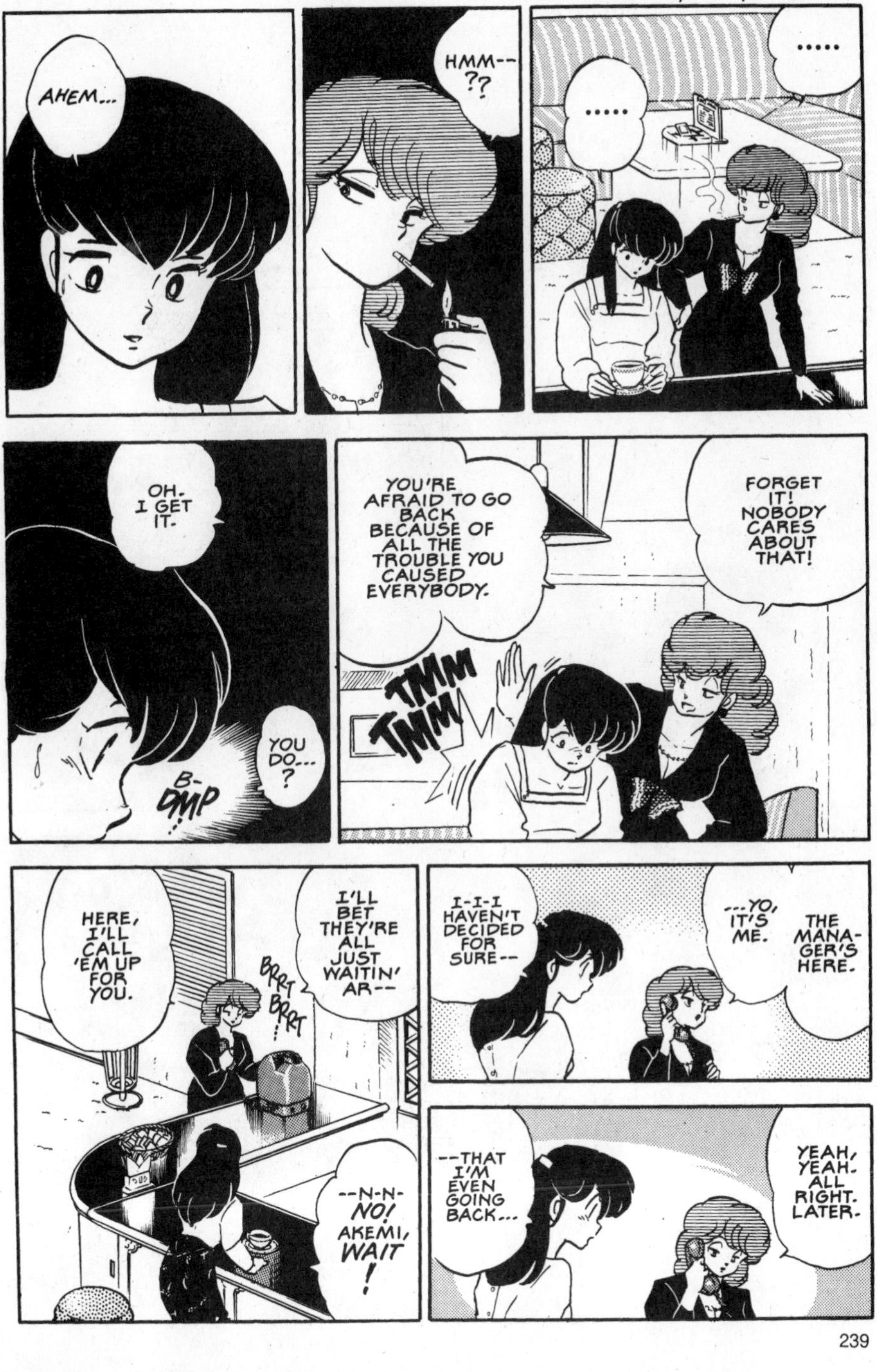
AHEM...
HMM--
??
......
......
OH. I GET IT.
YOU DO...?
B-DMP
YOU'RE AFRAID TO GO BACK BECAUSE OF ALL THE TROUBLE YOU CAUSED EVERYBODY.
FORGET IT! NOBODY CARES ABOUT THAT!
TMM TMM
HERE, I'LL CALL 'EM UP FOR YOU.
I'LL BET THEY'RE ALL JUST WAITIN' AR--
BRRT BRRT
--N-N-NO! AKEMI, WAIT!
I-I-I HAVEN'T DECIDED FOR SURE--
--YO, IT'S ME.
THE MANAGER'S HERE.
--THAT I'M EVEN GOING BACK...
YEAH, YEAH. ALL RIGHT. LATER.

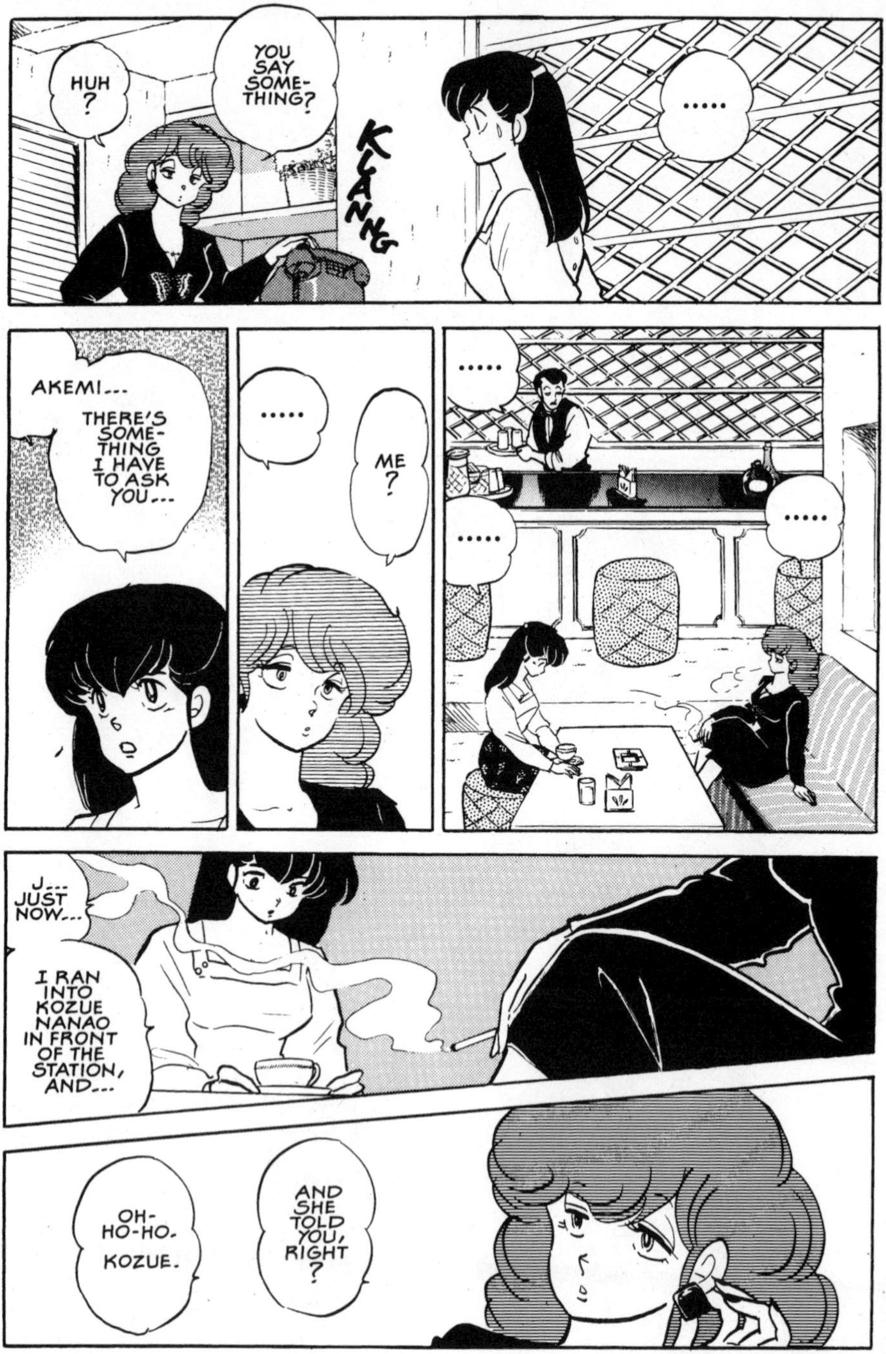
HUH ?
YOU SAY SOME-THING?
KLANNG
.....
AKEMI... THERE'S SOME-THING I HAVE TO ASK YOU...
.....
ME ?
.....
.....
.....
J... JUST NOW...
I RAN INTO KOZUE NANAO IN FRONT OF THE STATION, AND...
OH-HO-HO. KOZUE.
AND SHE TOLD YOU, RIGHT ?

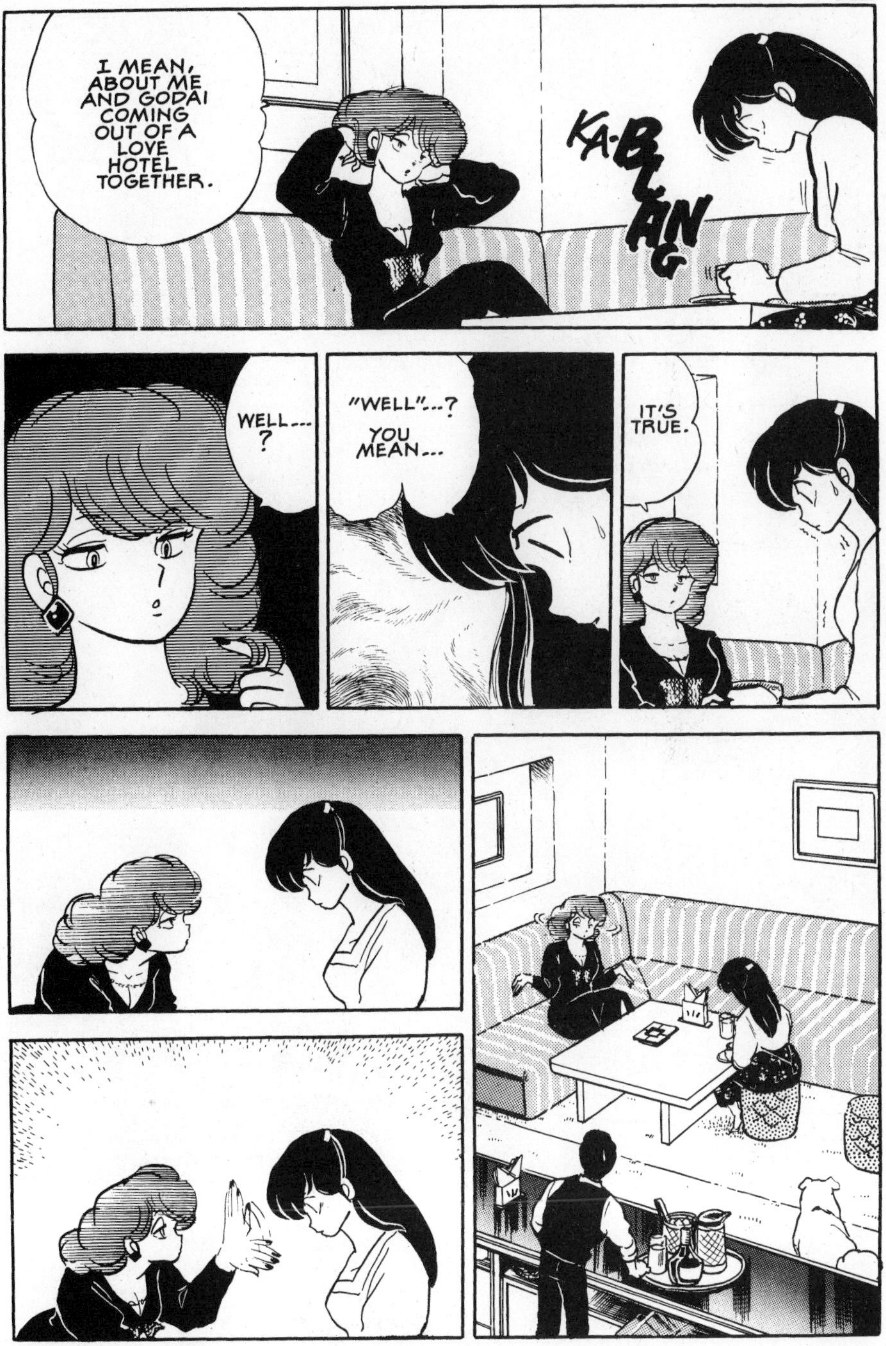
I MEAN, ABOUT ME AND GODAI COMING OUT OF A LOVE HOTEL TOGETHER.
KA-BLANG
WELL...?
"WELL"...? YOU MEAN...
IT'S TRUE.

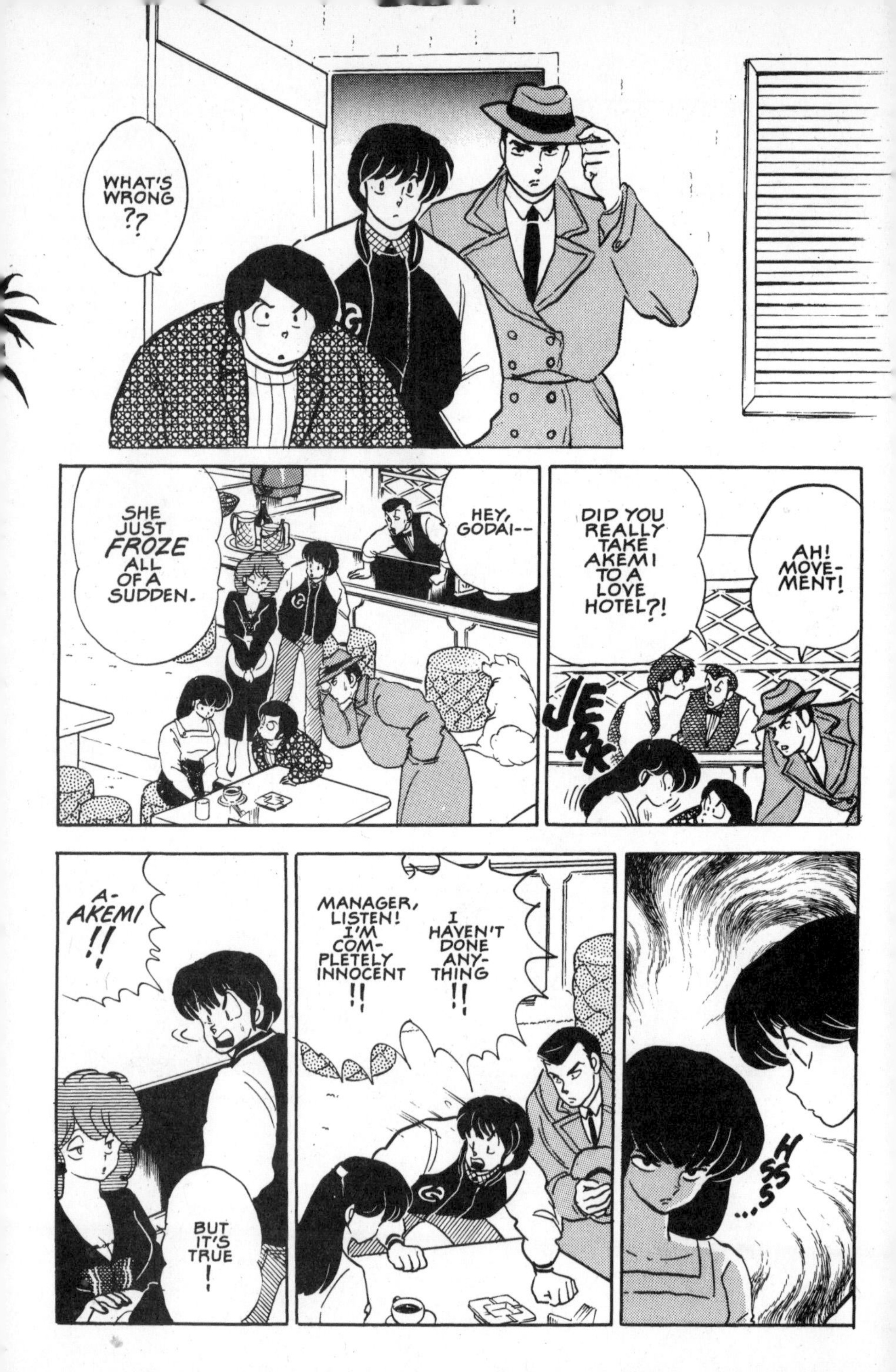
WHAT'S WRONG ??
SHE JUST FROZE ALL OF A SUDDEN.
HEY, GODAI--
DID YOU REALLY TAKE AKEMI TO A LOVE HOTEL?!
AH! MOVE-MENT!
JERK
A-AKEMI !!
BUT IT'S TRUE !
MANAGER, LISTEN! I'M COM-PLETELY INNOCENT !!
I HAVEN'T DONE ANY-THING !!
HSSS...

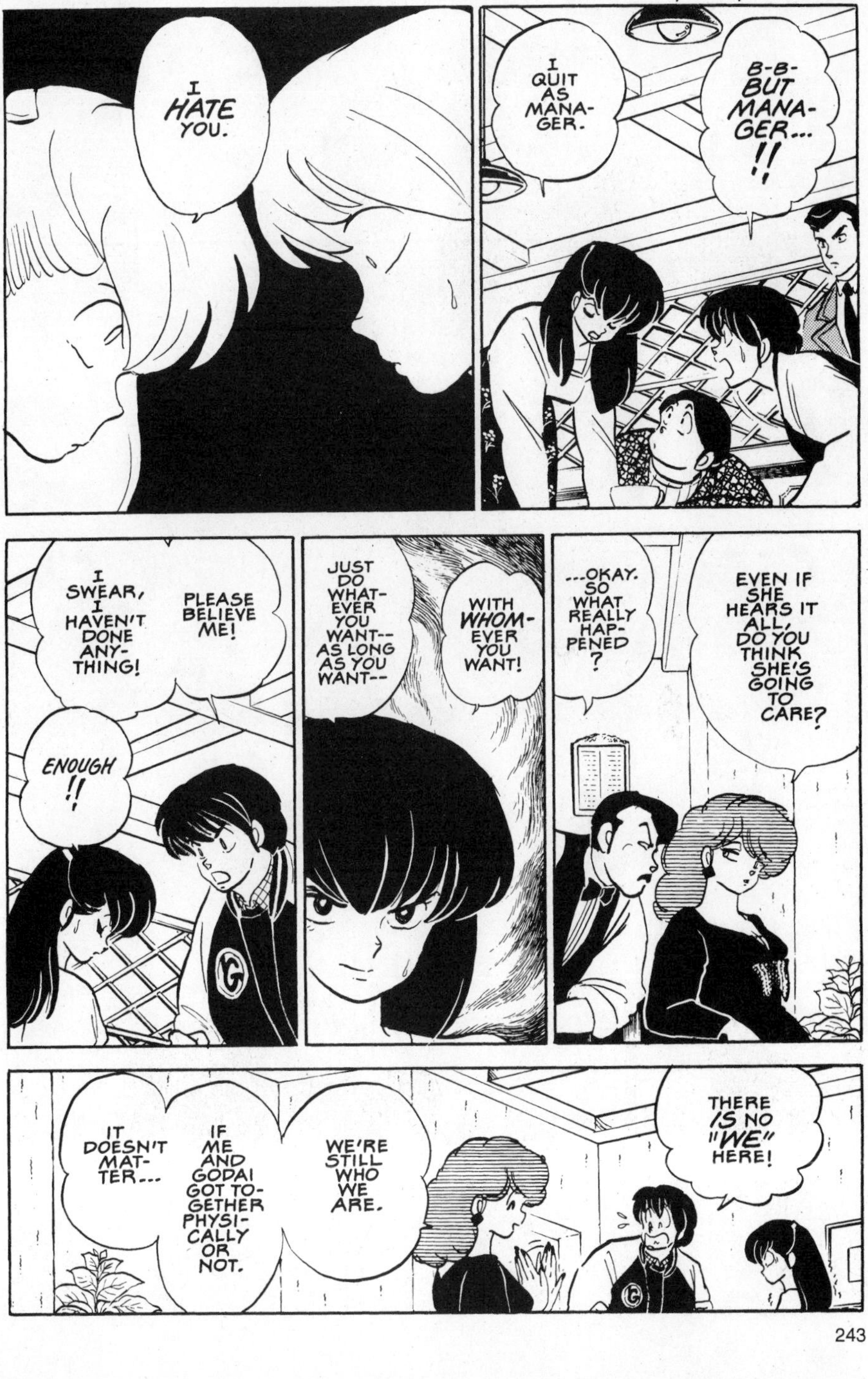
I HATE YOU.
I QUIT AS MANAGER.
B-B-BUT MANAGER...!!
I SWEAR, I HAVEN'T DONE ANYTHING!
PLEASE BELIEVE ME!
ENOUGH!!
JUST DO WHATEVER YOU WANT--AS LONG AS YOU WANT--
WITH WHOMEVER YOU WANT!
...OKAY. SO WHAT REALLY HAPPENED?
EVEN IF SHE HEARS IT ALL, DO YOU THINK SHE'S GOING TO CARE?
IT DOESN'T MATTER...
IF ME AND GODAI GOT TOGETHER PHYSICALLY OR NOT.
WE'RE STILL WHO WE ARE.
THERE IS NO "WE" HERE!

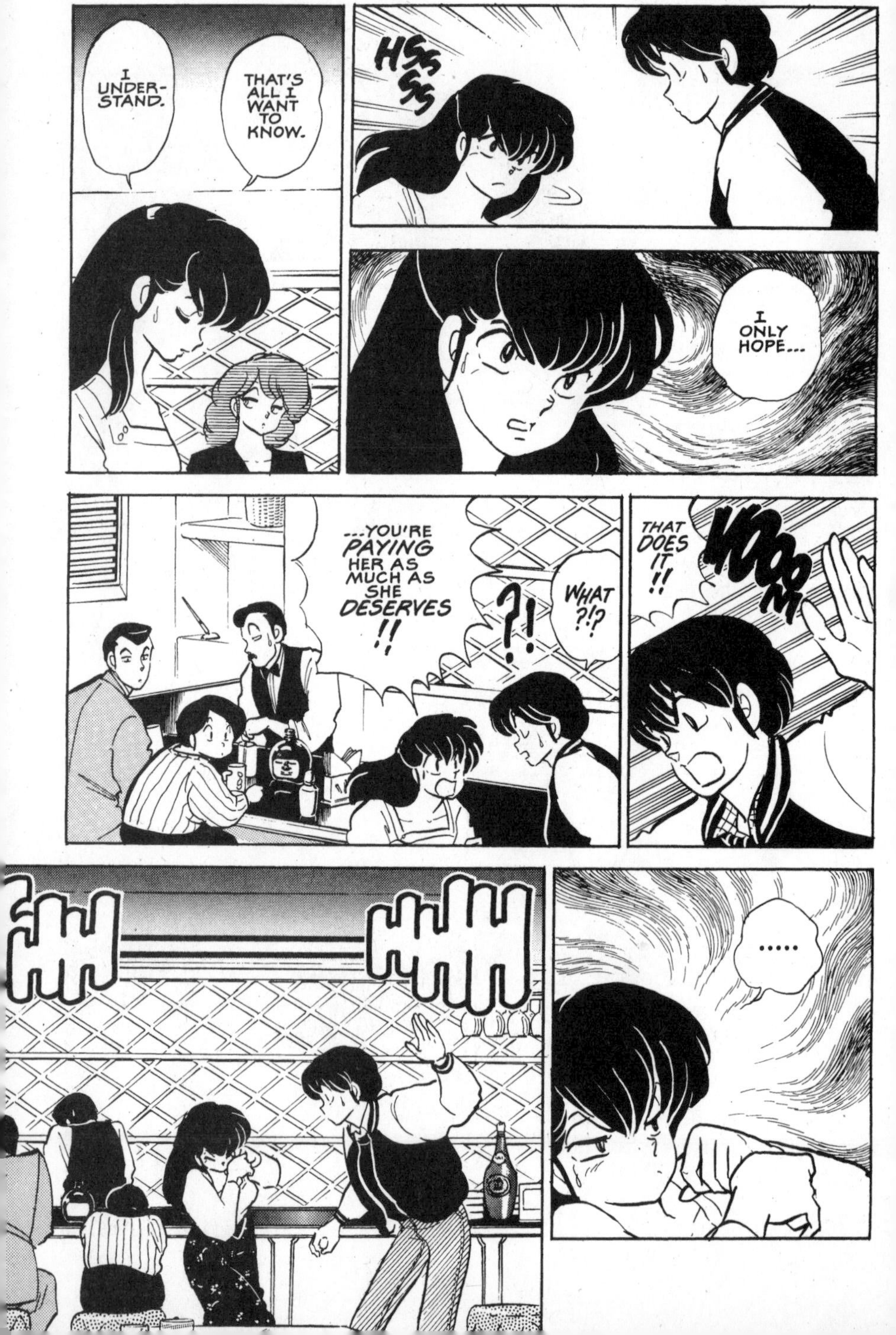
I UNDER-STAND.
THAT'S ALL I WANT TO KNOW.
HSSSSS
I ONLY HOPE...
...YOU'RE *PAYING* HER AS MUCH AS SHE *DESERVES* !!
?!
WHAT ?!?
THAT DOES IT !!
VOOOM
.....

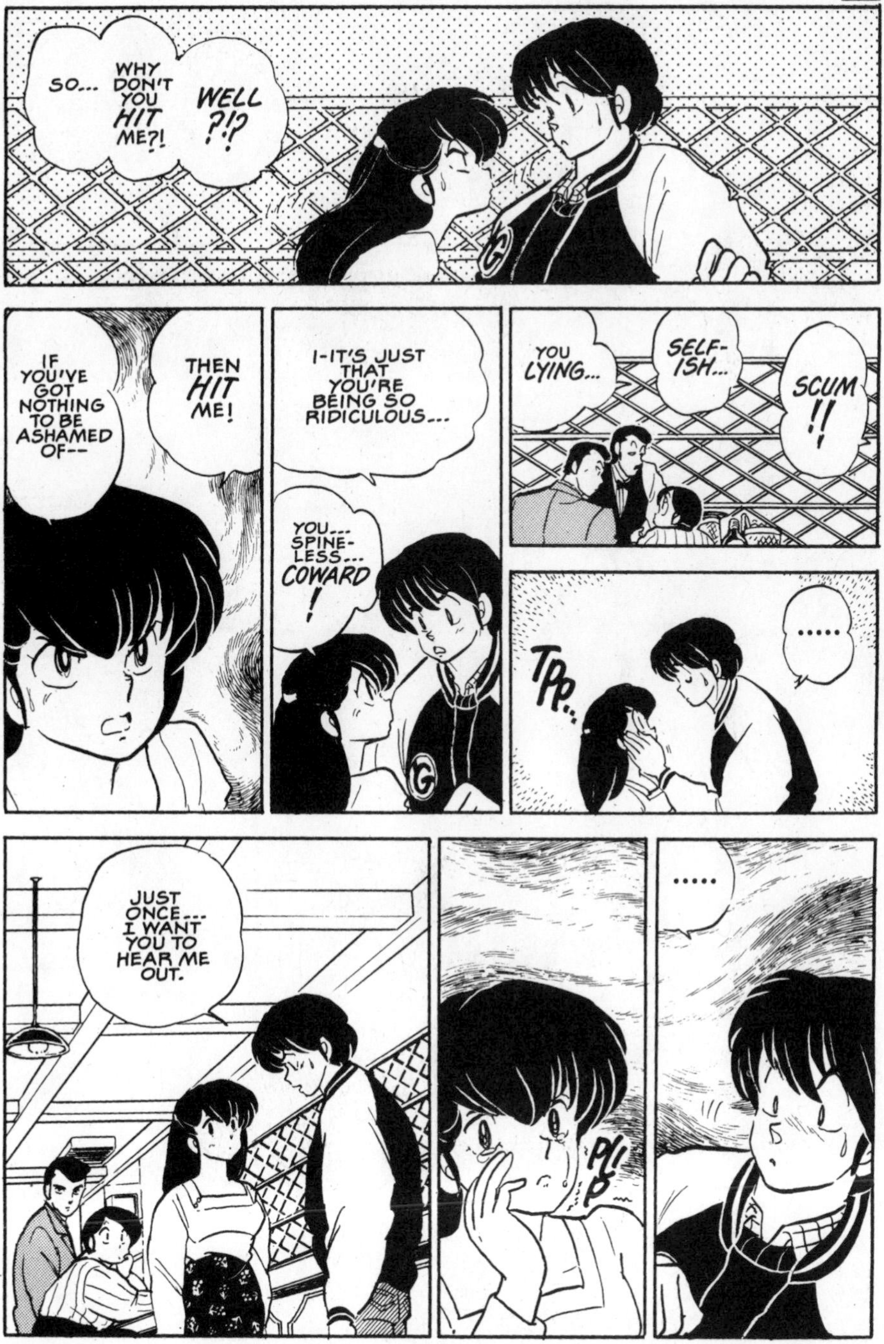
SO... WHY DON'T YOU HIT ME?!
WELL ?!?
IF YOU'VE GOT NOTHING TO BE ASHAMED OF--
THEN HIT ME!
I-IT'S JUST THAT YOU'RE BEING SO RIDICULOUS...
YOU... SPINELESS... COWARD!
YOU LYING...
SELFISH...
SCUM!!
TPP...
......
JUST ONCE... I WANT YOU TO HEAR ME OUT.
PLIP
......

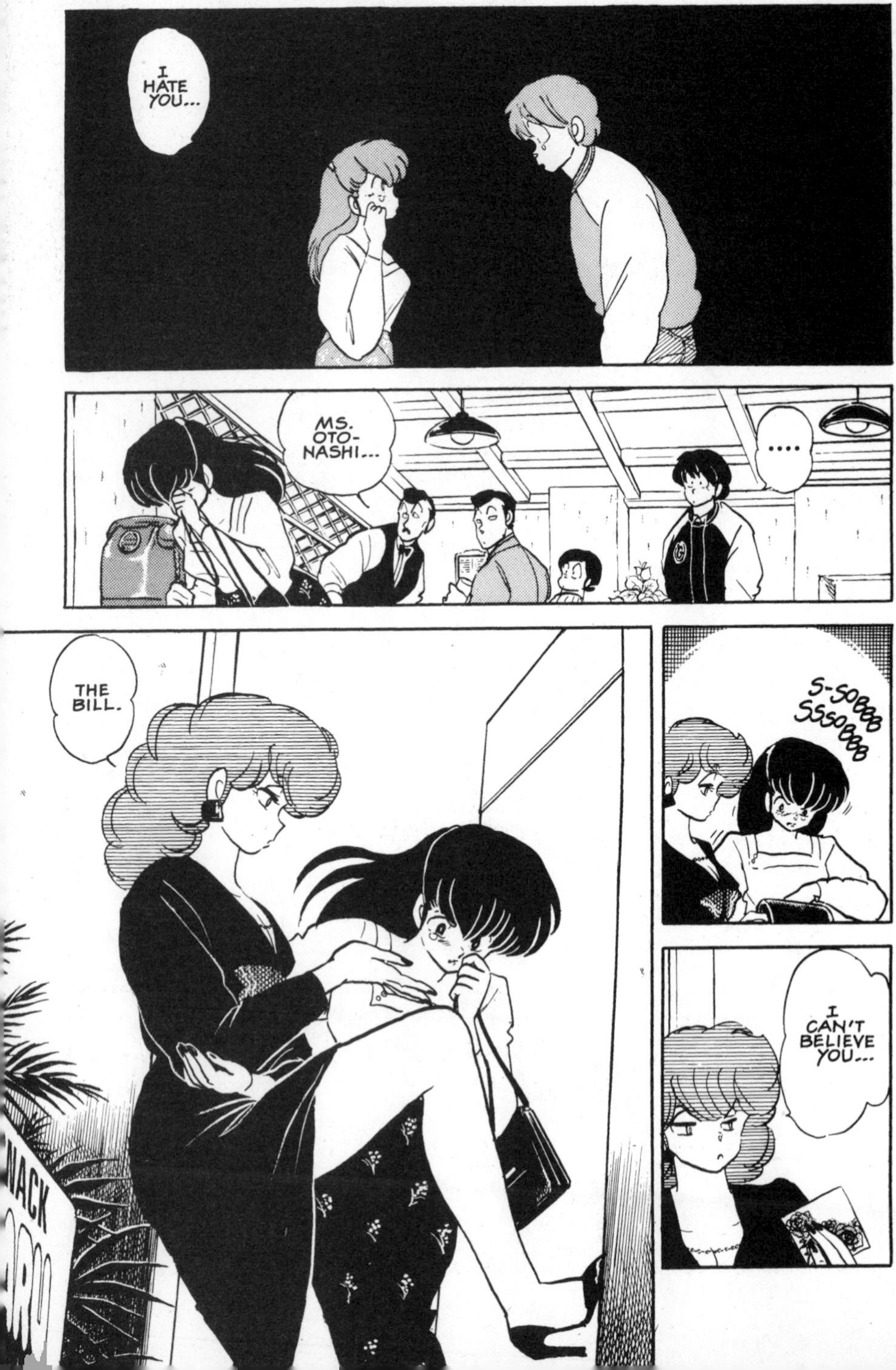
I HATE YOU...
MS. OTO-NASHI...
....
THE BILL.
S-SOBBB SSSOBBB
I CAN'T BELIEVE YOU...
NACK

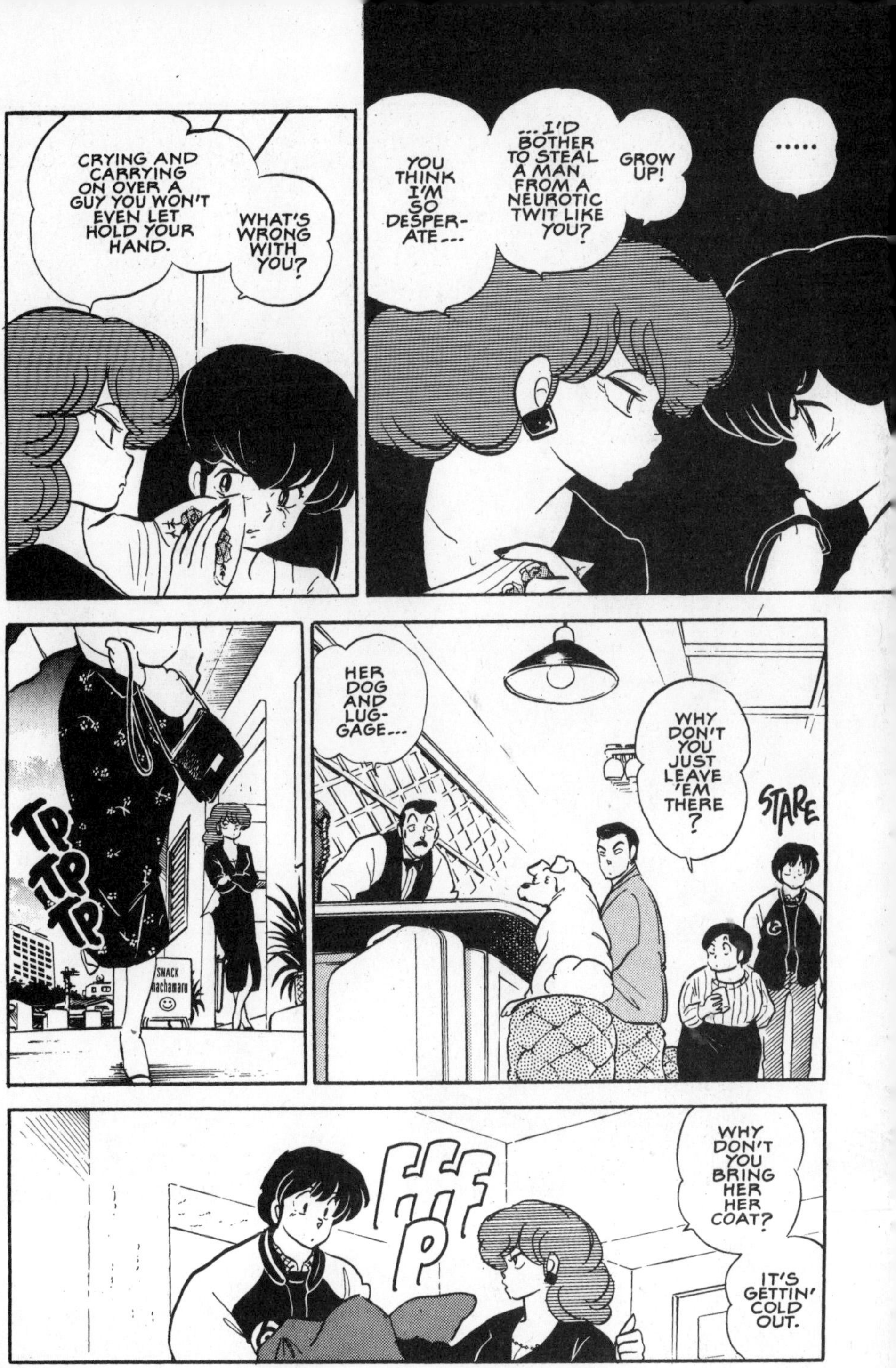
CRYING AND CARRYING ON OVER A GUY YOU WON'T EVEN LET HOLD YOUR HAND.
WHAT'S WRONG WITH YOU?
YOU THINK I'M SO DESPERATE...
...I'D BOTHER TO STEAL A MAN FROM A NEUROTIC TWIT LIKE YOU?
GROW UP!
......
TP TP TP
SNACK
Nachamaru
HER DOG AND LUGGAGE...
WHY DON'T YOU JUST LEAVE 'EM THERE?
STARE
fff
p
WHY DON'T YOU BRING HER HER COAT?
IT'S GETTIN' COLD OUT.

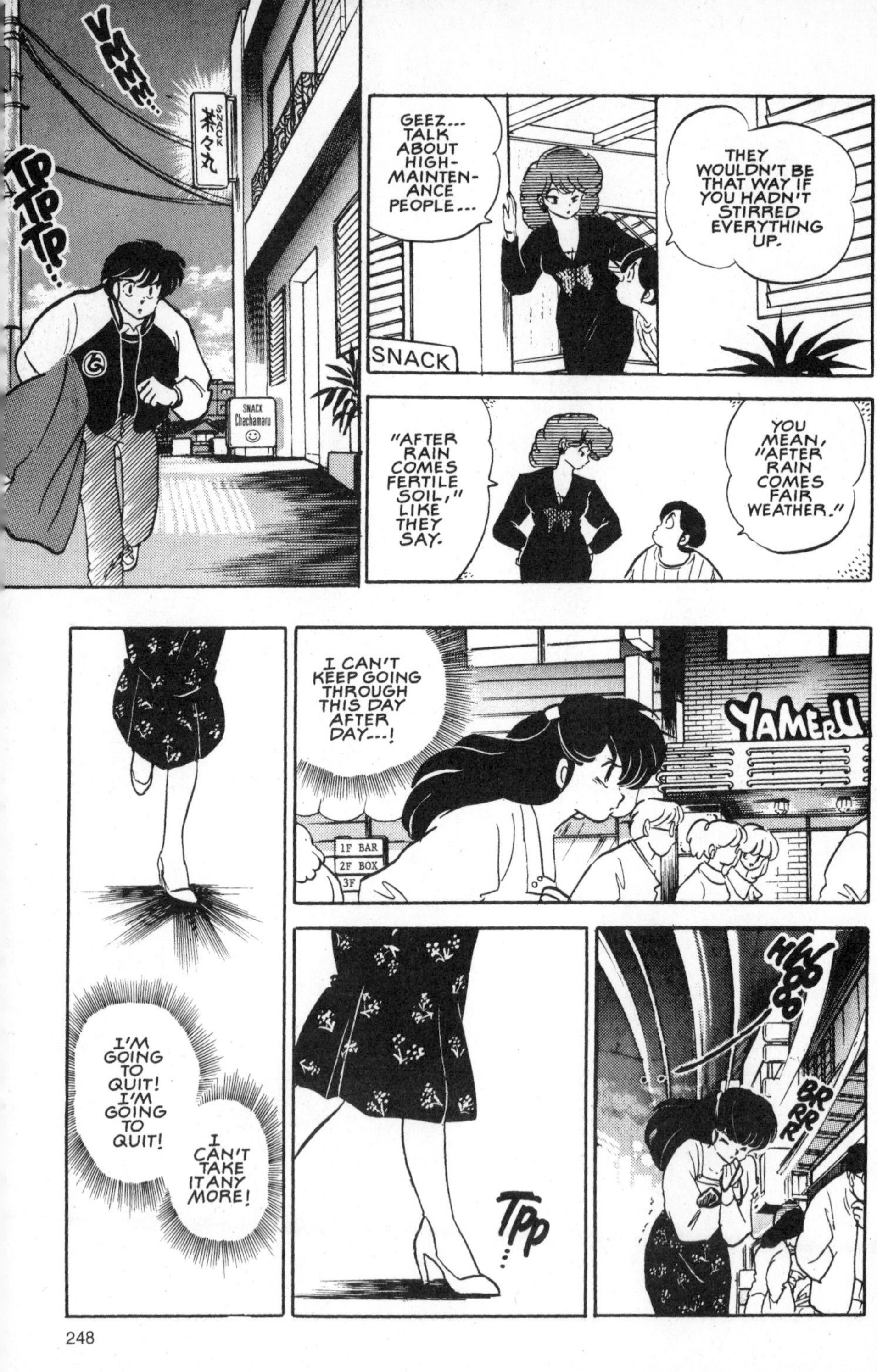
VMMM...
SNACK 茶々丸
TP TP TP...
SNACK Chachamaru
GEEZ... TALK ABOUT HIGH-MAINTENANCE PEOPLE...
SNACK
THEY WOULDN'T BE THAT WAY IF YOU HADN'T STIRRED EVERYTHING UP.
"AFTER RAIN COMES FERTILE SOIL," LIKE THEY SAY.
YOU MEAN, "AFTER RAIN COMES FAIR WEATHER."
I'M GOING TO QUIT! I'M GOING TO QUIT!
I CAN'T TAKE IT ANY MORE!
I CAN'T KEEP GOING THROUGH THIS DAY AFTER DAY...!
YAMERU
1F BAR
2F BOX
3F
TPP...
HWOOO
BRRR

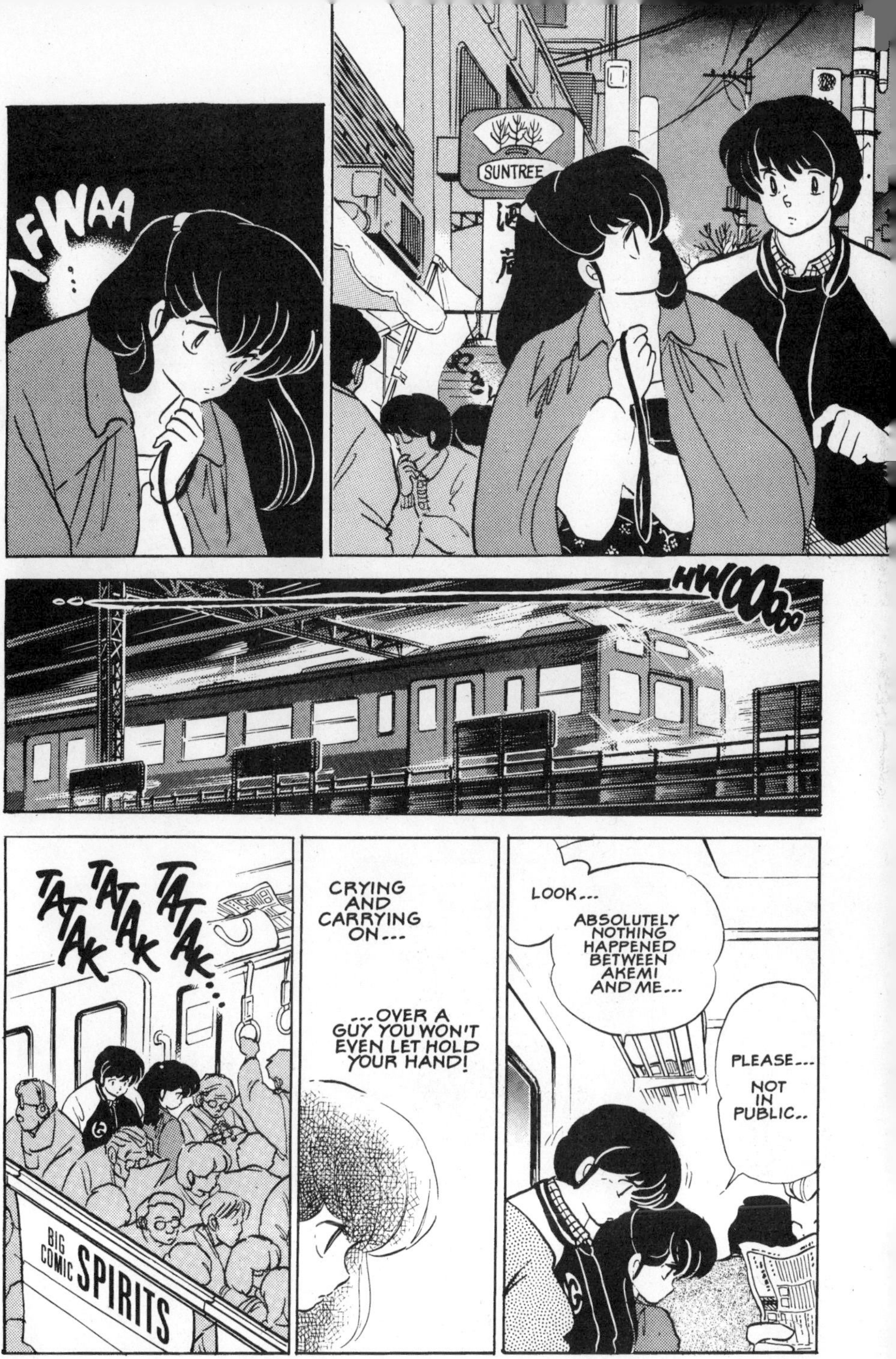
FWAA
SUNTREE
HWOOOoo
TATAK TATAK TATAK...
BIG COMIC SPIRITS
CRYING AND CARRYING ON...
...OVER A GUY YOU WON'T EVEN LET HOLD YOUR HAND!
LOOK...
ABSOLUTELY NOTHING HAPPENED BETWEEN AKEMI AND ME...
PLEASE... NOT IN PUBLIC..

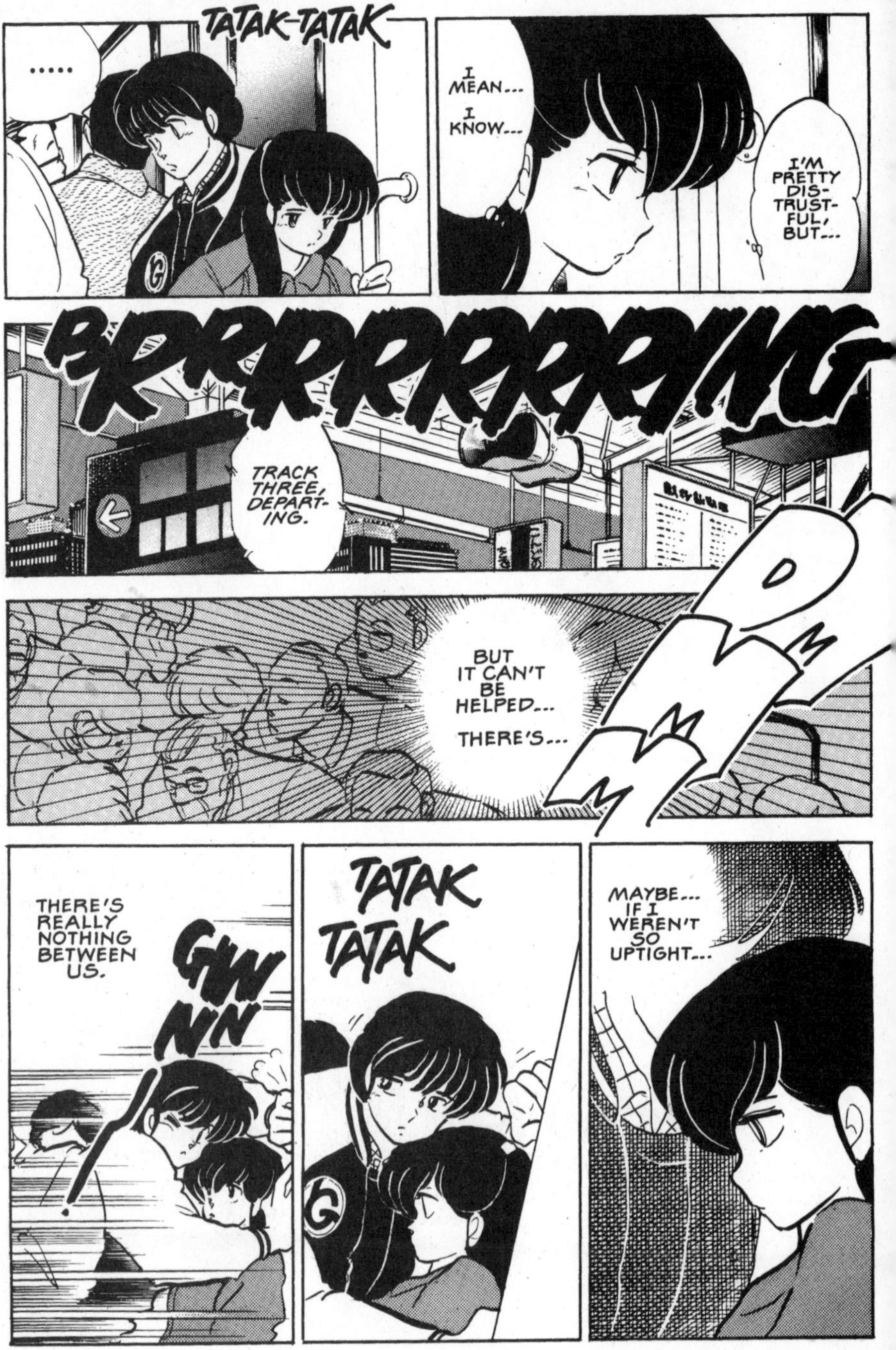
TATAK-TATAK
.....
I MEAN...
I KNOW...
I'M PRETTY DIS-TRUST-FUL, BUT...
BRRRRRRRRING
TRACK THREE, DEPART-ING.
DMMM
BUT IT CAN'T BE HELPED...
THERE'S...
THERE'S REALLY NOTHING BETWEEN US.
GWNN
TATAK TATAK
MAYBE... IF I WEREN'T SO UPTIGHT...

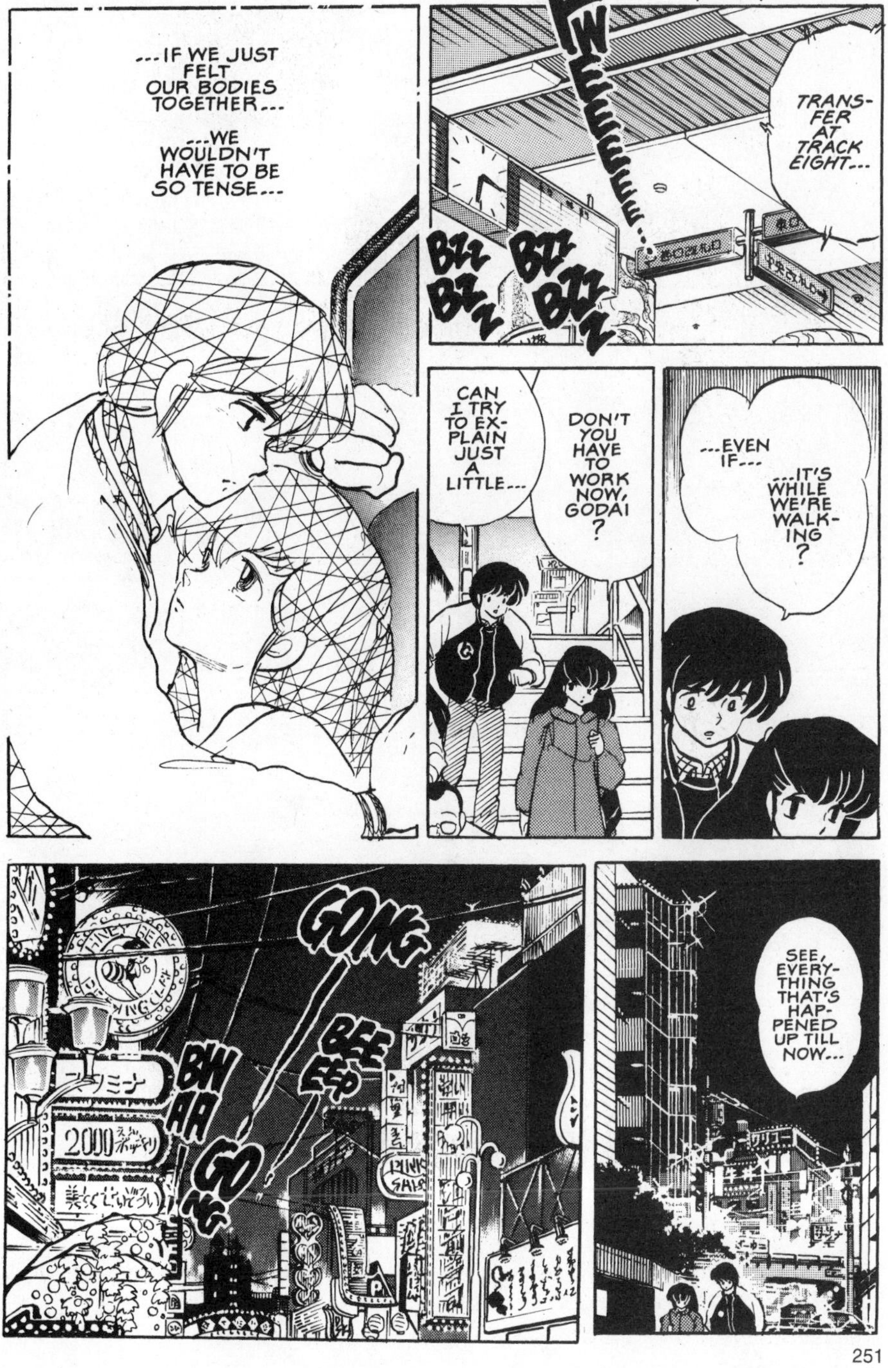
...IF WE JUST FELT OUR BODIES TOGETHER...
...WE WOULDN'T HAVE TO BE SO TENSE...
FWEEEEEEEE...
BZZ BZZ
BZZ BZZ
TRANSFER AT TRACK EIGHT...
CAN I TRY TO EXPLAIN JUST A LITTLE...
DON'T YOU HAVE TO WORK NOW, GODAI?
...EVEN IF...
...IT'S WHILE WE'RE WALKING?
GONG
BEEEEP
BWAAA
GONG GONG
2000
SEE, EVERYTHING THAT'S HAPPENED UP TILL NOW...

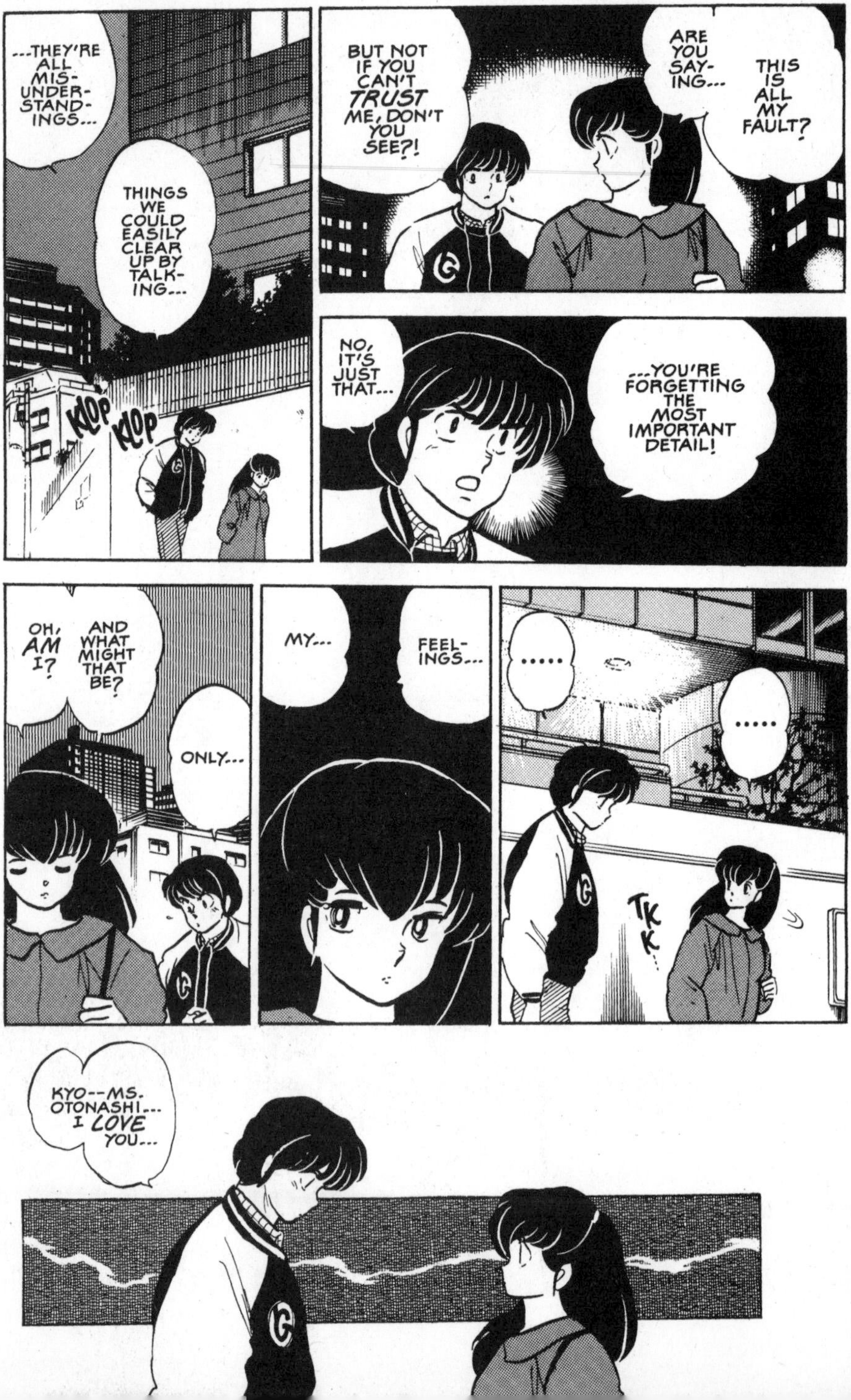

...THEY'RE ALL MIS-UNDER-STAND-INGS...
THINGS WE COULD EASILY CLEAR UP BY TALK-ING...
KLOP KLOP
BUT NOT IF YOU CAN'T TRUST ME, DON'T YOU SEE?!
ARE YOU SAY-ING...
THIS IS ALL MY FAULT?
NO, IT'S JUST THAT...
...YOU'RE FORGETTING THE MOST IMPORTANT DETAIL!
OH, AM I?
AND WHAT MIGHT THAT BE?
ONLY...
MY...
FEEL-INGS...
......
......
TKK...
KYO--MS. OTONASHI... I LOVE YOU...

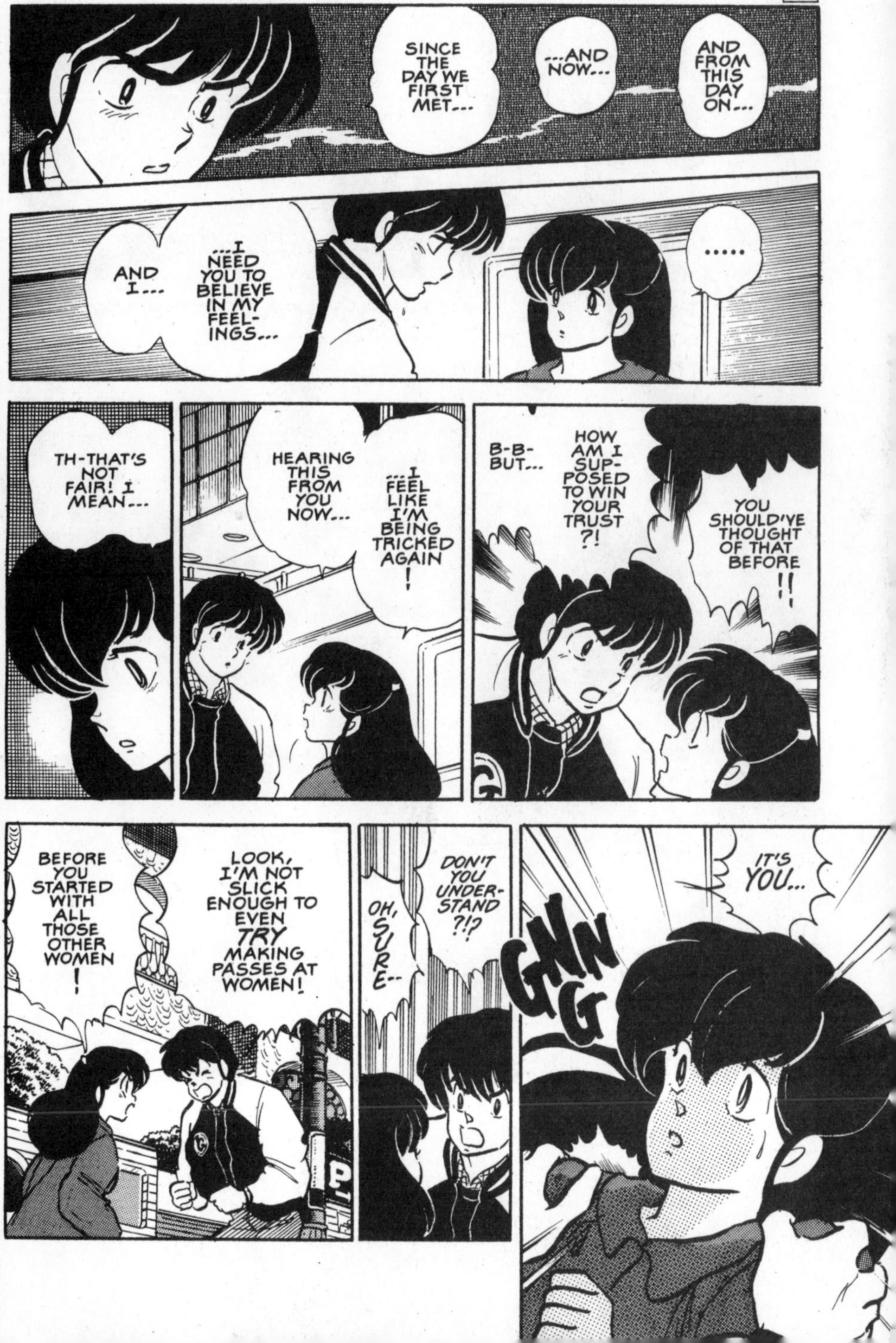
SINCE THE DAY WE FIRST MET...
...AND NOW...
AND FROM THIS DAY ON...
AND I...
...I NEED YOU TO BELIEVE IN MY FEEL-INGS...
.....
TH-THAT'S NOT FAIR! I MEAN...
HEARING THIS FROM YOU NOW...
...I FEEL LIKE I'M BEING TRICKED AGAIN!
B-B-BUT...
HOW AM I SUP-POSED TO WIN YOUR TRUST?!
YOU SHOULD'VE THOUGHT OF THAT BEFORE!!
BEFORE YOU STARTED WITH ALL THOSE OTHER WOMEN!
LOOK, I'M NOT SLICK ENOUGH TO EVEN TRY MAKING PASSES AT WOMEN!
OH, SURE...
DON'T YOU UNDER-STAND?!?
GNNG
IT'S YOU...

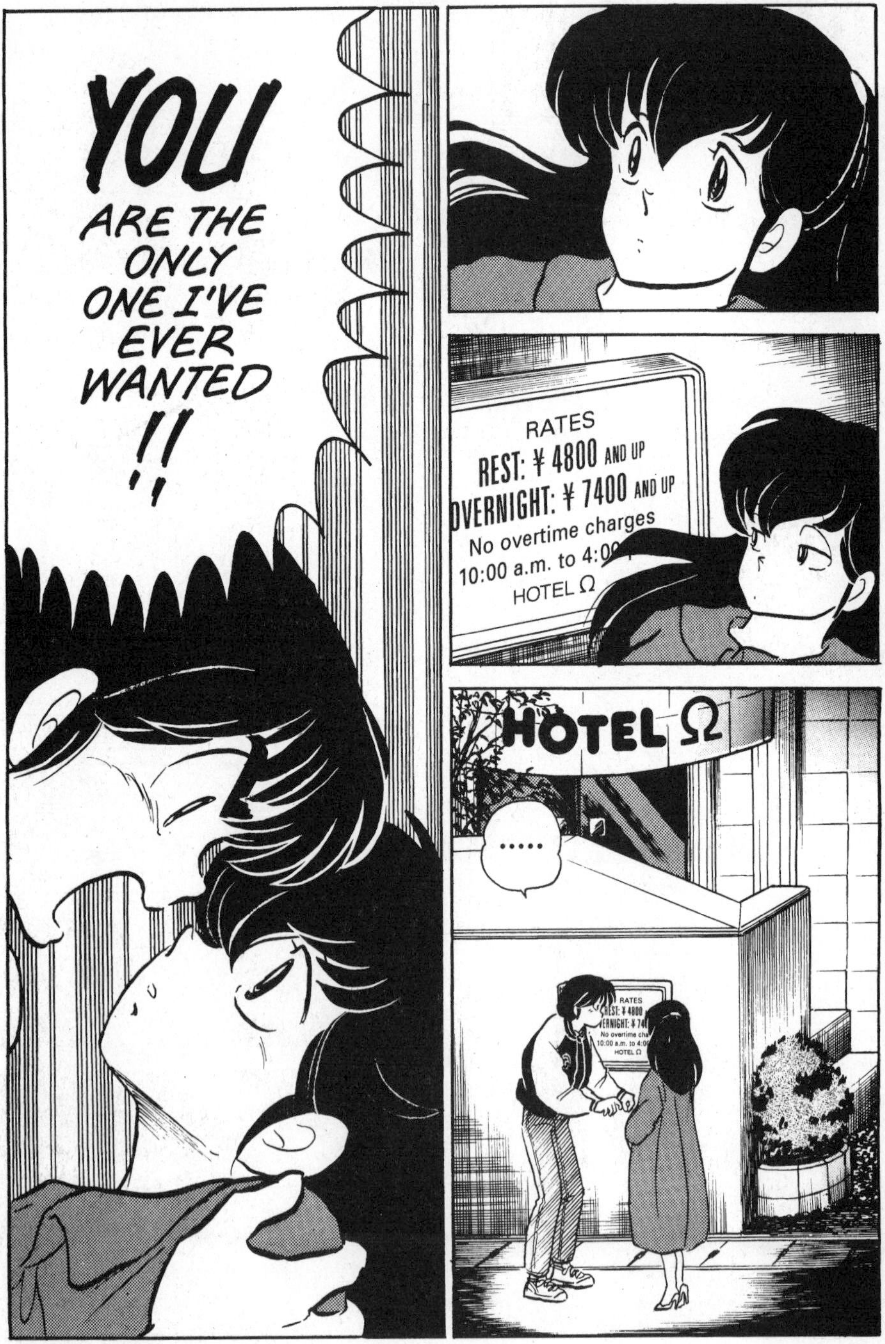
YOU ARE THE ONLY ONE I'VE EVER WANTED !!
RATES
REST: ¥ 4800 AND UP
OVERNIGHT: ¥ 7400 AND UP
No overtime charges
10:00 a.m. to 4:0
HOTEL Ω
HOTEL Ω
......

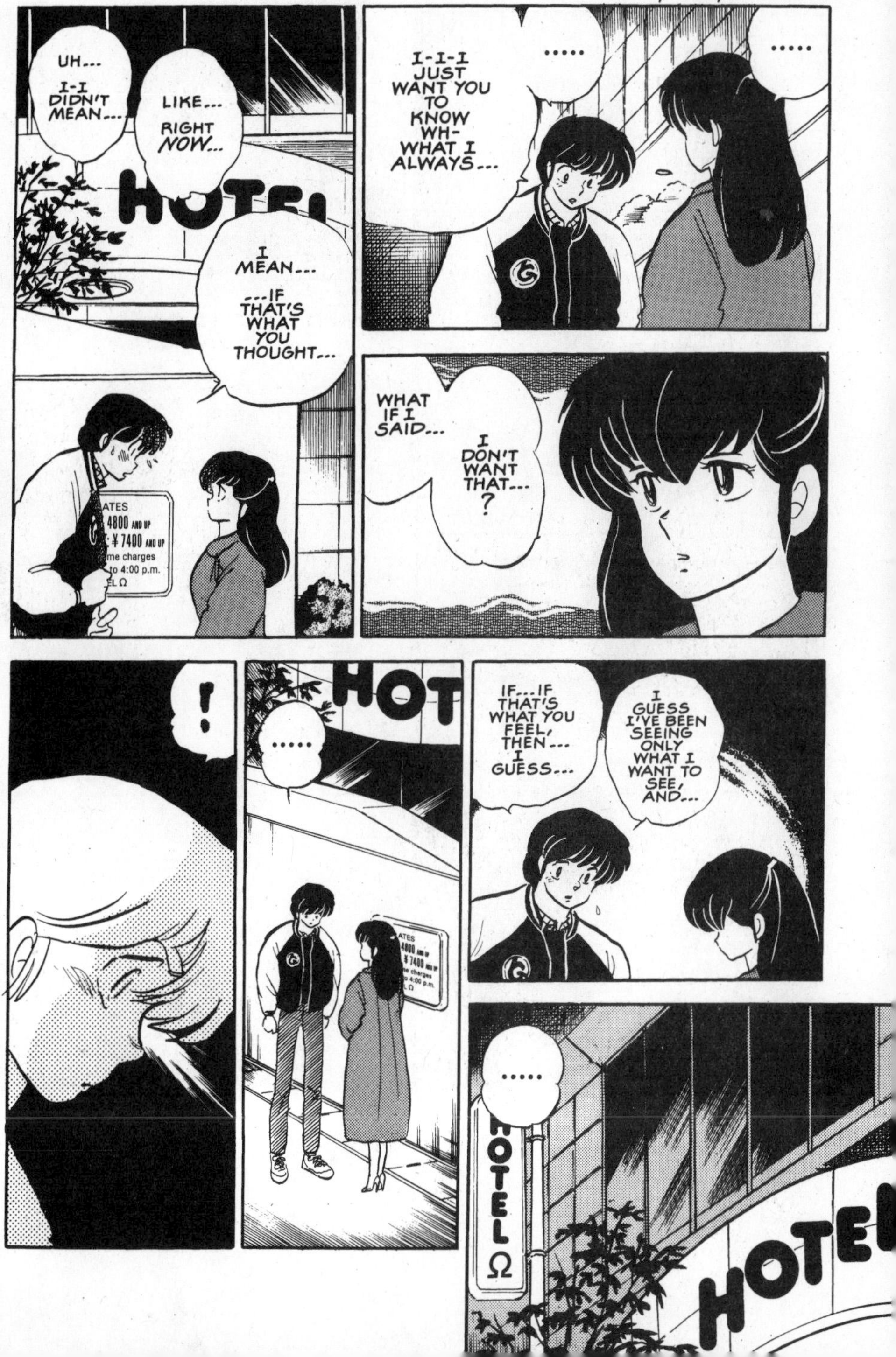
UH... I-I DIDN'T MEAN...
LIKE... RIGHT NOW...
I MEAN... ...IF THAT'S WHAT YOU THOUGHT...
I-I-I JUST WANT YOU TO KNOW WH- WHAT I ALWAYS...
.....
.....
WHAT IF I SAID...
I DON'T WANT THAT...?
!
......
IF... IF THAT'S WHAT YOU FEEL, THEN... I GUESS...
I GUESS I'VE BEEN SEEING ONLY WHAT I WANT TO SEE, AND...
.....
HOTEL Ω

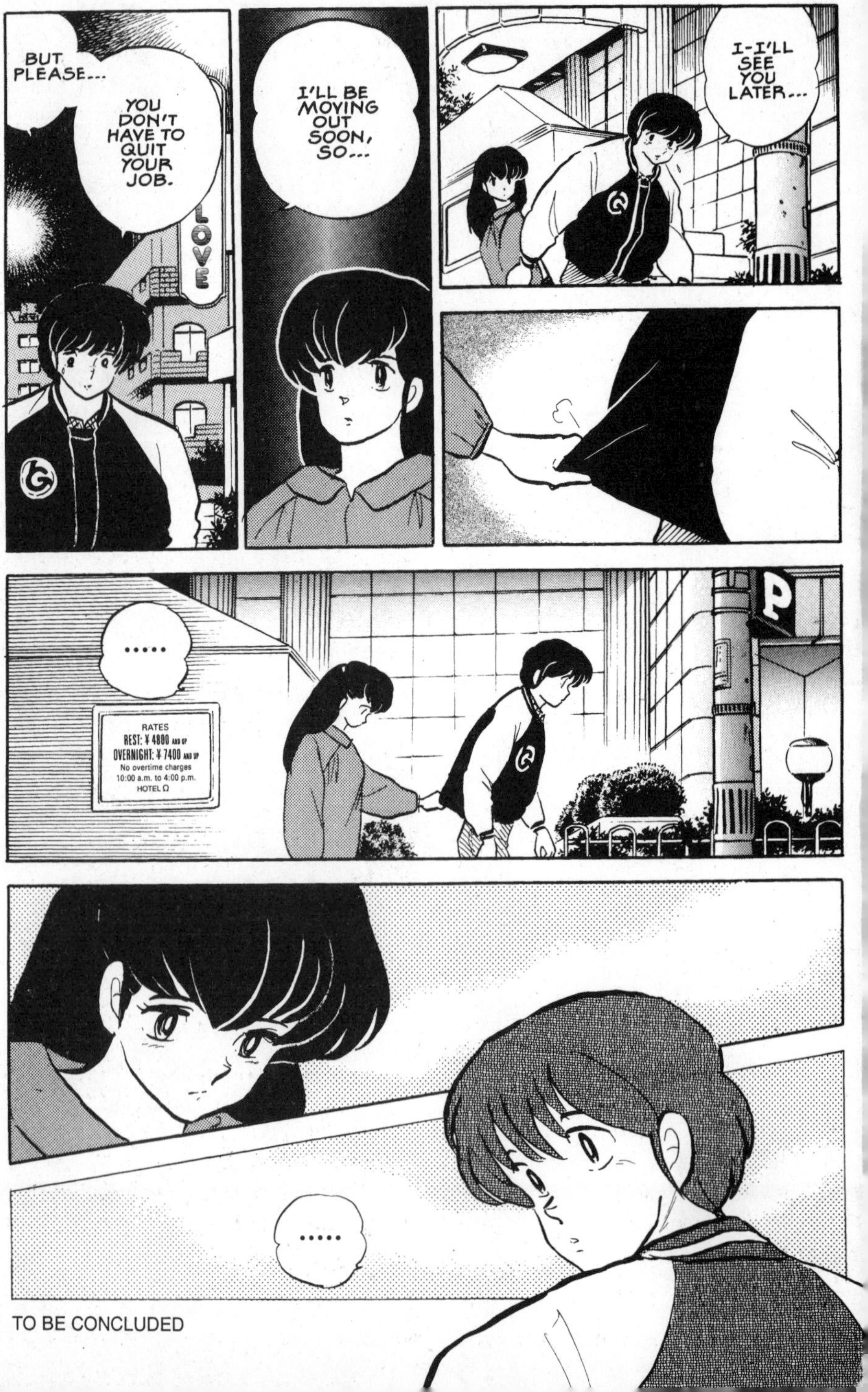
BUT PLEASE...
YOU DON'T HAVE TO QUIT YOUR JOB.
LOVE
I'LL BE MOVING OUT SOON, SO...
I-I'LL SEE YOU LATER...
......
RATES
REST: ¥4800 AND UP
OVERNIGHT: ¥7400 AND UP
No overtime charges
10:00 a.m. to 4:00 p.m.
HOTEL Ω
P
......

TO BE CONCLUDED